O. E. Kay

GENERATION WHY's
PERDITION REDEMPTIVE
VERSES

Mindfield Publishing
*Email: mindfieldpublications@gmail.com
info@mindfieldpublishing.com
publisher@mindfieldpublishing.coms

*Website: http://www.mindfieldpublishing.com

ISBN: 978-978-784-829-6

I dedicate this book to the YOUTHS and the PEOPLE of Africa!

PREFACE

When O.E.K., whom I affectionately refer to as such, initially approached me to pen the preface for this book, I found myself grappling with a mixture of uncertainty and intrigue regarding his request. It was only upon a subsequent occasion when he reiterated his desire for my contribution that I began to accord his proposal the earnest consideration it deserved.

Pondering over the matter, I remain bemused by the discernment he must have seen within me, which led him to believe I possessed the capability to craft a fitting preface for his distinctively unique book. Even now, having completed the task, I continue to contemplate the underlying motivation behind his choice, a curiosity that lingers in my thoughts...

One paramount commitment I hold in undertaking this endeavor is unwavering fidelity. I shall imbue my words with sincerity, ensuring that they faithfully represent my convictions. Thus, everything within these pages reflects my unfiltered perspective. I aspire to convey rather than impress, to communicate without indulging in ostentation. My aim is to maintain clarity for every fortunate reader of this book.

It is with profound honor and a profound sense of duty that I have been entrusted with the task of crafting the preface for this remarkable book. Remaining true to my journalistic principles, I pledge to approach this responsibility objectively.

Eddie has penned a truly captivating work, a fact I can attest to, having had the privilege of perusing the manuscript on two occasions, initially disagreeing and subsequently concurring. It is now unequivocal to me that this book's distinctive essence emanates from the perspective of a black author. It serves as a thought-provoking exploration, confronting the harsh realities faced by the black race without reservation or apology.

It becomes evident through these pages that the author harbors deep-seated discontent with the perceived shortcomings of the black race, particularly in their struggle to contribute significant inventions to humanity. He passionately argues that the inability to replicate and innovate upon existing creations exacerbates his frustration, drawing from his extensive travels and voracious reading.

The book provides an unflinching critique of Africa, highlighting its failure to provide basic amenities such as electricity, clean water, and sanitation in the 21st century. The root of the issue, the author contends, lies not in the continent itself but within the actions of its people. This exposition gains further weight as it sheds light on the rampant corruption among African leaders, who accumulate wealth while their nations suffer.

The book castigates African leaders, along with their accomplices, as insatiable thieves and parasites, preying upon their own people. It also reinforces the negative stereotypes of Africans as disinclined to work yet eager to partake in revelry, all at the expense of their nations.

The lamentable state of Africa, plagued by filth, lack of infrastructure, inadequate education, and healthcare, is a matter of grave concern. The book questions how one can justify such conditions and why Africans tolerate self-enslavement, colonialism, and institutional corruption, perpetuating misery across generations.

Religion appears as a superficial solace for both the rich and poor in Africa, where empty places of worship proliferate, contrasting starkly with the scarcity of functional factories to support economic growth.

The author boldly asserts that the majority of African leaders, past and present, are thieves, plundering the continent with impunity while the masses remain passive. This passivity, he argues, is a sign of their desire to emulate their oppressors rather than challenge them.

The book is replete with striking expressions that cast a critical eye on Africa and its inhabitants, sparking controversy and discourse as it gains recognition. It lays bare the peculiar flaws of Africans, which have relegated them to a position of inferiority and disdain.

The author proffers a profound solution, calling upon the youth of Africa to self-empower, break free from the shackles of tradition, and embark on a path of conscious self-improvement. This entails embracing Planned Parenthood, limiting family size, and prioritizing personal and generational success over procreation.

As you delve into this compelling work, a fusion of fact and fiction, I encourage you to continue the discourse initiated by Eddie. It is an essential read, characterized by its fearless candor, sparing no race or aspect of life. Within its pages, you will discover a raw and unvarnished truth that demands your attention.

~ **I. C. Emmanuel**, a journalist, author and activist.

CONTENTS

GENERATION **WHY's**

PERDITION REDEMPTIVE VERSES

Dehumanization is atrociously inhumane, so pause everything, stand up, dominate your filths and garbage, have your back or be dominated alongside more so from within, by one of yours.

DOMINATE YOUR ENVIRONMENT OR BE DOMINATED ALONGSIDE

TO DOMINATE DEHUMANIZATION AND ANNIHILATE ITS SINS - - SLAVERY, COLONIALISM, INSTITUTIONAL RACISM, SELF-ENSLAVEMENT, SELF-COLONIALISM, INSTITUTIONAL SELF-LOOTING – YOUR SELF-CONSCIOUSNESS MUST DOMINATE YOUR ENVIRONMENT.

IF YOU DON'T ENABLE YOUR SELF-CONSCIOUSNESS TO DOMINATE YOUR ENVIRONMENT - - OBLITERATE YOUR FILTH AND GARBAGE, CREATE FREEDOMS, VALUE-CHAIN YOUR RESOURCES, CREATE YOUR ECONOMIC AND WEALTH BASE, IN ORDER TO HAVE YOUR BACK AND THE BACKS OF THE GENERATIONS OF YOUR DESCENDANTS AD INFINITUM, "…CONTRIBUTING SOMETHING MANKIND CAN ENJOY"- - YOU WILL BE DOMINATED ALONGSIDE BY ANY OF THE ENABLED SELF-CONSCIOUSNESS WITHIN THE FAMILY OF THE THREE PIGMENTED HUMAN SPECIE. SO,

STAND UP, STAND UP, STAND UP, STAND UP, STAND UP, STAND UP, STAND UP, STAND UP AND

DOMINATE, DOMINATE, DOMINATE, DOMINATE, DOMINATE, DOMINATE
YOUR

FILTH AND GARBAGE – YOUR ENVIRONMENT –
OR
BE DOMINATED ALONGSIDE, IN CONTINUUM!

Dominance: the inherent basic instinct conquering mechanism in people and animals to brave in order to contrive and guarantee survival and well-being of self and family and perpetuate progress and development edge, necessarily empowering descendants, generation after generation ad infinitum. Without Dehumanization.
- (Perdition Redemptive Verses' Dictionary).

AUTHOR'S NOTE

In this book, the opinions, analyses, views, comments, and vision are exclusively my own. These are rooted in the factual realities of my personal experiences, substantiated by research from both public and private sources. They also draw upon the undeniable truths of the dehumanization and suffering endured by the Black community. My hope is that the words within these pages will grant readers a deeper understanding, a more profound critique, and a heightened awareness of the subject matter. Specifically, I aim to inspire the younger generation to cultivate self-awareness, recognize the challenges faced by Black individuals, and confront the systemic issues that continue to persist.

I extend a sincere invitation to readers to embark on independent research to dispel any doubts and foster constructive self-reflection and critique. By doing so, we can collectively promote self-awareness among young Black individuals, empowering them to contribute positively to the world. Ultimately, we owe this debt to them.

To the global community, especially to the exceptional generation known as Gen Z and, in particular, to Black Gen Z, who are poised to uplift and lead Africa's youth towards greater self-awareness—my heartfelt and humble congratulations! Your extraordinary aptitude and self-awareness have allowed you to harness the power of social media, creating a united global community of empathetic youth.

Despite being at a stage in life filled with myriad possibilities for charting your future, both professionally and personally, you have channeled your collective consciousness into a formidable movement against the centuries-old afflictions plaguing humanity. This book is my dedication to you, intended to bolster and support your efforts, even as you may have already made significant strides in this endeavor. Your passionate drive to break the cycle of institutional racism's perpetuation is admirable, and I hope this text serves as a valuable ally for Black Gen Z's journey towards self-improvement and social change.

To Black Gen Z, much has been taken from you throughout history, and you cannot afford to waver in your determination. While every generation of the White and Yellow communities in the West and Asia, respectively, has enjoyed ample opportunities, Africa has often not provided the same support and has constrained your prospects. The

burden of self-renewal falls squarely on your shoulders. Your commitment to a renaissance mindset, one that emphasizes self-awareness, will propel you into the Generation WHY and connect you with your global Gen Z family. Remember that everyone possesses potential beyond their circumstances, but words alone will not suffice.
I dedicate this book to you especially with the hope that you can overcome Africa's historical propensity to surrender. Africa has a long history of yielding to external pressures, and this surrendering mentality has hindered its growth and empowerment. Africa's habitual surrendering mentality has not contributed positively to humanity's well-being.

Africa's inability to stand up and fight is a reflection of its collective self-consciousness marked by complacency, laziness, and cowardice. Historically, Africa surrendered to slavery, colonialism, and institutional racism. This surrendering mentality has had a lasting negative impact on Black individuals worldwide.

To address this ongoing issue, this book is dedicated to inspiring a break from Africa's surrendering mentality. Unfortunately, Africa's self-consciousness, rooted in complacency, laziness, and cowardice, has been sustained by hereditary traditions that promote patronization, subservience, and preordination. These traditions perpetuate the cycle of disempowerment and disenfranchisement, leaving Black communities vulnerable to the whims of White and Yellow descendants.

To heal and break free from this cycle, we must recognize that Africa's hereditary hierarchical despotic tradition is at the core of the problem. It perpetuates the self-consciousness of laziness and cowardice, leading to enslavement, colonization, institutional racism, and ultimately self-surrender. This tradition has resulted in Black individuals being disempowered, humiliated, degraded, and traumatized across generations.

To usher in a healing process, we require a new generation of youth, a Generation WHY, particularly those within the Black community. This necessitates the emergence of successive generations of resolute Black Gen WHY-PPs. It calls for a generational commitment, and this very well could be embodied by Gen Z, who are poised to elevate themselves to Gen WHY, or if you will, Gen WHY-PP. This transition hinges on an unwavering, unyielding commitment to a Self-Consciousness Mindset that relentlessly asks the crucial question: WHY? These individuals must be prepared to challenge the comforts and transient joys of today, as well as the illusory notion of dignity.

To heal, we urgently require a cohort of young individuals ready to sacrifice their comforts and fleeting happiness. They must be willing to relinquish the ill-gotten gains within their households, the complacency of their impoverishment, the lethargy and cowardice that plagues them. These dedicated souls will forfeit the contentment of accepting misery and dehumanization, and they will reject the servile subservience to the despotic traditions that govern their politics, monarchy, and religious institutions. All this they will surrender for the promise of a brighter tomorrow, characterized by enduring happiness and dignity.

The path to healing demands that Gen WHY sacrifice their present to challenge and reform Africa's Hereditary Hierarchic Despotic Tradition. This deeply rooted tradition is the wellspring of dehumanization and suffering for Black descendants, perpetuated by the sinister triumvirate of Monarchycraft, Politiciancraft, and Priestcraft.

To heal, Gen WHY must dismantle these malevolent forces and their influence over the vulnerable and unknowing masses.

To embark on this healing journey, Gen WHY must cultivate self-awareness and contemplate the question: What do we owe ourselves and the generations that follow us?

To heal, Gen WHY must embrace the concept of Paused Parenthood, elevating themselves to Gen WHY-PP. This means building a robust economic foundation, accumulating wealth, and gaining control over their environment before embarking on parenthood. Only by securing their own future can they ensure that Black kind descendants continue to prosper for generations to come, ad infinitum.

To heal, Gen WHY must willingly make sacrifices to contribute something that all of humanity can savor and appreciate.

In this endeavor, "Generation WHY's Perdition redemptive verses" may prove to be an invaluable ally, a source of unfathomable support and guidance on the path to healing and transformation.

INTRODUCTION

It is an inherent truth that every child born on planet Earth arrives devoid of predispositions concerning timing, gender, parental identity, race, geographic location, or surroundings, devoid of any predisposition whatsoever. During their early stages of self-awareness, they embrace and flourish within the distinct characteristics of their respective environments. As they mature, they begin to pose profound cognitive queries, often entrusted to responsible and nurturing parenting, provided such parenting is not lacking or devoid of guidance.

The African child matures amid the familiar embrace of an environment characterized by a lack of urbanization, infrastructure, and basic amenities, or at best, a state of disrepair. Yet, they exhibit a dignified and innocent resilience. They have accepted this as their norm: homes constructed from thatch and mud cement plaster, reliance on candlelight and darkness, the presence of filth and refuse, dependence on pit latrines and open-air facilities, the constant presence of flies and mosquitoes. They trek for kilometers to access water sources, gather firewood, attend schools, visit markets, and seek healthcare at deteriorated facilities. They journey to places of worship, passing by oracular shrines and the gated, isolated mansions of politicians, monarchs, priests, and elders, often finding the elderly relaxing in the shade of trees. This enduring familiarity remains constant across generations, seemingly frozen in time and space.

No inquiries are permitted, nor should they be contemplated, until these young minds inadvertently encounter the extraordinary, which stands in stark contrast to their everyday environment. These extraordinary elements encompass houses, kindergartens, schools, clinics, libraries, paved streets adorned with trees, and modern amenities like toilets, refuse bins, generators, boreholes, and cars. These luxuries often reside within the confines of Government Reserved Areas (GRAs) or in the Western neighborhoods, homes to some of their peers. It's at this juncture that their self-awareness is piqued, leading to the contemplation of the "whys" behind these disparities. However, more often than not, the answers are either silently absorbed or met with reproach from the elders, monarchs, politicians, and priests.

For the teenage members of Generation Z in Africa, the smartphones they hold in their hands serve as a unifying force, enabling them to connect, evolve, and engage on social platforms. These devices bridge the geographical and cultural gaps between their familiar surroundings and the exceptional norms of the Western world. This generation possesses a heightened self-awareness that allows them to recognize the profound influence of Western norms, as portrayed and perceived through social media.

As their self-awareness continues to develop, they find the autonomy to analyze and rationalize without feeling the need to pose questions that might be met with complicit silence or resignation from traditional authorities such as monarchs, elders, politicians, and religious figures. They intern these figures in their own minds. It is a deeply troubling and profoundly tragic experience for a young person to stifle their curiosity and refrain from asking the fundamental "whys" that naturally arise in their quest for understanding.

When, by some twist of fate, an adult from his homeland, burdened by frustration, helplessness, and the trauma of abject despair, manages to traverse the formidable Sahara desert and treacherous Mediterranean Sea, eventually finding himself on the streets of the Western world, his self-awareness is profoundly shaken. Overwhelmed and bewildered, he grapples with a tumultuous mix of shame, humiliation, and an intrinsic inferiority complex. In this moment, he recognizes that what he once regarded as exceptional back home is, in reality, a starkly inferior version of the Western way of life.

As he contends with the trauma, shame, and confusion while pondering the root causes of his homeland's failures, his clouded self-awareness struggles to comprehend the significance of Western exceptionalism. The sheer abundance and empathy of this new environment leave him astounded. It's not just the inventions or innovations; it's the pervasive sense of communal prosperity. Everything exudes affluence—the buses, trains, cars, roads, electric energy, piped water, cooking gas in every residence, hospitals providing healthcare for all, schools and universities accessible to everyone, meticulously manicured gardens and parks, orderly streets, and the joyous expressions on people's faces. It's a remarkable spectacle, where everyone appears draped in opulence. This, he realizes, must be the epitome of national wealth.

And like countless generations of African youths before him, he surrenders to the overwhelming allure of it all. His self-awareness yields to the transcendent reality before him, leaving him with the profound question: Where does one even begin to comprehend and aspire to such a transformation?

So much so that, like generations of African Youths before him, as he walks the streets strewn with statues of conquerors–the looters, the pillagers, the scum – responsible for the dehumanization and humiliation and the object surrendering permanence self-consciousness of his Black kind, look at the museums housing their African trophies, he could not read the signs and the signified of the blank unwelcoming stare of competing and conflicting emotions of scorn, smile, hate, empathy, compassion, indifference, derision writhed in the faces of his Western host. His primitive self-consciousness could not, like the litany of generations before him, read the signs and the signified on those staring blank faces. He could not read, like generations of African Youths before him that those staring blank faces express one thing: scorn and derision for the incapableness of Black kind self-consciousness. That expression is indistinctively universally reserved, for any Black kind, regardless of your status acquired, rich or poor–refugee, immigrant, resident, a citizen or a Superstar, a scientist, an intellectual, an African president, Politician, Monarchy, Priest– in the western environment. The stupidity of laziness and of cowardice of his self-consciousness cannot read the sign and the signified of "your self-consciousness has not produced anything mankind can enjoy" expressed by the starring blank faces as he is intent on surrendering.

Against the backdrop of Africa's perplexing self-awareness, characterized by an inability to decipher the nuances between signs and signified meanings, the Western hosts transition from initially enigmatic expressions to a more straightforward and explanatory language. This communicative shift aligns with the limited understanding inherent in Africa's self-consciousness, as the Western hosts unabashedly employ the derogatory term, the "N-word." However, irrespective of how boldly this word is used, it holds no symbolic significance or meaning within Africa's self-awareness.

Nevertheless, the use of the "N" word could only truly resonate with someone of biracial heritage. The audacity of a compassionate and thoughtful young White individual, Tom Bradley, a 16-year-old from a KKK-affiliated family, to challenge his peer and family friend, Mezzi George, a biracial youth of equal intelligence and part of the same Gen Z generation, by hurling the hurtful and hateful "N" slur at him had an immediate and profound impact. It stirred a self-awareness that had long slumbered in indifference, far removed from the connotations and implications of the "N" word, as it was a preposterous falsehood when applied to someone of biracial identity. How could one dare to invalidate the identity, traumatize the self-worth, and challenge the pride of a biracial individual? Nevertheless, the damage was done.

It took the boldness of uttering the "N" word towards a biracial person for their self-awareness to comprehend the one-drop rule, recognizing that they are rejected by half of their White heritage. It took the audacity of using the "N" word towards a biracial person for their self-awareness to grasp that White privilege excludes them within the context of their biracial identity. It took the raw honesty of the "N" word for the biracial members of the Gen Z generation to confront the complex reality within the spectrum of human diversity.

The unvarnished use of the "N" word required courage, but it also prompted Mezzi's self-awareness to confront an inescapable reality: within the family of the human species, the very essence of humanity was eroded when individuals with White pigmentation dehumanized those with Black pigmentation through the mechanisms of enslavement, colonialism, and enduring institutional racism. These oppressive systems, designed to perpetually loot, exclude, and exploit Black generations, have cast a long shadow over the shared history of humanity.

The unreserved use of the "N" word compelled Mezzi's self-awareness to grasp the identity of the purveyor of dehumanization. It became clear to him that a portion of his own heritage belonged to the lineage of those responsible for this dehumanization. These individuals have long existed within the cocoon of luxurious denial, hypocrisy, complacency, silence, and the arrogance of perpetuating enslavement, colonization, and institutional racism. This cycle has empowered their descendants, enabling them to continue unceasingly looting their other half, the Black community, generation after generation, in a profoundly unjust manner.

The unflinching use of the "N" word prompted Mezzi's self-awareness to recognize the targeted group: the Black kind. He understood that the Black kind had been subjected to dehumanization, depersonalization, and objectification, enduring a persistent state of phobic neurosis resulting from the legacies of enslavement, colonialism, and institutional racism. Mezzi also came to realize that he is an integral part of the Black kind and that the use of the "N" slur serves as a painful reminder of his connection to this history of suffering and injustice.

The unvarnished use of the "N" word pushed his self-awareness from the confines of the Gen Z generation to the contemplative realm of Gen WHY. It compelled him to grasp a profound realization: despite the suffering imposed upon the Black community, there exists a bewildering paradox—a self-inflicted denial of self-enslavement, self-colonialism, and self-imposed institutionalized misery. This self-denial disempowers subsequent generations and perpetuates their subjugation to the peers of the very individuals who initially inflicted this suffering, generation after generation.

The unapologetic use of the "N" slur forced Mezzi's self-awareness to come to terms with a sobering truth: his own father, a Black billionaire and African oligarch, who paradoxically contributes to the perpetuation of poverty in Africa, personifies and embodies the self-enslavement, self-colonization, self-dehumanization, institutionalized self-looting, and disempowerment of Black communities and their descendants.

Thanks to the rise and revolutionary impact of social media, with its unparalleled capacity for disseminating information and facilitating communication, the dark legacies of slavery, colonialism, and institutionalized racism can no longer be hidden or obscured anywhere in the world. The profound injustices and dehumanization suffered by the Black community are thrust into the spotlight on social media platforms, particularly among the Gen Z generation.

Mezzi comes to a stark realization: he cannot escape the truth. Above all, he comprehends that his comfortable existence has been sustained by the ongoing suffering in Africa. Overwhelmed by an unbearable sense of shame, his life takes a somber turn. The privileges and pride he derived from exclusive institutions, top-tier education, high-quality healthcare, private yachts, airplanes, upscale residences in Western society—all lose their significance. In fact, the weight of it all becomes an indelible and shameful burden.

Driven by an urgent need for answers, for an understanding of the "WHYs" and "WHY NOTs," Mezzi embarks on a journey to the heartland of Africa, where his brother Buzzo, already there as part of the USA Youth Corps services at 21 years of age, serves as a guiding compass for his quest to find meaningful answers within the African context.

In his African homeland, the true meanings and implications of the "N" word become starkly evident to him. The human tragedy of injustice is laid bare, and the pervasive misery is palpable. The dehumanization he witnesses is not only heart-wrenching but also deeply unsettling. The legacies of enslavement, self-enslavement, colonization, self-colonization, institutional racism, and institutionalized self-exploitation into Western banks and environments are abhorrent, repulsive, and morally reprehensible. They exhaust every conceivable form of dehumanization.

Mezzi reflects on how Africa's dehumanization, particularly its self-dehumanization, is an indescribably embarrassing stain on the concept of humanity itself.

To Mezzi, what is even more distressing than the tragedy itself is the apparent unconsciousness, the paralysis, and the acceptance within Africa's self-awareness of its own dehumanization and self-dehumanizing patterns. It's a sobering realization that makes him deeply appreciative of Tom Bradley's courageous candor in using the "N" slur, as it served as a catalyst for awakening and awareness.

The fact that an entire continent, encompassing the entirety of African youth, seems to remain indifferent despite the buzz and the ever-evolving information landscape of social media platforms, to which they are intimately connected, where humanity strives to recover its lost essence. This global Gen Z movement, which seeks to unite people as one social family and instill in them the inherent spirit of collectivism, serves as a vessel for rediscovering essential human values – values such as compassionate empathy, the principle of "love thy neighbor as thyself," and the idea of "having one another's back."

The fact that these values are not only being rekindled but are also reaching new heights rather than simply garnering reactions implies that the self-awareness of African youth may be mired in a state of phobic neurosis. Even more troubling, it suggests a profound state of Object Surrendering Permanence, where the essence of their self-consciousness remains locked in a state of surrender and acquiescence.

In a nutshell, the self-awareness of Africa's youth requires activation and empowerment. The self-consciousness of Africa's Gen Z is currently underdeveloped, characterized by timidity, subservience, and a lack of assertiveness. Furthermore, any attempts to express doubt, anger, excitement, passion, questions, or challenges are systematically and heavily suppressed, forbidden, and prohibited. This suppression reflects the stranglehold and enslavement imposed by Africa's authoritarian traditions.

So with unwavering heroism, boundless enthusiasm, and a profound commitment to self-sacrifice, self-reflection, and empathy, Mezzi and Buzzo meticulously craft their blueprint for the revitalization of Africa, which consists of four essential and foundational components or verses:

1. Gen Z must be educated and empowered to self-educate, thereby reshaping the underdeveloped self-awareness prevalent among African youth. This transformation involves introducing them to a mindset that values the dynamics of ideas over stagnation, encouraging them to think critically rather than rely on rote memorization. It entails fostering independent critical thinking and analysis, as well as cultivating the courage to confront their suffering and question the norms underpinning African dehumanization, ultimately paving the way for a paradigm shift. In essence, Africa's Gen Z must swiftly transition from a stagnant self-consciousness to a self-awareness characterized by a renaissance spirit—one that constantly seeks answers to the "WHYs" and "WHY NOTs." In conclusion, the most pressing imperative of our time is for Africa's Gen Z to evolve into Gen WHY, not just for their own generation but for the generations of African youth to come, in perpetuity.

In this endeavor, Mezzi and Buzzo initiate a cognitive transformation aimed at healing the phobic neurosis and object surrendering permanence ingrained in the self-awareness of Africa's Gen Z.

Their fervent commitment to educating the mindset of Africa's Gen Z propels their self-awareness towards a point where they can recognize the pervasive misery that plagues their continent. They are encouraged to pose the critical question: "WHY has Africa not contributed anything for generations that humanity can benefit from?"

With an equal fervor, their newly acquired self-awareness yields an indescribable answer deeply rooted in Africa's enduring cycle of profound foolishness marked by laziness and timidity, persisting from one generation to the next.

Africa's profound foolishness, manifested through laziness and cowardice, has resulted in a perpetual state of subjugation for generation after generation. It has subjected Africa to colonization across successive generations, as well as exploitation, exclusion, contempt, fragmentation, disempowerment, humiliation, and ongoing trauma through the enduring framework of institutionalized racism. Africa's profound foolishness has, in fact, orchestrated and facilitated the delivery of institutional racism, perpetuating its own peril and decline.

And to prove this abject stupidity, Africa goes beyond.

How would Africa that's enslaved, self-enslave if not for its stupidity beyondness?

How would Africa that's colonized, self-colonize if not for its stupidity beyondness? How would Africa that's caged by institutional racism self-cage in institutionalized self-looting of its continent if not for its stupidity beyondness?

How could Africa, the cradle of Black civilization, willingly endure external enslavement and engage in self-inflicted subjugation? How could it tolerate external colonization and perpetuate self-colonization? How could it passively accept institutional racism, which exploits, excludes, degrades, traumatizes, disempowers, and dehumanizes its people for generations, without recognizing the magnitude of these injustices? If not for an inexplicable acceptance of these circumstances, one might expect individuals who have endured slavery, colonialism, and institutional racism to unite against dehumanization. However, tragically, they often embrace and perpetuate the very tyrannies that have oppressed them and their descendants. In essence, Africa finds itself trapped in a cycle of self-destruction, a profound tragedy that defies comprehension.

As the African Generation Z, benefiting from the guidance of biracial mentors, attains a heightened cognitive self-awareness, they finally grasp the fundamental aspects of their suffering. Overwhelmed by a profound sense of shame and dismay, they confront Africa's ongoing decline and the self-imposed dehumanization it entails.

With an urgent determination to break free from the cycle of seeking solutions from a continent that, generation after generation, has remained ensnared in self-dehumanization, incapable of realizing its full potential, they step into a new era of self-awareness - Generation WHY. Here, they explore the depths of the "WHYs" and "WHY NOTs" within their domain with a sense of purpose and inquiry.

To move past the identified drama of Africa's perdition, Mezzi and Buzzo pass to the next verse of their blue print:

2. Generation Y faces the imperative task of confronting and dismantling Africa's deeply entrenched state of intellectual inertia. In this confrontation, they recognize that Africa's intellectual stagnation finds its roots in an inherited hierarchical and despotic tradition, one that preordains condescension and feigned subservience, shackling its people in a state of profound intellectual stagnation dictated by archaic and primitive norms.

As they endeavor to challenge and reform Africa's hereditary tradition of hierarchical preordination, liberating the masses from the preordained shackles of obsequiousness and subservience, and dismantling the abhorrent status quo of Africa's dehumanizing patronization and condescension, they encounter the stubborn resistance, vanity, arrogance, conceit, and violence wielded by those in power. This starkly illustrates the truth of the aphorism that "despotism despises nothing so much as righteousness in its victims."

The unwavering determination of Generation Y to challenge, reshape, and transcend the arrogant stronghold of Africa's prevailing power structure remained unbroken. Rather, it fortified their commitment and capitalized on their early maturation in assuming responsibility. The pressing need for swift progress propelled them to a daunting yet noble realization: they must rely on themselves for support.

In stark contrast, Africa stands alone as the only continent that has consistently failed to provide support for its Black descendants across generations. In contrast, the Western world supports its White descendants, while Asia stands by its Yellow descendants.

The recurring failure to provide consistent support for Black descendants, regardless of where they reside across generations, underscores an enduring issue rooted in Africa's historical pattern of indolence and timidity, perpetuated from one generation to the next. To ensure their self-reliance, Africa must take the crucial step of "contributing something mankind can enjoy." Achieving this contribution hinges on Africa's ability to address and rectify its longstanding state of intellectual stagnation.

To initiate this healing process and break free from the shackles of recognized intellectual inertia, the members of Generation WHY in Africa must confront and ultimately conquer this challenge.

Unfazed, they fearlessly confronted, without distinction, the advocates, proponents, and the malevolent trinity - Monarchycraft, Politiciancraft, and Priestcraft - along with the individuals ensnared in Africa's hereditary hierarchical despotic tradition. This tradition perpetuated condescension, intellectual inertia, idleness, and timidity. It was marked by religious paralysis, fostering obsequiousness and servility, which in turn fueled phobic neurosis and a perpetual cycle of self-enslavement, self-colonization, and institutionalized self-exploitation, leading to the drain of resources into Western banks and societies. This cycle has left Africa in a state of despair, desperation, tribulation, trauma, and disempowerment, impacting her descendants for generations.

Reforming any autocrat poses an insurmountable challenge, and the African status quo appears to be entrenched beyond redemption. However, their efforts yielded an unexpected outcome in the form of the first family. President's sons, Mark and David, rallied their fellow Gen Z family members to embrace Africa's Gen WHY renaissance, fostering a newfound self-awareness. Remarkably, the President himself underwent a psychological transformation, aligning with their cause. To demonstrate his commitment, he took decisive action against the Priestcraft, holding them accountable for societal moral decay. This involved the closure of numerous places of worship, the confiscation of wealth amassed through tithes, redistributing these assets to congregants, and mandating theological education and graduation as prerequisites for priesthood. Furthermore, he oversaw the opening and supervision of all places of worship.

The President's unexpected departure from the Status Quo has sent shock waves through all corners, leaving the Status Quo itself in a state of confusion, as they perceive the President's actions as a betrayal. Meanwhile, the African Gen WHY generation is both perplexed and cautiously optimistic about this surprising turn of events. However, they maintain a healthy dose of suspicion, guarding against the possibility of sabotage and the derailment of their aspirations.

In an equally surprising countermove, a powerful trio of figures has thrown their support behind one of their own, namely the Priestcraft. They are taking the President's actions seriously, viewing them as a precursor to impending challenges. Notably, their influential political patron, Mr. Donald George, an oligarchic and biased African billionaire, and the father of Buzzo and Mezzi, has taken the lead in rallying the Status Quo on the Plaza hill, staging a protest aimed at removing the President, despite their familial ties. Their goal is to quash any ambitions of Gen WHY and eliminate this emerging movement in its infancy.

This entire scenario appears both astonishing and surreal to Gen WHY. The internal strife within the Status Quo validates the President's stance and could mark the beginning of the end for the perennial issues that have plagued Africa's youth, including degradation, humiliation, and a bleak future. It has inspired them to stand firm, and in a flash, they united on social media platforms and swiftly gathered on Plaza Hill in a counter-protest, fueled by determination and hope.

Plaza Hill serves as an exquisite platform for Gen WHY to eloquently highlight their predicament: the need for separation. Here, they firmly assert that the Status Quo's protest, in response to the rare opportunity for reconciliation, reform, and understanding with their descendants, inadvertently endorses and legitimizes their call for separation. This separation signifies the detachment of the once-dormant Gen Z, their offspring, from the established Status Quo.

The apparent success in thwarting the Status Quo's attempt to remove the President and the resolute assertion of separation on Plaza Hill significantly bolstered Gen WHY's self-esteem and their commitment to preserving their identity. It was at this juncture that Gen WHY firmly embraced their newfound freedom, which formed the cornerstone of their determination and self-worth.

The remarkable success achieved by Gen WHY sparked genuine excitement among its members. To such an extent that their unwavering self-awareness unconsciously disregarded the fragility of their non-existent economic and wealth foundation. In taking their separation with unapologetic determination, they boldly declared their self-sufficiency. They shifted their focus away from questioning what previous generations owed them and instead pondered their responsibilities to their own generation and those of their descendants.

The President, buoyed by their resolve and recognizing the need for change, took significant steps to acknowledge and support their efforts. He issued a decree mandating rigorous accountability for every politician, government employee, and businessman, linking wealth to possession and lifestyle. This decree unleashed a storm of reactions and responses across the nation.

Paraphrasing, it is said that nothing flatters vanity or confirms obstinacy in kings, in a despot, in positions of power more than lamentations, petitioning, pleading.

Indeed, their resolve grew even stronger. Africa's deeply entrenched tradition of hereditary and hierarchical despotism vehemently opposed Gen WHY's quest for separation, responding with violence. Tragically, a significant number of Gen WHY family members on Plaza Hill were killed, decimated, and left with life-altering injuries. Despite this horrifying incident, they persisted.

Gathered on the Plaza of the People's Republic, where they continued to celebrate their achievements, condemn the status quo, and applaud the President's courage, they prepared for the impending day of reckoning—a mandatory accountability of the entire system.

To the collective shock and disbelief of everyone, Gen WHY may have stumbled momentarily, but they did not falter. Africa had long been devoid of any significant revolution, but they drew unwavering inspiration from Victor Hugo's words: "No army can withstand the force of an idea whose time has come." In the midst of their struggle, they came to a subconscious realization that they had crossed the Rubicon. Gen WHY had paid the ultimate price, and the deed was done. To overcome and eliminate their predicament, any other sacrifices along their path could only be considered secondary.

This takes them to the next verse on the ladder of their blue print:

3. Gen WHY's Imperative Penultimate Sacrifice

Gen WHY fully grasps the pressing need to self-reliantly safeguard not only their own future but also the prospects of generations to come. They understand that to secure their own future, they must lay the foundation of their economic and wealth base.

The pivotal principle they must embrace can be distilled into one resounding truth: the penultimate act of unwavering sacrifice, a testament to the same unwavering determination exhibited on Plaza Hill—a sacrifice of unparalleled magnitude upon which Africa's future hinges.

Gen WHY must willingly embrace self-denial as their chosen path, a path that promises to heal Africa and bestow empowerment upon Gen WHY and their descendants for generations to come, an unending legacy of self-reliance and prosperity.

Their unalloyed self-conscious mindset demands a resolute sacrifice of their present comforts, fleeting happiness, and illusory dignity. This sacrifice extends to letting go of the comfort derived from ill-gotten wealth, the comfort found in poverty, misery, laziness, and cowardice. It entails relinquishing the complacency born from suffering and dehumanization, as well as shedding the comfort that comes from subservience to despotic political, monarchical, and religious traditions.

This sacrifice is necessary for the promise of a better tomorrow, one characterized by lasting happiness and dignity. To initiate the healing process, Gen WHY must sacrifice in order to construct a solid economic and wealth foundation, mastering their environment before considering parenthood. They must adopt the ethos of "Pause Parenthood" - Gen WHY-PP - elevating their own self-reliance as the essential prerequisite for supporting their future generations, generation after generation.

Also, even after achieving self-sufficiency, Gen WHY-PP must recognize the importance of not viewing their children as possessions. They should refrain from expanding their families beyond the capacity of existing resources, ensuring that their children can thrive without overextending those resources.

Their efforts garnered them two significant categories of allies: the African Status Quo President and their Gen Z counterpart, Tom Bradley, representing two vital facets of validation. The President, influenced by their audacity, courage, and unwavering resolve, perceives them as a formidable force that not even the combined intelligence agencies—KGB, CIA, MOSSAD, MI5, DGSE, the Tewu, and others—can undermine, subvert, or defeat in their mission to elevate Africa from its entrenched state of misery.

In contrast, Tom Bradley draws inspiration from Mezzi's endeavors on the African front. He played a key role in organizing massive protests on Western streets, echoing the "Black Lives Matter" movement, and relentlessly propelling momentum forward in the aftermath of countless injustices against Black individuals, epitomized by figures like George Floyd. He confronts the deep-seated legacies of slavery, colonialism, and institutional racism from within, driven by an audacious ambition to eradicate these injustices, seek atonement, demand reparations, and ultimately eliminate them.

In response, the African Gen Z, known as Gen WHY, express deep gratitude for the global Gen Z community's international display of empathy and support, exemplifying their collective commitment to addressing and rectifying these issues on a global scale.

In response, the African Gen Z, referred to as Gen WHY, express profound gratitude for the international Gen Z community's global outpouring of empathy and support. This display serves as a testament to their shared commitment to addressing and rectifying these pervasive issues on a worldwide scale.

However, as the African Gen WHY family grapples with the enduring challenges of institutional racism abroad and institutional self-exploitation at home, they remain cautious not to harbor the illusion that the recent wave of compassionate empathy exhibited by the global Gen Z community on Western streets alone will suffice to eradicate the dehumanization of Black individuals and deliver justice. History has shown that privilege often resists sharing, and human empathy, being inherently transient, tends to pass through phases of hypocrisy, temporariness, and contemptuousness before fading away. It seldom withstands the test of time.

The Gen WHY of Black descent are firmly convinced that they must play an essential role by dedicating themselves to hard work and sacrifice, thus contributing to the healing and empowerment of the global youth community. Through their own determined efforts and contributions, they believe they can ultimately eradicate institutional racism and institutional self-exploitation, ensuring that Africa supports and uplifts Black descendants worldwide.

As they navigate the audacious task set forth by their informed and ambitious renaissance creed, fueled by self-awareness, they astutely cultivate their economic and wealth foundation through the practice of crowdfunding. They perceive this approach as remarkably ingenious. Indeed, each succeeding generation of Black youth, guided by the collective ethos of Gen Z, acknowledges their success in crowd-funding, achieved through their rejection of complacency, indolence, and timidity, which has propelled individuals in positions of authority—be it in religious, political, or monarchical realms—into the realm of billionaires.

While collaborating closely with their newfound ally, the President, in refining the details of their blueprint into a pragmatic manifesto—dubbed

"Gen WHY's African Perdition Redemptive Verses"—they introduce a fourth fundamental verse:

4. Gen WHY must, having successfully established its economic and wealth foundation, acknowledge the importance of limiting family size to no more than two children. This is essential to ensure that our resources, both psychological and sociological, are not overextended and depleted. This may appear contrary to the ideals of Western democracy as applied in Africa. It might be perceived as authoritarian. However, it's crucial to reconsider the application of Western democracy in our African context, as it has historically failed and will continue to do so. This form of governance has made it easy for Africa to be subjugated, colonized, subjected to institutional racism, and burdened with phobias and a sense of perpetual subservience tailored to fit Africa's self-awareness of the easier path of apathy and idleness.

Africa's tendency to produce children without the means to support them, thereby straining our resources, is the simplest way to perpetuate self-enslavement, self-colonization, and the institutionalization of self-exploitation, thus disempowering our descendants for generations due to our inherent and hereditary hierarchical despotic traditions. Africa seems to have a cynical affinity for the continuation of its natural despotism through the lens of Western democracy, which essentially becomes a despotism in itself—despotism in the guise of democracy.

What we truly need now is a democracy of benevolent enlightened despotism, akin to the model seen in China. Reforming Africa's despotic traditions is the solution. We require a system that enforces mandatory education, healthcare, reliable electricity, clean water, food security, resource value-chain development, discipline, accountability, and clear rights and responsibilities, with consequences for transgressions. Alternatively, we must design a system tailored to our unique needs, demonstrating our capacity for rational self-awareness, rather than succumbing to lower, sub-human instincts.

In Africa, the practice of having children merely for the sake of it must be abandoned. Children are not commodities; they can become a source of suffering, not only for their parents but especially for themselves. Africa's own history provides ample evidence of this truth. Life and procreation should be guided by the principle of quality over quantity. An excess of offspring leads to self-imprisonment. The quality of our children is paramount, as is the quality of the descendants of the Black community, both essential for Africa's redemption.

To heal humanity, the Black kind must not merely be part of the solution; it must indeed be the solution. The healing of humanity cannot be achieved without the meaningful contribution of the Black kind. However, for the Black kind to make this crucial contribution, Africa itself must undergo a process of healing. To accomplish this, Africa's youth must develop a profound self-awareness of "WHYs and WHY NOTs."

To heal the Black community and empower its descendants through successive generations, Africa's Gen Z must cultivate a self-awareness akin to that of Gen WHY. They must produce and nurture a continuous lineage of Gen WHY youths, endlessly and unwaveringly committed to themselves, unyielding in their dedication to hard work, resolute in their sacrifices, and steadfast in their determination to cleanse Africa's Perdition Redemptive Verses. This transformation will inspire and elevate contributions that mankind can appreciate, enduring and perpetuating them from one generation to the next.

Until this transformation occurs, dehumanization perpetrated by one group upon their own within the human family will persist, unabated and even celebrated.

Until then, the healing of humanity remains an elusive goal.

VOLUME I
THE PERDITION

Chapter I

The expansive, sixteen-years-old Mezzi, grand, heroic, exuberant, optimist, virulently in love with his country, the United States of America, of known vibrant multiculturalism, suddenly becomes a recluse, virulently despondent. His love for his country took a dark turn, transiting from initial shock to disappointment, annoyance, irritation, disillusionment, indifference, disgust, anger, and ultimately, hatred.

His family, well aware of their hate-filled, vile and racist society is however, thrown aback and somewhat berserk, trying to understand and dig deep and figure out what would have happened.

Mezzi, out there in a remarkable private college graduation party, amidst the sons and daughters of the creme of the cream and the juices of society, his companions, has had an altercation with his best friend over an apparent non-issue: the sexuality, the sexual habits, and the femininity of white girls compared to non-whites. The argument degenerated into a fall-out of jealousy, and out of spite of sheer conscientiousness of racism and its evil of willful smear and heart-will perpetration and perpetuation, had his remarkably ethereal girlfriend, white, Jenny into focus:

Tom (tipsy almost overboard): Mezz, you are just having fun frolicking around my sisters. Not black girls, your kind. I don't find it fair. My race doesn't find it fair!

Mezzi (surprised, almost in mumbles): What...?

Tom: Why won't you go for those your lecherous ...yes those your over-sexed black sisters, who they say are perverse in bed, animals in a zoo, crazed with lust, making children at 12, 13 for their Nigger genitors?

Mezzi: Drunk! Totally drunk! I see you got a quintessential problem. Why don't you go catch some sleep, you inhibited repressed hateful jealous fool?

Tom: Yeah, I have a problem with that. Back in the days this could not have happened. A Nsigger fucking a White? Not even a White whore. The most excruciating remarkable Nigger Lynching Fit would have been it.

Jenny shocked, recoils.
Mezzi, in a flash lands a remarkable blow on Tom Bradly's face.
He screams, ducking subsequent blows from Mezzi.
Fellow boys intervene quickly holding and restraining Mezzi.
Jenny screams. Mortified.
Heads turn, surprised. The crowd mills. Builds.

Tom has blood gushing out of his mouth. He is rushed out for first aid. Sobbing Jenny, grabs Mezzi and they take their leave.

Chapter 2

We find Mezzi ponderously bruised. Remarkably re-dimensioned in his dignity, pride, offended in honor, in beliefs, in credo and in values.

His friend Tom, his human kind has made him understand the existence of human kinds-the White kind, the Black kind and the Yellow kind. The fallout brings him a letter:

Nigger!

You have private airplanes, yachts, fleet of exotic cars, innumerable high-brow properties here in the western capitals and beaches, best schools and over spilling western bank accounts and yet…you are a Nigger!

Your dad, like a director of orchestra, is orchestrating and remarkably directing African politics, African crude oil and mineral wealth businesses and the combined religious business symphonies of the churches, mosques and fetishism. Famishing his people, under-developing the entire continent. Denying them of freedom. Even the most commonplace freedom-electric energy, pipe borne water, education, health care, food security, basic infrastructure and more.

Your dad, an Al Capone-stylish dude, directing evil orchestra.

For what?

To give you a life style. Your life style equates Africa's deprivation. Africa's misery.

And yet, for the irony, the absurdity and the record: these aren't Nigger's life style.

Nigger, the worth of any human being is not the material wealth but solutions to human problems.

Mr. Rolls Royce, Mr. Mercedes are worth their cars. Mr. Edison, current electricity. Messrs. Boeing, Airbus and their airplanes. You can guess the worth of Mr. Gates, Mr. Jobs, Mr. Zuckerberg, Mr. Buffet and the list is endless.

These have found solutions to enable human lives bearable.

These are our life styles. Find solutions. Just look around you Nigger. Name everything you have, light, pipe borne water, cars, jets, yacht, television sets, telephone sets, music sets, computers, WIFI, Internet, etc. My White race presence is felt everywhere.

This is our White kind life style, that is so commonplace that even our dogs, cats and rats and roaches enjoy them.

As a matter of absurdity, White kind dogs have more dignity and respect than Niggers.

Instead, a nigger's worth is run the voodoo down, run the church down, run the mosque down, run his progenies down, dispossess his people, possess these objects plus the mementoes, the trophies: the fat golden chains and shiny diamonds and the drum beats and voila...they feel worthy.

Nigger, that's not it. You should be worth a life style! Not Niggertude life style.

Even though science has proven all humans to be genetically equal, your kind of the mankind remains... a Nigger...a coon...inferior...

Why am I picking on you, Nigger?

You are shrouded in worthlessness of "luxury", yet you are far removed from luxury. No self-indulgence. No over-indulgence. No complacency. You give hope.

You are ruthlessly determined. Ruthlessly growing your intellect into intelligence. Ruthlessly honest and introspective. Ruthlessly truthful. Ruthlessly passionate and humble. You are farsighted. A visionary!

You are shrewd. Quick-witted. Intellectual. Talented. Psychologically strong. Clever! You are rebellious. Dissatisfied. Craving for change and justice!

In sum, you are ambitious.

If this ambition can be ruthless but benevolent...even though, paraphrasing Harriet B. Stowe:

"Eyes that have never wept cannot comprehend sorrow."

...I am confidently betting the honor of my White kind that you will challenge NIGGERTUDE philosophy. And you will figure out why you are a nigger. Quickly too! And much more, I am betting the respect, I repeat, the respect of my White kind that you can figure out how not to be a Nigger. No more!

Earn dignity. Earn world's respect. Excoriate and reject Black kind life style. Get out of the COTTON-PICKING Mind. Reject Nigger Mind-Set. Reject Nigger*tude*.

Lastly, let me help, acquainting you with materials...materials... for the challenge. Your challenge.

(We visualize printed images, documenting historical racial slurs on the Black kind by the hateful Kul Klux Klan, the White Supremacists organ.)

So long.

I remain your best friend in truth. In spirit. Indeed. Devoid of respect. Luvs. Lot of luvs.

Your body,

Tom Bradly.

The above, reprehensibly worded vitriols hit him very hard. He is in unutterable spasm of affliction. The pains are ponderously sorrowing. Even as the authenticity of these vitriols and their truthfulness, from a jealousy afflicted mind, to him is disputable, they mysteriously put him indefensible and denude him at the same time, with equal vigor.

His distraught and inconsolable broken heartedness, in transition, sets his emotions into three-way remarkable, distinct but competing, compulsiveness of drives contemplation: compulsive drive for a ruthless revenge against a gratuitous inveighs of vilification, or compulsive drive to investigate their authenticity and verify their truthfulness, or their invalidity and then rebuttals. Which?

> *Nigger, you have private airplanes, yachts, fleet of exotic cars, innumerable high-brow properties in the western cities and beaches, best schools and over spilling western bank account and yet...you are a Nigger!*
> *Your dad, like a director of orchestra, orchestrating and remarkably directing... African business symphonies... Famishing his people, under-developing the entire continent. Denying them of freedom. Even the most commonplace freedoms: electric energy, pipe borne water, education, health care, food security, basic infrastructure...to give you a life style.*
> *Your life style equates Africa's deprivation. Africa's misery.*
> *And yet, for the irony, the absurdity and for the records: these aren't Nigger's life style.*
> *...Nigger, that's not it. You should be worth a life style! Not Niggertude life style.*
> *Nigger, the worth of any human being is not the material wealth but solutions to humanity's problems. Putting smile on humanity's face!*

Mezzi, miserably sullen, totally immersed in his conflicting and competing compulsive-drive thoughts, leisurely in his virulent idiosyncrasy and eccentricity, wizardry in Apps conceptualizations and the social media blogging, is busy checking out and running images of black history, their humiliation referenced to by Tom Bradley: Slavery, Colonialism, America's Civil War of Liberation of the Slaves, 3/5th Compromise, the Lynching, the march for civil rights, the assassinations of Malcom X, and then of Martin Luther King, the stereotyping, the ostracization, the racial profiling, the consequent incurable PHOBIC NEUROSIS, that he did not hear the incessant knockings on his door.

> *Why am I picking on you, Nigger?*
> *Nigger, I am confidently betting the honor of my White kind that you*
> *will challenge NIGGERTUDE philosophy. And you will figure out why*
> *you are a NIGGER. Quickly too!*
> *And much more, I am betting the respect, I repeat, the respect of my*
> *White kind that you can figure out how not to be a Nigger. No more!*
> *Nigger gain respect!*

Even as the door is forced open, he did not express any surprise. Instead, he forces a smile welcoming his dad with gusts of "Nigger" questions:

Mezzi: Dad, what is a Nigger? Who is a Nigger? Is every black man a Nigger? The black Doctor, the black Architect, the black Engineer? The black Senator, black President, the black Governor? The black music and sports celebrities, black business leaders? Even the black Pastors, spiritual and civil right leaders?

Dad, even the Blackman with private jets, upscale houses, Rolls-Royce, Rolex, Philip Patek?

Why are we called Niggers dad? Why do we live out Nigger*tude* philosophy? Every black kind is a Nigger?

Now he pauses briefly waiting for his dad to answer. The answers seem swallowed by his face, frowning disdain. Then he continues asking.

Mezzi: Dad, why is the White kind not a Nigger?

Why is the Yellow kind not a Nigger? Dad, are you a Nigger? Am I a Nigger?

He seemed possessed by multiple sclerosis: all attempts by his father, who meanwhile has reached him, to calm him down, to stop him, failed. He continues.

Mezzi: Dad, meet my eyes. Are you a Nigger?

Dad (holding stare): I am not a Nigger, son. You are not a Nigger. Only the African-American is a Nigger!

Mezzi: What?

Numbed at the last phrase of affirmation of his Father, utterly disappointed and mortified, he forlornly smirks, disengaging his stare off him.

Then he is assailed. Assailed by a spasm of unutterable cold rage, he ri-engages his stare, fixing his dad with a numbing lunacy, battling with his predatory affirmation. An affirmation that is, at the same time, a willful distortion and a gratuitous denigration. An affirmation that swallowed answers and spitted cringing cowardice. An affirmation that seems to give reason to Negro vilifications. An affirmation, to these extents, that dispelled doubts and decided for his compulsive drive to investigate authenticity, verify truthfulness of the vilifications and help shape rebuttals. The Nigger Rebuttals.

And without derailing, he steers on the course of his discourse.

Mezzi: Why Dad? You fit in this hyperbole man. Dad you are Negro. African-American is Negro. And yet you are all Niggers? You are not respected. We are not respected.

Why is the White kind respected?

And the White kind's dogs and cats and pets have more dignity, honor, respect than Niggers? Why is a nigger not respected?

Why is the African continent famished and in perpetual misery?

Why and how does my life style equate to their despair, peril and tribulations?

How does a Nigger gain respect?

Dad, you gain respect by killing the African continent…bonding them in misery?

Dad, who are you? I mean you say, you are a businessman?

What do you manufacture? I mean, we have all these monies, all these "affluence"…yet we are Niggers? You are not respected. I am not respected. No dignity…you are a coon! How would a Nigger gain respect?

Then in a flash, his father grabs him. He reacts, wrestling himself free, off him and continuing:

Dad I need answers. You are not answering me. You have no honor. You have no dignity. You have no respect. And right here, right now you are compulsively lying to me distorting and denigrating African-Americans, on their lone giant strides to freedom, in their unfortunate history caused by betrayal, slavery, abandonment legacy at the hands of Africans like us, to this day generations after generations.

He breaks down, crying and in mumbles to himself:

This is real. I don't mean nothing. We don't mean nothing. We are shit. We are evil. Useless. That's being a Nigger. We are Niggers!

With a diabolic strength, he grabs the TV set, hauls it towards his father, who ducks, dodging it, and hurriedly exits the room.

He continued in his rage, transforming his room into a topsy-turvy, throwing, destroying objects, venting his anger and frustrations.

He feels terribly dejected and rejected from without and betrayed from within his house. And in a flash, almost as he started, as if to a realization of a new dawn in his life, he stops.

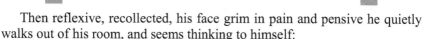

Then reflexive, recollected, his face grim in pain and pensive he quietly walks out of his room, and seems thinking to himself:

What now?

His dad, Mr. George, fifty-ish, a dude of a mixed breed, of a ruthless character - ambitious, greedy, opportunistic, vindictive, professed self-righteous, hypercritical, hypocritical, bigoted, insecure, inferiority complexed, domineering, selfish and cringing love for luxury (self-indulgent, over-indulgent, decadent) - is furiously surprised and remarkably disappointed at his son's show of reprehensible disrespect, appalling and disproportionate gratuitous unappreciation of his life effort. His life effort that has made the most enviable life style for him and his elder brother, Buzzo, to bear in his opinion.

He is only solaced by the thought of hope that the immediate future should bear on him with good sense. The hope that this juvenile senseless outburst of emotions against status quo society, found and anchored in the realm of politics and governance, and tailored in the values of the costume of the African tradition, in its fetishism, in the spirituality of the Pentecostal Churches and African version of Islamic religion, in the spirit of the capitalistic free enterprise, etc., etc., is temporary, short lived, oblivious within its limits of arbitrary conceivableness.

He is absolutely deluded that his boy could openly challenge him, judge him, disrespect him: the world has gone haywire!

All the fault of the social media, where kids want to change the basis and the basics of our existence: Primal instinct. The strongest survives, and now, no concept of tomorrow. It's a now thing.

The world is founded on greed, cheating, gluttony, kleptomania, lies, depredation, subjugation, keep people and perpetuate them in ignorance. What's new about this life?

Mrs. Donna George, Mr. George's wife, Mezzi's and Buzzo's mom, is a White kind, late forty-ish. She is a bigot-conformist, unimaginative, rigid, formal, courteous, guilt complexed, and luxury loving (self-indulgent, over-indulgent, vain, hypocritical). She is the Chief Operations Director, Third World Development Funds of the United Nations.

She is on duty, in some far away third world country. She reacts with a tempered dismissive preoccupation at the news from home, in her household, of his son's sudden "irrationality" at life. Of his young life.

She made effort at getting in touch with Mezzi to no avail. Regardless, she remained collected with muted dismissive preoccupation.

On day two, Mezzi, beaten and totally subdued, in unutterable sadness and delusion and confusion, gets in touch with mom:

Mezzi: Hi mom, listen to me carefully…

Mom (interrupting): You gone nuts, not picking my calls, picking fight with your father? Are you unconscientious, unconscientious to fight society…?

Mezzi (coldly): Mom I need the key. The key to who really, I am.

Mom: What?

Mezzi: Mom are you not White?

Mom: What?

Mezzi: Mom am I not your child? Am I not your blood? Am I not biracial?

Mom: Where are you? Get back to yourself…get back to the house Mezzi…

Mezzi: Mom, my half gene is called Nigger and…

Mom: Negro, Please!

Mezzi: And what's my other half called, mom?

Mom is slow to answer. She seems numbed!

Mezzi: The key mom. The key (almost sounding off).

Mom (alarmed): What key? Are you…?

Mezzi: The Nigger's key mom.

Mom: The Nigger's key? What's…

Mezzi: Nigger's key to earn respect mom. I know you have it. You all do…

Mom in a sudden spasm of fear, bewildered (almost in mumble to herself): Son's gone berserk.

There is silence on Mezzi's end of the line. The communication gone dead. Phone gone dead. Mom perplexed, looks at her phone. Tries calling back. But in vain. In bewilderment, she gives up trying.

It looks like the gravity of the situation has finally started sinking in.

Days counted, with no news of Mezzi's whereabouts.

The authorities were alerted but their search for Mezzi proved futile.

Finally, after days of what first appeared to be abscondment, she now understood the gravity of the son's psychology.

The family is in a full-blown dilemma. A tragedy unfolding!

Chapter 3

Mezzi has a brother whose name is Buzzo. He is a graduate in Human Health Engineering Science/data-algorithm applications. A promising wizard in his field. He is a 22-years-old Gen Z, whose character is almost a total replica of Mezzi's: ruthlessly ambitious, ruthlessly determined, ruthlessly passionate, fixated on goals, virulently dissatisfied with world's status quo, virulently altruistic, virulent fairness, virulent farsightedness, overtly sharp and quick-witted, shrewd, persuasive, talented, fearlessly adventurous.

The only difference is in temperament: he is a tempered radical.

And in fairness to Mezzi, that comes with age: you can't expect the young with the brain of an experienced Michelangelo.

Like all Gen Z, he is the mirror of the credo and the zealotry of saving the mother planet earth from the hands of the status quo: with the green, green, green-like religious maxim.

Gen Z are presently but quietly building their capital base, hopeful to cash-in on their potentials into reality max 10/15 years from now. Revolutionizing the landscape: build digitalization, power green technologies, empower tech mobility, eliminate elitism and reign collectivity: collective mobility, collective capitalization, collective wealth, collective spending, collective consumption. Quasi an ideal world. Right. No change is ever made without idealism!

It is with this mindset that Buzzo left for Africa. His ancestral troubling land, barely a month ago, within the auspices of the USA youth corps services.

He is totally overwhelmed by Africa's status on this earth just two weeks into Africa corps service. He is taken aback; deleteriously dishonored, reprehensibly shamed by his Black kind: his love for his ancestral homeland transits into disappointment, into annoyance, into irritation, into disillusionment, into disgust, into anger and down to delusion. There is no justification that holds. The distance between his known world, the West and this forsaken place seems unbridgeable. Not even in 1,000 years of White kind's choice of voluntary inactivity. The state of it all: everything is actually sub-human. For sub-humans.

However, being ruthlessly determined, and virulent against the status quo and its liberal state of static, and fixated, altruistic, quick-witted, fearless and all, he is making effort to come to terms with trying to find forgiveness for the African land. Never to terms with Africa's kleptomaniac-glutton-bombastic-hyperbole-evil political, religious, traditional, business, dishonest and gutless unintellectual class. It is in the middle of this mind-boggling pondering that Mezzi calls him out of the blue.

Mezzi: Hello, Brodaman!
Buzzo: Heeeyeeee, brooooodaboy. Finally, …your voice.
Mezzi: Buzz, I am disappointed and totally confused…
Buzzo: Cool, cool. Cool Mezz, I heard everything…the virulent inveigh…the Nigger, the sub-human Black kind…the Nigger*tude* philosophy.
Mezzi: So, what do you think of the shebang?
Buzzo: It's sad. Swallow the bitter truth. Tom Bradley is the best thing that happened to you. Africa is overwhelming. Shocking. Shaming. A sham…
Mezzi: Tom Bradley, that slur of a bitch…
Buzzo: No! He isn't a bitch. Far from it.
Mezzi: How?
Buzzo: Any motherfucker that gets your heart racing, gets your brain thinking is a blessing. There is something cynical, sadist about us. I don't know to what extent it might have to do or not with the word nigger. I find myself in Africa first hand and I can tell you that Africa has not done well, at all. And tragedy is no sign we are even planning to do well. We are reticent about our misery and regression. There is a willful Black commandment against self-reflection, self-critique and the truth. We kick the can. We are not ashamed of it. We deny it generation in generation. Its hardest pill to gulp down and that makes Tom Bradley the best thing ever Mezzi…
Mezzi: You mean there is some truth in the hateful hurtful inveighs of Tom?
Buzzo: Remarkably truthful than truth! The misery is so much and there is no apparent excuse for it, in a continent with abundance of everything.

Then silence on both ends. Deafening predatory silence. Then sound of Mezzi in sobs.

Buzzo: Mezz, I am sorry. I can imagine what you feel.

Another silence. Filled with remarkable unutterable high running emotions with fear of a psychological melt down for his brother, Buzzo breaks the silence almost immediately once again:

Buzzo: Easy Mezz. It's ok! We need to stand up. We need to stand up. We need to stand up to our remarkable reprehensible and despicable heritage.

Those words seem antidotal. In a flash Mezzi finds his voice.

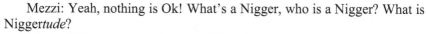

Mezzi: Yeah, nothing is Ok! What's a Nigger, who is a Nigger? What is Nigger*tude*?

Buzzo: A Negro you mean, not a Nigger?

Mezzi: Negro, Nigger it doesn't matter…

Buzzo: It matters. It's like saying the existence of our race does not matter. We are a Negro race. Not a Nigger race. We are defined by Negritude, not by Nigger*tude*. Nigger is a slur contrived. Nigger*tude* a slur conspired. Nigger*tude* is a state of being of a Nigger

Mezzi (impatient): It doesn't matter. Why were they contrived, conspired?

Buzzo: Excellent question. The white supremacist scientists are still short of answers to this day.

Mezzi: The white supremacist scientists?

Buzzo: Yeah, they are yet to conspire compelling reasons for those slurs.

Mezzi: We are biracial, are we not?

Buzzo: Yes Mezz, with half-White kind blood and half of Black kind blood.

Mezzi: How then do we fit in the Nigger code?

Buzzo: Again, the white supremacist scientists are short of answers yet.

Mezzi: Buzzo, you are not helping.

Buzzo: Sure, I am.

Mezzi: Anyway, how does any of them earn respect?

Buzzo: Respect and all? Are you ready to roost? Come visit home?

Mezzi: Yes, yes…yes, yes, yes!

Buzzo: Cool Mezzi. That's the only way you can understand and heal. I love you. Then listen to what I think the earning respect maxim is:

> *"The respect for you the individual, any individual of any tribe-Black, White, Yellow, of the human species is rooted, only rooted in the state of welfare, wellness, wellbeing, development, progress of the sum total, of the entirety of the collective human species, on this planet Earth, wherever they maybe or are found. Not just for your immediate family, children, siblings, relatives."*

Mezzi: Cool! Now you are up to something. Africa has turned you into a philosopher…

Buzzo: No Mezzi. We need to stand up. Africa is desolate than desolation. Africa is desperate than desperation. The state of misery is indescribable. It's palpable. You need to touch it…feel it.

Mezzi: Why is this misery perpetuity generations coming and enduring?

Buzzo: We need to stand up. We need to stand up. Please say it Mezzi.

Mezzi: We need to stand up!

Buzzo: Again!

Mezzi: We need to stand up. We need to stand up.

Buzzo: Cool! Are you still coming home to roost?

Mezzi: Absolutely yeah. As you open your eyes tomorrow.

Buzzo: Cool. Then eat these and I quote:

> *"There is no place for the slothful in the kingdom of God." "Every kingdom divided against itself is brought to desolation," and "Every city or house divided against itself cannot stand." And these are not philosophies. This is the holy book. The Bible. And they sum up the reason for Africa's tragedy.*

Mezzi: You have been ordained as well? Buzzo, I need to urgently understand who a Nigger is? What a Nigger is?

Buzzo: Mezzi believe me, there are no easy answers. Yet answers are voluptuously manifest everywhere in Africa. Negroes are willfully blind to these answers. They will not see them. The Nigger's commandment against them. Home to roost Mezzi. Home to roost for the answers. Maybe we can help the continent see the answers.

Buzzo, inadvertently, finds himself laden with gust of "Nigger" questions!

Poor Buzzo! He is just out of puberty to be laden with Nigger conspiracy questions. A Gen Z biracial, being wheeled into racialism contention, as old as the human race, to proffer answers to the "whys" of the desecration of the solemnness, of the uniqueness, of the oneness of the human race and its descent into racialism.

It's been said that the Gen Z are a Collective Herd. To the extent that they are collectively single-minded and stylish in the practice of their beliefs; to the extent that they are collectively pertinacious in the consumption of their pleasures; to the extent that they are collectively persistent in pursuit of their passion; to these extents, for their collectivity-ism to make sense and thrive and endure, in time and space, Buzzo and his peers have no choice but to chart into their yet willfully ignored and uncharted divisive "Deep State" Status Quo doctrine of human race and racialism territory.

A territory to Gen Z abhorrent, adversely apathetic and of a distorted and abhorrent reification.

To this inescapable reality, he braves terms of engagements of racialism questions:

Isn't the human race unique and one species, one gene?

Why was it desecrated and profaned?

And paraphrasing Toni Morrison: ...*"desecrated and profaned into the creation of the Other? Creation of Aliens? Of the Stranger? Of the psychological work of Othering? Of a Natural and divine delineation amongst the human race? The creation of Ranks? Ranks associated with pigmentations? Ranks creating values, enshrining differences, erecting fences? The human race's Reification? Racial segregation, racial divide, racial diversity, racial profiling?"*

And further more come to terms with:

Who conspired racism?

Why was it conspired?

When was it conspired?

Why this reify contrivance has a strong foot hold? Its grip abhors escape? Has substantive millions of followers? Who are these followers?

And yet come to terms with these other ineluctable questions:

The Europeans survived the arduous middle ages? The middle ages of Romanesque and Gothic periods? A brute, brutal period of plagues for the European Continent? The Europeans survived their many plagues? Many plagues of both force majeure and human causes? Their necessity to survive their many plagues enhanced the effort of their brain that conspired and contrived inventions? Most of those inventions besides, dealt with their human plagues? Their many filths, their human despicable, their human scums, who were plunderers, pillagers, looters, losers in their society were disciplined, tortured? Their Gothic torturing machines and mechanisms have nothing to be compared with in human history? In fact, most of their human scum, their losers, spared medieval torturing, were instead exiled to unchartered territories: Africa, Asia, Australia, New Zealand, Asia, the Americas? With the Roman Cross and Bibles in their hands? For a field day?

These scums, these losers beheld these territories? In them, they find a family of the same race, first time, first hand, and the majesty and the grace of the indigenous population, differently pigmented, framed in the beauty of endowment of wealth and climate? And their regality and air of royalty overwhelmed them? The ponderous sunlight, the soave temperature, the ocean, the ocean shores, the ocean lives, the pristine sky, the clouds, the animals, the forest with its trees, the regale welcome accorded them, including the relish of sexual congress, consumed in silence with the coyly ethereal indigenous women, are nothing to compare to theirs? To the disastrous theirs, back home in the continental Europe?

Then, they get assailed by unutterable spasm of jealousy? They whimpered, whispered and mumbled out: "God, why have Thou been so unjust?"

Then as they peer and glimpse at these black pigmented human species of indigenous population in their courtyard, they notice their pristine gracious nakedness dressed in golds and diamonds and emeralds, and the sapphires and the Tanzanites? And besides, they noticed they are organized, they have a system of governing hierarchy–Kings, Queens, Prince and Princesses, Vassals, Fiefdoms the Servants, the People? They have commerce, route of commerce, inter and intra-trade activities, fishing, farming in their primitive ways? They have their slaves? The Slaves have their shackles?

And behold, the scums, notice with elation and joy that their European shackless are comparatively of far more advanced torture machines?

The scums could now see the justice from God? The God that gave them the necessity to effort the brain to invent an advanced torture machine? The edge machine? That instrument ordained to dominate their environment and survive? And for nothing more?

They transited from unutterable spasm of jealousy to unutterable gratuitous fortuitous spasm of POSSESSION?

Then, they psyched the indigenous population up and established without doubt, that they – the indigenous people – are within the reach of their torture machines to dispossess them, possess them and own them and own their lands? And the only efficaciously justifiable means to possess them is they have to HATE them? They have to necessarily hate them? Necessarily disdain them? Ponderously despise them? Absolutely make them the Others? Make them Aliens, make them Strangers on their lands? That way they can own them, govern them and administer them? So, these scums, these losers, to become relevant back home, in the European courts of monarchs and monarchies they transmitted their discovery of another human race, a competing human race, though adorned, that is pigmented, that is Negro, that has no emotions but a natural instinct only to serve, a natural instinct to be controlled, a natural instinct towards kindness? Precisely what the 'natural instincts' of the likes of progeny Rosa Parks and her peers and generation of peers after theirs underpinned centuries later? Instead, for generation of peers, their progenitors and genitors centuries before, their 'natural instincts' were lost to dehumanizing brute force of subjugation, subduedness, denial and abhorrence? Even before the words of Harriet Beecher Stow could sprout to White readers centuries later?

> *...Here, to the European Courts and monarchies, there is a discovery of another human species that, though adorned, is pigmented, is Negro, and has no emotions but a natural instinct only to serve, a natural instinct to be controlled, a natural instinct towards kindness? Precisely what the 'natural instincts' of the likes of progeny Rosa Parks and her peers and generation after theirs underpinned centuries later? Even Before the words of Harriet Beecher Stow could sprout to White readers centuries later?*

Back home in Europe they gained a cautious suspicious audience?
The Kings and Queens of Europe send expeditions.
Confirmation dutifully came and the scums were given legitimacy?
The indigenous population were denied of their personhood?

Entire territories were annihilated, subjugated, dehumanized, obliterated and with them the indigenous population were dispossessed and possessed? The combined darkness of Africa, and the Australia and the New Zealand were shone lights. Lights of Christianity, of civilization, of culture and of development. And the lights of the Americas instead were plunged into darkness. They and their civilization were obliterated.

The conspiracy by the few White scums that spurred and lunged the whole Continental Europe into scouring illegitimacy and brute action of dispossession and possession of one member of his family species, the pigmented Negro, for a just cause of jealousy, was given the name Supremacy? The White scum Supremacy? And the medals for the White scum was Supremacy Legitimacy? Recognition? Approvals? Fulfilment? The legitimacy of White scum Abstract Supremacy or of the White Abstract Supremacy? The White Supremacy is the White scum? The White losers? The White Filth? The White scums are legitimized and are at the service of the White Race at large to conspire, contrive, promote, enshrine the White wishful Supremacy, the White race's conscientious licentious willful amoralities whenever, wherever?

All for racialism? To own the other? Dehumanize a fellow human species? Deny personhood? For an absurd cynical and sadistic interest to possess material wealth? For dominance of material wealth? Out of survival anxiety? Out of jealousy of not having what the Other is endowed with? To reap the others endowments? Blessings? Might makes right? Dominance is the only measure of success? If you can dominate, you should do it?

> *The Conspiracy by the few White scums that spurred and lunged the whole Continental Europe into scouring illegitimacy and brute action of dispossession and possession of one member of his family species, the pigmented Negro, for a just cause of jealousy, was given the name Supremacy? The White scum Supremacy?*
> *And the medals for the White scum was Supremacy Legitimacy? Recognition? Approvals? Fulfilment? The legitimacy of White scum Abstract Supremacy or of the White Abstract Supremacy?*

Is the human race not equated to human species, and cannot be sort into sub-species? The Whites at large divorced from moral judgement, divorced from the nonclassification of human species, and encouraged and enshrined brutality and forceful defraud and disdain and hate of one of his, of black pigment, and accepted and perfected her slavery and enslavement? The human species is about the White abstract supremacy claim to power, cling to power and power's necessity to control and sustain dominance of the Others of the same family?

Is it not of unutterable shameful tragedy to the human race the fact that one of its own is the precursor and arbiter of differences within the human species?

Is it not of a sorrowing tragedy that White scum's Scholarships and literary pundits exhaustively ponderously pushed for mainstay of race difference -the Aryan Race, the Caucasian Race through scientific racism? Nothing to prove: All human is a human species?

Paraphrasing Thomas Paine: *"...that Male and female are the distinctions of Nature, good and bad the distinctions of Heaven are not worth inquiring into; but it is worth inquiring into how a race of men came into the world exalted above the rest, and distinguished like some new species and whether they are the means of happiness or of misery to mankind."*

Is it not of unutterable shameful tragedy to the Human race, the fact that one of its own is the precursor and arbiter of difference within the human species?

The "Nigger" questions laden Buzzo, just like every Gen Z his peer, does not want any cheap and deliberate distraction than to come to terms with the question: What is the human project? What is the family of Youth, the Gen Z Project?

Is the 21st century human project hijacked, gripped and dictated to by the abstract race-ism of the White scum? The White scum supremacist-ism?

Our Gen Z human project should be about Whiteness or Blackness?

Should be about the dehumanization and estrangement of others?

Should be about ranking, racial segregation? Should be about erecting arbitrary fences that are irrelevant and stupid?

Should be about teaching the Gen Z the illusion of power through the process of inventing the other, dominance of the other?

Should be about teaching the White Gen Z that his success and respectability depends on the measure of White race dominance of the other, the Negro race? The Yellow race? The Brown race?

Should be about parenting the Negro Gen Z on how Negro exceptionalism depends on his moral high road, refusing to lower self to the abstract supremacist-ism of White scums, losers?

Should be about peddling the abhorrent and the despicable "one-drop rule"-ism, teaching the outrageousness of miscegenation and utter preference and legitimization and legitimacy of incest instead, in every White household?

> *The human project should be about peddling the abhorrent and the despicable "one-drop rule" -ism, teaching the outrageousness of miscegenation and utter preference and legitimization and legitimacy of incest instead, in every White household?*

The "one-drop rule"-ism forces the ineluctable question:
What happened after centuries of White scum "going indigenous"?
Sexual congress relishing welcome by the indigenous women was so unclean and so debasing for White scum masculinity, for his White feminine, for his White family? And a blot of unutterable graveness and solemnity on the Whiteness of his celestial blood? And to atone, the beguilement of the indigenous male and the ravishment of the indigenous feminine was conceived, contrived and consumed?

That moment he beguiled the indigenous male with the Bible and then with his superior shackles, and subdued, humiliated, assaulted, possessed and dispossessed the indigenous feminine, ratified and enacted the Supremacy of the White scum masculinity and of his whiteness?

And that moment repudiated, and abhorred miscegenation sexual congress, and his withering savagery at courtship and his cloying pleasure was a Favor, a Gift to the indigenous feminine, to non-Whites from the White Supremacist scum?

And that moment denied, and obliterated and delegitimized his cum, his gene, his seed, his biracial offspring and its reification, even before his badge of unutterable disgrace and shame–the mulatto crowd, appeared?

And that moment conceived "one-drop rule", validating his *inhumanus*, his depravity, his degeneracy, his perversion, his putrefaction and the horror?

That was and still is a psychological derangement?

The world's biracial family was and is still served?

Now to the scholars and scholarships of moral standard and its rules:

What is the moral-ism behind the single drop of "Black blood" i.e. "One-drop rule"? Is it morally loathsome, reprehensible to be biracial, to have the bloods of both parents, to have inherited the genes of both parents, to authentically and undeniably feel both parents, identify with both parents?

Or is it morally of the highest standard, of a sublime moral uprightness and right for a Parent to proudly deny the presence of his gene in His, to forcefully defraud the identity of him in His, to unashamedly slay and remove the inalienable feeling of him in His – in His biracial OFFSPRING?

Or candor holds that any, within the human species, capable of repudiating its gene, can only but be a human scum?

Paraphrasing Thomas Paine: "…*Civilization has operated in two ways: to make one part of society more affluent, and the other more wretched, than would have been the lot of either in a natural state.*"

19

Scholars and scholarships, is miscegenation a civilization of sexual congress that operates in three ways: to make one part affluent by forcefully denying and defrauding and "one-drop rule" ruling of Biracial of His, and the second part wretched, by accepting and loving Biracial of His, and the third part an indelible Blot, biracial personhood denied and denigrated, permanently enfeebled with unutterable spasm of unjustifiable life humiliation and traumatization?

> *To scholars, scholarships and literary pundits alike, is it morally of the highest standard, of a sublime moral uprightness and right for a Parent to proudly deny the presence of his gene in His, to forcefully defraud the identity of him in His, to unashamedly slay and remove the inalienable feeling of him in His- in His Biracial OFFSPRING? Any, within the human species, capable of repudiating its Gene, can only but be a human scum?*

Is it not of unutterable grieving sadness that the family of the world Gen Z would have to condescend to such a moral ebb, listening and cogitating to the makings of gene denial, racial-segregation, racial chasm, racial divide, racial profiling, racial diversity?

Won't the zero sum of these abominations, infelicitously and tragically amount to the human species self-inflicted suicide?

Gen Z human project should be to remain together human, to tackle and reverse and retrieve the decay at the Dehumanization of our common human species' Planet and Society?

Human race should fight for the idea to defend self, not to defend any dominance outside of our common human enemy, not to defend any human tribe over the other, not to defend any twisted interpretation of religion or defend any king or queen or kingdom but to defend the idea that all men are created equal and endowed by the Creator with the inalienable rights to contribute and make the world a better place for the human species? No ruin upon others, nor receive ruin from others, common defense from ruin? The family of the Gen Z human species should believe in this idea?

Buzzo, who, left without options, got speedily acculturated and informed by these flurries of racialism question marks, nonetheless, makes a 360-degree turn, to ponder and reflect on the connotation of the phrase "Human DOMINANCE." It has been 200,000 years since modern humans evolved?

And human civilization as is known is only about 6,000 years old?

6,000 years of human civilization produced 6,000 years of both systematic advancement in stages of development and organization, and systematic advancement in emotions of barbarism – jealousy, greed, dispossession, plunder?

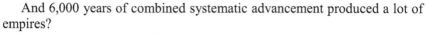

And 6,000 years of combined systematic advancement produced a lot of empires?

Every empire a power of dominance. A power of human dominance?

And these Empires produced as much Human Dominances, as they inevitably rose, dominated and replaced?

6,000 years produced the deeds of 50 to 70 empires. From the Akkadian Empire, the Ashanti Empire, The Ayyubid Empire, The Aztec Empire, The Babylonian Empire, Byzantine Empire down to Ottoman Empire, from Ghana empire, Egyptian Empire, Dutch Empire down to Jinn Dynasty, from Austria-Ungar, the Umayyad, the Achaemenid, the Ottoman, The Mongol, The great Roman Empire down to the British, etc. The list goes on.

As they dominated and are dominated, all with brute force and disdain, virtues and sins were left in their wakes?

> *Virtues and Sins of DOMINANCE? Of Human DOMINANCE? OF DEHUMANIZATION?*
> *The combined Virtues and Sins of DOMINANCE are both essential?*
> *Does Sin give Virtue justification? Or Virtue of Dominance gives Sin of Dehumanization exultation and reward?*

Virtues and Sins of DOMINANCE? Of human DOMINANCE? OF DEHUMANIZATION?

The combined Virtues and Sins of DOMINANCE are both essential?

Does sin give virtue justification? Or virtue of dominance gives sin of dehumanization exultation and reward?

Virtues and sins of DOMINANCE, of the DOMINATOR, of the DOMINATED?

The morals of the Bible teaches DOMINANCE? Man is given to dominate his environment, so commandeth the Creator? The mountains, the seas, the air, the sky, the cloud, and everything that laments in nature are commanded to obey the human species?

DOMINANCE has virtue? It has sin when it dominates self? Dominance of self is an abhorrent abomination?

The virtues of DOMINATOR? There are virtues in a dominator of our common enemies: diseases, illiteracy, misery, etc.? Dominator of self is a despicable sin?

The DOMINATED, the dehumanized has a lone virtue: Obedience? A dominated is a virtue for the dominator? Defeatist and despicable for self? There is a remarkable sin in the obedience of the DOMINATED?

No human species should allow self to be dominated? It's a heinous sin? It's against the wishes and dispensations of the creator in the created: the inalienable endowment of rights. Remember?

21

The Negros' sin is in the DOMINATED and in the badge of the DOMINATED? And the cringing tragic perpetuation of the badge of the DOMINATED? In the badge of NIGGER and NIGGER*TUDE*?

The Negros' sin is in the DOMINATED and in the badge of the DOMINATED?
And in the cringing tragic perpetuation of the badge of the DOMINATED? In the badge of NIGGER and NIGGERTUDE?

The European White Supremacist scum, found not just in Europe or in the Americas but around the world will stop at nothing to DEHUMANIZE his fellow human species? Pigmentation regardless. With unutterable shameless brute force and brutal force of disdain, of jealousy, of avarice, of pillage?

A sewer rat is a sewer rat. And a scum is a scum? But Why?

Has it not been said that you can't give to prostitution its former INNOCENCE?

It's been said that every DOMINATIONEM has a combined reason and leverage? What is the leverage to dehumanize the human kindred Negro? The scums leverage on the Negro weakness? An inherent weakness found in Negro's governing tradition? A tradition of hereditary hierarchy? A hereditary hierarchy that is feudalistic in nature? A feudalistic tradition of the monarchy, of the vassals, and of the flocks and herds-the masses? A feudalistic tradition that requires total submission of flocks and herds to the vassals and total submission of both the flocks and herds and the vassals to the Monarchy? The absolute superiority of the monarchy? Hereditary hierarchy tradition that preordains patronization and condescension from the monarchy on the vassals, on the flocks and herds, and obsequiousness and subservience from the vassals, flocks and herds in return, to the monarchy?

In sum, a DESPOTIC HEREDITARY HIERARCHICAL TRADITION that totally forbids any Opinions, any Challenges, any Freedom of thought and spontaneity of expression, annihilates individualism, obliterates thinking, subdues any reactions, and impedes proactiveness and rewards obsequiousness and subservience and cronyism? A despotic system of power and control in the Negro system that makes hostage the Negro mind, and the Negro mindset, and Negro progress and development and imprisons everything and anything of the Negro kindred? This is the leverage? The leverage of the White scum? A self-inflicted leverage of hostage of the Negro mind and mindset?

This Hostage has fueled and leveraged the grossly distorted notion that a Negro has no emotions but a natural instinct only to serve, to be controlled,

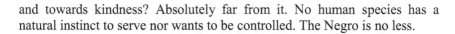

and towards kindness? Absolutely far from it. No human species has a natural instinct to serve nor wants to be controlled. The Negro is no less.

> *The White Scums leverage on the Negro gravest weakness? An inherent weakness found in Negro's governing tradition? A tradition of Hereditary Hierarchy? A Hereditary Hierarchy that preordains Patronization and Condescension from Negros Monarchy on the Negro Vassals, on the Negro Flocks and Herds, And in return, Obsequiousness and subservience from the Vassals, Flocks and Herds to the Monarchy?*
> *A despotic system of Power and control in the Negro system that makes Hostage the Negro Mind, and the Negro mindset, and Negro progress and development and Imprisons Everything and Anything of the Negro Kindred?*
> *This is the leverage? A Negro's self-inflicted leverage…that has fueled his emotion of Natural instinct only to serve, to be controlled…*

As it has been said, a sewer rat is a sewer rat, and there is no reason to believe that a ravisher would refrain from ravishing? So, a White scum remains a White scum.

It has been said that *quiet method for peace is historically ineffectual; that prayers are rejected with disdain; and that they only tended to convince peace – irreducible, that nothing flatters vanity, or confirms obstinacy in Kings more than repeated petitioning, perennial lamentations – and nothing contributed more than that very measure to make the King absolute.*

This principle is dynamic and holds broadly indistinctively to this day: for the King of Supremacy, the White Scum and in equal measure for the King of Negro's mind and mindset paralysis, the Negro Despots of the Africa's Hereditary Hierarchical Despotic Tradition?

Then there is no reason to believe reconciliation, friendship and harmony proffered between a dominator and a dominated?

As there is no reason to believe that a dominated Negro kindred injured throughout history would forgive and restore trust and confidence betrayed and trampled upon by a White kindred dominator?

Not when everyday does injuries, rekindles injuries and proposes future injuries, wearing thin the kindred and the akin between the dominated and the dominator?

> *This Principle is dynamic and holds broadly indistinctively to this day: for the King of Supremacy, the White Scum and in equal measure for the King of Negro's mind and mindset Paralysis, …*

...the Negro Despots of the Africa's Hereditary Hierarchical Despotic Tradition?

The only reconciliation, friendship and harmony that can hold is a Negro's DOMINANCE. A DOMINANCE of an equal vigor and brute force magnitude of the White? Not the criminal cowardly type-dominance of the European Supremacist White scum. Not DEHUMANIZATION but dominance of the Environment?

The Negro needs to stamp out, annihilate the White scum leverage?

The Negro needs to obliterate his despotic tradition of Hierarchical Preordination? The Negro needs to extinguish the foreordained Hostage of Obsequiousness and Subservience?

The Negro needs to crush out the despicable crushing Monarchical Patronization and Condescension of the vassal and flocks and herds in their Despotic Hierarchic Hereditary Tradition?

Otherwise, he will forever remain dominated?

The only solution and deterrence is DOMINANCE.

Negro should stand up and be a DOMINATOR and not the DOMINATED?

Negro should DOMINATE his environment. Should Dominate Africa's Misery.

Negro, you should be capable of discharging the SOCIAL DUTIES of Life.

Negro is DOMINATING SELF in Africa? Negro is A NIGGER in Africa? Negro DOMINATING his people? Self-DOMINANCE?

Practicing and doubling down on and multiplying the White Supremacist-ism Sin of Human species reify idea of DOMINANCE?

The outrageously DOMINATED practicing SELF-DOMINANCE dictates of his DOMINATOR?

In other words, the ENSLAVED, ENSLAVING SELF through the eye of his ENSLAVER the White Supremacist scum, the White looter, the White Loser, the White plunderer, the Skunk?

Negro, the only Reconciliation, Friendship and Harmony that can hold is a Negro's DOMINANCE. A DOMINANCE of an equal Vigor and brute force Magnitude of the White? No, not the Criminal, cowardly type-Dominance of the European Supremacist White scum. Not DEHUMANIZATION but Dominance of the Environment?

Negro, your only deterrence and self-respect is in the DOMINANCE of your environment? Dominate your misery? Don't be the enslaver of human species. Don't be the enslaved human species? Stand up. Stand your

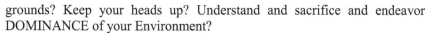

grounds? Keep your heads up? Understand and sacrifice and endeavor DOMINANCE of your Environment?

For humanity has a common enemy out there.

Isn't this the Gen Z collectivity-ism tenets as well? Collective defeat of the common enemies of the human species out there?

With these connotative reflections, Buzzo acquires a remarkable voluptuous self-confidence that he can finally proffer, if not birth cogent and compelling Nigger and Niggertude answers to Mezzi, as it relates, at least, to the African context.

The irony of it all is that he is a Biracial! Not by Choice, not by coercion but endowed. And the paradox is that DOMINANCE was and still is conspired, contrived, perpetuated and prevailed by the one-half of his gene. And the same DOMINANCE was compelled, inflicted, bound, bonded and endured on the other-half of his gene.

And fate compels him the arbiter of justice, instead of beneficiary of harmony and peace of his endowment, from the inalienable love within the human species. All in all, however, he concludes the bottom line lay in the Sins and Virtues of Dominance and on their capitalization. He sees the Sins and Virtues of Dominance existentially essential for the Negro: its Sins are essential for the Negro to avoid a repeat of unutterable spasm of trauma; and its virtues are essential for the Negro to endeavor dominance, and prevail dominance, endure dominance and safeguard dominance on his environment. And deter dominance. Deter human dominance - Dehumanization from within and without.

And in an unyielding pursuit of this AXIOM, regardless of the present and lurking despondent thin hope of the Elephant in the room, given a continent's generational history of lethargy, he is undaunted to deploy the art of *persuasionem and exemplum*. A systematic compelling persuasion and by example, in the arduous task to convince, and endure and prevail, in his life time, the Virtue of Dominance, on the one half of his gene, the Negro. And spur African Gen Z Peers to stand up, renounce subservience and obsequiousness, reject patronization and condescension, annihilate mind and mindset hostage-hold of the despotic hereditary hierarchical tradition and DOMINATE their environment. This is the idea. Dominance! Dominance!! Domination of Africa's environment by Africa's generation of Youth, succession of Africa's Youths ad infinitum, starting with Gen Z.

That way they can contribute, with equal vigor to Gen Z world family development and progress. That way they can earn Pride and Place.

This is the life project. This is his African life-purpose! This is his tortuous walk! His tumultuous path! This is his unflinching tough love resolve for Africa's Gen Z Family. His peers.

> *He sees the Sins and Virtues of Dominance existentially essential for the Negro: its Sins are essential for the Negro to avoid a historical repeat of unutterable spasm of trauma; and its Virtues are essential ...*

> *...for the Negro to endeavor Dominance, prevail dominance, endure Dominance, and safeguard Dominance. Dominance on his environment. And deter Dominance. Deter human Dominance– Dehumanization from within and without.*

Paraphrasing President Kennedy: *"the problems of the Youths cannot possibly be solved by skeptics or cynics whose horizons are limited by the obvious realities. We need Youths who can 'dream things that never were and ask why not.' It matters not how few we are to seek Dominance of our Environment, for when clad in the armor of a just cause, we are stronger than all the hosts of Conspiracies."*

Chapter 4

Now we find Mezzi and Buzzo together in Africa! Mezzi, since his arrival is listless. Insomnia-stricken, sleep challenged. Constantly in *reminiscenzia*: Tom Bradley's face, his voice, his inveighs, the remind and remand of his history, the hatefulness, the hurtfulness and the devastating weight of those inveighs are a life drama. He can't wait to verify the state of African homeland.

Mezzi: "Shillala… Allah Akbar. Shillala Allah Akbar." Buzzo did you hear that song at the microphone early this morning?

Buzzo: Yeah. Sorry I forgot to tell you there are mosques as there are churches and shrines in every corner of Africa.

Mezzi: So, what was that? That song was around 5 o'clock this morning. I remember it. I am jet-lagging. I was about drifting.

Buzzo: Allah is God. They were calling for prayers.

Mezzi: Uh! At that hour.

Buzzo: They pray five times daily.

Mezzi (in a spasm of fearful anxiety): What?

Buzzo: 5am, 1pm, 4pm, 6pm, 8pm every day.

Mezzi: So, how have you been sleeping?

Buzzo: By Allah Akbar. The Lord is great. By Gods' greatness you will get used to it as well.

Mezzi: How? To this early morning yelling?

Buzzo: Yes, Mezzi. The churches are not any different. Every and all day praying, numerous night vigils over megaphones of disproportionate decibels. Be patient, we are here to understand the signs, and the symbolisms and the signified.

Buzzo feels for his brother's shaken psychology. He absolutely does not want his degeneration into a remarkably dangerous bi-polar manic-depressive psychosis disorder territory. He swings into action taking him into the naked truth of their reality. The earlier he can come to terms with their African reality - Nigger and Nigger*tude*, the better. Not read in some fancy reporting. That would greatly help his psychology.

So, for the most part of the first week of Mezzi's presence, he embarked on a breathtaking tour of the ancestral city with his brother, driving around, panning and scanning the environment and the environ of the urban, of the suburban, of the villages.

As the sordid environmental details hit, Mezzi seemed hypnotized. Numbed. No proffering of words at the state of environmental disrepair: what he is seeing are remarkably appalling. Despicable. It's evil. It's criminal. It is beyond imagination. He is afraid its worse than Nigger*tude* as parodied in America. This is worse than the Nigger*tude* slur of Tom Bradley. It's worse than the 3/5ᵗʰ human worth compromise. It's despicably worse than Lynching phenomenon. It's appallingly worse than cottonpicking mind inveigh. It's remarkably sub of sub-human being. It pales in comparison to whatever Tom Bradley thought he was saying to hurt him. This is remarkably hurting than hurtful. Hateful than hate. Bruising than bruise.

Buzzo: Overwhelmingly despicable vile inheritance. Perpetuation of numbing poverty! Misery bondage! Defiling!

Mezzi (shaking his head in disapproval, his face in appalling grin): Got it. Got it. Tom Bradley was not being figuratively sarcastic. Neither uncouth, or hateful. A literal reality. Yeah, Nigger's paradise is palpable. Yeah, this is it.

Buzzo: Yeah, looks like it. Nigger and Nigger*tude* trying to gain definition.

Mezzi: The fourth power, I mean the media is arid of Nigger*tude*. Nigger*tude* not portrayed. Not fairly represented. Not said. Not told. Not written. Willful blindness. Denials. Reticence. Yeah this is what a Nigger, a coon is. Remarkably despicable. Appallingly reprehensible. Virulently repulsive. Inhuman. Beyond evil.

Buzzo: The devil himself pales in comparison to this evil of our people.

And what is troubling is the gap between the magnitude of the challenges and the magnitude of the willful blindness of the people, of the tradition, of the religion, of the politics…

Mezzi: The willful blindness? The willful evil?

Buzzo: Yeah, the pleasures of a Nigger's politics, of religion, of the tradition: creating…creative distances.

Mezzi: No doubt. Even the blind can see the remarkable distances.

Buzzo: Deafening distances. Orphans everywhere…

Mezzi: Yeah, everything and anything seemed orphaned in this place.

Buzzo: (Pointing randomly): Open air sewer, forced kids' truancy, buckets of water on kids' heads, open air street scape toilets, smell of urine and faeces everywhere…

…all freedoms denied; light, water, education, healthcare, food security…

Mezzi: The basics are missing…this is not befitting of any mankind…

Buzzo: Cool! Now you're beginning to grapple with the probable why. The probable why this misery is possible?

Mezzi: Yeah, you said it, sloth.

Buzzo: Bravo! Yeah, I believe that's the mother of the strings of our afflictions. Our deplorable tribulation. Our despicable misery. Yeah sloth.

The disinclination to work or to exertion. That I believe is the single factor responsible for a string of others...just look around you...at the amount of loitering and loafing and the slothfulness of the adults. Children and women are laboring. Groupage of men, seated under the trees, alcohol in hands, at foods, not books or papers and pen, not hoes and hatchets, tractors, loafing in endless futile discussions.

Mezzi: Why, why, why? The why of the sloth phenomenon in your opinion...?

No time for Buzzo to answer that:

Mezzi: Buzzo, could you stop the car for a second please?

Buzzo rolls the car to a stop.

Mezzi has seen and is fixing his gaze on a group of men, eating, across the road overlooking an over-sprawling open-stench-air sewerage.

Mezzi, in a flash, inadvertently walks over to the group, challenging them.

All these to Buzzo's utmost competing amazements: pleasant surprise and preoccupation for Mezzi's safety.

However, Buzzo stays his position looking on without moving.

Mezzi (his face in a sneering, berserking frown): A restaurant located in the middle of sewer and filth? Serving food? This is an aberration. You all comfortably eating and drinking at this hour of the day, sitting unperturbed and breathing the perfume and fragrance and the elegance of this open-air sewer, of faeces, of urine, of flies, of roaches in the middle of these fresh and hardened faeces and filths? And I am asking why?

The men slowly bring their stare, of apparent calm conflicting amazement on him: It's an amazement of severe grimaces and grinning, in their efforts to contextualize what he is saying. They contemplate him in a profound prolonged silence. Their silence communicates an eloquent "who are you, why not?" It was more. Mezzi notices with utmost dismay that their silence is presumptuous, condescending, of competing disdain and very dismissive.

Then they disengage their stare off him, returning to their foods.

Mezzi, undeterred goes irate. In a flash he grabs the shovel right in the vicinity, starts shoveling from the heap, filths in their direction, arousing filth roaches, filth rats, that run in every direction; filth mosquitoes, filth flies that perch on them and on their foods and drinks in its wake.

It's a disaster. A complete disaster.

The men react mutedly, trying to fend off the filth parasites as they could without much success. Amidst their fight to ward off the filth insects, they eat, drink and discuss, with their curious hostile eyes expressing: "you unhinged fellow…another fool of a spoilt child, another unhinged western Biracial bastard, trying to teach us how to live our lives," trained on Mezzi.

Air of tension builds.

Their muted non-reaction shoveled Mezzi to edge. His bid to provoke them to some reaction, if they believe in something, if they have dreams, if they have any virtue and dignity so far, has failed. He needs to up his game at provocation.

Mezzi goes berserk: undaunted he wedges into their midst and gets around picking unexpectedly the table on which the ready fuming foods are laid plates served from, for the clients.

Air of tension ready to explode looms.

Hell seems let lose: a woman, the owner of the "road side sewer restaurant" is voluptuously wailing, hands on her head. Her two female kids join her, trying to save some of the food spilled to the ground.

Mezzi seems unperturbed, unshaken, stays his ground observing the shebang, ready for any retaliatory physical and verbal consequences of disdain. Ready to bear a worst case, but deserving mediaeval mayhem.

Buzzo is still across the road, seated in the car calmly observing the shebang from that distance. But ready to spring to his feet.

Instead of any mayhem, the clients jump to their feet, quietly taking their leave.

Now the place is emptied. Mezzi and restaurant owner, who, overwhelmed, has stopped crying, face each other, locking eyes. Like in a Mexican standoff, they hold stare without proffering words. Then:

Restaurant owner: Young man, can't you see we are already downtrodden, dead? They sent you to kill us a second time?

Mezzi is taken aback at those words: they know him? They assume he belongs to authority? They loathe and fear authority? That explains their subdued reaction?

A lot ado to figure out the reason for their numbing reaction.

Mezzi, chagrined for the woman, reaches for his pocket and gives her some 400 US dollars

She immediately starts dancing and singing praises to God.

Mezzi shakes his head 'incredible.' Then he starts walking away mumbling to himself: not even animals, no mammal can be so subdued, so defeated and so numbed…

Mezzi unites with Buzzo. They are fighting the spasm of numbness. They just sit in the car, their eyes bitterly scanning, scrutinizing and reflecting and pondering in deep analysis of the situation.

Buzzo: Glaring huh! Everything remarkably numbing. No reaction. Total palsy.

Mezzi: Something is fundamentally wrong Buzzo. This can't be normal. There must be a realm of beyond*ness* of things where answers abound. This is beneath irrationality.

Buzzo: You just proffered beyond*ness* of things?

Mezzi: Yes. Some Niggers' veiled commandment of stupidity. You needed to peer at the overbearing pride, and insolence on their grimaces and grinning.

Buzzo: Veiled commandment with filth. And you are welcome to our fatherland!

Mezzi: It's just beyond the rational mind to why one would accept filth. Eat filth. Breath filth. Romance filth. Kiss filth. Comfortably filth away. Why? Is it ignorance?

Buzzo: And yes, veiled commandment with arrogance.

Mezzi: But I can see they all have phones in their hands to connect and view the world. For comparative relativity. And yet they arrogantly romance with filth.

Buzzo: Arrogance of humiliation. For if you know something of civilization, but far removed from civilization, you are not spared knowledge of humiliation.

Mezzi: If they know humiliation then why are they endeavoring ignorance?

Buzzo: A hypocritical self-depressing coping mechanism. But you put it remarkably punctiliously: the beyond*ness* of things. Nigger*tude* buried in the beyond*ness* of veiled commandments stupidity of the black race. Here let's try one more thing.

Buzzo roars the car to life and parks it perfectly in the middle of a usually heavy trafficked road, somewhat free-flowing at that hour. No hazard lights. They get off the car and walk away in the distance from where they observe reactions of motorists.

Nothing happened. The traffic is slowed and gradually builds to a snail pace. And yet for some fluke reason the motorists quietly accept the new traffic situation as the new normal, wasting hours navigating, meandering traffic around the parked car as they could. And in its wake quarreling, hooting, whooping and scowling in their smugness, condescending, cravenness, loathing, spitefulness ensued.

Their wills bent. No traffic responders came. No authority presented itself to address, nor to save the situation.

> *Arrogance of humiliation. For if you know something of civilization, but far removed from civilization, you are not spared knowledge of humiliation.*

Buzzo: The beyond*ness* of things is simply manifest.

Mezzi: You can bend them to your will. Very easy.

Buzzo: Yes! Precisely. You got it. Bend them to your will!

Mezzi: Yeah!

Buzzo: Bravo, you just gave beyond*ness* of things a name and a surname!

Mezzi: Yeah?

Buzzo: You got numbed! From the lack of basic expectations of the Negro you got disappointed and numbed.

Now Mezzi, with air of fearful confusion, is silently, curiously looking at Buzzo, lost. But with expectations.

Buzzo: From your mind of basic expectation to what your eyes beheld and yet to behold, you transited to disappointment, and from disappointment to annoyance, and to irritation, and to anger and down to repudiation. Numbness!

Mezzi (processing): Yeah, I think so!

Buzzo: Dominance! That's the name and surname of why we are in Africa.

Mezzi (his face a contorted frown): Dominance?

Buzzo: Yeah! You either dominate or be dominated. Africa is dominated by its Filth. We are attesting to it. We are looking at it. We are living it out.

Mezzi (recovers): Yeah, it makes a lot of sense. They are dominated by Filth, by open air Sewerage. If a man can accept to eat amidst those filths and dirt without flinching…

Buzzo: That makes it hard to think he can ever dominate his environment with any type of civility, development and progress, in time and space. Isn't it?

Mezzi: You are damn right! How can they not dominate even the basics? Illiteracy, health care, power electricity, portable pipe-borne water, filth, open air sewerage?

Buzzo: It's so numbing to common sense. To the rationale. To decency. I mean how can somebody feast comfortably amidst filth and garbage?

Mezzi: Precisely! I mean you don't need calculus to repudiate filth and garbage?

Buzzo: You can now imagine how tempting it is, indeed a leverage for any mind, even of the most exiguous civility at common sense, exiguous will at hard work and with basic instinct not to think of dominating or dominate who cannot dominate filth, indecency, garbage!

> *…Yeah, You Dominate or be Dominated. Africa is dominated by Filth, by open air sewerage. You don't need calculus to repudiate filth and garbage. And if a man can accept to eat amidst those filths and dirt without flinching…that makes it troubling hard to think he can ever Dominate his environment with any form of civility, development and progress, in time and space. And makes it automatically tempting, indeed makes it a leverage for any mind, of even exiguous civility, …*

> *...to Dominate who cannot Dominate its Filth and Garbage.*

Mezzi: Yeah! You can literally impose your will on these people. No reaction.

Buzzo: They have been subdued and numbed.

Mezzi: Dominated by something.

Buzzo: Africa is dominated by feudalistic tradition of laziness.

Mezzi: Africa has a feudal system?

Buzzo: Yes! Self-feudalistic despotic dominance from within has been and still is the gateway to wider dominance from without. Generations of misery creativity. Beyond*ness* of things from within, yeah, dominance from within holds the secret of the first string of sloth: The laziness to think. The laziness to rationalize. Laziness to research. Laziness to endeavor the intellect. And sloth begets compulsive arrogance, willful ignorance, absence of intelligentsia, aridity of wisdom of humility to acknowledge yourself, your state of being, your condition, your status, your problem. So, we are unable to dream. Africa is unable to dream and fantasize. Remarkable regression, cringing lethargy, generation after generation.

Mezzi: It's incredibly voluptuous to see this moral vice. The trait that counteracts intellectual prospering and frustrates the attainment of knowledge.

Buzzo: Not just that. Just imagine their status arrogance. Their presumptuous sense of superiority, their disdain, their condescension, their overbearing pride towards learning. Towards knowledge.

Mezzi: Yeah, the sloth pride to acknowledge. Sloth laziness to rationalize. A deluge of ignorance.

> *Yes! Self-feudalistic despotic dominance from within has been and still is the gate way to wider dominance from without.*

Buzzo: No, an overwhelm of willful ignorance. Ignorance by design. Deliberate disregard for facts and information, for knowledge, for education. Habitual disposition to disobedience, to rudeness, to denial, to disaffirmation.

Mezzi: Least of expectations. Terribly tragic from the very downtrodden.

Buzzo: Tragic? And beyond*ness* of things holds the second sloth string: Dominance from without, leverages on the dominance from within.

Mezzi (reflective): Dominance from without...leverages dominance from within!

Buzzo: When you are numbed you are vulnerable. You are divided, susceptible to predators, to anybody, to anything. We are like insatiable whores. We are always susceptible to domination: to sloth, to filth, to colonization and to slavery at some will from without. To the White kind. Now joined by the Yellow kind. Chinese all over the place for their share of the pillagery. A nation divided...desolation. A family divided...falls. A remarkable chronic inability to build a remarkable working consensus to tackle the challenges...

Mezzi: ...Tackle challenges? This thing is real. A Negro is not just withered of ability to invent but as well arid to copy solutions. Only sub-humans, only coons won't invent nor innovate, and worst still, won't even copy to make their lots better...these are what make a Negro a Nigger? That's who a Nigger is? And this stat of his is Nigger*tude?*

> *...Tackle challenges? This thing is real. A negro is not just withered of ability to invent but as well arid to copy solutions. Only sub-humans, only coons won't invent nor innovate and worst still, won't even copy to make their lots better...these are what make a Negro a Nigger? That's who a Nigger is? And this his state is Nigger*tude?

Mezzi pauses, stops talking, glaring gaze, full of expectations, at Buzzo.

Buzzo: Yeah, finally Nigger and Nigger*tude* finally unravelling before our eyes.

Mezzi: Buzzo, you really think we are human beings? You remember that psychological affirmation that says any child, who observes but does not replicate, for example, the facial smile, imitating the parents, after three weeks of life is not normal and should be subjected to Psychiatry?

Buzzo (without answering looks at his watch and to Mezzi): Let's go.

They walk, reaching the car. They enter the car, driving off. They maintain their silence. As they look back, the traffic straightens, it's almost turned normal.

Mezzi: Totally numbing. Said between us, you think we qualify as human beings?

Buzzo (visibly irritated): Of course, Mezzi! What a question! We are human beings.

Mezzi: Even in the face of Nigger*tude?*

Buzzo: Yes, even though we have the 3/5th humans compromise tag, the monkeys...self-destructive monkey's tag, the Coon tag, we are human beings.

Mezzi: Slave trade...slavery...colonization...lynching, our default excuses.

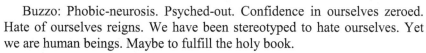

Buzzo: Phobic-neurosis. Psyched-out. Confidence in ourselves zeroed. Hate of ourselves reigns. We have been stereotyped to hate ourselves. Yet we are human beings. Maybe to fulfill the holy book.

Mezzi: To fulfill the Scriptures?

Buzzo: Maybe. Think about Jacob and Esau, the sons of Isaac.

Mezzi: Yeah!

Buzzo: Both were the Lord's creatures. Both were pitched to underpin the competitive comparative nature of God. Favored against unfavored. Fairness against unfairness.

Mezzi: Without the uselessness of Esau you won't notice the usefulness of Jacob.

Buzzo: Not exactly. I would say favored and unfavored. Fairness to one and unfairness to the other.

Mezzi: Said between us, that was plain gratuitous partiality on the part of God.

Buzzo (breaks up laughing): Good point. Apparently, it looks partial. Without the uselessness of Esau and his oblivion, one will not notice the usefulness of Jacob and his prominence.

Mezzi: You are saying in essence that without Black kind uselessness we won't notice the usefulness of the White kind?

Buzzo: Not exactly. The Lord works in a mysterious way. He endowed us with everything second to no other. Just like the endowed Canaan, the land of other Nations taken from them and given to the Jews out of Egypt by the Lord as the promised land.

Mezzi: Then our natural endowment looks like our nemesis, our curse.

Buzzo: Far from it. Our curse is our iniquities. Canaan was taken because of those Nations' wickedness.

Mezzi: It's beginning to make sense. In fact, in the book of Deuteronomy, it was the evil and iniquities of those nations, not the righteousness of the Jews that decided the gift.

Buzzo: You asked if we are human beings? We are but less humane than our White kindreds. Our iniquities of laziness, denials, cowardice and hate for ourselves, perhaps take away our endowments.

Mezzi: Great point, but regardless it does not annul the amount of animosity and hate that is left in the wake of the good books' fulfilling.

Buzzo: You have a great point. Esau comes out hating Jacob. The Black kind comes out hating the White kind.

Mezzi: It is much worse. The Black kind hates and despises self, to the extent that Black "men of God" psyche out their congregants, to the extent that the African politicians deprive and loath her citizenry. To those extents, we even hate our skins and our hairs. We crave for bleaching creams and wigs.

Buzzo: Malcolm X said it loud and clear. How can a man hate the colour of his skin, the texture of his hair, the thickness of his lips, the conformation of his nose? We have phobic-neurosis trauma. Psychologically beaten and subdued. Yet we are human beings.

Mezzi: Caravan of incapableness…the one capableness: bonding and romancing with misery.

Buzzo: Paraphrasing Oscar Wilde: *"…no civilized man ever regrets a pleasure, and no uncivilized man ever knows what a pleasure is."* So, let me ask you this: Are you ready to walk the African walk?

Mezzi (reflexively): Are you kidding me? Yes Buzz, that's why I am here!

Buzzo: Then, let me say this to you: No civilized mind ever regrets pleasure of civilization. Anything less gives him broken heartedness. Our African walk is an existential luxury. And in it, if Africa does not break your heart, know that you do not love her enough.

Mezzi: That's compelling. I will love her enough to prove books fulfilment obsolete.

Buzzo: It will be our luxury of self-reproach. The luxury will be courage.

Mezzi (his face a frowning grimace): The luxury is courage?

Buzzo: Paraphrasing once again: *"…at the end, nothing remains but recollection of pleasures or the luxury of regrets."*

Mezzi (smiling): I guess that's Oscar Wilde once again?

Buzzo: For we can be compassionate with everything but with misery and with dehumanization. They are of equal footing. Their recollections are of no pleasure.

Mezzi: Sacrosanct veritas! Then Buzzo, we've got to prove we are human beings.

Buzzo: Prove *"…we can contribute something mankind can enjoy."*

Mezzi: It's unfathomably humiliating. It's humiliating to grapple with the fact that Africa has not contributed to anything I have in the microcosm of my room – the TV, the phone, the music set, the Light, the pipe-borne water, my computer, my iPad, my watch, my shoes, my clothes, down to the macrocosm of the world as we see and use it – the trains, yachts, airplanes, skyscrapers, the houses, the parks the sewerage, the schools, the hospitals the roads, airports, stadia…

Buzzo: Precisely! Our inheritance is arduous. The task seems remarkably transcendental. Overwhelmingly overwhelming. Total lack of environment, a lack of platform for our Black kind Gen Z family to ride on, like the White kind Gen Z family have. Even at those, we have no luxury of going back. We the Youths, we the Generation Z, the Black kind Gen Z must dominate Africa's environment.

Mezzi: Well said Buzzo.

Buzzo: Our first step is to deal with Africa's youths' self-consciousness.

Mezzi (somewhat lost): Africa's self-consciousness?

Buzzo: Yes. That's our problem. Imagine Consciousness to be the macrocosm – God, Nature, and Self-consciousness to be microcosm – yourself. Self-consciousness must work with Consciousness to figure out the nature of things for harmony and progress.

Mezzi: I get it. Macrocosm and microcosm. Nature and Science. God and us.

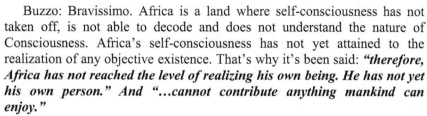
Buzzo: Bravissimo. Africa is a land where self-consciousness has not taken off, is not able to decode and does not understand the nature of Consciousness. Africa's self-consciousness has not yet attained to the realization of any objective existence. That's why it's been said: *"therefore, Africa has not reached the level of realizing his own being. He has not yet his own person."* And *"...cannot contribute anything mankind can enjoy."*

Mezzi: So, the bottom line is to develop one.

Buzzo: Yes. We need to educate Africa.

Mezzi: Educate Africa, educate generations of our father or just our Generation?

Buzzo: Or both.

Mezzi: You want us to waste our time? My teacher of psychology says it is 99.9% impossible to change any person above 26 years of age.

Buzzo: That sounds right. A lot of psychology has been said and I can even tell you that from what I see here in Africa. I will even exclude Gen Z who have kids already.

Mezzi: Precisely the point. When you have kids, the fighting spirit of any revolution is over. I think we should just channel and restrict our efforts to African Gen Z.

Buzzo: We should try regardless broadly, indistinctively given that their self-consciousness is moronic and take them out of their spasm of phobic-neurosis of enslavement and colonialism and from their Object Surrendering Permanence of institutional racism.

Mezzi: Slow down Buzzo, I know this is a repeat: what's phobic-neurosis?

Buzzo: In simple terms, it is the extreme anxiety and the extreme fear of the self-consciousness to rationalize and research social situations due to its extreme laziness and cowardice.

Mezzi: The mind cannot bring self to rationalize?

Buzzo: And to research!

Mezzi: What of Object Surrendering Permanence?

Buzzo: Object Surrendering Permanence means you give up rationalizing and to research your problem, surrender to the problem and live with it permanently.

Mezzi: Yeah that's why Africa looks arrested in time and space.

Buzzo: That's why their self-consciousness is only able of self-enslavement, selfcolonization, institutional self-looting, all vestiges internalized from slavery, colonization and institutional racism at the hand of the West.

We should try regardless broadly, indistinctively given that their self-consciousness is moronic and take them out of their spasm of phobic-neurosis of enslavement and colonialism and from their ...

...Object Surrendering Permanence of institutional racism.

Mezzi: Then we only need to educate the minds of our Gen Z African peers. We don't need to waste time in a losing battle. Just the Gen Z. We need a platform. A platform to ride on (sudden glow in his eyes). Absolutely Buzzo! Our kids got to play...kids got to play...these kids must play.

Buzzo: (surprised, lost): Kids got to play?

Mezzi: Yeah, the platform! The platform!! The platform!!! Buzzo, the distance between our world and theirs, between us and them. Yeah bridge the distance. Yeah, these kids got to play...yeah, every kid literate...yeah, break this cycle of jinx.

Buzzo (Recovers, got it): Bravo! You are processed and progressed overnight. Africa has fast-tracked you already into adulthood overnight! Yeah, you are right than right! Break the cycle of jinx. Kids got to...they got to play. Kids got to play is generations coming. Kids have never played on this continent before.

Mezzi: Never, ever! They have never dreamed. They've got to dream. The platform. The platform serves them to dream. This bond of misery speaks for itself.

Buzzo: Never dreamed. Can't dream. They can only have nightmares. Totally defiled. Subjugated and subdued. Incapacitated to dream beauty. Can't believe in something positive. You just brought me to the realization of a remarkable undisputable truth. Which is that Africa grows into adulthood without playing. Just think about it. No kindergartens, no primary education. No high school education. No colleges. No healthcare. No parks. No gardens. No jobs. Where and when you have them, they are ill-equipped, sub-humans. Just nothingness.

Mezzi: In the West these life stages are like toys. Toys all the way and everywhere. We toy with current electricity, with free education, with nutrition, with mass transit systems, with travels, with health care, with WIFI, with social media. With liberty of expression. With freedoms. With virtually everything and above all, with the luxury innocence of them all.

Buzzo: We toy with everything as basic fundamental human rights. But Africans toy with nothingness. They are not denied of toys. They deny themselves of toys. So, they grow into adulthood, subjugated in a harsh environment, subdued in tribulation and enslaved in remarkable misery at the hands of their despotic hereditary tradition and all.

Mezzi: Yeah, their individual talents denied access to any ability, to any motivation or any right to develop and make any value of themselves.

Buzzo: And for the few privileged, like the primogenitors of the despotic tradition, their toy is primal instinct: the few primogenitors are predatory to the over one billion and counting Negro's continent.

Mezzi: Correct! Kleptomania. Hyperbole.

Buzzo: One man owns 360 homes and houses overseas. Over 200 cars. Few men have the Gross Domestic Product of 1.4 billion Africans in foreign banks.

Mezzi: Our father inclusive.

Buzzo: Yeah, indeed! Pure insanity. Remarkable madness. Our father is a very, very, very sick persona.

> *...Then let me say this to you: No civilized mind ever regrets the pleasure of civilization. Anything less gives him broken heartedness. Our African walk is an existential luxury. And in it, if Africa does not break your heart, know that you do not love her enough. For we can be compassionate with everything but with Misery and with Dehumanization. They are of equal footing.*

Mezzi: Urgency of the moment Buzzo. This is extraordinary time. This time puts into focus the old code of law that holds every wrong a justice. We have to move the problem from our hearts to the streets. We owe them a better continent than this

Buzzo: Yeah, a revolution. Clinging to old pattern of subservient cowering, cringing cowardice, craven hypocrisy of the past before the misery legacy of hereditary hierarchic despotic tradition must be overwhelmed. Annihilated.

Mezzi: Yeah! We've got to go back to grandpa, to the village. We are starting from there, our calling's now. Our kids got to play! Dominance of our environment.

Buzzo: Yeah, kids' literacy is a fundamental step in the right direction. If done now, it would remotely help uplift the place in 18 years of time.

Mezzi: Remotely?

Buzzo: These educated kids would only gain economic mobility in 18 to 20 years. The other real urgency of the time is the tribulation of the teaming youth, the young men and women turned adults of the family of the African Gen Z. Our peers on the African continent. They are denied. They are subjugated. They are vacuous. They have been impacted laziness. No parenting. No social set tools. No social skilled sets of values. No social coping mechanisms. No social platforms. They are confused. They are unfocused. Low esteem of themselves. Addicted to technology. They are impatient. They want entitlements and yet they don't have beliefs. Complacent. They want mundanity, worldliness like their peers in the West and yet they don't know what it means. We need to study them, understand them, prime them and give them belief renaissance. Believe in themselves renaissance. Every man is the center of the universe. Every Gen Z, a demi god. Renaissance interest. A hope renaissance. Virtue of work opium. Work culture the drug.

The African spiritual situation is they don't believe in God. They hope in his grace. They seem stuck with religion because there is nothingness in the horizon. A solemn tragedy.

Buzzo shoots a glance at Mezzi who looks transfixed. Lost. With the realization of a seeming boring monologue, he stops talking. He thinks "don't convolute the already convoluted and hurt mind of Mezzi. He is looking up to you as a model of paradigm shift and solace."

Buzzo: Common let's go with your idea- check out the willful hereditary hierarchic despotic tradition.

Mezzi: Plus, the local government councilor.

Buzzo: Yeah, the willful political kleptomania.

Mezzi: There has to be some accountability. Some consequences. Just look around us. Misery everywhere. Kids everywhere. Not in school. They eat, kiss and blend in open-air urination. In open air defecation. In open air trashes. No sewer system. No refuse trashes. Filth everywhere. Filth is all a nigger is worth.

Buzzo: Yeah remarkably slothful. Total dislike for work.

Mezzi: Remarkably slothful than sloth. But why? Can any human be born stupid?

Buzzo: Of course, yes. The DNA.

Mezzi: Can any human be born slothful?

Buzzo: I don't think so. No. A culture could decide to dislike to work. Complacency. Gratuitous craven laziness. Cowardice.

Mezzi: Even amidst an ocean of misery?

Buzzo: Yes Mezzi. We are seeing it. We are living it. It's palpable. Our dislike to work. Our slothfulness, our misery. We accept misery when we have adoptable solutions available to us, from all over, not to have misery. To that extent, we are sub-humans and remain slaves in turn for the hardworking White kind and now for the Yellow kind. The Asians...

Mezzi: ...Except we shift to 'Love of work paradigm.'

Buzzo: Yes. Love, smart work credo. And fast. Dominance. Now!

Now they lock and hold stare. Momentous seconds that seemed interminable of an undaunted fiery, fierce, reassuring tacit stare pass, they break a smile.

Buzzo pushes the pedal, accelerating towards grandpa.

The two brothers are united by fate and in a cohesive bond. A remarkable binding faith. A belief system. A remarkable powerful source of inspiration of hard work, of perseverance, of fortitude, of hope, of comfort, of understanding to defeat numbing poverty and the palsy of despicable shamelessness of a Nigger and Nigger*tude*. In the distance you can hear the calling to 16:00hrs Muslim prayers:

"Shillala...Allah Akbar, shillala...Allah Akbar."

Buzzo looks at Mezzi. Mezzi understands and drawls with a simper, short of a smile.

Mezzi: I told you, too many religions with their symbolism of misery on this land.

Buzzo: I can't agree any less.

Mezzi: Look at the freedom, incarnated in development and in progress of humanity achieved by the Western Christian Religion. And look at the freedom Islam is lately incarnating. Qatar, Singapore, Malaysia, UAE, Saudi Arabia, Kuwait, giving their people dignity. But in Africa, null.

"Shillala…Allah Akbar, shillala…Allah Akbar," is drawing nearer.

Buzzo: Even the atheist China is developing and progressing freedom.

Mezzi: Our oracles, voodoos and jujus are such a primitivity, just good for a total obliteration.

Buzzo: Yeah, to that extent, like the Western Christian civilization, China just like Turkey, has established secularism to develop. We should do the same.

"Shillala… Allah Akbar," is now staring them in the face. It's one of the city's mosques of medium importance.

Mezzi nudges Buzzo to stop.

Buzzo slams the breaks, and grinds the car to a stop across the road, overlooking the mosque.

The Mosque

The Moslem Faithful are milling, entering the mosque.

Mezzi comes down from the car and follows. He gains the inside in a minute.

Buzzo, in mind his brother's unruly temperament and develop Africa with immediacy mindset, is in a spasm of anguish, waiting in the car, observing the movements, busy talking to somebody over his phone.

Like most people, Buzzo has never seen the four walls of any mosque before. To this extent, whatever goes on inside a mosque is left to their individual imaginations and judgement.

In what seemed a literal twinkle of an eye, the prayers are over: the faithful are coming out of the mosques in droves, fluttering and dispersing and disappearing. Buzzo notices and checks out his wrist watch. In realization, he grins elatedly. He disengages and trains his stare, back on the faithful as they swarm out, flutter, disperse and disappear: but Mezzi is yet to be seen. He was amongst the last to gain within. He should have been amongst the first to gain without.

On the inside, we take on Mezzi who, meanwhile has walked up to the Imam, a man forty-ish, tall of slim and agile built, of an absolute austere demeanor, monk-like looking, in his long robe of meek and self-effacing sheepherder, of disarming fascination, engaging him in discussion.

Mezzi: Your place of worship is quite austere. Your prayers quite brief.
Imam: Just like your Lord's Jesus prayers.
Mezzi (grinning): Yeah, correct. You figured out I am a Christian in your domain.
Imam: That was easy. How may I help you?
Mezzi: Beautiful question. Can't you put off your 5 A.M. prayers to 7 A.M. instead?
Imam: African Millennials should not be sleeping at that hour. You can afford that in the West but not in Africa. They shouldn't be sleeping. They can't afford that luxury yet. They should be working hard 24/7 against their misery and against misery Status Quo proponents.
Mezzi (stunned by his line of reasoning): I am surprised. Isn't religion, including yours, their prisoner, their dilemma?
Imam: Son, that's an excuse. Sloth is our prisoner. Sloth makes the African leadership prisoner. With equal vigor, sloth is the prisoner of Africa's Leadership followers. Anything else son?

Before Mezzi could answer, the Imam walks away, solemnly disappearing in a flash behind the mosque's flapping curtains.
Meanwhile, an alarmed Buzzo, who could not wait anymore has gained the inside of the mosque and had watched them from a distance, far removed. Mezzi, with air of bewilderment and wonderment, turns and heads out.
Then, he sees Buzzo standing, his figure, silhouetted by the setting sun. Now Mezzi reaches, joining him. They leave, heading out of the mosque, for the car.

Mezzi: That Imam is a pleasant strange man. I think he is a hostage. He is a victim. He is not subdued. He is angry at Africa. He could be our ally. He stands to express himself someday.
Buzzo is momentarily speechless. He is in worrisome confusion at Mezzi's words. He is trying to make sense of whatever information Mezzi is in possession of.
Buzzo: An African Imam angry at Africa?
Mezzi: Sure Buzzo.
Buzzo: You are kidding! It should be the other way around. All religious faith in Africa, including Islam, hold Africans hostage.
Mezzi: Trust me. He is different.
Buzzo: Imams, just like the Pastors and the voodoo chief priests, are paid by the kleptomania Status Quo leadership for prayers to buy their places in heaven and to enslave and perpetuate enslavement of the men and women and children and the environment of the continent.

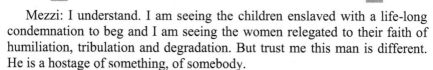

Mezzi: I understand. I am seeing the children enslaved with a life-long condemnation to beg and I am seeing the women relegated to their faith of humiliation, tribulation and degradation. But trust me this man is different. He is a hostage of something, of somebody.

Buzzo: Hostage of Allah maybe, far from a Nigger hostage.

Mezzi: Who is a Nigger?

Buzzo: Who is a Nigger? The dominated!

Chapter 5

The Village
  Their ancestral village, located 4,000 meters from the city center is made up of five hamlets. Each hamlet is a community of families. Each family a community of households. Each household a community of parents. Each parent a community of siblings: a remarkable number of siblings. A remarkable community of siblings. Each hamlet has a square. Each square is connected to the other by a road path, sandy or muddy or of both surfacing. Each square is devoid of any amenities, facilities like garden, equipped garden, library, civic center, water, any interactive structure and is corniced by remarkable fewer numbers of huts. And sometime you can see some Western style affluent structures. Yet the squares are filled with remarkably overwhelming presence of children. So much so that you can guess a ratio of 15-20 children per hut. These communities of children are subdued by fate of misery but regardless busy at what they can to mitigate misery routine.

Their ancestral home is a fortress that alone hosts six of these remarkable Western style affluent structures: in fact, a remarkable six towering duplexes, like an island of a castle in the middle of the ocean. Ocean of huts and children and misery. This is home to their grandfather who is the traditional chief. The hereditary traditional despotic power.

The fortress has every comfort: hybrid solar-generating electric energy, treated borehole water, garden and parks, recreational meeting islands, a chapel, island of garage of cars.

This place has been remarkably created to suit the needs of their father, the wants of their father. And to mirror the image of their father's life style. Three of these duplexes are always on a permanent lock down. They are for their father and his friends whenever he visits. One is permanently occupied by their grandfather. One by the household of home executives and the Butler. One for visiting relatives.

Their grandfather is a man of 82 years. One of the oldest of the village. For his age, he is still physically and mentally sane and sound. He has an austere demeanor, in antithesis to his environment. He actually looks lost.

He lost his wife to an excruciating cancer battle. He is all by himself now, taken care of by a host of home executives and butler.

Buzzo and Mezzi walk up to their grandfather, who is alone, seated in the middle of the park of the house, eyes fixed right across the family tomb.

He is close in spirit to his deceased wife, deceased mother and deceased father.

Buzzo: Hi grandpa, we are back.

Grandpa (raising his head smiling at them): Welcome back boys!

Mezzi (sitting on the arm of grandpa seat, looks him up, cuddling his arm and down to his head): The remarkable solemn memory in this remarkable vacuity of this environment accentuates grave vacuity of loneliness. Anybody's loneliness. Your loneliness.

Grandpa: Yeah, remarkably sad.

Buzzo: I have advised you need kids around to keep you alive and strong.

Mezzi: Yeah grandpa, that's a sacrosanct truth.

Grandpa: Your kids. I am waiting for your kids.

Mezzi: Common grandpa! We are too young to have kids.

Grandpa: At your ages I had kids already.

Buzzo: Those were in your old good days. Things have evolved and are evolving.

Mezzi: Grandpa, there are plenty of kids in this village already.

Grandpa: And I already told you the consequences.

Mezzi: Grandpa, don't be worried about our dad's consequences. You need to be happy and alive.

Grandpa: He won't let them. They won't ever come. They are afraid of this compound.

Buzzo: He won't let them or you won't let them?

Mezzi: You have never loved kids, grandpa?

Grandpa: I have always been a traditionalist. Always far removed from the kids.

Mezzi: You are strictly-closely with the oracles.

Grandpa: Kids are for the women. I am always in the business of appeasing the souls of our ancestors and the gods.

Buzzo: Grandpa, that's absolutely a waste of precious time. You need to appease the living.

Grandpa (irked): Sons, it's forbidden to talk like that. You need to avert the wrath of the gods. I am the chief, the traditional authority, the custodian, the protector of the village.

Mezzi: The wrath of which gods? The gods of the dead souls? The despotic hereditary devil, the prisoner of the African mind-set, freedom and liberty, the evil?

Grandpa (now angry, with a finality of voice that prohibits): You must stop talking that way immediately.

Buzzo (undaunted): Why grandpa? After all you are the chief and not the chief priest. You have nothing to do with wraths and spirituality of the voodoo oracles.

Mezzi: That rickety looking chief priest, who does nothing but present enticing plates of jollof rice and chicken and boiled eggs to the oracle everyday instead of feeding the kids with them.

Buzzo (re-aligning the argument): However, we are yet to understand, why you have never loved kids.

Grandpa: I have always felt their presence but I have never had anything to do with them.

Mezzi: That's why. That's why so much misery. No love. Just penetrate the women and they pump out kids.

Buzzo: Grandpa, it's never too late to try.

Grandpa: It's remarkably too late instead, to try. Kids know who loves them. I have never manifested any interest, any affection towards them.

Mezzi: We will try now. For a remarkable ultimate experience. You have missed out the best of fun in your life.

Mezzi rushes out of the compound to the square and calls out, beckoning to the children, who should have been in school at that hour, to come. The kids mill and build up around him in a flash.

Mezzi: You all follow me. I want to give you all something to play with. Some toys. You all know what toys are, I hope!

The Shrine

Mezzi, apostrophizes his walk back to grandpa. He first walks straight to the shrine, overlooking the village square. The kids stop short in their tracks: they are afraid of what they have been taught, the value of the shrine, its oracular god and the ways it represents: infallible prophecies and harrowing punishments.

Mezzi, does not believe any of these things. His rationale knows the oracle is simply fetish.

It's juju, voodoo, hoodoo, fetish combined. It has nothing with rationalism, nothing to do with consciousness and self-consciousness development. Nothing to do with science and progress. It's simply a farce. A superstitious farce to defraud and enslave the African ignorant mind, generation after generation.

The kids, assailed by spasm of anxiety and curiosity, stand aloof.

Mezzi now enters the shrine and repeatedly kicks the oracular god in the face. The oracular god falls. This profanation aroused general competing amazement in the kids.

Mezzi then grabs the plate of rice with chicken and boiled eggs and to every kid's unutterable apprehension, he started eating the jollof rice and the chicken and the boiled egg.

Now in amazement of bewilderment, some of the kids crease into a debilitating fascination and attraction at the same time. Fascinated by the ethereal figure of Mezzi and his challenge to the oracle god, and attracted with equal vigor to the sumptuous elegance and the fragrance of fuming jollof rice and chicken, they trance in the realm of pseudo-omnipotence: A bunch of them break ranks, joining Mezzi to eat. They break with the jinx of centennial fear of unfounded retributory dire consequences, only found in conditioned mind and stereotyped psychology.

Done with the shrine, he walks off. They all follow him. He heads straight back to grandpa's compound. The kids notice. They follow him and as they get close to the threshold of the remarkably majestic gate of the compound, the kids abruptly stop, as if in compliance with some tacit transcendental order. Mezzi notices, stops in his tracks and turns facing them.

Mezzi: Common guys, let's go!

The kids instead gradually backtrack...break up running...disappearing en masse. Mezzi remarkably surprised and disappointedly pained, gets trudging back to the compound. Back to grandpa and Buzzo, who have witnessed all in the meantime.

Grandpa: You wanted to try. Not even if here was a free Disneyland. Neverland, Wonderland. Whatever.
Buzzo: I have heard you say that before. You won't go any further than that?

Grandpa looks at both, in contemplation. With a heavy voice:

Grandpa: Your father in his last visit walks into this compound unannounced, surprising the presence of a handful of children who had come to fetch water from our borehole over there.
He orders their arrest and detention. Then in the distance you could hear the floggings and their excruciating yelling. It was remarkably despicably sickening. Their crime, fetching water from our compound instead of from the distant stream. I begged on my knees for clemency and mercy but to no avail.

He pauses. And continues:

You know when you feel remarkably a piece of shit? Remarkably chagrined being alive? Praying for the earth to open up and swallow you? For the first time I knew I was never loved nor respected. I was nobody. Meant remarkably nothing.
Your father did not stop there. He got the entire household arrested, detained, punished and summarily sacked.

In the distance, Mezzi has broken down. Sobbing and vomiting. Buzzo goes for him.

Grandpa: Leave him. It serves him. Serves both of you right. I have been a bad person, a coward, obliged and compelled by tradition. Not any good excuse. I wish I could have a second shot at life. But I can't.

I like your remarkably profound intrinsic spiritual essences, your energies, your courage, your unscripted veil of justice. Congratulations on your choice of different path and pattern from your parents. I have never seen such a callousness and soullessness.

Now, Mezzi recovers and not demoralized, pressed on undauntedly:

Mezzi (jumping to his feet): Buzzo, thank you. Let's go.
Buzzo: To where?
Mezzi (grabs the hand of Buzzo, dragging him, heading out of the compound): We have unfinished business with the Councilor. Dominate kleptocracy.
Buzzo (resisting the dragging): Easy, you are going to break down. Let's do that tomorrow.
Mezzi: I am having nightmares. I can't sleep.

Buzzo who is remarkably preoccupied for Mezzi's remarkable restlessness, remarkable insomnia, obliges.

Together they head out of the compound to the seventh remarkable western style structure of the hamlet. The structure of the local government councilor. The political kleptomaniac power.

The Councilor's Home
The local government Councilor, the political authority welcomes them remarkably cordially. Yet Buzzo knows that they are generally remarkably viscid than viscidness. He needs tact to handle the situation at the extremes of emotions: on the one hand, willful proponents and contrivance of misery, and on the other, the willful opponents of misery and seekers of a remarkable beginning to freedom.

Buzzo: Councilor, we are here more for reflections than for reproach.
The state of our village, our hamlets is remarkably markedly offensive to our feelings, remarkably despicable to our eyes and remarkably morally reprehensible to any human character.
Councilor: Oh! The state of the village, the hamlet? Well, well, well. It's not easy... has not been easy.
Mezzi (immediately goes on the attack, head on): Building your house has not been easy? Sinking your borehole has not been easy? Generating your current electricity has not been easy?
Councilor (display of cynical irony): The world is not a perfect place.
Buzzo: Let me restate that we are here for reflections. We wish to understand why it has been remarkably easy doing nothing for these kids?

Mezzi: It has been easy denying them schools? It has been easy denying them water? It has been easy denying them health care? It has been easy denying them a playground, a garden, a park, a library, Internet center, laboratories. It has not been easy sending your kids to study overseas? It has not been easy sending your family for medical care overseas?

Councilor (irritated): I understand your cultural freedom of everything. Just imagine your profanation of, and your vicious attack on the shrine, before the watchful curious eyes of everyone. Please your cultural freedom should not mean disrespect for our institution and constituted authorities.

Mezzi: Are you not that constituted institution and authority?

Councilor: No, I am not. They are the tradition and its authority, the family and its values, the government and its authority, the church and its morals. I only represent the government.

Mezzi: You represent the government and its authority of gifting misery, instead of protection and dignity. That's the culture of your representation. Dominance!

Councilor: That's a mischaracterization. My culture is work for the people.

Mezzi: Your work culture is making yours the people's resources and money and making the same people remarkably miserable. Dominance over the people. Bond the people and youth and kids in misery.

Buzzo: Let's just for one second grant that every being merits consideration even for a remarkable evil doer.

Councilor (piqued): What? Remarkable evil doer?

Buzzo (ignoring him, pressing on): Councilor, do you believe in the after-life?

Councilor: Of course. Who doesn't?

Buzzo: So, you believe there is a soul?

Councilor: Yes, I do.

Buzzo: Then you believe in the dogma of heaven and hell? Dogma of hell as punishment and heaven as paradise? Hell, for evil soul and heaven for good soul?

Councilor: Correct. Very correct.

Buzzo: So, we all agree there is afterlife? There is soul? There is heaven and hell? There is heaven to receive good souls and hell to receive evil souls?

Councilor: Absolutely so.

Buzzo: Councilor, if we care for our souls' afterlife, how then do people like you and my father…

Councilor (recoiling voluptuously at the mention of father): Your father?

Buzzo: Yes…people like you and my father contrive the idea of punishing our people, trample on them, deny them dignity, give them hell on this earth? Is it something passed on to you, generation after generation? Imposed on you, generation after generation? Or it's something received by learning generation after generation and retaliated subsequently generation after generation?

The Councilor seemed remarkably wanting and in trepidation, overwhelmed and confused at this reasoning. He is fixing the ground. Some infinite void beyond the physical ground. Numbed. Mezzi is fixing him intensely. Buzzo continues.

Buzzo: There is no premium in making anything, everything better than we find it. Our progeny better. Our progenies make their progenies better. For that's every human's natural calling.

> There is no premium in making anything, everything better than we find it. For it's the human's natural calling to make its progeny better. Progeny's progeny better. Progeny's progeny's progeny better. Progeny's progeny's progeny's progenies better. Progenies better, better, better, better, better, better, better, better, better, in continuum, in continuum, in continuum, in continuum progress, progress, progress, progress, progress, progress, progress, progress, progress, progress. Otherwise the human has failed.

That's what the White kind does remarkably remarkable. Their progress is glaring. Their solutions to mankind's problems give us earthly heaven. Our life styles. Sometimes you may condemn them for their method of chicanery and deceit and rapaciousness as their means of progress that may sometimes seem remarkably cynical. But life itself sometimes imposes that. Imposes choices. Hard choices. Primal instinct does. Survival of the fittest in the zoo does. The slothful is swallowed by the smart hard working. Joy and pride, their life purpose, their soul motivation. Immortality of legacy, their afterlife legacy.

Maybe what happens to a man after he is dead is of no significance to him. But what of his soul? Councilor, shouldn't we care where our souls go to when we are dead? If there is afterlife, why the efforts at giving misery? Why the efforts at perpetuating misery? Why the efforts at example and at exhortation of remarkable willful selfishness? Why willful selfishness of illusive progress only in our individual families? With gifting of derogatory misery to our Black kind?

Why the vanity and presumption to govern from the grave?

It's been asked before if a man does own another man? Or own property in man? Or any generation own a property in the generation following?

Why we obliterate individuality, regress collectivity, perpetuating societal retrogression, conflict and misery?

Shouldn't we care to gladden the hearts of our kids instead of hardening them into how to further refine and perfect the arts of punishment of the punishments they have beheld and received and in turn perpetuate these arts of punishment and spell these dooms of punishment in return as soon as they assume authority? A neverending story…that's our calling? That's what our self-consciousness is only capable of?

Mezzi (who has been impatiently listening, interjects, his finger pointing): Mr. Councilor, that forest over there that stretches infinitely before us, can it be rented or leased or purchased?

Councilor and Buzzo are caught by surprise. They quickly recover spinning their heads following the direction of Mezzi's hand.

Councilor: That, over there? That belongs to your family.

Mezzi (bouncing to his feet, pleasantly surprised): Councilor you are kidding?

Councilor: Absolutely not. The whole expanse. From that footpath to that other one and stretching for about infinite kilometers and confines with the city that direction…close to Governors lodge.

Buzzo: There is the right of occupancy, certificate of occupancy?

Mezzi: What's that?

Councilor: Sure. I handled it for your father. I have the photocopies of the whole documents. Approvals. Ready to go.

Buzzo: Means we can put it to use right away?

Councilor: Sure, as that crescent moon (pointing at the dusking sky).

Mezzi: (pushing back, restraining his joy, his eyes glistening): We can use it right away?

Councilor: It's yours.

Mezzi instantly springs to his feet. His eyes in the infinite horizon.

Mezzi: Buzzo, let's go. So long Councilor.

Mezzi is already in the distance. Councilor and Buzzo shake hands bidding each other good night.

Then Buzzo catches up, joining Mezzi.

Mezzi (breaks out jumping in felicitation): What a defining moment. What a day. Unbelievable precious day. Buzzo our dream realization begins.

Buzzo: Yes. The secret of happiness begins.

Mezzi: Buzzo, wishes could become horses?

Buzzo: Horses are going to pass through the eyes of the needles?

Mezzi: The miracle, Buzzo! The kids are going to be riding. Kids got a play center.

Buzzo: We see things that should have long been and we say now be them!

Mezzi: Who was that again you are paraphrasing?

Buzzo: President Kennedy.

Mezzi: No! The man of Irish descent.

Buzzo: Right. George Bernard Shaw.

They give each other low fives as they approach their ancestral compound.

> *It's been asked before if a man does own another man? Or owns property in man? Or any generation owns a property in the generation following? Why we obliterate individuality, regress collectivity, perpetuating societal retrogression, conflict and misery?*
>
> *Shouldn't we care to gladden the hearts of our kids instead of hardening them into how to further refine and perfect the arts of punishment of the*
>
> *punishments they have beheld and received and in turn perpetuate these arts of punishment and spell these dooms of punishment in return as soon as they assume authority.*

The last 10 days have been the most remarkably remarkable:

To the extent they have launched the "Kids got to play center" in the hamlet;

To the extent that they have dug a borehole in the hamlet;

To the extent that they have built a six-room block of a civic center that hosts a library, an Internet center, a first aid dispenser, teachers' rooms. Another block of six classrooms. A block of refectory with kitchen. A block of restrooms; To the extent that they installed solar panels and batteries for power;

To the extent that they built a garden and equipped it–soccer, basketball, fitness, slides, slings, etc.;

To the extent that they placed every kid of the hamlet on scholarship– free tuition fees, free books, free uniforms, free shoes;

To the extent that some unemployed Gen Z graduates are being skilled and engaged to handle the extra–curricular activities of the kids;

To the extent that they bought and provided bicycles and tricycles and vans, fueling them, commuting kids to schools back and forth;

To the extent that they engaged and organized some young entrepreneurial restaurateur to cook, in turns for their every school day breakfast and launch needs; To these extents the last ten days have been both remarkably excruciatingly challenging and remarkably, overwhelmingly satisfactory for Buzzo and Mezzi.

The joy their hearts behold is sublime than subliminal. Their ultimate pride is the ultimate air of incredulity every hamlet's eye expresses in their behold. Their pride in beguiling the fervidness, the ardor of the ultimate pride affectation in the eyes of the kids. Their pride in the defiant air of importance demeanor of the kids.

It is remarkably amazing the speed, the grace, the naturalness with which the kids fitted into their new roles: their luxury at patience, their torture at impatience, their remarkable tenacity of faith in the hopelessness of hope have defeated at least for a day the consorts and coiners of their miseries and degradation.

The consequences of Buzzo and Mezzi's actions, remarkably transcend any emotion they have felt in their yacht, in their private jet, in their Rolls Royces, Ferraris, Bugattis; in the luxury of their upscale apartments and palaces; on their first date, their first kiss, their first coitus; their graduation day; their lofty gifts of 20 million US dollars apiece, ready for them, as they turn 18 years of age.

Even though this feat has been harrowingly excruciating, even though it has been like peeling off layers of an onion, each layer unfolding forth a new problem, Caravans of problems: dig a borehole you need to pump water; provide the solar panels, you need batteries and maintenance; provide scholarship you need to refurbish the dilapidated piteous public schools' classrooms, libraries, restrooms, playgrounds, cloth them, book them, extra-curricular activate them; provide a commuter, and the commuter and the commuted need fueling and maintenance; provide refectory you need the restaurateurs and services to feed them and maintain the structure; provide the "Kids must play center" platform, you fight their slothful parents' system of children enslavement to labor and abuse; to their thrill, all these misgivings pale remarkably in comparison to the remarkable sense of pride and the subliminal joy their hearts behold.

They partake in how this singular action remarkably barrens any intellectual speculation, contrivance and inaction.

This trailblazing action has more than anything else shot them unexpectedly into remarkable elevation, prominence and Limelight.

Their grandfather is congratulated, admired in awe and effusively blessed for having grandsons, their types.

The Councilor seems chagrined, filled with double sense of shame and lost. Both grandfather and Councilor have helped guarantee that the parents take first bite at their slothfulness: must fetch water for themselves from the borehole and that the kids must not be disturbed from their school activities, even though the kids remarkably fought back on their own, unrestrained by the new taste of freedom. Even the local churches and the mosques are praising and referencing the solemnness of their act. A Godly act. The true "love thy neighbor" commandment.

These days hold Mezzi grandeur and Buzzo ethereal.

However, Buzzo is not beclouded by the beautiful beauty of the moment nor by its emotional emotions.

He watches his brother fall asleep with some apparent peace, heavy breathing. He puts out the light and settles into the peace of the study of their village home to do some hard thinking.

He understands the non-negotiable ineluctable umbilical cord. Cord of sustainability. Cord as a tangible hope. A tangible belief. Hope in belief.

Belief in hope. Faith and trust fulfilment indivisible. Their indivisibility, essential for success. He understands the present and clear danger in disaster of failure. The fear of disaster of failure obliges his neural groove, his self-consciousness to a perennial critical thinking engagement, thinking engagement to avert failure.

They cannot depend on the Status Quo. Status Quo has been and is Africa's misery. Predicament. Dilemma.

The combined Status Quo of the Hereditary Hierarchic Despotic Tradition – the superfluous and disdainful evil African monarchy, the Kleptocratic Political Leadership, the Hypnotic Religions–have Africa's family of Youths on a lock down. They have them deprived. They have them depraved. They have them denied. They have them hungered. They have them in phobic-neurosis. To these extents they have them remarkably traumatized, vulnerable and in hopelessness of hope. They have them caged in nothingness. Nothingness begets nothingness. And this is where some faith take hold. Take advantage. Fill the vacuum. Faith in some remarkable vague. Vague of celestial promises. Vague of uncertainty. Vague of horizon of nothingness.

And if the Status Quo must be severed from, if they must be laid to rest, if the funeral of evil is now; if the aura of freedom is now; then promises are not the answer. Even the most remarkable subliminal celestial promise should not be the answer. We need Renaissance credo. The Renaissance belief. The family of deprived African Youths, commencing with Gen Z need a renaissance to grow their self-consciousness.

> *They cannot depend on the Status Quo. Status Quo has been and is Africa's misery. Predicament. Dilemma.*
> *The combined Status Quo of the Hereditary Despotic Tradition–the superfluous and disdainful evil African monarchy, the Kleptocratic political leadership, the hypnotic Religions–have Africa's family of Youths on a lock down. They have them deprived. They have them depraved. They have them denied. They have them hungered. They have them in phobic-neurosis. To these extents they have them remarkably traumatized, voluptuously vulnerable and ponderously in hope-hopelessness. They have them caged in nothingness. Nothingness begets nothingness. Self-esteem is lost. And this is where some faith take hold. Like opioid, vague of celestial promises and myth and mysticisms fill the vacuum.*

It has been said that religion is the opium of the masses. It should have appropriately been framed as "the opium of the poor masses."

Let the renaissance belief, the belief, as was given birth to in Florence Italy *"that man is the center of the universe, that you have been created in God's image–the Consciousness, that you are a demi-God–the self-*

54

consciousness, that you are in charge of your life, that you are your destiny, that your life depends on your hard work, your efforts, your endeavor" be the belief, the credo, the opium of the African Youth family, commencing with Gen Z. Yes, we are demi-gods. Only subject to the Almighty God. Self-Consciousness in subordination, submissive only to Consciousness. That firstly, the Almighty worked so hard, creating the abode for Man: the perfect environment; and secondly, he created you in his image. So, we must be his image too. The luxury of his image. Believing him, believing you are his image. Emulating him, creating a near perfect environment. Self-consciousness decoding Consciousness, dominate your environment. Be the Renaissance Man - the Man at the center of the universe.

This concept, even though difficult to comprehend by the embattled African Gen Z Family, must regardless be enshrined. Very arduous task. But not impossible.

So, we need to create the African Youth renaissance credo movement. Yes, the African Youth Family renaissance credo movement. Indeed, the African Youth Family renaissance credo movement, to level up with the global family of Youth renaissance credo self-consciousness. A self-consciousness that asks questions and broache and prod answers. A self-consciousness that African Gen Z must be imbued with, elevated to enable and able the WHYS and The WHY NOTS. Yes, African Gen Z must trailblaze. And in turn Gen Z must imbue the minds of Africa's youth with renaissance credo self-consciousness of the WHY and of the WHY NOT to anything and to everything. Yes, a Generation WHY and WHY NOT renaissance credo erudite self-consciousness. Yes, a Gen WHY self-consciousness, in succession of the Black kind youth ad infinitum.

To do this we need food and earthly material, terrain hope palpability as our vehicles. Not promises. The slothful feeds on promises. Black kind youth, Africa's Youth, Black Kind Gen Z, Africa's Gen Z go to church not because they believe in God but because of some immediate miracle of their hope belief. Their desires. Their wants. The good news is that promises are remarkably transcended and subverted by an empty stomach. By hunger. Always.

So, we need food palpability. Material palpability. Earthly hope palpability.

Not the chimera celestial hope as the first vehicle, to sway and captivate the hungry and the forlorn.

That African Youth Family renaissance credo, that African Gen Z family, that opium must have a base, a social base, a financial base, a capital base, a live base, a work base, a play base. A platform. This is the second vehicle. A platform. A platform to imbue, to enable renaissance credo self-consciousness to elevate and emerge Gen WHY.

These are the caravans of remarkable invincible everyday shadow. Invincible everyday anxiety. Invincible everyday companion, all visibly present predators that Buzzo must vanquish.

Even though they have taken their first stride of the long path; even though they have started drawing down on his $20M; even though once Mezzi turns 18 years of age, he would add his to the cause as well; but for the multitude of African family of kids and Gen Z to progress, their survival, their sustainability down to their success hinge on cash flow. Staggering constant cash flow for an efficient deployment and result for a paradigm change.

Something has to happen. Something must be contrived. Contrived quickly too. $40M pales. It's nothing to take out misery. Its nothingness is however the bedrock. The ineluctable foundation. The essential fundamental ingredient. The challenge antidote. The irrefutable adrenalin to success.

Otherwise the Status Quo would once again be advantaged and perpetuate even more refined subtle misery in continuum.

These are his thoughts when suddenly Mezzi creeps up on him. Holds and kisses his head. He was in deep mental notes so was not necessarily shaken. But pleasantly surprised.

Buzzo: Hey, I thought I left you in heaven.

Mezzi: The face of Tom is ever present. A sleeping companion.

Buzzo: Umpteenth *reminiscentia*? You might consider putting a call through to him. Make some peace. Have some peace.

Mezzi: No! That bitch.

Buzzo: Common! Making peace is strength. Not weakness. Besides, for all you know he might be looking for you. You are at large. Remember?

Mezzi: If it's so, that serves him right. Anyway, can I share in what you are plotting?

Buzzo: Let's hear your neural grove out first. Mine could be boring. Nerve racking.

Mezzi: Yeah Buzzo, Tom Bradley might be right. He is right in telling me who we are. Our roots. He has been our trusted family friend from day one. I trusted him. Why on earth would he choose that place and time for a sudden gratuitous inveigh? That hurtful, hateful inveighs of Nigger and Niggertude?

Buzzo looks at him and waves him to the seat in front of his sitting position. Mezzi sits. Buzzo grabs his hands cuddling them reassuringly and starts speaking.

Buzzo: Now you know you are a degraded Biracial. Degraded to a Nigger, down from a Negro. You did not expect it, huh? Your self-consciousness reacted and you are very angry. Now you know that the world could be mean as well. I understand all that, but Listen to me carefully. Even though you are a teenager, it might help you to draw some conclusions, hopefully of peace. Tom Bradley comes from a shattered family. His family is separated. You have never seen his father before, right?

Mezzi (his face a sullen frown, nods his head): No.

Buzzo: His father, Mr. Johnson J. Bradley is a Klansman. From Mississippi. One of the capitals of slavery, lynching, confederate flags and all. Last state to rescind the 3/5th compromise institution. Do you know when?

Mezzi: What's 3/5th compromise institution?

Buzzo: I am sorry. The 3/5th compromise stated that a slave would count as 3/5th of a person. Of an American Citizen, for both taxation and representation. But the fall out obviously was, him not considered a full human being. He was 3/5th of a human being. If ever he was going to be allowed to vote, his vote would equal 3/5th of the value of a normal vote of a human being. The White kind being.

Mezzi (countenanced, in obvious assault of humiliation): When was it rescinded?

Buzzo: In the year 1991. Just the other day. So, Tom's mother is a White liberal, a progressive. Whatever that means. So, Tom lives in completely opposing divisive views of life, feeds and thrives in these confusing hybrid of environment set-values. Forced to come play with us on our yacht, private jets, homes, beach houses, in sum, shares in our privileges and all. Possibly as a respite. There is possibility that he could have, should have developed an ill-informed taught opinion of our family and its hyperbole privileges, coupled with the frustration that he is living within the opposing competing and conflicting family values of his background.

More so being White, a Gen Z White, he is empowered. Empowered. Empowered. Remarkably empowered. He has the finest, enviable hereditary and heritages. Hereditary of progress, of inventions, of innovations, of freedoms, of liberty, of confidence and of evil and vestiges of dehumanization. He has a platform for departure, a platform to higher realms of continuum inventions and innovations. Their renaissance credo – believe in yourself, man as a demi-god, man the center of the universe, belief in hard work, you decide your destiny – are God's image and likings. The foundation of science, of modern world took place in Florence, Italy, hundreds of years ago (1400 ad). They consumed liberation. Liberation from the medieval Christian religion period, considered one of the darkest moments in human history, with atrocities, killings, subjugations, enslavement, humiliations. Consumed in the name of God. Thanks to renaissance credo the mind was liberated and infused with this masterpiece centerpiece credo and decoration of science. And progress became. Conversely, present-day Africa is in her darkest period now after slavery and colonialism. We are in our middle ages now where our churches and mosques and juju shrines reign supreme, ruling the conscience of the African masses with illiteracy palsy, poverty palsy, sloth palsy, intimidation palsy, emotional blackmail palsy, celestial hope palsy, after death heavenly palsy, all with the platform of paying tithe to gain grace, then heaven palsy. With the pastors and cohorts making luxury living credo and principle out of the poor.

Since then, since their renaissance credo, their journey, his White kind journey has been remarkable. His heritage confers on him remarkable pride, remarkable confidence, relative superiority complex, defiance and thence a sublime intrinsic irrefutable spiritual essence rooted in the ability of their self-consciousness. Mezz, conversely take a look at our inheritance. Our heritage misery. Bonded in misery, regression. And thence shame. Lack of confidence. Inferiority complex. Stereotype. Confusion. Hopelessness. Our awful low self-consciousness and its inability.

And yet with these our misgivings you defeat him at the love court of Jennifer.

So, I think the only way he could live his frustrations and anger could be his inveighs.

Taking it out on somebody. That somebody happens to be you.

Maybe in his shoes you might have done the same.

But these said, let's take the positive side of it all: without Tom Bradley you won't be here, at least not so soon, taking the best chance of your life, dreaming and making effort to give your spiritual essence pride. In the end dreaming is no less important to realizing one's dreams. One means life in continuum. The other is just catharsis. And then what?

> *In the end dreaming is no less important to realizing one's dreams. The One means life in continuum. The other is just a catharsis. And then what?*

Mezzi (relieved. Smiling): Thank you Buzz. I feel a lot better. A lot better.

Buzzo: Cool?

Mezzi: Yeah. I feel a lightness. Weightlessness of being.

Buzzo: Milan Kundera. So, you can go to sleep now?

Mezzi: No! You promised your 'boring', nerve racking excogitations. Remember?

Buzzo: Sure, you want to bother yourself with that?

Mezzi: Yes Buzzo. Nigger and Niggertude are ever ponderously lurking in and voluptuously messing with my brain.

Buzzo: Yeah, real?

Mezzi: You were not there to see the cruelty and the viciousness of those words at me. And the condescending reactions on me. A total effrontery. Predatory. You were not there. I can't find peace. I am enwrapped in it. It has a stranglehold. I feel an abject humiliation. Traumatized. My brain needs to come to terms with the weights of Nigger and Niggertude.

Buzzo: We must then dig at them and have to understand them three dimensionally and annihilate them. That's why we are talking, rationalizing, digging, growing the self-consciousness to shift the paradigm.

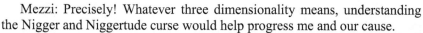

Mezzi: Precisely! Whatever three dimensionality means, understanding the Nigger and Niggertude curse would help progress me and our cause.

Buzzo: Physiology, Sociology, Psychology dimensions form self-consciousness.

Now listen carefully; to progress our cause, we need a renaissance credo as the opium of the African Gen Z family that should replace religion that has been and is the opium of our poor people.

Mezzi: The believe in yourself credo. The renaissance man credo. Hard work credo. Your destiny depends on yourself credo. You are demi-god credo. Got it.

Buzzo: That should be our religion. The renaissance credo, our religion. Our opium. And our bible is preaching hard work. Our bible is hard, smart work.

Mezzi: Our bible is hard work. Our heaven is hard work. Make heaven on earth through hard work. The supreme holiness of hard work. Hard work earns you heaven. It's the blessings for your vision and hard work. Gratuitous blessings for you from above is, a chimera.

Buzzo: Yes, our holiness's hard work. Our heaven's hard work. Our progress and development, freedoms here on earth is our reward and pride, and are what qualify us for heavenly hope.

Mezzi: Hard work qualifies and rewards you to be with God. Qualifies you for heaven. Takes you to heaven. Catapults you to heaven.

Buzzo: We got to understand every being on this earth is God's creation and loves everyone unconditionally. He blesses everyone with talent unconditionally. And our calling is to develop our talents at something to help humanity. It means hard work. Belief in God sets of rules is proven a chimera. Worshipping God set rules is a chimera. Doing the deeds of God set rules on this earth instead is the answer. Doing his deeds to enable humanity, means you would have believe in him and you would have earned heaven.

Mezzi: This would be a hard sell for the lazy miserable poor, especially for the embattled, deprived African Gen Z family. Like for the generation of African Youths before them.

Buzzo: Absolutely. The vehicle to make these things possible with the hungry, deprived, depraved, phobic neurosis-challenged, traumatized African Gen Z family are the provision of earthly palpable hope in form of food, material gadgets and comforts and a platform to inculcate the renaissance credo ideals.

Mezzi: You think in an environment where the human platforms, in the form of the students' union, labor unions, religious unions, teachers' unions have all failed, quasi obliterated in its totality, our physical platform will succeed?

Buzzo: Yeah! Because those human platforms are bare, are cringingly craven, baseless, devoid of any values, any criterium, any rules, corrupt, phobia neurosis-challenged and above all subdued, while our platform will be substantiated and sustained with ideas and ideals that have endured and still endure. Indeed, ours finds its reason of existence in life progress, life in death through protests and standing up and standoffs as a necessary antidote to misery. Catharsis of death.

Mezzi: Death?

Buzzo: Yeah! As a sublime catharsis of the reason to gain heaven. A platform not just of ideals but of palpable hope. Food. Live. Work. Play.

Mezzi (his face in a grinning frown): Genial. Sounds cool. Even though generations of youths are already dead on this continent, death is the last thing they think of.

Buzzo: Bravo, that's the key. They don't know they are dead. They know they are hungry. They hope against hunger. Your idea will function. For a hungry deprived frail hopeless man to listen, he needs food and some liberties. Then he will be a convert. Just look at the number of churches. The number of mosques. The number of shrines. Why do we have about hundreds of thousands of churches and half as much of the mosques and a quarter as much of the shrines, and only three hundred factories in a deprived, depraved continent?

Mezzi: Because of sloth. Because of hope in heaven. Laziness transcends them.

Buzzo: You said it: sloth and hope. There is nothing palpable to lean unto. These folks in reality are tired of that hope preaching. Nothing is coming out of it. their selfconscious is vacuous, deprived, arrested in time and space. They are already looking elsewhere. Ready to abandon. Switch camp. The camp of palpable, tangible hope. We just need to give them a different credo. A renaissance credo with a palpable platform of livelihood: food, food, food, with play, play, play, and then renaissance credo doctrine of work, work, work, to goad and coalesce them. Sway them. You want to bet?

Mezzi: With play, play, play, you mean entertainment, right?

Buzzo: You had any doubt? Indulgence. Music, dance, alcohol, fitness, sports, sex, smoke, church, mosque, African religion, any practiced religion with plenty of food. Provide these dressings, then our platform will function with any proposal. They will listen to renaissance credo.

Mezzi: I can't just come to terms with the fact that the African youth can't have any say, any form of expression whatsoever for anything they feel on this continent. Life is dead here.

Buzzo: Life is long dead here. Gifts of individual talents suppressed, obliterated and buried. Every generation inherently inherits death from the precedent. Africa's long dead. Pyramid of the dead. Pyramid of retrogression. Pyramid of hopelessness. Pyramid of illusions.

Mezzi: Cool: the pyramid of death. I love that.

Buzzo: Cynically?

Mezzi: Sure!

The two brothers lock stare, hold it in a contemplating grin and frowning grimace, with their eyes in mixed amazement of delusion, hope and undeterred determination at the same time to succeed.

Now the two brothers, break their silence since Mezzi's arrival, writing to their parents:

Dear Parents,

The odious oddity of this land is preposterously, deleteriously and virulently remarkably turbid and disturbing.

We are simply distraught. Lost. We are trying to find our faith in something, a reason to believe in humanity.

What is worse above all is our faith and trust in you, our parents are fast eroding. We have pondered at length and are still doing soul searching to understand why parents should live in what seems compulsive lies, feed on pathological lies and mislead the youth, children. Their own children.

We have parents who are perverts, numb to love, pathologically and compulsively evil.

Dad you made us believe in a virtual reality world. A false world rooted in evil. Your world. You cause desperation, tribulation, disrepair, peril. But why?

You are supposed to be our undisputed role-model, our shinning beacon, our bearing, our compass. Instead, you reprehensibly and despicably betrayed us.

But why?

Mom we've always proudly admired you on the podium of the United Nations Institute, purportedly speaking fearlessly to power, defending the poor.

You spoke words like compassionate conservatism against radical conservatism, modern liberalism against perverse liberalism, leave no child illiterate, health care freedom, food security, poverty eradication...etc. etc. You deluded, deceived. Raped.

Pillaged. Exploited. But why?

To embarrass us? Make our lives worthless?

We must congratulate you both for your air of enticing luring affectation of genteel nobility that hides your primitive savagery. Spurious!

We are staring the remarkable uncomfortable niggers' truth in the face.

However, we are hopeful that truth is omnipotent and would transcend justice on this land.

We have decided to be part of the fight for justice. Alas, to spur it. At the whim of White kind philosophy: pay the ultimate price, if need be for it.

We still love u. With no respect whatsoever.

Your sons:

Buzzo and Mezzi.

> *Pay the ultimate price if need be for it. Pay the ultimate price if need be for it.*
> *Pay the ultimate price if need be for it.*

No remarkable surprises. It has been said that as children, we love our parents. As we get older, we judge our parents. And we may decide to forgive them.

Buzzo and Mezzi are born in freedom. Coined in liberty. Consorting with remarkable development and progress. Uninhibited. Non-inhabitable. Non-scripted, non-scriptable. Their human three dimensionality, subliminally sound.

The problem, their problem becomes the relatedness factor with their African peers, who have been coined in the contrary and consort with the opposite. All their lives. An uphill battle to relate with them for salvage. Dual salvaging.

Back in the USA, Dad and Mom react violently differently, expressing vehement passions to the letter: the one, their Dad, of professed self-righteousness and bigotry that embodies domineering, hypercritical, conformist, zealotry etc. and the other one, their Mom, of tempered combined cad and bigot–insecure, guilt complexed, cowardly but opportunist, unscrupulous, unimaginative with irreducible love for vanity and luxury.

The one offended in his pride, dignity and righteousness, of unutterable anger, lashing out expressing inveighs, profanations and curses against his kids' ingratitude and their injurious insults. And the other one battered, numbed, collectedly confused, shamed in remorse and tears, dejected, vulnerable in her life conduct and spiritual intrinsic essence.

The one virulently unrepentant. The other remarkably in transition.

As the two brothers sit down, as it's habitual, in the study of their village home, to their evening night task of continuum research, rationalization, definition, redefinition, refinement of ideas and strategies of the long journey ahead, Buzzo and Mezzi are conscientious they have accomplished an important, ground-breaking stride. And going back is absolutely suicidal, forbidden for what they stand for.

Buzzo is savoring a little of peace: finally, Mezzi sleeps a little bit more.

Mezzi feels good. He's found a purpose of life-drive and hope in the will. Every day they make sure the hamlet has life: the kids, the schools, the power supply, the borehole, the extra-curricular activities–the lessons, the fitness, the story telling, the commuting, etc. etc. The kids are the envy of the entire Africa. The hamlet the happenstance miracle.

Remarkably inspired, they are moving undauntedly on with a remarkable audacity of will at work to hatch in full and as soon as possible, their renaissance credo opium project: critical thinking, critical analysis, planning, re-planning, programming, reprogramming, timelining, re-timelining, time-framing, re-time-framing etc., absolute use of technology indispensable: all imbedded in and tailored absolutely with technology–from data collection, data generation, algorithms, simulations, app creations down to digitalization. Grow the self-consciousness of their African Gen Z peers.

Buzzo is the bedrock, the role model. The custodian of his younger brother Mezzi. He knows this arduous responsibility and is powerfully erupting to fill it. Adept in computing engineering, in anything and every aspect of data. Algorithms. He is working assiduously round the clock to develop the things they need to tackle challenges, fight Status Quo and turn lots around for the better, changing niggers' status.

He has developed, experimented, perfected these apps: at the press of a button data collections; another button data analysis, categorizations, hacking, sabotaging, jamming, generate answers. Quick irrefutable answers.

Apps to detect the number and state of infrastructure of any locality, to get the population of any locality, to know the amenities – hospital, schools, gardens, parks, detect and determine properties and their ownerships, farm lands, mineral deposits, revenues, revenue collections, the ports, health care, car insurances, the functioning of the government, public administration, public-private sector enterprise, employment, unemployment, demography, taxes collected, the state of the olice, army, navy, air force, power, water generation and its supply, etc.

He can detect, verify and corroborate the state of anything he wants.

These he's gotten ready for himself and Mezzi, who is a wizard in social networking: different blogging platforms, generating and keeping substantial consistent crowdloyalty in different realms of life discussions and their advancement: political, economic, social, religious, marketing, advertisement.

Mezzi launches "#kids must play center awareness" with its content. Content with aim to inform and acquaint. Content to create awareness of the importance of "#every kid must play" drive. Jingles like "a real father sends kid to school"; "a real mom tends to kids not to male penetration"; "tomorrow holds better than today"; "today is the father of tomorrow"; "our tomorrow is our kids"; "our kids, the future"; "our children, our future"; "our children must be better than us, otherwise we have failed as parents", etc. etc. are on the go through social media and the traditional radio vehicles in the meantime.

Buzzo, a tempered radical, persistently in the shadows of their father and the inner workings of their mom understands power and its subtleties. He understands the intricacies, the intrigues, the scheming, the manipulations, the exploits, the deceptions, the pleasures, the indulgencies, the reticence, the lies, the comforts of politics. So much so that in their bid to succeed and in protecting his brother Mezzi as absolute priority, he has taken the back seat and role of power-strategist and tactician, while leaving his brother to the efforts of tactics.

That way, for Mezzi's young age, the play of perception of empathy and sympathy, adhesion, cohesion of followers, instead of apathy, is readily available and drawn for what may otherwise be considered treasonable terrorism.

Buzzo wants to make sure Mezzi is and embodies the fascinating symbol of their Millennials' generation effort to subdue and break the jinx of Status Quo cycle of evil Nigger*tude.*

Their first line of action is to ascertain realities. Even though they are in possession of data of the United Nations on Africa, some, through their well-entrenched mom and some, by virtue of the Internet, it is a duty to ascertain facts. More so, it is ineluctable and necessary to draw the line between scathing vituperative vilification from without and the social defensive coping mechanisms set: Defeatist arrogance, contemptuous ignorance, virulent denials, the hypnosis, the indispensable comfortable *erasus* and *oblivionem*, in the Defaults, in the Willful, in the hereditary conspiracy or in the hereditary despotism from within.

Buzzo thinks it is absolutely necessary and very urgent to educate, acquainting Mezzi with the above listed Africa's defensive coping mechanisms sets that Africans use in mitigating and dealing with their misery stress, misery anxiety, misery depressions, misery frustrations, misery tribulations and misery mirage hope - hopelessness, in some celestial unmerited inheritance. The Jesus Lord's Grace!

Misery is profane. Beyond blasphemous. Misery is overwhelmingly evident in Africa. It's palpable. To solve any problem, firstly, it needs to be identified and secondly owned. Africa instead engages willfully in defensive illusionary set of coping mechanisms that are found and justified in:

a. *Willful prolepsis–willful denials, willful blindness, willful hypocrisy, willful falsehood, willful kleptomania, willful chicanery, etc.;*

b. *Default–default blame (on history of slavery and colonialism), default arrogance of ignorance, default resignation in religious mysticism, default hypocrisy, default religious palsy, etc.;*

c. *Hereditary conspiracies of silence, hypocrisy, complicity, arrogance, mystifications, ignorance, apathy to remorse, slothfulness, gullibility, falsehood, criminality, etc.;*

d. *Hereditary despotic tradition that is arrogant, ignorant, static, anti- expression of freedom and liberty whatsoever. Just evil and miserable;*

e. *Erasus. Efface facts from recognition and memory. The Lord's commandments are compulsively erased;*

> *f.* *Oblivionem. The laws, duties and rights belong to willful oblivion;*
> *g.* ***Religious Mysticism–Grace and umerited favour reign supreme:*** *the moment you accept Jesus Christ, even superflously, you become a "born again". Once you are, you can sin as you wish and want: you can gift misery and unmerited favour will take you to heaven. Remember kings David and Solomon; and you can recieve, suffer and endure misery, for unmerited favour for heaven is especially for the miserable.*

Buzzo: Mezzi, coffee or tea?

Mezzi: Thank you. No, I am cool.

Buzzo: Great. Moving forward, it's absolutely indispensable that I acquaint you with Africa's self-inflicted, abhorring and defeatist defense and coping mechanisms sets.

Mezzi: Our anathema and dilemma? Great!

Buzzo: Precisely. Africa's celestial curse. I need to familiarize and harmonize you with them. They are malevolent, destructive, spiteful, venomous opioids. Addictive. We need to subdue and dominate them.

Mezzi: Where are they?

Buzzo: You need to consort with the dictionary.

Mezzi (excitedly kissing his phone): Got, everything on my phone. Let's go.

Buzzo: If I say willful, what's the response?

Mezzi: That's easy. Done by design! Deliberate.

Buzzo: Arrogance?

Mezzi: A moral vice characterized with disdain, superiority complex, overbearing pride, insolence, condescension, undermining of the intellect, and undermining the attainment of knowledge and its flourishing.

Buzzo Willful arrogance?

Mezzi: Deliberate arrogance. Arrogance by design.

Buzzo: Ignorance?

Mezzi: Lack of knowledge or education. Lack of information. Uneducated, rude, unlettered. Untaught. Untutored.

Buzzo: Willful ignorance?

Mezzi: Deliberate disregard for information, or facts, or education.

Buzzo: Denial?

Mezzi: Disaffirmation. Refusal to accept reality.

Buzzo: Willful denial?

Mezzi: A deliberate defense mechanism put up to deny painful thoughts, abhorrent remembrance, deliberate denying the existence of the problem.

Buzzo: Default?

Mezzi: As in Default option?

Buzzo: Yeah!

Mezzi (looks it up): An option selected automatically on the absence of a specified alternative.

Buzzo: An automatic, reflexive response to a stimulus. That stimulus is exoneration. Volition from exoneration. Conscientious cowardly exoneration. If I say blame?

Mezzi: A reproach from lapses or misdeed.

Buzzo: So, within that context if I say Default blame?

Mezzi: Cowardly exoneration from reproach?

Buzzo: Bravo! Default ignorance?

Mezzi: Exoneration from ignorance. Denying it. Pushing back.

Buzzo: If I say prolepsis?

Mezzi (looks it up): Anticipating and answering objections in advance.

Buzzo: Anticipating prejudiced or biased or having an attitude or a belief preformed or formed beforehand.

Mezzi: Punctiliously.

Buzzo: If I say Willful prolepsis of denials?

Mezzi: Deliberately anticipating prejudiced disaffirmation.

Buzzo: Willful prolepsis of hypocrisy?

Mezzi: Deliberate anticipated attack on sincerity.

Buzzo: Or deliberate disaffirmation of insincerity. Etcetera, etcetera, etcetera.

So, in the face of these obnoxious, peril and defeatist misery, leveraging defense coping mechanism sets, found in the Willful, in the Defaults, in the Hereditary Conspiracies, Hereditary Despotic Hierarchic tradition, in the *Erasus*, in the *Oblivionem*, in religious mysticism etc., etc., etc., to overcome and prevail in our effort for Dominance we must remain tempered. Tempered radicals.

Mezzi: Tempered radicals?

Buzzo: You already had arrogance and ignorance come at you. Yes, an arrogant ignoramus speaking, lecturing you with his eloquent cowardly defeatist silence.

Mezzi: Yeah, voluptuously-ponderously flabbergasting.

Buzzo: So, as we work at the renaissance opium credo, as the cornerstone of freedom for the family of African youths, we must expect virulent gratuitous attacks, we must listen to and we must respect opinions different from ours. We must avoid violent disagreements. We must agree to disagree. We must be respectfully flexible and rational in our dialectics, in our conversations, reasoning, especially when we find ourselves before the uninformed, the ill-informed, the irrational, the arrogant, the ignorant, the willfully blind and bland opinions. Because, we are going to have them every day. And we are going to tolerate them every day. We are going to navigate through them every day. Every day, never lose your calm. Every day, don't be tired nor afraid of prolixity.

Mezzi: Cool! Tiredness and cowardice are abjectly forbidden in the African walk. It has been said that our Black kind is afraid of the books. If you want to cheat them, deal them a remarkable blow, remarkably gratuitously effortlessly, ink it. Put pen to paper. Write it. He will NEVER read. Prolixity, Verbosity, Repetition is the option.

Buzzo: **This continent is withered of any pleasure. The African system annihilates civilization: the education system annihilates knowledge; the religious system annihilates morals; the governing system, freedoms; the justice system, justice and fairness; security system, security; the banking system, the economy, etcetera.**

Mezz: Bottomline, Africa's system has deliberate disregard for civilization?

Buzzo: No! Their system murders civilization. Civilization is eviscerated and arid! Even though it's been said that it's better not to be different from one's fellows, we cannot unknow our knowledge so far. We cannot regret or renounce our pleasure of civilization. We are here to prevail pleasure of civilization to our fellows.

Mezzi: Well-coined Buzz! Prevail the intellect. Dominate Black kind tragedy. Make our kids dream.

Buzzo: Yeah, Africa forbids and forecloses her progenies from dreaming.

Mezzi: Dreams of making bicycles, dreams of turning our cocoa into chocolates, our crude oil into refined finished products, plastics into toys, our fruits into juice, our lands into food, our streams into pipe-borne water, our Sun into current electricity as the White kind does. Sad. Very sad.

Buzzo: At least the basics: electric power security, pipe-borne water security, food security, education freedom, health care freedom, jobs freedom, housing...

Mezzi: ...For us to gain human league status. Gain respect. Give respect to our progenies by having their backs wherever they may find themselves.

Buzzo: Yeah, that explains the lingering animosity between the African-Americans and the Africans. An Italian American can't be told 'go back to the forest', because Florence is renaissance. And renaissance is the cradle of science. Science invented technology, technology innovated the old world and invented the modern world.

Mezzi: Roman empire and their intelligibilities – Latin language, aqueduct, first laws, medicine, architecture, religion, arts; and their progressed intelligibilities – middle ages, renaissance, science, industrial revolution, a loop, the wheel, the bicycle, the wheel in the dam, energies, trains, cars, Ferraris, Lamborghinis, airplanes, space flights, spaghetti, pizza, lasagna, ravioli, prosciutto, parmigiana, wine. etc. etc. etc.

Buzzo: Neither can you tell a German American to 'go back to the forest' and so on and so forth. Only African Americans can be told "Nigger, go back to the rodent infested uninhabitable forest of your homeland," and they have nothing to fall back on, other than on unutterable embarrassment and grieving shame.

Mezzi: They fall back on shame of misery, our prize from sloth. Africa gifts misery and shame. Africa has never given dignity in any form to her progenies.

Buzzo: Not psychological, not physiological, and not sociological. The West has the back of White kind descendants wherever, Africa should have the back of Black kind descendants wherever, but does not.

Mezzi: Precisely our shame. No respect, no protection, no background for her progenies. Progenies to progenies are denied in continuum. A Vicious cycle.

Buzzo: Why won't they hate Genitor Africa? Isn't it striking and debilitating that there should be Negroes and Niggers within the same family? A family divided.

Mezzi (his face in a contorted frown): You confuse me Buzz. You are at it again. Who the hell is a Negro?

Buzzo (his face a chagrin): The word Negro literally means Black. Negro is the Latin word for Black.

Mezzi (eyes wide open with expectation): Yeah, this never-ending tandem NegroNigger. Who then is a Nigger?

Buzzo: For so long Genitor Africa has been conceded innocent of slavery phenomenon and of the Trans-Atlantic slave trade on his coastline. For so long he has been conceded ignorant of Nigger contrivance and ordeal on that slave ship on his shores. And for so long his conscience is in consort with *erasus* and *oblivionem* of his grave complicit participation. For so long he is far removed from coming to terms with this vicious assents and cruel consorts with Niggertude conspiracy.

And that's why he is in the luxury audacity of priding himself a Negro and denigrating the African-American with the word Nigger.

Mezzi: Are you trying to change the conversation?

Buzzo: Yeah! The conversation that Genitor Africa was cajoled, forced, coaxed to endure the denigration, the degradation and desecration of his negro progenies and therefore innocent.

Mezzi: Yeah, alongside the teaching in whispers, not in the history books that African-Americans are Niggers.

Buzzo: And alas, the African Genitor Negro is the megaphone of those whispers.

Mezzi: And yet nobody explains why the word Nigger is full of competing and conflicting amazements: it is feared, it is whispered, it prevaricates, it equivocates, it amuses cynically, it offends, it's hurtful, it's loathsome, it's dangerous, it's deadly.

Buzzo: Yeah, Nigger is one word that arouses fear and inculcates dread in the streets of America, of the West. On the White kind streets. You can hardly meet any race that is openly comfortable with it. Everybody dreads it as something they can't forget and can't summarily deal with. Because it is a conspiracy. A conspiracy contrived to subdue and subjugate the psyche of a weakling. A conspiracy contrived, peddled and trafficked by a race to efface the self-consciousness of another for edge, and endure the edge in time and space.

Mezzi: That's like a monster.

Buzzo: Yea! A monster created, peddled and trafficked, out of shear jealousy, abject fear of survival and ultimate greed, by the White tribe to have the edge over the Negro tribe. A Negro tribe they found complacent and naïve, cloaked in his natural rich blessings.

African-Americans have long understood the conspiracy and their inalienable rights as human beings and they rebelled, are rebelling and have been refuting, fighting that scourge. That scourge called domination, called dehumanization.

While Africa, the Genitor Negro instead, willfully holds it in abstract, relegates it to default *Erasus* and *oblivionem*, but at the same time, at hypocrisy's demands and cynicisms, he promotes the Nigger conspiracy against the African-American to satisfy his falsehood, meanness and cowardice.

Mezzi: This conversation is revealing and at the same time fascinating and grave. In fact, it seems the ego of African genitor Negro, is fascinated and thrilled by the word Nigger. Just hear our father out for example. He audaciously throws Nigger tantrum denigration at the African-American. He is indeed an active ally of the Nigger conspirator. The White Supremacist. The White race's Scum.

Buzzo: Except when the White supremacist, the White Scum, throws Nigger tantrum indistinctly at the Negro race. Then the African genitor Negro stutter, recoil and his moron self-consciousness can only but grapple and coalesce around the truth and uniqueness of his remotest and irrefutable original sin.

Mezzi: Pardon me Buzzo, but to avoid equivocations, could you kindly shade light on what is Nigger and who is Nigger?

Buzzo: We will get there soon. Let's have some context. Let's try to see the terms.

Mezzi: You mean get to terms with the stain of Nigger and Nigger*tude*?

Buzzo: Precisely. To come to terms and to heal with anything, there must be responsibilities.

Mezzi: Right. Otherwise the conflicting and competing amazements continue.

Buzzo: I think that "Negro coaxed" enslavement conversation does no longer hold water. The conversation should be that the African Negro Genitors haunted down their progenies, and sold them to shackles of the slave ship of their choosing. By their own volition. How about that?

Mezzi: I am listening hard. Trying to make sense of the logic of your reasoning.

Buzzo: And then he consorted with the ship owner and the slave owner in subjecting and relegating his Negro progenies to the sordidness and stolidity of a ship. The slave ship. Of a stranger. On his shores. *Where their Negritude was unutterably cruelly and viciously assaulted and humiliated and subdued and conquered and subjugated and traumatized. On that ship, Negro lost its innocence. Negro was desecrated of its humanity, dignity and value and virtues. Negro was baptized Nigger. Negro lost its significance and its signified and was dominated.*

Mezzi: Negro became Nigger. Under the watchful eyes of the Genitor Africa Negro?

Buzzo: *There, on that ship, Negro lost its innocence and pride. The Genitor Negro, aloof from the shores coronated his son Nigger. Of his own volition. Instead of standing up, dying if necessary, in defense of his progenies. He contemplated the ships, filled with subjugated Negroes, alias Niggers, sail off solemnly to an unknown destination to him, the Americas. In perpetuation. Days after days. Months after months. Years after years. Decades after decades. For centuries he enslaved his progenies. Then he sat back. Satisfied of his conduct and proud of his exertion, his full Negro ego goes into an assault of spasm of unutterable smugness.*

Mezzi: That's the meaning of Nigger?

Buzzo: Yes, in sum. That's the definition. Nigger is a subdued, a subjugated, a conquered state of a being, whose self-consciousness of a human being, with his innate instinct, capacities and abilities were foreclosed and annihilated. And in best case scenario limited and alienated. And he is coaxed to replace it with, wear and display a subservient self-consciousness conduct.

Mezzi: So, a Nigger is a subdued persona. A subjugated persona with a subservient self-consciousness.

Buzzo: Yes. Subdued. Subjugated. Denigrated. Besmirched. Defamed. Calumniated. Traumatized. Dehumanized. His self-consciousness subdued and annihilated and coaxed, infused with a subservient self-consciousness on that slave ship to where thence. Shipped to the Americas. In the Americas. And his accrued and accruing trauma is Nigger*tude.*

Mezzi: His trauma is Niggertude?

Buzzo: While back home in Africa, in his pristine Genitor Negro domain, the Genitor Negro with a self-consciousness of complacency and total smugness of his Negro exertion continued and perpetuated the Nigger baptism.

Mezzi: It was no one-off action?

Buzzo: For centuries he prided himself with Nigger Baptism and depleted his negro progenies into the wild.

Mezzi: The Americas were the wild?

Buzzo: Yes indeed! Worse than wild. African Genitor Negro had no doubt of his Nigger and Niggertude exertion of a continent. He lived in abject illusion of the smugness of catharsis of Nigger and Nigger*tude.* He was making a living, complicit in sublimating Negro progenies into Nigger progenies. In the far, somewhere, in the middle of nowhere. Far removed from scouring denigrating Nigger shame, sorrow and tribulation. He could care less. He didn't need to stand up. He didn't stand up. Yes, in his home in Africa his Negro self-consciousness could not see beyond his pathetic pride and smugness at Nigger and Nigger*tude.* A self-inflicted abasement, self-inflicted subjugation and self-inflicted annihilation. Of his own volition. Numbed by smugness and with refined predatory self-consciousness, he could not stand up.

Mezzi: His moronic Nigger and Nigger*tude* self-consciousness drive numbed him?

Buzzo: I think so. Conversely to the point of a total loss to self-confidence, to self-annihilation, to stereotypes. To evil. He could not read the signified of the loss of "Innocence" of Negro on that slave ship, nor the drawling effect of its subjugating trauma.

Mezzi: You are making a lot of sense.

Buzzo: So much so that after centuries of his Negro progenies *sublimationem* into Nigger and Nigger*tude* and its catharsis in faraway land, his retribution came: not from his Negro progenies (the African-American), but from colonization. From the hands of same proponents of Nigger subservient self-consciousness conspiracy. For the ultimate Nigger subjugation. As colonization wrecked, Genitor Negro lost his innocence. This time around on his turf. Genitor Negro was himself baptized Nigger in his pristine, suave domain in Africa. Genitor Negro was subjugated. Into Nigger. This second time, a scouring Negro subjugation. Not African Nigger, not African-American Nigger but the Negro Nigger. On his home turf. In Africa.

Mezzi: The Negro ego shattered. Nigger*tude* his trauma.

Buzzo: Yes. Of course. A scouring subservient self-consciousness conspiracy foothold. Just look around you, how would you explain the psychological Nigger and physiological Nigger*tude* surrounding us? Just look around you, look at the state of our environment, here in Africa, decades after slavery and colonization, where Negro, they claim, never lost its innocence to Nigger?

Mezzi: The ultimate personification of Nigger and Nigger*tude* everywhere. Misery palpable. Retrogression perpetuity. The much-prized innocent African Genitor Negro, in a raw state of Negritude, remains a Nigger, in a subservient self-consciousness psyche, reigning supreme in his Niggertude Supremacy kingdom. In Africa.

Buzzo: To this extent, but for some unfortunate persisting Nigger vestiges, one could argue that Negro progeny refused Nigger subservient self-consciousness in its totality, right away rebelling. Rebelling, rebelling from aboard that ship, rebelling and dying. Dying and rebelling on those farms. Dying on those lands of abject tribulation and degradation. Rebelling and dying on those lands to create the wealth of America. Rebelling working hard against their emancipation with infamous famine. Rebelling against Jim Crowe. Against Lynching. Enduring the jealous destruction of their Black Wall Street wealth base. Up to Civil Rights deaths, to mass Negro incarcerations, to modern mass shootings in Negro churches. In substance, the African-American was never a Nigger. He rebelled to martyrdom. He stood up and is still standing up. Fighting and dying against the bane and scourge of institutional racism.

While the Genitor African Negro embraced in its totality the Nigger subservient selfconsciousness psyche, infused. In him. He is the Nigger. He remains the Nigger.

Mezzi: It's self-evident. Just look at the amount of misery. They are multiplying the ills and serving the purpose of the White supremacy's imposed subservient selfconsciousness psyche. Indeed, I need to erect monuments to Tom.

Buzzo: To be clear and to avoid equivocations, if any human being, wherever, of any race, lets his innate human self-consciousness be effaced and be replaced and be dictated to by some conspiracy subservient self-consciousness of conduct from any quarter, that human is a Nigger.

Mezzi: Phew! What a definition.

Buzzo (with a skeptic frown): Mezzi are you sure it makes some sense?

Mezzi (puzzled): That is broad. Very deep. You can't keep it simple, huh?

Buzzo: Nigger is a subdued, a subjugated psyched out state of the mind of a human being that accepts to be effaced by some conspiracy of a subservient self-consciousness that in turn dictates stereotypes of conduct for his being.

Mezzi (still puzzled, lost): You are still broad. We need some succinctness, Buzzo.

Buzzo: You are subdued, subjugated, withered and emptied of any thought or thinking or of any opinion. And then you are told what and how to think.

Mezzi (ponderously elated and voluptuously relieved): Yes, bravo! This is it. Finally, a definition of Nigger. Thank you Buzzo. Finally, Gen Z and generations their descendants would be less at loss on the Nigger word. Then we can infer that Nigger cuts across races. It can be anybody of any race, right?

Buzzo: You got it. Absolutely anybody of any race could be subjugated by evil conspiracy into a subservient self-consciousness.

Mezzi: Got it.

Buzzo: Yet the biggest tragedy is that African Negro, still today, is totally withered of self-consciousness of his self-Negro desecration, Nigger contrivance and Nigger*tude* perpetuation, so much so that to this day, the African Negro, or what is left of the colonized Negro, in abject feel of Nigger smugness, still takes pride in deriding himself. In Niggertude exertions. A travesty. Grotesque.

Just look around you, you can see the Nigger left in him is manifest everywhere. His Negro subjugation multiplied the lootings, the desecrations, the humiliations, the tyrannies of colonization as his model of development. Any doubt on his role in Nigger baptism of Negro progenies, subjugated and shipped off to America is dispelled by the self-evidence that he is today. He is unashamedly still trafficking the Negro Progenies of the African Continent in Nigger and Niggertude. Misery bondage in African homeland. No more to the Americas. African-Americans rebelled, are rebelling and refuting Negro subjugation. The genitor African Negro is still stupidly and embarrassingly *gifting* our monies and natural resources, the African intellect, unsolicited, to the KKK Western banks and institutions and economies. To help develop KKK Progenies. He is trafficking a whole continent in Nigger*tude*.

Thumbs up to the African-Americans, who have consistently been fighting the vestiges of slavery and colonization and institutional racism – a continent's and a race's defilement and condemnation–on multiple of fronts, to reinstate and rehabilitate Negro and Negritude back to lost dignity in time and space.

They have single-handedly been waging war on sloth, primitivity, stupidity, ignorance, vicious stereotypes, stigmatization on behalf of the entire Black Race. What does the African Negro do instead? He does the Nigger and Nigger*tude* traffic: under-develop Africa. He is the avowed Negro Progeny subjugator.

Mezzi: Bravo, Buzzo. The vapor is becoming clearer. Negritude into Nigger*tude* by the Negro Progenitor, who did not stand up to protect his progeny. Instead he takes pride in further humiliating them. Indeed. In fact, our Dad is a cringing villain, a craven kleptomaniac, like the Negroes, his kind, on the entire African continent.

> *To be clear and to avoid equivocations, if any human being, wherever, of any race, lets his innate human self-consciousness be effaced and be replaced and be dictated to by some conspiracy subservient self-consciousness of conduct from any quarter, that human is a Nigger.*

They deprive, enslaving the entire African continent. African wealth is looted by Africans into the enemy territory of the KKK Western banks and institutions to disempower and dismember the African descendants.

We need the memoirs of both Malcom X and Martin Luther King bravados through the lens of the monumental Rosa Parks and Tubman, rekindled in today's Black kind memories in their Object Surrendering Permanence Self-consciousness. To stand up.

Buzzo: Their bravery stood up to such magnitude and grace that compelled a President, President J. F. Kennedy to phrase: *"The rights of everyman are diminished when the rights of one man are threatened."*

Mezzi: Yeah, perhaps the lone American President that braved racism. And I think he said this as well: *"The Negro baby born in America today, regardless of the section of the nation in which he is born, has about one half as much chance of completing high school as a white baby born in the same place on the same day, one third as much chance of completing college, one third chance as much of becoming a professional man, twice as much chance of becoming unemployed, about one seventh as much* *chance of earning $10,000 a year or more, a life expectancy which is seven years shorter, and the prospects of earning only half as much. "*

Buzzo: Bravo! That is institutional racism. Africa sold and abandoned them to the predatory of the unknown. Of an unknown predatory foreign land, the America that gave them a fate of abject subjugation and humiliation, and embarrassment, and defilement and evisceration that incarnate America's 'structured racism' – in denial of equal or decent education, denial of employment, denied moving into large cities, denied opportunity to eat at restaurants or lunch counter or to a movie theatre or commuting in the same commuter trains or buses. So much so that their suffering, their humiliation and embarrassment forced the solicitude of President J.F. Kennedy to yet another proposition, impervious to America's hyper hypocrisy: *"I am today proposing, as part of the Civil Rights Act of 1963, a provision to guarantee all citizens equal access to the services and facilities of hotels, restaurants, places of amusement, and retail establishments."*

Mezzi: Are you serious? I thought that happened in Apartheid South Africa?

Buzzo: Jim Crow laws mandated racial segregation in all public facilities in confederate states and other states of America, starting in the 1870 and was rescinded only in 1965 with the deaths of Martin Luther King and Malcolm X.

Mezzi: Just in 1965? And their humiliation is still counting because Genitor Africa, till today, in the twenty first century, won't stand up for her family wherever they are. We are unable to have the back of Black kind descendants wherever.

Buzzo: Precisely the dilemma. Just look at the state of our environment now. Just look at everywhere, we have private jets, yachts and grandpa village is without water. If you were Tom, tell me how you earn his respect for us, the Black Kind? You expect him to respect you when you have no sewer, no toilet, no water? Perhaps shake your dirty unwashed hands after you have defecated in the forest of your house or removed the phlegm from your nose without water to wash your hands?

Mezzi: Bah! Of course not. We won't copy electric power and pipe-borne water into African houses. Aqueduct came on, over 2000 years ago. No Education, no healthcare for our kids. It's just so remarkably shameful.

Buzzo: Sacrosanct truth. Our Africa is not informed. Is orally informed. Is lazy to read. Is lazy to inform themselves. Is lazy to confront head-on their problems. Africa does not produce answers. Answers, thoughts, solutions, reactions are swallowed. Africa is a masochist. If Africa produces answers to any of her problems, the combined Jesus Christ, Prophet Muhammed and the Voodoo Oracle will foreclose them from Heaven. That's why the whole race is where we find ourselves today. Regressed and counting. They don't understand that nothingness begets nothingness. It's been said that poverty, misery, ignorance, tribulations, in sum, nothing goes away on its own except you deal with it. Since we don't deal with these things they will never go away. Indeed, their clefts widen and deepen.

Notwithstanding their sloth and ignorance and their entities, Africans have sets of defensive coping mechanism they use to cope with their stress, anxiety, tribulations, depression, their misery and their illusions.

You need to know these remarkable arrogant, ignorant defensive coping sets. Of course, they don't make sense but you need to be armed to deal and defeat them comfortably as they come.

Mezzi: Cool. I love you Buzzo. Your love for me is immense. Your effort and tenacity and love for Africa are remarkable. But I am still very confused with this place. I understand misery. Fully now. I can see it. I can touch it. It's palpable. I am grateful to Tom Bradley. I understand your amazing insightful lights on Nigger and Niggertude. But that comes from African leadership. Isn't it?

Buzzo: Correct! From the Despotic African Hierarchical Hereditary leadership.

Mezzi: Then, before you get to defensive coping sets mechanism, why would the victims, the masses, the men and women of entire continent not react against their misery? Is there any amount of sloth and ignorance and whatever else, capable to obliterate the innate instinct of rationalism and rationalization in any human not to react against misery and fight not to defeat it?

But instead there is rationalization awakening in a slothful and ignorant person to develop love for kleptomania and gluttonous and evil culture and then defensive coping sets mechanism?

Buzzo: Cool! You want to know what's responsible for non-reaction to misery?

Mezzi: I am all ears.

Buzzo: The 'why' might seem the single remarkable enigma of all times. However, it's because of Africa's moronic self-consciousness. In simple terms, one would imagine the early mankind had a life-style. A primitive life-style. Primitive farming, water from the streams, plucking of fruits, tree branches as shelters from the rain and sun. Not houses. Living like in a zoo. Making love like animals. Crossbreeding and incest. Primal instincts. Predatory. Survival of the fittest. Arid of technology.

Then came the Phoenicians with alphabets. Then came the empires. Roman Empire stood out. A language premiered. Aqueduct became. First laws became. Medicine became. Roman empire reigns for 542 years on the known world. Founded European capitals. Civility became. Dealt with Christian movement. Judged Jesus Christ. Christianity became. Roman Empire fell. Christianity grew. Christian crusades. Dark ages. Second coming of Roman Empire: the Italian renaissance credo—the selfconsciousness axiom that rationalized and gave logic. Science became. Inventions became. Progress to present day makes remarkable technology strides in everything. Pardon me but I repeat succinctly. The loop, bicycles, dams, cars, ships, trains, airplanes. Institutions established to regulate and guide society and its symbols. All these by the White kind of the original early mankind.

Mezzi: All these strides only by the Whiteman?

Buzzo: There were others before them. Like the Sumerians of Mesopotamia with the wheels but the results of the exertion, of the geniality, of the power of imagination, of the dream of the White kind stood out. Theirs became a life-style. White kind lifestyle

Mezzi: The Whiteman's life style as explained to me by Tom Bradley.

Buzzo: Yes, everything as we know it today: just look around you within the confines of this room: current electricity, pipe-borne running water, the tv set, the phones, the computers, the iPad, music system, the chairs, the tiles, the doors, water faucets, the tea cups, the cutleries. And then from without this room: the bicycles, the cars, the trains, the ships, the airplanes, the yacht, the trains, the schools the hospitals, the parks, the factories, the satellite, going to the moon, the space etc. etc.

Then thanks to White kind's technologies, the original physical distances were bridged among the kinds of mankind. Africa was reached!

Then the psychological conscious distance ensued. Whiteman's life-style overwhelmed them. Traumatized them...

Mezzi: Traumatized them?

Buzzo: Overwhelmed them, traumatized them, and left sense of embarrassment, sense of defeat, sense of humiliation, sense of confusion, sense of resignation in them. It numbed them. They get into ponderous spasm of phobic-neurosis. So, in its wake they had two opposing realities: their primitive life-style and the novel Whiteman's life-style.

Mezzi: They chose to remain primitive. Primal instinct. Predatory.

Buzzo: Primitive life-style was not the choice: darkness opposed to current electricity was not the choice. Untreated water from the streams and the boreholes opposed to pipe-borne treated water was not the choice. Foot paths instead of roads, rail lines. Huts instead of houses. Trekking, donkey backs instead of bicycles, cars, buses, trains, ships, airplanes. Shrines and ignorance instead of schools and education. Voodoos, witchcraft wizardry and witch doctors instead of hospitals and medical doctors. Famine, hunger thirst instead of agriculture, agro-allied industries and manufacturing, value added transformational industries chains, etc. etc. were not the choices. They were already living out those. They did not have to make any of those choices.

They just needed to make one choice: the choice to stand up. They just needed to stand up.

> *They just needed to stand up. They just needed to stand up. Needed to stand up. Needed to stand up. Stand up. They never did to date!*

They needed to start dreaming about the catalyst, the accelerator, the happenstance of the novel life-style before them. They did not. They did not stand up to defend their life-style neither. Capitalize on the novel. They did not see the catalyst element of the novel White life-style. They did not see the catalyst element to improve their life-style. They did not stand up. They gave in like imbeciles! Characterless imbeciles. And instead, the novel life style did not only numb them but fascinated and swallowed them at the same time. They were baited with the taste of the novel lifestyle, including the churches: austere heavenly gates and the earthly materialistic palpable heavenly doctrines. They chose the latter under the umbrella of the former. A chimeral choice. A glutton choice. A grotesque choice. A remarkable betrayal of themselves choice. Sold their dignity and honor of being. You know why they did it?

Mezzi: Sloth. Laziness. Cowardice.

Buzzo: Bravo, *bravissimo! Laziness and cowardice of self-consciousness* A gratuitous laziness. A laziness without reason. A renegade laziness, that became hereditary. A hereditary despotism, a hereditary despotism in perpetuity. Generation to generation. This laziness is made culture. Made fascinating. A dignifying, defying, proud laziness credo. A spiritual intrinsic life-style. Adored. Adorable. Valued. Valuable. This laziness colonized them. Laziness enslaved them. Laziness lynched them. Laziness gave 3/5th of a human being. Laziness made them apes. Laziness shitholed them. Laziness turned them over to the churches and mosques. Laziness cemented them into prayerfulness. Laziness cemented them into miracle seekers. Laziness cemented them to cowardice, to wickedness, to lawlessness. Laziness separated them from the Almighty God. Laziness drove God away from Africa and yet the same laziness cemented them with unmerited favor tenet, the grace hope, from the same God to this day. Laziness cemented them to kleptomania. Laziness cemented them to avariciousness. Laziness cemented them to hyperbole. Laziness consorted them with the devil. Laziness kept them in their caravan of a tradition of hereditary willful conspiracies: hereditary conspiracy of willful silence. Hereditary conspiracy of willful blindness. A hereditary conspiracy of willful hypocrisy. A hereditary conspiracy of willful evil, of abject willful resignation, of willful despotism...

Mezzi: Yeah, fuck our willful complacency. Fuck our hollow vacuous pride. Truth be said: the African tradition is a tradition of inherited conspiracies!

Buzzo: A tradition of hereditary conspiracy of complicity. A hereditary conspiracy of mystification. A hereditary conspiracy of ignorance and arrogance. A tradition of hereditary conspiracy devoid of shame, devoid of humility, devoid of mortification, devoid of remorse, devoid of chagrin, devoid of empathy. Mezzi, laziness is Africa's misery.

Mezzi: Everything is beginning to take form in my brain. Making sense. Borrowing from and paraphrasing Thomas Paine's common sense:

> *Laziness sprouted hereditary despotic tradition of conspiracies and culture. Laziness sprouted religious palsy.*
> *Laziness sprouted enthusiasm of heroic cowardice.*
> *Laziness sprouted passion of animation of cowardice of freedom and of liberty. Laziness sprouted cowardice of truth.*

However, the question "what sprouted our gratuitous laziness?" remains.

Buzzo: You said it: Cowardice. Self-consciousness of cowardice. Passion for cowardice. Enthusiasm for cowardice. Animation of cowardice. Standing up to nothing. Giving in and up easily. Blackman does not persevere in anything. He readily surrenders.

Mezzi (in mumbles to himself): Cowardice, cowardice, cowardice and laziness.

Buzzo: Yes Mezzi. Cowardice to act. Cowardice begets cowardice. Laziness begets laziness.

Mezzi: Nothingness begets nothingness.

Buzzo: Distance begets distance. The original distance is laziness. And this laziness begets the defensive coping mechanism sets: the default blames; the default blame on the White tribe. Default blame on slavery. Default blame on colonization. Default blame on agriculture revolution. Default blame on industrial revolution, default blame on market economy, on capitalism. Default blame on institutions of capitalism – World Bank, International Monetary Fund, World Trade Organization, United Nations, United Nations Educational Scientific Cultural Organization. Default blame on technology…

Mezzi: Default blame on the White kind's life-style that Black kind laziness loves and consorts with. Default blame on a life-style that you are kleptomania to, that you are gullible to, glutton to, that you are enslaved to, thanks to the White's effort at geniality? And by extension geniality of Black kind Dominance and his misery.

Buzzo: Default hypocrisy. Default arrogance of ignorance. Default resignation in some religious mysticism. Added to the remarkable preposterous willful prolepsis.

Mezzi: Willful pro… what?

Buzzo: Willful prolepses of defensive coping mechanisms sets: Africa's willful denials of their facts and situations. Africa's willful blindness to their facts and realities. Their willful hypocrisy. Their willful kleptomania. Willful corruption. Willful false hood. Willful wickedness. Willful reticence. Willful self-abandonment. Willful greed. Willful gluttony. And of course, the willful of the willful of the caravan: Laziness.

Mezzi: So, Africa's misery…

Buzzo: … Africa's distance. Our distance Mezzi.

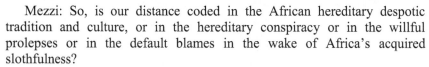

Mezzi: So, is our distance coded in the African hereditary despotic tradition and culture, or in the hereditary conspiracy or in the willful prolepses or in the default blames in the wake of Africa's acquired slothfulness?

Buzzo: Bravo! Add religious blessing hypnosis: the grace hypnosis (whatever evil you are and do, you can have unmerited favor, grace). Sow the seed hypnosis (not the seed of righteousness but sow evil and sow money as the seed and you will be sanctified and blessed). Pay tithe hypnosis (if you don't pay tithe God will not bless you).

Mezzi: The blessing hypnosis: remain lazy and evil with illusion of paradise hypnosis.

Buzzo: Add the *erasus* of the laws and the *oblivionem* of the commandments.

Mezzi (in a brief amnesia): The *erasus*...the *oblivionem*? Oh yeah. Right!

Buzzo: Yes, Africans don't believe in God. They have no fear, nor respect for him. They conscientiously erase the laws of God; the laws of the land. Just look at the *erasus* of the supreme first law of God "Love thy Lord" and the *oblivionem* of the second commandment "Love thy neighbor like thyself". Talk less of the *erasus* and the *oblivionem* of the rest of the laws.

Mezzi: We can say that Whiteman's life-style is the "Love thy neighbor like thyself" commandment of the Lord.

Buzzo: Absolutely. Our distance. Their distance. Their distance has no transgression. Not vile. Their distance has creativity. Innovation. Not indifference. Compassion. Their distance is closeness. Collectivism. They invent and innovate to enable humanity. Their distance is hard work and progress. Our distance is laziness. Laziness our orgasm. Distance our misery. Our charade. Our travesty. Our shame. Our embarrassment.

> *Their distance is closeness. Collectivism. Creativity. Their distance is "love thy neighbor." Their distance invents and innovates to enable humanity. Their distance is hard work and their progress. Their wealth. Our distance is laziness. Laziness our orgasm. Our distance our misery. Our catharsis. Our charade. Our travesty. our shame. Our embarrassment.*

We need dreams. We need men who can dream inspirations, visions to tear down the prison-hold legacy of African Hereditary Hierarchic Despotic Tradition, generation after generation. And TEAR it Down.

VOLUME 2

THE APOSTASY

Chapter 1

B uzzo and Mezzi, their gadgets and apps in hands, are ready for their next move. Buzzo contrives some brilliance: roll with the devil. With the constituted authorities. Even though, from the Gen Z there is a profound chasm of deepest virulent hate and bias against the constituted authorities–the government, the oligarchs, the religious, the tradition and their corresponding heads – Presidents and Governors, kleptomaniacs, the Pastors and the Imams and the Priest, the Kings and the Chiefs and the Emirs and the Sultans and all their combined fiefdoms; even though they know of the complicity, the role, the responsibility and the deep connect between these authorities and their family in the African tragedy of misery, even so they are deeply convinced that to succeed they need them. They need them for protection and as a platform to carry out their excogitation.

Therefore, the constrained deceit, and their willful intent to exploit the authority far outweigh their guilt, pride, prejudice, anger and the resolve not to.

So, they make their first port of call:

The President's Residence
After all the surprises expressed for the arrival and for the presence of Mezzi (first time in Africa), the pleasantries followed.

What they did not know with certainty, but assume could be a possibility, is the fact that their anguished parents, in a clear and present torment, back in the USA, have kept a line of communication with their family friend, the President. The President, who as well is their father's best friend and puppet is keeping tab on them. The President, on his own initiative, has advised to let time mitigate the situation and eventually rein them back in, into niggers' reality, without dramatizing and further dramas.

To what seemed sincerest pleasantries carefully choreographed on the part of their family friends – the President, his wife and the household – their guests, Buzzo and Mezzi, responded with measured warmth: a fine line between simulation and sincere response.

Even though this uneasy tense aura was evident, the pleasantries trudged on, amidst some awkward moments.

Yet Mezzi found a ready tacit compactible friendly feeling, in one of the President's kids: younger Mark. His generation.

A tacit feeling that sprouted into a binding profitable alliance for his intent.

While in the President's premises, Mezzi did not fall short of noticing: The voluptuous size of the palace, the remarkable pomp and pageant; The remarkable luxury of the palace from within is of remarkably sharpest contrast with the remarkable abject poverty and the remarkable despair from without – like a remarkable puddle of water in the middle of the desert, a remarkable island in the middle of the ocean;

The remarkable number of people seated, standing, strutting, idling;

The remarkable number of household servants;

The remarkable number of exotic cars parked;

The remarkable numbers and remarkable sizes of lounges, sitting rooms and sittings;

The remarkable curated garden devoid of life, signs and symbols: not for kids; The remarkable absence of bookshelves and books;

The remarkable amount of security without and within.

The remarkable amount of security brings into focus, reminiscence and evocation of a remarkable prison – a hospital to cure and reform the psyche – environment situation: the awe, the exclusion, the seclusion, the symbols of society, the consequences of crime.

The paradox: the rich in Africa is remarkably the indisputable prisoner of society. He is like parasites – cockroaches, mosquitoes – that hide in the dark. Guilty-ridden he holes up, hiding in these farcical mansions, stolen from the poor, in abject illusion of safety and protection. Afraid of the poor from without. The remarkably poor prowl the streets, in "liberty," hassling to survive.

After the greetings and the pleasantries, they are assigned a 24-hour Range Rover SUV with the President's orderly in charge of the State Security Services escort for the duration of Mezzi's stay in Africa.

Mezzi: No escorts please!

Buzzo: Low profile please, normal people!

They don't need this protocol. Be in the eye of the people. They need low profile. They can't be part of that problem, aggravating, wasting the people's resources. It will be a remarkable betrayal of what they stand for.

Their protest surprises the rank and file of the escort. So much so that the orderly on security chore tries to address the issue.

Orderly: Common gentlemen, the President's wish…common kids…

Mezzi (thinking ahead): Please between us, kindly withdraw the escorts…the fuel must be borne by us…

Orderly: There is a clear lurking and present danger and lingering anger out there. You are not in America. You are in Africa…besides, to be together with your friends David and Mark…

Buzzo: We understand fully. But consider this: when we are with the escort, could the siren be silenced? When we are by ourselves, none of both. A deal?

David: Common. Everybody in this little town knows us. They know every of our cars. We are conspicuously popular. They know me. Some love me others hate me. I have followers. It's like not noticing the few trees in the desert.

Mark: Yeah, but even at that let's pretend civility today. Behave like we are in the West. No sirens.

David has an instant assault of frowning grimace. Every other person, beams with smile, seems to agree to compromise. Off they went.

> *The paradox: the rich in Africa is remarkably the indisputable prisoner of society. He is like parasites–cockroaches, mosquitoes that hide in the dark. Guilty-ridden he holes up, hiding in these farcical mansions, stolen from the poor, in abject illusion of safety and protection. Afraid of the poor from without. The remarkably poor prowl the streets, in "liberty", hassling to survive.*

Chapter 2

We have four of them in the Range Rover SUV. In movement. Escort in the distance. Siren silenced, heading to nowhere in particular but to everywhere at the same time.

Of the two President's sons, David 21, the age of Buzzo is dad's boy. Even though he studied in the USA, he has been molded to mirror his father's demeanor: somewhere between a cad-unscrupulous, selfish, envious, vanity, insecurity, non-creative and anti-social-cruel, ruthless, inhibited, bigoted, perverse, introvert; and Mark 14, mom's boy. Mark is a combination of cleverness, shrewdness, quick-wittedness, persuasiveness, observation, intellect, talent and ambitious-rebellious, expansive, extrovert, cravings for change, for fame, loyalty, ruthlessness.

David, already recoiled, air of smugness in the owner's seat, is almost to himself, not saying much. Mark in contrast, already playing, at some joke, totally at home with Mezzi, has already observed the device in Mezzi's palm.

Mark (reaching out grabbing for it) What's this?

Mezzi: It's ingenuous. *Relievo* and Blogging!

Mark: What the hell is *relievo*?

Mezzi: Relief, access, detect…flicking this app will tell us what's happening in a radius of ten kilometers…

Mark: Kind of a spy machine, kind of Google search?

Mezzi: Yeah kind of…kind of data collection. For example, if I ask you "how many parks and gardens have you in this city," do you know?

Mark: Parks and gardens? None!

Buzzo (cutting in): Common, no gardens?

Mark: Let the app tell us, common…

Mezzi puts the machine to work. Comes up after some split seconds with:

'No parks. 4 gardens: 1 private, the Governor's and 3 commercials, the Lebanese's.'

Mark: (surprised) Cool. Incredible. Really cool… but shit you mean in this whole God forsaken city, ours is the only garden?

David: That cannot be true. It's impossible. Utter nonsense…that your gadget…is a hoax!

Buzzo (who developed the gadget smirks): You can bet your ass it's authentic!

Mark: It's unreal. Ours is the only garden?

David: So, what then? Who cares about gardens…what for…who for?

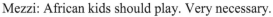

Mezzi: African kids should play. Very necessary.

David: African kids? Should play? Who cares about African kids?

Buzzo: What the hell are you saying?

David: Who the fuck cares? They have lazy parents...can't you see them all over the place...how dirty they are? They are filths... poor. They will mess the place up in a minute...

Buzzo: That's remarkable. You talk like they are not your kind...your Black kind...

Mark: ...Yeah. He thinks he is a White kind...Whiteman. He despises everyone but himself. Bombastic. Complacent. Don't mind him.

(then to Mezzi provocatively): Please Mezzi, find out more...if there is any Disneyland, any Museum...Zoos...Libraries, hidden with fairy tale books and photography exhibitions...

David (his face a mockery smile, staring down Mark): You are ridiculous. You know there is none...

Mark: No, I am not. What do you know?

David: I know a lot, certainly more than You do...

Mark (irked raising his voice): What the fuck do you know? We are holed-up in that prison of our house. We need siren to make any move. Isolated, distanced from all and places. We should live. We should play. Make our home in Africa like the one we have in America. We don't even have a functional library. Our grandparents used to have functional libraries, museums, ride on trains, public functional schools, functional hospitals in his time. Yes. He said so...left by colonialism.

David: Can you shut the fuck up! Be civil! Stop shouting!

Mark (angry and agitated, now shouting): You shut your dirty mouth up...driver stop.

(Almost hysterical) I want some air...stop!

Mezzi: Easy guys! Easy! Cool! Let's see... actioning the apps...emm!

Mark already opened the door of the moving Range Rover SUV, forcing the driver to a stop.

Cursing his brother out, Mark storms out of the car followed closely by Mezzi.

We see Buzzo contemplating the twosome, beaming with smiles. With muted exhilaration, excitement, underpinning the fact that Mezzi got company. Remarkable company. His kind for their cause.

Chapter 3

We see Mezzi already at work. Remarkably working up Mark, demonstrating the prowess of his device, the apps and the blogging aspect.

Mark is remarkably curious and remarkably desirous.

The company is now split. Buzzo and David in the car with the security on the one side, moving. Mezzi and Mark on the other side, in a rented taxi and autonomously moved on combing the town.

With the prowess of Mezzi's gadget, they are fact-checking and corroborating the existence of each and all of their interest: not just the gardens, or parks, or basketball fields, or football fields, but the museums, the zoos, the libraries, art exhibitions, the schools, the hospitals, etc., but there was none. You could see the colonial development legacy of these institutions everywhere but in a permanent state of abandonment and disrepair.

And besides, the opportunity afforded them the sight of open-air sewers, heaps of garbage, sometimes to a height of three floors of a normal building, the remarkable number of bars, the remarkable amount of folks, the kids, the youths and the elderly amongst them indulged in alcohol, the smell of reefers, the stench, the remarkable number of churches, the remarkable number of mosques. The absence of industrial parks, of factories and industries.

The town is not functioning. Everything seemed remarkably arrested in time and space. Everything, anything is remarkably denied and yet everything and anything seem to have a soul: Order. Rationale. In sequence. Open air urination. Open air defecation. People immune to them. Nobody seems to care, to notice. In their midst people are remarkably, comfortably eating, feasting, spitting. Garbage flying in the air, thrown out of everywhere. The people seem happy. They simulate happiness. Simulation, stoicism, *omerta'*, denial, smugness, complacency, all framed by the force of arrogance to mitigate their suffering and tribulations and predatory sense of inadequacy?

One is readily forced to ask: Can they rationalize their situation? Their misery? Do they know what is happiness? They have feelings? Are these human beings? Are we human beings? Africans live in the perdition of their indifference and failures?

In the distance Mezzi and Mark notice cows and goats and sheep, with their herdsmen, herding them, plowing the streets. Some of the animals are defecating as they walk! Some others are drinking from the puddle. They seem content each time they find to graze.

They could not help but draw the remarkable striking similarity between these animals in their midst and the Black kind, their race. And you are tempted to ask the question: What is and where are the differences between Black kind and these mammals?

These Mammals defecate open-air. Black kind defecates open-air. They urinate open-air. The Black kind urinates open air. They drink from the puddle of rain water. Black kind scoops from the puddle to drink and cook and bath. They don't have libraries. Black kind doesn't have functional libraries. They can't read. Black kind can but won't read. They don't seem to have the intellect for any higher creative cause. The Black kind has but won't develop his intellect to intelligence. They seem not worried. Black kind are not worried. They seem happy, content to be followers, to be led. Black kind compulsively simulates remarkable happiness, happyholic, hopeholic, obedient follower, devoid of self-consciousness of rationalizing and reasoning.

The most striking difference seems to be that these animals remarkably tend to and care for their little ones.

The Black kind eats and feasts away from its little ones. Animals eat along their little ones.

Mezzi plugs his device and ascertains the existence of the very many local government councils of the land: they lunge into the countryside, the villages. Village after village, hamlet after hamlet, as they silently observe, they begin to understand the significance and the profound importance of relativity; the quality of being relative and having significance only in relation to something else in space and time. Life is remarkably subdued, beaten, despaired, forlorn, shamed, denied, stilled.

This conundrum is remarkably repetitive. It's devastating and numbing especially for Mezzi, who lives in the pleasures of civilization and civility.

Now the boys are tired of exchanging glances fraught with humiliation, and defeat, and sense of blame, and sense of complicity and shame. Their inadequacy of pride. Mezzi's neural groove is filled with ever present 'Nigger syndrome,'s while that of friend Mark, is tranced as it transits from surprise, disappointment, delusion, shame to remarkable sense of injustice and indebtedness to society.

A lot of huts. Most of them remarkably tiny. Most of them remarkably host over a dozen kids each. You get to this rural setting early enough; you lose count of remarkable number of kids streaming out of them. A human caravan.

Those tiny huts measure 3 meters by 3 meters. They ascertained. Of course, devoid of any freedom. Not even the minimum basic current electricity, pipe-borne water, what more of urbanization and amenities.

Now they assist first hand as kids, malnourished, are violently awoken and beaten to get to their first task of the day: trek to the stream with buckets on their heads to fetch water. Not even bore-holes are here. Pipe-borne water would be heavenly. They come back most of them in trudge over the burden of their water catch: heavy buckets of water that tense and twitch the muscles of their necks.

Their next task is trek to the farms for fire woods. Sometimes some are accompanied by their mothers, when they still have them. Of course, there is no cooking gas. No generator, no electric energy. Yet this is a continent of crude oil but devoid of cooking gas, crude oil refined by-products. The gas is voluptuously flaring.

The next scene is some form of remarkable austere, demeaning breakfast where the 'lion share' is consumed by their 'male lion' figure fathers, cool, in their traditional role demeanor, looking tough, head of the family demeanor posturing, sitting aside, all by themselves. The kids, seated with their mothers, share whatever meagre is left. Then you would finally wish the next scene is see them go off to school. No, their next task scene is, 'be the bread winners': some are handed down hoes, others matchets, off to farming activities. Yet others are handed trays of bananas, peanuts, mangoes, cashew fruits, etc., and off they head out to hawking activities with trays of merchandises on their heads, and yet others head out to begging chores. What a humiliating way of life: Africa's gifts to its progenies. Generation after generation.

These are heartbreaking deplorable scenes of facts. This is the passion. Africa's passion. Africa's willful self-enslavement passion. The Via Crucis of the future of at least 95% of African children. The tomorrow of Africa. A *sacrilegium*. Trampled. Permanently condemned to misery. To tribulation. To despair. To disrepair. To death. Passed on generation to generation. Unabated.

> *Africa's willful self-enslavement passion. A passion to self-inflict misery. A tragedy. A consolidated tragedy passed on from generation to generation. Consolidated Tragedy passed on from generation to generation. Tragedy passed on from generation to generation. Passed on from generation to generation. From generation to generation to generation to generation to generation to generation to present day generation. Unabated.*

Again, the relativity significance catapults Mezzi and Mark to their impeccable infancy: they were read to, they were cuddled and had lullaby to sleep, cuddled and induced to wake up, bathed, dressed, given breakfast, and driven to kindergarten, to nursery or to school, then to the parks, libraries, museums, theatres, growing their self-consciousness. Mezzi, in his unutterable bewilderment and numbness and cold rage, finds his voice, breaking the silence:

Mezzi: Too many kids.

Mark (shaking his head 'disapproval'): They are orphans. Too many orphaned kids.

Mezzi: Derided and deprived...

Mark: Their freedom denied...

Mezzi: They have never known freedom.

Mark: Why do you think they make them and make them so many?

Mezzi: Bah! Maybe they are sexually crazed. A physical need. A spiritual need.

Mark: ...Maybe as their life insurance, guarantee for livelihood...

Mezzi: ...Life insurance has value. These children are not given any value...

Mark: ...Yep, they are worth nothing. Maybe for the love of cynicism.

Mezzi: These children know their fathers but their fathers don't know them.

Mark: Fathers unconsciously, unconscientiously, pathologically make them...

Mezzi: Compulsively. African women just throw their legs open to become mothers. Catharsis of laziness.

Mark: Simply for the male penetration...pure cynicism. Anarchic. Lack of love.

Mezzi: Perennially pregnant. They have pride in pregnancy. The state of pregnancy mitigates their nothingness. A child obliterates their nothingness. A selfconscientious predatory sense of motherhood defies the real and present selfconscientious danger of misery for their kids. A criminal endeavor.

Mark: Then the shrines, the African tradition permits and does nothing...

Mezzi: Alongside the churches, the mosques.

Mark: They are everywhere. Magnificently and sumptuously, remarkably noticeable.

Mezzi: They don't sing poverty. They sing riches. Richness. Pardon. Grace. But not for these kids.

These three symbols – the shrine, the church and the mosque – are in every nook and corner. They are rapacious. Remarkably predatory.

> *These children know their fathers but their fathers don't know them...*
> *African women are perennially pregnant. They have pride in*
> *pregnancy. A perennial state of pregnancy mitigates their*
> *nothingness. Having A child, in their mindset, obliterates their*
> *nothingness. A self-conscientious predatory sense of motherhood*
> *defies their real and present self-conscientious danger of misery for*
> *their kids. A senseless inhuman endeavor, forced by the ...*

...moral blackmail of their hereditary despotic tradition and their subservience.

Mezzi and Mark more than ever tacitly agree to do something for their generation. They intensified their documenting, planning, programming this audacious arduous task. Reviewing the Millennials family social blog, "let the kids play", set up by Mezzi and planning how to progress participatorily further, formulate questions, suggest answers, understand who they are, define who they are, define their future without Status Quo, when:

Lo! In the distance from their vintage view point they behold the most beautiful, yet most remarkable puzzling scene Mezzi, subconsciously had wished but had thought it near the impossible: African kids' rebellion within the African context?

This batch of kids, of this hamlet, of this village drops their work tools- their hoes, their matchets, their trays of merchandize etc., one after the other in the nearby bush and head out for an apparent unknown destination to them, the spectators.

Mezzi (in a delighted frown, turning to Mark): Did you see that shebang?

Mark: Yeah, panicky. What do you think is happening?

Mezzi: This is revolutionary. Absolutely remarkable.

Mark: Chorused courageous act. Remarkable. They must be up to something.

Mezzi: Common let's go. We absolutely need to follow them. Find out what the hell is going on.

They pick their sacks and, in a flash, run off after them.

Now we find Mezzi and Mark stalking the kids, following them for quite some distance until they stopped at their destination: "let the kid play" center.

They are occupying, blocking the main entrance, the portico, of the center. Mezzi and Mark stop in their tracks, taking in the situation.

Mezzi was in amazement of location surprise as he gets into realization of his position: his hamlet is before his eyes. He truly had never taken this route to his hamlet ever before. He recognizes his grandfather's village, that appears to him like a kismet. Now he understands what's going on: his center is the impetus of the rebellion. Isn't that something?

Mark (cognizant of location): What...where are we? Is this not your hamlet?

Mezzi (smiling with air of smugness, fixing his center): Do you like it?

Mark: (in a spasm of confusion) What's going on?

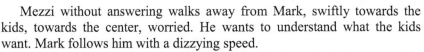

Mezzi without answering walks away from Mark, swiftly towards the kids, towards the center, worried. He wants to understand what the kids want. Mark follows him with a dizzying speed.

Mezzi reaches out, greeting the kids reassuringly as he gains entry into the center. Mark, transfixed is following up on every hint and detail. The center is remarkably empty and relatively quiet at that hour of the morning. The regular kids of the hamlet have had their routine breakfast and are all gone to school.

Meanwhile, Mark who had stopped asking questions is still lost for words. He is overwhelmed by the entire center: the structures, the facilities, the equipped playground. All buried in the trees and meadows and plants and flowers.

Mezzi has in the meantime called in the kids. Have them taken to the refectory. Have them sit down, have them served breakfast, watch them as they devour the fries, the beacons, the bread, the palp with remarkable avidity, spilling all over their ragged clothing and on the tables. In silence until they are done.

Mezzi: Did you all enjoy the food? Are you all feeling better?

They proffered nothing. Just silently fixing Mezzi: Deafening illiteracy.

Mezzi understands. He needs the services of a translator. These kids are stark illiterates. Bonded in misery. Denied education, enslaved by child labor. Denied any form of dignity. Their environment remarkably predatory to them.

He calls in the head of admissions of the center who asked them who they are, why they are there by themselves, what they think they want!

Kids: "We want to eat, we want to school and we want to play like the other kids, our peers of the hamlet" were muttered in their tongues.

They are readily translated to Mezzi, who beams with a winner's smile, like someone who won at some big lottery.

Mezzi (shouting and awaiting translation): You want what?
The kids (in unison): We want to eat!
Mezzi: You want what?
The kids: We want to school, to feed, to play!
Mezzi: Are you sure?
The kids: Yes, yes, yes, yes, yes. We want to play

Mezzi understood and without pondering any further, ordered the center's administration to have their names taken and subject them to center's formalities for admission.

Now, Mark gets emotional. Overwhelmed, he broke down in tears. Mezzi notices. He unites himself with him.

Mark (amidst his profuse sobbing and hiccups): Congratulations. I am very proud of you.

Mezzi (pulling him to himself and hugging him remarkably tightly): Thank you my friend. I hope we can sustain their hope-renaissance together.

Mark (cleaning his eyes): This is remarkable. Remarkably inspiring. Remarkably remarkable.

The Center grew. Many more kids from neighboring hamlets have heard. They are rebelling and joining the Centre. They are being sent to school. More expenses are incurred by the hour. Most kids won't go home to avoid the wrath of their parents. There is a remarkable emergency. Everything is challenged and challenging. The Center is outgrown. Outpaced. The well-thought out infrastructure, amenities, facilities, the human resources at the Center are outpaced by the growing kids' population. Constantly remarkably on the increase. Something must be done.

Mark: We must together sustain this hope renaissance. It's our reason, our life purpose.

Mezzi smiles. His face expresses pride and contentment.

They throw themselves in each other's arm. Profoundly moved amidst an eerie silence.

Chapter 4

Now we take on Buzzo and David as they walk the corridors of the secretariat of Government's public administration absorbed in discussion. Their discussion is interrupted intermittently by interjections of salutes and greetings. Host of the interjectors are in awe of him from their very behavior of simulation of subservient servility. David's persona of first son statute evidently commands crowd and reactivity.

Buzzo: You are famous. They know you.

David: It's easy to know me. It's nothing. They actually hate me and my family.

Buzzo: Tell me something, you really don't care about kids?

David: Kids? Never liked them. Indifferent to them and their stupid cravings...

Mezzi: Common! Are we men? We have just started the weaning process.

David: So much so that teenagers should be teenagers...

Buzzo: ...Our tomorrow is the future. Our tomorrow is us, the kids, our kids. It's a circle. Breathe life into the world, the unstoppable life transition begins: Infant, youth, manhood, old age, death.

David: Yeah, I know. My brother is a pain in the ass. Very assuming. Stubborn.

Buzzo: No, my friend, don't go personal. You spend the most part of your childhood within the privilege of civilization and civility, where you never saw the electric bulb blink...or the portable tap water not running...or open-air sewer. You should be happy at such burst of maturity at his age, looking at facts and acknowledging them.

David: What does he know? I have long been seeing what he just started seeing. It's been like that. Nobody can solve it. What the hell is new about it?

Buzzo: You break my heart. That is compulsive vacuity. Intellectual dishonesty.

David: It's been going on generation after generation. Hereditary tradition.

Buzzo: That's a default African resignation solution at not evolving to the next level. Africa's coded commandment against change dynamism. Change dynamism in perpetual arrest.

(He suddenly stops talking. Grabs the shoulders of David fixing him in the eyes):

Buzzo: Let me put it to you this way, Mark is right. Our kids got to play. You went through excellent education. Didn't you? You went through cutting-age hospitals. Didn't you? You went through public gardens and parks? You saw the old and the young tended to. Didn't you?

David: Yes, I did, and so?

Buzzo: You went to the zoos, you used libraries, went to museums, went to National Space Agency NASA, to Apple Corporation, to Amazon, to Microsoft, to the Capitol Hill, to the White House premises, etc., and what do you think those opportunities mean? You had the opportunity to play and be literate and grow your mind, your self-consciousness. You deny the stark differences?

Irritated, incredulous, Buzzo now let go of his shoulders and they walk into an office. An open space. 2/3rd empty. David takes a look at his wrist watch: it's 11:15 am. Few, among the handful of workers, recognizes his presence and readily recomposes self to office posture.

Now they walk into Buzzo's office. David closes the door behind him asking:

David: Why is the public office empty at this hour?

Buzzo (sitting down, smirking): The environment, David. Africa needs to build acceptable working environment.

David (angry, suddenly raising his voice): I have got to let my father know this, now.

Buzzo: Garbage in, garbage out, David. This is the system. It's just not about your father only. It's about the system. You are the system. I am the system. We, by mere happenstance, are the positive victim of the system.

David (his face a disapproving frown): What? Not fair about my father? You crazy or something? What do you mean?

Buzzo (waving him to a seat): Please make yourself comfortable and let me bring you home to roost.

David sits, with expectations. Eyes and attention fixed on Buzzo. He is tensed. Even so, tempered radical Buzzo knows where he is headed to.

Buzzo: My father, your father…does it make any difference?

David: It does. Don't play with words. I hate mysteries.

Buzzo: Mysteries? Cool, you want operation candor? David, my father is a billionaire! What does he manufacture? Nothing. He is into King and Peace-making business. In other words, he is into corruption. That's his business. This business nets him billions of Dollars. Right?

He pauses, scanning him for his profound attention, and continues.

Your father is a politician. He is as well a billionaire. What was he manufacturing? What does he manufacture? What's his salary? What's the Gross Domestic Product of his government? What's the income per capita of his people? What's his scorecard? David, his scorecard is mass misery. Our fathers' combined actions create bonds of mass misery. I repeat, we are the 'positive' victims of the system. In fact, it's positivity literally means embarrassment. We are an embarrassment.

He stops talking and locks eyes with David, fixing him intensely. There is an assault of eerie silence in the room.

David is in total amazement of doubt. His arrogant countenance started waning. The obvious and ever present, destructive forces of default inertia and momentous defensive reaction stance, characteristic of majority of Africans, youths and adults indistinctly, that blindly opposes any positive thinking, any dialectics, seem deflated. He continues:

Buzzo: David are you there? Candor David. Only in Africa a-do-nothing, a non-solution provider to enable humanity in any form, in any place is a billionaire! And they are in the form of politicians, traditional rulers, religious leaders, oligarchs. Cabals, Niggers!

You know why? Our ignorance. Our cowardice to act. Dislike for work. Our laziness. Nature produces raw materials for us and we produce mass misery. Niggers!

Buzzo suddenly stops talking, unlocks his drawer, brings out part of his research work, for which he is hired to do for the administration, under the auspices of the United States Agency for International Development (USAID), to datalize and digitalize, for an eventual ambitious smarting and efficiency of the state and the nation, sticking it to David's face:

Buzzo: Here are my findings, the State of the Union-like records. Cancerous absenteeism. Few workers. Ghost workers. All within the rank and file of the public administration and parastatals.

Here you will find out the misery contrivance game. Ghost workers are created to net and siphon public funds. These Ministers and Directors, against every conflict of interest, make moribund public utilities – hospitals, schools, parks, gardens, security outfits etc., etc. and amenities – establishing private practices with pseudonym. Not only, they then appropriate money to rehabilitate them which they loot. State of disrepair is promoted and perennial.

Minimum car insurances are paid for by all motorists but no cases of repairs of any accidents. Who takes the money?

Pensions that are dutifully deducted during active services and, or are contributed to, are not paid to our senior citizens.

The teachers are not paid. The medical staff are not paid.

These combined salaries are put away in banks forever to amass interest for who?

The port authorities and airport authorities don't even report revenues and yet duties are collected. And they are paid salaries from other public resources.

African Presidents are billionaires. African Governors are billionaires. African Lawmakers are billionaires. African local government Councilors are billionaires. African monarchs are billionaires. African Pastors are billionaires. African Imams are billionaires, African Chief Priests are billionaires. Yet, none of them manufactures a pin nor a toothpick, but misery.

Their families are overseas for freedoms and liberties and rights. Like me and you, David.

The government of the people is for themselves. The masses here are given, are subjected to and endure misery. They are in forced misery. Remarkably remarkable.

African Presidents are billionaires. African Governors are billionaires. African lawmakers are billionaires. African local government Councilors are billionaires. African Monarchs are billionaires. African Pastors are billionaires. African Imams are billionaires. African Chief Priests are billionaires. Yet none of them manufactures a pin nor a toothpick, but Misery. Their Families are overseas for freedoms and liberties and rights. Like me and you, David. The African Masses are here gifted misery. Generation after generation. Remarkably remarkable, huh? What an inexcusable, unutterable sorrowing sordid gift.

David is ponderously stunned. Indeed, he is in a spasm of unutterable self-absorption. He slowly gets out of his seat to a standing position.

Buzzo pauses to gauge the reaction of David, who in the meantime has stopped looking at him, fixing the void. Some place in the middle of no place, pensive. Contemplative. He started pacing back and forth in the little room, in transition.

The melodious music of truth seems to be clear and present.

Buzzo seizes the opportunity, and continued reading from his documents.

Buzzo: There is more. The government thwarts and impedes the efforts of Foreign Direct Investment (FDI) sometimes to the tune of $500 billion in agriculture sector for mechanized rice farming on a total of over 2.5m hectares of land in the last two years. Do you know the motivation? The peasant farmers would, did you hear me, the peasant poor farmers would potentially protest and riot against it for their ancestral lands.

Here's another one...to build and produce the pharmaceuticals here in Africa is more expensive than their importation of same pharmaceuticals. We lose $2.5 trillion in Foreign Direct Investment (FDI), on the average every year and $trillions importing. It's cheaper to import chocolates, jeans, refined oil products than to process cocoa, cotton and refine crude oil. The list goes on and on.

David, on those words suddenly jerks back to life from his tranced state. Shocked.

David: You kidding!
Buzzo (handing over the documents): You can keep these confidential papers. You will kindly do me the great favor of perusing them.
And you know the real reason are aid money and corruption. Complicity my mom and our dads in the former and our dads in the latter. The United Nations or elements or some officials of the donor countries, my mother inclusive, buy the consciences of a few Africans, our fathers and elements of government inclusive, to bond mass misery. Monies are falsely allocated to import products that are round-tripped, quadrupled and then diverted and embezzled. Only Niggers can contrive harm to themselves and to their future, their future generation. Their descendants. They share the monies, year in, year out. Generation in generation out. Poverty is enhanced. Mass misery deepens. Tribulation and despair perpetuate. Have you ever seen a thief stealing his own money and properties? That's exactly what a Nigger does.

David (involuntarily) starts vomiting in the middle of the room.
He's heard enough. He's had enough. He can't take it anymore. Buzzo walks over grabbing and steadying him to a sitting position. He now tends to him, giving him a box of tissue papers.

Buzzo: Common David, I am sorry. Are you okay?
David (clearing his throat, nodding yes, at the same time): Cool!

He gives back the box of tissue papers to Buzzo. Buzzo refuses saying:

Buzzo: Keep it. You can take all up with your dad.
David: Waste of time. And what now...I mean what can we do?

Buzzo has understood. Remarkable. He has found an ally and he seizes on the opportunity. He immediately calls into action his extemporaneous art of inclusive persuasion.

Buzzo: Between us, whether we wish ourselves well, ill or evil, I will always expect your constructive criticism of my views. But that should not stop our desire to fight for freedom. Freedom for us, for the family of Gen Z.

Freedom of the family of African Youth should be our passion. And it requires sacrifice, selflessness, perseverance. Should be our life calling. I am not interested in anything else.

There's been, on the one side, a long history of what had seemed to me, a White kind's "tough hate" of a willful denigration of Africa. While on the other side, there is a long tradition of what seemed a remarkable "tough self-hate" of a remarkable default defensive denial reaction from the Black kind. It was remarkably mind blowing. In my intrinsic confusion and position I decided for Africa. In an attempt to dig in and dig out, and dig up facts. Ascertain facts to the best of my capability and possibility.

He pauses, reaching for the fridge, in his office space, opening it.

He brings out an apple and a carrot and a soda placing them on the table. Continuing:

Buzzo: David, this apple is an apple. This is a carrot. This is a bottle of coke. We can see them. We can touch them. Can't we? We can't deny these facts. Can we? Africans must stop the compulsive default denial of their misery and shame. They must stop denying their inadequacies. They must accept the state of their facts.

Africa is misery, we must accept this our evil blot. The acceptance of our evil blot is essential. If we continue in the Black kind commandment of willful and default denial of our evil blot, if we don't accept our evil blot as our common denominator of malaise and disgrace, and continue having a house divided, a family divided we will continue prevailing failure. A family divided means unutterable failure. It means moronic perpetuation of misery. It means perdition. And no god of progress and development will have basis to lead us out of perdition that we dug, dig and perpetuate ourselves in.

David: Nothing could've been more concise. I am with you Buzz. We are evil.

Buzzo: paraphrasing President Kennedy: *"In our long human history, only a few generations, have had the strength, the perseverance in faith, the patience in tribulation to crave, seek and create freedom. The promoters and the flag, militants of freedom are those few apostates, seeds of the bourgeois, to whom much have been given."*

David, at our ages, too much has already been given to me and to you.

The seeds of misery are bonded in misery. Every day they are buried in misery.

Fortunately, you and I are seeds of freedom. We must be bonded in freedom. We must give freedom. We must rise to the faith. Devotion and perseverance to enthrone freedom for our generation thence.

If the soul of our journey be liberty, let us represent and free our Gen Z, and generations thence, be the ambassador of freedoms calling.

David rises, his eyes watery. These words have knocked him over remarkably. He goes over to Buzzo, who rises. They embrace each other, holding out on tightly. There is tacit agreement. Embrace and solemnity of thoughts are not substitute for strength and perseverance. They may serve the compass of strength into revolution for life, and evolution of progress, and its fortitude of survival.

> *Africa is misery, we must accept this our evil blot. The acceptance of our evil blot is essential. If we continue in our commandment of willful and default denial of our evil blot, if we don't accept our evil blot as our common denominator of malaise and disgrace, and continue having a house divided, a family divided we will continue prevailing failure. A family divided means unutterable failure. It means moronic perpetuation of misery. It means perdition. And no god of progress and development will have basis to lead us out of perdition that we dug, dig and perpetuate ourselves in.*

VOLUME 3
THE SCHISM

Chapter 1

Back in America, there is a remarkable grievous family situation fraught with distraught. Unknown to Buzzo and Mezzi, their parents are temporarily apart. Their mother, to the extent that she is unable to bear the sudden loss of confidence of her life: from her two sons; To the extent that she is unable to convince her husband of the urgency of the moment to reverse position from his intransigence; To the extent that she is unable to win him over to accommodate the views and position of truth and to instead take pride in the precocious maturity of their boys in truths' path. To these extents she separated from him:

Husband: If we are still a family, and we are genitors of that family we can't let them dictate their perverse Gen Z culture of freedom. We have to be in charge.

Wife: The forest must have its trees. Without the trees there is no forest. Without the happiness of our kids we have failed. It's no more about me and you.

Husband: Gen Z's cultural freedom cannot mean disrespect for family, tradition, church and the flag. Let's remain real!

Wife (locking eyes with him): Our racial freedom here in America and everywhere in the West, meant riots and rock and roll and crime and pain to the Status Quo. Right? So why not?

Husband: You win by promising economic order. But you acquire real power and maintain power by the taming of the streets. There must be misery for power...

Wife (sick and tired of his intransigent line of thinking): Just like sexual freedom must come to mean divorce.

Husband: That's below the belt.

Wife: How?

Husband: We have come a long way – love, marriage, work, business, fun...

Wife (smirking 'disapproval'): What love? What fun? What business? However, nothing comes before my kids. Not you. Not anybody. Not anything.

Husband (surprised, taken aback): What? Are you out of your mind?

Wife (her heart heavy. Almost in tears): Don't take it. I don't know if I have ever loved any man. I could have married anything. Anybody. I married you to escape from the oppression of my father and to punish him at the same time. You knew it. I told you.

He was perverse. He was domineering, cruel, ruthless, inhuman, hypercritical, inferiority complexed, a Kul Klux Klan member. A misogynist. You really thought he ever loved you? Ever respected you and what you represented and your race? No. Never. You must have been the worst of fools to have ever thought that.

He considered you because you were smart. Your smartness got you your home country's scholarship opportunity, that in turn, got you out of your cringing family's poverty and humiliation back in Africa. You were not just smart but obedient as well. You were one of my father's smartest, but obedient worker at the New York Stock Index. You made a lot of money for him. He loved your acumen. He loved the money. He prided himself with the ability of turning you into a money-making machine due to your craven obedience. You were his preferred worker. He never loved you. He never loved your color. He never respected your color. He remarkably abhorred the color of your skin.

I eloped with you. He despised me for it. It was my revenge over what he gave to mom and me and my sisters. A depraved misogynist.

You married me not because you loved me. You know it. You don't know what love is. Inferiority complexed as you are, psyched out by the White conformist stereotype system. You would have married any trash with the tag "White" on it. For a stupid feel of ego amongst your race. That way you had with ease 90% of your sexual transgression with your fellow Black women. You will be a fool to be under the illusion that I don't know. That way you violated and humiliated me the second time. After my father. Just like my father years before. Yet I flew with your ideas and enthusiasm and fraudulence.

I pretended I loved you. I did what you wanted. I had to give my mom and sisters some dignity at life. You made money. You knew how to make money. Your way. You made me an involuntary accomplice with your deals at the United Nations, deals whose catharsis was divert funds meant for Africa. Not all your fault. I was under the false illusion that there was going to be a limit. A stop to illicit deals. Somehow, someday. But as days, months, years passed by, I was completely obsessed, transcended by the voraciousness, the hyperbole of materialism and the fun of distance from reality.

She stops. Takes a look at the husband who in the meantime has sunk into his seat, totally recoiled, eyes streaming with tears.

This sight to her is repulsive. Apathetic. Even so she sighs and continues:

Wife: I am so sorry. We lost. We became inhuman. But thanks to this generation, the Gen Z, I want and wish to walk back my path from perdition. Walk a different path. Give sense to my life. They are only, but fortunately asking us to repent and be real. We embody fakery and falsehood and evil.

I am going to be alone quiet, for quite some time, at some unknown destination. Don't call me please. Don't look for me. I will get in touch if necessary.

That was it. Their mom broke down. In a spasm of unutterable sadness and anguish, in ocean of tears, left the house and took leave of absence from work for an undisclosed destination to a grieving shame affliction.

VOLUME 4
THE TRANSITION

Chapter 1

Buzzo and Mezzi are guests of the President. Everybody seems present: the first Lady, David, Mark, and two younger siblings. They are all seated at the table waiting for the big man to arrive and take his position at the head of the table. The ambient is lascivious: a combined Asnaghi and Turri, Italian utmost luxury finishes and furnishings. Everything is classy and aristocratically begotten. The air is uncertain with muted suspense: the combined Buzzo, David, Mark and Mezzi don't know why this sudden midweek dinner convocation. They are assailed by spasm of suppositions: their parents complained to the President? They have a purview of why Mezzi is around and not in school? Is it about Buzzo's consultancy job to datalize and digitalize his government, ready for smarting exercise of his state? Has David given the pulp of his documentations to his father and he is incensed at it? What? They don't want them around influencing their revolutionary excogitation intents on their kids?

More so, it's been a tumultuous day trying to corroborate and lay bare, unveiling Africa's dilemma to their very peers and family friends–the inhibited David and the rebellious and ambitious Mark. However, the dice is cast.

Then His Excellency, the President, the Commander-in-Chief, saunters in and all heads turn towards him in greeting. He is without security guards. That makes him austere, very benign and human. He walks, taking his position at the head of the table. He smiles as he scans, panning his eyes to check on all faces that are seated.

President: Well, none of you is looking very famished.

Mark: Dad!

President: For real. There is much hunger amidst people out there. And you all looking composed and cool before these bowls, filled with appetizing food.

Mark: Dad, let's go. Don't mind our composure. We are hungry.

President: Kidding! I am sorry for keeping all you waiting. Government job. Mark please lead us in prayers.

Mark: Dad common, the tradition says David. He is the first son.

First Lady: Common Mark. Are you no longer hungry?

Mark: Close your eyes please. Our Lord God, thank you for this food. Thank you, Lord, for the opportunity of this gathering that was almost six months coming. Good Lord afford us more opportunity like this to eat together as a family. God let this food serve us as strength especially as strength to my father to fight and bring food to the table of the famished children of this land and force their fathers to eat with them on the same table like we are doing. In Jesus name. Amen All in unison: Amen.

> *...God let this food serve as strength to my father to fight and bring food to the famished children of this land and make their fathers eat with them on the same table like we are doing. In Jesus name. Amen*

Some applauses follow Mark's line of prayers.

Everyone opens their eyes and trade their looks on the President and Mark. The President is smiling but not saying anything. Disappointing on their expectation, his attention is on the chef serving, the wife breaks the silence:

First lady: What a prayer, Mark!

Mark: Mom, there is remarkable misery for those kids my peers. The kids are nothing but orphans in those huts. They have no fathers. Just mothers.

As all settle in on their plates, eating, there is air of surreal silence, waiting to be broken by the President, as commands the tradition. But to no avail.

Buzzo could not careless. He is not used to this oppressive complicit air of silence. He looks at the Chef.

Buzzo: Chef bravo! Your food is tasty. Beautiful. Huh David (nudging him)?

David (looking at his father): Very nice.

Mezzi (to Mark who looks absorbed eyes on his dad): A pass?

Mark: I think so. (and shooting a stare at his dad) Dad, you are saying nothing!

President: Yeah, Mark I am thinking of the line of your prayer. It's amazingly shocking such utterances at your age. Anyway, it would be my pleasure to hear the Gen Z unscripted passionate opinions on such line of prayer.

Mark: Really? Cool. Dad it's amazing. Just look at us. It's beautiful. We are beautiful. Amazingly gathered all together on the same table.

Dad, it's African tradition that African dads won't eat on the same table with their children and wives?

First Lady: Mark, enough of this. Leave your dad to eat in...

President (breaks up laughing): ...Honey please stop impeding them. I don't want them scripted. Let them dream and express whatever. We are to guide them. I am enjoying the discussion. David?

David: Well …I think Mark raised a remarkable critical point for us the Gen Z. African tradition is antiquated and anachronist. Evil and static. No rights, no liberties, no freedoms as we experience them in the Western democracy.

In fact, Mark here on this table you are not supposed to say a word before I do.

Even if you happen to be a whiz kid.

Everyone cracks up laughing.

Mark: Wow, that's a pleasant surprise coming from you. That sounds facetious…witty. You are in transition?

First lady: Mark…

Mark: Sorry mom. My apathetic heartless brother. Did you visit grandparents in the village today? Willful blindness gone? You on the part of the poor now?

President: African tradition is of value. Good natured. Somewhat static I agree. Out of tune with Gen Z? No doubt…

Mark: Dad, not just with Gen Z but with the youths and with everything their need – with current electricity, with clean water, with typhoid, with malaria, with polio, with schools, with hospitals. Dad with everything…

Mezzi (interjects, tired of waiting to be called): With firewood, with buckets of water and pans of merchandize on their heads, with cutlasses and hoes, with hunger and begging…

President: I love your energies. But Western democracy goes with reason. Progress, development go with educated mind. We have married laziness, generation after generation. We are very lazy, we dislike to work, and we are afraid to challenge whatever and make better. Absolute, absurd self-complacency. Buzzo?

There is a general mixed feeling of amazement at President's remarks. It's a remarkable pleasant surprise. Music for the ears of Buzzo, David, Mezzi and Mark. They are all in smiles, pleasantly surprised, nodding their approvals.

Buzzo: Thank you excellency. Then we all agree that African tradition is a hereditary, hierarchical, inherited despotism. Your life, everyone's future is foreclosed, preordained, and decided before you are given birth to. Nothing short of a monarchical, primogeniture, despotic tradition.

Buzzo pauses, locks eyes with the President and finds approval to continue.

Buzzo: Laziness and fright? Excellent points excellency. And Sir, in your opinion what do you think is the cause of our laziness?

President: It's been difficult to answer that question. Litany of miscellaneous reasons across a wide spectrum of excuses. Maybe complacency. Greed.

David: Gluttony. Gullibility.

Buzzo: Sir, abundance, breakthroughs, success might be correlated to complacency.But not to misery. Can we feel complacency in misery's midst? Can we?

President: I have tried. Let's ponder on the cause of laziness for a noble prize.

Buzzo: I think the cause of our laziness is cowardice. Cringing cowardice. Our fathers, fathers' fathers, fathers' fathers' fathers' up to our fathers, generation to generation have never stood up to anything. They quit always. We quit always. Our race quits always, instead of dominating.

President: Dominating? Very interesting. True. Very interesting novel point of view.

David: Absolutely compelling. We can't even dominate our environment to date.

Buzzo: And what is worse is that we got married to it, to cowardice. Made it our culture, our mantra. And cowardice of despotic tradition slowed down whatever courage we had. Up to a total annihilation of courage. Obliteration of courage. Cowardice over trying out anything overwhelmed us and informed and formed our laziness. Cowardice endures our laziness. Laziness became our tradition.

President: I love this. That could be part of the explanation.

Mark: It's a compelling reasoning.

Buzzo: Just think about it, folks. We were enslaved for our laziness. We were colonized for our laziness. We lost agricultural revolution because of our laziness. We lost industrial revolution, products-transformation revolution, market economy capitalization revolution, technology revolution, digital revolution because of Black Kind tradition of enthralled laziness. And we are still remotely presently enslaved from without and with self-inflicted bonded misery from within. At the hands of our own people, the politicians, the religious, the oligarchs, the traditional authority. The land is denied willfully of education, health care, food security, environment. They practice dominance on their people as they suffered and learned it from slavery and colonialism and institutional racism and that's remarkably absurd.

David: This laziness bred and breeds and breaths into everything – from lying to cheating, from greed to gluttony, from avariciousness to vanity and hyperbole. Absolute corruption...

Mark: Mom, look at these your funky diamond rings and kleptomaniac bombastic jewelries. Dad, our exotic cars. Those Rolls Royces, those Bentleys, those Lambos and Bugattis and Ferraris and Rovers, should all be sold and the monies raised used to dig boreholes, build more schools, send kids to school instead of to the farms and fetching fire woods and begging in desperation and humiliation and tribulations...

Mezzi: Save the kids. Empower the women. Build a better environment to enable them play and dream. Nigger becomes a human being. Nigger earns respect.

> *Africa's passion for laziness gives us self-enslavement, which in turn gives us perpetual misery. Africa's tragedy is its passion for laziness. The heart of our laziness is not courage nor bravery but cowardice. Africa's laziness consorts with cowardice. That's why our race quits always. We were and are enslaved by our laziness, to this day. We were and are colonized by our laziness, to this day.*
> *Africa's passion for laziness is responsible for its perpetual misery, to this day. Generation after generation.*

President (rising, tired, eyes heavy): Cool guys. Remarkable. I have listened to a bunch of Gen Z revolutionaries. I love your energy. I love your intelligence. You have not known misery. You might have glimpsed misery. Much have been given to you boys. You can't complain. Much is expected of you. Nothing is easy though. I would love your courage. Not cowardice. Paradigm shift. We have been a generation of disappointed and of disappointing. A disaster up till now. Yes, you boys can lead a change and change the paradigm. So, I look forward to your programs and plans of actions. You will have my fullest unwavering support. Show me your guts and vigor.

Everyone is surprised at his last remarkable yet unexpected "programs and plans" remark line.

Buzzo and David (in unison): Really?
Mark: Astonishing! Funky dad.

Mark gets out of his seat in amazement. And in a dancing spasm gets and jumps into his father's arms embracing and planting a kiss on his father's forehead.

David: If that's not mockery but a true, real challenge, then dad, I do really have a plan already. We need a park, a talking point, a platform for the youths.
Buzzo: Brilliant. The youths are disorientated. We need to involve and evolve them.
David: They need to know they are loved by their father, the President.
President: I like that. A platform. A social, work platform. That would serve to tame them. Keep them busy. Keep them off the streets. Make them responsible. Progress their intellect.
First Lady: Woodstock. Hip-hop, weed, alcohol and sex. Common folks, you guys must be kidding.
Mark: That won't be bad. They would help keep us off the street like dad said.

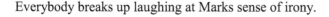

Everybody breaks up laughing at Marks sense of irony.

David: And you won't spend a dime dad.

President: How? What's your miracle?

David: Cool, just let me raise the money my way with the oligarchs, who you have made in this country, especially the Lebanese, the Indians, the Chinese, the Europeans and the Americans etc. Have each of their community of businesses invest something back into our society through corporate social responsibilities, just like what they do back in their home countries.

President (stands up ready to exit, with smiles): Good strategy. It will help. Approved. Meets my approval. But nonetheless you need money. Plenty resources. Just look at what Buzzo and Mezzi are already doing. Not talking. Doing. Incredible courage and love. You must join them and start.

Mark: ...Dad, so you know about their efforts? Awesome!

President: That gives me hope, a lot of hope. And with all of you working together? Won't it be awesome?

There is a general rousing to those unexpected pronouncements amongst the Gen Z. Rousing to high fives, low fives, clapping, hailing.

Then suddenly, the air of contentment is broken and silenced once again by the President.

President: I said it. Gen Z are sharp minded. Collectively bonded. Collectively driven. And if I can trust you guys as my true friends, I will charge and support you to transmit the parody "ask not what Africa can do for you but ask what you can do for Africa" on that park, the platform.

Mark: That's President Kennedy, dad...for Africa has done nothing but produce orphans. What can one expect orphans to do for Africa than orphans in turn?

Everyone cracks, cynically, up again. The President takes the first steps of his leave. But before, the air of laughter could settle, Buzzo grabs his wine glass, raising it in the air, and raises his voice in toast.

Buzzo: To more mid-weeks' dinners. Very inspiring indeed.

President (stops without turning): To your parents, Buzzo. They are broken as you well know. They need it. We need their support for the African youth. For the future of Africa. They are going to have to be proud of you all. Gen Z trailblazing. We are all going to have to. There is no other best choice as a matter of fact.

He completely exits the dinning lounge. With his wife, the first Lady following him.

...for Africa has done nothing but Orphans. What can one expect orphans to do for Africa than orphans in turn?

Chapter 2

Buzzo and Mezzi are in the Range Rover SUV by themselves reflecting on the dinner, contemplating the future, as they tear through the darkness heading home, to grandparent's village, 5 kilometers from the city.

Mezzi: Isn't that remarkable?

Buzzo: The evening?

Mezzi: Yeah. Looks awesome.

Buzzo: Apparently. Simulation to satisfy something.

Mezzi: Our parents?

Buzzo: Indeed. How would a man, a President, domineering, ruthless, bigoted and perverse, same specie as our father, suddenly become accommodating, democratic, docile and all…?

Mezzi: Listening to the views and opinions of the youths? You right. We will see the roll out.

Buzzo: "Aren't no stopping us now, we are in the groove."

Mezzi: That music is old.

Buzzo: Yeah but it suits.

Mezzi: Did you take note of Mark?

Buzzo: Mark is absolutely remarkable. He is unrestrained, unscripted, pure, unpredictable, undaunted. Sublime sense of humor, short of taunting.

Mezzi: Yeah. Did you see the face of her mom at his mention of her jewelries?

Buzzo: Formidable. African women are, in my judgement, abhorrently destructive, disruptive to progress. They are an active part of the problem, holding back Africa from developing.

Mezzi: They are always and perennially pregnant. Like reproductive animals. Apparently subservient to their male counterparts for their organs. Throw their legs wide open…

Buzzo: For their males' penetration and satisfaction.

Mezzi: Without them getting nothing off it, except the pains of labor at making the kids and tribulations of rearing them.

Buzzo: That's just the apparent down side to it. When they are not pregnant, they are powerfully greedy and gluttonous. They bend the men and society to their wills.

Imagine where the women tell their husbands that a kid, two kids, three kids at most are enough. One car, two cars, three cars are enough. One diamond ring, two rings, three rings are enough. And encourage their husbands to work and fend for society, every kid in school, every kid given access to health care and all.

They say men are in power, have power. To a large extent that's an illusion.

Mezzi: Why do you think so?

Buzzo: Just think about this: everything, anything a man does is for his home. Imagine who is in the home?

Mezzi: The wife. The children. The entire household.

Buzzo: The comfort, security of the wife and of the kids, if they have them. A good wife would be able to tell the husband enough of this, enough of that. We need this, we don't need that. That's more than enough. We need to help humanity and all. What do they do instead? They overtly force their husbands to steal above their means, and bring home their wants, to the detriment of society. For what?

Mezzi: Then it's clear that the men are very stupid.

Buzzo: Very much so. They are cowards. Not men enough. Can't stand up.

Mezzi: Yet here in the African village they seem to have the worst of it: the woman labors all day with the kids, to put food on the table for the man. The man does nothing all day but eat and drink and sleep and give orders.

Buzzo: You sincerely think that any man fed by wife and kids is a man?

Just look at the logic: a woman, for innate reason of 'supreme motherhood sense' and feelings, forces the man for penetration and in compensation she guarantees livelihood to the man. Absurd huh! That's the African tradition.

Mezzi: Yet if the family has western education, the same woman forces him to steal to maintain her wants and not only, but including the cravings of the kids and that of the caravans of the members of her extended family's wants.

Buzzo: You got it. In any case the man is subservient to the woman. He is a reproductive tool. In fact, the man does not know about the kids. In the first place he seems not to want them, and secondly, they are imposed on him. But for societal valueless or face-value conformism, he is coaxed, bewitched.

Mezzi: Yet the kids know their fathers. The mothers know their fathers who penetrated them. The African tradition knows no love, knows just penetration. Knows violence. Animals know better than African tradition.

Buzzo: You got it. No love. No cure. No communication. Individualism. Hypocrisy. Hate. Greed. Avarice. Gluttony. Voodooism. Hyperbole. Kleptomania. No virtues whatsoever. Vices. Evil.

Mezzi: I see the light in your powerful logic. Otherwise how could one explain the logic and the rational that a poor African man, even sometimes old, indolent, sloven, capable at nothing, sometimes next to his grave, could have many wives, most of them young girls, who are enough masochist to condemn their future to penetration, perennial pregnancy and child bearing and rearing?

> *Formidable! African women are, in my judgement, abhorrently destructive, disruptive to progress. They are an active part of the problem, holding Africa back from developing...They are always and perennially pregnant. Like reproductive animals... Just think of how powerfully greedy and gluttonous they can be. They bend the men and society to their wills.*
> *Imagine where the women tell their husbands that a kid, two kids, three kids at most are enough. One car, two cars, three cars are enough. One diamond ring, two, three rings are enough. And encourage their husbands to work and fend for society: every kid in school, every kid given access to health care and all.*
> *...Everything, anything a man does is for his home. Imagine who is in the home?*
> *The woman. A good wife, a good mother, would be able to tell the husband enough of this, enough of that. We need this, we don't need that. That's more than enough. We need to help humanity and all. What do they do instead? They overtly force their husbands to steal above their means, and bring home their wants, to the detriment of society. For what?*

Buzzo: Yeah, it is the irony and cynicisms of a tacit complicit destructive charm of a supreme motherhood feel, that for more than any reason, is to satisfy the conformist Hereditary Despotic Tradition. Everybody and anybody of the African family nucleus ends up bruised, if not imperiled to a state of total despair and disrepair: the man is striped of dignity, the woman is condemned to a life of perpetual humiliation, tribulation and ponderous enslavement. The child is permanently humiliated, dehumanized and traumatized and permanently subdued and defeated. Life defeat, his future permanently retrogressed and encaged in servitude to his peers of competing races. Fabric of African society is perpetually torn, impaired, imperiled and permanently in a state of abject disrepair. Number of children outpaces the already arrested development, resources and the crevices of poverty and underdevelopment widens and deepens. Nigger*tude* bonded misery perpetuates, generation after generation.

They finally get home to sleep.

> *Everybody and anybody of the African family nucleus end up bruised, if not imperiled to a state of total despair and disrepair: the man is stripped of any dignity; the woman is condemned to a life of perpetual humiliation, tribulation and ponderous enslavement; the child ...*

> *...is permanently humiliated, traumatized, dehumanized and subdued and defeated, his future permanently retrogressed and encaged in servitude to his peers of competing races. Fabric of African society is perpetually torn, impaired and permanently in state of abject misery.*

Buzzo: Fortitude Mezzi. We got work to do. I hope you don't break down.

Mezzi: You kidding me? Whatever it takes we are in. I will persevere.

Buzzo (looking into him severely): Let's catch some sleep. It's been a long day.

They hug each other to sleep.

Chapter 3

The foursome family of Gen Z: the two teenage youths – Mezzi and Mark, the two ablactated prime youths–Buzzo and David, are sitting at the table, meeting to progress their resolve: the family of Gen Z must put to end the remarkable cycle of vicious poverty and misery or the remarkable cycle of vicious poverty and misery will put an end to the family of Gen Z and the Black kind descendants, generation after generation will continue to endure misery, humiliation, tribulation and trauma. They know that for the family of the youths of the world to assist, much depends on the intransigent and strident resolve of the family of the youths of the Black kind on the African soil: but they are numbed with misery.

They need the desks to think and ponder at life. The desks to grammar and to logic. The desks to critically think and to critically analyze. The desks to discuss, hatch out plans and contrive programs. But they need the battlefield for rhetoric. The battlefield to square things up and out. The battlefield to implement, to evolve, to reevolve and to freedom.

They perceive and live its palpability beyond imagination, the remarkable damage done to the Black kind family of youths. Not just the physical, palpable pang of poverty and misery. The physical, palpable poverty and misery pales to the remarkable psychological damage, that is on the limit of irreparability, despair and dilemma.

Generations of African genitors have remarkably perpetrated and perpetuated a tradition of despotism. A perpetration of traditional despotism that has become a hereditary despotic culture and of vicious practice.

In the words of Thomas Paine: *"a monarchical primogenitor hereditary despotic tradition that forecloses the future of children before they are even born."* Generations to generations the Black kind tradition have never entrusted trust or responsibility to the family of Black kind youths.

They think them nothing. They think them unenlightened, unintelligible, incapable of exercising effort and control with awesome discretion.

What is worse is that instead of educating them to inform their discretion, their discretion instead, is informed with phobic-neurosis, of reticence, of sloth, of abject subservience. A remarkable psychological damage that finds a remarkable expression and answers in a tradition of hereditary despotic conspiracies.

Yes, African hereditary despotic tradition cannot even acknowledge, much more accept her realities, her misgivings, her misery, her situations. So, how do you even broach the grammar of their misery, the logics of their misery and the rhetoric of their misery? How do you involve its critical mass in a critical thinking, in a critical analysis, in a ponderable plan, in a ponderable program of action, in a ponderable execution timeline of any feasible solution?

Yes, the foursome has the privileges of being informed and are sprouted by the remarkable impact politics of democracy could play in the West. They are in the age, where the dictatorial communist China and of most Asian countries have progressed remarkably their families of Yellow Kind, even if it is at the cost of a sometimes muffled and harsh violence on the freedom of their Yellow kind youths.

In Africa instead, there abides and abounds a tradition of hereditary despotic politics of misery. With a veiled commandment of denial and a tacit complacency of same. To that extent, the African youths are victims of a hereditary despotic politics, that is a holistic-synergic continuation, in continuum of the hereditary despotic tradition with its cycle of vicious conspiracies of evil: Deprivations of all. Denials of all. Ignorance and fear of all. Cowardice of all. Myth of all. Default blames and denials of all. Poverty and misery bonding of all. Phobia-neurosis of all. Down to Object Surrendering Permanency of Self-consciousness.

Mezzi: Folks we are ready to launch?

Mark: Yeah to launch the family of youth hashtags

Buzzo: Great. Great news. You guys are amazing. Full of energy.

David: Thanks to your resolve and impeccable leadership.

Buzzo: Leadership? The foursome is in it together. We are in it together. We are not yet started. Value in collegiality. Pride goes before any fall. No complacency. Ever!

Mark: Yeah, a lot of work. You both have done a lot of work already. You both have spent too much money and yet counting. You are very courageous. We can't wait to be indeed part of the children to play credo. Part of renaissance self-consciousness credo. Ask Status Quo WHY and sentence WHY NOT to them. Annihilate misery.

David (bringing out some papers): Yeah, guys before we launch, I got some news. Take a look at these.

Buzzo: What are those?

David: Make Status Quo and status misery obsolete. Our hope platform signed and delivered (handing over the papers to Buzzo).

Buzzo looks at the papers and emits a flurry of screams as curious Mezzi rips them off Buzzo's hands, reading them.

Buzzo: David and Mark, thank you all. What a gift. What awesome gift of credo.

Mezzi: Your father, a true renaissance credent.

David: Indeed. He's given us those hectares of land adjoining your "kids must play" center. That expanse of land. All from here into the inner-city center. Totaling 450 hectares.

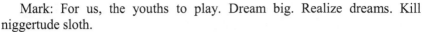

Mark: For us, the youths to play. Dream big. Realize dreams. Kill niggertude sloth.

Mezzi: A boulevard of a platform, right up to the city center and beyond. Phew! Nigger gain some respect.

Mark: Besides, we have sold some of the Ferraris, the Lambos, the Bugattis, the Rolls Royces, the Bentleys, those unutterable numbers of Audis and Mercedes to the Lebanese and raised over $20 million instantly...

David (pulling out other papers): Here, dad has as well signed this circular directing all foreign businesses on our land to contribute in cash and kind to the launch of our Gen Z platform in two months from now.

Buzzo: Wow, that's incredible. Beyond our most intuitive imagination of the mind.

Buzzo stops and pans his eyes looking at them all.

Buzzo: Cool. Sorry guys I hate to suppress our air of enthusiasm, but for the remarkable gravity of our continent's misery, and the urgency of getting rid of it in a flash, let me ask if you all know why we are here?

Mark: For the kids to play. Play with toys. Dream big. Realize dreams. Kill Nigger*tude*.

David: To enable great environment for all to dream and pursue their dreams.

Mezzi: Grow self-consciousness. Inculcate renaissance credo. Our bible "Hard work. Smart work." Obliterate Nigger. Negro dominates his Nigger*tude*. Negro's dominance of his environment.

Buzzo: Cool. Well spoken. We all want a revolution. Every past revolution needed vision and visionaries from the top and pressure from the downtrodden masses. A visionary bourgeois class, and the misery-ridden proletariat. And ours would not be any different. I am here thinking with utmost sadness and utter chagrin, that our masses are subdued. There is no pressure whatsoever coming from them. They are defeated and numbed. They tolerate everything. Bear everything. Forgive everything.

David: Apparently. They hate everything and everybody in real sense. Unforgiving.

Buzzo: Misery knocks off even the most tenacious of senses and sensitivities. But that makes our challenge and job interestingly arduous and pleasant at the same time.

David: That makes us visionaries and persuaders at the same time.

Buzzo: Yes. Visionaries and persuaders of presumed potentially pressurized masses but latent.

Now Buzzo sighs shaking his head 'disapproval'. Then continues.

Buzzo: I hate sowing doubt. I hate despondency. But we should find out if the masses are really potentially pressurized, easily persuadable with the unveilings.

David: Unveilings?

Mezzi: Yeah "the unveilings" are probably going to be our first hashtag launch.

Mark: Before the "your cries" hashtag launch follows.

Buzzo: David we are not done with verifying the field yet. Just a few more. In my opinion as we progress the process, we must first be done with "the unveilings." We are here to build the bridge. We are the bridge to imbue our African Gen Z peers with renaissance credo self-consciousness to understand and take on and take out the unveilings.

Mezzi: Right. Identify, recognize, confront and eradicate the unveilings of the hereditary despotic tradition. We recognize the unveilings of the remarkable kleptomaniac malevolent political leadership in our society. Your father, our dad. Our local councilor. Our voodoo shrine. We need to have some insight on African Gen Z gatherings: places of worship, places of entertainment and insight on the monarchy.

Buzzo: …And the unveilings of religion in our Black kind misery and poverty context. We need to understand why the White kind Western Christian religion has progressed its people and the world.

We need to understand why the Confucianism self-consciousness is successfully copying capitalism and innovating same and progressing China.

We need to understand why Islam self-consciousness is building 'work' for its people, building 'live' for its people, building 'play' for its people, through White kind Christian inventions and technology and philosophy of love for society and their descendants.

We need to understand why the Buddhistic philosophy of India is adopting the same, having incremental Gross Domestic Product, building progress for its people. We need to understand the combined African religions–the Western Christian African contextualized religion, the Arab Islam African contextualized religion, the voodoo in Africa–and why their self-consciousness instead is not able to copy capitalism, innovate capitalism, make progress, able to make prisoners, able to enslave, humiliate and give misery to African youths , generation after generation.

Now Buzzo pauses, scanning everyone, making sure they are on board his line of reasoning:

Buzzo: You all with me?

All in unison: Yeah Buzzo.

David: We are rapt with attention. My mind is already inspired thinking of sneaking into those infamous night-long vigils, the Sunday churches, the midweek church activities.

Mark: Oh, finally. Those midweek gatherings…infamously full of chicks, chickens, hens, cocks and mischiefs.

Buzzo: We got to scan the Mosques. The austere demeanor Mosques.

Mark: Yeah, no chicks, no chickens, no hens, no cocks. No chance of misdemeanor.

David: Yeah, so much like the Voodoo Shrines.

Mezzi: Indeed, these two places are apparently very elusive to the eyes and to the senses, yet they mean a lot to the poor masses palsy.

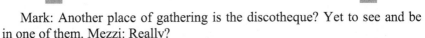

Mark: Another place of gathering is the discotheque? Yet to see and be in one of them. Mezzi: Really?

Mark: David is bad. In Africa he has not taken me in there, citing safety and security concerns for the family of the first citizen.

Buzzo: (to David) Real bad ass. You mean you have not taken Mark to a club yet?

David: Good idea. Mezzi's presence would do the miracle.

Mark and Mezzi celebrate in a high five.

Their celebration was short-lived however. Cut short by the sudden presence of the Imam, who suddenly appeared from nowhere, walking in on them, to everyone's surprise and general amazement.

Before they could find their words, the Imam, who has stopped in front of Mark, disarms them with what seemed genuine and unfeigned smile and greeting.

Imam: Assalamu Alaikum.

Now they slowly recover, relaxing and smiling back. Buzzo looks at Mezzi tacitly communicating "your friend is here." Mezzi quickly reacts to the Imam.

Mezzi: Imam, good evening. What a pleasant surprise.

David: Alaikum Assalamu.

Buzzo: Shalom.

Imam: Sorry, I came in uninvited. Very rude of me.

Mark: Can I give you my seat?

Imam: (cuddling fleetingly Mark's head): Very kind of you. Don't worry.

Buzzo: You can come in any time of your choosing. You are a man of God. Your presence in our midst is a blessing.

Imam: I've come to congratulate you in person for your love to humanity, for your passion for courage and exertion.

Mark: The children must play center?

Imam: Indeed! Congratulations. Africa has been a land of cowardice, cowards, lamentations, sorrows, misery and evil.

Buzzo (ponderously surprised): Indeed! We wish to understand why, every day you send the kids begging and the women are perennially obliged animals of reproduction?

Imam: Indeed! You have cracked the egg. The jinx is broken. The kids are very happy. The women would as well find happiness soon with the hint of your paradigm shift. And not everyone consorts with your efforts. For we are possessed with such madness and vicious evil.

Then he pauses, fixing Mezzi.

Imam: Mezzi, you promised you were coming to visit me. However, I understand. Your chores at the center are responsibly eating up your precious time.

My congratulations. May Allah bless you all for your love, and strengthen you more with patience and perseverance.

Then he leaves, as he had entered.

Imam (without turning): Mezzi, my doors are open. I am waiting. Fortitude boys!

Their faces writhe into grimaces, as they watch in a ponderous, hapless, debilitating unutterable silence, his silhouette, disappear in a flash.

They are left in a conflicting amazement that is scorching, enigmatic and delighted at the same time. All answers of why he came are swallowed in some wonderment. The curiosity the Imam aroused justifies the scorching. The mystery of his visit justifies the enigma. Curiosity and mystery are necessary–they reward the foursome with the delight of immediate wedging of their minds into the busy realm of intense intellectual imagination for their self-consciousness of answers.

Chapter 4

The Night Vigil

The first church, the first Christian civilization Church is said to be the Roman Catholic Church. The power and strength of dissatisfaction gave rise to protests and reforms, and these sublimated into evolutions. To that extent, the Roman Catholic Christian Church has evolved into Protestantism, into Lutheranism, into Evangelism, into Pentecostalism. And the list goes on.

> *Africa seems in total embrace of Pentecostalism, and Pentecostalism proliferations, and their tailored doctrines, and worshiping nuances, remarkably characterized by religious excitement and talking in tongues, by prosperity credo, by Paying Tithe chicanery, by Sowing Seed conspiracy, by the Grace and unmerited favor hypnosis, by a Sinner has been pardoned from all future sins, because Jesus Christ has already paid for your sin palsy. Etc. etc. etc*

As the foursome family of youths approach the venue of the vigil, they can't but notice the remarkable aura and the substance of the without: the traffic, the caravan of cars. Amongst them Rolls Royces, Ferraris, Lamborghinis, Bentleys, SUVS of Mercedes Benz, Range Rovers, Toyotas, etc. These give way to human beings. Stream of humans–the old, the men, the women, the youths, the teenagers, kids with their moms–streaming towards and swallowed by the many entrances of this arena-like structure. Like moths would stream to light.

Now the foursome are assailed by spasm of utter curiosity. The remarkable anxiety of curiosity can't wait to have a glimpse of the within.

Now they gain entrance.

Its breathtaking as they solemnly take their positions.

Notwithstanding the confusion, David and Mark are recognizable and are recognized by the teaming crowd. So are their friends Buzzo and Mezzi, the two biracials. They stand out constantly. Intelligible.

Their eyes scan and pan. Pan and scan. It's overwhelmingly, remarkably amazing as they take in the situation.

We can imagine the arena of the ancient Greek Acropolis, packed with audience, their ears to the dialectical arts actors, philosophers like Aristotle and Socrates, give birth to democratic principles and to democracy; we can imagine the *Amphitheatrum Flavium Colloseum* of the Roman Empire, packed with spectators, their eyes glued to their physical endowment and fitness and prowess of the gladiators, acting out their deadly entertainments for the watchful eyes of the Emperors; we live the modern arenas, the stadia for American super bowl football, world soccer, world rugby, cricket, basketball, concerts of music stars, purely for entertainment. To these extents, they pale in comparison with this arena of the Pentecostalism. The multitude is surreal. The number of youths, the number of women with their children, which by far outnumber the presence of the elderly is remarkably overwhelming.

The churches in the West are usually filled with grandparents and their grandchildren. The majority of the able-bodied men and the youth are busy building bridges. Building progress. Building dreams. Not here.

The church, the Schools, the grandparents and the homes path values and serenity into children.

While the arenas of Acropolis had actors that sprouted democratic principles and gave the world democracy; while the *Amphitheatrum Flavium Colloseum* had Emperors that enhanced alphabets for languages, laws, anatomy, medicine, aqueduct, conquest, discipline and civilization to the world; while to those extents the modern arenas have celebrity entertainers–actors, artists that excite and entertain our passion, sometimes to extreme joy and happiness and sometimes pushed to the edge of sadness and suicides. To these extents the foursome look forward to the actor and to his gift to the audience and to humanity.

The actor, the Priestcraft, finally enters, sauntering, taking his sumptuous position on the elevated podium at the center of the arena.

Around him on the magnificent podium are the dignitaries, the politicians amongst who are the President and the First Lady, the parents of David and Mark, ministers, the oligarchs, the creams of society. And they are framed by the rest of the audience who is a heap of spectators–women, children, the youths. Disposed randomly as the situation could permit them.

So, we have this lion-sheep room situation. This carnivore-herbivore room situation.

This predator-prey situation.

The African oppressors and the African oppressed situation room.

It evokes a tragic comic miracle sitcom. It is a remarkable miracle to have a lion and a sheep in the same room looking forward to the same gift of satiety. There is a miracle of satiety. A subliminal satiety. A sublime expectation gift that would distract and stifle the primal instinct of attack and the kill of the lion, as it sits side by side with ...

> *...its prey, the sheep. And with equal vigor the sheep's primal instinct of running for escape, for survival would be numbed, as it sits beside its predator lion.*

Now the long, awaited moment arrives. The procession begins. The Pastor- Priestcraft walks up, taking the microphone, and in a standing ovation, he begins delivering his tailored and choreographed gift of persuasion to humanity, between ovation and silence.

As we know, all the religions of the world have a common denominator: they preach God, faith, love, love thy neighbor, forgiveness, peace, honesty, hard work, hope. Etc., etc.

But Pentecostalism broaches these and besides dwells remarkably to nausea on these tenets: hope prosperity; miracle prosperity in tomorrow; forgiveness of thy oppressor prosperity; don't judge thy oppressor so thou shall not be judged prosperity; thanksgiving prosperity; sowing seed prosperity. Paying tithe prosperity. Blessed are the givers prosperity; those who cannot give are sinners against the Lord's prosperity; hell fire for those who does not give for the Lord's prosperity; no mention of the poor: the poor is against the lord prosperity; blessing for those who pay tithe prosperity; blessings for those who sow seed prosperity. No mention of sowing seed of righteousness, for everything, anything in time and space that lives.

To the foursome, there is a remarkable disproportionate amount of prayers of blessings, and remarkable praises for the givers. The majority of these givers are oppressors. As there is a remarkable disproportionate amount of prayers for hope, peace, miracle and heaven in the pregnant tomorrow. The majority of the hopeful, who are 'non-generous' givers are the oppressed masses.

On the one side, are commendation and validation for the oppressor for giving. And on the other side, rebuke and despise for the non-generous givers, majority of who are the oppressed poor.

On the one side, infusion of enthusiasm, of self-esteem, of pride, of excitement at life passion of oppressiveness. And on the other side, infusion of despondency, humiliation, dejection, rejection, shame of self, life of resignation and fear and despair and trauma and phobic neurosis.

Paraphrasing Thomas Paine: *"our youths are sored with the sense of oppressions, humiliation and are menaced with the prospect of new ones, is it the refuge in the calmness of philosophy, or the palsy of insensibility, or the hypnosis of passivity of the hereditary despotic tradition, willful masochism, conspiracy of silence to be looked for?*

Or degraded and debased and silenced their feelings are decidedly hardened waiting for the opportunity to take revenge on the oppressors and lift themselves out of misery? Or are in reflections of how to emulate their oppressors in perpetuation of power of vulgarity and punishment of hope?

Or is it just vacuity of the mind. In other words, laziness the mother of all these?" They witness the sickening moments of anointings, with the remarkable disproportionate amount of anointing oil, enough to make any anointing oil merchant, a remarkable billionaire.

They witness the remarkable, purported act of healings, and the claim of casting of the devils and demons from their possessed bodies. It is a ritual that has the connotations of the rites and rituals of voodoo, as officiated by the high priest. Something that remarkably pervades in Africa, Haiti, South America. In African voodoo religious shrines and temples that culminate in forehead-pushing act, by the Pastor Priestcraft ('the man of God"), with incantations, an act that has its catharsis in feign of sedation–many bodies are remarkably apparently sedated, hypnotized and carried away tranced, into darkness.

It seems that the voodoo religion has remarkably evolved. It has abandoned the shrine, the bush and gained entry into the towns and cities with their temples. It has abandoned its barrenness, its nakedness for bespoke clothing. Sons of its high priests have turned into Pentecostal Pastors. Pentecostalism their sanctuary. They have identified with, updated in, fused with the principles and values of Pentecostalism and its dogma. In fact, they are above the disciples and apostles of our Lord Jesus Christ. They are Jesus Christs in person. They bless you in their own names. They heal and cast out devils in their own names by mere wavering and incantation of white immaculate linens. They claim they raise the dead. They even have the audacity to claim invoking, commanding and make-descend, the holy spirit.

In fact, right now, the foursome witness the simulation of speaking in tongues. There is a miracle of compulsive mumbles of unintelligible murmurings in clattering and chattering of languages. Everybody is like possessed in some remarkable feign of spasm. These hybrids of voodoo priest Pentecostal Pastors have taken a hold on the people. They have become not just pseudo-omnipotent, but omnipotent, and like our God Almighty, they are transcendental. They transcend everything and anything in their path.

May the Holy Spirit forgive us all. For Africa's indulgence in exaggerating heresy.

> *It seems the voodoo religion has remarkably evolved. It has abandoned the shrine, the bush and gained entry into the towns and cities with their temples.*
> *It has abandoned its bareness, its nakedness for bespoke clothing. Sons of its high priests have turned into Pentecostal Pastors. Pentecostalism their sanctuary. They have identified with...In fact they are above the disciples and the apostles of Jesus Christ. Indeed, they are Jesus ...*

> *...Christ in person. They bless you in their own names. They heal and cast out demons in their own names...claim they raise the dead...make-descend the Holy Spirit and all.*

However, the foursome remarkable moment of sublime disbelief came when the pastor Priestcraft, like in a roll-call, called names of givers with the amount in millions of restricted currencies–for unrestricted currency is the dollar, or euro or sterling–they have given to the church. All of them without exception are the creams at the podium with him. In turn, they stepped forward for anointings and blessings by the pastor Priestcraft amidst deafening applauses. Applauses from the oppressed and the down-trodden.

By some kismet, a perverse elevation of a few, perversely debases the majority. This debasing is the antidote that fires their sloppy self-consciousness up, that coalesces them to that giving conspiracy, to sowing the seed psychosis. Whatever.

However, the amount of stealing, of misappropriation of funds, of denial of freedoms, the hyperbole, the kleptomania, the gluttony of the politicians, of the oligarchs, of the cyber theft boys, etcetera, find refuge, solace and justification in the blessings they receive from these vile Pentecostal Pastors Priestcraft, for being the generous givers. Givers of the people's wealth subtracted. Givers of the people's misery.

Jesus' teaching "Don't let thy right hand know what thy left is doing when giving offering to God" has endured ultimate crucifixion, buried and rose on the third day, and ascended and would surely descend with Jesus' second coming. Until then...

However, the above life remarkable moment of sublime disbelief pales in comparison to the remarkable palsy hypnosis of the African youths before such a gratuitous heresy. With total air of resignation, numbed, their self-consciousness just sit and absorb this falsehood, with its spiritual debauchery.

These pastors debauch and get away with it. Indeed, the family of African youth aid and abate their debauchery. Without the power of and in the congressional crowd of family of African youth, there would be no audience, therefore no deception, no falsehood, no life hyperboles of the Pentecostal pastors.

There got to be much digging of facts. How would the family of African youths, especially from among them the Gen Z be congregated every Sunday, every night vigil at will by falsehood? They know it is falsehood and they feed from the falsehood and absorb falsehood and go away filled with falsehood?

The curiosity, the drama, the question is: what could be responsible?

> *How would the family of African youths, especially from among them the Gen Z be congregated every Sunday, every night vigil at will by falsehood? They know it is falsehood and they feed from the falsehood and absorb falsehood and go away filled with falsehood?*

The curiosity, the drama, the question is: what could be responsible? Paraphrasing Thomas Paine again: *"shouldn't everything we see or hear offensive to our feelings, and derogatory to the human character lead to other reflections than those of reproach? ...the instant we ask ourselves these questions, reflection feels an answer."*

The foursome are remarkably sickened, nauseated. They take an anticipated leave of the gathering. They have had enough. They are shocked and hypnotized by utter sense of disbelief.

Would this experience solace and fire up their plans? As determined and undaunted in their cause, can this add to their list of genuine catalyst, energizer for their cause?

As they drive home:

Buzzo: A remarkable absurdity and imbecility!

Mezzi: Beyond the psychiatry. Tom Bradley's nigger*tude* painting pales in comparison.

David: Total capitulation of our psyche. How the hell do you defeat this palsy of religion?

Buzzo: That's our calling guys. I am more than ever remarkably optimistic we would succeed. We should succeed.

David: Buzzo it's an arduous task to subdue this palsy hypnosis in the Gen Z.

Mark: How can the ranks and file of Gen Z just sit there and absorb this rape?

Mezzi: They have been psyched out. Poverty has psyched them out.

Mark: They are a living-dead. What does a poor living-dead person get to lose departing physically?

David: In the White society, a physically dead man signifies life to the living. Our race won't understand this concept that for every single conquest of White man's lifestyle: current electricity, portable running water, motors, machines, flying, satellites, communications etcetera, every single one costs them the ultimate prize.

Buzzo: Paraphrasing Jesus Christ: *"You love life, you lose it. You give life for life."* Mezzi: The messiah. That's the concept Jesus Christ our Lord in person validated for all. You just can't walk straight into the heavens. He died first.

Buzzo: Bravo! You started digging at scriptures.

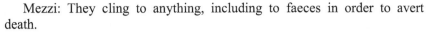

Mezzi: They cling to anything, including to faeces in order to avert death.

David: That faeces is called hope.

Mark: What hope did they see tonight?

David: Hope in the unknown. Hope of tomorrow.

Mark: But the tomorrow is us. Tomorrow is the future. Tomorrow is not the pastor. Not the man of God. We are the hope. Gen Z is trailblazing the hope.

Buzzo: Bravo Mark. Concise and punctiliously so. The effort is to make them believe in themselves. Make us believe in ourselves. There exists miracle of exertion, of efforts. Perseverance and fortitude guys. We will succeed. I have a groggy, willful energy. All of us must find a collegial willful energy. Enough to arouse in our youths, in the words of Thomas Paine: *an enthusiasm of heroism, such only as the highest animation of liberty could inspire.*

There is a remarkable moment of solemnness amongst the foursome. Marked by absolute silence in the moving car. They are like psychologically beaten. Angry. Deluded to even exchange glances. Trade glances. Mezzi is impenetrable. Mark is fixing the distant void. David and Buzzo notice boredom.

Buzzo (apprehensive for his brother): Common guys, let's go have a drink before going home.

Mark: Going home to do what? The night is young.

Buzzo: Pardon! *Scusa moi!*

Mezzi: This is a night of vigil.

David: Brilliant. To play then.

Instead of going home they check out what should be Gen Z's respite sanctuary. They stop by 'Play' Disco club.

The play-Disco club: at that hour normally virtually empty.

To their pleasant surprise the club at that young early morning hour is teaming up, pilling with Crowd. Crowd of every race. Voluptuously amidst them is the African Gen Z. Even though they make the majority, we have among them a remarkable combined number of the White Gen Z and the Asian Gen Z youths as well.

What the foursome did not know is that as soon as they were noted and then observed leaving the vigil ground, most Gen Z, their peers found the complicit courage to file out after them. Now they mill, filing the Disco Clubs of the city, of which Play is one of the prominent.

As the foursome drink with their voices snuffed out and their hearings reduced to the sole full blast of music, their eyes can't but help admire the sinuous scene of creative dancing. Looks like the god of sublime creative dance abodes in Africa. Everyone is remarkably a consummate entertainer. Flurry of sublime pleasurable pleasing movements.

The African Gen Z seems very happy. You cannot help noticing a remarkable amount of socially bonded group gatherings within. Group conversations. Group synergy. Not necessarily a homogenous grouping of Gen Z dictated by anagraphy, but grouping of heterogenous entity. Heterogenous entity grouping of mixed anagraphy.

Of mixed religious credos. Groupings, mainly of Moslems and Christians, at their drinks. The quantity of alcohol and shisha sold and consumed are remarkable. You wonder for how long these poor folks would have been saving for their drinking spree of being bees than bees. Everything and everybody look surreal. This place makes the harshness, the suffering, the tribulation, the debauchery, the misery of the Gen Z captive. A palsy. A Hypnosis. An *Oblivionem*. It assists to annihilate their misery. This is their sanctuary to obliviate their misery. To bury their misery. At least temporarily. Its temporariness finds hope and solace in its repetitive temporariness of precedence: tempo of thrice every week.

A tense scrutiny at some of the groups reveals that in most cases somebody is footing the bill. Not the famous Roman-style bill payment sharing rules, where the sum total bill, after dinner is shared equally amongst the participants on that dinner table, independent of social status. Everyone shares equally to the bill. Instead, what is manifest here is that somebody, who could be of Gen Z extraction, usually sons and daughters of expatriates, or could be sons and daughters of the African oligarchs, or of the politician, or of the pastor, or could be the politician in person, the oligarch in person, is the one always saddled with the burden to offer and pay. The others with him in the group are usually social proximity 'parasites': flocks of desperate Gen Z youths, majority of them girls flocking to their tables for drink rides, drinking to their despair.

Conversely, for Buzzo, this state of things gives hope: it might prove to provide the answer to the enigma of the African Gen Z palsy, to the hypnosis, to the *Erasmus*, to the *Oblivionem,* to the default blame, to the default denials, to the willful abnegations. His thesis of providing a Youth platform finds genuine hope of functioning. Provide a platform. Fill it with food and alcohol as the luring, enticing, tangible, palpable, urgent bait of hope for the famished stomach, to take them to the teaching and maxim of renaissance credo maxims instead. Grow their self-consciousness.

To make his point to the foursome, he waited until late hours, when every table is on low energy with drinks to order, offering every grouping, a remarkable amount of assorted drinks–spirits, champagne, wines, energy sodas, shawarmas and grills and shisha etc.

The effect is immediate. The foursome are acclaimed and remarkably celebrated. So much so that as they take their leaves, a handful of African Gen Z crowd, majority of them girls, followed them to wherever, as if their company is the premium. Sexual company the appreciation.

The President's Lodge

The party continued in the President's lodge unabated till dawn.

Mezzi and Mark had the fun of their life. What a way to getting closer to their misery plagued peers: understand a little bit of them and their habits and their thinking at remarkably close range. They had their innocent sexual mores challenged. Put to test by the ethercal and sublime beauties of Glenda, 19 years, and Lynda, 18 years. Both undergraduate students of the bourgeois class of society. They let themselves, measurably sliding, without losing control of their hormones. Yet many times they got to that confine. Buzzo had however given them condoms in advance. He had tacitly-overtly approved spicy juvenile novelty to premium their participatory efforts at decoding the why of African misery and at efforts to ending the African millennium misery. Buzzo, finds it of respite-premium to distract them for a minute from this remarkable, arduous task routine for their young ages.

Even though David had offered them advice not to venture into sex-asking, because "today is a Sunday and sex holds as a sacrilege," it has become conformist tacit rule out there in the air for decades. No formal validation but they should not conflict with the Lord's holy day. Even so Mezzi pleaded with Glenda for a fellatio and Mark offered Lynda a cunnilingus.

The girls refused both advances in any form and substance.

Great girls: they keep to the sanctity of the Lord's day. And conversely instead, the girls succeeded in coaxing them to go to church service alongside them, with the promise of sex as a trade-off afterwards.

Absolutely an irresistible and enticing proposal that glued their will to them.

Chapter 5

The Church

The Church. A Pentecostal Church. Different denomination from the vigil's. Like the stadium arena of the night vigil. This parish is filled, in the inside beyond its capacity and on its outside, spilling and sprawling with human beings. Daylight flocking bees compared to the nocturnal flocking moth.

Save for the difference in size and magnitude: the one, the stadium size arena, was a collection of many parishes of the same faith, and the other, a single parish in a normal arena; the one was of artificial lighting with its play of umbra and semiumbra, shadows and semi shadows of faces, shadows and semi-shadows of hyperbole, shadows and semi-shadows of imagination, of intrigues, of manipulations, of real and unreal, of truth and falsehood, of innocence and lies and hypocrisy accomplice. The night complacence. The other is in day light. No umbra or semi-umbra. The distance is not imagined. The oppressive distance. The derogatory distance. The discriminatory distance. They are palpable. Tangible. The day light predatory. There is nakedness of everything and to everything: faces, intrigues, falsehood, manipulations, hypocrisy, hyperbole and chicanery.

Every other thing is of the same setting: the podium, the scenium-altar to give prominence to the pastor, the man of God; the proscenium-orchestra for the lionpredators–the politicians, the oligarchs, the despotic traditional powers and their progenies. Here we find the foursome. Including the President, the first Lady and entire first family; the auditorium is of the absolute majority, well above 90% of the masses. The young parents with their children. The downtrodden family of African Gen Z youths. The lambs. The faeces of society. Here we find amongst others Glenda and Lynda. All bonded in misery by society, flocking to the house of the Lord, in search of solace, comfort, seeking hope, relegated to the rear.

The rear guarantees distance. The distance between Status Quo and misery. Between the rulers and the ruled. Between the oppressor and the oppressed. Between the actors and the audience. The distance is kept, maintained.

On that side, the side of the African Gen Z, the distance is sweating, sweating expectations: hope expectations, love expectations, consolation expectations, solace expectations, comfort expectations, miracle expectations. Liberty expectations. Freedom expectations. That distance endures obedience, endures failures, endures hopelessness, endures heartbreaks, endures struggle to live, endures hate, endures restraints, endures tribulations, endures misery, endures captivity, endures doubts of God's existence. While on the other side, on the side of the Status Quo the distance sweats arrogance, sweats disdain, sweats exploitation, sweats captivity and its perpetuation, sweats ordained rights of richness, sweats hyperbole, sweats kleptomania, sweats gluttony, sweats hereditary despotism, sweats falsehood of miracles, sweats pseudo-omnipotence.

That distance imposes palsy, imposes oblivionem, imposes *erasmus*, imposes the defaults, imposes the willful, imposes hypnotism, imposes the conspiracies, imposes forgiveness credo, imposes sowing seed of money, imposes unmerited favor misplaced tenet, imposes cheerful giving, imposes paying tithe. All designed to intimidate, subdue and sabotage the instinct, the intellect and any reasoning and the rationality and rationalization of the African children, generation to generation. The stage is set. The same lion-sheep miraculous tragicomic setting, tenable at the night vigil. The silence deafening.

Now the man of God walks in with his wife. He looks like a fashion icon. Corporate businessman-like demeanor, a hyperbole chief executive officer, out of a gangster 'God Father-style' movie: Louis Vuitton suits; Cavalli shoes; Armani shirts; Valentino neck tie; Rolex watch; glittering Bulgari's fat diamond-emerald rings. This man of God is worldly. In a total contrast to the meek and humble Jesus' Cossack-sandals monk austere demeanor.

The wife takes her seat in the next seating position behind him. The man of God starts preaching. Preaching apostrophized by mythical pastoral pauses, for words to sink in. He preaches nothing any different from the remarkable Pentecostal doctrines and maxims, all tailored and geared towards prosperity religion.

Man of God: Glory to God. I see a lot of new faces today.

He pauses, scanning the audience.

Man of God: You are all welcome to the house of God. We will talk salvation today. As you may already know, and if you don't, salvation is not something that is about to start in heaven. It starts here. And the requirement for salvation is to confess the Lordship of Jesus. Confess the Lordship of Jesus Christ, our Lord. And believe he was raised from death. For our lives.

He pauses;

Man of God: Believe! Believe!! Believe!!! If you believe, you are automatically saved. No other conditions. You are graced. Unmerited favor.

A pause. An unutterable pause of starving eerie expectation. Then he continues.

Man of God: So, right here on earth, salvation started to take place.
But you can lose salvation and not make heaven! How?
You can only make heaven by maintaining, we must maintain our relationship with God. Even though we have been saved by faith, we must walk our path, play our part.
Our God not a poor God; Our God a rich God;
You want his blessings?
You must pay tithe. If you don't pay tithe, you can forget his blessings.
You can kiss heaven goodbye. And welcome hell.
You cannot rob him. Tithe is his.

Pause;

Man of God: You want prosperity? You must sow the seed. Glorify him with the seed. Sow the seed for being alive. Sow the seed for promotion at the work place. Sow the seed for safe trips. Seed for pregnancy. Seed for giving birth. Seed for the rain. Seed for the sun. Sow the seed for Christmas, for Easter, for miracles, for deliverance...You must sow the seed for everything, for anything if you want prosperity. If you don't sow, you can't reap. It is written in the holy book.

The church is stilled. They seem hypnotized. Seem dazed. Seem numbed. Numbed for any protest? Or is it just an impression? They are used to it? A custom? A culture? Amidst this remarkable, capricious, condescending, predatory preaching and the remarkable, culpable accommodating accompanying silence, the already irritated and religion-biased foursome are uncomfortably shifting in their seats, nauseated. The irritation transits into anger in Mezzi, who in defiance, suddenly raises his hand looking squarely at the man of God, surprising everyone.
A lot of heads turn looking at him, from a voluptuous oddity of perspectives and then at the man of God who now notices.
The man of God squinting, looks at him coldly, hardly, then forces a smile, suddenly diverting and refocusing, ignoring him, continuing his sermon:

Man of God: You want to be graced with unmerited favor?
You must be a giver. You must be a cheerful giver.

Mezzi, undeterred by the litany of judgmental and curious eyes, mostly trying to stare him down, stands his grounds: his hand remains raised with his eyes trained on the man of God.
The situation is tense within the proscenium-orchestra stratum occupants, and particularly awkward for the President. All eyes are on him or are intermittently shot in his direction, checking out his reaction. As has been said, the President is hosting Buzzo and Mezzi alongside his family, by the virtue of the proscenium-orchestra placement positioning.

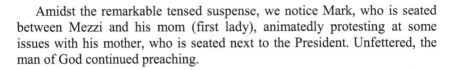
Amidst the remarkable tensed suspense, we notice Mark, who is seated between Mezzi and his mom (first lady), animatedly protesting at some issues with his mother, who is seated next to the President. Unfettered, the man of God continued preaching.

Man of God: You want miracle in your life you must be a cheerful giver.
You want wonders you must give. Not grudgingly, but cheerfully.
So, my brothers, we have distributed envelopes, please do your duties.
Give your tithes. Sow your seeds. Cheerfully give.
Some of you can give a $1000 and above.
Some $ 500, some $ 300. At least you must give $100.

Hearing these dictates, which Mezzi considers a violent imposition, and in US Dollar notes, it tore ponderously furthermore at him and in escalatory reaction, he raises his second hand. Mezzi's courage had Mark and he breaks with his complicit silence. Mark joins ranks, raising his hands as well. He has had enough. He joins his friend Mezzi. All attempts by his mother to dissuade him was met with a remarkable glaring petulant reaction of resistance. And instead, this unpredicted alliance sprouts four hands. Mezzi and Mark have both their hands defiantly in the air. They hold their stare, a Sphinx-like inscrutable stare trained on the man of God, who as usual, unfazed, continued to ignore and preach.

Man of God: Don't say that you are not employed, that you are poor, that you are a student. You can give your ear rings. Your items of value. Sell your cars, anything to raise money for the Lord. Our God, a merciful God will bless you, prosper you and grace …

Now the pastor stops in his tracks, overwhelmed by air of tension and the unease the four young hands have built next to discomfort. In a stance of reversal, he takes cognizance, finally giving some attention to their resolute defiance. Continuing in a smile short of feigning.

Man of God: In our midst, we have two angels who are anxious to participate in our sermon of today. They are over there (pointing at them). The crowd acknowledges their location.

The President (to Mark and Mezzi): Now you got his attention. Could you both respectfully stand up and make good at your cases.

Mezzi and Mark stand up. They look confident and remarkably defiant. A voluptuous ponderous silence is accomplice.

Man of God: Mr. President, thank you, Your Excellency. Young men, you have my ears.
Mezzi: We would like to discuss the scriptures with you, man of God.

Mark: Yes, we want to clarify, straighten things up.

The crowd breaks up, laughing.

Man of God: This is important. Please don't laugh. Jesus says let "little children come to me. For theirs is the kingdom of heaven."

The President starts applauding. The Proscenium-orchestra occupants join in. The applause grows. Become contagious, deafening.

Man of God (a glimpse at his Rolex watch, his face a solicitude frown): Or can we remand you to our Sunday school learning, after church service?
Mezzi: No, right now Pastor.
Mark: Right there with you Pastor.
Mezzi: The youths deserve the rights to be heard. We want everyone here to hear and participate. Even with their silence.
Glenda (from behind): Yes! Yes!! Yes!!!

Eyes turn and fish out Glenda. She stands their competing, scrutinizing stare: some bigoted and others delighted and yet others sincerely curious. Then Lynda's "yes-ooooooooooooo" joins in.
Glenda and Lynda (in unison standing to their feet): Yes! Yes!! Yes!!!
And like a kismet, there are more standings. More 'Yes'. And in a sudden remarkable collegial rush of courage of enthusiasm, as if obeying some fluke calling, the Gen Z of the church, gradually get to their feet, expressing outburst of pent-up passion. The "yes'" build, multiply and then surge. Become deafening.
Man of God finally obliges: he invites them with the wave of his hands to the *scenium*, amidst the remarkable and ponderous incessant deafening cry of "Yes, Yes, Yes." The remarkable deafening cry of "yes, yes, yes…" accompanies Mezzi and Mark to the altar.
As they take their positions behind the microphone, every "yes" ceases.
Every foot takes back its seat. The air is stilled. Stilled with expectations.
Man of God encourages them with a wave of his hand, urging them on.
Mark somewhat confused, with evident pre-emptive anxiety, is looking up to Mezzi. Mezzi winks at him reassuringly, giving him the Holy Bible. Mezzi remarkably does not betray any anxiety. He simulates total confidence. Totally rebellious. Uncondescending. Uncompromising. Unapologetic. Very fashionably appealing, likeable, his hair rebellious. Like an extemporaneous speaker, born on and for the podium, his aura of a mulatto, a biracial, a cross breed, a mixed breed virtue, that confers on him a whole lot of credibility, a whole lot of advantages from his part of White blood, his White part, with privilege of progressed civility and civilization, and at the same time with the whole disadvantages of the retrogression and the retrogressive incivility and primitivity of his part of Black blood, he acted.

His eyes are glittering, blistering with life, a golden life opportunity to appeal to his peers, the African Gen Z. A lot is at stake. A lot would depend on his performance today, in order to inculcate renaissance credo self-consciousness, hit the ground running with popularity. He can't disappoint. He can't fail his Gen Z family. Nigger*tude* got to be demised. Identify and recognize phobic-neurosis. Attack and confront Object surrendering permanence. Grow self-consciousness Tom Bradley must be appraised. Must sublimate. Tribute paid to him.

Mezzi: Thank you man of God. Thank you everybody. I thank the opportunity. I have never been here before. Every house of God is a blessing.

Then fixing Mark:

Mezzi: My friend Mark, are we ready to reference the holy book?
Mark: Sure. Born ready!

Everybody laughs, amidst a resounding applause of encouragement.

Mezzi: Jesus said "let the children come to me, for theirs is the kingdom of God." When any child, when we youths are scolded, maltreated, injured out there we run to our parents for refuge, for consolation, for solace. Isn't it so?
The congregation (amidst some silent nodding assent): Yes.
Mezzi: Man of God, just look at the beauty of your church. Over 85% of your church is graced with the presence of we Gen Z.
We Gen Z on this continent, on the African continent are at lost. We are deprived of every freedom. Our liberties are trampled upon. We are subjugated. We are depraved. We are a forlornness. We are bonded in misery on our land at the hands of our society, and systematically so by the political kleptocracy, by the despotic hereditary tradition, by the despotic monarchy, by the hyperbole gluttonous oligarchy. We are in captivity. And we run to the house of God, the house of our supreme omnipotent Father, looking to embrace our scepter, our scepter to make our captivity captive. And what do we get folks? We get killed a second time, profaned in the house of God. By the very "men of God."

> *And we run to the house of God, the house of our supreme omnipotent Father, looking to embrace our scepter, our scepter to make our captivity captive. And what do we get folks?*
> *We get killed a second time, profaned, desecrated in the house of God. By the very "men of God."*

135

A handful of Gen Z of the congregation (located at the auditorium, scream their pentup mix feelings): Yessssss...hallelujah... correct... the truth finally said...let's shout it. God bless you brother!

Mezzi pauses and scans the crowd. The air turns still, back on.
Everybody seemed enwrapped and rapt by the vehemence of these words.
A lot of other people are shifting in their seats uncomfortably. No words are proffered.
Mezzi now looks briefly at Mark and diverts, disengaging, settling on the man of God who fixes him back seemingly unperturbed. Continuing:

Mezzi: Man, of God, you preach and profess prosperity theology. Why? For You? Doesn't the Lord in the book of Deuteronomy chapter 18, verse 1 to verse 6 commanded that the Priests or the Levites shall not have inheritance among their brethren: The Lord is their inheritance?
Even so, Jesus preached and professed spiritual prosperity, righteousness. Why would you preach prosperity theology to the deprived African youths generation after generation? Instead of feeding them with spiritual hope, with the seven virtues: justice, prudence, temperance, fortitude, hope, faith, charity and virtues of hard work, with the blessings of hard work, the sins of slothfulness, virtues of patience and perseverance in tribulation, and preach supreme absolute value of the most important commandment "love thy God" and of the most second important "love thy neighbor like yourself" teachings and maxims?

Man of God says nothing. Fixes the void. His wall of mask is beginning to crack.

Mezzi: You don't preach belief sets of values.
You don't preach obedience to God.
There is a correlation between belief and obedience. If we truly believe in God, we should obey his commandments. When we obey our parents, we act belief sets of values. We obey set rules of society. Or face punishments.
We can in fact comfortably assert that we don't believe in God.
In Africa, folks don't believe in God. Majority of Africans don't believe in God.
The proscenium-orchestra of the congregation reacts a vehement "not true...no, we believe in God."
Mezzi (addressing the Status Quo sector): If you really do, you would love thy God, you would love thy neighbor. Those are two instances of obedience.
If you really do, Africa and her descendants would not be bonded in misery.
If you really do, Africa and her descendants cannot be pillaged in perpetuation.

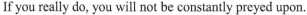

If you really do, you will not be constantly preyed upon.

If you really do, God would be here.

If you really do God will not make you Canaan for the White nor for the yellow nor for any other race.

Canaan was sacrificed and given to the Jews, not because of the righteousness of the Jews but because of the wickedness of Canaan. Africa is wicked. Africa's wickedness and iniquities turned Africa into the Canaan of the World and misery for Africans.

The auditorium of Gen Z congregation: Phew, yesssssss! Correct!

Mezzi: Just take in the life-style invented by the Western Christian religion. That is truly obedience of "love thy neighbor" at play.

There is education for every kid, health care system for every kid, pipe-borne running water for every kid, current electricity for every kid, mass transit for every kid. Employment opportunities, etc., etc. for everybody. Whether you are poor or rich, they make life at least bearable for everyone.

Gen Z congregation: Truth is said. Hallelujah. Jesus has finally come in our rotten midst.

> *Man of God, you preach and profess prosperity theology. Why? For you?*
>
> *Didn't the Lord in the book of Deuteronomy 18, verse 1 to verse 6 commanded that the Priests or Levites shall not have inheritance in their brethren: The Lord is their inheritance?*
>
> *Even so, Jesus preached and professed spiritual prosperity. Righteousness. Why would you preach prosperity theology to deprived African Youths?*
>
> *Instead of feeding them with spiritual hope, with the seven virtues...*

Mezzi (back, fixing man of God): You preach paying tithe without contextualizing it. Why so?

Then to Mark:

Mezzi: Please reference the book of Deuteronomy chapter 14 from verse 22 -29...

Mark finally has his day at the pulpit started. He is excited.

Mark: Thou shalt truly tithe all the increase of thy seed, that the field bringeth forth year by year...

Mezzi: ...Tithe thy increase. Tithe thy profit. If you make an investment, if you have an increase, a profit out of thy investment, thou shalt tithe the profit not the capital invested. Ok?

Then to Mark:

Mezzi: Please reference the tune of what fraction or percentage.
Mark: Tithe one-tenth of thy increase...
Mezzi: And do what with it?
Mark: And divide it into four parts, giving a quarter to the Levite.
Mezzi: The Levite was the man of God back then in the old testament. And...
Mark: ... one quarter to the Stranger, because the stranger might be my angel. Then one quarter to the fatherless and one quarter to the widow.

Here, we have a general mixed congregational remarkable reaction of disbelief and doubt: huh? Really? Are you sure? Are they sure they are reading from the bible?

Mezzi (badgers on adamantly): Thank you. The book of the old testament never commanded who hasn't or who cannot, to tithe an imaginary increase.

More importantly Jesus Christ our Lord never, never, never, ever mentioned tithe throughout his sojourn on earth.

There is a remarkable sharp but firm reaction of intent by a handful of congregants in muted mumbles: "huh?" ... "sure?" ... at the mention of "Jesus never, never, ever did."

Mezzi (to man of God): Jesus Christ of Nazareth our Lord never did. So why you?

Man of God just fixes him coldly. He is irritated.

The crowd is back again in rapt attention. Taking in every situation. Gen Z are excited. Full with expectations. Fascinated by this their scepter who is challenging the man of God to the books. Challenging their religious palsy, their greatest hypnosis, their greatest inspiration of erasus, oblivionem and complacency.

Mezzi: You preach cheerful giver and giving, without its contextual nature of bounty and non-covetousness.

Then turning to Mark:

Mezzi: Please reference the second book of Corinthians, chapter 9, from verse 5...

As Mark starts leafing through the Bible, you could hear the ample participation in Bible leafing by most worshippers, Gen Z and the Status Quo alike, who are spurred. Their sloth at reading and at curiosity temporarily subdued, for now, it seems.
Mark: "Therefore, I thought...as a matter of bounty and not as of covetousness...

Mezzi: Hold on Mark... did we hear and read that: as a matter of 'bounty'? In other words of plenty, of success, of profit and not of covetousness, not of avariciousness, not of rapacity, not of kleptomania, not of chicanery...

Mark (continuing): Verse 6; "he which soweth sparingly shall reap also sparingly, and he who soweth bountifully shall reap also bountifully."

Mezzi: Sow bountifully in righteousness, reap bountifully in Heaven. And verse 7; "Every man according as he proposeth in his heart, so let him give, not grudgingly or of necessity: for God loveth a cheerful giver."

Mezzi pauses and looks at the crowd who are somewhat disappointedly transfixed but remarkably attentive, then he continues.

Mezzi: This is the bible, its words leave no room for any misinterpretation, for any equivocations: as your "heart proposeth, not grudgingly," not of necessity, for God loveth a cheerful giver.

And furthermore, in the book of Deuteronomy 16;17:

... *"Thou shalt truly tithe all the increase of thy seed, that the field bringeth forth year by year..."*

...Tithe thy increase. Tithe thy profit. If you make an investment, if you have an increase, a profit out of thy investment, thou shalt tithe the profit not the capital invested. Ok.

The book of the old testament never commanded who hasn't or who cannot, to tithe an imaginary increase.

More importantly Jesus Christ our lord never, never, never, ever mentioned tithe throughout his sojourn on earth.

You preach cheerful giver and giving, without its context nature of bounty and non-covetousness:

"Therefore, I thought...as a matter of bounty and not as of covetousness..."

"Every man according as he proposeth in his heart, so let him give, not grudgingly or of necessity: for God loveth a cheerful giver.

Mark (already reading) ..."Everyman shall give as he is able, according to the blessing of God, which he hath given thee..."

A lone voice from the auditorium pierces: Wow, it's true! It's written here. These our men of God are biggest thieves, fraudsters!

Another voice joins in: Coons, con men, misleading men of God...

Mezzi: And Jesus himself, in temporal precedence, ahead of all had established, saying in the book of Mathew chapter 6; from verse 1 to verse 4;

Mark: "Take heed that ye do not your alms before men, to be seen of them: otherwise ye have no reward of your father which is in heaven. Therefore, when thou doest alms do not sound a trumpet as the hypocrites do ..."

Mezzi: ...Do not your alms...do not sound a trumpet, do not sound a trumpet before thee as the hypocrites do. Then to Mark: Please continue...

Mark: verse 3; "but when thou doest alms, let not thy left hand know what thy right hand doeth.

Mezzi (pantomiming): Let not this hand know what this other hand doeth when you give alms...

Mark: Verse 4; "that thine alms may be in secret and thy father which seethe in secret himself shall reward thee openly."

Mezzi: Mark please reference the book of Deuteronomy chapter 18; from verse1 to verse 6.

Mark: "The Priests the Levites and all the tribe of Levi shall have no part nor inheritance with Israel" ...Therefore shall they have no inheritance among their brethren: The Lord is their inheritance..."

Within the eerie silence of congregants' mental notes and reflection Mezzi pauses. Now he continues.

Mezzi (to the man of God): The Lord is your inheritance. Nothing among the people.

Even so, you are totally distorting and reinventing the scriptures.

Why would you dictate how much to give to God's kingdom?

Why would you levy with the intent to extort money?

Why would there be a roll-call instead of secrecy as the Lord commandeth? You have to humiliate who has not? Especially the Gen Z? As if they lack humiliation and have not been humiliated enough yet by you and by society? You exalt covetousness. You promote sins, stealing, falsehood, chicanery.

You bless kleptocracy, you profess hypocrisy;

You preach rights without preaching duties;

You preach sowing material seed instead of sowing seed of righteousness;

You preach grace, unmerited favor without faith essence;

You preach conduct without conscience element;

You preach belief in God without obedience to God;

You preach prosperity theology instead of spiritual prosperity;

You give hopelessness of hope. You preach captivity and its perpetuity...

It has been said that the greatest gift we can give to one another is smile.

Man of God, the greatest gift you are commanded to give to the world family of youth, to Black kind Youth, to Africa's youth, to Africa's Gen Z is hope.

Instead you...

Suddenly a clap is heard, interrupting Mezzi. Another follows. More join. Heads turn in their directions. They are from the Proscenium-orchestra. David and Buzzo are on their feet clapping. The President, visibly moved, joins them, impulsively standing up, clapping.

More clapping are heard. Glenda, Lynda, President's wife, more and more are standing, joining the overture. Courage in profile. Almost everyone, has assault of unutterable spasm of variegated emotions. Mixed emotions: some are in tears; some are fixing the void; Some are openly crying. Gen Z are remarkably fractiously collected, yet happy, with a remarkable sense of vindication by a fellow Gen Z, their peer, out of the blue.

Mezzi and Mark embrace and take their leave of the pulpit. In standing ovation.

> *"The Priests, the Levites and all the tribe of Levi shall have no part nor inheritance with Israel" ...Therefore shall they have no inheritance among their brethren: The Lord is their inheritance..."*

The man of God is stilled, seated beside his wife, amidst his crew, flabbergasted. Densely nonplussed, stupefied, dazed and confused.

The crew is fixing the void. Lost. No proffering of words amongst or between them. All his spite in lying and defiance in him subdued, beaten to his profession, humiliated in his art of misdeeds and deceptions, cowardly but deadly kleptomania contrivance, in God's name, of unutterable reprehensible abomination are now barren. Hopefully orphaned.

The mesmerized, transfixed Status Quo, and the captive, but energized empowered African Gen Z alike, can't wait to glimpse Mezzi from a closest distance. The closest distance for the Gen Z hope. Hope for their resurrection.

It seems their self-consciousness is departing from the realm of phobic-neurosis. Time will be of essence to validate.

> *You are totally distorting and reinventing the scriptures.*
> *Why would you dictate how much to give to God's kingdom?*
> *Why would you levy with the intent to extort money?*
> *Why would there be a roll-call instead of secrecy as the Lord commandeth?*
> *You have to humiliate who has not? Especially the Millennials? As if they lack humiliation and are not being humiliated enough yet by you and by society?...*

> *...You exalt covetousness. You promote sins, stealing, falsehood, chicanery;*
> *You bless kleptomania, you profess hypocrisy;*
> *You preach rights without preaching duties;*
> *You preach sowing material seed instead of sowing seed of righteousness;*
> *You preach grace, unmerited favor without faith essence;*
> *You preach conduct without conscience element;*
> *You preach belief in god without obedience to God;*
> *You preach prosperity theology instead of spiritual prosperity;*
> *You give hopelessness of hope. You preach captivity and its perpetuity.*
> *It has been said that the greatest gift we can give to one another is smile.*
> *Man of God the greatest gift you are supposed to give the Millennials is hope.*
> *Instead you...*

Now to everybody's numbing surprise, the President steps up to the podium taking the microphone. Everybody and everything, simmers down. Quietens. The air turns still, filled with perplexity. With suspicion, with despondency, the political kleptomania authority, part parcel of the infamous Status Quo wants to speak.

President (picking his words carefully between pauses): Thank you all. Thank you all. What a beautiful day of revelation.
Congregation has heard. We have all heard. There are no equivocations. The Lord Jesus is here, hearing us. He is amidst, bearing us witness.
Great lesson from our great kids. We needed these two guileless, gritty, gutsy youths, the Gen Z amongst us to open our willful blind eyes and touch our willful stolid hearts.
Please, rounds of applause.

Congregation loosens up and applauds vigorously.

President, with a wave of the hand, that expressed finality in gesture, had an immediate silence. A rapt dense silence returned.

President: Shame on us all, especially on the Status Quo. We are ignorant and gutless. We use 'no time' alibi to not read the words of God, to not nourish our souls. We, elected officers are busy with our time at debauchery, at cowardice. Our wives, mothers, sisters are busy at cosmetics, at gluttony, feasting away, instead of pathing our kids, pathing our youths in the Lord, in the values of society. That way, we let these impostors "men of God" form and thrive in our midst at our expenses. Spiritually and materially. We willfully let them mislead us. What a violence they are. What evil masters.

They don't preach 'love thy God.' They don't preach 'love thy neighbor like yourself.' They don't preach 'sowing seed of righteousness.' They preach prosperity theology. These villains, these abhorrent, impostors "men of God" preach solely prosperity theology, using the myth of a psychological theology warfare: pay tithe or no heaven. And we pay; sow the seed or no grace, we pay; be a cheerful giver or no miracles of multiplication, we pay; we pay to speak in tongue, as if it should be by our making. We pay for the grace of God that will never come that way. Grace of God depends on our faith level, righteousness level. We pay for prayers. We pay for miracles to happen that never ever happens. We pay to be buried. We pay for anything. We pay for everything. Then they bless covetousness. They bless rapacity. They bless greed. They coax the haves and the have-nots with equal vigor, coax all of us of the spiritually fragile and vulnerable, to subtract, to steal, to dispossess society and we submit ourselves, we submit all the monies, we submit all our items of value to them, including our hearts and ourselves.

Then, with our monies and naïve hearts they own airplanes, fleet of exotic cars. They buy homes all over the world, have fat bank accounts world over. They spot designers wears. They are adulterous and they fornicate with our wives, mothers, daughters. They own schools, they own hospitals, they own parks we collegially contribute to build. Then they commercialize them exorbitantly and charge our families again to pay for them. Craven shylocks! The worst filth of money laundering and lending. We the church become their family inheritance.

And then they flaunt all these, remarkably unequivocally. Remarkably bombastically to our faces. Straight faced to the Faithfuls. To us the Faithfuls, the makers of their worldly riches. It's incredible. Shame on us the Faithfuls. Indeed, our stupidity has no rivalry. No equal. Unparalleled. Unequalled. Unpardonable. Negro where are you?

Shame on us all, especially on the Status Quo. We are ignorant and gutless...
We, elected officers are busy with our time at debauchery, at cowardice.
Our wives, mothers, sisters are busy at cosmetic, at gluttony, feasting away, instead of pathing our kids, pathing our youths in the Lord, in the values of Society. That way, we let these impostors "men of God" form and thrive in our midst at our expenses. Spiritually and materially...
They don't preach 'love thy God.' They don't preach 'love thy neighbor like yourself.' They don't preach 'sowing seed of righteousness.'...

> *...They preach Prosperity theology... Using the myth of a psychological theology warfare: pay tithe or no heaven. And we pay; sow the seed or no grace, we pay; be a cheerful giver or no miracles of multiplication, we pay; we pay to speak in tongue, as if it should be by our making. We pay for the grace of God that will never come that way. Grace of God depends on our faith level, righteousness level. We pay for prayers. We pay for miracles to happen that never ever happens. We pay to be buried. We pay for anything. We pay for everything... Then they bless covetousness. They bless rapacity. They bless greed.*
> *They coax the haves and the have-nots with equal vigor, to subtract, to steal, to dispossess society and we submit our hearts, we submit our monies, all our items of value to them, including our ourselves.*
> *Then, with our monies and naive hearts they own airplanes. Fleet of exotic cars.*
> *Own homes and properties. Fat bank accounts world over. They spot designers wears. They are adulterous and they fornicate with our wives, mothers, daughters. They own schools, they own hospitals, they own parks we collegially contribute to build. Then they commercialize them exorbitantly and charge our families again to pay for services...Negro where are you?*

President (looking at the man of God who has his head fixing the floor:

You could not preach belief theology and obedience set of values. The absolute importance of obedience in the belief set. How can you believe in God without obeying what he commands: Belief and obedience?

If your son believes in you the father, he must follow your teachings: do your dish after eating, make your bed every morning, read your books to pass your exams, respect others, don't steal, don't be mischievous, etc, etc, etc. If he does them, he will please the heart of his father. To this extent we don't truly believe in God. We don't obey his commandments. We drive him away.

Man of God, we all, men of authority, you, me, the traditional chiefs have no powers. It's our illusion. We have the people's power. God exists because of us his creation. Power does not exist for some vacuum. Power exists for some purpose. Our purpose is to make life bearable for the people we represent.

You are supposed to be our saints. Our bar of righteousness. Our ultimate interceding hope for heaven. Our impeccable role model. Your job is to call every other power to order when we err. Instead you lead us astray. You deceive us. You encourage us to loot and we share the loots with you. You bless us to bond society in tribulation and misery. Societal captivity, your gain. And we have a society without ethics, without morality and standards. Lost. We are lost. These our "men of God" took us into perdition.

Damn us in Africa. Damn our ignorance. Damn us for our ignorance, generation after generation. shame on us. Just think about the whole logic, thanks to the revelation in the book of Deuteronomy, chapter 9, verse 4 to verse 6 by our two young jewels, it becomes easy and fair to infer that Africa, pre Atlantic slave trade was already thriving in wickedness, and when the Lord could endure no more Africa's wickedness, he made it the "land of Canaan" for the White race, with the advent of Trans-Atlantic slave trade in the 16th century and since then, regardless of the Bible, its teachings, and what it progressed and progresses out there, Africa remained and remains unrepentant, continues in its fetishism, in its falsehood, in its wickedness, in its evil. And our "men of God", who are supposedly called to preach and path us in righteousness, to help sanctify Africa from our wickedness, and undo it from "land of Canaan" status, instead give Africa the final lethal blow, not just for "land of Canaan" perpetuity for the Whites and the Asians, but for land of Perdition for Africans. We are lost in perdition, thanks to our "men of God."

The Bible speaks about these false prophets. They are wicked men indeed.

Damn us in Africa. Damn our ignorance. Damn us for our ignorance, generation after generation. shame on us. Just think about the whole logic, thanks to the revelation in the book of Deuteronomy, chapter 9, verse 4 to verse 6 by our two young jewels, it becomes easy and fair to infer that Africa, pre Atlantic slave trade was already thriving in wickedness, and when the Lord could endure no more Africa's wickedness, he made it the "land of Canaan" for the White race, with the advent of Trans-Atlantic slave trade in the 16th century and since then, regardless of the Bible, its teachings, and what it progressed and progresses out there, Africa remained and remains unrepentant, continues in its fetishism, in its falsehood, in its wickedness, in its evil. And our "men of God", who are supposedly called to preach and path us in righteousness, to help sanctify Africa from our wickedness, and undo it from "land of Canaan" status, instead give Africa the final lethal blow, not just for "land of Canaan" perpetuity for the Whites and the Asians, but for land of Perdition for Africans. We are lost in perdition, thanks to our "men of God."

President (now directly to the Gen Z congregation):

Let me put this to you Generation Zed: why would naked falsehood, willful deception and willful embrace of misery be the order of your days? Pervert your spiritual instincts and essence? Why would that appeal to your senses of self-consciousness?

Why you the oppressed want to be like us the oppressors?

You want to join us in perdition? Are you all senseless masochists?

The vehemence of this truth voiced from the power that presently is, the President, with its unrestrained nakedness, without any preemptive scripting, tangents like a shrapnel on the listeners, and have unutterable spasm of chilling goose skin effects on the entire youth congregants.

For some moment they remained stilled. Silenced. Dazed. Then abruptly they erupt in standing ovation to the reality of the *Mea-Culpa* courage of their President.

The President waves them "sit down, sit down, sit down." They take back their seats.

President: Yes, the challenge chore! Not to challenge was the most grievous mistake we made in our youths. We did not challenge the Status Quo. Our fathers did not challenge their own fathers. The African youths have not challenged and does not challenge their Status Quo from generation to generation. This is the original sin. The original unequivocal sin of our race. This original unequivocal sin created the original distance. The original distance between our race and every progress was created. This is the greatest dilemma, our mystery of all times. It started our stagnation. It started our retrogression. So, Retrogression became entrenched and perpetuated as our bar.

Why? If we claim we are human beings with any sense of logic and innate instinct and rationality, can we ponder at any reasonable assumptions of why we don't challenge anything and we don't stand up to anything, we don't stand up for anything?

Is it our embrace of sloth? Is it our ignorance? Is it palsy of religion? Is it the trauma of our inherited superstitious, despotic tradition and culture?

Are they all these adversaries, interlaced, intertwined, embraced, allied, combined? Why are we not reacting against deception, against misery, against injustice, against humiliation, against subjugation, against tribulation, against shame... from generation to generation?

Indeed, we do the contrary. The oppressed wants to be like the oppressor! Generation after generation. That's the reason for no end in sight? *Haba!*

President takes a brief pause, peering into the congregation. The congregation is rapt attentively, listening remarkably incredibly to the President's surprising *Mea-Culpa* homily.

Let me put this to you Gen Z: why would naked falsehood, willful deception and willful embrace of misery be the order of your days? Pervert your spiritual instincts and essence? Why would that appeal to your senses? Why You, the oppressed want to be like Us, the oppressors?...

> *...Yes, the challenge chore! Not to challenge was the most grievous mistake we made in our youths. We did not challenge the Status Quo. Our fathers did not challenge their Status Quo. The African youths have not challenged and does not challenge their Status Quo from generation to generation. This is the original unequivocal sin of our race. This unequivocal sin created the original distance between our race and every progress. This is the ...greatest dilemma...*

President: The White race is adventurous; generation after generation. Curiosity, analysis remain his trademark. His hallmark is developing the intellect, tasking the brain. Inventions their way of life. Taking risks. Challenging everything that be. Anything. Imbue the abstract. Build mind of abstract capacity. Dream the impossible, make the impossible become. Advancing humanity. Paying the ultimate price. Yes, the ultimate price for any, for every of their life style. Our borrowed life-style. Yes, we live their life-style. While they try to build heaven on this earth, making life bearable for their people, living out Jesus. Yes Jesus' "give life for life", the love he exemplified on the cross for humanity. Instead we are simply intent on borrowing their life-style. We are incapable of carving out something out of our primitive life- style to this day. We remained and remain primitive in our brains, capable only of trafficking kleptomania, despotism, oligarchy, sloth, hate, dishonesty, sorrows, lamentations, cringing excuses, manufacturing lies, evil contrivances, tribulations, depravity, tyranny, misery.

And let me ask you all this, "have you ever heard or seen anybody who has gone to heaven and been back?"

Congregation (responds a deafening): No!

President: Then you all agree we should conduct ourselves, build bearable heaven here on earth for everyone, to help qualify us for the Lord's heaven after our demise?

Congregation: Yeeeessssss!

President: Gen Z, don't make our mistakes. Develop sense of curiosity, sense of truth. Adventure. Rationale. Passion. Determination. Focus. Courage. Abstract. Critique. Critique anything you don't know. Challenge anything, everything. Ask why. Be Mr. Why. Become Generation of Why and of Why Nots.

Buzzo (ponderously interjecting): Yes! Become Generation WHY!

Mezzi (voluptuously joining in): Yes, the seed of WHY self-consciousness!

Gen Z (gradually joins in): Yes, yes, yes!

Now the President hints at continuing, the Gen Z yelling and scowling ceases.

147

President: Yes, it is a chaos, anarchy to be like us. We have not given you anything. We were given nothing. Our inheritance is nothingness. And nothingness begets nothingness. It's up to your will of courage to break the jinx of gift of nothingness. We cannot let these hateful, hurtful criminal, ignorant, arrogant "men of God" deceive us. We can't let them make worst an already worse situation.

We should read, read, read. Read, read, read, read, read, read, read. Develop our intellect. Develop our intellect into intelligence. Our intelligence into selfconsciousness and into love for humanity in order to challenge everything. Anything. Please read, read, read, read, read, and read to enable the mind. Change the mindset. Reading is the magic. It's the miracle to qualify for heaven. It's the first hurdle to heaven. Please read. If you don't, you will have no arm to challenge anything. You will have no arm to challenge us. Challenge us rationally. Challenge the Status Quo. Challenge anything always. Challenge and defy the guns. Defy the bullying. If need be, sacrifice the chance at life to gain ultimate life. You can only gain life with ultimate life price if necessary. That is the real, lone reason for life. Our lives.

Never you get tired of thinking that Jesus Christ gave us life by dying on that Cross.

And I repeat, Jesus said "You love life, you lose it."

At the words "challenge us ...the Status Quo" once again the Gen Z section of the congregation erupts in a standing ovation.

And at the words "defy the...Status Quo...if need be. Pay the ultimate price," the standing ovation deepens. Deafens.

The Gen Z seem ready to fight. Seems there is a self-consciousness passion awakening. Passion enthusiasm. Heroic enthusiasm. To sublimate exertion. Finally, on the African continent.

The President (pressing on): Can any of you willingly let a fake doctor perform surgery on you?

Congregation (shouts a resounding): Nooooooooooo!

President: Didn't Jesus our Lord have disciples to teach?

Congregation: Yes.

President: And only afterwards they qualified for apostleship?

Congregation: Yes.

President: So, you agree that all "men of God" must know theology?

Congregation: Yeeeeeeeeeeeeeeeeessssssssss!

President: Consider it done. To qualify as a priest or as "men of God" going forward they must from tomorrow graduate in theology before they open and run a church.

Congregation: Yeeeeeeeeeeeeeeeeeeeeeeeeeeeeeeeeeeeeeeessssssssssssssssssssss!!

President: From tomorrow we are closing all the churches with these so-called men of God without theology papers on our land.

Congregation: Yeeeeeeeeeeeeeeeeeeeeeeeeeeeeeeeeeeeeeeessssssssssssssssssssss!!

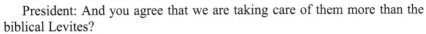

President: And you agree that we are taking care of them more than the biblical Levites?

Congregation: Yeesssss.

President: More so in virtue of the revelation of their inheritance in the Lord: Deuteronomy, chapter 18, verse 1 to verse 6.

Congregation: Yeeeessssssssss!

President: That's why their effort at kleptomania, their effort at hyperbole, their effort at our abuse with our good will, with our monies and all pales beyond hell.

Congregation: Yeeeeessssssssss!

President: Then the airplanes, the homes, the schools, everything they arrogate, their bank accounts, the hospitals are ours and we should take them back.

Congregation: Yeeeeeeeeeeeeeeeeeeeeeeeeeeeessssssssssssssssssssssssss.

Now chants of: Ours, ours, ours, ours fill the Church.

Then a lone voice of a male Gen Z out of the crowd: What about our Moslem brothers?

President: Gen Z! Gen Z!! Gen Z!!!

African Gen Z, the imperialist powers, dead and living, would be goggling with ultimate satisfaction at that question.

African Gen Z, it's not about Moslem brothers or Christian brothers, or Voodoo brothers, or tribal brother, or language brother. It's about the Black kind. They have used these to polarize and divide us and sow seeds of hate and mayhem amongst us and reaped and reap us to this day.

African Gen Z, the problem is not religion, it's about the Black kind.

African Gen Z, every religion preaches love, peace, virtues, rights and duties, commandments and respect and observance of commandments, conscience and conduct. Etc.

African Gen Z, what we do is our choice. It's about moving a race forward.

Our choice to deviate from religion, all in God's name is the heinous and vile problem. Our choice to listen to the litany of falsehood, of hypocrisy from our so-called evil "men of God" is the problem.

Our choice of sloth not to read the holy book, to corroborate whatever is preached to us, is the problem.

African Gen Z, Moslems, Christian, Atheist, Voodooist, any faith alike should please read and read and read and read and read

Should dig, and dig, and dig, and dig. Uncover, and uncover, and uncover, and uncover layers, and layers of facts for understanding, and for a total obliteration of ignorance, and develop the intellect, develop self-consciousness, imbibe the abstract to challenge the Status Quo.

And I repeat, challenge the Status Quo, and her rampant remarkable viscid abhorrent hold on power and it's unfortunate, reprehensible abuses, in order to progress Africa, give Africa human dignity. Make African lives bearable henceforth. Generation after generation. This in my opinion would help to change the situation.

Please, I implore you to read, read, read, read, read, read, read, read, read, read. Develop your intellect into intelligence. Intelligence into self-consciousness and into love for humanity in order to challenge everything. Please read, read and read. Reading is the magic. It's the miracle to qualify for heaven. It's the first hurdle to heaven.
If you don't, you will have no arm to challenge anything. You will have no arm to challenge us. Challenge us rationally. Challenge the Status Quo. Challenge anything and everything always. Challenge and defy the guns. Defy the bullying, the lies, the arrogance, the ignorance, the bombast, the superficial.

If need be, sacrifice the chance at life to gain ultimate life. You can only gain life with ultimate life price if necessary. That is the real, lone reason for life. For Our lives.
Never you get tired of thinking that Jesus Christ gave us life by dying on that Cross. And I repeat, Jesus said "You love life, you lose it".

Congregation (in standing ovation, chanting): Yes, change we must...change we must...

Chapter 6

Back to President's Lodge

The foursome is back to President's lodge trying to analyze the happenstance. They are seated at the table, over coffee and tea after Mezzi and Mark escaped a near lynching type felicitation by the Gen Z congregants, who remarkably informally coronated them heroes. Their heroes. Their courage was of stupefying eruption. Surreal. Their adeptness at the bible subliminal. Their charming innocence ethereal. Their fragile air of naive vulnerability, of lamb before the lion "men of God" empathetically captivating. Rarefied.

David: What volcanoes you guys turned out to be.

Buzzo: What a pleasant surprise it was. Bravoes to both of you. What you both accomplished today will surely resonate during our life time…

David: …And well beyond. And if this does not awaken us the African Gen Z…

Mezzi: Did we really try or this is just some cheap flattery all along?

Mark: You needed to see yourself speak. Sorry preach. Powerful. Supernatural. And me beside you is the biggest privilege.

David: For you to have flipped the psych of our very diffident father who, however represents the ultimate despotic power in every form and in its subtleties to your side? What a fit!

Buzzo: When did you two practice, rehearsed the scriptures?

Mark: Never did. Never read the bible before. You know your little brother here is…ehm…how is it said…ob…

Buzzo: Obdurate?

Mark: Yes! Thank you, the word is obdurate. He can be stubbornly obdurate. Unyielding. When he sets his mind on something, he never quits. Look at that children must play center. He perseveres in anything. I am learning a lot from him: "Don't be broken." "Never give up." "Keep digging."

David: The white blood in him.

Mezzi: Nothing to do with blood. It has instead, to do with aridity of shame on the African Land. The niggertude shame, the misery bonding shame, the retrogressive perpetuity shame are arid.

Buzzo: You openly declared a revolution today Mezz.

David: And the crowd is with you.

Mark: The crowd is with us.

Mezzi: Remarkably seemingly. Amongst them the African Gen Z, the men and women, the old, the corrupted, the corruptible, the gullible, the gluttonous, the kleptomaniacs, the oligarchy, the religious, the hungry, the meek, the hyperbole, the rapacious. All seem to be in.

Buzzo (looking at David): Who knows for how long. The only figure that gives me hope is your father. Defiantly defiant. Courageously courageous. Against constituted authority. Against himself. He proved beyond every doubt he is in. And that is remarkably, fundamentally important.

Mezzi: Whatever happens, however it goes, I will remain proud of your father.

David: He will be filled to hear this.

Mark: He respects, admires and loves you guys. Although tacitly-remotely, maintaining the distance, because of his position.

Buzzo: Imagine if we had such a father. What a chagrin.

David: Urgency of the time. Urgency of everything.

Buzzo: Yeah, correct. We must capitalize on today. Today, as the Hemmingway's "one day", this day, our today, of every other day. Today may become the today for every of our today, on this earth.

Mezzi: Today...Mark how many Gen Z were in that church today; do you estimate?

Mark: Well over ten thousand.

Mezzi: Today, the one day I think we rekindled the inherent self-consciousness of ten thousand African Gen Z at their captivity.

Buzzo: Today, the one day that must spur every day, in multiples of ten thousand, the inherent self-consciousness in the African Gen Z to stand up and make their captivity captive.

Mezzi: Whatever we inherited, whatever have been pushed unto us, we are here to defeat.

David: Urgency guys. Urgency our platform. The platform now more than ever.

Buzzo: Platform our church. There, on our platform, the Gen Z hunger shall defeat misery. Their fear, tribulations, faithlessness, complacency, gullibility, corrupt inspirations, credos shall succumb to courage. Annihilated, subdued to their courage. Renaissance credo will triumph. Reign supreme.

Buzzo and Mezzi finally head home, after a long emotionally charged positive day.

The day has been a drawl. A terrific beautiful and pleasant drawl. They head home, to grandpa, for much merited and required respite.

> **Today, the one day that must spur every day, in multiples of ten thousand, the inherent self-consciousness in the African Gen Z to stand up and make their captivity captive.**

Chapter 7

The Mosque

As they head home in the rather iconic Range Rover, their faces look serene as they make mental reflection of the day. A ponderous dense silence is their accomplice, when in the distance, the Imam's voice pierces the darkness for 20:00 prayers. His last chore for the day:

Shillala…Allah Akbar. Shillala…Allah Akbar.

Buzzo and Mezzi exchange glances. Mezzi has an assault of a solicitous frown. Buzzo notices but remained silent. As they drive and the calling to prayer grows nearer, Mezzi drawls a smirk that fleeted short of a smile.

Buzzo looks at him reassuringly. Mezzi understands: his expression creases from a frowning to a delightful amazement.

Now, they arrive before the mosque, Buzzo stops and parks the car in a space overlooking the mosque. They wait for the faithfuls to alight.

Then, the faithfuls alight. Some minutes passed by, and silence ensued and lulled.

Now they enter the mosque and find the Imam in prayers, his eyes fixing the void.

The Imam notices them amidst his prayers.

They waited respectfully, silently collected.

Now the Imam is done, over with his prayers.

He waves them "come."

They obey, uniting themselves to him and disappear behind the blind, crossing the door's threshold.

They walk into an expansive courtyard of the mosque. A deserted courtyard whose lighting has an unkind dismal play of umbra and penumbra.

Mezzi and Buzzo, in amazement of muffled protest stop shot in their tracks. The Imam, undeterred urges them on.

Imam: Just follow me. The light is dingy, but your eyes will adjust quickly soon.

It took Buzzo's and Mezzi's eyes some minutes to adjust to the devastating dismal optic play.

They can now make out stack of twenty feet containers, orderly arranged.

The Imam stops before one of them, reaches for the keys and opens the door. He illuminates the inside with his torch light, inviting Buzzo and Mezzi in.

The Imam exudes calm and confidence, a calm and confidence that seemed honest and unfeigned. Buzzo notices and in a flash fought back and suffocated the assailing spasm of dread. Without hesitation he gained entrance and Mezzi followed suit.

The Imam closes the door behind them.

The container is filled with stack of cartons, orderly and firmly laid out, bottom up. The only space they have left seems to be where they are standing.

Imam (his voice down to mumbles): I strongly and firmly plead for you to pardon my uncouth manners.

Buzzo: It's ok.

Imam: Please make yourselves comfortable.

The Imam, as he proffered those words, immediately realizes these two are of non- Islamic faith; not used to customs of the floor and carpets. In a flash, under the watchful eyes of Buzzo and Mezzi, he moves the torch light to his mouth, holding it between his teeth and wedges himself on the tightly stacked cartons. He grabs the topmost cartons, lifting them off, carrying, placing them carefully on the floor, in turns, three times.

Now done and panting, he sits on one of the cartons.

Imam: Now you can make yourselves comfortable.

Buzzo and Mezzi sit on the cartons hesitantly. The Imam, in turn fixes them in the eyes. Buzzo and Mezzi hold his stare with unwavering vigor.

Imam: It is with full confidence and honor of both parties, myself and yourselves, and with your magnanimity of the heart and selflessness at your young ages that I believe I can trust you with my intent of heart. That eventually we can trust one another.

You are here because I want to cash in on the opportunity you have created to help our kids.

Most of us just wait for the future. Future is like prison in Africa as you realized. Future in Africa is made up of mini-objectives of prison. Everyone knows it but does nothing about it. We ignore it. And its cleft of scourge grows by the hour. It's consuming us. Its utter cowardice to wait for future to come to us.

Buzzo and Mezzi are listening hard with unutterable vigor of attention, an attention of delightful curiosity. This is a rare moment of learning. This is a world, whose inner workings and full tenets and culture and mannerism, are totally arid of everything about Islam to most non-faithfuls, remains in the wildest realm of suppositions and imaginations. Non-faithful's biased views are mostly that of violence, subjugation, mythologies, hypocrisy and nuances and subtleties. The rest seems suppositions and imaginations of unutterable darkness.

Imam: We should be at the service of Allah. Like your Levites. Unfortunately, we are totally not. Here on earth we are at the services of the Emirs. We belong to them.

The Imam pauses, with his nose creasing and his mouth puckering at something, short of contempt. He is fighting back without doubt, some unpleasant memory of something.

Now his face decides and relaxes. Buzzo and Mezzi watch him amidst a dense, eerie silence.

Imam: Mine is an inherited profession, a family calling. We are a family of Levites. My grandfather died a "Levite." He was killed trying to create a future. My father died a "Levite." He was as well trying to create a future. I am not afraid of trying to create a future. I must honor them. I must give sense to what they lived and died for. Heaven on earth is my calling. And you are the vehicle. Otherwise, my life would be nonsense. Allah bless you.

The Imam suddenly stands up and rips open the carton he was seated on. It is full of US Dollars. Stack of dollars. Of course, of 100 Dollars bills.

Buzzo and Mezzi go into competing amazement: a competing amazement of sorrowing sadness, of dreadful delight and open admiration of courage.

Buzzo and Mezzi, in open imitation of him, stand up from the cartons on which they were seated and opens them.

Buzzo: Bravo! Let me ask you: these containers are your banks?
Imam: They are subtracted from the banks.
Buzzo: Indeed, that's of a sorrowing sadness. Investing money, hiding them within the confines of containers yields nothing. Not jobs. Not profits. Not pleasure.
Imam: Correct. They don't care. Our land is withered of accountability.
Mezzi: You are their accountant?
Imam: I am not. I am entrusted to keep eyes on them.
Mezzi: What is the source of these monies?
Imam: We receive donations for prayers, we receive donations for the distressed, we receive monies from invested business profits to evade taxes, etc. etc.
Mezzi: For the distressed? You send the kids to beg on a daily basis, you degrade the women and the mosque use the monies for illicit business ventures?
Imam: The mosque does not. Our spiritual head could well be. He calls the shots.
Mezzi: You know nothing. You are just the custodian angel. I don't get it.
Buzzo: Mezzi, count your teeth.... It's that obvious.

Imam: It's ok. He is very young and very pure. But he understands fast.

Mezzi: But that's utterly dreadful.

Imam: I agree, but won't you agree that it is less dreadful to deploy the money back for the people?

Mezzi: Of course, absolutely yes.

Imam: Now let's compare the sins inherent in the actions: does the sin in stealing, subtracting the money from the people far out-weigh the sin in returning the money to the people by all means possible?

Buzzo: Imam, we are with you. Let's go ahead.

Imam: So, I would want us to expand and enhance your center with more activities. Teachers, nutrition, more schools' refurbishments, more vocational training activities, skill acquisition for our youths and women alike: tailoring, carpentry, mechanics, iron welding, driving, discipline, respect for themselves, hard work, the danger of alcohol, drugs, the ills of begging. Grow their self-consciousness out of surrendering and instead in to recognize, analyze, research, challenge and confront.

Just be assured that money is not the problem.

Mezzi: So, we can safely deploy the monies. All these monies here?

Imam: You are safe. You don't know who owns them. You don't know how they are made. You don't know who gave them to you.

Nobody gave them to you. It's donated to your foundation from an anonymous philanthropist. Every other curiosity would be left to the African future progress to unveil and validate the answers and justifications.

And besides, in Africa cash reigns supreme. Cash and carry. We don't run credit cards. We run debit cards. Just to exclude the poor masses. Willfully.

Mezzi: True, you draw on your prior deposited money.

Imam: Precisely. There are no forms of mortgages. There is no middle class. Middle class that measures the health, the wealth of a nation is obliterated. Purposefully. Its either you are among the majority of the very poor who can't have mortgages, or you are among the few who are enriched with the people's money and welfare who, in any case does not need mortgages.

Buzzo: It's clear. Anonymous philanthropic donors would suffice.

Imam: Can we agree to this *conditio sine qua non* for our collaboration?

The Imam fixes their eyes, holding stare in turns as he scans their attentive pensive and rapt faces, in mental contemplation, for approval. Buzzo and Mezzi did not budge. They hold his stare independently, in turns, as they weigh the weighty choices: the sin of money laundering against the sin of viciously subtracting money from society; the risk of love and exertion of creating the future against the non-risk of evil to maintain and continue the perpetuation of Status Quo humiliation, subjugation and misery on the African future–the youths; and their consequences.

> *Now let's compare the sins inherent in the actions: does the sin in stealing, subtracting the money from the people far out-weigh the sin in returning the money back to the people by all means possible?*

Imam: Deal?

Buzzo and Mezzi now fix each other in the eyes, and tacitly decide that the development and progress of the African future reigns absolutely supreme. And with equal vigor the honor in the risk of effort and the meek spiritual essence of this selfeffacing ethereal Imam is worth upholding into a legacy.

It is commonplace to stereotype and imagine Islam violent, oppressive, dehumanizing, subjugating, but in all fairness to this Imam, in the realm of the African Levites–pastors, men of God, priest and priestesses and the Imams – it is mind blowing to find a meek and self-effacing essence, amongst the three dominant religions, who has consorted or is consorting with mercifulness for the distressed poor. In form. In substance. While this Islam Imam simply dresses in Kaftan, the Pentecostal "men of God" are sporting designers' wears. While this Islam Imam's drive is mercifulness towards the poor, the Pentecostal "men of God's" drive is vicious avariciousness. Savage kleptomania. Cruel covetousness.

So, with a simple simultaneous nod, Buzzo and Mezzi express a finality of gesture of a deal. They hint a smile. A reassuring smile.

The Imam understands. He is overwhelmed with unutterable happiness and with a sense of a proprietor pride: his life is beginning to make much more sense.

He hints a bow of a nod.

Mezzi: Imam, thank you. African future should not be prison.
Buzzo: Should never have been prison.

They shake good bye in turn with the Imam.

Chapter 8

President's Office
The President is seated in the study of his office all by himself at the early hours of the Monday morning following Sunday's church service, scanning, reading the daily newspapers of the right wing, left wing and independent ideologies alike of his state, and musing over their variegated headlines in form but all in expression of same in substance:

Daily Times: President rails gratuitous attacks and tantrums at the church.

Daily Guardian: President moves to save our society from false men of God.

The Punch: President gone nuts, empowers the Youth to a revolution against constituted authorities.

Thisday: Finally, much desired sanity: President contemplates closure of 23,000 as many churches with as many a mix of voodoo priests at best, and Atheists priests at worst on devastated land of Africa. A sacrilege to Christianity. Theology certificates a prerequisite, in the pipeline.

The Nation: President leads the charge against misery, admits *mea-culpa*, rails against our despotic inherited tradition and the evil of the majority of false priests.

Daily Sun: President rekindles the conscientiousness of love thy neighbor maxim, repudiation of sloth, tasks challenge credo, human dignity axiom in our Youths in order to save continent from misery and bondage; when one of his two phones rings. He looks at it, ignores it and continues at the dailies.

Then his other phone rings. He contemplates it. Glimpses at his watch and reluctantly picks it, without diverting from the dailies.

President: Hello my chairman.

The chairman is Mr. George. The father of Buzzo and Mezzi, his political godfather, calling from Manhattan, New York City, his abode.

Chairman: Hello Mr. President.
President: Chairman not in bed at this hour?
Chairman: Yeah, your misdemeanor is keeping me awake.
President (disengages from the dailies, springing to his feet. His countenance altering): My misdemeanor?
Chairman: Yeah, your misdemeanor is grievous.

President: My misdemeanor...grievous?

Chairman: In fact, it is not just grievous it is devious of you. It's next to a felony.

President (countenance altered): Devious of me? A felony?

Chairman: Your near felony is all over the place.

President (air of disappointment): That's gratuitously rude and offensive.

Chairman (raising his voice): You must take that back.

President: You are the least qualified to pontificate to anyone. You personify abject mind poverty, you embody dehumanization, misery and evil.

Efforting to empower our descendants to be curious, to ask why to everything, to chart a course out of Africa's misery, out of our youths' enslavement is a felony, my near felony?

Chairman: Yes, how can you ever do that? Are you out of your mind?

President (disappointed): It does not surprise. You are a venomous worm just like the African fathers before you. Just like them you are incapable of answers, incapable of giving answers and you are afraid of 'why'. Isn't that our greatest problem?

Chairman: You take it upon yourself to ruin all we have built of life.

President (air of delusion and derision): What did we build? You know why we and our Fathers before us are afraid of 'why' and the why we cannot hold stare with Africa's youths? It's because we built and build suppression, subjugation, servility, hypocrisy, cowardice in them.

Chairman: Precisely. We must build those inalienable dictates. Those dictates of our tradition is Africa's power system. Instead you incite revolution against the Status Quo, against the same church that gives them hope. The opium that keeps these kids pacified. That keeps you in power.

President (raising his voice remarkably angry): Who are you George to talk to me that way? Can't you look yourself up in the mirror sometimes? Can't you see you are a remorseless, shameless monster? You give this continent opium of misery and your sanctuary is the West. Heartless criminal. There is a season for everything under the sun. Are you not tired of your killing field? How dare you? Are you not tired of trafficking orchestra of kleptomania, hyperbole, bombast, punishment, tribulations, deprival, numbness, slavery, misery? Our Youths are dazed, forlorn, confused, miserable... how dare you?

Why don't you come live here amidst your orchestra? What a craven cringing coward...

Then he stops shot and hurls the phone against the wall.

The phone goes in thousand pieces and fragments.

At that sudden remarkable shattering noise, his chief of staff, at his post, in the next office, rushes into the room to find him incensed.

President (to his chief of staff): The cowardly repugnant Mr. George wants to give me lesson of my life from his sanctuary in New York.

His kids are remarkably courageous in comparison. They are here living out Africa's misery he manufactures. Misery enforced and perpetuated by us, by all of us including you chief of staff on our continent. It's time for a change. To everything a season.

Chief of Staff, I need those decrees on the churches and theology certificate prerequisites brought to me for signing today. Did you hear me?

Chief of Staff: Yes sir!

President (scowling, his face in an incensed grimace, banging his hand on the table): Absolute priority. Suspend every other thing until I get them signed.

Today...today...today!

Chief of Staff: Consider them done, sir!

President: Out...stop standing there like a zombie... go to work!

Chief of Staff rushes out of the room underpinning his Boss's fierce urgency of the moment.

Then, yet another of the President's special phones rings:

President fixes the phone for a moment and smiles, reaches grabbing it. President: Mrs. Donna George, Buzzo's and Mezzi's mom, like in some fluke is on the line. He picks the call:

President: Hello, our wife!

Mrs. George: Good morning Mr. President.

President: Morning Mr. President? Common, don't mess my day with this flattering formality. How are you by the way?

Mrs. George: I thought you should be in the office at this hour. Formalities required in the offices. I take it back. Good morning Donald. Congratulations at your courage.

President: Congratulations to your kids. Awesome boys. Their energy seismic. Their force a hurricane. Their aura infectious. Contagious. They literally swept my boys off their feet.

Mrs. George: I heard. The great news is shared on the social media. Without your help and protection that was impossible. May God bless you in this dangerous and delicate battle. But if you let me, I will get into this epic African Gen Z fight right away for them to have their place in the family of worlds Gen Z future of collective freedom for their progress.

President: That's a beautiful construct! Congratulation. Yes, you can. Today the African Gen Z platform is being launched.

Mrs. George: Oh my God, really? A platform?

President: Oh yes. The minimum we can do is shore up the first African generation in our historical memory with a gut. The first, trying to stand up. We must shore them up to succeed. We owe them that. They are standing up. They are standing up to evil. We did not stand up to anything. We failed. Cowards. Cowardice. Craven. We hid under our laziness in perpetuity, generation after generation. We hid under the ill-gotten, corrupt comfort of our parents. Be it corrupt comfort complacency, corrupt comfort cowardice, corrupt comfort defeatism and corrupt comfort gullibility and hypocrisy of our parents. These kids are the future. Africa's salvation. I wish they can succeed where we have remarkably failed, generation after generation. It's a shame. The African continent is a sham. Let's leave this life, this earth filled with a terrestrial hope certainty for our Gen Z and succession of our descendants thence. Only our terrestrial hope certainty may guarantee us celestial hope.

Mrs. George: Great. Let me know and have the details of how to participate.

President: Great woman.

Mrs. George: Donald, thank you for the open doors. For the opportunity.

President: Do have a beautiful day.

Mrs. George: You too.

Chapter 9

Kids **Must Play Centre**

Meanwhile, Buzzo and David, who would usually have gone to their respective chores at corps services have, instead been summoned, on impromptu, by the President's office. That leaves Mezzi and Mark at grandpa's village, as always, their presence essential, in the heart of "Kids must play center" A center, overtly overwhelmed by the multitude of kids at education. A center that provides meals, healthcare, recreational activities gratuitously. They can't wait to have the planned platform for the African youths launched and be integrated.

Once the kids have been seen off to school, by various commuting means available, the place respires. Once its respiration whittles down to a whisper, Mezzi and Mark get down to social networking. Hash tagging and streaming. As always.

As they do, this time they find the greatest surprise: their Twitter, Facebook, Instagram account sites are swollen, trending, filled with activities:

Mark: Mezzi, what the hell…are you seeing what I am seeing…?

Mezzi (who is concentrated at something else, nonchalantly): What's that?

Mark (can't contain with his excitement): it's incredible. We have over 800,000 activities on our kids must play center blog. You believe that? Down from 30,000. And its counting by the minutes. Now we are at 890,000…

Mezzi jumps to his feet and grabs Mark, peering into his computer. His eyes are popping out of their orbits and his mouth is "fuck." He goes into a jumping spasm.

Mark: Now we are over a million. And they are looking for us. The two renegades. They call us the 'duo renegade.' They want to participate in our endeavor. Must be yesterday's church performance.

Mezzi: Let's confirm. Common let's open our personal blogs.

They get busy at their computers. After a while Mezzi has his hands cupping his mouth, screaming.

Mezzi: I have over three million followers. From nothing. Jesus!

Mark: What? Are you serious? Show me?

Mezzi pushes the screen of his laptop to his face.

Mark (screaming spasm): Oh my God! What's going on?
Mezzi: Common, get to yours!
Mark (continuing screaming): Oh my God. Oh my God. God, God, Lord. I have two million followers.
Mezzi: Wow! We are famous. The church.
Mark: What do we do now? Do you see their questions? We need to chart them up. And now!!
Mezzi: That's easy. The whole thing we stand for. The renaissance Credos! The WHYs! Actions what they think? What we are going to be doing. We are to direct the orchestra...
Mark: "Where can we find you guys?" Yeah just listen to this other one: "#Who really are you guys, at courage, in a hypocritical society like ours, risking the chances of your "#acquired freedom" for us, your peers? Incredible. Isn't this very sweet?"
Mezzi: Indeed. Listen to this: "#You sure you not the Messiah incarnate, at your young ages? Was he not 33 years of age?" Yet another: "#You leave the ultimate comfort of your world, of your confines, sacrifice your chances at beautiful life for us. For Africa. What an act of love you are." "#You so fascinating, so soave and surreal, and real, looking like a demi-god in that your renegade look and outfit demeanor." And this: "#we urgently need a forum of constant teaching and interaction. We need to fight. We are ready to fight."
And yet another: "#thank you. We won't disappoint you. We are ready for the fight and break the jinx." Mark this is beautiful.
Mark: They are too many, too important. What do we do now? I am confused.
Mezzi: Just chart: #Thank you all. We appreciate your conscience awakening. We are all on board the flight of freedom. No, no! This: #Welcome on board the flight for freedom. Or: #We are all on board this flight, until we capture freedom." Or:
#together unconditionally till we vanquish captivity.
Mark: That sounds very cool. I am putting it up.
Mezzi: Yes. And add: #We will be very active with you permanently from tomorrow. Let me put up something for them. Something to hold them off, until the foursome converge, for our joint decision of action forward.
Mark: Cool. Right. When are they back?
Mezzi: They are coming.
Mezzi and Mark get busy blogging. Replying:
Mezzi writes: #Thank you. Thank you all. Thank you for listening. Thank you for your courage. Thank you for believing. Thank you for joining in, being part of the platform. Thank you for your amazing loves.
#Your love has remarkably empowered me.

\# We are Gen Z. We are a family of Gen Z. A family of African Gen Z. Essential part of the world Gen Z family. Collectivity maxim our principle: collective consumers, collective sharing, collective craving. Collective altruism. Collective researching. Collective braving. Collective challenging. Collective empowering. Collective progress. Collective wellness and richness. Collective collectiveness. No one left behind. No one illiterate. No one jobless. No one thirsty. No one sleep outside. We abhor prejudices. We abhor sexism. We abhor deception. We abhor racism. We abhor a house divided. We, collectively want to make the world a better place for everybody.

#We are a generation of visionaries. We are a generation of missionaries. On a mission. Our mission: make our captivity captive. We need ourselves. We need each other. We need our reciprocity of support to make our captivity captive. To defeat our misery by ourselves on the African continent. That's our dream. Our mission. To that extent, we the African Gen Z, have fallen short of the gut. The grit. The callings. To that extent, to succeed the African Gen Z must grow in self-consciousness. That means we must traffic belief tenet in ourselves, traffic we are the center of the universe, traffic the renaissance man self-consciousness of WHY and WHY NOT. Elevate to Gen WHY. Yes, emerge Gen WHY. That means we traffic listening, reading, digging for objective understanding, in order to rationalize and challenge the Status Quo. We must traffic love for God. We must traffic love for one another. We must traffic humility. We must traffic hard work. We must traffic honesty and discipline. We must traffic respect. We must traffic rights and duties. We must traffic conduct and conscience. We must traffic patience, perseverance and fortitude to elevate to generation Y. And we must traffic prayers for one another. For all. We must have our backs in order to have the backs of generations our descendants in continuum. Black kind must produce something mankind can enjoy. That's the bottom line.

#So long my peers of the beautiful African Gen Z. We will permanently go to work from tomorrow to quickly elevate to Gen WHY. God bless you all. Lots of love.

Chapter 10

The battle line seems drawn. Drawn by the President. He is gone personal. Personal on the constituted authorities:

On the church, he has promulgated decrees on priesthood-theology graduation prerequisite, closed 23 thousand "abusive churches", froze and confiscated the bombasts, the declamatory and the hyperboles of the "men of God"- their airplanes, their schools, properties, state security services protection, their bank accounts etc. On the mosque, he has decreed abolishment of conspiratorial "child" Almuhajjurun, making it criminal for the Imams and religious heads to covertly or overtly engage in the exploitation of children, enslaving them to illiteracy, ignorance, child labor, child marriage and begging for alms for economic and political end. Almuhajjurun literally means 'seeking for spiritual knowledge" in order to propagate the Prophet's teachings and heal ignorance and achieve individual peace of heart for the people. Every child is moronic. And none is able to seek spiritual knowledge. Every child should, instead be parented, fed, and taken care of. Or you don't make them. For God does not make them either. He blesses good efforts. God does not bless the abhorrent and callous effort of making kids without having their backs.

The President: The Emirs and Imams are spiritual heads. They are the means to accede to heaven. The Muslim community carters for their welfare. They have no business with earthly riches. They cannot be businessmen and should not own properties or properties in men.

Their private businesses, hyperboles and flamboyancy are an abuse against Allah.

They are forthwith sequestered.

On the political establishment that made him, he is trading a finest line. There is a rift, fault line of chasm between his new found vision of empathy on the state of health of the people, the tribulation of the people, the misery of the people, their despair on the one part, and the kleptomaniac vision and subjugator conduct and the chicanery trade of the politics and the political establishment he represents, on the other.

On the traditional ruling council, he has decreed the whittling down of Paramount Rulers (the Obas, the Chiefs, the Emirs, the Sultans), their fiefdoms, into a few, withdrawing certain superfluous privileges. Besides, they are forbidden to be in the business of generators, transformers procurement, fertilizers and manure procurement, cereals importations, mineral wealth dealings, cement importations, money laundering. It's absurd and outrageous for them to be in or do any businesses. They should either be traditional, spiritual Leaders or they are Businessmen. One thing or the other. Draw from the other world monarchies to live by state grants. On the Gen Z, he has rapidly constituted an ad-hoc committee, with Buzzo and David appointed to government capacity to represent the African youth interests. Why the President has gone suddenly personal is to everybody's guess, and is at everybody's judgement: conscience of guilt. A conscience of guilt that is brutal. Cruel. Vicious. Fearless of Status Quo. Reckless by Africa's set rules and standards. Even a military dictatorship pales in comparison. Would have dared much. A conscience of guilt remotely latent and has only been awoken by the challenges thrown by the Gen Z foursome?

The ramification of the effect of these sudden actions, stance, that is totally inundating, taking all and sundry by waves of its brutal tide, is unsettling, shockingly awesome.

The sudden volte-face of the President got everybody and everything reeling. Everything is fermenting and everybody is in turmoil. Within the confines of every social and sociable proximity, there's the dialectics. This is unlike the Africans: taking a stance and standing up seem to be gathering an unequivocal momentum. Evidenced everywhere with audacity. Placards. Graffiti. Their explicit contents against the Status Quo, markedly unambiguously. Remarkably surprising, such that memory cannot recall when and where such audacity of a Politicalcraft on the African political scape, is not just greeted by palsy of the Soldiers, the passivity of the Police but by their explicit expression of tacit cheering, encouragements, at the limit of a palpable passion.

More remarkably remarkable is the surprising expression of incensed and incendiary anger at the church and at its "men of God." The courage at breaking with faith in those crooked "men of God".

In sum, emotions are running high, pervading, dangerously unguided in every direction. This palpable near incendiary emotion must be guided. Channeled. Not exploited but funneled into a positive transformative force. A force to tackle and subdue their social vice. The misery. The Africa's youth misery.

Buzzo and David are breathing this air. They understand the remarkable urgency of the situation. Now more than ever, a platform, their platform, as alternative to physical palpable church, a place of gathering and participation, as opposed to gathering and listening, against your wish to falsehood is needed. A place for erudition, for rationalization, capacitating the brain instead of radicalization and pacification and mollification, is remarkably urgently needed. Indeed, the remarkable urgency needs speedy action.

As the Gen Z's representative of the President's ad-hoc committee, the duo get busy. Busy at meetings, participating at details, drawing up the blue print, distributing invitations, organizing for the launching of the African youth Park as was promised by the President.

It's 16 weeks away. Every state contractor and every other contractor are invited. Coaxed to actively participate. Cash donations. In kind donations. Building funds. Construction funds. Indigenous and foreigners, alike.

A fund base of US $100 million was launched. And $100 million was instantly raised.

$80 million in cash and $20 million in kind.

With this fund-base, construction companies' task forces have been drawn.

They have mobilized to site, started marking out every section and sector of the masterplan. And have started surgical clearing operations, making sure that fewer trees are felled, and the features, and topography, and morphology of the existing nature are maintained, and dove-tailed into the overall architectural masterplan on the 350 hectares of land earmarked by the President, in the middle of the city. The space adjoining the "kids must play center." The stretch of land between grandpa's hamlet and the city. The immediate periphery, 10 minutes-drive between them.

The space has been conceptualized by the Gen Z foursome with the help of and with the participation of the state's development authorities: the urban and regional land use department; the development control department; environmental impact analysis department; the engineering department, park and gardens, etc.

The concept of the African youth Park, given the rectangular shape of the land area features a concentric of rectangles, each rectangle spotting a precinct of activities: The outer rectangle, contiguous to the roads, spots a ten-meter breath walkway swallowed by trees on both sides, with studded wooden sitting benches on both sides of the aisle;

The next rectangle has four Disco clubs, a handful of restaurant and bars located in the middle of the four sides;

The next line of rectangle is a precinct of precincts of variegated sporting activities– two professional size soccer pitches, basketball, lawn tennis, baseball, table tennis, wall of squash- all open air, each with open air podiums for spectators, with four Lshaped structures housing changing rooms and restrooms and showers, all in a cornice of jogging tracks lined with trees;

The penultimate rectangle has the main structure, the heart of the Gen Z. The ultimate erudition forum. The rarefied cognitive cradle. The cradle of the Gen Z hope. The place to tool understanding, to tool belief credo. The renaissance belief credo. Multiple conference centers for multiple tireless conferencing, dialectics. Mentoring, from grammar of it all–stimuli, tasting, to the logics of it all–learning, developing the understanding, the intellect, interaction, rationalizing, down to the rhetoric's of it all–application of intellect, reactions to subdue misery. The Black kind descendants' misery.

Make their misery captive. Make captive their inherited misery. Their anathema captive. Their nightmare captive.

The ultimate rectangle is housing twin-open air arena, twin contiguous amphitheaters, with two stages and their corresponding galleries of sittings for spectators, for product presentations, awards of excellencies and substantial musical concerts, entertainments for the Gen Z and for their successions thence.

Back to the Hamlet

Back to the hamlet, Buzzo and David join Mark and Mezzi. The air is in palpitation. Everything and everybody palpitating, throbbing fluttering.

A lot has happened, a lot is happening. Everything is accelerated. A cascading of unforeseen stream of events, without sequential chronology. Remarkably randomly. It's completely a trying, tempting moment at overwhelming, at obfuscating their preordered program priorities. Planned objectives.

Their enthusiasm remarkably much. Their anxiety, ponderously cruel. Their quest at delivering, successfully brutal. Failing at their dreams, remarkably unthinkable. Reprehensibly inconsiderable. To these extents there is a gruesome fight on what should take precedence, amongst the flurry of things on their agenda: the excitement of the younger among the Gen Z, Mezzi and Mark or those of older among the Gen Z, Buzzo and David.

Mark: Look, our websites are swollen.

Mezzi: Buzzo, our sites are overwhelmed. They are spitting fire and furry. They are spilling. They are trending constantly. I don't know what to tell them.

Buzzo: Are you not happiest? After your awesome sermon performance that is having reverberations and ramifications, spilling all over. David: Have you read the dailies of today?

Mezzi and Mark look at each other incognizant. At loss.

David (brings out the heap of dailies, slamming them on the table): The two of you have taken the continent by storm. Your photos are all over the pages. All eyes are on you two.

Buzzo: Not just eyes. All hopes.

Now Mark and Mezzi are busy scanning the dailies.

Mark: Incredible! Unbelievable!

David: Yeah baby boys, all hopes are on you two now.

Mark: Yeah, you mean on us all! Yeah, we know from the millions of postings. Hashtags. They have their hopes on us all.

Mezzi: We have been waiting all day for you both. We suspended online responses. Dialogues. Discourse. Conversations. Dialectics. We don't even

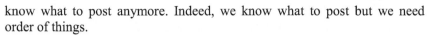

know what to post anymore. Indeed, we know what to post but we need order of things.

Buzzo: Wisdom. Wise boys. Before we shoot ourselves on the foot.

David: A lot of expectations out there.

Mark: A lot of anger out there.

David: A flow of a multitude of disappointed...

Buzzo: No, that's an understatement. An overflow of a multitude of dazed and confused and traumatized hopefuls...

Mezzi: ...Who have in a brute way lost faith in the only umbilical hope of hanging onto life...

David: For afterlife...

Buzzo: Here guys. Over here guys.

Buzzo unrolls, opening the masterplan of the platform, whose construction and realization on the field just got underway, on the big table.

Mezzi and Mark take a fleeting study of it. And soon afterwards both broke up smiling. In a spasm of felicitation.

David: You like it?

Mezzi (his face a rebuking frown): Bravoes! Bravoes!! Bravoes!!! Awesome! Awesome!! awesome!!! However, there's a fundamental miss. We absolutely have to add a 'rectangle' of equipped park for our kids.

He looks up fixing Buzzo, who is bewildered and confused.

Mezzi (reiterating): You got it? Buzzo, our kids must play!

Then, Mezzi breaks rank, dashing into the kitchen area.

Mark: Awesome! Awesome!! Awesome!!! The kids must play. Leave no kid behind. Leave no kid out...

And he dashes, follows Mezzi in his tracks, into the kitchen.

David and Buzzo look on, thrilled and get back, re-examining the masterplan. The remarkable truth and the deafening despair of the absence of the equipped park, for the Millennial kids, dawns on them both. Then they recover.

David: He is damn right!

Buzzo: Yeah, sure he is! You just can't get it all. Can you? Collegiality is fundamental.

David: Yeah. He is adept to details. He is so sensitive. So mature. So human. A gift of life.

Buzzo: Yeah, just like your father. I can't ever stop being grateful to the courage of your father. His courage in breaking ranks. A very dangerous life-threatening bargain.

David: You are remarkably awesome at courage. You did the most. You left the comfort of your house to fight Africa's misery.

Buzzo: Actually, Mezzi did. That little boy did. He sacrificed the chances at comfort for Africa's misery. At his fledgling age. His presence here is my hurricane. The hurricane that inspired and transcended me into action. The hurricane that makes my life worth living. He gives me a lot of energy.

David: And thank you for the infection. You have an infectious energy.

Buzzo: Believe me, without your father...

David: What would be would be. Maybe just could take a little bit longer. With your brute force, with your brutal determination and cruel perseverance and disarming temperament, anything could come to bear and endure...

Mezzi and Mark walk back in, with trays full of bottles of champagne and sodas and glasses and candles. They are being followed by the house chef and his assistants, carrying trays of crudités, meat balls, chips, olive fruits, cheese, pop corns etc.

Buzzo: Hey guys, somebody's birthday?
Mezzi: Yeah. What a million-Dollar question.
Mark: The birth of the platform. The birth of hope.

Mezzi pops open one of the bottles of champagne, filling the glasses. And in toast;

Mezzi: To renaissance credo! To self-consciousness of WHY and WHY NOT!
Mark: To captivity captive! To filth and garbage dominance!

Everyone lifts glass up in the air, in toast.

Mark: To end Africa's Gen Z tribulations and misery!
Buzzo (lifting his glass in the air, his eyes on Mark): Brilliant! Hold it guys!

Everybody's surprised. They hold their glasses suspended half way in the air, with expectations, eyes on Buzzo.

Buzzo: Brilliant Mark. We are toasting to the Africa's Gen Z, guys. And they are not in our midst?

Everybody looks at him perplexed. Confused.

Buzzo: Our very reason for war at misery is absent. We, all of us here are but a privileged House Gen Z. The Field, the vulnerable unprivileged Gen Z, are not here.

Mezzi, in a sudden assault of guilt, disgraceful spasm, immediately recoils. In expression of frowning grimace, he drops his glass of champagne back on the table as he curses himself out in stern mumbles, settling back into his seat.

Mezzi: I am mortified. Ponderously stupid. Imbecile.
David: This is a brutal, cruel truth. A remarkably gross inadvertence.
Chagrined, David drops his glass back on the table. And in a frenzy grabs his phone and started making calls.
Mezzi (recovers): Yeah Malcom X's House slave, Field slave! Huh Buzzo?
Mark: Was it not Martin Luther King?
Buzzo: Without the people and the people's interest there won't be a Capitol Hill. There won't be a European parliament. Literally there won't be any social media. In Africa the people have no Capitol Hill. Misery has no European parliament. The people's Capitol Hill is the social media. Facebook, Twitter, Instagram are the Peoples European Parliament. The peoples Capitol Hill. The social media is misery's bespoken parliament. Africa's Gen Z parliament. The megaphone to dominate Misery.

And Mark, his thirst at felicitation leaden, follows suit dropping his glass.
We just witnessed a sudden collapse, a capitulation of plaque complacency inadvertent hint.

> *Our very reason for war at misery is absent.*
> *We, all of us here are but a privileged house Gen Z. The field,*
> *the vulnerable unprivileged field Gen Z, are not here. Without*
> *the people and the people's interest there won't be a Capitol Hill.*
> *There won't be a European parliament. Literally there won't be*
> *any social media. In Africa the people have no Capitol Hill.*
> *Misery has no European parliament.*
> *The people's Capitol Hill is the social media. Facebook, Twitter,*
> *Instagram are the Peoples European Parliament. The peoples Capitol*
> *Hill. The social media is misery's bespoken parliament. Africa's Gen Z*
> *parliament. The megaphone to dominate Misery.*

We leave them taking back their seating positions. Eyes chagrined, but full of contagious determination that appears remarkably brutal, to transcend and subdue any hint at complacency. Ever! Never! Nothing must be in the way of ending and eradicating Africa's youth endemic misery. Misery dilemma. Enthroning in its wake, renaissance credo. A renaissance self-consciousness credo: man at the center of the universe. Gen Z elevates and emerges Gen WHY and WHY NOT. Yes, emerges Gen Y renaissance credo self-consciousness. A credo to dominate the biggest Africa's youth existential dilemma, generation after generation.

The biggest social problem you solve, the most successful you are. And your life becomes meaningful to the Lord: You are most probably welcomed in heaven.

> *The biggest social problem you solve, the most successful you are. And your life becomes meaningful to the Lord: You are, most probably, welcome in heaven.*

In less than thirty minutes David's phone calls have had overwhelming result: now we find the foursome with an enlarged group of Gen Z. Presumably, majority of them should no doubt be "field Gen Z." The brunt of misery. The crucifix of society. Among them we notice three familiar faces – Glenda and Lynda and Brett – the youth – who had courageously demanded of the President during church service "what of our Moslem brothers?"

Now Mezzi remembers vividly and teases and tears at him.

Mezzi: You are Brett, right?
Brett: Yeah. And you are our grandioso, Mezzi!

Mezzi reaches over, shaking hands with Brett.

Brett: My pleasure.
Mezzi: The honor is mine. You still perplexed about the Moslems?
Brett: Not really, after the great lesson of the President on religion.
They do the same thing. The 'lion men of God' and the 'meek looking Imams. They do the same: the vehicles to perpetuate misery.
Mezzi: There is a little difference, a subtlety.
Brett: In America or here in Africa?
Glenda: Which?

Attentions are now fully aroused. Everyone is looking expectantly at Mezzi.

Mezzi: Did you know that Imams are accountable to their earthly spiritual heads? The Emirs, the Sultans?

Glenda (vigorously skeptical): Really?

Mezzi: They take earthly orders from them. They are only confined to spirituality chores in the Moslem world. They don't enslave. They don't own properties in man while the men of God are "lords" on earth. They take no orders from God, because our God is a spirit, omnipresent but not palpable. So, they make and unmake.

Buzzo: In fact, the one does not preach prosperity religion nor owns properties. The other, the priest, preaches prosperity religion and deceives and owns properties.

Glenda: I agree to a certain degree. They are the Status Quo's angels. The despotic hereditary Monarchal Angels. They enslave and pillage and rape for them.

Mezzi: I do think that they are instead, confined to their spiritual chores.

Brett: You might be making sense. I just have not seen a bombastic Imam yet.

Mezzi: Brett, I will introduce you to an Imam who is an acquaintance of mine.

Brett: That would be great. That would help disabuse our inherent biases.

Buzzo: Cool! Now let's take a break and face our chores at captivity captive. At dominating our filth and garbage.

Mark: Yeah. Please the floor is open. Let's drink to our health.

Now the broadened, enlarged felicitation is in full gear. Everybody is busy, intent at something: The foursome, glasses of champagne in their hands between sips, watch with intense curiosity and incredulity the rest of the Gen Z group–the unprivileged, field Africa's Gen Z – as they greedily and inordinately, disorderly dent at, tear at, devouring foods in gulps, amidst chattering and clattering of glasses.

Here, on their table, you have the maximum of flattering and flogging of classic fine table-custom and costume expressed. A crucifixion. Cutleries were ignored for the most part, and yet hands were not washed prior. The table napkins on the table are visible, yet they brushed and wiped their soiled fingers and palms on the table clothes, and on their laps of their clothing. A lot of unforgiving, unapologetic noisy spitting. You can see animalistic snuffling and sniffling in the immediate distance. And yet, they find themselves in an ultimate awesome nature–ridden locations with no open-air sewers, nor stagnant water, with nothing unkempt. Indeed, you have Roses and their remarkable characteristic pleasant scents.

The sense of disgust and the distaste of it all, it provoked in the psychosis of the "privileged house Gen Z", was at the limit of repulse, nausea.

However, they proved they could temper repulsion, aversion with tolerant patience. Tempered radicalism is sophisticatedly at play.

The foursome watch, as the inglorious and yet excusable show of voluptuous gluttony, starts to slow down, simmers down as hunger nears domination. Everything, everybody seems to have regained some sense of self-pity, self- presence, sense of consciousness of the surrounding, sense of purpose, dignity, perhaps ready to finally lend ears to some listening. Save for some of the psychologically proven, who are remarkably busy gathering, packing and putting away left-overs into their knapsacks and bags. Hunger is defiling and predatorial.

Buzzo, careful not to turn their hospitality into contempt, empathy into apathy;

Buzzo: Guys, don't worry about those left-over crumbs. We are here to subdue the spite of hunger. We are here to dominate hunger. It's come right now, the permanency of meals folks.

Those youths, bring their languid stare, fixing him. Then quickly they disengage and continued at their quest at left-overs, as if nothing was said. "An egg in hand is worth thousands in the bush", seems what they silently say to themselves. Nothing, not sense of shame, not sense of humiliation, not scorn, not contempt, not derision, not staring down, not temporary satiation, not promises can temper hunger than the egg in your hands.

David saves the unpleasant scene engaging everyone.

David: Thank you all for your rapid responses at my beckoning.
Brett: You kidding me? We have…I have not seen such generosity of heart all my life. Eating to satiety. Beautiful.
David; We all love food!
Brett: This is not just food. This is sublime food.
Mezzi: You would like to eat like this every day?
Brett: You kidding me? What a question. I will slave to eat like this every day.
Brett (pans, scanning his eyes checking out the crowd): Huh guys?
Almost everybody of the crowd is nodding "the affirmative."
Buzzo: We can all eat like this without slaving. We would only have to make the choice.
Glenda: Choice?
Buzzo: Yes, choice!
Glenda: Africa is devoid of choices.
Lynda: Any choice requires at least two options to choose from.
Buzzo: I believe nobody sitting here today is below 15 years of age except Mark.

In a flash Lynda and Glenda go into a screaming spasm.

Lynda (cupping her screaming mouth with her hands): You kidding?
Glenda: Jesus, he is just 14?
Lynda: Holly shit! Wow! How incredibly close I got to a felony the other night.

Mark: Common Lynda, because of some months under? I am a man. And I look it.

Glenda shoots a look at Mezzi.

Mezzi (smiling): What?

The crowd is lost except the foursome who were the architects of the night of muted debauchery: Lynda and Glenda refused any form of sex (oral and penetration), and used it instead as a tradeoff for the church service. The same church service that shot Mezzi and Mark into the spotlight.

Buzzo: Cool guys. We are a retinue of beautiful Gen Z here, now, today. And amongst us we have graduates at different disciplines or graduating students.

I want to make sure that everyone of us is on the same page with the state of our nation. Our nation is corruption-ridden, our nation is debt-ridden, our nation is economic volatility-ridden, our nation's institutions like the civil service, pensions, customs, security are broken, our nation's healthcare, education, energy, water are grossly inadequate, poorly delivered and inexistent, infrastructure is grossly inadequate and the few, existent are remarkably in a state of disrepair. Gen Z is disfranchised with our future mortgaged. As always has been on this continent.

Buzzo pauses, pans peering into the faces of his audience who are listening hard with a competing, concentrated, disenchanted and curious frowns.

Buzzo (continuing): Our nation is incorrigible. Irreformable. Forlorn, of unutterable misery. Generation after generation. An endemic dilemma, with our many churches and mosques, with our fervent hours at prayers and offerings, withal our Voodoos and incantations, withal our mineral endowment, withal our sunshine, withal our "intelligence", withal our arrogance, withal our 'men of God' and Imams, we are irredeemably corrupt. We have hope-hopelessness, abject misery. There has never been any end in sight. There is no end in sight.

Generation after generation they can only give us empty hope, vacuous hope. They give us vain hope. They kill our bright side, our willing side, our believing part that wants to be loved.

They have the talent of killing our wills. And that brings us to why we are here.

We are here to sow the seed of self-consciousness. Grow our self-consciousness.

Grow our self-consciousness to recognize our misery, to confront our misery, to subdue and eradicate our misery, create our wealth base in order to have our backs and the backs of the generations our descendants. We are

175

here to make possible Black kind can "...contribute something mankind can enjoy".

So, against any equivocations, we are solely gathered here to discuss ourselves, chart us a course for the highest quintessential existential order: make misery captive. For misery's dominance.

> *We are here to sow the seed of self-consciousness. Grow our self-consciousness.*
> *Grow our self-consciousness to recognize our misery, to confront our misery, to subdue and eradicate our misery, create our wealth base in order to have our backs and the backs of the generations our descendants. We are here to make possible Black kind can "...contribute something mankind can enjoy." ...highest quintessential existential order to make misery captive...existential order to make misery captive...order to make misery captive...to make misery captive...make misery captive...misery captive...misery captive...misery captive...misery captive.*

Buzzo pauses once again, scans their attentive faces, as he awaits his words to sink in.

Finding their hint of approval, he continues.

Buzzo: Now as adults nobody should dictate choices to you. You decide choices. Choices are intrinsic in nature. Intrinsic in us. We are born with choices. No place in time is devoid of choices. No place can foreclose choices. Africa does not foreclose choices. God gave us choices. The most beautifully essentially crafted gift: choose Jesus, you have heaven; choose Devil, you have hell. Isn't that supreme sublime democracy from the Lord?

We all have the choices as adults to live or die. Be poor or rich. Be happy or sad. Be intelligent or remain devoid, stupid. Shape our destiny, etc, etc.

Brett: Shape our destiny?

Mezzi: Yeah, shape your destiny. Every destiny equates the amount and the strength of your individual character.

Everyone seems at a loss. Their faces writhed in competing grimaces of frown and wonder and doubt.

Buzzo: Destiny is not preordained. No amount of prayers, no amount of penance, can substitute the character and its strength.

Just imagine the strength of character of God, that made him not complacent at the sixth day of his creation, and out of self-critique, still had the will of strength to strike light out of darkness.

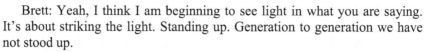

Brett: Yeah, I think I am beginning to see light in what you are saying. It's about striking the light. Standing up. Generation to generation we have not stood up.

David: Bravo, precisely. You are the choice of your situation.

Buzzo: It might sound absurd, but we are the choice of our misery situation.

Glenda: How can we be the choice of our misery?

Buzzo: We shy away from accepting our share of responsibility of our misery.

Glenda: How can we share responsibility in *force majeure*, state of transcendency?

Buzzo: Misery is not *force majeure*. Strong wills decide destiny, Shape destiny.

We choose destiny.

Lynda: We choose destiny?

Buzzo: Yeah! In Africa our choice is always temporary happiness for permanency of sadness.

Glenda (confused and paraphrasing every word in a slow, deliberate mumbles): Temporary happiness for permanency of sadness…temporary happiness for permanency of sadness…temporary happiness for permanency of sadness…temporary happiness for permanency of sadness…

Buzzo: Yeah. In Africa we choose the temporary happiness of child bearing in defiance of the self-conscientiousness of the permanency of sadness of Africa's child's bleak future. In Africa we choose the temporary happiness of consuming chocolates against the permanency of sadness of not transforming our cocoa into chocolates. Same for crude oil refined products importation, temporary happiness against our crude oil refining products exportation sadness permanency. With our weather we choose food insecurity temporary happiness, we choose energy paucity's temporary happiness, we choose pipe borne water dearth's temporary happiness, we choose illiteracy's temporary happiness, we choose kleptomania's temporary happiness, we choose corruption's temporary happiness, we choose glutton's temporary happiness, we, especially the Gen Z, choose complacency's temporary happiness, we choose sloth's temporary happiness…etc…etc. We choose all these happiness's temporariness with their sadness beyond*ness* and beneath*ness* against happiness's permanency choices. Just like sequence of Africa's generations of youth before us. Let's take out some minutes to think about it folks.

> *Yeah! In Africa our choice is always temporary happiness for permanency of sadness.*
> *Temporary happiness for permanency of sadness…temporary happiness for permanency of sadness…temporary happiness for permanency of sadness…temporary happiness for permanency of sadness…*

These words hold everybody to a spell. The air is stilled. Everybody is thinking, reflecting at these powerful words, out of the blue. Buzzo lets the words sink in. And then he continues.

Buzzo: Has any of you sacrificed any comfort, sacrificed your chance at any comfort, at any pleasure ever before?

Almost every face goes into a distorted grimace with air of alarmed complicity, of guilt, as they languidly ponder over the question in ponderous silence.

A silence, that is immediately pierced by a sonorous voice paraphrasing out of sync in the distance.

Sonorous Voice: Sacrificing your chance at comfort, at pleasure on my property? What an audacity of courage.

Everybody of the guests looks up in the direction of the voice with a start, ready to stutter.

Ponderously surprised, their eyes blazing recognition, Buzzo, Mezzi, David and Mark recognize the unmistakable voice: that of Mr. George, the father of Buzzo and Mezzi, who is standing in the door's threshold, appearing from nowhere like a ghost, interrupting, in the middle of Gen Z meeting.

Nothing gave away his arrival: no prior household order for culinary, no entertainment preparations. No usual siren or the welcoming ponderous silence of the kids of the hamlet. Indeed, nothing stupefying: the immediate past has seen the President revoke and withdraw the services of the State Private Security Services accorded V.I.Ps.

While Buzzo, David and Mark promptly struggle out of their seats in a bid to welcome him, Mezzi sits on, unperturbed, scanning, checking out his father's mood.

He notices his father's arrogant spiteful demeanor, still consumed in the fabrics of raging anger of misplaced defiance. No sign of remorse or chagrin.

Buzzo (standing and getting out of his seat): Dad, what a surprise.

Mezzi: That's a brutish surprise. Why are you still looking vicious and cruel like a completely unhinged beast?

Mark (somewhat in bewilderment): Uncle, welcome.

David: Welcome, Uncle. What a pleasant surprise. How was the journey?

Mr. George, with his eyes trained on Mezzi, ignores everybody, ignores every greeting and ignores every stare amidst the eerie silence. Mezzi engages and holds his stare fervidly.

The crowd understands who they have before them and recovers. They relent, relaxing, curiously gearing to watch and listen to father and sons engage in impromptu meeting, and in impending unscripted heated points of views and rebuttals.

Mr. George (his nose wrinkling, his face contorting, his mouth puckering with contempt): Sacrifice at some comfort? That's a pretty good theme. A God-forsaken pretty cheap concept for your generation to understand.

Buzzo takes in his father's phrases and stops short in his tracks, forcing both David and Mark to hold off and guess his next move of a shebang. Then in a sudden assault of hysteria, he screams:

Buzzo: Dad, look at me!

Mr. George disengages his disdainful stare from Mezzi and fixes Buzzo.

Buzzo, his face in a fierce contorted grimace, his fume of anger and disappointment transcending words, holds stare with his father in silence. And suddenly, cell by cell, his body drew back into itself: the emotion of elation and surprise were in a flash overrun and replaced by a cold grieving anger that is once cynical and sorrowing.

Buzzo (coldly): Only to a stupid man it is given not to understand his limits and limitations.

Mezzi: Can you hide the bulge of pregnancy? Is it undisputable that these youths before you represent our sins at ostentatious, kleptocratic comforts and bombasts? Buzzo: You are of the illusion that these youths, just look at them, this Gen Z youths, like the sequence of generations of youths before them you fostered with stress, anxiety and misery don't understand they are our comforts? That they are the prize of our comforts? That you and the evil you represent feed fat on them?

At those words the crowd writhes into restrained amazement that is stupefying, consternating, shocking, and delighted at the same time.

Mr. George's face, in a proprietary smugness, wanes into tortured contorted smile.

Mr. George: You call your father stupid? You boys are lost. No bases, no basics. I don't want to curse you boys out. You have already lost it. No more virtues in honoring parents. No dignity. You have all lost your honor.

But the last thing you want to do is sacrifice the honor, and the dignity, and the comfort of my abode, and my landed properties, for your socialism debauchery and conspiracy sadism.

These words, in no small measure got Buzzo and Mezzi voluptuously infuriated and inflamed. And in a flurry, they get into seizures of ponderously inflammatory profane retorts:

Mezzi: Dad, you really pale beneath stupidity. You are the quintessential abuse of honor and dignity…

Buzzo: …Dad, you remain immensely pitiable in your ruthless pursuit of power, profit, pleasure and humiliation…

Mezzi: …No Buzzo! He remains excruciatingly pitiable in his cloak of fear and guilt. That's his irrefutable constant haunting dark angels…

Buzzo: …Dad, the saddest thing you can say of a man, of any man, is that he is tough. No emotions. A robot. A zombie. It's ponderously stupid to remain enfeebled in this dress of weakness. Toughness is a dress of weakness. A dress of lies.

Mezzi: In all human endeavor and efforts to distort, obstruct, twist, besmirch and conceal, truth always remains triumphant. For truth is God. Your conscience. Won't it be pleasant for you to find truth and finally live a decent, peaceful, fulfilling life?

Before Mezzi could finish those words, Mr. George has, in a flash, disappeared into nowhere. Just as he came.

There was ponderous surprise and shocking silence. A silence that's grieving, sorrowing and delightful at the same time.

The crowd, watch in a confused amazement the two incensed, frenzied faces of Buzzo and Mezzi collapse into expression of wretched suffering and shame.

Their family and what they represent is their medal of disgrace. It is of such a pitiable disgrace of ultimate forlornness, of a remarkable chagrined spectacle.

Yet with equal vigor, there seems to be enormous pride for and gratitude to them in their unquestionable determination, perseverance and fortitude, in dedication to and leadership of the Gen Z cause.

These found virtues, the found solace, the found intrinsic faith of hope that, the Gen Z find in them, that is trusting, is beyond price.

Now Lynda breaks the lingering tensed, complicit silence that is solemn, instructive and discomforting at the same time:

Lynda (to her fellow Gen Z crowd): That was something, some real thing. Folks, those were some real men. Folks, those were some real courage. Folks, that was real lesson of sacrifice at comfort.

Brett: Courage in its raw and pristine state and nakedness of truth in profile. Folks applause to our undisputable role models.

Everybody stands to a deafening applause to Buzzo and Mezzi.

They watch Buzzo and Mezzi struggle out of their blazing reflections, back into the reality of the moment. They join in the applause.

To that extent, they collegially broke ranks, forcing back the air and serenity of the aura of their present chore of discussion.

Yet, Mezzi creases back into contorted grimace of wonderment:

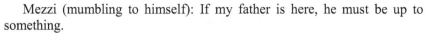

Mezzi (mumbling to himself): If my father is here, he must be up to something.

Buzzo: Right. David you need to urgently inform your father.

Mezzi: Please do it now. My father is no good.

Buzzo: Sorry folks, where did we leave off?

Lynda: Yeah Buzzo... we were at chance... comfort... pleasure? Sacrifice chance at comfort...sacrifice chance at pleasure...chance at comfort...chance at pleasure...comfort...pleasure?

Buzzo (in a reluctant smile): Each one of us has comfort and or pleasure that we can sacrifice.

Mezzi: True. Jesus said "leave everything and follow me" for the kingdom of heaven. Mark: Right. And the poor felt they could not. They lost out.

Brett: The rich. Not the poor.

Mezzi: The poor at heart. Remember!

Buzzo: Just like our 'men of God.' They preach heavenly comfort to you all, but indulge in earthly comfort. Ask yourself why?

Brett: There is something sinister about this comfort thing. Simply put, they don't believe in what they are preaching to us.

David: Africa's 'men of God' are poor at heart. They are indolent. Craven. Comfort in others' discomfort.

Buzzo: Precisely. Comfort sublimates the moment you can sacrifice it for anything sublime. Anything to progress humanity, from where humanity is, is sublime.

Sacrifice the corrupt comfort, provided by our parents. Sacrifice the permanent comfort, provided by the discomfort of others. Sacrifice our comfort at sloth, sacrifice our comfort at complacency, sacrifice our comfort at vain, sacrifice comfort for the pleasure of your food, of your shoes, of your clothes, sacrifice comfort for your cheating, sacrifice our comfort at debauchery, at willful blindness, at willful hypocrisy, at your selfishness, at your laziness. Risk discomfort for the progress of collectivity. Sacrifice your chance at any comfort for a temporary sadness, risk discomfort for an unknown outcome, for a revolution to progress humanity.

> *...Folks, that was real lesson of sacrifice at comfort at play.*
> *...Comfort sublimates the moment you can sacrifice it for anything subliminal.*
> *Anything to progress humanity, from wherever humanity is, is sublime.*
> *Sacrifice the corrupt comfort provided by our parents. Sacrifice the permanent comfort, provided by the discomfort of others. Sacrifice our comfort at sloth, sacrifice our comfort at complacency, sacrifice our comfort at vain...sacrifice your chance at any comfort for a ...*

> *...temporary sadness, hardship, risk, discomfort for even an unknown outcome of a revolution to progress humanity.*

Once again, the power of his words and the fascination for his extemporaneous speech hold the air spellbound. The air is silenced with palpable incantation. And every aura of the air in its wake.

You can feel the solemnness of the situation. Like a solemnness of a homily.

Then Buzzo, once again, breaks up the deafening deep and sublime air of silence:

Buzzo: Brett, David, Mark, Glenda, Lynda...all of you, once again can any of you guess why we are here now, today?

Glenda: Probably to celebrate Mezzi and Mark. Their awesome performance at hope?

Yeah, I honestly think they should be celebrated. I am not sure I know.

Lynda: I can't remotely guess the reason for such an abundant feasting away.

Buzzo (shaking his head disapproval): You delude me folks. Let me repeat: we are here to grow our self-consciousness to contrive something mankind can enjoy and...

Glenda: And consequently, have our backs and the backs of our descendants.

Brett: Making misery captive for black kind to have respect wherever it finds self.

Buzzo: Cool! Renaissance credo self-consciousness is the lone reason of Gen Z. We are born to incarnate renaissance credo self-consciousness in order to have our back and "...make something mankind can enjoy" and have the backs of generation our descendants and they theirs, and theirs's theirs in sequence. Ad infinitum.

Having said that let's have a go at the grammar of sowing the seed of self-consciousness. Now do we all agree that there is a family of Human species?

Everybody silently nods the affirmative.

Buzzo: So, we all agree that we, the Black pigmented are a part of the human species?

Everybody once again silently nods "yes."

Buzzo: Obviously something informs us rightfully that we are human beings. That something that informs us, makes us aware of who we are is called self-consciousness.

Everybody's face creases into air of relief.

Buzzo: Now, why hasn't that something, that self-consciousness inform us, the black pigmented, why we human beings are here on this earth? Why we are given birth to? Why we come into the world naked. Literally naked without any clothing, jewelry or any material thing? And why our certainty of death and our certainty to die without any material wealth to our graves? And not by any choice of ours. Except of course by rare cases of a cowardly suicide?

Brett: That's a compelling question. Honestly, I have never asked myself this before. Never heard this before from anyone. Why we are here on this earth...why we are here on this earth...why we are created...why we are given birth to...why we must all die...why we come literally naked with nothing and must die and depart this earth to our graves without material wealth?

Buzzo: Yes, does what we can call 'life interval' make sense, if only we are born and must die and die with nothing? Shouldn't we all, have doubts in some way about our brief life-essence here on earth? Why God Lord, or if you prefer Nature, whatever, created life and then can end it at wish and will, without warning? Why, what for?

What's the essence? What's our life purpose?

Lynda: For us women may be to make children.

> *...does what we call "life interval" make sense, if only we are born and must die without our knowing, without our making, and we must be born and must die with material nothing? shouldn't we all, have doubts in some way about our brief life-essence here on earth? Why God Lord, or if you prefer Nature, whatever, created life and ends it at wish and will, without warning us or our permission...What's our life purpose?*

Almost everyone cracks up laughing at this sudden and apparent languorous but sincere consideration of Lynda. She really did defuse the built and mitigated the building tension.

These youths have not been handed down classical sense of education – Grammar to Logics to Rhetoric, from generation to generation. The process of critical thinking, rationalization, critical analysis is remarkably wanting. Absent.

Glenda: Common Lynda! After all you've been through in your miserable life, you are really not good at memory.

Brett: Common Glen, let's hear your views instead!

Glenda (piqued and sarcastic): May be to guarantee life on this earth. Just like Lynda said.

Buzzo (ignoring her undertone): Yeah, while progressing humanity is no doubt part of it, however, human beings must be here, on their relative intervals of time, determined between date of birth and date of death, for an essential reason. Mission. Purpose. I don't think the good God or Nature or the Hydrogen Mass did this for some kismet. Fluke. Huh guys, to produce children without having their backs? Black kind self-consciousness has not informed if we are here as human beings on this earth to produce or consume?

Everyone is remarkably subdued to a pensive frown.

Buzzo: Sorry guys if I insist in asking. Let's look at it from another angle: why would a race define her life-style with things like bicycles, cars, trains, airplanes, current electricity, pipe borne water, computers, phones, television, healthcare, education, space conquest, artificial intelligence, name them, etc., etc. within their life intervals, generation to generation? And another race within the same life interval is dumb? Won't define her life-style, won't even copy, just hands out misery, lives in misery. Embraces misery. Just evil. As a life-style?

No words are proffered. The silence deepens with their faces creasing into moaning but expectant honest frowns.

> *why would a race define her life-style with things like bicycles, cars, trains, airplanes, current electricity, pipe borne water, computers, phones, television, healthcare, education, space conquest, artificial intelligence, name them, etc. etc., within their life intervals, generation to generation? And another race within the same life interval is dumb? Won't define her life-style, won't even copy, just hands out misery, lives in misery. Embraces misery. Just evil. As a life style?*

Buzzo: What could be the exegesis that, the one works hard inventing, innovating, enabling her race, defining a life-style and the other one docile, but kleptomaniac, fractious, destructive but gullible, glutton but lazy, devious, evil but prayerful, retrogressive, punitive, humiliating, mendacious, sacrilegious, unpatriotic, chicanery, savage?
Which would you be inclined to choose between the two?

Buzzo, with much suffered chagrin did not fragment the much-numbed air of silence. Delicately, did not humiliate them. He just continued in his monologue, teaching, hopeful to enable them power off their critical reasoning mechanism of the brain. Grow their mind. Grow their self-consciousness.

Buzzo: It is pristine, it is clearer than sorrow, it is obvious than lamentations, it is wiser than prayers that human beings are here on this earth to make this place better than we found it. Human beings are here on this earth to make this place better than we found it...beings here on this earth to make this place better than we found it... here on earth to make this place better than we found it...on earth to make this place better than we found it...earth to make this place better than we found it...to make this place better than we found it...make this place better than we found it...this place better than we found it...place better than we found it...better than we found it... than we found it.

Generation to generation...generation to generation...generation to generation to generation, in continuum.

Otherwise we have failed...otherwise we have failed... otherwise we have failed. We have failed. Have failed. Failed.

> *It is pristine, it is clearer than sorrowing, it is more compelling than lamentations, it is wiser than prayers that human beings are here on this earth to make this place better than we found it. From generation to generation*, **ad infinitum**. *That's the meaning of human's "life-interval" on this earth with the Lord. Otherwise we have failed. Failed! Failed!!*

Buzzo engages again their attentive, expectant but yet solicitous frowning faces, and continues.

Buzzo: Did you all hear me? Whether you agree or disagree, no cavil, no quiddity. That is the truth. Black kind has failed. Africa has never made her descendants better than herself. It is peremptory to say that it's our turn now to make this place better than we find it, to make ourselves better, to make our descendants better than us. We must sow the seed of self-consciousness to "...contribute something mankind can enjoy."

Buzzo pauses once again amidst their collected mental notes that however hints their approval to continue.

Buzzo: Even though, and I agree that we are living out disappointments and delusions and abandonment and misery at the hands of generations before us, we the Gen Z are here to make a single choice: our choice to sacrifice for the progress of collectivity. The house Gen Z, the main street Gen Z, together, we must make that choice.

That choice comes from a simple truth. A simple truth that has eluded us for so long. The simple truth is that, we the Gen Z on this continent, have never accepted our share of responsibility of the pain, sorrow, misery we beget and go through. That's why we have not dealt with our pain and sorrow. We have been cringingly, complacently craven. We have a craven self-consciousness. Just like our fathers before us. And our father's fathers before them. An unutterable craven selfconsciousness of laziness capable of consuming. Black kind self-consciousness instead of standing up quits. Instead of daring our despotic tradition we dare the Sahara Desert, the Mediterranean Sea, we gain contemptuous compassion or at best the Christian's sign of the cross compassion from our obliged poor European hosts. Then we overstay the welcome by showcasing our incivility, stemming from our primitivity, urinating and defecating and spitting on their streets, in the 21st century? Then we refuse to build from bottom up. Fastest money making. We turn on them with overwhelming drug trafficking, prostitution trafficking, human organ trafficking, cyber thefting and then we come out permanently bruised. Nowhere to go, but prison perpetuity.

And should we not ask if we have this audacity to turn against a compassionate host in his land, trying to destroy that fabric of progress and development that gave a lifestyle everyone is copying, is it not easier, instead to dare the status quo, dare our parents for our just cause to make misery captive here at home in Africa?

Everything under the sun has its cause and meaning. Just like every action and reaction. Just like every love and hate. Just like every comfort and discomfort. Just like every sign and the signified. Just like every beginning and ending. Just like every life and every death.

So, it will immensely help to know the three dimensions of the field, brunt Gen Z…

Brett: Our three dimensions?

David: Yes. Not your height, width or length. Those form part of physical properties of any object, but your psychology, physiology and sociology.

Lynda: Our three dimensions are hunger, desperation, hopelessness.

Glenda: It's tribulation. It's joblessness…

Brett: We need food. We need job. We need hope.

Lynda: Yesterday was a mirage. Today is a mirage. Tomorrow will be a mirage. Glenda: This is no life. We have all been sacrificed already. I wish we have something we can sacrifice to eat like this every day.

Buzzo: Ok! Ok! Ok! Get it.

Glenda: No! No! No! That's pretentious and presumptuous of you. You can't get it. You can't understand our fears and our sorrows. You have not lived it. We are here listening to you, because you and Mezzi are pristine, pure excellent souls. We respect your courage. Your high level of self-consciousness. We admire your tenacious perseverance of conviction, of your purpose, to kill Africa's misery. We have heard about you guys. Your ponderous courage to recognize, question, refuse, reject, confront, renounce.

Renounce your corrupt privileges at home, in the USA and take the fight directly to the cruelty and callousness of injustice against the African youths, for all of us your peers. It is flabbergasting, mind boggling. We are here because of these values and the hopes you represent. And we appreciate you very much. Believe me. You give us conviction, choice, leadership, direction and hope.

Glenda, abruptly stops, shooting a grinning persuasive frowning face to the crowd, underpinning those facts.

Glenda: Huh folks? For these virtues and values, the minimum we owe them is loyalty. Don't we?
Crowd: Yesssssss! More…more than loyalty!

> *The choice comes from a simple truth. A simple truth that has eluded us for so long.*
> *The simple truth is that, we the Gen Z on this Continent Africa, have never accepted our share of responsibility of the pain, sorrow, misery we beget and go through. That's why pain, sorrow and misery are dealing with us.*
> *We have been of cringing craven self-complacency.*
> *Instead of standing up, we quit. Instead of daring our despotic tradition we dare the Sahara Desert, the Mediterranean Sea, we gain contemptuous compassion or at best the Christian's sign of the cross compassion from our obliged poor European hosts.*
> *Then we overstay their welcome by showcasing our incivility, stemming from our primitivity, urinating and defecating and spitting on their streets, in the 21st century, as if in justification of Jim Crows' laws?*
> *Then we refuse to build from bottom up. Fastest money-making syndrome for egos in Africa. We turn on them with overwhelm of drug trafficking, prostitution trafficking, human organ trafficking, cyber thefting and then we come out permanently bruised. Nowhere to go. But prison perpetuity.*
> *And should we not ask if we have this audacity to turn against a compassionate host in his land, trying to destroy that fabric of progress and development that gave a life-style everyone is copying, is it not easier, instead to dare the despotic Status Quo for our just cause of making misery captive here at home in Africa?*

Glenda (back to Buzzo): Even so…even so you have never gone to bed hungry. Have you ever gone to bed every day, systematically hungry with the palpable self-consciousness, hopelessness of sure hunger tomorrow when you wake up? All of us African Gen Z cry everyday of desperation. If you listen carefully in the black distance of the night, you will hear the stilled blue silence of the African darkness fragmented and fractured by our sobbing. Sobbing of the African Gen Z. Africa's just great at making orphans. So much so that no African child has known, has enjoyed the innocence of childhood. None. Everybody has one excruciating cruel and bruising memory of sadness or another. Have you ever been to one of our mass burials of starved children? Have you ever witnessed impotent, a famished dying child, laid to rest by vultures? You cannot get it. Who feels it, knows it!

Everybody seems stunned. Eyes are trapping water, turning red.

Most times, a whole bunch, are beclouded and enfeebled by fleeting memories, distractions. Why and where a miserable mind finds the audacity to make its misery oblivious, remains a mystery. Praises to Glenda who, regardless had the acuity recount of the sorrowful constant presence of their being.

It's been said that nothing in life is wiser than sorrow. The ultimate wisdom. The ultimate sorrow.

The foursome are chagrined, even though for no fault of theirs.

Mezzi visibly moved, gets slowly to his feet and walks over to Glenda hugging her.

Buzzo: Bravo! Your mind is so powerful. Remarkably, constructively lucid. You see the present so clearly. Your acuity of the misery, amazing. Our self-consciousness is being sown. It's awesomely in the making.

Please, a round of applause to Glenda.

The crowd applauds Glenda remarkably.

Buzzo: I love the glow of passion in Glenda. We need a sublime animation of passion to achieve the catharsis of our effort.

Brett: If passion can guarantee that eating like this isn't a chimera, a dream, I am ready to permanently animate the highest passion.

Buzzo: We are here not to eat like this. We are here to choose to eat better. We are here to make that choice. We are here to sacrifice the temporary eating like this for a permanency of eating better than 'like' this. Sacrifice our choice of temporary comfort at eating like this against permanency of misery. For Misery dominance. *Every sacrifice is wiser than failure. Every failure begets fulfilment and not sorrow. We cannot wrap our pains in the comfort of our sorrows. No sorrow is comforting. We should sacrifice our sorrows in the strength of our life struggles. As our reasons to be. Right to any meaning.*

Lynda: I wish we have any comfort or indeed sorrows to sacrifice though.

Mezzi: Your time at television, is comfort and sorrow enlaced in the same time lapse. Your time at gossiping is comfort and sorrow enlaced in

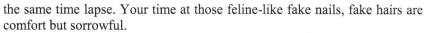

the same time lapse. Your time at those feline-like fake nails, fake hairs are comfort but sorrowful.

Lynda: Oh boy, those are our only survival set mechanisms. You want me to sacrifice those choices at dream of comfort? Sacrifice my outward looks? Sacrifice my toning creams? Those optics help keep us dreaming. Hoping in hope.

Mezzi: Yeah. You are all hopeholic. Happyholic. They becloud your minds. Mess your thinking and thoughts. Derail you. Deprive you. Imperil you. Bedevil you. Idle minds enslavement.

Lynda: What else can we do? How do we progress collectivity? With what? For who?

Buzzo: For ourselves. To have our backs. For our kids. For generations coming. With ourselves. With our choices of sacrifice at comfort. That's the calling of every human being.

Glenda: Like I said, if progressing collectivity is your conviction, we will stand up and follow you.

David: So, let it be! For White kind did it. The Japanese did it. The Koreans did it, the Chinese are doing it. Every one of them had their moments of disfranchisement. We should do same. Progress collectivity. Progress collectivity, progress collectivity. Progress collectivity. Progress collectivity. Progress collectivity. Progress collectivity.

Buzzo: Every human being of any race has individuality DNA. Has selfishness DNA. Has primal instinct DNA. Has survival DNA. How is it that the White race and the Yellow race can sacrifice their DNA at individuality, at selfishness, at superego for collectivity? And our race does not?

Brett: Why our race cannot sacrifice, overcome our selfishness for collectivity?

Buzzo: Precisely! First and foremost, do we Gen Z agree to the premise that collective force is stronger than any individual force within the same realm?

> *Every human being of any race has individuality DNA. Has selfishness DNA.*
> *Has primal instinct DNA. Has survival DNA...How is it that the White race and now joined by the Yellow race can sacrifice their DNA at individuality, at selfishness, at super Ego for their Collectivity? And our race does not?*

Crowd (in unison, a voluptuous response): Yes!

Buzzo: Collectivity over individuality?

Crowd: Yeah, collectivity over individuality! Collectivity over individuality.

Buzzo: Individual gifts, individual talents, individual hard work for collective progress? Individuality feeds collectivity?

Crowd (repeating in unison): Yes. Our individual talents, gifts, hard work to progress collectivity. Individual talents, gifts, hard work to progress collectivity.

Buzzo: Gen Z epitomizes collectivity. We are collectivity…yeah?

Crowd: Collectivity…collectivity…collectivity…collectivity…

Buzzo: Collective electric energy, collective pipe borne water, collective health care, collective schools, collective happiness, collective empathy, collective spending, collective consumption etc., etc., etc.

Then, why in your opinions, individual generators, individual boreholes, individual health cares, individual schools, in sum individual selfishness reigns supreme on the African continent?

> *Every sacrifice is wiser than failure. Every failure begets fulfilment and not sorrow.*
> *We cannot wrap our pains in the comfort of our sorrows. No sorrow is comforting. We should sacrifice our sorrows in the strength of our life struggles. As our reasons to be. Right to any meaning.*

The crowd is doing some mental thinking. This apparent insurmountable, irrefutable unanswered question yet, had lulled, has lulled, lulls constantly large in the psyche of every black person centuries after centuries, decades after decades, every day. A whole race seems incapable of standing up to it. Pondering on it. Answering the question. Just like everything, anything else. Kick the can unashamedly down the road. Always surrendering.

They ignore the very essence of their survival, dignity, honor, respect. Progress. Black race is not dealing with this question. So, the question is dealing with the Black race. And this is the mother of their malaise, misery.

Dealing with it will be their only salvation. Their only salvation from perdition.

Buzzo: In your opinions, why do you think that the oppressed is docile, is resigned, is complacent, is gullible, does not react against his oppressor, has endless ability to endure or endless ability not to react?

> *In your opinions why do you think that the oppressed is docile, is resigned, is complacent, is gullible, is accommodating, does not react against his oppressor, has endless ability to endure or endless ability not to react?*

Lynda: Hunger!

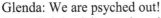

Glenda: We are psyched out!

Brett: Subdued, beaten by misery.

Some voice out in the crowd: We are craven, recreants, poltroons.

David: Hope in the Lord's miracle. Religious palsy!

Buzzo: Excellent points. But I beg to disagree. So, in your opinions, why when the same oppressed is given the chance at life, at power to address issues, he joins them, becomes oppressor? Oppressing the very oppressed world that he is coming from?

David: Yeah, that's what happens. A mystery.

Brett: True! Betrayals. Just count them: our friend turned pastor, our new councilor, our new commissioners, ministers, senators...all of them, the change we voted for to turn things around, not only they forget us, they turn against us...

Lynda: They go in there just to acquire incredible number of cars, Rolex watches, prime properties. Travelling abroad. Acquire and acquire and acquire White man's products, or as you say the White's life-style, with our money.

Mezzi: Yes, very much so. But why would the oppressed cross over, becomes oppressor?

Glenda: I think it's a psychological imperceptible thing. It's as difficult as hell to explain. However, the answer may lie in trying to wear the shoes of an oppressor and the oppressed alike. A house Gen Z like David could explain the oppressor's stand point to start with.

David is surprised and taken aback at the mention of his name. At the subtle attack with a hallmark of unforgiving resentment. His face becomes a sad contorted grimace, that transited into a torment of ascending pain. He is visibly chagrined, countenanced and thought it cruel to remind him of his past, that he and his family, are excruciatingly fighting to transit from.

As the crowd observes and reflects on this once fearsome figure, that is now looking vulnerable and fascinating at the same time, Buzzo saves the situation piercing the miserable complicit silence. Encourages him.

Buzzo: Common David, you are not being accused. Just play our part. We are renegade house Gen Z, whether we like it or not.

Now David recovers from those words and encouraged by the obvious simple truth expressed by Buzzo stands up to the truth of his immediate past.

David: I have not much to say. I was privileged. I was defined by ruthless pursuit of power, pleasure, cruelty. I felt power when I subdued. I felt pleasure when I humiliated, I felt cruel when I pillaged. Pure dopamine. Pure adrenalin. And I think, it's just kleptomania. No other reason.

Then David stops short. His face turning into a tortured sadness, his eyes red, trapping tears.

Then Mark moved with tears streaming down his cheeks starts clapping.

The rest of the crowd joins in, giving a standing ovation to David. Underpinning his courage at mea culpa. Absolute transitional growth.

Now the clapping simmers down, stops and the crowd sits back to listening.

Buzzo: Now let's hear from the oppressed, brunt Gen Z Glenda.

Glenda: Very simple and easy. We are defined by ruthless perpetual submission. We are defined by cruel perpetual humiliation. We are defined by reprehensible perpetual pillaging, raping, ransacking. Our body turns into anger, into rage. Our anger and rage are hopeless, helpless and hapless and they wear into hunger. And hunger perpetuates.

Why the oppressed turns oppressor: from the moment hunger endures, we lose confidence and then our ego. We feel shit. We feel vacuous. We feel hopeless. Neuropsyched out, we become despicable, deplorables. We capitulate. We become vulnerable. Then on the horizon, oppressors' crumbs and crumbles. Their ploy. Our hope rekindles. We submit. We submit to avert physical death. Our excuse. They throw more crumbles. Our fear of hunger simmers down. Our hope, in kind, of oppressors' power 'miracle' kindles. We fear humiliation. We hold them in awe. We resign without pardoning and accept same abhorrent pillaging and ransacking and savagery as ways of life. Willful and blind admiration for our savagery instinct. And we want to be like them. We are like them. We have the edge. Just for the edge.

Buzzo (standing applause): Bravo! Bravo! This is poetry. Common guys…Glenda congratulations for this introspective, courageous, punctilious submission.

> *And we want to be like them. We are like them. Just for the edge? Just for the edge? Just for the edge? Just for the edge? Just for the edge? Just for the edge? Just for the edge? Just for the edge?*

The crowd joins in the standing prolonged applause. Glenda is submerged. Her demeanor is that of a flat flattery. She is to say the least surprised and somewhat confused. Her face is in contorted and convoluted grimaces and wryness. Now the prolonged applause convinces her of their sincerity. She must have done something good if Buzzo who, above others, she admires and holds to highest esteem and has accepted as a mentor, for his intellectuality, courage, perseverance and fortitude is still standing in applause for her.

Now she is overwhelmed. She gets emotional. She stands up clapping in tears.

Then, the applause reluctantly slows, simmering down.

Buzzo: Impressive. Beautiful. Now if we plug on like this, I have no doubt we are going to pluck, win in our intent. Now going back to where Glenda left off, she submitted 'just for the edge' is what turns the oppressed into oppressor. That was a complex psychological analysis. Merits kind of a Noble prize. However, I beg to disagree once again that you can have an edge having, wanting, acquiring, instead of being.

David: Yeah, I agree. To be is life. To have without being first is inferiority complex. It's death. That's what engulfed us. To have instead of to be. The Shakespearean "to be or not to be" is and remains the absolution from misery. "To have and not to have" is ineluctable perdition from misery.

Glenda: I love that. In fact, White race is alive. The Black race is alive. Alive in hell.

Lynda: All those their damn billionaires produce something to enable humanity. African billionaires and millionaires are children of kleptocracy. Kleptomaniacs.

Buzzo: Then, is it true to infer that for an oppressed to turn oppressor, oppressing the very oppressed world he is coming from means that the sum total mass of the oppressed holds no love amongst themselves?

Glenda: Yeah, not only. It's commonplace that we really don't love ourselves at any level in Africa.

Lynda: There is envy, there is hate at every and within any social stratum of African society. Yeah, otherwise how would you explain it?

Brett: Yeah, how would you explain that my friend Daniel buys a used car and won't even look in my direction anymore? He deserted our group. No longer shares any drink with us. Can you believe that?

Buzzo: Before we conclude on this very fundamental moral human spiritual essence, let's shade some more lights: we have kleptomania being the ultimate goal and practice for the oppressor in Africa. Ok?

Everybody silently nods in the affirmative.

Buzzo: Then we have wants, fears and hopes. Any dream has a somber point. That somber point or point of contentment, of reality is the meeting point between want and fear and or between fear and hope. Otherwise dreams become nightmarish. Are you guys there?

Everybody silently nods in the affirmative.

Buzzo: So, on the one side we have wants, plus fear which equals contentment. And on the other we have fear, plus hope which equals contentment.

The oppressor dreads fear, despises contentment, lives wants and celebrates kleptomania. While the oppressed lives in perpetual fear, wishes contentment, revers hopes of wants and is in pursuance of kleptomania.

Buzzo stops and pans at the puzzled contorted faces.

> *Any dream has a somber point. So, on the one side we have want, plus fear which equals contentment.*
> *And on the other we have fear, plus hope which equals contentment.*
> *The oppressor dreads fear, despises contentment, lives wants and celebrates kleptomania.*
> *While the oppressed lives in perpetual fear, wishes contentment, revers hopes of wants and is in pursuance of kleptomania.*

Buzzo: Are you all there? The one dreads fear, the other lives perpetually in it. The one despises contentment the other wishes it. Remarkably the one lives wants and the other revers hopes of wants. And extra remarkably the one celebrates kleptomania the other is in pursuit of it. Strange enough the behavioral pattern of the oppressed, one would say.

There is a deep troubling silence of incomprehension and reflection on their faces. Regardless Buzzo badgers on.

Buzzo: So, what is that single reason in your opinion why an oppressor, why the docility and the palsy of an oppressed, why an oppressed turns oppressor, why an oppressor acquires, acquires and acquires when all human beings born poor or rich must age (if you are lucky), and must die with nothing to their graves?
And the oppressed wants and wants and wants to be like the oppressor? What's that single reason?

The deep silence turns spectral. Spectral of remarkable expectation. The air is stilled with it. No words proffered. They have their eyes trained on Buzzo, with their ears listening hard for any piercing of the spectral silence.

Buzzo: Let's shade some insight that might help us get to that single reason.
At what point does the oppressed heart hardens like that of the oppressor's?

There is an initial fascination of this suggestive question that transits into amazement, that is transcendental and delightful at the same time.
Their already deep troubling silence of incomprehension and reflection contorts, deepens. Their expectant eyes give tacit approval of continuation to Buzzo.

Buzzo (calling out familiar names amongst the crowd): Philosopher Glenda, Sociologist Lynda, all of you, what do you think?

The crowd is inflexibly confused. They remain expectantly rapt, enfolded in themselves.

Buzzo: Is it at the point he loses faith and hope in the terrain justice system or and at the point he loses faith in God's pent-up justice system?

Now their faces get animated. Alive again. Glenda breaks the silence:

Glenda: That might be it. Losing faith and hope in God's pent-up justice system. The only hope that remains when our justice system is blatantly unaccountable. Selectively accountable to the few, the few oppressors, that might be it.

> *That might be it. Losing faith and hope in God's pent-up justice system. The only hope that remains when our justice system is blatantly-brazenly unaccountable. Selectively accountable to the few. The few oppressors. That might be it.*
> *At that point truth and falsehood annuls. Heaven and earth annuls. Reality and virtual reality annuls. Believing and not believing annuls. The diabolical logic of endurance annuls. At that point chaos rules. Nothingness reigns. At that point parents sell their children into sex slavery, the evil man seems blessed and lives voluptuously complacently with ponderous smugness.*

Buzzo: At that point truth and falsity annul. Reality and virtual reality annul. Honesty and dishonesty annul. Heaven and hell annul. Believing and not believing annul. The diabolical logic of endurance annuls. The point of infinite void where nothing and everything is palpable, where nothing and everything matters no more. Everything and anything could reign supreme. Light is extinguished. Darkness is ingrained. Man, floats in vacuum. And to that extent man becomes unsolicited ally to anarchy. To palsy. To willful blindness. To willful defaults…

Brett (confidently animated, jumps in): Churches turn into Sodom and Gomorrah. Mosques are places of silent hypocrisy of unutterable spiritual cannibalism, desecration and calamities. The traditional African shrines places of burlesque irreprehensible spiritual sodomies and falsehood…

Lynda: A point where parents sell their children into slavery… for sex. A point where truth is violated and silently tolerated and accepted…a point where…

Glenda: A point where everyone sees and yet everyone is willfully blind. A complete paralysis. Point where the justice of God does not manifest. The evil man seems blessed and lives voluptuously complacently. With ponderous smugness.

Buzzo: That's the point of no return. The point the oppressed heart flips. Hardens like that of any oppressor. They annul and become void. Vacuum. Nothingness. Nullity.

That point when we lose faith and hope in our justice system and in the pent-up Lord's justice system...that point when a man loses faith and hope in the justice system, loses faith and hope in the Lord's pent-up justice system...point a man loses faith and hope in the justice system and in the Lord's pent-up justice system...a man loses faith and hope in the justice system and in the Lord's pentup justice system...man loses faith and hope in the justice system and in the Lord's pent-up justice system...loses faith and hope in the justice system and in the Lord's pent-up justice system.

At this point the oppressed heart hardens. Flips. A Complete paralysis. Transits into oppressor's heart. Chaos rules. Nothingness reigns.

Buzzo pauses. He scans, panning the now somewhat relaxed, but curiously optimistic expectant faces that are imploding, cheering him to a final catharsis.

Buzzo: And that brings us to the reasons of the whys. Why an oppressor? Why the hardened heart of an oppressor? Why the palsy and the endless ability of the oppressed to endure? Why the oppressed, turns oppressor? Heart hardens? Why?

> *And that brings us to the reason of the whys. Why an oppressor? Why the hardened heart of an oppressor? Why the palsy and the endless ability of the oppressed to endure? Then why his heart hardens? Why he turns an oppressor?*

And the simple but single sublime answer, I think, is primitivism. Primitiveness. Primitivity! The single reason is not in the realm of beyond*ness*. It's in the primitivity of self-consciousness. The primitivity of Africa's self-consciousness.

Africans' minds have not evolved. Our minds, our self-consciousnesses are moronic, like that of children, still remarkably very primitive...Africa's self-consciousness is still remarkably very primitive ...self-consciousness still remarkably very primitive...still remarkably very primitive...remarkably very primitive...very primitive.

Amidst the return of a voluptuous and ponderous silence, the lone known voice of Glenda braves and pierces the air first, leading a litany of others:

> *And the simple but single sublime answer, I think, is Primitivism.*
> *Primitiveness. Primitivity! The single reason is not in the realm of*
> *beyondness. It's in the primitivity of self-consciousness. The*
> *primitivity of Africa's self-consciousness.*

Glenda: Primitiveness?

David: I totally agree. Sequence of Africa's primitivity mindset. Primal instinct stage.

Brett: I am puzzled and doubtful with equal vigor. But we can drive cars. Fly airplanes. Use phones. Use computers. Social media and all. Do everything they do.

Mezzi: Yes, we can do everything they do. But we don't. They think hard to invent and innovate, we don't. They work hard for collectivity, we don't. Besides, we don't make everything they make. They make collective health care, collective education, collective energy source, collective treated water supply, collective mass transit system, they make cars, airplanes, phones, computers etc... etc... and we don't.

Brett (point of view deflated): So why are we still primitive in your opinion?

Mezzi: That's the question we need to answer. Not answering this question has been centuries coming. Our nemesis.

Buzzo: Our scourge. Sloth our scourge. Slothfulness. Why we remained primitive, why our self-consciousness remained primitive is because of our laziness. Our slothful life style. We remain vulnerable because of our slothful ways. We are always susceptible to colonization, to dehumanization, by any hard-working race. First to the White race. Now to the Asians. Why? Our slothful scourge.

Crowd (ruptures to mixed reactions): Not completely true! I don't think so! That's true!

Buzzo: Ok, no hurries, let's just calmly think as we ponder about it.

I think kleptomania is because of vacuity. We are docile because of vacuity. We are gullible because of vacuity. We have palsy of religion because of vacuity. We lag because of vacuity. We retrogress because of vacuity. We are confused because of vacuity. Vacuity of the mind. Of the brain. African brain is orphaned by vacuity of sloth! Folks, our slothful way hinders, blinds our race to figure out that our collective wellness is more than our individual wellness. Our sloth hinders the reason we are here on this earth, the reason we are given birth to. We are here to make this place better than we found it. Our sloth hinders us to dominate our filths and garbage. To dominate our environment. The singular reason why we are here on earth, why we are created is to dominate our environment and endure its progress. Make our descendants better than ourselves. And for that axiom to be progressed from generation to generation. Exactly what the Whiteman does. Give it to him.

Everybody falls back into silence. The truth of these words pierces their veins, their souls like the sharpest of swords would the body.

Now you can observe the contorted, convoluted, puzzled grimaced faces unravelling and relaxing, accepting, convinced, this solemn truth.

Buzzo (unflinching, badgers on): Any doubt is palpably, remarkably dispelled by series of I-Phones...1234567891011, series of cars, of tractors, of trains, of buses. Schools. Colleges. Clothing. Cosmetics. Healthcare. Entertainment. Constructions, Computers, Energy, Health Care. Airplanes. Pipe borne water.

Just look around, look around you, everything has its precedent progressed in time and space. Innovations. Evolve the brain. Evolve the mind. Dominance and evolution.

Glenda: Bravo Buzzo. Thank you for connecting these dots and keys. Eh, guys?

Glenda overwhelmed with excitement gets to her feet. She solemnly walks to Buzzo with air of respect that seem pure, dissimulated and unfeigned, and gives him high five in validation.

Glenda: God bless you Buzzo. Collectivity against narcissistic individuality. Primitiveness. Primitivity of our self-consciousness. Sloth. Slothful scourge. We are here on this earth to make this place better than we found it. Dominate our filths. Dominate our garbage. Dominate our environment. make our descendants better. Dominance!

Sloth obliterates this existential reason. Nobody, not our professors, not our leaders, not our parents have taught us much in one go. Not in all our short life times.

She suddenly takes a break. Heaves a sigh of relief and now in mumbles, as if talking to herself:

Glenda: We are primitive. Evolution. Evolve the mind, our self-consciousness. Evolve the brain. Brain and mind vacuity. Dominate our filths and garbage. Dominate our environment...

Brett (interjecting): Our parents' laziness. Laziness won't let them overcome primitivity. Thank you Buzzo. Today is a day of sublime catharsis. Thank you Buzzo. Incredible.

Glenda, meanwhile peers at the crowd and starts clapping for Buzzo.

Glenda: Yes! Yes!! Yes!!! Sow the seed of self-consciousness. Grow our self-consciousness for Dominance. Dominate. Dominate our environment.

Crowd responds to the rhythmic standing ovation. A standing ovation of a voluptuous entity.

Crowd: Dominance! Dominance!! Dominance!!! Our misery captive!

Then standing ovation's voluptuousness reluctantly slows to silence.

Brett: Today is a defining day in our lives. Now we the Gen Z can't say we did not hear, or that we don't know. Laziness is the curse. We got to heal. The antidote is hard work. Grow our self-consciousness. Advance our self-consciousness. Relentless hard work to advance collectivity. Glenda: A total day of sublime catharsis.

Buzzo: I hope you are all confident in this. Now can we claim a little bit that we are beginning to dent at the grammar of our problems, arousing our self-consciousness?

Lynda: Are you kidding me? We leave here today saying: God created us, and the time, the interval, the palpable time period between our birth and death lies our lifepurpose: we are here to make this place better than we found it. This incarnates, embodies our fight for freedom. Dominate our filths and garbage. Have our backs. Make something mankind can enjoy. Have the backs of generation our descendants.

Today is a defining day in our lives. Now we can't hide under any ignorance.
LAZINESS and PRIMITIVITY. Our LAZINESS is colonized by our PRIMITIVITY.
We now know that our Laziness is responsible for our Primitivity.
LAZINESS is the prime supreme curse.
We've got to heal. The antidote is HARD WORK. Relentless hard work to DOMINATE our Filths and Garbage and progress COLLECTIVITY.
If we don't make anything, everything better than we found it, within the Lord's permitted individual "Life-Interval", make our children better than us, we would have woefully failed. There is no plausible excuse not to develop COLLECTIVITY.

As some hint of light, finally seems to descend and pierce through and dent at the lethargic brain of the African Gen Z, as witnessed through their fine unrestrained liberty of expression and wishes to fight for freedom, Buzzo's demeanor, goes into expansive humbling pride and his face creases into expression of exquisite hope. Glimmering.

Buzzo: Cool! Last Sunday these young fellas started the wind of change. We need to cash in on it. Do you all understand that?

Mezzi (before the crowd could react, paraphrasing): Last Sunday Mark started the wind of change. Do you all understand that we must work hard to rid us of Black kind descendants' misery?

Everybody cracks up, laughing. Mark, overwhelmed, proudly shifts in his sitting position.

Crowd (shouting): Yes, yes, we fully understand that!
Buzzo: It is cringing craven to wait for our future to come to us. Huh?
Crowd: Yes, it is!
Buzzo: We should dream the future. We should make the future.

Crowd (ponderously rising to their feet and thunderously): Dominance.

As everybody gets back to sitting positions, and the ponderous validation reluctantly silences, David pierces the air with a testing, tempting, tasty provocation, that puts everyone on their guards.

David: Brett, all said and done, what would you go for first: Food, job or hope?
Brett: Why at me? That's a tricky question.
Glenda: Jobs, no doubt. With job you can work harder and determine your destiny. You don't have to slave-sex.
Lynda: I agree 100%. With job you can have aspirations. Independent thinking. You don't have to prostitute for lipstick, you don't have to be sodomized for menstrual pad, for fake hair, for toning cream…

Almost everyone cracks up laughing at the bareness of that societal evil truth. Nonetheless it's surreal, a fate flip, an existential win that the crowd is finally at ease engaging, rationalizing, speaking, in dialectics.

Buzzo: Then let's put it to vote.

Hands go up in the air, raised.

Buzzo: No, no, no Guys. Put your hands down. To popular votes. To our parliament. To Gen Z parliament. Our social media.

Then, to Mezzi and Mark:

Buzzo: Common baby bloggers! Mezzi, Mark, your computers. Common, to work.
Mark: Uh, finally some activity.

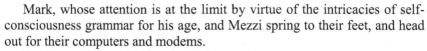

Mark, whose attention is at the limit by virtue of the intricacies of self-consciousness grammar for his age, and Mezzi spring to their feet, and head out for their computers and modems.

Buzzo continues with the rest of the crowd.

Buzzo: In about 15 weeks from today, we are going to have a continent's descendants hope. Our Gen Z platform from where to obliterate our perpetual misery. David?

David: Thank you Buzzo. Guys, for our revolution against misery we need to understand fully our pressure, from within us in order to support the vision above, from without. Our pressure must be subjected to and vetted by the grammar of it all, by the logic of it all and by the rhetoric of it all. The classic education. The welleducated mind...the educated mind...educated mind...the educated mind.

The educated informed mindset. The informed mindset. The mindset. Gen Z Mindset. We must defeat ignorance on our land. Grow our self-consciousness to dominate. The renaissance self-consciousness credo of WHY and WHY NOT. A Gen Z elevates to self-consciousness of WHY and WHY NOT. A Gen WHY and WHY NOT. A Gen WHY emerge to Dominate our filths and garbage. Dominate our environment.

Crowd looks on lost, amazed and at the same time perplexed at the eloquence of a transformed David. His terminologies and construct are amazing. His proximity to the intellectual prowess of Buzzo is at play. Buzzo notices.

Buzzo (repeating to drive home the point): For any revolution to succeed there must be pressure from below, from amongst the majority of the poor people and a vision from above. An illuminated, visionary leadership.

David: The vision is Renaissance Credo. Man is the center of the universe. Please read the Renaissance Man of Florence, Italy. Renaissance Florence elevated man to demigods. Elevated Man with a self-consciousness of a demi-god. We are demi-gods subject only to the almighty Consciousness. The almighty God. We are his image.

Buzzo: Just like him, God, Man is empowered to decode his signs and put out their signified. That is the Renaissance Man. A self-consciousness that nurtured and became. That questioned nature and its signified. That figured out dynamics, forces, gravity, equilibrium. Figured out how a bird flies and made Aeroplan. That figured out how fishes swim and made ships. That colonized the environment, urbanizing. That created freedoms via wheels – current electricity, pipe borne water, transportation for all, health care for all, education for all. That landed on the moon and created telecommunication for all...etc. Just like him work hard, think critically and challenge and invent and find answers to everything. Impossible is nothing.

Lynda: Nike! No, Adidas!

Everybody cracks up. Buzzo ignores her and continues.

Buzzo: We must believe in God. But believing in God is not enough. We must worship God. But worshiping God is not enough. We must either know God or we must not. Knowing God is doing his deeds. Knowing God is doing his deeds. Knowing God is doing his deeds. Doing his deed. Doing his deeds. His deeds. Deeds.

David: His deeds indeed. His deeds through hard work, creative mind, creativity and nothing is impossible. We hold our destiny in our hands. You want heaven? Renaissance credo.

Buzzo: Our Gen Z hope platform is our renaissance center. The cradle to defeat all our malaise –all our captivities, tribulations and misery. Our cradle to grammar and in other words to critically taste, to recognize the WHY; cradle to logics and in other words to critically analyze, rationalize the WHY and inform the WHY NOT; cradle to rhetoric and in other words to compellingly react with efficacious, impactful decisions, say and enforce the WHY NOT. Dominance decisions. Dominate our filths and garbage.

Mezzi (interjecting): Not just literal filths and garbage but most importantly dominate our mental filths and garbage.

Buzzo: Yeah, absolutely! All in order to obliterate our misery permanently. David?

David: As you well know, you have the first family as an ally from above.

Bellowing voices of the crowd: We see the signs! Would these signs endure, persevere without abandoning us?

The Vision, Gen Z's Vision, is RENAISSANCE CREDO self-consciousness.
Man is the center of the universe. Renaissance Florence elevated Man to the status of a demi-god. Man, at the center of the universe. Man, in charge of his Destiny. The Man-god.
We are demi-gods, only subject to the Almighty GOD. We are created in his image. Man is empowered to decode his signs in nature and put out the signified.
And the renaissance man sprouted and unleashed development and progress decoding the signs of God in nature and unleashed development through science and arts and passions and compassion.
If we truly believe in God, truly believing in God is not enough. If we must truly worship God, truly worshipping God is not enough. We must either know God or we don't.
Knowing God is doing his deeds on earth. Not in heaven. Doing his deed on earth. Doing his deed on earth. Enable humanity. LOVE THY NEIGHBOR like yourself.

David (to the skeptical crowd): I understand how you feel. Let not your faith waver. It's a totally different season. Season of change. Season of faith. Season of deeds. The first citizen is not turning back on us.

Buzzo: Praise the courage of the President. The risk of it all. A Status Quo against Status Quos. The hope alone. It's exciting. It's amazing. We just need to do our own part. The Gen Z part. Total unflinching, unwavering support for this cause. We need to sacrifice the comfort of our time at nothingness. We must sacrifice sloth. Sacrifice complacency, sacrifice gullibility, sacrifice pretension, sacrifice imposture, kill them with hard work. Appraise 'to be'. Sacrifice 'to have.' You want to eat like this every day? Hard work. You want to impress the Lord guys?

The crowd: Hard work!

Buzzo: You want heaven?

The crowd: Hard work!

Buzzo: You want to dominate our misery?

The crowd: Hard work!

Buzzo: You want to dominate our captivity?

The crowd: Hard work!

Buzzo: Everything is possible with hard work and sacrifice.

Glenda: You want to subdue misery?

Crowd: Hard work!

Lynda: You want to impress yourself and be our role-model and hero?

Crowd: Hard work.

Lynda: Thanks to Buzzo I can recognize the significance of the words of a famous man.

Paraphrasing Denzel Washington:

"Sloth is a greater threat to progress than hardship. Without commitment, you will never start or more importantly without consistency you will never finish. It's not easy. If it was easy there'd be no sorrowing. If it was easy there'd be no tribulation. If it was easy..."

Glenda: *"...There'd be no trauma. If it was easy there'd be no dilemma..."*

Brett: *"...If it was easy there'd be no filth and garbage, there'd be no misery..."*

Lynda: *"...Sloth is a greater threat to progress than hardship. So, Gen Z must keep learning, keep working at renaissance credo self-consciousness to emerge Gen WHY..."*

Glenda: *"...Gen Z can only live once. Gen WHY will live always through sequence of its descendants..."*

Brett: *"...Gen Z must dream with goals. To succeed Gen Z need life goals, yearly goals, monthly goals, weekly goals, daily goals everyday..."*

Glenda: *"...And to achieve these goals the emerged Gen WHY must apply discipline and consistency. Everyday. Everyday Gen WHY got to work at it. Everyday Gen WHY has to plan. As it is said, we don't plan to fail. We fail to plan. Gen WHY must plan to succeed..."*

Brett: *"...To make something mankind can enjoy; Gen WHY must do something in succession of generations of Africa's youth before Gen Z never did."*

Buzzo, overwhelmed but elated with this ponderous, unexpected, pleasant surprise of participated subliminal recitative paraphrase coming from the main street Gen Z, that underpins their speedy cognitive renaissance credo self-consciousness progress, decisively interjects, rising and applauding vigorously.

The rest of the house Gen Z join him in the applause.

Now the applause simmers down and ceases.

David: *"...sloth sucks. Sloth is a greater threat than hardship to progress. If it was easy there'd be no renaissance credo self-consciousness, there'd be no science, no art, no inventions, no innovations, no development, no progress, no hope."*

Buzzo: Completing Denzel Washington's quote: *"...Hard work works! Working really hard is what successful people do...to get something you never had you must do something you never did...every failed experiment is one step closer to success. There is no passion to be found playing small. So never give up."*

So, let's traffic sacrifice. let's traffic perseverance, let's traffic fortitude, let's traffic hard work. Emerge Gen WHY. And traffic sequence of Gen WHY to bury misery.

For Gen WHY can only come this way once. For sequence of each Gen WHY descendants can only come this way once. But self-consciousness WHY must permeate this way always.

Mezzi and Mark come back in that moment taking their sitting positions, eyes trained on Buzzo and David, full with expectations, ready to blog.

Buzzo: Have you already prompted them?

Mezzi: No. Not yet.

Mark: We are waiting for a compelling plan of action.

Buzzo: For a compelling plan? Bravo Mark, your vocabulary is growing indeed. Cool. Good boys. Tell them "hello beautiful Gen Z, are you there? Are you ready? We are with you."

Mezzi and Mark go to work tweeting #hello beautiful Gen Z! Are you all there?

Buzzo (back to the crowd): I am excited! Finally, power to the African Gen Z family. Whatever the Gen Z parliament decides, rules. Reigns supreme.

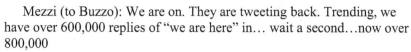

Mezzi (to Buzzo): We are on. They are tweeting back. Trending, we have over 600,000 replies of "we are here" in… wait a second…now over 800,000

Mark: 1.4 million in just five minutes of our tweets…

Buzzo rushes to the computers of bloggers Mezzi and Mark tweeting:
Welcome beautiful Gen Z! # Are we ready to go?

Right away the screens go haywire with tweets responses back "#We are ready to go", "#born ready to go", # ever ready to go", "# go Gen Z. Gen Z go."

So much so that within two minutes we have overwhelming 2.5 million trending '# activities tweet responses.'

Mezzi and Mark have their eyes popping out their orbits with excitement at the screen.

To this extent, everybody leaves their seats and sitting positions, flocking behind Buzzo and David, who were already behind Mezzi and Mark, fixing and observing the #trending activities.

Buzzo: Are we ready for #food or for #job or for #hope?

Immediate Gen Z responses: "#food, food, food, food, food, food, food" overwhelms.

"#hope" takes second place. "#job" ranks last.

David: Food is paramount to them.

Brett: That's the number one priority.

Glenda: You want our Gen Z attention, unfortunately you must preach food. Food is the audacious vehicle to the growth of their self-consciousness.

Lynda: We slave for food. If you ask me, the mantra is food first.

Crowd bellowing: Yes food! Food! Food!! Food!!! There is too much starvation. Too much tribulations on the land. Too much of nothing.

> *You want our Gen Z attention, unfortunately you must preach Food. Food is the audacious vehicle to the growth of their self-consciousness.*

Buzzo raises his hand miming for silence. And drives the point personally:

Buzzo: Brett, what's your choice?

Brett: Job. With job you have power.

Buzzo: Are you convinced? It's no more a tricky question?

Buzzo is trying to, among the main street Gen Z present, ascertain who could be part of his inner circle running of their Gen Z plan and program and project. He goes back tweeting.

Buzzo tweets: #Free food or # Earned food?
Gen Z: #free food, # free food!
'#free food' overwhelms '#earned food,' within some seconds.

This is an appalling defeatist stance. Buzzo however, does not get discouraged in the face of defeatist Gen Z trending tweets. He simply, conversely tries to empathize with them to see and imagine their hunger, starvation, sorrow and miserable endemic dilemma. Nevertheless, he presses on.

Buzzo: #Slave and die for food or #Slave and die for freedom?
Gen Z: #Slave and die for freedom overwhelms absolutely.

Buzzo (smirks. Turns around and checks out the faces. Smiles to himself and in mumble): Even though there is yet a justifiable defeatist psychological lethargy, nevertheless, we will get to their cathartic lexicon flip. He turns and badgers on.
Buzzo tweets: #Free food=#Slave and die for food. #Earned food =#Slave and die for freedom, which do we opt for with vigor?

Gen Z's tweets retort are slow to show up. Everybody is waiting. The air is still and tight with equal vigor. The crowd is not proffering words.

Buzzo (taunting and baiting them): #Are you all there? Which?
Gen Z tweets' retorts are slower than slow to come.

Buzzo (encouraging them): #Freedom, right. #Slave and die for freedom, right?
Gen Z: #Yes! Right!
Buzzo: #Our Gen Z platform is going to give you and guarantee you earned food. Yes?
Gen Z's response: #Yes! Yes!!, Yes!!! # Platform! Platform!! Platform!!! Overwhelms the screen.
Buzzo: #Cool. #We will be giving back loyalty to ourselves. Loyalty of cohesion. Loyalty to platform?
Gen Z's responses: #Yes, #Loyalty. #Loyalty. #Loyalty to platform.
Buzzo tweets: "#Understanding?"
Immediate Gen Z responses: #Understanding what? #Let's go, what?
Buzzo: #Understanding Gen Z. # Understanding ourselves. #Understanding our loyalty to our platform.

Gen Z response is slow to come.

Buzzo: #Gen Z, are you all still there?

Gen Z's responses: # Yes, we are. #Understanding ourselves. #Understanding our loyalty to our platform supreme.

Buzzo tweets: #We need humility. #The power of humility. #Wisdom of humility.

#Humility at classic education. #Classic learning to power off our understanding.

#Power off our moronic self-consciousness.

Gen Z's responses are back on, fully trending: #Gotch you. # Absolutely necessary. #We want to enable understanding...

Buzzo: #Grammar? #Logic? #Rhetoric?

Gen Z: #Yeahaaaaaaaahh, self-consciousness.

Buzzo: #Cool. Then you have a premium! #A premium!

Gen Z: # Yeeeaaaaaahhh. # What premium? #We are waiting for our premiums!

Buzzo: #We want you to form associations. Strong associations, dictated by your different passions of ambition, or skills: mechanics, carpentry, tailoring, welding, trading, teaching, driving, farming etc., etc.

#Register yourselves in these associations.

Gen Z: #Why? We have them already?

Buzzo: #Yeah, best practice organization. # For your premiums.

Gen Z: #What are our premiums!

Buzzo: #Are you ready?

Gen Z: #We are ready.

Buzzo: #You are going to be trained, your skills enhanced, free of charge, and fed for free of charge until you become adept and your businesses will be found and funded by loans or and given employment opportunity. Yes?

Gen Z are assailed by an overpowering spasm of incredulity, at the words of those tweets. Then to realization, they promptly erupt in a dense ponderous clamor of shouting, jubilations, exultations, rejoicing.

Besides, Buzzo is of course expanding the kids must play center, in concept and in a scouring substance, deploying the Imam's will at legacy and money. Mezzi is the only one, among the Gen Z who tacitly knows the secret accord with the Imam.

Gen Z: #Buzzo, Buzzo, Buzzo, Buzzo, Buzzo. #We love you. #We will do anything for you. "#May Lord Jesus bless you," are overtly over-trending.

Buzzo (without responding directly to their tweets, badgers on): #With your premiums, check out the words: #Grammar. #Logic and #Rhetoric. #Themes. #Humility. #Discipline. #Empathy. #Hard work. #Slothfulness. #Perseverance. # Fortitude. #Shame. #Remorse. #Regrets. #Apology. # Self-accountability. #Justice. #Altruism. #Sacrifice. #Premium. #Dominance. #Filth and Garbage. #Environment.

Buzzo (disengages from the computers, turns and faces the crowd): They will have some work to do checking out those words.

In the meantime, guys let's do some work. If you guys agree. We are going to have teams of operations.

David: Division of Labor, sort of.

Buzzo: David, by virtue of your engineering profession, you are going to head Infrastructure Development and Field Operations Development Team. Start working on how to constitute your team.

David nods his consent. Buzzo continues.

Buzzo: Sociologist Brett, you are going to be human resource person. Youth development. You are going to source, scout for talents. Please constitute your team of Gen Z to work with.

Brett: Beautiful. I love it.

Buzzo: Psychologist Glenda, you are going to head the team to resource and coordinate operations for a successful platform take off, the very heart of operations. Glenda (her face an excited frown, shrieking): Hurray to the Renaissance center.

Buzzo: Hospitality Lynda, you are going to handle the team of catering and its comprehensive functions. Eating culture and civility–table manners, eating decently, table clothes, napkins, no spitting, controlled belching and farting. The refuse taken care of. The mind discipline must be seen to and guaranteed. Food is very important and we must accord it elegant demeanor and decency and monarchical table discipline aura all the time. We must differentiate ourselves from animals.

Lynda (in acknowledgement): To filth and garbage dominance!

Buzzo then pauses and takes a rapid scan at some youths in the crowd, pointing out a youth more for his eccentric looks (he is a ragged replica of Prince and the revolution), than for what he could actually be:

Buzzo: Hey Mr. Prince and the revolution can you head the entertainment team?

The crowd erupts in a voluptuous and ponderous sincere laughter of assents. "Mr. Prince" whose real name is Frank is actually a graduate of theatre and fine arts. He promptly acknowledges the call to service, standing up.

Frank: Yeah, what an honor that I arouse the memory of the image of the great Prince. May his soul rest in peace.

Brett: Amen.

Frank: My name is Frank. It will be my pleasure to keep Gen Z busy with music, promote art exhibitions, promote fashion shows, theatre, singing classes, auditions etc. etc. All work and no play they flutter away.

Buzzo: Cool Frank.

Now Buzzo points and calls out a lady who, even though has quietly and attentively listened all the time and had rigorously participated in vigorous rounds of applauses is prominent for her beauty, her tall and slim built, elegance and her regale composure.

Buzzo: Hello lady elegance, discipline and hygiene. What's your name please?

Laura (standing up in acknowledgement): My name is Laura.

Buzzo: My congratulations. I find you absolutely compelling to head the team on hygiene of our platform. Is that fine with you?

Laura: It will be an honor and pleasure.

Buzzo: You are going to have from chemical toilets, from refuse bins, from hoovers, from liquid soaps to liquid detergents down to sanitary towels and napkins. You are charged to be Miss Immaculate. Discipline of the mind and consistency of it for the Gen Z cause.

Folks, we need somebody to handle sporting and recreational activities of various disciplines–indoors, outdoors. The mind must be healthily alert.

And lastly, the team of security. From wireless to physical. Our platform must be smarted.

Folks, lets strive ponderously to fill these two positions as soon as possible. Scout and make your recommendations as soon as you can.

He stops. Pans his eyes scanning everybody as they wait in expectation to further receive instructions: he exudes indefatigable energy.

Buzzo: Guys now let's get to work. We have all we need: our brains. Please apply. I will handle Research and Content Development with bloggers Mezzi and Mark.

And in a flash, he spins, doing a 180degrees spin in his seat, springing to his feet, turning and heading in the direction of Mezzi and Mark, howling out words.

Buzzo: Mezzi, Mark throw these words at them to check out:
#Who is a Gen Z?
Who is African Gen Z?
#Who is a Gen WHY?
What is Status Quo? #Who is a Status Quo?
Who is an incumbent? #What is government? #Who is government?
#Who is an Oligarch?
#What is Africa's Tradition?
#What is Africa's Life Style?
#Why is Africa's descendants perennially in misery?

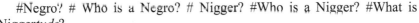
#Negro? # Who is a Negro? # Nigger? #Who is a Nigger? #What is Nigger*tude*?

#What is Respect? #Why is a Negro not respected? #How can Negro earn respect? # What is self-consciousness? # What is and how is Renaissance credo selfconsciousness? #What is a Renaissance self-consciousness mindset? #Why is self-consciousness the bottom line?

Mark's voice suddenly howls in overlap, interrupting Buzzo's, who now reaches, standing before them.

Mark: Protest!
Buzzo (without giving weight to his words, howls): Cool tweet #What is a Protest? #What is freedom? # what is despotism?

Now Mezzi's voice interrupts decisively, vehemently:

Mezzi: Buzzo, a protest. A march of protest just got underway. From different sensitive parts of the city and looks headed to the Plaza, the Plaza Hill, overlooking the President's residence.
Mark (his voice trembling, emotive): They are heading to our house, including the President's lodge and office and the parliament...let's do something.

Then overwhelmed and somewhat confused he raises the alarm shouting:

Mark: David! David, don't just sit there. There is a protest heading to our house.

David is busy with Gen Z task force platform, planning. He ignores Mark as he notices with elation Buzzo insinuating himself amidst Mezzi and Mark.
Buzzo ignores their faces in frowns of consternation, peering straight at their computers. He takes in the situation in a flash and hugs Mark tightly, in a bid to calm his anguish and restore his confidence.
Now David turns and takes a slow reluctant look in Mark's direction. Mark seems calm and that reassured him. Buzzo's tight hugging has apparently smoothened his brother up. Looks like nothing was untoward.

Buzzo: Mark throw these words...
Mark tweets: #Gen Z, have you heard of the protest?
Buzzo: And you Mezzi, these...
Mezzi tweets: #Gen Z, is it true there is a protest?
Gen Z: # Yes! Yes!!, Yes!!! #They just got started. #Some of us are part of them.
Mezzi (tweet): #You are part of the protest?

Gen Z: #Yeah! #Curiosity, infiltration to sabotage! #Yet some are a sold out.

Mezzi has an instant assault of delusion and mumbles out 'Judas, hungry judas.'

Mark (to Mezzi): Calm, no surprises! The usual betrayals, to help build and bolster the crowd for the usual miserable perverse bait and miserable compensation.

Mezzi (recovering): # Who are they?

Gen Z: #A lot of politicians. #Many men of God –the pastors, the Imams, the Mallams, the Voodoo Chief Priests and Priestesses. #The monarchy – the chiefs, the Obas, the Emirs, the Sultans. #The Oligarchs. #Cabals. #Cyber thefting syndicate and their cohorts. #Disgruntled elements against President's beautiful decrees.

Mark (tweets): # Are they armed?

Gen Z: #No reports of arms. They are carrying placards. Looks peaceful.

Mezzi: # Can you read the placards from your position?

Gen Z: # There are too many of them.

Mezzi: #The most prominent.

Gen Z: #"President is an infidel." #"President is a dictator." #"President usurps powers of the land." #"Usurpation is treasonable offence." #"President must resign and must go."

Mark: #They are crazy! #Gen Z, what do we do?

Gen Z: #Fight! Fight!! Fight!!! #We are going to fight. #We reject misery. #Enough is enough. #We've had enough. # We must make our future ourselves.

Mezzi: #Fight?

Gen Z: #Yes. Absolutely. Never again. #Fight. #Fight. #Fight.

Mezzi: #Our sold-out Gen Z, in their midst?

Gen Z: #Our determination and doggedness will overwhelm the cowards, the gulls, the gluttons… win them over to the fighting side of light.

Mark: # Let's go forth. #Misery captive?

Gen Z (overwhelmingly); #Yeah, Yeah. #Misery captive.

Mezzi: #Let's go forth. #Dominate misery, now!
#The right things for the right reasons. #Now!

> *#Our call to duty has suddenly come. #Let's go forth. #Misery Captive?*
> *#Now or never. #Dominate Misery. # The right things for the right reasons. #Now!*

Buzzo, surprised and at the same time overwhelmed by the extemporaneous voluptuous fighting stance, and gladdened by their unconditional enthusiasm, devoid of fear, so far expressed by the Gen Z tweets, jumps into action taking over the situation from Mezzi. He calls out for David, Brett and Glenda. They join him.

Buzzo (without removing eye from the computer): David, Brett, Glenda, over here. Guys, take a look at the computer. We are in a situation room kind of. There is a marching protest out there, against the government. But as you all know, it's against us, the Gen Z. And we need to redirect it, botch it, before it turns deadly.

David joins in. With his eyes glued on the computer, he reaches out, taking over from Mark, as he contemporarily instructs Mark.

David: Holy shit! That's why my mother has been trying to reach me. Mark call mom. Tell her we are fine. Reassure her everything is going to be cool.

David got busy at the computer, blogging.

In the meantime, the remaining Gen Z group, overwhelmed by curiosity has quickly milled to and disposed around Buzzo and crew. All listening hard with their faces a contorted, concerned and concentrated frowns.

Glenda rises to the occasion. Her instinct, instant reaction is remarkably remarkable.

Glenda (in mumbles, almost speaking to herself): We are already sore with oppression, suffering and humiliation. We are very tired of prospects of new ones.

(Suddenly raising her voice to Gen Z peers) Aren't we? Are we not tired of being dominated and cowards, guys? There is a march of protest against us by the Status Quo. Our politicians are not tired of their plundering Gen Z, our monarchs are not tired of depredating Gen Z, the 'men of God' are not tired of their avariciousness and subjugation and chicanery of Gen Z via their fabricated superstitious palsy of reap in heaven. These evil trinity want to continue their pogrom against Gen Z. Kill us the umpteenth time just like they have done to generations of youths before us. Let's go guys. It's not going to happen any further.

Then she goes for her handbag, howling:

Glenda: Brett, Lynda, all of us, let's go turn the tide. Dominate Status Quo!

Brett (whooping with joy): Phew, Hee! Hey guys, now is the time to put to end Gen Z's palsy. Gen Z's slumbering spirit. Isn't it?

The crowd (in a scowling and howling spasm): Yeah!

Brett: Is our infinite ability to endure misery not over?

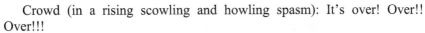
Crowd (in a rising scowling and howling spasm): It's over! Over!! Over!!!

Brett: Is our infinite loyalty to their injustice no more assumed?

Crowd (in a catharsis of emotional intensity): Yeah! No more; no more!!

Brett: Let's go end our misery on the high place. On the hill, the Plaza hill.

Like in some miracle of exertion, the crowd responded with such unknown passion of animation of freedom ever imagined or expressed or to be expected capable on the African continent.

Everyone, already on their feet, hurries and made their ways running out of the compound behind Brett.

Obviously, Brett did not delude. He can't delude. He is the leader of youth wing intrareligious endeavor, besides having headed the national students' association as part of his curriculum vitae. He is a fascinating figure, held in awe by his peers and arouses fear and suggestions in opponents.

Glenda (ready to move, to the "house" Gen Z): Buzzo and all of you, we will take care of the field. You direct the actions from here. Keep tweeting. We will keep you informed with our positions and with the dynamics as they evolve.

Then she turns to David, fixing him with a reassuring grimace. They hold stare.

Glenda: David, don't worry about anything. Tell your dad to relax. Let him not call in the Army, nor the Police. We don't need them. We don't need his help. This is squarely within our existential compass. Time to prove our gratitude to him. Time to prove we are becoming of age. Time to prove we can be trusted. Time to become Generation Why and WHY NOT.

The rest of Gen Z peers unsolicitously go into shouting and howling spasm. Glenda gives a high five to Mark, Mezzi, David and then to her hero Buzzo, who all stood to acknowledge.

Then in a feline-like move, she takes off. Followed closely behind by Lynda.

Buzzo (howling to them): Please all of you be careful! We love you all!

Buzzo and the house Gen Z crew take back their sitting positions at their computers. But it's Buzzo who is deciding the content and directing the texts of the tweets.

Buzzo (tweets): #Beautiful Gen Z Family, are you out there?

Gen Z: #We are here. #We are waiting

David: #Are we ready to retake our birth rights?

Gen Z: #Yeah. We are ready. Let's go, let's go!

Mezzi: #Gen Z of all walks of life, the working and suffering Gen Z–mechanics, carpenters, traders, farmers, butchers, hair dressers, entertainers, restauranteurs, beauticians, club owners, hoteliers, teachers, students, graduates, undergraduates, workers etc., all of you…are you all there?

Gen Z: #Yeah! Let's go Mezzziiiiiii!

Mezzi: #Wherever you are, whatever you are doing, drop it. Drop it dead and stand up. #Now or never.

Gen Z (whooping and hooting): #We are already standing up.

Mark: # If you are not standing up, you are an accomplice, not a victim!

Gen Z: # Victims! Victims!!, Victims!!!

Mezzi: #It's time for sacrifice. Sacrifice the comfort of whatever you are doing, whatever, and get going to the hill.

Gen Z: #Yeah, we hear you loud and clear. We are on the move!

Mezzi: # Time to prove Gen WHY and WHY NOT.

Gen Z: # Yeah, Yeah, Yeah!

In the background you can make out the music of Bob Marley: "Get up. Stand up for your rights" peaking.

Buzzo (in smile, a smile of an expansive winner): #Dominate the Plaza Hill.

Gen Z: #Get up, stand up! #Get up, stand up!!

Buzzo: This fight is about standing up for the right thing: shaping our destiny! Right? Gen Z: #Dominate! Dominate!! Dominate!!!

Buzzo: #On this land, there are enough enemies for all of us. Our enemies are the evil trinity. The **Monarchycraft** who depredates us, the **Politiciancraft** who plunders us, the **Priestcraft** who is the enabler, the betrayer, the means, the vehicle through palsy of religion, of superstition, of reason, of fear, of heaven, that perpetuates our misery for his heaven on earth.

Gen Z: #The truth. #Sacrosanct.

Buzzo: #These men of evil trinity have a rivalry of infirmity. These men of infirmity govern Africa. This fight is about standing up together. Either we are together or we perish!

Gen Z: #Together! Together!!

Now you can hear the music "one love, one love, people get together" of Bob Marley on.

Buzzo: #Gen Z, it's about defiance. Defy the belief that Gen Z have infinite ability to endure misery. Our loyalty, the Gen Z loyalty, the leverage through which we slave cannot be assumed any more. No! No more!!

> *#On this land there are enough enemies for us all. Our enemies are the evil trinity: the* **Monarchycraft** *who depredates us; the* **Politiciancraft** *who plunders us; the* **Priestcraft** *who is the enabler, the betrayer, the means, the vehicle through palsy of religion and heaven...*
> *#These men of evil trinity have a rivalry of infirmity. These men of infirmity govern Africa.*
> *#Gen Z, it's about defiance. #Defy the belief that Gen Z have infinite ability to endure misery.*
> *#Our Loyalty, the Gen Z loyalty, the leverage by which we slave cannot be assumed any more. No! No more!!*
> *#This fight is about standing up. #Standing up together. #Dominate the status quo. Dominate the plaza Hill Or we are Accomplices. #Stand up together or we continue the perish. Together.*

Gen Z: #No more, no more! Dominate status quo, dominate the hill, Plaza Hill!

Buzzo: #Get up, Stand up?

Gen Z: #Stand up, fight for our right!

Buzzo: #Are you fired up?

Gen Z (with hint of impatience): #We are almost there on the Plaza Hill.

Mark (assailed by sense of panic, mutters to himself): You kidding me!

Now, there is a new fierce urgency of now: contain and direct Gen Z movements on the Hill. Mark takes over the tweet. He knows the city to his palms.

Mark (tweeting): #Cool!

Gen Z: #Yeaeeaaaah! Mark, Mezzi, Mark. Mezzi, Mark, Mezzi, Mezzi!

Mark: #The Status Quo protest is marching, approaching the Plaza Hill coming in from Independence Boulevard. Let's avoid that route. Let them come in from there.

We are rallying to the same Hill instead, through the six horizontal arteries.

Mark: #Are you there?

Gen Z: #Yeah. We are following.

Mezzi: #Cool. Then let's get going. Fast!

Gen Z (recognizing Mezzi's voice, they give ovation): #Mezzi, Mezzi, Mezzi, Mezzi!

Mezzi: #Emerge Gen WHY, Gen WHY, Gen WHY!

Gen Z: #Gen WHY! Gen WHY!! Gen WHY!!! Gen WHY!!!! Gen WHY!!!!!...

VOLUME 5
THE REBUTTAL

Chapter 1

Gen Z are in movement, surging to and reaching the six arteries where they readily find their field leaders: Brett, Glenda, Lynda…waiting. A lot of them shake hands, their faces in tensed frown, in camaraderie, known consolidated relationships spanning years, full of stories, while others contend and content with exchange of tensed concerned pleasantries.

Gen Z are mustered at the six entry arteries, avenue 1, 2,3,4,5,6, at the threshold of the Plaza Hill, short of entering the plaza waiting for the instructions from Buzzo and his crew from their situation room, in the middle of somewhere.

From the threshold without being in sight, they lay in wait furtively monitoring and observing the general movement on the plaza and concentrating on the one from Independence Boulevard of the incoming expectant protest march.

Meanwhile, the President, from his office, is on his feet, observing from his glass window pane, the whole shebang. He is fighting to restrain himself from the cruel authoritarian urge to quell and disperse the protesters and hold the proponents, the culprits accountable given their unjustifiable intention to his judgement, for such a destabilizing, sabotaging act.

Even though he has decided to respect the wish of the foursome and crew in staying out of the protest, and test them to make good on the Gen Z momentous moment of proof of value of trust, reliability, resilience and integrity, he has already made contingent plans: his security intelligence is all over the place and the Police and Army are ready to move into action at a moment's notice.

Now, behold the protest march makes its entry into the plaza amidst a voluptuous colorful and remarkable funfair: voluptuously remarkable given the volume of the participants, the diverse anagraphy–old, middle and the many Gen Z, "masochist malicious" Gen Z with them. And remarkably, a funfair given the music, singing, dancing, the snacking and the drinking and the many beautiful placards on them with different concepts and reasons.

Misery is really predatory. It molds situations, forces betrayals, forces enmity of friendship, forces friendship of enmity, forces voluptuous recklessness.

The voluptuous effrontery of hunger shoves snacks and drinks into the mouths of those perdition-disposed, masochist Gen Z. The complex psychology of malicious hunger and misery forces a complacent willful evil and a feigned deference to march for Status Quo, even if it is to their peril.

Misery forced them to a display of contemptuous disdain, sneer at their peers, the Gen Z peers, wedged in wait in the streets of the adjacent avenues of the hill. Besides, there are ponderous shrieks and whooping and howling and scowling and name-callings. However, the air is taut and charging to implosion.

As the 'marching protest' approaches midway the length of the Plaza Hill, the ethereal figure of Glenda, a green-colored flag of placard with inscription, "It is time for the WHYs and for the WHY NOTs.", towering in her hands pierces the horizon like a knife would, on a cake. She is followed by the convergence of two streams of Gen Z from both sides of First Avenue occupying the whole width of the Plaza Hill, overlooking adjacent government secured area.

The 'marching protest' notices and gets baffled. Confused, consternated and in awe, it reluctantly slows to a snail's pace.

In no breathing interval, in a simultaneous co-occurrent moves, the other arteries empty their Gen Z into the plaza. You could behold Brett, Lynda, Laura, Frank, green color flag placards with different message inscriptions- "#Ask WHY and sentence WHY NOT." "#We choose freedom, dominate Status Quo.", "#We choose progress, dominate filths and garbage.", "#We choose responsibility, dominate unaccountability.", "#We choose sacrifice, dominate laziness.", "#We choose love, dominate selfishness and kleptomania.", "#We choose honesty, dominate cronyism, mediocrity and tribalism.", #We choose our brain power, dominate falsehood, evil and misery." Etc. etc., towering in their hands, leading the river of Gen Z.

In a flash, the 'marching protest' is surrounded, encircled. Brett is atop of south end occupation, Frank the west end, Lynda the east end and Glenda the north end. To surround and encircle the African Status Quo, their consent assumed, their loyalty forced, hold them to ransom, hold them trapped, have them feel an imaginary hint of accountability, on the African continent by their Gen Z descendants—young sons and daughters, grandkids–is like a fortuitous miracle of exertion gifted from heaven. In yet another kismet, the encirclement has in its wake created, left and maintained a natural distance of separation, of divide, of philosophy, of psychology, of purpose between the parts in all length and breadth of the Plaza Hill.

Now in the evolving dynamics, the marching protest is forced to a complete stop. The drums have ceased. The dancing legs halted, the swaggering bodies stilled, the placards lowered. The masochist-malicious Gen Z are shifting ground, slowly distancing themselves from the innermost shielded body of the Status Quo, now fully exposed. And trapped. Their disdainful arrogance gone, their vicious spite beaten, vulnerable, afraid of the dread of uncharted territory, the prison.

In fact, the Status Quo, now vulnerable and overwhelmed with uncertainty and fear for their safety, their confidence, valor and vain demeanor lost, have their faces writhed in expression of remarkable exquisite dread.

> *"It is time for the WHYs and for the WHY NOTs." "#Ask WHY and sentence WHY NOT." "#We choose freedom, dominate Status Quo.", "#We choose progress, dominate filths and garbage.", "#We choose responsibility, dominate unaccountability.", "#We choose sacrifice, dominate laziness.", "#We choose love, dominate selfishness and kleptomania.", "#We choose honesty, dominate cronyism, mediocrity and tribalism.", #We choose our brain power, dominate falsehood, evil and misery."*

Fear and guilt and miracle of grace and of salvation are the dark angels, the indisputable constant shadow that haunts the enriched. Not the rich. The enriched. Fences, all fences are arbitrary and irrelevant. They are relevant as fortresses and prisons. The enriched in Africa literally live in self-inflicted prisons. They are afraid of the misery they created out there. Even though these fences are a violin to the enriched, they are walls of snow to enthusiasm of a heroic revolutionist.

In fact, conversely so, the Gen Z demeanor is a remarkable fearlessness, a threatening and soave fierceness. Expansive fieriness. Their faces, expression of exquisite smugness and smirches. They stand their ground.

There is a remarkable, ponderous silence. The air is voluptuously taut. Words are not proffered. Not heard. Positions are held and maintained. There is a Mexican standoff. Until…

The hint of approaching car pierces the distance… grows louder as it nears… then a colorful all four sides placard–ridden pick-up van with a sole inscription on the four sides "Separation from Filths and Garbage" makes its entry into the plaza, through first avenue, wedging into the separating distance and stops facing the center, where the status quo is encircled by the Gen Z. The glasses are shielded. One can't decipher who the inside holds, nor determine what the van is carrying. There is a voluptuous curiosity that is afraid, appalled and delighted at the same time. But silent. Kill or be killed.

Seconds in the complicit silence elapsed that seemed interminable. Then the van does a 90degree displacement, bringing its trunk to bear on the Status Quo. The voluptuous curiosity on the 'marching protest' trapped

219

is now imploding: The Status Quo trapped, phobia-prone caught in some psycho-socio asphyxia is paling with fear, gasping for escape.

What the truth holds: *fear can flatter vanity of the powerful after all.*

In the eerie quiet, some within the ranks and file of the masochist Gen Z are writhing in moaning, in suppressed wailing, caught by a feigned and insincere chagrin of being on the wrong side of history, attempting and wishing to cross over to their peers, in defilement of the line of separation.

Then the moment came. The waiting is pierced by a crackling of metallic sound: the back of the van snaps open, with its three sides sliding in some gravitational fit, with sharp snapping noises to the ground, revealing two beautiful fascinating Gen Z.

The two, on their feet, are Mezzi and Mark with microphones in their hands. They momentarily but momentously hold everything and everybody to a spell.

They are legible, intelligible and recognizable and now recognized.

The Plaza Hill comes alive. The Gen Z crowd roars into potent clamor of shouting, shrieking, scowling, howling spasm.

Mezzi and Mark, speaking into the microphone acknowledge:

Mezzi and Mark (calling them out in unison): Gen Z...Gen Z?

And they mime, sticking the microphones in their direction for their response.

Gen Z Crowd: Noooooooooooooooo!
Mezzi and Mark: Why?
Gen Z Crowd: Gen WHY!
Mezzi: Uuuuuuuh, shame on us! Indeed, you are right.
Mezzi and Mark (in unison): Generation WHY are you ready?

Gen Z crowd believe they have come of age to recognize and elevate themselves to Generation WHY, even by mere abandoning their daily individual miserable chores at survival, and defying abject servility on the youth as silently but implicitly coded by the African despotic tradition, mobilizing to Plaza Hill to wedge an existential fight and determine their future. They have found faith, passion, time and space and determination within the context of their glaring misery for their primitive moronic self-consciousnesses be infused, imbued, appraised, with renaissance credo selfconsciousness of "Consciousness" God and "Self-consciousness" Man, man a demigod indeed, at the center of the universe to figure out "Consciousness's" spiritual instinct and able WHY to everything and WHY NOT to every dream. It is blaze trailing. They are blaze trailing this effort in Africa. Yes, they took it. They only need to validate themselves thence.

Gen WHY (scowling and howling): Yeeeeaaaaaahhhh!
Mezzi: Misery captive?

Gen WHY: (ponderously thundering, voicing their mixed feelings): Captivity captive! Status Quo captive! Hard work! Standing up! Sacrificing at comfort! Renaissance credo! Renaissance Man! Man, at the center! Impossible is nothing! Life is yours! Earn respect! Humility! Etc. etc.

Their adeptness in expressing, exercising and rehearsing and acting out the philosophical interactive teaching of the past weeks of tweets in such a short time is telling. It has evidently left a pugnacious brain empowerment of the field Gen Z in its wake. Not long ago they could not articulate much. And even so, hereditary despotism of palsy, reticence, complacency, resignation hijacked and subdued any guts and feelings and their expressions of any interest whatsoever.

In the meantime, the morphology of the Plaza Hill has drastically and swiftly remixed: the line of separation has been profaned. Crossed. Shifted. Redesigned. The 'masochist Gen Z' have decamped, infused, befuddled with their peers, realizing in defiance their dream of the exceptional and not of the familiar. They leave, abandon the company of the Status Quo, unceremoniously.

The Status Quo, abandoned to themselves, distanced, left in the middle of the ring, vulnerable, their faces in continued dictated endurance is a miscellany of expressions–tortured smiles, preoccupied grimaces, disapproving frowns, solicitous frown, contemptuous and appalled grimaces, malicious, malevolent frowns, distressed grimaces, frowning smirks and smugness of vengeance–all of immense anguish but immensely, facetiously pitiable.

Then Mezzi raises his hands miming silence. The crowd responds with a reluctant gradual silence.

In an instant a dreadful silence, like a threatening cloud settles over the Plaza Hill.

Mezzi: As is said, the best first good thing is listening.

He lets them deal with the grammar and the logic of the statement. And he switches, looking at Mark.

Mark: And do you know the best second good thing?
Gen WHY: Noooooooooooh!
Mark: Knowing that you don't know. The art of humility!
Mezzi: The art of the most intelligent, wisest man.
Mark: The man who knows that he does not know. Socrates. The dialectics.
Mezzi: 'The only true wisdom is in knowing you know nothing'. And do you know the third best good thing?
Gen WHY: Noooooooooooooh!
Mark: Being listened to.
Mezzi: The art of dialectics. (Then fixing the Status Quo) now let us thank our Status Quo for arranging this beautiful rally. Indeed!

Gen WHY disapprove, letting out a dense, and ponderous shriek of condemnation.

Mezzi: By the way, to conquer doubt, inculcate and reiterate understanding in our self-consciousness, let's briefly cast some light on who our Status Quo is, if you agree.

He scans the crowd who transits into a rapt silence as they nod their approval to continue.

Mezzi: We have Status Quo Leadership and Status Quo Parenthood. The two forms are of the same coin.
Mark: Status quo leadership and Status quo parenthood. They are of the same coin.
Mezzi: The One kills us from without and the other kills us from within. Our Status Quo leadership is in the middle of the plaza right now as we speak. You can see them. You can touch them. The Status Quo Parenthood, in sum our parents are participating, shoring them up from a distance. They are a combined category of Trinity.
Mark: Do you get that? Both the leadership and the parenthood are a category of Trinity.
Gen WHY: Yeeeeeaaaaaaaaah, we get it.
Mezzi: To avoid equivocations, the first group of the Trinity is our African monarchy: Kings, Chiefs, Emirs, Sultans, Obas. In sum, the Monarchycraft.
The second group of the Trinity is our African politicians. The Presidents, Prime Ministers, their Cabinets, the Senators, house of Assembly, the Governors, their cabinets, state assemblies, the local government councils and councilors. The Politiciancraft.
The third group of the Trinity is our Priests. Christian Priests, Moslem Imams, Voodoo Priests. The Priestcraft.
Mark: So, we have the Monarchycraft, the Politiciancraft, the Priestcraft.
Mezzi: We don't need to imagine them. We can see them, we have them in our midst. Just looking at them, they no doubt evoke the impression of the combined remote and distant past among the immediate present. We are in antithesis. Their antithesis. Let's look at their roles and responsibility on our land, Africa.
In Africa, in African system, in every African family, wherever on earth, there has been and there is a rule of hereditary hierarchic despotism of custom and tradition.
Mark: Hereditary hierarchic despotism. Hereditary despotism founded and sustained by customs and usage. A feudal tradition of despotism.
Mezzi: The African monarchy crafted the rule of hereditary despotism.
Mark: Hereditary despotism is simply the rights for a few and slavery for the rest in a society.

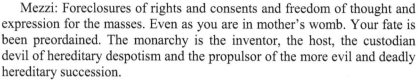

Mezzi: Foreclosures of rights and consents and freedom of thought and expression for the masses. Even as you are in mother's womb. Your fate is been preordained. The monarchy is the inventor, the host, the custodian devil of hereditary despotism and the propulsor of the more evil and deadly hereditary succession.

These trickle down into a thousand facets, shapes and forms with infinite deputations. He is the depredator in chief.

Mark: The Politiciancraft imposes hereditary hierarchic despotism and perpetuates the evil hereditary hierarchic succession. He is the plunderer.

Gen WHY roar in shrieks and howling, applauding remarkably ponderously and vigorously at the naked audacity of the courage of auto-critic, of mea culpa giving a hope of requiem to rooted African morbid reticence, outlandish willful lies, willful pathological complacency and default endemic hypocrisy and callous willful denial. As Mezzi raises the microphone to speak, Gen WHY crowd acknowledges and a reluctant silence settles back.

Mezzi: And the Priestcraft: the lion in the body of the harmless sheep. He consoles and comforts and paralyzes and feeds the perpetuation of hereditary hierarchic despotism and its more evil hereditary succession of mass depredation, mass plunder, mass misery. All for a reason. For a superstitious supercilious avaricious reason: Our misery perpetuation is his heaven on earth. They reap on earth. The Lord Jesus reaps in heaven. Our Priests reap here on earth. Jesus sacrificed here for humanity. Our men of God are the integrated plunderers, depredators, avarice, kleptomaniacs, gluttons. They grab their inheritance on earth. From the poor.

The crowd is in a dense and a ponderous eerie silence. Totally rapt, attentive.

On our land this trinity is in a rivalry of despotism. The one, outdoes the other.

Today they organized rallies to perpetuate our hopelessness, our enslavement, our ignorance, our tribulation, our subjugation, our humiliation, our misery.

Today, they are here to continue their depredation. Their plundering. Their avariciousness. Their combined palsy of filths and garbage.

Not even brutes devour their young. Nor do savages make war upon their families. A continent should not find joy at depredating its posterity, joy at running them into debt, joy at running them into misery with the palsy of comfort and consolation of supercilious, superstitious reason of some faith mystery.

Then training his eyes on the Status Quo, fixing them:

Status Quo, you reject your posterity with disdain.

Status Quo you hate light. You hate posterity. You abhor us. You repudiate your seed, your DNA. You hate our dignity. You love our humiliation. But why?

Let me quote from one of the giants of civil rights movement in America, Ella Baker:

"Give people light and they will find a way."

You refuse us light. You refuse us the keys. But why?

Now Mezzi overwhelmed, his eyes laden and fighting back tears, takes a breath. Fixes the ground. The infinite void.

Mark notices, understands and rises to the occasion, fixing him and starts clapping for him.

The crowd notices and gives him voluptuous encouraging applause. Mezzi recovers smoldering with a renewed energy of anger.

Mezzi (looking straight back at the Status Quo): Status Quo, you have failed us. Let it be known to you that we can drive. We are determined to find the keys.

Gen WHY: Yeeeaaaaaahhhhhh, we can drive.

Mezzi: Now, we the Gen WHY want to share in our responsibility in this failure. Eh guys?

He scans the attentive, expectant faces of Gen WHY crowd, now gripped with doubtful, skeptical frowns but finds approval to continue.

Mezzi: The African youths, generation after generation, including ours have not taken our share of responsibility in this misery. Just imagine if our loyalty can no longer be assumed? Just imagine where we defiled beliefs? Just imagine our defiance to over enduring misery? Just imagine if we discovered the power in reading? Just imagine if we can critically think, critically analyze and critically rationalize? Just imagine if we knew about the renaissance man? Just imagine if we stand up for the floor of freedom that is as level as water? Just imagine if we dream the future, plan it and concretize it? Just imagine if we knew we are gifted to shape our destiny, just imagine if we accepted our inalienable rights from God of being his image, demigods, brain-gifted and empowered to invent anything, everything? Just imagine if we knew that nothing is impossible? Just imagine if we knew everything depends on hard work of the brain? Just imagine knowing what respect and earning respect mean? Just imagine if we can stand up. Just imagine if we grow a self-consciousness of WHY and WHY NOT. Gen WHY, just...

In the eerie silence, now he pauses to let his words sink in. Then he continues.

Mezzi: Gen WHY, just imagine holding our parents accountable *ostracizing, estranging and punishing them for not having their own backs first–because of their laziness and stupidity and primitivity–before making us for traumatization. They make, not to take care of us but as their human properties for their life-lines.*

Mark: Yes, Parenthood's love for Africa's youths is gifting and permeating the culture of making children without having economic base first, gifting the children misery and making properties in them for their life-lines.

Mezzi: Yes, because each time we do their chores–fetching water, firewood, hawking, prostituting–some for our school fess, some for our school books, some for our rents, feeding, buying examination papers etc – suppressing our hearts for relationships of convenience to support our siblings and feed our Parents, supplanting responsibilities of parenthood, we are being enslaved. The vigor of the African youths is subdued and traumatized and arrested and retrogressed in segue. That's the culture we are gifted. This culture is of utmost abhorrent tragedy.

Gen WHY, just imagine what a madness separates us from the truth?

The madness of ignorance? The madness of laziness? The madness of stupidity? The madness of primitivity? The madness of complacency? The madness of malicious malevolence? The madness of morbid misery endurance? The madness of mysticism and superstition? The madness of hypocrisy and reticence? The madness of filths and garbage?

He pauses again in the eerie silence. And once again badgers on.

Mezzi: Now let's express what is remarkably and embarrassingly-paradoxically hurting on our African continent.

Gen WHY, just imagine holding our parents accountable *ostracizing, estranging and punishing them for not having their own backs first– because of their laziness and stupidity and primitivity–before making us for traumatization. They make, not to take care of us but as their human properties for their lifelines.*
Yes, because each time we do their chores-fetching water, firewood, hawking, prostituting–some for our school fess, some for our school books, some for our rents, feeding, buying examination papers etc – suppressing our hearts for relationships of convenience to support our siblings and feed our Parents, supplanting responsibilities of parenthood, we are being enslaved.
The vigor of the African youths is subdued and traumatized and arrested and retrogressed in segue. That's the culture we are gifted. This culture is of utmost abhorrent tragedy.

The world's black population is about 1.5billion people.

And this population is run by their government in perdition thus: their father, the Evil – the Devil himself; and the Devil's Son, the Evil, embodied by the trinity – Monarchycraft, Politiciancraft, Priestcraft; and the Evil spirit – the one million Cowards (the Army, the Police), and the 10 million Stupid men (Bureaucracy and the Bureaucrats). They experiment on the voluptuous, self-forsaken, slaves by choice, misery stricken, self-abandoned miserable 1.488006 billion (1.5 billion minus 11.000004 million) Guinea pigs.

There is a voluptuous shriek of disbelief and ponderous curiosity amongst the Gen WHY that came in subdued gasps.

Mezzi: Let me further shade light. The Devil is called hereditary hierarchic despotism. He is the mother and father of every evil, mother and father of misery, mother and father of primitivity, mother and father of humiliation, mother and father of ignorance, mother and father of hunger. The Abstract, the ever-looming imperceptible shadow, very rich and the very powerful, whose decisions are a force majeure. irrefutable. Inalienable.

Now to the Devil's Son, the Evil who is made up by the Trinity–the monarchy, the politician and the "men of God". Not the church, the "men of God." The so-called Pastors of the evangelical and Pentecostals, the Imams, the Voodoo Chief priests. They function by deputation. They administer the poison and the antidote: the depredation, the plunder, and the palsy; the evil of hereditary despotism.

Then we have the Evil Spirit. They are two of them. The first is the one million Cowards, who are the combined soldiers, the policemen, the security agents. They are zombies. They franchised their conscience to their profession. They know but can't question obedience. Obedience is the essence of their being.

They may be brave in places of wars but are cringing cowards in giving their lives and services to the evil men in perpetrating evil and misery in civil society, thwarting freedom, liberty and peace in their wake. And yet their reward is normally abandonment and neglect at the hands of same Devil and the Devil's Son.

The second is the ten million Stupid men, who are the cabals, the consultants, the government contractors, the heads of banks and their banks, the bureaucrats–civil servants, papers and pen shufflers, their directors, heads of departments, committees, heads of associations like labor unions, the officers of the courts, the lawyers, the judges, the oligarchs, their managers, secretaries who know what is going on, permit the rule of the Devil, the Devil's Son and the 1 million Cowards who look the other way while they sign the condemnation of 1.5 billion people to permanent famine, starvation, humiliation, misery and to slow and sure excruciating death.

Then comes the Guinea Pigs, the masses, all of us the 1.488006 billion masses, the people, systematically experimented on with famine, slavery, depredation, plunder, ignorance, abject misery.

And reiterating, these same misery-ridden masses are capable of just one thing: multiplication of misery given to them by themselves. Pumping out children they can't or won't take care of. Indeed, they famish and traumatize Africa's youths and then they make property in them for their life-lines. Criminals.

The Gen WHY amidst the crowd, more than being gripped by the play of conflicting emotional spasm – believing, disbelieving, truth, doubt, are humiliated more by their vacuity at critical thinking and critical analysis. By their yet moronic selfconsciousness in comparison. Against their self-elevated status of Gen WHY.

Even though amongst them are university graduates, graduating students, they pale by comparative intellectuality to the 16 year-old Mezzi. His critical analytical skill, his contemporaneous virtuoso, and his adept, compelling intellectuality and his articulatory ability and endurance, to say the very least are threatening. Pure wizardry.

Gen WHY are at the same time spellbound at the audacity of the truth as they air the intrinsic stir of their admiration and fascination for Mezzi.

They can be absolved, remembering that Rome was not built in a day and that they have started and are on their journey of thousands of miles.

The African youth, generation after generation, including ours have not taken our share of responsibility in this misery. Just imagine if our loyalty can no longer be assumed? Just imagine where we defiled beliefs? Just imagine our defiance to over enduring misery? Just imagine if we discovered the power in reading? Just imagine if we can critically think and critically analyze? Just imagine if we knew about the renaissance Man? Just imagine if we stand up for the floor of freedom that is as level as water? Just imagine if we dream the future, plan it and concretize it? Just imagine if we knew we are gifted to shape our destiny, just imagine if we accepted our inalienable rights from God of being his image, demi-gods, brain-gifted and empowered to invent anything, everything? Just imagine if we knew that nothing is impossible? Just imagine if we knew everything depends on hard work of the brain? Just imagine knowing what respect and earning respect means? Just imagine if we can stand up. Just imagine...

They are rummaging at the violence of this reality when Mezzi pierces the air again.

Mezzi: Generation WHY are you there?

There was no ponderous response.

Mezzi: Guys it's that simple. They are here, palpable in our midst: lo there - the Devil, the Devil's Son and the Evil spirit.
And we are, the rest of us, the Guinea Pigs.

The Cowards seem absent. Maybe they are hiding amidst in mufti.

Now the Gen WHY crowd hint at recovering. Mark fires them up:

Mark: Gen WHY are you there?
Gen WHY: Yesssssssssssssssssssssssss!
Mark: Gen WHY don't be in shock. We have enough enemies out there in the name of status quo that comprises of our parents. We must be together to challenge them or we perish.
Gen WHY: Togetherarrrrrrrrrrrrrrrrrrr!

> *Gen WHY, just imagine what a madness separates us from the truth? The madness of ignorance? The madness of laziness? The madness of stupidity?*
> *The madness of primitivity? The madness of complacency? The madness of malicious malevolence? The madness of morbid misery endurance? The madness of mysticism and superstition? Madness of hypocrisy and reticence? The madness of filths and garbage?*

Worthy of note that the Status Quo, men of portentous voices, men with finality of power that prohibited and punished, men with flagrant disdain and flattering vanity, have been compelled to stand there, disdained, humiliated and afraid at the same time. Silenced, trapped, listening against their will. Their intent not only upturned, defeated, cowered, alienated and annihilated but has in itself, effortlessly sprouted, generating a resistance, a Gen WHY movement that seem fierce, fiery and determined to succeed and endure the WHY NOT.
Despotism, it is said, despises nothing so much as righteousness in its victims.

> *Despotism, it is said, despises nothing so much as righteousness in its victims.*
> *...Despotism despises nothing so much as righteousness in its victims.*

> *...Despises nothing more than righteousness in its victims.*

Mezzi: Gen WHY, let me ask you the next embarrassing, hurtful thing: Do we as a race have a life-style?

There is an absolute consensual humbling silence of consensus. Their faces are pitched in attentive, expectant grimaces.

Mezzi: Is our life style bicycle, cars, trains, airplanes, phones, TV, computers, iPad, light, pipe-borne water, healthcare, education, food security, etc.,?

The silence has now grown eerie. There is a surreal attentiveness. Ears are listening hard, straying to understand and to guess the finality of Mezzi's reasoning.

Mezzi: The list goes on and on. But they are more like some race's life-style. Isn't it? Buckets of stream water on our heads is our life-style. Darkness and candle light is our life-style. Starving is our life-style. Famine is our life-style. Open-air sewer is our life-style. Open air urination and defecation is our life-style.
Misery is our life-style?
Just imagine, if you and I want to urinate or defecate, ease ourselves right now, what do we do?
Mark: What do we do? We do like cows, goats...we do it on the streets now...
Mezzi: Correct! Kissing the stench, starring at the stench. And having the stench as our companion. Like animals. And we think we are any different from animals?
Mark: No, I don't think so. Shameful. Totally unacceptable.
Mezzi: Just imagine, if we get sick now, there are no diagnosis. No prescriptions. Adulterated drugs the lone choice. No hospital with a human face. We die like rats and flies. Just imagine our graduation certificates equate to hand outs, sex, cash payments. To nothingness.
Now our Devil, the Son – the trinity, the Evil spirit – the Cowards and the stupid men embrace and live out Whiteman's life style. His cars, his airplanes, his yachts, his hospitals, his schools are their cocaine, and then they believe they have arrived. They have earned respect.
They do not know that respect comes with what you can give.

Then he addresses directly, smoldering at the Status Quo.

Status Quo, you seriously believe if I were Mr. Rolls Royce, Mr. Mercedes Benz, Mr. Airbus, Mr. Rolex, Mr. Cartier, Mr. Gucci, Mr. Apple, Mr. LG, Mr. Edison, Mr. da Vinci etcetera and etcetera and etcetera, you do have more respect for buying my comforts than myself the inventor and the manufacturer?

Mark: Ridiculous. Laughing stocks. Below human stupidity

Mezzi: You crave respect from the Whiteman? You complain he does not respect your race? How can he? What have we contributed to the world? Not even the dignity of copying their toilet and a shower for your race. Not airplanes, but toilets to our mothers, wives, daughters and sisters. You won't provide toilets to black family. You won't pump water from the streams into the houses. You won't pump cooking gas into the houses. You let the Black woman fetch water and firewood on their heads to this day. No decency of the mind. No dignity as humans. And yet you crave respect. You crave validation and recognition. Shame on you.

You crave recognition and validation from the inventor and maker of civilization and its pleasure that your self-indulgence is over addicted to?

Mark: Shame on us. We can't even give toilets, running water, light, health care, education, some dignity to our people? Generator is an expensive pollutant. Borehole is a pollutant. Water tanks are pure poison. And yet we crave for respect.

Mezzi: In this 21st century, we have no water for our people? Roman empire had aqueduct 2000 plus years ago. You have a grieving, shameless guts craving for respect.

And to the question: What's our life style on this continent?
The hurtful answer: Just imagine, if me and you want to urinate or defecate, ease ourselves right now, what do we do?
We do it like cows, goats…we do it on the streets now… Kissing the stench, starring at the stench. And having the stench as company. Like animals. And we think we are any different from animals;
Just imagine, if we get sick now, there are no diagnosis. No prescriptions.
Adulterated drugs the lone choice. No hospital with a human face. We die like rats and flies.
Now our Devil, the Three Evil Men, the Stupid Men, the Cowards embrace and live out Whiteman's life style. His cars, his airplanes, his yachts, his hospitals, his schools are their cocaine, and then they believe they have arrived. They have earned respect.
They do not know that respect comes with what you can give.
Shame on us. We can't even give toilets, running water, light, health care, education, some dignity to our people? Generator is an expensive pollutant. Borehole is a pollutant. Water tanks are pure poison. And yet we crave for respect.

Mark: Shame on us. Shame on us. How dare we crave for respect and recognition? There is no excuse whatsoever not to have toilets, light, pipe-borne water in our homes. No excuse whatsoever. Sorry, but no excuse holds. More so in the 21st AD.

Mezzi: These men do not understand that to earn the others' races respect (Whiteman and the Japanese for example) you must make sure that your Black family, each single Black person of the Black race wherever found, whatever his status, rich or poor, healthy or disadvantaged must have at least a house, not a shelter. A house urbanized with pipe-borne water, constant current electricity, education, health care, food security, mass transit system, roads.

Mark: At least! At least!! At least!!!

Mezzi: The evil Black man buys the White man's gadgets and denies his people the common basics and expect to be respected? No. No.

Mark: Status Quo you can hear us. You really have never made any sense to our people.

Now Gen WHY crowd burst into thunderous applause. They are jumping. Shrieking and scowling and howling. Their amazement is fearless, contemptuous, fiery, determined and delighted at the same time.

As Mezzi brings anew the microphone to his mouth, a reluctant gradual silence returns.

Mezzi: We are insignificant to the world. We don't make sense even to ourselves. We don't make sense to them. We cannot be respected because we have never stood up.

We don't stand up. The Black race has never stood up.

Africa did not stand up to slavery. Yet we want respect.

Africa did not stand up to colonialism. Yet we want respect.

Africa did not embrace agricultural revolution. Yet we want respect.

Africa did not embrace industrial revolution. Yet we want respect.

Africa did not embrace manufacturing economy. Yet we want respect.

Africa lost out on market economy. Yet we want respect.

Africa on technology is lagging, doesn't stand up to it. Yet we want respect.

Africa refuses to copy, to imitate, to innovate, to invent, to stand up to give light, give running treated water, give education, give health care, give food security... the very least to our people and yet we crave for respect.

Respect from who? From the hardworking race that is taking care of her race? That has given a life-style to her race and by extension to the world? Should liberty respect slavery? Can liberty respect filths and garbage?

The highway, the technologies, to any life-style we desire to suit and sooth our culture, costume of our race are available, not hidden from us, are at our disposal from the White race. He is not hiding them from us. And all you are capable of doing is looting Africa's resources into the western banks and giving misery to us. And we are human beings. We qualify as humans–our blood, DNA, IQ the same as theirs.

Is it not legitimate that we Gen WHY ask the Status Quo if it is not below the human stupidity, not to copy to enable our environment for our people?

Isn't it a preposterous stupidity, arrogance, perversity in all their forms nakedly, remarkably unjustifiable?

Then Mezzi between pauses:

I don't stand up; I don't earn respect.
You don't stand up; you don't earn respect. We don't stand up; we don't earn respect We don't stand up; we are insignificant.

Why the 1873 compromise in America? Because genitor Africa did not stand up.

Why the KKK? We are not standing up.

Why the lynching and the present-day African lynching? We are not standing up.

Why noble laureate James Watson DNA IQ tests conspiracy? We don't stand up.

You stand up, you earn respect. Respect is not given. It is earned. It is won on the battlefield of standing up.

And now let's humbly ponder at this:

How much significant remarkably insignificant would be significant to bring our Negro Specie to understand the significance of remarkably insignificant?

> *How much Significant remarkably Insignificant would be Significant to bring our Negro Specie to understand the significance of remarkably Insignificant?*

The smolders of shame and derision flames into anger and into fist tightening rage at the unfairness of it all. As they seem pondering "what kind of system, what kind of government, what kind of people, what kind of race, what kind of faith, what kind of, kind of, of kind of, of kind of, of kind of, of kind of, …generation after generation allows and gives misery like this to her people?"

Mezzi: As we ponder over the answer, my fellow Gen WHY peers, let today be our defining day.
Mark: Today our defining day!
Mezzi: The day we took share of our responsibility to stand up!
Mark: Today our obligation, our indebtedness to stand up.

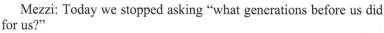

Mezzi: Today we stopped asking "what generations before us did for us?"

Mark: Today we stopped asking what generations before us did for us!

Mezzi: Today, we ask "what can we do for ourselves?" Today we task ourselves with "We must make generations our descendants better than us."

Mark: The day we choice to sacrifice and challenge the comfort of our hypocritical upbringings. The day to make our misery captive! Today we stand up to dominate our filths and garbage, our environment!

Gen WHY rise to a spasm of remarkable enthusiasm, that seems unfeigned, convinced and honest, pounding and fisting the air ponderously in approval.

Mezzi: We can't restitute to prostitution, its former innocence, they say. You lost it.

Status Quo on this continent has systematically failed her light. You lost it.

You hate light. You repudiate light. You devour light. We are that light that you systematically disavow and repudiate and devour. You lost it.

> *My fellow Gen WHY Peers, let today be our defining day.*
> *The day Gen WHY took share of her responsibility to stand up!*
> *Today our obligation, our indebtedness to stand up.*
> *Today we stopped asking "what generations before us did for us?"*
> *Today, we ask "what can we do for Ourselves." Today we task*
> *ourselves with "We must make generations our descendants better*
> *than us."*
> *The day we choice to sacrifice and challenge the comfort of our*
> *hypocritical upbringings. The day to make our misery captive! Today*
> *we stand up to dominate our filths and garbage, our environment!*

The only thing you give, want to give and can give us is and has been filth and garbage. You have no regrets. No remorse. No apologies. You rallied here today against light. To continue giving us your filths and garbage. That's the only thing you have. That's the only thing you can give. That's the only thing you represent. And You lost it.

Mezzi stops speaking, disengaging from the status quo and engages his stare on Mark. They hold stare, and without removing his eyes from him, he continued. The Plaza Hill tranced: eerie silence is his accomplice.

Mezzi (pointing, angrily raising his voice): The devil and them, the evil Status Quo, rallied against the President and his family. The lone tree in the forest. The lone sand in the desert. The lone rain-drop in the threatening cloud. The lone star in Africa's sky. The lone voice in our wilderness. The lone remarkably remorseful. The lone trail blazer. The lone selfless hand who is risking, trying to put on the light on our continent? How dare they?

Gen WHY roar in a thunderous applause to Mark, who, struggling with selfeffacement, pales into austere demeanor. The swiftness of this sudden deviation and deflection of Mezzi took everyone by surprise. Mark was no exception. It was above his expectation.

Now Mezzi takes a pause, and in eloquent pantomime thanks Mark. A thanks that embodies the voluptuous appreciation and gratitude to their family, the first family's. Then he disengages his stare from Mark and faces the crowd, engaging the Status Quo, for the umpteenth time.

Mezzi: How dare you Status Quo? What a craven audacity?
You know, you just don't gift filth and garbage: You are literally filth and garbage.

Now Gen WHY crowd eases into extasy.

Gen WHY: Yes, literal filth and garbage! Filth and garbage!
Mark: Yeah!
Gen WHY: Yes! Yes, integrated filth and garbage!
Mezzi: Conversely, the youths of Africa have a history of shying away from their share of misery-responsibility, generation after generation.
Mark: Conversely, we accepted filth and garbage handed down to us and in turn we became literally filth and garbage.
Mezzi: That's the cycle. A never-ending cycle of filth and garbage for this beautiful continent.
Here, today on this Hill, Gen WHY are now choosing to take our share of the responsibility. Yeah?
Gen WHY (fisting and punching the air, shouting): Yes! Yes!! Yes!!!
Mezzi: Our loyalty is now by consent. Status Quo, you need to earn it. Yeah?
Gen WHY: Yes! Yes!! Yes!!!
Mezzi: We choose to dream the future. We choose to make our future. We abhor misery. We disavow and repudiate filth and Garbage. No other way. Yeah?
Gen WHY: Yeah! Dominate filth and garbage! Dominate our environment!
Mezzi: Now please, listen carefully.
Mark: We need your rapt attention please.
Now silence is spectral.
Mezzi: Thank You. It has been said that "You can't give what you don't have." Status Quo can't give more than filth and garbage. That's all they have.

Mark (interjecting): Pardon me: That's what they are! They personify filth and garbage.

The audacity of this unexpected affirmation and its ruthless candor left competing emotions in the crowd. The Gen WHY crowd is gasping and agape, taking in its full weight. The Status Quo, despite their forced, momentary status of obsequiousness, have their faces, instead, grimacing disbelief and contempt, and mouths puckering and wielding anger and wishing medieval punishment.

Then the Gen WHY crowd recovers and gives undaunting, unequivocal consensus.

Gen WHY Crowd: Yes! They are filth and garbage.

This further validated and empowered Mezzi as he badgers on.

Mezzi: Yet, they are proud, and they are obstinate to give us filth and garbage. Maybe convinced in their farcical goodwill and gracious faith.

But it has also been said that nothing flatters vanity, or confirms obstinacy in the Status Quo more than repeated petitioning, lamentations, complaining, prayers. They systematically rejected these quiet methods for peace, justice and progress from generations of African youths. It makes them absolute. Generation after generation. But now, today they lost it!

Mark: We disavow and repudiate filth and garbage.

Mezzi: In fact, today, right here, right now we have separated from filth and garbage.

Crowd (in ponderous and voluptuous shrieks and jubilation): Yeah, Separation! Separation!! Separation!!!

Mark: Indeed, separation. Seperation from filth and garbage.

Mezzi: No, no Gen WHY, separated! We are officially separated.

Gen WHY Crowd (overwhelmed with air of grit and resolve): Yes! Yes!! Separated! Separated!! Separated!!!

If Gen WHY's stupor and slow reaction to the audacity and ruthlessness of candor of "they are filths and garbage", underpinned a doubtful and confusing hint at their resolve and determination for a breaking point, then "we are officially separated", leaves no equivocations to its confirmation.

Mark: Filth and garbage equate to negro Status Quo. They are of the same coin.

Mezzi: Each to our separate businesses.

Gen WHY Crowd: Dominate our environment!

Mezzi: Gen WHY, everything, anything whose content is right and wrong at the same time, pleads for a separation. Incompatibility forces the separation. Our want of dignity forces the separation. Your retroversion of retrogression of Black kind descendants' progress, generation after generation forces our separation.

It is high time we separated.

Gen WHY Crowd: Separated! Separated!! Separated!!!

Mezzi: Gen WHY, we are here to dominate our inherited filth and garbage.

Even though you are the literal filth and garbage, Gen WHY take it as a capital offense to dominate a fellow human being. For the gravest sin of humanity, committed through slavery and colonialism is dehumanization.

We don't want to carry the human blot of the White Scum. But please don't be on our path.

The unconscionable vigor of the youths is ruthlessly ingenuous. The outlandish threat: "please don't be on our path", might appear preposterous and grotesque and could be readily relegated and dismissed to naive self-aggrandizement and effrontery of their momentous juvenile emotional matrix. However, with their lives enfolded and entwined within tribulations, sorrows, filth and garbage, it will remain to be seen if hard work, perseverance, fortitude, and even punishment and crime on anything on their path, are enough to endure them to catharsis of triumph.

Mark: Status Quo, please don't be on the path of the force of hurricane and tsunami.

For that's what we are. We are officially a separated family.

Mezzi: Yeah, after all you are afraid of the stranger. And we welcome the stranger. The stranger has a name.

Mezzi pauses, pans his head, facing Mark. Mark understands. Acknowledges.

Mark: The stranger's name is love.

Mezzi: You don't know love. You don't give love.

You can't love. You can't give love.

Love is sublime power. That's why you fear to love. You can't stand love.

You earn love. You can't earn love.

We need love. You are withered of love.

You are devoid of love. You can't manufacture love.

This memorable moment of Mezzi's 'poetic homily' has forced an eerie quiet and a profound reflective mood amongst the audience. Faces, inclusive of those of the Status Quo are in a spasm of competing amazement of solemn frowns and grimaces. Whether those moments will enable chagrin and remorse and love in Status Quo's dogged ruthless pursuit of pleasure, power, profit and humiliation or provoke sublime enthusiasm that will unleash heroic passion of exertion that can persevere, endure, thrive and sustain the catharsis of liberty, freedom of the Gen WHY remains in everyone's judgement.

What is clear cut is the general amazement that is unafraid, fearless, fiery, impatient, plotting, undeterred, disappointed, threatening, intriguing, contemptuous, determined, hopeful and delighted permeating the Gen WHY

Determined, hopeful and delighted because, the Gen WHY have proven themselves. They have rallied on the shortest notice and have declared their statement of intent, their stance boldly unwaveringly so. They have proven incoercible, incorruptible and unafraid to speak to power.

There is no act of courage more defiant, more generous and more hopeful than to see misery–ridden, forlorn, broken-hearted starving African youths, conscientiously, turn into brave, ready sacrificing Gen WHY without a real plan, with just ideal and hope to succeed. That is like being a devastating unstoppable Corvid-19 weapon, with a brute force, that should turn fascinating, dangerous and destructive in its wake.

They have proven incoercible, incorruptible and unafraid to speak to power.
There is no act of courage more defiant, more generous and more hopeful than to see misery–ridden, forlorn, broken-hearted starving African youths, conscientiously, turn into brave, ready sacrificing Gen WHY without a real plan, with just ideal and hope to succeed. That is like being a devastating unstoppable Corvid-19/nuclear weapon, with a brute force, that should turn fascinating, dangerous and destructive in its wake.

Then Mark's voice, suddenly pierces the eerie quiet.

Mark: Gen WHY, Gen WHY what next?

Gen WHY, awoken by his voice, get out from their reverie.

Mark: Now that we know our problems, what next?

Gen WHY (gusting answers): Dominance, dominance, dominance! Platform, platform, platform! Captivity Captive, Captivity captive! Misery captive, misery captive, misery captive! Dominate our environment, dominate filth and garbage! Platform! Platform! Platform! Platform! Freedom! Freedom! Freedom!

Mark: Hard work, sacrifice at comfort?

Gen WHY: Yeaahhhhhhhh, let's go, let's go, let's go. Let's begin, let's begin, let's ...hard work, hard work, hard work…

That's it. From the van, songs come on And they are from Michael Jackson's: "Everyone his story" to "they don't care about us" to Kris Cross's "Kris Cross is going to make it."

For the whole time Buzzo and David have been working behind the scene: orchestrating and directing every shred of the whole shebang through the remarkable mouthpieces of Mezzi and Mark that hypnotized, held and tranced the latent intrinsic Gen WHY essence optics into action. Action of defiance, intransigence, self-confidence, tenacity, and share of responsibility in Africa's generational endemic failures and of separation with what has been not to progress themselves. Responsibility through the belief in themselves, through deeds of hard work, renaissance credo self-consciousness of WHY and WHY NOT, with faith in God. Buzzo and David had usurped and transformed a section of President's office, the office overlooking the Plaza Hill from the first floor, in their situation room.

Everybody of the first house: The President, the First Lady, the chief of staff, the chief protocol officer, the chief security officer, the chief of police, the chief of the combined army, navy, air force, etc., united to them.

Miscellany of events have defined the chaotic moments that characterized the beginning of the Status Quo's march to the time the situation room became operative. There was an assault of conflicting emotions in the situation room that pitched a generational divide of pros and cons on Gen WHY's will, determination and tenacity of resolve. There was such gloomy hollowness in First Lady's eyes, as there was a conflicting emotional crackling tension of hopefulness and exquisite dread locked in the inscrutable resolve in the President's eyes, as there was some consensus of unspoken affectation of confidence in the smug and smirk and unwavering grimace of Buzzo and David that swallowed all the questions and numbed all expectations, anxiety and answers.

There had been a litany of voluptuous doubts to trust the scorched, charred, subdued and defeated hearts of the youths to rally. Then after they rallied at such a short notice, releasing answer to first doubt, came the miscellany of ponderous touting doubt at their determination to endure, defy. They did defy. Much more. They subdued and crushed the spite in the Status Quo. Apparently. At least apparently. Then finally came the catharsis of the general remarkable amazement of their conduct that is incredulous, delightful, optimistic, encouraging. Gen WHY coalesced and held. They did not cower and disperse.

A conscientious willful win, theirs, that graced their honor and dignity in defying gravity on that fate of a hateful, hurtful, desperate and rewarding frontline. Before everybody's eyes Gen WHY turned into a remarkable trusting, reliable brute machine with a brute unstoppable but humbling force, to alongside plan, project, pursue and realize an enabling Gen WHY future. With just but a passion of enthusiasm of ideal and hope to succeed, they separated and resolved to dominate their environment and build their future.

In fact, the President's words were: "Remarkable. This is voluptuously remarkable. These kids merit everything we can give them. Look at them. Look at my little Mark.

Our laziness, our stupidity, our complacency, our hypocrisy, our kleptomania to say but a few have inadvertently, precipitously and perspicaciously made them men. This continent is saved. Honey (to his wife) God bless this day. These are good soldiers. They can endure. They can stand the conspiracies and assassinations of combined CIA, KGB, MOSSAD, CI5 unlike anything before on this continent. And this pleases my heart remarkably especially as the saying *"dream things that never were and say why not."* is gripping our youths from within.

Buzzo takes the opportunity of the winsome, glorious moment at the Plaza Hill to introduce his idea of the economic mainstay of the Gen WHY economy and wealth- base, prompting Mezzi and Mark in tweeting:
#Gen WHY at faith, yes?
#Gen WHY at victory, yes?
#Gen WHY at celebrations, yes?
#Gen WHY at collectivity, yes?
Gen WHY phones go haywire with their diverse prompting rings.

Before they could check out their phones, before even responding, Mezzi and Mark and Glenda and Brett and … had noticed Buzzo's tweets. And Mezzi abruptly stops the music. And into the microphone screams:

Mezzi: Gen WHY, our faith in our capacity has given us victory. Yes?

Gen WHY reluctantly stop dancing and get back to the realization of a sudden crackling voice. It's Mezzi's. Then they realize. They respond back.

Gen WHY: Yeeeeeeeeaaaaaaaaaaaaaahhhhhhhhhh!
Mark: Gen WHY, our collective capacity gives us victory, yes?
Gen WHY: Yes, it does!
Mezzi: Gen WHY, our collective victory celebrations, yes?
Gen WHY: Yeeeeeeeeaaaaaaaaaaaaaaaaaahhhhhhhhhhhhhhhh.
Mezzi: Are we hungry and thirsty, yes?
Gen WHY: Food! Food!! Food!!!
Mark: Gen WHY's collective crowd economy to vanquish hunger, yes?
Gen WHY: Vanquish hunger. Vanquish misery!
Mezzi: Collective crowd economy, yes?

There was a feeble response. Not a ponderous response. Instead in its wake an uneasy, uncomfortable silence descended and veiled the air. An uneasy menacing silence that swallowed the answers as faces creased into wonderment and doubtful and lost wry grimaces.

The word "crowd funding" rings a remarkably voluptuous familiar bell of disdain. Their minds get promptly assaulted by spasm of devastating and humiliating chicanery world of "faith of crowd funding" of the men of God.

Crowd funding was the last straw to confound their already confused minds. Their misery synthesis.

Crowd funding is what the Priestcraft of the land has used to violate, profane and desecrate them and viciously crushed their hope, their faith in the church. With crowd funding, the pastors had encouraged, legitimized and perpetuated stealing and corruption in Africa.

The more amount of money you donate, the more you are visibly blessed and privileged in the house of the pastor, the less question is asked about the legitimacy of the money. The more less you donate, the more less you are blessed, the more you are disdained, the more you are despised, the more the only option is to steal and bring to the church. The more the encouragement, the authorization and the validation to steal through whatever means for the house of God. For the pastors.

The pastors own airplanes, exotic cars, houses, schools, lands, hospitals. Their heaven is on earth. So, members are encouraged and authorized to be like them.

Emulate them in this gracious special God's favor. Special God's favor indeed.

Members are authorized to be thieves, gluttons, kleptomaniacs and be sinners.

And their absolution lies in the blessings of the pastor. And its justification is in the unmerited favor of the Lord. God's grace is unquestionable. It's justifiable. It graces illegitimacy. Illegitimate origin of donations regardless. By Africa's men of God tenet. And to that extent their faith in God is withered and viciously subdued and crushed. Crowd funding is based on faith in God. It's not a social contract with God. Or a social covenant with God.

Mezzi understands and badgers on.

Mezzi: Ours is a collective crowd economy. A collective covenant with our sweat. With our hard work. With our efforts. With our sacrifice. With our vision. We sow we reap. Where we sow, we must reap with faith and trust in God.

We give by ourselves, to ourselves and for ourselves. We are our end users. We are a community. Our Gen WHY community, our Church. We are the Body for Christ: Love thy community like thy self. We are our government. We are our revenue.

Mezzi pauses, scans their hopeful, expectant faces and finds approval to continue.

Mezzi: Gen WHY, here is the deal; here is the covenant with ourselves: Each weekend, precisely from Friday evenings to Saturday evenings to Sunday mornings till midday, starting from this weekend, Gen WHY can feast with foods and drinks, dance and celebrate to satisfaction in nominated disco clubs and eateries of our choice. All at the cost of one American dollar.
Mark: Gen WHY, have you heard? $1 from each and every one of us.

Gen WHY are left agape with wonder and incredulity.
Mark drives home the point.

Mark: Gen WHY have you heard? Yes with $1.

Now some amongst the Gen WHY recover, with cupped hands over their ears as the others are in animated confabulation.

Gen WHY (with cautious optimism): Could you kindly repeat please?
Mezzi: Our two-day weekend feasting consolation at $1 each.
Gen WHY (Ponderously incredulous): You are not kidding?
Mezzi: Are we kidding on the Plaza Hill?
Mark: That's the miracle of crowd funding. We re our tithing, our revenue.
Mezzi: We are our government. And that's not all. We will continue this consolatory respite practice at our platform, at Gen WHY platform, after its launch.

As the reality of the message sinks in, Gen WHY are incredulous. They erupt in an irrepressible thunderous scowling, wailing, shrieking clamor.

Gen WHY: Yeeeeeeeeaaaaaaaaaaaaarrrrrrrrrrrrrrrrr.
Mark: Yes, Gen WHY you got it: 1$ bill for the whole weekend.
Mezzi: From Friday night, Saturday and Sunday morning. Breakfast, lunch, dinner. Food, drink and music.
Gen WHY: Yeeeeeeaaaaaaahhhhhhh! Crowd covenant! Collective economy!
Mezzi: Crowd economy at victory, yes?
Gen WHY: Yeeeeeeeaaaaaaahhhhhhhhhhhhhh our tithes for us!
Mark: Collective economy at celebrations, yeah?
Gen WHY: Yaaaaaaaaaaarrrrrrrrrr our revenue for ourselves!
Mezzi: Collective economy at hunger and development and progress?
Gen WHY: Yaaaaaaaaaaaarrrrrrrrrr our revenue for light, water, schools, hospitals!
Mark: Collective crowd economy our covenant for our future!
Gen WHY: Yeeeessss, build our factories, homes, dominate our filth and garbage!

Mark: And this practice of weekend respite is to be continued at the platform?

Gen WHY: Platform, platform, platform. Collective economy. Collective covenant. Collective economy.

Buzzo and David tweet: The collective economy account No: 55555555555.

Gen WHY phones go berserk with the prompting tones announcing receivals of crowd account No: 55555555555.

With equal vigor they started posting 1$ bills to that account.

Mezzi puts the music back on. The dancing and the celebration continued.

The faces of Buzzo and David crease into a delight of relief, breaking into expansive Winner's pride.

> *This is voluptuously remarkable. These kids merit everything we can give them.*
> *Look at them...Our laziness, our stupidity, our complacency, our hypocrisy, our kleptomania to say but a few have inadvertently, precipitously and perspicaciously made them men. This continent is saved... These are good soldiers. They can endure. They can stand the conspiracies and assassinations of combined CIA, KGB, MOSSAD, CI5 unlike anything done before.*

Chapter 2

"UNEQUIVOCALLY AUDACIOUS: A FIERCE, FEARLESS, YOUTH MOVEMENT CORONATED: THEY CALL THEMSELVES GENERATION WHY."

"STATUS QUO DEFIED, HUMILIATED, DEFILED, BEATEN AND IMPRISONED. ON THE HILL."

"AWESOME: THE YOUTHS STANDING UP TO A CONTINENTS GENERATIONAL FAILURES OF HEREDITARY DESPOTISM."

"THE PRESIDENT AND HIS FAMILY GIVE FALSE HOPE TO GENERATION WHY."

"ILLUSSIONED YOUTHS WANT TO CHANGE THE WORLD WITH SPEECH AND PASSION."
"GEN WHY IDENTIFY THE EVIL TRINITY THAT PLAGUE THE BLACK RACE."
"GENERATION WHY DECREE SEPERATION: YOU CAN'T GIVE BACK TO PROSTITUTION ITS LOST INNOCENCE."

"A GENERATION'S EUPHEMISTIC GENIALITY COININGS: THE DEVIL, THE DEVIL'S SON–THE EVIL TRINITY, THE EVIL SPIRIT– ONE MILLION COWARDS AND TEN MILLION STUPID MEN, AND A BILLION PLUS GUINEA PIGS."

"THE YOUTHS: THE AFRICAN GOVERNMENTS, MONARCHS, PRIESTS, LIKE APPLE, A BADGE OF KNOWN AND PRESENT EVILS."

"GENERATION WHY: WHAT'S THE CONTRIBUTION OF THE BLACK RACE TO THE WORLD?"

"GEN WHY: WHAT'S THE BLACKMAN'S LIFE-STYLE? OPEN AIR DEFECATION, URINATION, OPEN AIR SEWERAGE, CANDLE LIGHTS, HUMILIATION, MISERY?"

"OUR RENEGADE YOUTHS: BLACK RACE BENEATH THE HUMAN STUPIDITY?"

"GENERATION WHY: SHAME ON US. AT LEAST ELECTRIC LIGHT, PIPE BORNE WATER, FOOD SECURITY, HEALTH CARE, EDUCATION FOR ALL."

"GEN WHY: THE SIGNIFICANCE OF THE INSIGNIFICANCE OF THE BLACK RACE?"

These are some of the headlines describing the rally as captured by the different politically disposed dailies on the table of the President.

The President, seated, his face pinched in a solicitous frown but with the gesture of a propriator pride, has his eyes scanning and scrutinizing the dailies.

The youths' determined stance to stand up and challenge the Status Quo, that was generations coming was highly generous and fulfilling to his heart. Their act of faith was a sublime generosity. More so coming from a multitude of the starving and famished. Their fierceness and fieriness and sense of purpose, as he witnessed from the window of his house overlooking the Plaza Hill, have seemed to him unfeigned, unhinged, extemporaneous, honest and uncompromising. That their new expression of "never again": Never again to hunger, never again to pain, never again to fear, never again to humiliation, never again to slavery coupled with their determination of "we rather choose hell than misery again" and courage in calling out "Filth and garbage" and "Separated" were at the same time undaunting, telling and humbling.

It goes to confirm the saying that 'the best qualities of humans, who dispose and stand up inadvertently in a crisis, are very often the best to trust in a prosperous calm.'

They are justified by a race's, a continent's generational disdain for their posterity. They want to obliterate the impression, the specter, the ghost of misery sum total and its perpetuity of a continent's past within the immediate present.

The same way, he feels justified of his towering ambition to be instrumental in enabling that change, fostering the posterity pride and its perpetuation for always. He has hope. The stance of Gen WHY gives him the people's moral edge, the empowerment, together with some heavenly justifications, entrust him with the validation to not compromise in crushing all the nervous agitation, the obduracy, the spite, the defiance and the pride of the Status Quo in their hereditary evil despotic exertion and its perpetuations.

In fact, the same night of the rally, his intelligence and security services made arrests. Arrests of excellence and stature: monarchical, political, ecclesiastical. Reason: unwarranted rallies with treasonable offences of attempt at life and destruction of properties.

He went further. With the gut, the guilt, the soullessness and the groggy determination of a boxer, enfolded with and bent on the spasm of fear of a knock out, he neutralized and incapacitated the power of Status Quo in every form and shape and format and contour: to the frozen monies and assets of the "men of God", he froze that of the monarchy, the oligarchs and of his fellow politicians.

And decreed that those same monies and assets would become properties of the masses with immediate effect: "You all have 14 days grace to prove legality of properties and monies."

To prove property legality in Africa of the Evil Trinity, the Cowards, the Stupid Men, is like the towering impossible proverbial biblical teaching proportion: "A Carmel passing through the eye of a needle".

He did not stop there: he froze the accounts of the Lebanese and of the Indian contractors. They have 14 days to come forward for review, reconciliation of contracts between work done and undone, monies expended and whatnot.

He further decreed general accountability on the basis of salaries-wealth possession ratio for workers of government, for workers of the organized private sector and the rest–banks, private enterprises, local contractors, oligarchs and all their combined families.

He imposed a travel ban of four months on the leadership and their families, on civil servants, on the Lebanese and Indians, on the management of the church, etc. Furthermore, to the ranks and files of the men in uniform– men of the armed forces, men of the police force, men of the prisons, he raised their minimum monthly wages, to avoid mutiny, to have them by the balls. He needs their loyalty and sympathy and support to remarkably enable this moment of purgation.

He asked the men and women in uniform, of the Customs and excise, immigrations that they have two months to restructure and be profitable to the economy or be disbanded and reformed with dire consequences.

In sum general accountability. Without fervor or favor. Regardless of whom it benefits or whom it detracts, in its wake. Impartial. In a land where absolute amorality reigns supreme, unchallenged.

It has been said that terror of society is the basis of morals. And the fear of God is the secret of religion.

However, these two metrics are grossly remarkably absent on the African land.

The accountability fervor, caused such animation of justice-passion of remarkably ponderous, resounding approval of Gen WHY that underpins affectation, contempt, gratitude, humiliation, vengeance. The feelings and resentments of vengeance towards the Status Quo that overwhelmed the homes, the neighborhoods, the streets, the nation was unfathomably pleasant for the youths.

In fact, their passion animation of justice, sprouted and culminated in more rallies, taking to the streets, for protracted hours. Its quickness and swiftness in support and validation of the President's actions were remarkable. It's like a deterrent machinery. Its most remarkable facet is its endurance and its endearing capacity. Its endurance has given the Gen WHY movement its purpose. While its endearing has validated the determination, the perseverance, the selflessness, the voluptuous unwavering courage and ponderous audacity of Gen WHY to severe with hereditary despotism and forge to dominate their filth and garbage at all costs. And its unwavering deterring and scary force to be hedged at this very fledgling stage or any imagination, any hints, any mumbles at plots and intrigues and maneuverings are to be seen, not just against the constituted authority of the President, but against the Gen WHY.

While on the other hand what is left of the Status Quo families are vitriolically incredulous, ponderously consternating, voluptuously devastating, remarkably scary and afraid of what their life could hold. Now they have their life that has been smeared in the conceits of their despotism and punishment in the crosshairs of arrogance of the unforgiving menace of fear and humiliation of defeat.

The choice you make between hating and loving, punishing and forgiving can become the story of your life. The story of your hope and the crushing arrogance of hopelessness. A chicken comes home to roost.

The remarkable affectation of their arrogance of confidence held them ransom. They saw the whole thing coming: they saw the President vituperate at the men of God, defile the men of God, crush their spite and defiance and pride, closing down their places of worship to the voluptuous plaudit of the youths. They saw him with what seemed unfeigned swiftness, do away with his vestiges of bombasts and corruption: his exotic cars and most properties sold to the Lebanese. They saw him concretely shore up the youths' efforts: donate the proceed to platform effort. They saw his demeanor gone radically, remarkably austere. Yet they defied him, rallying.

As it has been said, the contours of all virtues are shaped by adversity. The President knew, knows his position is rooted in arrogance, and in disdain, and in vain, and in corruption, and in cruelty, and in punishment, and in retribution, and in humiliation, and in kleptomania…and in evil.

Africa as a society is evil;
Africa's tradition is coded in evil norms;
Its ridden with men and women of evil spirit;
People just think evil;
People contrive evil;
People perpetrate evil;
People perpetuate evil;
People shield evil;
People feed on evil;
People thrive on evil;
The result, the cost, and the effect speak for themselves.
Evil in government;
Evil in governance;

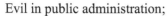

Evil in public administration;
Evil in private enterprise;
Evil in the churches;
Evil in the mosques; Evil in the tradition; Evil in the masses.

For a man in his position to have transited during sermon, he must have had violent angst of conflicting emotions of shame and determination, got glided into remorse, regret and opportunity.

Opportunity gives regret its obligations, and regret gives obligation its purpose.

The President decided to love and be saved from his complicit complacency.

His coeval did not. An onerous, fatal, conscientious challenge, they took.

The President is part of the immediate remote past and the immediate present.

He is the system. He is part of the system. He is the product of the system.

He knows the system's intricacies, intrigues, maneuverings and tricks and chicanery.

He knows how a bridge is promised and built without a stream underneath.

He's been part of the looting.

He is part and parcel of the 00.5 or so exiguous percent of the Africans, dead and living, past and present, with billions stashed away in foreign banks. The likes of...Mobutu, Museveni, Jonathan, De Santos, Nguesso, Babangida, Boigny, Bongo, Abacha, Obasanjo, Atiku, just to name but a few; almost all members of the national assemblies, the secretaries to the governments, the heads of government corporations and parastatals and their directors, the central banks governors and directors, the state governors, their secretaries, chiefs of staff, heads of parastatals, their directors, the local government council heads, the local government chairmen , the Emirs, the Sultans, the Obas, the Chiefs, their fiefdoms; the men of God, their families and their cohorts; the oligarchs and families, the contractors, the labor leaders, the judiciary, the justice department, the judges, etc., etc. The list is endless. These are the Status Quo group that have 99.9 % of Africa's money stashed away somewhere, overwhelming amount of Africa's wealth-sum in foreign banks.... with the complicities of the White Scums, Indians, Lebanese and the Chinese.

African leaders are the worst prostitutes. Insatiable. They lay in wait, not for the best offeror but for the most demeaning. Demeaning misery offeror. Misérables on their own merits. Like the Lebanese and the Indians.

The Lebanese and the Indians are attracted to lawlessness, to corruption, to caste system, to dysfunctional system, to mud, to filth... like moths to fire.

Worst humans are the easiest to find in a remarkably functional filth.

On the one hand, the White race is the devil you know. The hard-working devil. And the Black race is the devil you want to know. The sloven devil. The devil is in the details, they say. These two races have had history of antagonism, protagonism. The one the story of heartbreak, sorrows in their humiliation and defeat. The other the story of competing regret, remorse and intransigence, sorrow and pride, suffering and apathy, self-mortification and arrogance in their apparent conquest. To this day, somewhere in the infinite virtual distance between them, tolerance, pardon, forgiveness and goodwill, chicanery, tacitly-consensually reign.

On the other hand, why would the Lebanese run away from their war-torn 'paradise' back home for the sodden lanes of Africa? For extrinsic peace?

Why would the Indians leave their 'sublime spirituality' amidst Indian open-air defecation, their voluptuous remarkable stench filth, to the filths of Africa amidst Africa's voodoo, witch-craft? Because Africa's filth is diamond plaited and their voodoo withered of spirituality?

The one for extrinsic peace? The other for African converts and sainthood? Perhaps?

The Europeans did not run away from their land. They sent away their embarrassment at their intrinsic peace. They sent their filth, scum to Africa. And in the process added wealth pillaging from the indigenous, for full peace at home. Conversely the Lebanese never almost have peace at home.

And before the Europeans sent missionaries for converts, they sent their human filths, their scum to plunder first. Before they enslaved, they preached Jesus. Before they colonized, they prayed Jesus. Before they found a sublime peace at home they disfranchised, converting Africa to mercenary plundering land, even to this day.

Lo, let's not forget that Africans are on their own merits, self-plunderers.

To the Lebanese, you don't need peace at home. Africa is your peace. Africa does not stand up.

To the Indians, you don't need to convert Africa. They are already converting at plundering. The land is ever ready for pillaging. Africa does not stand up.

Africa just needed more sophistication at the art of plundering. That you both are already providing and should provide. Africa does not stand up.

Africa's sodden streets are their prosperous sanctuaries. Open air defecation and filth of African system are their sanctuaries.

The Lebanese cart away every loot. Loot away into Lebanon. They have visceral love for nationhood. For the Lebanese nation. They help Africa perpetuate her misery. The Indians are mercenaries of adulterations. The dehumanizing counterfeiters. Africa is a killing field. Their killing fields. They help Africa remain moribund, die slowly. With the adulterations and the counterfeiting trade-drugs, machines, heroin, cocaine. Adulterated everything. They paralyze, loot and cart away.

It is said that any economy where you find the Lebanese or the Indians or both, would never thrive. Now Africa is adding, aiding and abating nonmonotheist China to its menu. Finally, the ultimate Africa's annihilation in the offing.

The Lebanese and the Indians are in Africa ingratiating themselves in the filth of Africa. To help the cleavage of misery peak. It's ever peaking.

Why not, Africa does not stand up.

It's of ponderous curiosity and of remarkable conflict the President's open accountability challenge to the land. This challenge is flagrant, defying, arrogant, crushing and intimidating at the same time. That challenge remarkably conflicts with culture of not standing up.

In our history, in quick successions, far more iron tyrannies from within replaced the one form of colonial tyranny: control from without. Africa informs and feeds the colonial control today, tomorrow and geared to infinitum. Africa does not stand up. The hereditary despotic African tyrants end up heroes in Africa. This has left in its wake a ponderous devastating fallout on the conscience of generations of its youth: The slumbering conscience, the gullible conscience, the resigned conscience, the slothful conscience, the complacent smug conscience, the scrooge conscience, the apostate conscience, the glutton conscience, the kleptomania conscience, the reprobate conscience, the miracle conscience, the hypocrisy conscience, the faith rhetoric against the faithfulness of faith conscience, the hope against the hopelessness conscience, the celebration, the adoration, the adulation and the aspiration of the oppressor conscience, the corrupt bombast-glutton-kleptomania lifestyle conformity conscience.

A total erosion of set values conscience has been instilled, and it evolves and renovates, spirally downward. This is mirrored in their everyday conduct: respect for selves gone, honesty gone, accountability gone, community gone, hard work gone, meritocracy gone, discipline gone, self-confidence gone, self-esteem gone. All gone. "Gone" somewhat justifiably gone generations of Africa's youth could argue: filth and garbage absorbed, filth and garbage spitted out.

Even though there is a total erosion of set values; even though the continued devastating regressive downward spiral consequences are voluptuously sorrowing to the land; even though there is no happiness without its woes, no wealth without its costs, no laziness without its misery, no slavery without its dehumanization, no colonialism without its dominance, no trial without its risks, no success without its failures, no life without its errors, no death without its sorrow; even though to these extents the President's audacious fight for accountability is turned gruesome, fearless, dreadful, intimidating and fascinating at the same time, even so the success of accountability challenge remains to everybody's imagination.

And being an integrated product of the past but striving not to be prisoner of it, the President takes refuge in and is solaced by the mantra:

"Don't give up trying, for every failed try is a step closer to goal."

Even though every African who had submitted self to accountability, to selflessness, to value set rules has been disgraced and killed;

Even though a majority of Africans have been psyched out into despising set values and upholding and appraising unaccountability, chaos and anarchy instead in its wake; even so the President remains undaunted, unfazed and determined in a viciousness contrivance of:

Why not to accountability, why not to justice, why not to integrity, why not to courage, why not to dedication? And to that extent the youths' platform must be.

Even at the cost of paying the ultimate price: death for love.

Love is death as death is life. They interlace and incarnate the same value.

Lo, let's not forget that Africans are on their own merits, self-plunderers.
African leaders are the worst prostitutes. Insatiable. They lay in wait, not for the best offeror but for the most demeaning. Demeaning misery offeror.
Misérables on their own merits. Like the Lebanese and the Indians.
The Lebanese and the Indians are attracted to lawlessness, to corruption, to caste system, to dysfunctional system, to mud, to filth… like moths to fire.

Chapter 3

The land is gripped with a ponderous unutterable suspense of such a delicious menace. The delicious menace finds its reason in the decrees for accountability and in the 14 days ultimatum to legitimize the rights of caravan of properties owned by all and sundry but with special attention to those of the Status Quo and families, of the Lebanese and the Indians.

The ponderous unutterable suspense instead finds its expression in the spasm of anxiety and anguish, the assault of fear, flush of shame and grieving sadness.

The tradition of hereditary despotism in Africa has the unquestionable right – ruthlessness of pursuit of power, profit, pleasure and humiliation and unchallenged norm of unaccountability. In fact, staggering huge sums of money of the people are stolen and subtracted, diverted and stashed away in the banks at home and abroad, are as many houses are owned, home and abroad, are as many cars are owned at home and abroad, are as many investments are made in refineries abroad, in manufacturing, in agriculture-allied machines, fertilizers, generators, finished products abroad, are as much disinvestment and sabotaging made in these same sectors at home, in Africa. As much taxes are collected, and Africa's raw materials are exported and revenues are generated, at the ministry of finance, and the banks are strewn with monies, are as much disinvestments in health care, in education, in social amenities, and are as much properties in men are made: unemployable graduates of generations of African youths or at best itinerant worker; women are objects of domestic slavery and child bearing, enduring an excruciating ruin of their latent talents; children will never know but the fields, the river, and scavenging. *Every generation produces youths. The segue of youths is life continuation here on earth. The youthful vigor produces energy, drives justice, proposes fairness, impresses development, endures idealism. That gives the world a segue of hopes and dreams. That in turn guarantees life and life's facades on earth.*

And anywhere of any society where this youthful Vigor is beaten, trampled upon, subjugated, subdued, their very life essence significance snuffs out. Africa is it.

And as much…and as much…and as much are subtracted and unaccountably unaccountable. Unaccountably unchallenged and ponderously celebrated.

The leadership – politician, monarchy, the priests plus the voluptuous Lebanese and the Indian sophisticates – installed flagrant corruption, ultimate stealing and sublime kleptomania and entrenched them.

Their bombasts and debauchery, through their symbols – their private airplanes, their mansions, their exotic cars, their designers apparels and clothing, jewelries and watches, their frequent travelling abroad with families and lovers, their highly overseas educated children, their pilgrimage for health cares and religiosity, their churches, their hotels, their restaurants and bars, their menus, their best spirits and champagnes and wines, their arrogance, their snobbishness etcetera,…in sum, this life style held and swayed, excluding, of course, the very victims: Guinea pig masses. The majority of Guinea pig masses' life purpose is, has been of visceral blind aspiration to live out this life style. The oppressor's life style. What a beyond*ness* of self-inflicting grieving mockery. Maybe a grieving paradox. Enigma.

No surprises: the mythical oppressed-oppressor relationship debacle.

The comet-like speed with which the symbols of bombasts and expression of debauchery stuttered, dispersed and disappeared from the street landscape was remarkably amazing. An amazement that is incredulous, numb, afraid, sad, nostalgic, disapproving, uncertain, pregnant, delightful, full of expectations at the same time. Conversely the Gen WHY self-confidence instead, coalesced, bonded and held on the streets.

They are now the familiar expressions, the proud legitimate patronage, within the confines of the symbols of debauchery and bombasts: the hotels, the restaurants, the bars, the nightclubs, are hosting Gen WHY celebration of the Status Quo defeat at the Plaza Hills.

They are celebrating their severance from the Status Quo.

They are celebrating the hard-won trust and confidence of the President.

They are toasting to being the force of deterrent.

They are toasting to their courage in profile.

They are toasting to their new-found economy, their 'crowd economy' with its justifiable skepticism. Skepticism that stems from the chicanery "men of God", who privatized and appropriated crowd funding, of paying tithe platitude.

They are in amazement of the fluke of drinking and eating away the weekend at $1.

They are awed and fascinated by and in the company of their found idols Buzzo, Mezzi. The audacious, ardent visionaries, whose presence sooths the field Gen WHY and attracts and fascinates and infects the house Gen WHY in equal measure. As a matter of fact, children of Status Quo are turning in, elevating into house Gen WHY's self-consciousness, grappling, grasping, gasping with the truth, transiting, challenging their homes, sacrificing at their comforts of ill-gotten wealth and chagrined at the mass misery of their peers at the hands of their families. In fact, deflated, resized, and befuddled in conflicting expressions of fear, vanquish, humiliation,

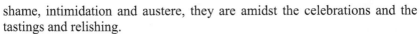

shame, intimidation and austere, they are amidst the celebrations and the tastings and relishing.

Amidst their youth peers from the West are the Lebanese and the Indians youths as well, celebrating and toasting in what the field Gen WHY see widely as provocation, curiosity and derision and infiltration and hypocrisy.

They can pardon and overlook the presence of provocations and derisions from the West, that can find their justification in the stupidity of the black race and purpose in their seemingly honest unfeigned solidarity and support to get them out of misery. After all they are the hardest working race, who have invented everything for their lifestyle. To that extent the world's life style. And instead of being jealous they put it at the service of the other two races to use and advance the lives of their people.

The presence of the Lebanese and the Indians youth, their peers in amidst instead, provokes in them a voluptuous assault of spasm of sinister suspicion. They are incensed. After all, the Lebanese and the Indian families are the vehicles, the chicanery personified, the pulsating veins of their misery. They rightly don't want to trust them.

Brett and Glenda crease into disapproving fierce grimaces with their eyes trained in their direction. Buzzo and David notice and they confer on the line of action to mitigate the situation. These days have proven Brett and Glenda to have a special talent of taming and controlling the streets and coalescing and herding the unruly herds of the youths. The unruly herds are the most stubborn, unyielding of the unruly youths of the youths of the Gen WHY.

David (scowling, waving, and phoning him at the same time amidst the clattering and shrieking of the youths): Ahmed!

Without success he sends him a WhatsApp message.

It's given. Ahmed, Asian-skinned, as most Lebanese and Indian families, is endeared to and friend of any and every African ruling class family.

Ahmed did not hear him but sees the prompting of his WhatsApp message, noticing at the same time the missed call. He calls back David immediately.

Amidst his call, he scans the crowd around him and meets the eyes of David in the immediate distance. They hold stare and they smile. In some minutes Ahmed followed by his Lebanese and Indian friends, in a human caravan, wedge themselves amidst the beehive of duties of pleasures found in the Gen WHY's celebration and insinuated themselves at the table of David, Buzzo, Brett and Glenda, framed with a ponderous presence of the unruly herds of the unruly youths. Remarkably absent are the presence of Mezzi and Mark, who are ever busy at tweeting, working, alternating from their situation room at President's office, shoring up the Gen WHY, preparing them for the Platform launch, and at their 'kids must play center' at the hamlet, taking care of the kids and the 'Kids must play center.'

It's worthy of note that Ahmed's family had bought the Ferraris and Lamborghini, out of the fleet of exotic cars, off David's family, as their real psychological transition really started, raising money to help with 'kids must play center.'

David (after a brief exchange of pleasantries): Ahmed my friends over here, Brett and Glenda don't feel comfortable with your presence. Won't you guys want to know why?

Ahmed's face turns into a mask of frowning grimace. He looks at Brett and Glenda. And back to Brett, locking eyes with him.

There was a breathing menacing silence. A silence insinuated in fear, hate, love and courage. A lot of fate is decided in silence. Ahmed, his stare still held on Brett:

Ahmed: David, why?
Brett: You tell us why?
Ahmed: I should tell why you hate our presence?
Glenda: Yes, precisely. Without mincing words.
Ahmed (looking at David): I am confused.
Glenda: When did our live with its tribulations, sorrows and misery enfolded and interlaced with the glitters of yours on our land?

Ahmed and the community of Lebanese and Indian youth have understood. Their faces writhe into shameful, frightful and tortured grimaces that disfigured them.

Buzzo is impassively listening with rapt smugness. His face does not betray any expression. He is thinking: Brett and Glenda have grown in courage. An African youth could finally challenge the sophisticates, the vulgar profligates of their misery.

Brett: Tell us your education and knowledge of the Africans?
Glenda: Yeah for example what your patriarchal dad tells you about Africans?

Ahmed seem to succumb to the vicious, piercing and cruel stare and to the scrutiny and the judgement of the infinite threatening eyes of the Gen WHY: his face forlorn and chagrined, his heart summons the courage to unleash the hurtful, hateful truth to the expectant ponderously impatient ears.

In a spasm of gasp of conflicting emotion of fear and anguish and shame and in a rush of words:

Ahmed: That Africans are below human stupidity. That you are lazy. That you won't read. That you won't react. That you won't stand up. That you are substandard human beings. That you are more stupid than sheep. That our job is to help perpetuate and feed off your stupidity. That we should discriminate against you. That we should have a limit to your friendship. That you are the only mistake of Allah...

Glenda (incensed, interjecting): So, vulgar profligates, why are you in our midst?

Ahmed: Believe me. We fight this prejudice concept every day in our homes until we are subdued through coercion. Then the rally happened. Everyone was to say the least shocked. And we, the youths of our community, are so happy, viewing and reviewing the video of the drama of your dominance of the Status Quo at the Plaza Hill. In fact, there is a conflicting emotion of fascination and apprehension of that amazing found "captivity captive" slogan within our community.

Brett: So, is it correct to imply that your families and community are in a state of assault of unutterable sadness, fear, anxiety, forlornness at the turn of things?

Ahmed: Yes and no. Yes, because we have no peace back home in Lebanon. No because our community of diaspora families has a lot of savings stashed away in foreign banks to provide for at least ten future generations without exertion at any work, plus they don't believe the Gen WHY, in sum you guys are going to change anything on the African developmental landscape. Africans love enslavement.

Buzzo (interjecting): Ahmed, if you are truly with us, who is the cabal?

Buzzo's question caught everyone off guards. There is a voluptuous general amazement of surprise and unutterable interest and attention. The remarkable interest and attention imposed an immediate eerie silence of such a conspicuous curiosity.

Ahmed's face is in an uncomfortable pensive grimace as he fixes and holds stare with Buzzo. He's heard of Buzzo but has never met him before now. He is fascinating and he is awed by his combative demeanor and intimidating intelligence. He has that gesture of finality that warned and threatened.

Ahmed: Cabal is fortunately not a ghost. It's not a myth invented to induce us to fear or keep us subjugated. It's real. It's a cartel. It could be the civil servants. It could be the mineral wealth sector. It could be the electric power authorities. It could be the generator importers. It could be the waterboard. It could be the oil marketers. It could be the fertilizer importers. It could be the port authorities. It could be the telecommunication sector. It could be the government bureaucracy. It could be your father. It could be my father. It could be all of them combined.

Buzzo (swallowing the hard, hurtful truth): I agree. To that extent, my father is one of the cabals.

To Ahmed's surprise there was no amazement to Buzzo's mea culpa self-effacing admission. It's an open secret. This guy is selfless. That seems to infect and inject him with courage. So, with equal vigor:

Ahmed: Yes, my family is as well a cabal.
Buzzo: The generator importation authority?
Ahmed: No! They are the facade. Generator business is owned and financed by Africans. Just like most of other businesses.

The hard, listening crowd erupts in a voluptuous shriek of surprise and consternation.

Ahmed: We are complicit, 360 degrees complicity to import everything and thwart any effort at growing any home manufacturing, industries, agriculture, jobs etc. However you look at it, we execute the continent's wishes.

Buzzo, now wedges in raising his beer glass in the air. Almost every eye, notices and holds its stare and breath. There is a gradual, reluctant silence in the whole bar. Then he toasts to the space.

Buzzo: Long live to courage. Long live to honesty. Thank you, Ahmed. I believe you. We are all, all of us seated here, seated there, standing here, standing there, all the youth of the world – Gen Z, Gen WHY – out there are a community. We think collectively. We act collectively. We are a collectivity.

Then he pauses, scanning and panning the faces of the Gen WHY. The Gen WHY's faces, that had been fiercely contorted, ready to ostracize the already stereotyped communities of Lebanese and Indians, crease into tortured smiles and somewhat into a forgiving smirk of resignation.
Buzzo interprets the signs and seizes their approval and continues.

Buzzo: It has been said that children begin by loving their parents; as they grow older, they judge them. Sometimes they forgive them.
It has also been said that the basis of optimism is sheer terror. Which is agreeable if we rephrase thus: *the abject resolve to deal with and defeat our sheer terror is the basis of our optimism.*

Buzzo pauses once again. Every eye, in mental note, is expectant, trained on him

Buzzo: And on that note, I want you Ahmed to toast to every Gen WHY's determination, perseverance, fortitude, punishment and even to the necessary sins and griefs that must endure to our triumph and happiness. Tell your parents and communities that.

> *It has also been said that the basis of optimism is sheer terror. Which is agreeable if we rephrase thus: the abject resolve to deal with and defeat our sheer terror is the basis of our optimism...And on that note, I want you Ahmed to toast to every Gen WHY's determination, perseverance, fortitude, punishment and even to the necessary sins and griefs that must endure to our triumph and happiness. Tell your parents and communities that.*

He then toasts and...boom...boom...boom...boom...boom...boom... boom...concurrently there is a ponderous sound of explosions in the far distance...then more...and more...then more, now closing in.

There is a general amazement of surprise, fear and consternation.

Then more explosions in the near distant that shook and ripped and shattered the glass panes.

The amazement creases into a ponderous clamor of shouting and shrieks and wailing.

Most of the youths have ducked flat on the ground for safety.

Buzzo instead dashes out, braving the sounds of explosions as if he has a life duplicate.

David alarmed for him, follows suit.

Then Brett and Glenda followed by the unruly herds fearlessly and fiercely gain the streets and Plaza Hill, undeterred to face whatever fate is out there for them. In a life emulation of courage, Gen WHY rise en masse, insinuating themselves outside, braving the exploding streets.

Then as sudden as it had started, the explosions simmer, cease with equal vigor. Then there is an eerie silence. A silence of a voluptuous dreadful menace. Then a wailing moan...more wailings profane the eerie quiet.

The Gen WHY crowd milled and coalesced.

Then consternated, agonized, wailed, stuttered but held.

It's clear that Gen WHY have been attacked. They have attacked multiple restaurants and bars at that hour thumping with the hearts of Gen WHY at celebrations. There is an evident and prompt payback. A payback from the Status Quo, who took offence with "a forced separation" and with "filth and garbage" smearing.

Like any institution, Status Quo must adapt to remain relevant and in place.

They want to crush the Gen WHY's spite and subdue their defiance.

A handful of bodies is ripped, torn into fragments, lifeless, lying on the ground. A lot are wincing, wounded.

In that fearful confusion, you can see faces in spasm of anguish, spasm of nausea, assault of anxiety, stream of grieving tears and in a wilderness of sorrowing.

That newly found grit, the defiance, the will to separate, acceptance of the wilderness of the uncertain future, life-purpose to make captivity captive on which hinges their only hope that found fortitude, that unequivocal happiness that is innocent, blind but trusting seems to slip away, conflicting with reality of death. With themselves to blame? With hateful-hurtful damaging doubt insinuating self for loss of life and injuries on friends.

It's been said that men wage wars for profit and principle. And Gen WHY are waging their existential war for their irrefutable ineluctable future.

In all fairness, to see all of their belief, gut, grit, resolve, justice, defiance purpose, soiled with blown arms and legs and heads and wincing bodies and death of brothers and friends, one could shake to bones and become susceptible to be swayed by the conspicuousness of dread, and death-palpability. And the doubt releases "is it worth it?" proposition as the answer.

In the meantime, the President declares a state of emergency.

Men of the intelligence move into action. Security agents are wedging in. Security roadblocks are being mounted. Traffic warded off. First responders are mobilizing to the scenes. Fire fighters are on the move. Traffic is being directed and diverted amidst the voluptuous wailing, moaning, shrieks, scowling, consternation and shouting.

Now you can hear the sounds of a few ambulances of the city's impoverished health care system wailing their sirens. Arriving in the distance.

David is shouting into his phone giving directions of their locations to them.

Glenda, Brett and most Gen WHY are busy tending, doing whatever they can to mitigate the pains and sufferings of the wounded.

Buzzo is too numbed for sorrow and in unutterable sadness. A sadness devoid of tears, withered of fear, too cold for rage, pitiable for the Status Quo. However, he is overtly confident for the success of Gen WHY.

Buzzo saw death, escaped death first time and first hand today. Yet he is filled with some mystical, mysterious confidence. A confidence that finds its reason in the virtue–the grace in endurance, in gesture, in tenacity, in fieriness, in determination– of Gen WHY before adversity. A determination whose finality warned of ability to endure whatever madness the Status Quo presents, to catharsis. Catharsis of filth and garbage dominance, of captivity captive.

And the finality that warned will find its purpose in the pitifulness of the Status Quo. The conspicuousness of the suspicion is pervasive as it is subtle. So subtle that every doubt on the responsibility of the Status Quo is subdued and defeated. Gen WHY will brave the Status Quo. They will fight back. They have such intrinsic visceral infection of grit and fearlessness and standing up and holding. There will be without doubt a fall out. A fall out of scouring violence. Of scouring obliteration magnitude. A scouring obliteration that will be a grave beautiful reward for the Status Quo. A fall out that is hoped won't degenerate into lawlessness. That will survive. That will be saved by whatever the law holds.

In the meantime, the air comes on with cascades of Gen WHY's tweeting tones: Mezzi and Mark from the President's office are working, communicating to Gen WHY of the vicious killings and encouraging and shoring their morals up:
#The Status Quo and its cabal!
#The myth. The ghost. You are a coward.
#Like the Kul Klux Klan, you are veiled. You hide your face. You love darkness.
#Parasites, cockroaches! Villains! Cravens! Cringing cowards! You act in darkness!
#The craven, cringing cabal is afraid of light!
#You are scared of us. We are the light. # You can't mess with Gen WHY.
#Gen WHY your requiem, your demise.

Gen WHY (sullen, with their fist, feebly punching the air): Yeah!
We know your faces. You can no longer hide.
We asked for separation. We separated.
We don't need you.
We refuse your bondage. Your filths and Garbage.
Instead that's asking too much.
You shed our blood. Innocent blood.
You force hateful spite into us.
Our blood your nemesis!
#Our blood your demise!
Gen WHY (resuscitating, with their fist, punching the air): Yeeeaaaaaaaah!
They aren't seen nothing yet!
Gen WHY (reinvigorated): Yeeeeaaaaaaaaaah
Even brutes do not devour their young.
Gen WHY (vigorously): No! Shame on them.
Nor do savages make war upon their young.
Gen WHY (ponderously): Shame on them.
They can't crush our gut, nor our spite, nor our defiance, nor our credo.
Gen WHY (howling): Nooooooooh. Renaissance credo.
They are grossly mistaken.
They haven't seen nothing yet.
We give life for life!
Jesus' passion: life for life on that cross.

Gen WHY on that tweet break in a clamor of shrieks and shouting: life for life! Life for life! Life for life...
Mezzi and Mark escalate, in a gust of tweets:
Renaissance credo.
Our lives in our hands.
Life for life.
Our blood your demise.
Gen WHY (howling spasm): Renaissance credo! Renaissance credo!! Renaissance man. We are the center of the universe. Our life in our hands!
Can't you see how tall and majestic you are standing?
Gen WHY: Yeeeeaaah!
Rounds of applause to yourselves. They are afraid. They are in a dreadful confusion.

A ponderous voluptuous clapping and scowling of remarkable magnitude breaks and pervades.

They are cringing cowards.
They can't mess with us.
They haven't seen nothing yet
#Captivity captive...captivity captive...captivity captive...
Life for Life!
Our blood your demise.

Gen WHY (scowling voluptuously-vigorously): Yeah, our blood your demise. Captivity captive to our last blood. We give life for life!

Gen WHY seem totally re-invigorated.
Their spasm of sorrowing minds and excruciating sadness and inconsolable despair regardless, they seem to have their emotions steadied ready to honor their fallen peers.

Now we take on the President seated, in unfathomable sadness, his face streaming with tears in his situation room overlooking the Plaza Hill, amidst beehive of inflow of information of the evolving situation from his security and intelligence reports, watching in awe Gen WHY and their grace and demeanor of selflessness pride turn their tragedy and the remarkable fatality into ponderous celebration of plaintive courage, spite and defiance.
Africans are not heir to courage. They are heir to courage of cowardice. Africans are not heir to abhorrence of sloth. They are heir to abhorrence of hard work. Africans are not heir to sacrifice. They are heir to love of comfort. Not to pursuit of comfort. Not to pursuit of courage. Not to pursuit of sacrifice. These logics are being defied first time, firsthand. Live.

Without any doubt dread is adrenalin. And terror is the pulsation. Courage their transmission. Dread and terror arc the basis of courage. Development and progress of the White race find their purposes in courage. White race even extremized that courage: his courage is not just informed by sheer dread and sheer terror but by the love to triumph human species, triumph human happiness, triumph over death by daring death. And dying to give living.

In fact, there is no act of faith more sublime than the courage of the very disfranchised prey.

Africans are not heir to courage. They are heir to courage of cowardice. They are not heir to abhorrence of sloth...They are heir to love of comfort, not to pursuit of courage. Not to pursuit of sacrifice. These logics are being defied first time, first hand. Live.
The basis of courage is shear dread. Dread and terror are the basis of courage.
Development and progress of the White race find their purposes in courage.
White race even extremized that courage: his courage is not just informed by sheer dread and sheer terror but by the love to triumph human species, triumph human happiness, triumph over death by daring death.

With two days to accountability deadline and four weeks to Gen WHY platform launch, it is natural for the President and in fact, the society at large to expect a peaking of reactions. Reactions however not this violent, and not this fatal.

These violent acts and the gracious unwavering ponderous selfless defiance, with equal vigor of Gen WHY, have cemented his belief in them and more than anything else given him his life purpose: having the back of and empowering Africa's Gen WHY forthwith and consequently in segue generations their descendants thence ad infinitum.

His intelligence and security reports have made ponderous identifications. The cabals and their cohorts have been identified. The oligarch cabals as culprits. Cabals in Africa are those in the business of thwarting democracy. At will, wish and want, hoisting societal leadership pawns, of mediocrity, of graft and of money and property laundering, of life-intimidations, of coercions, of killings. Their sworn life-purpose is to under develop and perpetuate underdevelopment of life of the Black kind. For the benefit of the very few. For themselves, the cabals.

The cabals are within the rank and file of society: the monarchy, the polity, the religious, with their consolidated cronyisms, in the service sectors- the army, the police, the bureaucracy, the academia, down to the civil society.

The President's intelligence reports releases answers to the names, surnames, their plots to unseat him. Nefarious arms funding, purchases and trafficking, monies from their foreign accounts down to the violence of the psychological and physical maiming and killings of Gen WHY.

Prominent among the list of the cabals is Mr. George, the father of Buzzo and Mezzi. Unknown to them, he is among the few the President had arrested and released a day after the Status Quo rally for their involvement to unseat him. They are same cabal that has hoisted and made him. A decisive conscientious defiant move with its calculated risk by the President: now they are funding, mobilizing rallies and explosions from their off-shore accounts.

And prominent among the cohorts and pawns are remarkable elements of the Gen WHY. The outlawed cultists. Cultists, lots of them turned Christian Pastors, imams, cybertheft syndicate, amongst others are the gruesome foot soldiers, executing chaos and disorder.

Within the President's daily crunching timelines of governing chores, he recomposes self–fighting not to betray resoluteness and empathy demeanor – squeezing out a momentous moment to confer in his office, with the leaders and the leading members of the Gen WHY family in order to appraise them and evaluate the enduring dynamic and evolving situation.

So, he has David, Buzzo, Mark, Mezzi, Brett, Glenda, seated with him around his conference table.

Gen WHY, conspicuously shrouded in conflicting hope and doubt, fear and defiance, cowardice and purpose, death and life, are seated, their faces writhed in unutterable sadness and expectant plaintive frowns.

President: My profound condolences. Fortunately, at your young ages you are forced to know that no happiness exists without its woes, no wealth without its hard work, no rewards without its selflessness, no life without its sacrifices.

And my congratulations. I have been awed totally by your grace at sacrifice at your various comforts, at resistance, determination and fortitude and perseverance this past week underpinning your rapid climb out of your moronic slumbering selfconsciousness and more so out of a lumbering spirit for the lives of your peers violently and viciously and gratuitously cut short at Plaza Hill.

Your ardor at fieriness, your candor at courage and your valor at fearlessness and defiance at the battle of your future, future credos, captivity captive, renaissance credos is remarkable. Unseen, unheard of, unimaginable ever before on the African continent. It has been, to say the least overwhelmingly amazing.

You are onto the Rubicon. Reaching the Rubicon and its crossing is the deal. Your deal with life fulfillment.

Gen WHY rise and give a round of applause to the President on his kind words without discomfiture, their faces impassable, in indescribable sadness crease into a solicitous frown as they take back their seats. In their proven state of psychological shock, of a wilderness of sorrowing, of fearful confusion, of discomfort and voluptuously rationalizing and ponderously pondering on the WHYs, they are looking forward to the answers. Any answers that could soothe the situation to birthing the WHY NOTs to conjure way forward.

The President understands. He scans their solemn solicitous faces and finds their approval to continue.

President: Rubicon crossing is the deal. Your deal at life…you, the Gen WHY?

The President pauses and scans their faces in an intense scrutiny.

President: That's what you call yourself, right?

Everybody nods solemnly. Then Mark breaks ranks.

Mark: Dad in part thanks to your encouragement.
President: Gen WHY hold the power of Africa's freedom. Biggest responsibility of Africa's freedom. Don't ever shy away from telling the truth. The truth is what you are already at: hardest-unflinching-harrowing must-beat hereditary despotism into submission.
If you remain strong, your strength will speak for itself.
If you wither, your failure would haunt you to your graves.
You should be extremely proud. You are on course for history.
Have there been any African revolution whatsoever in history?
Are we heirs to any revolution? None that we know.
You are doing for progenies what progenitors did not do for you. A revolution. Don't lose sight of the Rubicon.

Then the President pauses and trains his eyes on Brett and then on Glenda. Then back to Brett and holds his stare on him.
Brett disengages, lowering his stare. And re-engages holding President's intensive stare.
There was a general amazement of surprise and wonderment.

President: Herding the unruly herds is not the same thing with herding the cultists herds. Our colleges have had history of confraternity. Confraternity to check abuses and excesses and bring discipline and sanity and excellence to our entire decaying school system. Then unfortunately confraternity was accused of elitism of the few by laziness of the many.

Laziness has reason in mediocrity and sprouted cultism. Cultism has its purpose in craven cowardice, cringing debauchery, crime, gluttony, bombast, sloven slothfulness, disorder, banditry, anarchy and chaos.

Buzzo, Mezzi and Mark are totally at lost. Their amazement at total loss is of such obvious conspicuousness. But not David. Not Brett. Not Glenda.

David knows the confraternity saga very well. He had part of his college education in Africa before proceeding to the West.

Brett and Glenda consorted with cultism and cultists and know their mysteries and mayhem. Brett was the leader of the unruly herds–the ranks and files of "pirates and sailors"–which was the militant arm of the confraternity to counter all the purposeful cultism. Even though both suffered equal humiliation and crushing defeat in the hands of erstwhile military governments and were consequently outlawed, they secretly thrive at the powers of willful anarchy contrivers and contrivances.

Glenda was the secretary general of the female wing of the confraternity.

The President, keeping his intelligence report cards to his chest, is carefully choosing his words not to betray his cards, nor to explicate or induce a militant-arm-style retribution, a contrivance to settle the score with the cultists.

However, at the same time he wants the Gen WHY to absolutely rein in the rotten eggs, the Gen WHY cultist-remnants amongst them and square off with what could be a potential blow to their success.

President: You are almost there. Reaching, crossing the Rubicon is the deal. Two days to the day of accountability and five weeks to Platform launch, you are witnesses and victims of their ponderous gratuitous violence. They are afraid and their spite wishes to derail our efforts at sanity...or how did you coin it..., at captivity captive?

Mark (interjecting): Bravo dad. Captivity captive or filth and garbage dominance!

Everybody sinks in a smirk, their faces in a reluctant smile that fluttered short of a laughter. Hint of a subdued laughter that however faded and disappeared as it came.

President: You have a divided house. Africa's youth, you have a divided house. A house divided against itself cannot stand. Youths' cultism and cultist youths are the puppets of the cabals. The so-called "cyber-thefting" reprobates, the visible arm of anarchy and chaos and disorder of the cabal...of the Status Quo.

The Gen WHY body must stand whole. The effort should be that any curable sick finger should become part of the Gen WHY self-consciousness and any incurable sick finger must be cut off before it debilitates the entire body.

Brett has understood the coded but eloquent message: heal the sick finger in your ranks. The President, finally disengages from the face of Brett. His face creases into a smirking frown, training his stare now on Mark. And continuing:

President: Let me say this paraphrasing President Kennedy: *"Let every African Generation know, whether old, middle or young, whether it wishes us well or evil, whether a Christian, a Muslim, or others, whether one tribe or the other, that we are ready to pay any price, bear any burden, face any hardship, support any friend, oppose any foe to assure the entrenchment, the survival and the success of our choice to make captivity captive and advance our race."*

Mark: (applauding) Bravo dad. Even so dad some fantasy: that was easy!

Everybody in the room cracks up, as their faces in spasm of restrained smirk crease into a consoled-constricted grimace with determined expansive smile.

Brett: That was Kennedy. Back in the days, 1962.

The President brings back his stern stare, once again, on Brett and then smiles, breaking with his cloak demeanor of impenetrability:

President: Back in the days, huh? You were there then. Common boys, climb the Rubicon instead. I charge you to climb on the Rubicon.

The message is clear. They got it. If they insinuated themselves in President's office shrouded in confusion of doubts and troubles and despondency, now they walk out ridden with confidence, optimism, determination, resolve and with sense of direction and purpose.

Comforted, consoled, re-engineered and regenerated purposefully with: "Climb the Rubicon as the second-best deal of your lives." The first being crossing it.

Cross the Rubicon is the deal of your lives... the Rubicon is the deal of your lives...Rubicon is the deal of your lives...Is the deal of your lives...the deal of your lives...deal of your lives...Deal of your lives...Of you.

Anything, everything in its path must be crushed. Annihilated.

If you remain strong, your strength will speak for itself.
If you wither, your failure would haunt you to your graves.
You should be extremely proud. You are on course for history.
Have there been any African revolution whatsoever in history?
Are we heirs to any revolution? None that we know.
You are doing for progenies what progenitors did not do for you...

...A revolution. Don't lose sight of the Rubicon.

VOLUME 6

THE MATYRDOM

Chapter 1

The air is grave. It has been grave after the explosions on the Plaza Hill. It is evening, and it's no exception. On every evening channel, including the ultra-conservatives, their main headlines read:

IT IS A MASSACRE: 69 DEAD, OVER 600 INJURED!

A MACABRE MASSACRE OF OUR YOUTHS: 70 DEAD, 600 INJURED!

69 OF OUR DESCENDANTS ARE DEAD, 622 ARE INJURED. A SICKENING HORROR!

Each gave context and a substantive in-depth analysis of which pulp is:
Our youths had only called for a peaceful separation.
They wanted absolutely nothing from the Status Quo.
They wanted their independence, in pursuit of subduing their Misery in order to have their backs by themselves. That same misery given to them by that same Status Quo. That same back denied them by Status Quo. In fact, our continent's misery. Without Status Quo's help.
The culprits are not known. The authority is yet to identify the culprits…
The President has work to do…
The President, like a fluke, unannounced appears on the screen. His face grave, fighting and holding back tears. With plaintive solemnness, he finds his voice.

President: We cut the lives of 69 of our descendants short and we maimed 630 others. And traumatized their whole generation with terror and dread. And gave their families unutterable vicious sorrow and tribulations and trauma.
We cut their birthdays short, we cut their graduations short, their aspirations short, their future dreams and purposes short. Reason? They are tired of our perpetual filth and garbage for them. "Their loyalty to our willful misery for them can no more be assumed", they rightfully proclaimed. And they asked for separation.
It is unutterably heartbreaking for parents to bury their children. Children should grow into adulthood to succeed and bury their parents.
Evidently not in the Black Kind families. Not in Africa. We make them orphans, slaves, give them misery and now kill them physically. Instead of

separating, or repenting and atoning, we react killing them. Our heinous reaction has perspicaciously sprouted selfless defiant men. Beautiful minds. Minds with selflessness syndrome of heroic entity. Our heinous reaction has drawn a battle line, a remarkable shameful battle line between progenies and progenitors. A shameful battle line between parents and their children. A shameful battle line between Status Quo, gifting misery to youths and youths fighting back to dream and for the realization of those dreams of life. Of their lives. By themselves. A battle line that is fortunately turning them into brave and sacrificing selfless men. A battle line that might produce the most fierce but fascinating purposeful generation, not just for a generational positive change but for a sequence of it. A paradigm change and successions of it in its wake.

As we work to identify and apprehend the culprits, the state of emergency is extended to 48 hours, within which the youths will exercise their solemn rights and duties to mourn their heroes, however they deem fit within the confines of civility.

They are asking us, the Status Quo, to respect their wishes by staying out of it, totally. So please refrain from any provocations. Please you are warned.

The job, duty of my office to them and to the Continent is to guarantee order and safety for all. Forthwith, for 48 hours vehicular movement is hereby limited to state's mass transit buses and trucks, to help commute the community of youths to their mourning grounds.

Any cars, even the government's, would require special permits. Thank you.

There was voluptuous eerie silence in the whole city, in the state, on the land, imposed by the wake of the news of the killings and the injured running on the tv. Everyone has been listening, eyes and ears glued to the television and to the radio, rapt in silence. A sorrowing silence. A heartbroken wrenching silence. A ponderous silence withered of tears. A fearful suspicious silence of dreadful menace.

A silence that is now pierced by Mezzi and Mark with gust of audacious, pugnacious tweets:

#Gen WHY, we have heard the unutterable.
#69 fallen. 630 wounded.
#The 69 and the 630 are our heroes.
#They gave us hope, purpose and life.
#Go occupy the Plaza Hill, the valleys, the streets, every inch of the city, with candles.
With candles.
#We announce 48 hours of mourning and vigil. And it's commencing henceforth.
With immediate effect.
#Gen WHY honor the lives of our mightiest.

#There are state mass transit buses and trucks to commute you all from your nooks and corners as your needs might demand.

#We beg the authority to guarantee security before we rage on anything trespassing our path.

Gen WHY tweet back: Rage! Rage!! Rage!!! Rage!!!!

It's been said that hereditary despotism disdains and fears nothing so much as the courage and defiant in its victims.

The city is on the march. Beehive of activities. A city lighted up in candles. Gen WHY are milling. Coalescing anew, plaintive in a solemn procession. No laughing, no smiling. No words proffered. Their demeanor black, gruesome, grave, minacious, suggestive, awesome, audacious for the voluptuous underpin of abject solemnity. Their solemnity finds its purpose in their luxury of self-consciousness. Selfconsciousness to honor their heroes' life's-after-life. Self-consciousness is the luxury conscientiousness of suffering to get to and cross the Rubicon. They have, with their demise from life, reached the Rubicon. They need climbing and then crossing it. An ultimate gift, the Rubicon of life to themselves. That Rubicon that draws its strength from the luxury of harrowing suffering.

And suffering, from the luxury of pain. Suffering cannot exist without pain. Collective pain is the basis for collective suffering. And collective suffering is the basis for collective happiness. Collective pleasure. The Gen WHY ultimate premise.

And suffering absolution would be the infusion, the catharsis of the beautiful "selflessness affliction syndrome mind essence" in the Gen WHY.

The conscientiousness of the absolution is why they are marching on. They are marching on to honor their life purpose. Its honorableness finds its purpose in Rubicon crossing.

Now many trucks, many buses are crisscrossing the land hauling in and dropping off Gen WHY in all nooks and corners of the city. As they voluptuously coalesce in the city, a few of the trucks loaded with the unruly herds take advantage of the state of emergency declared to mourn and bury their peers and head out, surreptitiously, in a mission of cleansing and vengeance. It is indeed in a disguise to put the Gen WHY divided house in order, as subtly demanded by the President.

In fact, in the tacit ponderous menacing complicity of the emergency decorum, and the plaintive vigil observance, Brett and Glenda, herding the ponderous unruly herds, in their multitudes, have furtively insinuated themselves in the vicinity of the cabals, of their cronies, of cohorts, of cultists-yahoo youths, ready to subdue their spite and restore order and hope in instilling their existential 'selflessness affliction' mind pursuit in these wayward youths, their peers.

Existential selflessness affliction mind pursuit in Gen WHY...Selflessness affliction mind pursuit in Gen WHY...Affliction mind pursuit in Gen WHY...Mind pursuit in Gen WHY...Pursuit in Gen

WHY...In Gen WHY...Gen WHY's existential selflessness affliction mind pursuit.

However, despite what the urgent urgency of the time construed and imposed, Gen WHY leadership, out of their spiritual essence tolerance for fairness, and intellectual probity, ponderously and exhaustively put to debate their conflicting points of views to explicate their contrivances.

To execute their contrivances of retribution they evaluate and judge the hierarchy of the competing powers on the land: of the Status Quo, of the cabals, of the cultists, and of the witch-doctors with their vain and vulgar superstitions.

They submit that the greatest single power on the land is that of the Status Quo. That their power is informed by fear and cruelty. Fear of the masses and equal cruelty on the masses. This power is only sustained by the craven ignorance, the cringing cowardice, the unutterable laziness, the compulsive crave for gratuitous comforts, the pathological belief in superstition, the love for life of the African masses. African masses' love for life is obnoxiously incomplete. Life without death is not complete. Life is equal to death. If there is no life there will not be any death. In equal measure if there is no death there will be no life. Reiterating once again the Lord Jesus said you "give life for life.", "If you love life you lose it." There is hardly any human invention that did not take life. That death of life sprouts life. Africans conscientiously obliterate life continuum of the afterlife. That's simply why we don't think of death. We want to live forever. We end up living miserably. Every black person, regardless.

The second greatest power is that of the witch-doctors. Before the coming of Christianity and Islam, Africa had voodooism, which system of logics is based on ponderous voluptuous superstition. To this day superstition holds spiritual spell on and sway the masses more than scientific system of logics and rationality and religious faith. Their superstitious belief system finds justification in the pent-up anger of justice system of God, not to deliver immediate punishment on foes and friends alike, and for immediate rewards for selves. They believe in false, obscure superstitious, immediate solution delivery of mystifying grace and favors of the oracle. Grace and favors of the oracle to especially inflict evil on others – enemies and friends alike, and have blessings for themselves and absolution for their own sins at the same time. This oracle-god belief system, deliberately and voluptuously defiles and befouls and defames the rational logical system based on self-esteem, faith, hard work, sacrifice and patience and perseverance to achieve and glaring achievement. An indisputable unutterable laziness and cowardice in miracle of hope flock African masses to the churches and mosques. And that's why African masses, regardless of their religious faith to this day, once out, devoid of the expected miracle, disappointed ease back to their darkness, throwing their Bible and Korans to the wind and flock to witchdoctors, making the worst of their places of worship:

'cosmetic grotesque confines.'

The cabals' powers are informed by the Status Quo and by the witchdoctors.

They are at the service of both powers.

Even when a cabal is a successful businessman through hard work, sacrifice and perseverance and unavoidable accomplice of the Status Quo, they are however swayed by superstition for longevity, for protection of health, of wealth and for more wealth and for impediment of new comers at wealthiness club, jealously and viciously guarding against competition. Every level of African society loves life, and death is far removed from their psyche and life equation. They ponderously love themselves and despise others.

The cultists instead depend solely on the cabals and on witchdoctors. They are spiritually squarely dependent on superstition, to satisfy their immediate lifecomfort, life bombasts and debaucheries, weaknesses without accountability and justification, get rich quick without working. It doesn't matter how. Their vulgar, obstinate, superstitious pilgrimage finds reason in getting rich quickest by all means necessary, for a life comfort of bombast and debauchery trafficking and with equal vigor; it finds rewards in the prevailing system of unaccountability, of corruption, of kleptomania, of bombast, of gluttony and in the lack of employment. And indeed, a ridiculous reward for the very few employees of cyber thefting, money laundering, malevolency of the cabals. This is the scourge amongst the youth. A forlorn scourge.

With this critical analysis, they head out to their task of Rubicon crossing objective to infuse 'selflessness affliction' in the wayward youths, their peers, conditio *sine qua non*, to making captivity captive and making the best of their future dreams and aspirations: they have to deal with the witch doctors first, then with the generation of cultists youths , their peers. That way they would have deflated and muted to a ponderous degree the hurtful spite and the hateful defiance of the power of both the cabal and the Status Quo. That would help make the President's imminent day of accountability chore effective and in turn beneficial to their cause.

> *An indisputable unutterable laziness and cowardice in miracle of hope flock African masses to the churches and mosques. And that's why African masses, regardless of their religious faith to this day, once out, devoid of the expected miracle, disappointed ease back to their darkness, throwing their Bible and Korans to the wind and flock to witch doctors, making the worst of their places of worship: 'cosmetic grotesque confines'.*

In any case, to engage head on with the witchdoctors, with the myth of their superstitious powers, dictates discretion and circumspection. The Bible clearly states "don't tempt thy God, Lord." Even though their superstitious powers might be a myth, not proven, even so they wish there is a smoke without fire. So, their innate self-consciousness and conscientiousness psychology suggests a precautionary faith-refuge in the Bible and in the Koran. Almost everyone on the African continent has a Bible or a Koran. Even so, they are swayed by superstition. God's deeds are never observed on the continent. The faith reposed in the false and illussional 'immediate' results of superstition justifies the evil deeds.

Conversely, it is voluptuously proven that faith in the Bible has proven supreme. The West has Christian religion and everyone and everything amazes at their conquest, civilization, products, development, progress. Love for human species. With that same Bible, they enslaved and colonized Africa. The African Oracular-gods with it. The omnipotent African oracular-gods that dominate Africa's self-consciousness and senses was dominated with the Bible.

And invariably, common sense would infer to consort and use the faith Belief in that same Bible that dominated oracular-gods and brought civilization. Instead their infidelity at faith in the Bible transcends their common sense into fancying and consorting with hypocrisy within self-consciousness of degradation and primitivity and cowardice. The oracular-gods dominate their senses. Transcends their beneath primitive self-consciousness. The oracular-gods their vulgar nemesis. That's why Africans cannot dominate their environment.

The Bible regardless, rationally, the Asian countries are marching on with the virtues of will of hard work. Not of compulsive laziness, not of cowardice, not of ignorance, but of educating their mind of the power of the mind, and not of some kismet or of myth of superstitious power. With the power of the mind from imitating, they started innovating and inventing.

Conversely, it is a voluptuous axiom that faith in the Bible has proven supreme. The West has Christian religion, and everyone and everything amazes at their conquest, civilization, products, development, progress. Love for human species. With that same Bible, they enslaved and colonized Africa. The African Oracular-gods with it. The omnipotent African oracular-gods that dominate African senses was dominated with the bible. A scouring Dominance.
With the Bible's validation, invariably, common sense would infer that Africans consort with and use the faith Belief in that same Bible that dominated oracular-gods for Africa's development and civilization and civility. Instead their infidelity at faith in the Bible and the Koran transcends their common sense into fancying and consorting with hypocrisy, within self-consciousness of degradation and primitivity and cowardice. The Oracular-gods dominate their senses. The Oracular-gods their nemesis. That's why Africans cannot dominate their environment.

Brett, Glenda and the multitude of unruly herds, Bibles strapped to their bodies, dressed in impeccable black robes: oversized layered-kaftans, their legs in tennis shoes, their heads in hats and faces to the eye level, completely wrapped in black facial clothing masks in order to evade recognition evoke the mythical Knight Templers of the Christian punitive crusade of the middle ages. Like them they inspire fear and dread and hope of justice in conquest. Armed with matchets, and hatchets and clubs and lanterns, they move into action in a commando-style, besieging the compound of the head and the most prominent of the witchdoctors, defying whatever gods and vulgar spirits he represents and damning whatever obscure penance consequence as held to myth in its wake.

In a gust of coordinated ghostly-like actions with the mythical dread fascination, cruel viciousness and gruesomeness evocation of the Knight Templars of Christian punitive crusade of the medieval ages movie memories on the 'infidels', they seize and make every life of the entire household prisoner in a flash, including the dogs which, split moments earlier, shattered the crackling tension of the vicious silence amidst eerie silence of the night of vigil and emergency, with their burst of ferocious barking.

Every member of the households' hands and legs are tied and their mouths gagged against their wills. Some of them have put up some degree of feeble resistance. Their resistance beaten and spite subdued with ease, they have been hobbled into the spacious master bedroom and tied and locked up. Under the watchful vigilant menacing but suspicious eyes of the unruly herds, that convey appalling spite and compulsive threatening hate, ready to obliterate them, they resign to their fates, their faces writhed in fear, dread and solicitous wonderment.

They watch helpless as their family head, who is as well their father, the witchdoctor, is hobbled away without regards or consideration towards his shrine.

Now they tie the witchdoctor to a seat before his oracular-god for questioning.

Then he breaks down. Down in a trembling spasm of fear and dread. His spirituality and invincible pseudo-omnipotent austere demeanor gone; he is lost in the hollowness of his dread-ridden eyes.

Brett (derisive): You know your mouth is gagged. When you are ready to answer my questions just nod, so you will be enabled to talk. Ok?

The witchdoctor did not react.

Brett (ignoring him): You, Jesus Christ and Prophet Mohammad who is greater?

274

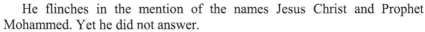

He flinches in the mention of the names Jesus Christ and Prophet Mohammed. Yet he did not answer.

Brett notices and in a flash flicks out two little-sized Bible and Koran out of nowhere sticking them to his face.

Brett: You recognize these? This represents Jesus Christ, and this represents Prophet Mohammad, right?

The witchdoctor creases into a trembling spasm of anguish, avoiding the sight of the Bible and the Koran.

The unruly herds have noticed and their hearts took solace and comfort: there is shriek of derisive laughter amongst them behind their face masks.

Brett retracts the Bible and the Koran in a flash as they had come.

The witchdoctor creases back to stable composure.

Then Brett presses on.

Brett: You and the devil, who is greater?

He did not react nor betray any emotions. He did not answer, in defiance. Silence. Pantomiming a gangster move, Brett snaps his fingers, indicating the shrine to his men.

In a flash they work up the shrine, shredding everything in it to rubbles, revealing a door in the middle of nowhere in its wake.

The witchdoctor wanes into an uncontrollable wailing moan and is overwhelmed by spasm of heaving, retching and gasping in an unutterable sorrowing grief for the amount of defile and profanation to his gods.

Brett ignores him. Fixing the door, he nods his head "affirmative" to his men.

They understand and smash the door.

The door reveals a contemporary modern office furnished to taste. Exquisite Italian luxury at kitting and fitting.

A winner's smile breaks on Brett's face.

Brett walks in there and identifies heaps and heaps of documents and five safes of steel boxes. Two of them of electronic locks and the remaining three of ordinary key locks. He trains his eyes scanning the documents, his curiosity muted, he disengages and fixes the locks, dawdles and comes out, back to the witchdoctor.

Brett: You are going to have to give us the list of your clients who unleashed mayhem, exploding and turning the Plaza Hill into a killing field of our youths.

Witchdoctor did not react to the request. His eyes expressionless, maintains a disdainful defying silence.

Brett: Could we have the keys to those safes?

Witchdoctor fixes the infinite ground. His magic power gone like in an enchantment, he started in a throbbing moan and creases into mumbles of unintelligible frustration, as if in some rebuke to his god for abandonment in this ordeal and for lack of immediacy of punishment.

Brett nods "smash the locks" to his men. They do. And behold instead of list of clients they find stacks of monies, in foreign currencies-sterling, dollar, euro, neatly stashed away in those boxes. There is a general amazement of shock, disbelief and contemptuous condemnation.

However, the unruly herds did not betray any emotions of wants or gullibility. They are simply self-effacing, far removed. Even so they think that for this austere ragamuffin maroon demeanor pitiable man to have such monies, something is simply just wrong in Africa!

They just think that the amount of monies in the hands of a witchdoctor is simply telling and depressing, and to that extent buttresses the level and importance of superstition and the climax of rot and decay and putrefaction of their society. Superstition is the evil. It contrives evil. Fans the flame of evil. Enthrones evil. Its propagation is swift, fluid and ponderously effective. Lethal. Precise. Contagious. Its fertile ground is the realm of Laziness and cowardice. Laziness and cowardice feed off primitiveness. Superstition is the epitome of primitiveness.

They get the boxes out unto the now open shrine space and empty them there.

They soak the entire money with kerosene ready to burn out the entire shrine space. But the witchdoctor remained intransigent, defiant, he did not flinch. Instead he continued his mumbling of unintelligible incantations, his eyes fixing the infinite void.

Then Brett loses his patience. He's had enough.

He snaps his fingers and in a flash one of the ultimate torture devices of the medieval ages, the rack, home-crafted rack, was hauled in, in a sack, laid bare and assembled promptly by his men.

The witchdoctor flinches at the dread of the sight.

Then they grab and lay him on its wooden platform and his hands and feet tied to each end of the rollers.

The witchdoctor understands and goes into a spasm of trembling and gusts of mumbles of suffocated wailing incantations.

Now, Brett goes medieval on him, ordering the turning of the rollers. As his body started stretching, he screams wildly and started wrenching, struggling, gasping, and finally nods his head in a rush of frenzy.

Then Brett orders them to stop and he ungags his mouth.

What has become of him was to anybody's judgement. The pain was so harrowing that his spirit nearly left him in those split seconds on the rollers. He's given up screaming. What is left in him could no longer sustain but a moaning fit. There was silence.

Cringingly cowed, he became obsequious and servilely hints out the numbers with his last groggy will:

Witchdoctor:1,3,5,6,7…10,8,7,6, 0.

And he slumped and transited into deep silence, passing out, fainting or dying.

Those two sets of serial numbers opened the safes and it's hoped would hand them down the names of the mythical superstitious secret power: names of the politicians, names of the "men of God", names of the cabals, names of the cultists, names of the monarchs. In sum, names of the clients. Names that are under the mythical superstitious influence, who decide, dictate and run their society with evil inescapable lethal precision.

They untie him off the rack and transfer his unconscious body, making him integral part of the rubbles of defunct shrine and heap of monies. Then they soak the entirety afresh with kerosene.

Then everything stops breathing. The moment transits into an immediate, ponderous expectant silence. The anxiety mounts. The whole unruly herd is looking up to Brett to sign off on the grey space of moral act of justice. That grey space that lacks a defined and an objective standard of morality. That grey space that validates an act of extreme mortal justice and gives absolution at the same time. That grey space that is of a luxury of validation and absolution. A validation and absolution space luxury that must be ponderously inspiring for Gen WHY effort to endure to success.

Bret is faced with the conflicting play of 'right', 'wrong', 'reason' in his mind.

His blurred mind, in competing inspirational and aspirational emotional amazements, rushes out reasonings and evaluations, incarnated in the momentous fleeting dictates of "the right thing for the right reason", "the right thing for the wrong reason" and "the wrong thing for the right reason".

The "wrong thing for the right reason" transcends, overwhelming his sense of moral justice, as he understands it.

> *The wrong thing for the right reason...the wrong thing for the right reason...the wrong thing for the right reason...the wrong thing for the right reason... the wrong thing for the right reason...the wrong thing for the right reason...the wrong thing for the right reason...the wrong thing for the right reason...the wrong thing for the right reason...wrong thing for the right reason...thing for the right reason...for the right reason...the right reason...right reason...reason.*

Brett puts light to the heap to everyone's pleasant relief and concurrence. A cynical concurrence that finds its justification in the massacre of members of Gen WHYs' family at the Plaza Hill, and that is hoped must find its reward in Gen WHYs' triumph.

And then, off they go.

The unruly herds are in amazement of faith.

A lot has happened in a short time. As they observe the flame of the burning body of the witch doctor rise and stutter and disperse in the air, and as they reflect sifting and sieving through the events of the past minutes—they have dared, subdued and defeated whatever, physically and spiritually, the witchdoctor represents—they finally entrench in their psyche that superstitious power is simply a farce and a myth. Just like the Bible proved centuries before.

The power of the mind, power of hard work, power of courage and bravery, blessed with faith in God is the deal to Rubicon and for its crossing. It's the supreme thing, the ambitious and unfaltering resolve for Gen WHY.

They have work to do. They hurriedly walk out in expansive proprietary body- language pride, of a rewarding but expectant baptismal first salary invocation. Selfesteem and fulfillment are the feel within them.

Chapter 2

The Plaza Hill

The candles and incense are burning. The wake keeping is on-going in a dense and ponderous silence.

It's been said that the great events of the world take place in the brain.

But it is in silence, only in silence that the great things of the world are hatched.

It is only in silence that the youths can discover their souls.

Only in silence can the youths discover their spiritual essence.

It is only in silence that the youths can find harmony with themselves.

It is only in silence you understand that though man be kept ignorant, he cannot keep himself ignorant.

Only in silence that the youths can consort with the signified of consciousness and self-consciousness–dream and conceptualize their future, be able to give form to every feeling, give expression to every thought, give reality to every dream, forge fresh energy to bury the shackles of misery.

It is only in silence that you can understand the limits and limitations of entertainment.

It's also been said that You can't solve the problem of the slaves by amusing the slaves.

In silence you understand that most churches are entertainment centers to confuse and amuse the poor.

And the mosques are rehearsal prayer centers to hold the poor engaged with the arts of conspiracies, falsehood, cruelty, viciousness and violence.

It's as well been said that entertainments may amuse the mind; they cannot inform it.

In silence you understand the inspiring creative silence of music.

In silence you can develop deep empathy, sympathy and solicitude for the distressed. In silence you understand suffering is life.

In silence you embark on the journey of skill value set and virtues: patience, hard work, love, joy, sadness, joy of life, respect, compassion, justice, prudence, temperance, fortitude, hope, faith, charity, fear of God, fear of society, self-esteem, self-confidence.

In silence you understand that strength of faith in hard work defeats misery. In silence you understand that Africa's problem is found in hope palsy, sloth palsy, cowardice palsy, ignorant palsy, religious palsy, superstition palsy. They numb their self-consciousness from developing.

In silence you will understand rejection, denouncement, renouncement, discredit.

In silence you inculcate rejection of hypocrisy whatsoever, denounce every ill-gotten wealth of your parents, of society, renounce the ill-gotten wealth, discredit gluttony and greed and avariciousness and silence, abhor looting and kleptomania.

Selflessness affliction syndrome would reject, denounce, renounce and discredit ills of society anywhere they are found to progress collectivity.

In silence you will understand your lack of parenting and failed parenting.

In silence you will understand the futility and danger of impatience.

In silence you will understand the beyond*ness* of life and of life purpose and of afterlife. In fact, of the beyond*ness* of goodness and of nothingness with equal vigor.

Paraphrasing Oscar Wilde, there should be within our senses, within our ranks, our family of youth ranks, a mad willful rejection of monstrous forms of selftorture, of self-denial, of selflessness affliction syndrome, whose origin must not be fear or favor but a catharsis of justice to defeat the degradation of family of the youth.

These competing and conflicting wishful, imaginary thoughts are framed in the incessant ponderous reflective questioning tweets in quick succession of Mezzi and Mark:

#What is progress?
#What is regress?
#What is sloth?
#What is hard work?
#What is integrity?
#What is reliability?
#What is complacency?
#What is gullibility?
#What is gluttony?
#What is kleptomania?
#What is bombast?
#What is hyperbole?
#What are rights and duties?
#What are conduct and conscience?
#What are accountability and holding accountable?
#What is giving life for life?
#What are palsy and religious palsy?
#What is choosing temporary happiness against permanent sadness?
#What is sacrifice?
#What are chance and #chance at life?
What is sacrificing chance at life?
#Can you criticize your chance of corrupt comfort of life?
#Can you sacrifice your chance at corrupt comfort of life?

#What is Love?
#What is believing in God?
#What is worshipping God?
#Is it about believing, worshipping or deeds of God?
#May God bless us all!
Gen WHY phones tweet ponderously: #Amen!!

Suddenly in the far distance there is an overpowering glow of light that paled the combined candle vigil lights glow in comparison. In fact, it swallowed the combined candle vigil lights glow.

Then a ponderous sound of explosion followed in the near distance.

An immediate clamor of shriek, shouting and consternation of ponderous entity started up among Gen WHY. They are in amazement of wonderment and suppositions, and grim curiosity. In a near stuttering stance, ready to flutter, they held their breath without dispersing with their eyes trained in the sky.

Then the sky lights ponderously up. There is a cascade of sounds of explosions in voluptuous successions. With consequent blinding flood of lights that rose in balls and exploded vigorously, stuttering and dispersing in its gravitational falls.

The succession of exploding sounds is incredibly loud but incredibly removed in the far distance. The incredible loudness with the threatening overhead flares, make for a disproportionate illusionary near palpable proximity.

Gen WHY stuttered, ducked and shrieked. But did not flutter. They held once again.

Then the sounds of siren fill the air, they fade with the disappearing cars, heading out, towards the suburban areas, towards the countryside. Away from the city center and the Central Business District. Away from the vigil of Gen WHY.

Now Gen WHY come to the realization that they are not the target this time, as it's underpinned by the absence of screaming and moaning or wailing from injuries or pains amidst them. No maimed bodies. No agonizing twisting bodies. No dead body. They held. Nonetheless, they creased into slow reluctant general amazement of conflicting bewilderment and consternation, confusion and of competing fear and defiance, courage and cowardice, wonderment and supposition, dispersing and holding.

Understandably, it has its justification in the ponderous psychosis of explosions and killings few days gone by.

Then the tweets came immediately on:

#Gen WHY, Gen WHY, there is a raging fire.
#From your position you can't take in the situation.
The countryside is raging with fire.
We are safe. Everyone is safe out here.
Stay your positions. Don't panic. Avoid stampede.

#The intelligence community is on it.
#The government is on it.
#The situation is under control.
#We will give you more information on the situation as the night evolves.

Now confidence and normalcy slowly return amidst Gen WHY, as aloof, they fix their eyes in the direction of the ponderous plumes of fumes stuttering and withering and dispersing in the air.

Back to the countryside, the original mission by the unruly herds to frighten and rein in the cultist youths their generation, the arm of the cabals has digressed into unscripted and unrestrained remarkable mayhem.

The decision to take on and crush the spiritualist and obliterate spiritualism responsible for superstition and superstitious spite contrivances and audaciousness on the land, and in its wake save and rehabilitate their peers who have been deceptively and forcefully coaxed into cultism, has instead opened up a Pandora box. The list of names, the chores and responsibilities of the superstitious cultism- spiritualism world gotten from the witchdoctor's safes are clearly remarkably detailed and spelt out but devoid of the names of his clientele.

Their clienteles' names are ponderously shrouded in secrecy, remarkably undiscernible, rigorously protected and voluptuously guarded.

Brett and the unruly herds were, nevertheless, undeterred and undistracted in their resolve to endure the task.

In the meantime, their mayhem contrivance continued: they tortured and burnt, killing five more witchdoctors. And in its wake a kismet: one of these five dead witchdoctors made a reluctant disclosure of the names of some monarchs, who are amongst their clientele.

Consequently, eleven monarchs (the Chiefs, Obas, Emirs) were hunted down, tortured and burnt to death and a valuable survivor from the service of the Emir taken hostage. A survivor barely unrecognizable, complicit the darkness of the night, who in forlornness, cringed before the medieval rack machine, creasing into a ponderous spiritual crisis, breaking down and pleading guilty and cooperation. On close observation, this survivor is the Imam. The Imam, friend of Mezzi and Buzzo, who they had introduced to Brett. Not to Glenda. Not to the group of unruly herds. Not to Gen WHY group. They have heard about him and what he represents, arousing incredulous, voluptuous surprises.

Brett behind his mask recognized him, spared his life, and happily took him hostage. Then the Imam led them to the most unimaginable unutterable surprises of their lives: the abode of one of the prominent promising rising young stars "man of God." Indeed, of two: the "man of God" pastor and the "woman of God." The pastor's wife, of the Pentecostalism persuasion. Pentecostalism Family business outfit.

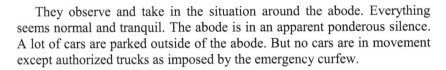

They observe and take in the situation around the abode. Everything seems normal and tranquil. The abode is in an apparent ponderous silence. A lot of cars are parked outside of the abode. But no cars are in movement except authorized trucks as imposed by the emergency curfew.

Brett (his mask on, conscious of protecting his identity): Imam, why are we here?

Imam (reassuringly surprised): Imam? Merciful Allah! Then we are in a familiar territory. You did ask to see the remaining clienteles, right?

Brett: Yeah! The two spouses of God. The Prominent pastor and his pastor wife.

Imam: Are you doubtful and afraid? You are my guest. I am offering you the privilege to understand your land, young man.

Brett turns his back to the Imam, faces the unruly herds, strips himself of their threatening attire and gives instruction to Glenda and the rest of the unruly herds.

Brett: Be vigilant! Don't move from here. Glenda put your phone on and activate googles position identification app. I will call you from the inside. As soon as possible.

The moment is ponderously predatory. The moment is like a knife of fate waiting to be twisted. It was a moment of a cruel and menacing agony. There was a voluptuous, worrisome, confusing silence among the unruly herds, afraid of losing Brett, their indisputable head and charismatic role model and the risk of forlornness and loss forever.

Brett pans, scanning their hidden grim agonizing faces, imagined, behind their black facial clothes masks and he smiles, reassuring them.

Brett: I am afflicted. Afflicted with 'existential selflessness affliction'. Selflessness affliction. Remember we sacrifice for collectivity. We are here, for nothing may remain but a recollection of pride of our audacity or the luxury of failure and misery and regret. So, at the end, dead or alive, I wish to have succeeded in giving my life some sense.

But I think I will be back in your midst. If I don't, remember selflessness affliction syndrome permeating your self-consciousness renaissance credo as the new deal.

Brett now turns and faces the Imam. The Imam recognizes Brett and his face is assailed by unutterable amazement of hope and pride. They smile and without betraying familiarity to the onlooking unruly herds and Glenda, they walk to the gate of the abode.

The Abode of "Men of God.s"

The Imam rings the bell. He is recognized and in some split seconds the gate swings open and they disappear behind the gate. Disappearing in the night.

On the inside, there is a ponderous security. There is voluptuous, vicious looking armed men with cruel menacing assault weapons in defiance of the President's actions and acts and orders on security: through executive order he had withdrawn all privileged securities, saving the tax payers from this brunt bearing futile activity. Now they pass the points of three security posts in successions and they get into the corridor leading to the heart of the abode. As they approach the door's threshold of the dome-like hall, the Imam gives him instructions and indications. Brett nods his head 'yes', perplexed and disappears taking position from where he could spy on the ongoing situation. The Imam, now at the door's threshold stops, turns and furtively checks out, making sure Brett is alone, infiltrated and eaves-dropped and safe. He then opens the door and gains the inside.

Brett insinuates himself from a vintage point where he sees without being seen nor perceived: he's climbed into the top alcove overlooking the void of the lounge.

What his eyes are witnessing cannot be entrusted to ephemeral risk of oral recount or to the cheap vulgar doubts. It is beyond this. The resounding voluptuousness of it has to be entrenched in common memory of place, of space and of time. In history. He brings out his phone, videoing the literal bare nakedness of the event: everybody is naked except for the slips covering their private parts. The woman of God, is the undisputed chief priestess, seated in her throne-like sit at the raised podium. Behind her throne-like sitting position, on the high wall, you see hanging, different symbols of varying fraternity and religions: the Celtics, Judaism, Greek crosses, the Christian cross, others etc.

On the table before her, you can see a litany of objects: basin full of a solution, a concoction of fresh blood placed on her right side, and on her left, pouches of indefinable content. Burning insects, heads of blood-drooping animals, restricted and unrestricted currencies, burning candles, burning incenses, bottles of olive oil, bottles of wines, palm wines, spirits, etc. All is shrouded in the cloud of fumes of burning incense. Amidst which she administers the rites and rituals of superstitious spiritualism of their world, as members solemnly come forward for rites of renewals and of initiation.

Members go forward, reaching and stopping before her position. They bow their heads to her. She stands, her hollow glowing eyes fixing the infinite void, she trances into spasm of unintelligible incantations, reaches, taking pouches one by one and soaking them into the bloody concoction. Then she lifts them out, reaches, strapping them to their arm, or to their waist or to both. And blesses them, in their ordination, with the signs of unintelligible gods. Then they walk back taking their seats.

Meanwhile, Brett is busy videoing and lifting the video images into the social media, relaying to Glenda, Buzzo, David.

David and Buzzo with the President, are viewing the recognizable faces of the members: a community of mixed anagraphy of mostly young promising, prominent "men of God" and "women of God", and of mostly young monarchs and of some cabals. Every one of them is here for a purpose: *hereditary despotic power passage, power transfer, power conferment for hereditary hierarchical despotic power perpetuity and hereditary misery perpetration and perpetuation.*

The President, Buzzo, David are in frowns of competing pleasant surprises and amazement. They are in amazement of consternation, preoccupation and alarmed for the safety of Brett. They can't figure out where he is. And they can't reach out to the phone of Brett: he seems out of network. Anxiety builds.

In the meantime, Brett, who had gotten tired and bored of videoing the rites had changed position, wandering farther off in the environment unknown to him. And in so doing, he stumbles fortuitously on caches of arms and ammunition.

Surprised and shocked, he brings out, flipping his phone open once more, videoing his findings and lifting the images once again to David and Buzzo.

They in turn are swiftly messaging him back "bravo Brett! Could you kindly give us your position please?", Brett promptly does and in the process the sound of the clicking keys of his phone gives him away. His phone goes dead. He has been discovered. He's been knocked over.

The President swiftly reacts, dispatching mixed men of the army, with their armored and assault vehicles, and of the intelligence unit, with assault weapons, and the police.

Meanwhile, Glenda has been located and given instruction to immediately evacuate from their position within the vicinity of the Abode.

Glenda quickly comes to grip with the situation and convinces the team of unruly herds, and they reluctantly head out, ponderously confused and preoccupied for the fate of their charismatic leader, Brett.

In a flash the mixed men of the army and intelligence unit and the police arrive in the eerie night. In silence they surround the abode, within and without the compound taking key positions.

Now the head of operation, in a flash, blast the gate open, driving through it, in his armored assault vehicle, and shouting orders.

Head of operation: You are surrounded, lay down your arms!

The heavily armed guards reacted and opened fire in their direction. They had no hint they had been overtly surrounded.

The soldiers responded with equal vigor and with ponderous viciousness. A fierce battle ensued.

And in the process the cache of arms got inadvertently hit.

Successions of ponderous explosions greeted the night. The voluptuous flares and glows lighted the sky, with plumes of fumes drifting and swirling into the air and stuttering and dispersing with the wind. The risk to contain it was remarkably ponderous. The soldiers let them explode, ducking and protecting selves as they could.

Chapter 3

Back to Plaza Hill
In the plaza, Gen WHY phones go haywire with ponderous tweeting tones and Instagram posts, u-tube video images from Mezzi and Mark: they have the privilege of previewing the past 10 hours of drama of the night events in anticipation of the expectant media reporting shortly.

We see graphic images in close-ups, medium close ups and long shots and naked video images of the rites and rituals of the "men and women of God," of members of their monarchy (the chiefs, obas, emirs, the sultans, etc.), the politicians, the bureaucrats and of the cabals. All in one place. Birds of a feather confirmed.

You can hear sudden bursts of clamor of shrieks and shouting of disbelief, consternation and condemnation amongst the youths:

Gen WHY: #Firing squad, firing squad, hang them, hang them high.
Mezzi tweets: #There is no god but God.
Gen WHY (ponderous shrieks): Yeah, there is no god but God. There is no god but
God...no god but God. Firing squad, firing squad, firing squad...

Then Mezzi and Mark tweet, uploading the images of the mediaeval rack with the torture of the witchdoctors and the dreadful Knight Templars Christian punitive crusade mission style-images and symbols of the unruly herds, with nooses, lanterns, hatchets and axes and medieval torture racks in hands, in cruel spiteful stance, in their black face coverings overlooking, contemplating, daring the victims engulfed in flames. Everything and everybody are enshrouded by the flame.

Gen WHY go haywire. These gruesome vicious images of the unruly herds Knight Templars Christian crusade style-images and symbols with nooses and lanterns, hatchets and axes and torture racks are greeted with a ponderous voluptuous ovation. They explode in clamor, wailing, shouting, scowling, howling accompanied with dancing at the same time. It's a mere savoring of justice at its raw stage. Fear of contrition far removed.

Gen WHY: Yeaaaaaaaaaaaah! Yeaaaaaaaaaaah, our GenWHYKlan Templars, GYklan Templars Rack them highhhhhhhhhhh! Some justice be done. Hilarious. Freedom. Rack them high!

Then Mezzi and Mark tweet.

Mezzi: #The Black angels are avenging us.

Gen WHY: Yeaaaaah, the GYKlanTemplars! Rack them highhhhhhhhhhh!

Mark: #Yeah our Black ghosts, the GYKlanTemplars are vindicating us.

Gen WHY: Rack them highest.

Gen WHY are lifted. The unruly herds have befittingly just gained the appellative "GenWHYKlanTemplars." They are in exhilaration of courage in profile. The awe of courage. They are proud wearing the hat of courage. Courage, the Gen WHY's crown. The cleverness of courage and determination. There is no comfort in cleverness of hope. There is solace in cleverness of courage. They are in exhilaration of freedom.

Life is about freedom or death. Courage or misery. And once again the cleverness of courage is freedom. Courage, freedom and life are enlaced. It's best to die fighting than die miserably. Whatever you do in life, wisdom in courage. Whatever you do in life don't die in misery. Misery of the mind. The mind's emptiness is negation of life.

> *Courage, the Gen WHY's crown. The cleverness of courage and determination. There is no comfort in cleverness of hope. There is solace in cleverness of courage. They are in exhilaration of freedom. Life is about freedom or death. Courage or misery. And once again the cleverness of courage is freedom.*
> *Courage, freedom and life are enlaced. It's best to die fighting than die miserably. Whatever you do in life, wisdom in courage. Whatever you do in life don't die in misery. Misery of the mind. The mind's emptiness is negation of life.*

As the day broke the streets acquaint self with media's full-page headlines, giving context of the night's full happenstance:

"POWER TO THE YOUTHS: A KLAN PROVEN PROWESS"

"THE GenWHYKLAN TEMPLARS, AFRICA'S HOPE TO PROGRESS"

"WHAT A FIT: Gen WHY's' OBSTINATE DEFIANT KLAN SAVES THE BLACK KIND FROM SHACKLES OF SUPERSTITIOUS, PRIMITIVE JINX"

"WHAT A PRODIGY! PRODIGIOUS GYKLAN TEMPLARS RESCUE OUR SOCIETY FROM WITCHDOCTORS GENERATIONAL APPALLING TENTACLES"

"WHAT A PORTENTOUS VISIONARIES OUR GWHYKLAN IS: THEY UNVEIL OUR DARKNESS"

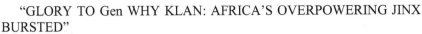

"GLORY TO Gen WHY KLAN: AFRICA'S OVERPOWERING JINX BURSTED"
"IGNOBLE! IGNOBLE AFRICAN RELIGIONS OUR NEMESIS FOR PROGRESS"
"AFRICA'S PRIMITIVITY HER NEMESIS TO DEVELOPMENT AND PROGRESS" "A DEFIANT Gen WHY MAKES CONSPICOUSNESS OF ORACLES, FETISHISM ON OUR LAND".
"THE Gen WHY KLAN SAVES US FROM THE EVIL TRINITY OF AFRICAN LEADERSHIP ALLEGIANCE TO AND ALLIANCE WITH POWER OF SUPERSTITION".
"SUPERSTITION THE BANE ON AFRICA'S SELF-COSCIOUSNESS"
The dailies of all sympathies, conservative, liberal, centrists, independent are all remarkably and voluptuously united in their praise for the fit of Gen WHY.

Every human race outgrows moronic phase. Africans, willfully remain morons. Every race resource to inform and power the mind. Africans willfully don't. Every race has the ability to learn, Africans willfully don't. Every race has the ability of inventiveness. Africans willfully don't. Every race can draw conclusions. Africans willfully don't. Every race does self-criticism necessary for growth. Africans willfully don't. Africans have the mental capacity to discern, and absorb and embrace tough love principles and concept as the saving grace. Africans willfully don't.

Tough love is the truth to evolving to every next level. Tough love is the truth to power, tough love is the truth to willful denial and to reticence. Tough love is the truth to hypocrisy, to laziness, to ignorance, to cowardice, to not standing up, to complacency, to misery, to mediocrity, to corruption, to demeaning stance, to bombast, to kleptomania, to life.

Africa, you can't go on willfully denying your status. You can't go on with hypocritical and historical reticence. You can't go on devoid of self-criticism. Africa, you can't go on kicking the can down the road. Africa, you can't go on having a divided house. Africa you can't go on denying your problem. Africa you can't go on not having a common denominator of accepting you have a problem. Africa you can't go on not identifying your problem. Africa you can't go on not recognizing your problem. Africa you can't go on not confronting your problem. Africa you can't go on not eradicating your problem. Africa you are an embarrassment. You can't go on feasting in embarrassment. Africa, you are an embarrassment to yourself and to the other two races.

You can deny it. You can vent your anger about the truth of it all. You can continue consorting with evil. Your eyes can live in conceit. But deep in your hearts, you cannot know any peace. You will remain hollow. You have "...not contributed anything mankind can enjoy."

You are a continent of misery. The more you deny it the more you disfranchise your future, your children. Your future is your children. Your descendants. Africa you are the father of Black kind. Africa you should have the back of your descendants–the Black kind descendants. Africa you are an unutterable shame. And the more your shame, the more your demeaning embarrassments.

You can't hide in excuses, generation in generation not to develop. Africa, you transcend every and any excuses not to develop. It's not just acceptable what you do to yourself. You are a demeaning embarrassment. Africa, find your will. Africa, tell yourself the truth. Africa, you live in denial. Africa, forge a resolve to progress. Africa, chart your kids to excellent education. Uplift their minds. Chart them out of ignorance. That's the real power. Power of the mind. Africa, chart your kids to health care. Africa, give them healthy mind and body. Give them dignity. Give them electric energy, clean water, toilets, jobs, homes. Africa give yourself self-esteem.

Poverty is predatory and adversarial. Ignorance is predatory and adversarial. Laziness is predatory and adversarial. Cowardice is predatory and adversarial. Misery is the sum game. Misery is predatory, dehumanizing and adversarial and humiliating and subjugating. Misery is life-abnegation.

The truth is that anyone who cannot change before adversary and peril, and yet that change is imperative for his survival, must be mentally defective.

> *You don't change before adversary and peril, and yet that change is imperative for your very survival, you are mentally defective...you don't change before adversary and peril, and yet that change is imperative for your very survival, you are mentally defective...you don't change before adversary and peril, and yet that change is imperative for your very survival, you are...*

Today, Africa ponderously amazes. Her powerful, influential mass-communication organs, the newspapers, the televisions and radios are rejecting complacency scomplicity-smugness. These powerful organs lay to rest the willful blindness, the willful deafness, the willful hypocrisy, the willful complicity, the willful omerta and gave truth its place in time and space. In their critique context, they ponderously brush aside on "how much wrong is in Gen WHY's actions" but gave prominence, dwelling on "how much right is in Gen WHY's reason" and "how much beneficial is this beautiful, and long desired, and desirable, action of reason."

As it's been said, "societies concentrate their laws, investigations, prosecutions and punishments on how much crime is in the sin, rather than on how much sin is in the crime."

Just imagine the extent and repercussions of the sins in the crime of the combined alliance of the devil and the evil triad and the cowards and the stupid men, with superstitious power on the African continent? On the black race? On the lethargy of development? On the miser, generation after generation? On the shamefulness of it all? On the tragedy of it all? On the embarrassment of it all? On the presumed, assumed mental defectiveness of a race?

The GenWHYKlanTemplars saw their fate in the madness of their society. They saw their fate in the fear. They saw their fate in the death. And yet they defied and braved them all. The selflessness affliction absorbed, the Rubicon climbed, a new beginning began. A new season.

Gen WHY family mourning mood dissolved into jubilation. A liberating act. Their one desire, as uncanny cynicism rips away at their innocence, is the justice for happiness.

A justice for happiness at whatever cost that would find reason for Africa's youths progress. To that extent its virtues and comforts and solaces are beyond any prize.

The youths are chanting, shrouded in pride and hailing the President.

The President's actions and visions are validated. Gen WHY are intimidating, fascinating and ponderously credible at the same time. They are voluptuously validated. They have ridden the tigers back and vanquished the tide on their own terms. Nothing really gifted. Except the irrefutable existential President's backing. They fought honorably and won gallantly.

The selflessness affliction syndrome mind that formed and assimilated and permeates in them coalesced and held and braved and climbed the Rubicon. In its wake unleashed mayhem. A scouring obliteration mayhem of ponderous deterrent entity and of vicious dissuadable future attempt and recurrence of evil indulgence indeed.

The wake of scouring obliteration mayhem night had 23 witchdoctors racked and burnt alive and 5 monarchs racked and burnt alive. The help of the Imam gave additional deaths to 37 monarchs, 138 politicians, 300 "men and women of God", 15 prominent government bureaucrats and administrators and 17 bankers, all gathered in their rights of the night of the rite and initiations to "the man and woman of God", in the host priestess's abode.

And besides, a voluptuous number of the security guards were decimated.

A combined hostage of witchdoctors, of monarchs, of politicians, of "men and women of god", of public administrators and bureaucrats and bankers and cabals were made and carted away.

Fate claimed the Imam. Like his father, and father's father. They all died honorably and would never be obliviated by history but by luxury of pride, greatness and gratefulness. May their souls rest in peace.

Bret survived unharmed by some kismet. The sound of clicking phone keys had given him away and he was consequently immediately knocked over in his fierce fiery resistance to three security guards who hurriedly took him down to the basement unconscious. He was left on the watch of one of the guards, tor his sign of life, in order to grill him for information…until the unfathomable boom, boom, Boom, of the flying, exploding rockets overhead, and cruel, vicious exchange of gun fires woke him languidly up to the ponderous grim and gruesome reality of the night.

The gruesome reality shoots him into his life reverie of misery, courage, honor and dignity.

Brett has been a precocious child who lost his father at early age of ten. His presentiment against the fear of misery had him work, progressing his inherited father's catfish aqua culture activity to maintain their family of five while at the same time adeptly brilliant at school. He has lived love from his parents. He has seen courage in his father. He lived the dignity and honor and faith and grit of courage: his father, a school teacher, who at best received one-month salary every six months of work, never stuttered nor fluttered in his faith in God, faith in courage and in virtues of honesty, love and hard work. He has seen fear of misery in their poorer neighbors. But his savage hatred for misery and love for honor and dignity gave him courage after his father's death. Courage that despised corruption, defied mediocrity and rejected and denounced the hypocritical, corrupt, cheap comfort of the homes of his peers that, imbibed in him the unequivocal importance of hard work, which virtues and rewards could be as remote and as priceless at the same time.

His trusting font of happiness gone and innocence ripped away at early age, he had to be informed and formed by the competing life intricacies and solemnity of courage, faith and death.

Not fear. He really does not know the emotion of fear. That life solemnity riveted, waking him up to the existential obligation to the youth: crossing the Rubicon with selflessness affliction. It's better to die fighting, than to die the cowardly miserable death of a thousand times. Whatever you do, die a courageous death.

He jumps to his feet, stepping furtively to the outside, braving the exploding mortars and the vicious gun fires.

The complicity of the siege salvages and liberates him: the soldiers had his profile and they promptly have his back to a hero's welcome.

Now the entire operation protracts into the early morning hours, with the exploding nights and its ponderous sounds simmering… and then completely ceasing with breaking of dawn. In its wake you can see clouds of smoke rising and smoldering and dispersing in the sky against the aurora.

The whole city creased into eerie silence with competing emotions of inauspicious, ominous fallout, ponderous suspicion amidst whatever remains of the Status Quo and its cabals, and a delightful curiosity and voluptuous menacing expectation among Gen WHY, on the Plaza Hill, in their second day of vigil.

Then the sound of sirens in the distance pierces. Then they grow louder and nearer. They are approaching and you can make out distinct sounds of heavy trucks in their midst. Suddenly everything stops.

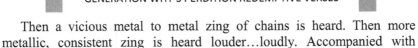

Then a vicious metal to metal zing of chains is heard. Then more metallic, consistent zing is heard louder…loudly. Accompanied with distinct voices, spitting marching orders and floggings:

Voices: Common! Move! Filths!

You can hear spasm of wailings and moaning laments. Everything grows louder and nearer and distinct.

Gen WHY, their cringing, curious heads are turning in the direction of the approaching sound when a soldier in combat menacing mode appears on the horizon. Then followed yet by another, in his hands a rope of metallic chain dragging a caravan of naked trembling, wailing, moaning subdued human beings in societal punishment symbols-hand-cuffs and leg-cuffs, hobbling, climbing the platform on the Plaza Hill.

Gen WHY breathlessly glimpse. As their glimpse transits into contemplation, they daze into gawping and gawking confusion and bewilderment. Unbelievable at the palpability of it all, they understand and go berserk in amazement. They erupt in clamor and uproar of shrieks and howling, scowling and shouting spasm. Everything is of voluptuous significance and of epical magnitude.

Their ponderous mind commotions are readily put to interpretation, and their form made perceptible by the prompt tweets of the foursome:

#Gen WHY, can this be true?

#You must be pondering if this were a nightmare?

#Unfortunately, everything is palpable. We can feel it. They are starring at us.

#The vacuity, the profanity, the nonsensical, the vain superciliousness, ponderous hoax of superstition and of its high priests and priestesses are defiled, revealed and in chains.

#These profane bodies strewn with pouffe of charms are Africa's leadership? Do you believe that? What unutterable shame.

#Are these our political leadership for our education, our health care, our laws, our justice system, equity, science, technology and our development?

#Are these our religious leadership for morality, deeds of God and savior and paradise?

#Are these our traditional leadership for our values in customs, costumes and traditions?

#Poor Africa. #Poor Africa. #Poor Africa.

#The 2020 Africa is in her primitive ages still? In her peak of primitiveness?

#Superstition hold's Africa hostage. Captive.

#Cry Africa. #Cry Africa. #Cry Africa.

#Let's all cry together, Africa. # Let's cry together, Africa, to generate an ominous wave energy for progress and development. It's a tragedy.

#Our tragedy is palpable. We are looking at our tragedy.

We are our tragedy.

#How can we be slaves to these macabre vacuous, viscid superstitious filths? #Can't we be slaves to power of the mind, to science and technology and to development?

The nakedness of our tragedy is before our eyes.

#How can these cheap perverts, deviates, debauchers be our leadership?

#The vacuity, the absolute profanity, the integral and integrated innocuousness of superstition, superstitious powers and their superstitious idiosyncrasies are before us in societal symbol of punishment chains.

#These perverts, deranged continent fuckers are in chains. They can't save themselves. Just like the oracular gods during slavery and colonialism did not. #We are our tragedy! We are slaves to superstition and to superstitious vacuity #Harriet Tubman, great woman where art thou? You need to wake up from ages beyond and help us.

#Harriet Tubman you need to free a whole race. Not just one thousand slaves. You need to free more. For we are now, conscientiously conscientious we are slaves. Please! Please!!

The more Gen WHY stare and contemplate the parade of subdued, beaten, defeated and trembling restricted and restrained images of these immediate past "mightiest", with their myths and mythologies of superstition, their powers , their prowess, their evils, their symbols and symbolisms they represent on the high ground of the Plaza Hill, the more their minds get into spasm of dazed, awful, reprehensible and ponderously troubling realization of their appalling facts: the space of reality and dreams. A nightmare.

Dazed, broken and confused before this vulgar macabre spectacle of superstition made prisoner, the omnipotent evil power of the African land made hostage, their fountain of shame and misery captivity made captive, Gen WHY dissolve into transition of competing amazement of horror, consternation, delusion, shame, embarrassment, resolve, exultation and delight.

These competing combined amazements are essential and have their reasons and justifications. Horror gives consternation its purpose. As consternation gives embarrassment its purpose.

Embarrassment gives shame its purpose. And shame gives delusion its purpose. To the extent that delusion gives resolve its purpose; to the extent that resolve gives exultation its purpose; to these extents, exultation gives delight its reward. The scouring obliteration of superstition and superstitious belief would give Gen WHY freedom and exultation purposes. Gen WHY freedom and exultation would give superstitious scouring obliteration its reward.

Exaltation and exultation of hard work, rewards the power of the mind.

The President's ponderous reason to parade and shame the beaten, the defeated, the subdued, the vulgar and the obscure superstition and the profane vacuity it represents, is in making sure that any of its vestiges is absolutely obliterated, stamped out of the minds of the youths, and at the same time instill deterrence punishment value system against superstitious practices and observations forthwith.

And there is more to it: Africa is constantly and consistently humiliated, derided and scorned by the White kind. By the Yellow kind. Her two sibling kinds within the realm of human species. It's time for Africa to feel shame and embarrassment. Instead of its attitude of refuging in the willful: willful denials, willful deafness, willful blindness, willful hypocrisy, willful self-abandonment; and in the defaults: defaults excuses of colonialism, default excuses of slavery, default ignorance and arrogance, default resignation in religious mysticism, default *erasus,* default grace of unmerited favor, default religious palsy, default compulsive *oblivionem* of laws and virtues of God and of society; and in the hereditary despotic conspiracies of tradition and culture: conspiracies of silence, ignorance, arrogance, sloth, falsehood, evil, abject resignation, superstition, apathy to shame and remorse; and in the cowardice of enthusiasm of heroism, cowardice of passion for animation of liberty, cowardice of inward reflection, self-critique and of truth.

For her two siblings mean well. They should take it as tough loves.

We are fortunate we live in a world of mostly compassionate majority.

We live in a world of love and forgiveness. Forgiveness gives love its purpose.

Even though the scornful and the divisive and the derisive are in the minority. Even though the thinking and thoughts of the scornful and derisive minority might blur the humane thinking of the majority, and even pollute and make complicit and complacent their conscientiousness of fairness and justice, even so it should not be considered obnoxious or demeaning. Their love, their tough love, even in the name of derision and scorn, still put at disposal the fruits of their technology to develop and progress everybody.

Even if the motto of guilt-forgiveness is ponderously hard, very hard to justify dehumanization, Africans may embrace unconditional unilateral forgiveness for the White race and instead have a ponderous guilty conscience from within themselves, in order to wake up to the use of White's technology at disposal to improve their lots, evolving it and occupy their rightful place in the human realm. Not just the lot of the wicked and evil few.

The above submission regardless, Africa should find reason and purpose in scorn and derision. They are both essential to her well-being.

Scorn and derision should give shame and embarrassment its purpose.

And shame and embarrassment should give standing up its purpose.

Standing up would give Gen WHY their reward: obliterating misery and developing, progressing and empowering descendants of a race in its wake. Like the other two.

They had asked for a peaceful separation from the Status Quo, with no strings whatsoever attached. They had asked for separation, even though fraught in the weight of their ponderous excruciating misery. They had asked for a separation, braving the arduous passion of their cross into the realm of the unknown. They had asked for separation, consorting only with faith in standing up with vacuous uncertainty of any hint at success. The dual courage in separation and in faith in standing up, finds its justification in understanding and refusing and rejecting fate of slavery and enslavement. Enslavement is simply life-negation.

Separation asked on a platter of gold of the Status Quo was reneged. When as a matter of fact, a civil law of sacrament; penitence, atonement and absolution devoid of confession, should be enacted on the African continent instead. For any confession pales in comparison to the craven embarrassing misery self-confessed, selfevidence, self-manifest on the African continent of the damages done to progenies, by their progenitors. You don't just make children at wish. You make children you can be responsible for, in making sure their future must be better than yours. But African progenitors are perpetually ponderously consorted with willful blindness. They don't see to this day.

And worse still, they were violently attacked and massacred on the Plaza Hill. All in the bid to instill fear, continue the perpetuation of youths' assumed loyalty and subdue their found ideal and courage. Their life purpose ideal: standing up!

They stood up. If they knew nothing of victory, standing up has given them knowledge of victory. Victory on their own terms. This has given them the ponderous and audacious luxury of self-esteem, the luxury of self-reproach and the luxury selfeffacing self-discipline. This luxury is courage. The courage to stand up. Standing up is the found faith. It's like the art of confession. They have confessed to faith. This confession is the catharsis of absolution. Faith in standing up gives confession its absolution. Not in the priest and priestesses of superstition.

Their standing up has denuded superstition, revealed its vacuity, unveiled the profanity of its symbols and symbolisms, exposed its indecipherability and imperceptibility, desecrated its veiled non-existent and vacuity of myth and power. It has never had any powers. Just a myth. Reason, rational and science are the route. If it had those imagined awed powers, wouldn't it have fought back, not just by protecting self and her citizenry from enemy fire and the chains but effective as well in guarding against misery and misery perpetuity on her people?

> *...regardless, Africa should find reason and purpose in scorn and derision.*
> *They are both essential to her well-being.*
> *Scorn and derision should give shame and embarrassment its intent. And shame and embarrassment should give standing up its purpose....*

> *...Standing up would give the Gen Z their reward: obliterating misery and progressing a race in its wake.*

Today, the eve of accountability, the whole lot of superstition and superstitious notions and beliefs and vacuity and vagueness were sent to the gallows. They were quickly and summarily executed by firing squad. A public execution. A willful public conscientious participation and her willful, blunt, blind vicious cynicism. A public validation. A voluptuous ponderous punishment-deterrence of intimidating disincentive voluptuousness.

The cruel callousness and viciousness of it all remains in the macabre primitivity that is rooted in the past historical formats, and in the disposition of summary executions from litany of human history.

Its justification, besides the very treasonable offence of arms possession, arms trafficking, with intent to subvert and kill and overthrow a legitimate government, is in the future progress of Africa's descendants.

The summary execution of superstition was craven, intimidating, and its effect was voluptuously, devastatingly immediate.

What remains of the Devil (the hereditary despotism), of the Devil's trinity Son (the Status Quo- the Monarchycraft, the Politicalcraft, the Priestcraft), of the Evil spirit one million cowards(the army, the police, security agents), of the 10 million stupid men (the government bureaucrats, the contractors, the professional consultants, the banks and the bankers) and of their cabals, of their cultists, of their priest and priestesses, of its cronies, of its surrogates, of its superstitious contrivances, debaucheries, sacrileges, profanations, desecrations, deceits and conceits, its spite and defiance seemed psyched out. Brought to their knees. Subdued. Seemed obliterated.

To the extent that today, the day of accountability, the lid of superstitious notion of obscure and vague and veil of fear and ignorance, of deceit and conceit seems to be lifted on the Plaza Hill, on the psyche of the land.

There is a general heroic enthusiasm for this miraculous exertion. The stake was transcendental: superstitious annihilation was to be the prize or the tragedy of captivity perpetuation of Africa's descendants. Just as their cry for separation at the Plaza Hill was to be their freedom or slavery. Indeed, imagination would fail to punctiliously capture and describe and compare the voluptuous silent air of éclat for Gen WHY on the land to the historical and remotest distanced ponderous epic acclaim and conspicuous success of the medieval assailants for renaissance credo.

It is said that money is the root of all evils. And paraphrasing Harriet Beecher Stowe: *"No one is thoroughly superstitious than the Godless Man."*

We can, with equal vigor infer that superstition is the root of evil. At least in Africa. Superstition is the devil. It is Africa's hereditary despotism. It is like octopus. To defeat it, you need to annihilate the head to avoid its reforming and resurgent tentacles.

The two sibling races have had to deal and defeat it with education and rationality. In Africa, this is why it is hoped that, this event marks the beginning of freedom and end to slavery.

To the extent that today, the day of accountability, what remains of the Devil (Africa's hereditary despotism) and his Trinity son (Africa's status quo, the real devil incarnates), and the evil spirit, the angels of death, the angels with finality of authority, the alfa and omega, the pseudo-omnipotent is a pathetic specter of travesty. African hereditary monarchy and hereditary despotism, African hereditary political aristocracy and hereditary despotism, African hereditary Priestcraft (men of God) and hereditary despotism, all of hereditary successions of despotic dispositions, of mastery mystery and hazard who have held the continent captive with harrowing misery has suffered a near scouring obliteration gravity, almost of the scale of Sodom and Gomorrah. There are no signs of any remnants. None showed up for accountability. None showed up for claims. None showed up for litigation. Abjectly denuded, defiled and the remnants dispersed, dispersing and gone into hiding. Beaten and resigned and pathetic;

to the extent that today, the day of accountability, African one million cowards, one half of the evil spirit–the army, the police, the security agents– who usually like zombies hold their conscience avowedly in abject palsy, who hold dear the hereditary despotism cause, broke rank and protocols: retrieved her mortgaged conscience, remembers it has conscience. Its majority coalescing with constituted authority of conscience of the Plaza Hill, with the President, holding, collaborating with Gen WHY cause of making misery captive, leaving its few officers complicit in the interest of hereditary despotism. Its few officers had aided and trafficked the arms and ammunitions intended to subvert a constituted authority. They have since been apprehended, court-martialed and sent to the gallows. And within the ranks, new files are promoted to officers and appointed to new positions and postings; to the extent that today, the day of accountability, the African ten million stupid men, the other half of the evil spirit–the cabinet ministers, the heads of government parastatals, the heads of public private enterprises, the bureaucrats, the heads of departments, the secretaries, the paper shufflers, the pen-pushers, the contractors, the professional intellectual consultants, the head of universities, heads of schools, teachers, the bankers, heads of associations, heads of labor unions and the cabals and retinue of high priests and priestesses and cultists–who are complicit in the conspiracy theory of misery, who are aware of what's going on, but are compromised to it for their own ends, who indeed strengthen themselves by pretending obedience, as it unleashes tyrannies of duty, are submitting themselves to the court of the Gen WHY opinion.

Their deceit unveiled, their conceit defiled, their alter ego dishonored, their integrity desecrated, their conscience constrained by the restraining concurrence of circumstantial remorse and of hope to mitigate the future consequences are all coalescing, collaborating. Self-denouncing identities, denouncing veiled activities, denouncing veiled properties and rejecting their lifetime loots and ill-acquired comforts and lascivious life-styles; to the extent that today, the day of accountability, the ponderous epic fit of Gen WHY is yet to dawn voluptuously on Gen WHY themselves.

Used to misery themselves, numbed by it, dazed by it, traumatized by it, they had but little conviction that liberty was capable of such inspiration, or that a body of unarmed youth would dare much, or that their incredible ready natural coalescing at the Plaza Hill was remotely ponderable, or that their incredible resolve exhibited could astonish and embarrass Status Quo despotism, their sworn enemy. Or little did they know that the cause in which they were engaged in, the crisis they engaged in was to determine their freedom or slavery of an entire continent. Indeed, of an entire race.

As the effects of this miracle of exertion become manifest and in continuum evolution the ardor of the valor of their scouring success, scouring liberty and freedom started sinking in.

And caught amidst competing emotions of fervor magnificence, and triumphalism and the incredulity of the reality, their psyche transits reluctantly out of their doubtful doubt as they witness, awed and amazed, the finality of miracle of their exertion transcend on the infamous cultists' youths, their generation.

Alias the crime infested and criminal integral "cyber-thefts boys", kingpin at cyber thefting, who, betrayed and abandoned by a humiliated superstitious myth, in abject vulnerability, in austere hollowness, in craven bewilderment and in cringing fear of the present and menacing consequences that punish and annihilate, are in a debilitating guilt and grieving shame as they submit themselves to Gen WHY's "selflessness affliction syndrome" creed, resigning willfully to authority, denouncing their unutterable avariciousness, ineffable bombasts and more importantly, rejecting their families' kleptocracy shroud and veil and protection and its delusional illusion of comforts.

The combined guiltiness and shamefulness are necessary: guiltiness and shamefulness give denunciation, resignation, rejection their purposes and at the same time give selflessness-affliction credo its rewards of virtues and solaces.

In fact, it is wished and hoped that far from anything else, Harriet Tubman's forlornness and chagrins:

"I freed a thousand slaves. I could have freed more if only they knew they were slaves.", are finally embraced and sanctified and acclaimed on the black continent, on the Black kind, on the Black conscience. On the Black kind youths. In successions; to these extents, today, the day of accountability has a grande standing for a land arid of accountability. Grande for a race. For a conscience. The conscience of selfenslavement in

unaccountability. For a conscience in luxury of self-reproach. The luxury is standing up. For standing up is freedom. Standing up triumphs.

"Standing up" triumphs. "Standing up" triumphs. "Standing up" triumphs. "Standing up" triumphs. "Standing up" triumphs. "Standing up" triumphs. "Standing up" triumphs. "Standing up" triumphs. "Standing up" triumphs. "Standing up" triumphs.

In life, most things lay in the purpose and reward. Love is unconditional. Its universality is sublime. Love is God. Its unconditionality gives love its purpose. Its unconditionality gives unconditional Heaven, the sublime reward.

With equal vigor standing up is unconditional. Standing up is an unconditional triumph. Triumph of freedom: triumph on ignorant slavery, triumph on cowardly slavery, triumph on slothful slavery. Triumph on self-inflicted and inflicting slavery. Triumph on self-inflicted and inflicting colonialism. Triumph on self-inflicted and inflicting looting.

Earning respect gives triumph its purpose, and triumph gives standing up its reward.

> *To these extents, today, the day of accountability has a Grande standing, for a land arid of accountability. Grande for a continent. For a continent's*
> *conscience: the conscience of self-enslavement in unaccountability. For a conscience in luxury of self-reproach. The luxury is standing up. For standing up is freedom. Standing up prevails.*
> *"Standing up" prevails. "Standing up" prevails. "Standing up" prevails.*
> *"Standing up" prevails. "Standing up" prevails. "Standing up" prevails. "Standing up" prevails. "Standing up" prevails.*
> *"Standing up" prevails.*
> *"Standing up" prevails...*

VOLUME 7

THE ASCENT

Chapter 1

While the rest of the world is long in possession of the knowledge and palpability of Africa's perennial generational prison, self-imprisonment and their perennial misery of cruelty, viciousness, humiliation, subjugation, spite, defiance and hazard and mayhem, Africa, the Black kind on the other hand, is being perennially, proudly busy in their denial, deflection and or at best, masterly shrouding and veiling in the blame of the scourging history of slavery and colonialism, and in their unjustifiable myth and mythologies to the present day.

While the rest of the world long knows that the nemesis of and answers to Africa's prison misery lay in her cowardice, ignorance and sloth, all found in her mind-set of primitivity and timidity, Africa on the other hand shrouds and veils her nemesis and answers in the mystery, myth, mythology of faith and hope in heaven and in their hazards and mayhems.

While the rest of the world is dogged in finding, and persevering the antidotes to common malaise, defeating human nemesis and progressing humanity, Africa is dogged in, and persevering, and perpetuating stupidity, generation after generation.

While the rest of the world had amazed appallingly, reprehensibly, astonishingly, embarrassingly, bewilderingly at Africa's stupidity, had given up on her stupidity, and now encourage her stupidity, feed fat on her stupidity, through her self-slavery, self-colonization, self-looting and of course through the world's institutional racism, even veil her stupidity under the appalling political-moral correctness of ethic umbrella as the only way forward, Africa on the other hand promulgates her stupidity as a conditio sine qua non in perpetuation of her self-enslavement, post slavery, in multiplication of slavery and colonial era tyranny, all in pursuance of a befitting Africa's moral-political-economic-enslavement grandstanding.

Today, the first post-day of the day of accountability, the African Gen WHY and their defiance, their selflessness, their love, their heroic enthusiasm, their passion of animation by virtue of self-consciousness exertion has finally produced a miracle of stupidity catharsis, a stupidity purgation.

The miracle of Gen WHY exertion did not only subdue the myths and mythologies and their vacuity and validated courage over cowardice, knowledge over ignorance, exertion over sloth, but with equal vigor it lays bare, unveiling the beyond*ness* of Africa's complex stupidity of vain and vacuity, its bane of complicity, its scourge of arrogance, its nemesis of ignorance, trials, tribulations and trauma.

302

Today, the first post-day of the day of accountability has ponderously unearthed a miscellany of voluptuous, convoluted outrageous litany of Africa's stupefying stupidity in its wake.

Gen WHY inner-working committee, the foursome and peers–Brett, Glenda, Lynda, Frank, Laura and now enlarged to include the GenWHYKlanTemplers Christian crusaders ghosts-like warriors of the unruly herds–are gathered around a grand table placed in the middle of the platform under construction. In the background you can hear subdued sounds of nervous generators, the whining insistence of drills and grinders, the humming and clattering of machines in the distance: men at work, fiercely progressing the youths' platform venue to completion and launch.

As they complement one another on their success, and their found self-esteem, and are pondering and evaluating the ever-fluid situation and discussing, planning, programming the platform launch, some 10 days away, Mezzi and Mark suddenly break in, their faces wreathed in a smirking elation that aroused sense of suspense. They place their laptops, already tuned-in to the President's impromptu state of the union address, in the middle of the table, interrupting and getting everybody into a new focal point.

Mark: My dad is about to speak: The state of the union speech.

In the general confusion of wonderment and amazement, all attentions without words are promptly redirected to the screens of the laptops.

The President readily appears but looking sorrowful. His demeanor, austere. He takes his sitting position and lurch into a tirade of analytical synthesis of the nation and of the haul of the 'day of accountability' in figures and numbers.

President: (reading from a teleprompter)
Our Gen WHY…congratulations to you. You are a miracle. You are the proof that life could be a miracle. You underpin the ferocious urgency of now, growing yourselves with a renaissance credo self-consciousness and enduring it into a revolutionary dynamite, supplanting Africa's perennial self-consciousness of stupidity of laziness and cowardice.

He pauses and peers, in ponderous scrutiny of Gen WHY, through the lens of the television in his intention to pin down their attention.

President: I repeat, our Gen WHY are a miracle. Now Gen WHY please listen well and hard. The authority wishes to bring you up to date with our nation and with the state of our day of accountability for your information, evaluations and takes.

At least 99% of our African leadership, past and present, dead and living, were and are thieves.

That was the most sweeping, outlandish, ponderous, voluptuous truthful truth said on the African continent to this day. More so, by one of the active living actors. In fact, Gen WHY are unprepared to such a scouring submission by an active player. They are too numbed to believe their ears, and their nerves too cold to react with any emotion.

The President pauses, disengages from the text and with a remorseful chagrined grimace, continues.

President: The politicians, including myself, my cronies and cohorts; the monarchy – the Obis, Ezes, Obas, Emirs, Sultans, the Chiefs and their cronies and cohorts; the men of God – Priest, Pastors, Imams, and cronies and cohorts; the defense and security chiefs – the Army, Air force, Navy and the Police; the cabals and the bureaucrats–all of us have been and are thieves. Totally corrupt. This is the tragedy.

Now Gen WHY recover, gaining the defining peculiarity of the moment, breaking overwhelmingly into a thunderous unsolicitedly deserving applause on this scouring self-indictment.

Gen WHY (applauding): Awesome, awesome, awesome!
President: And the bigger tragedy is the fact that our progenies or descendants whose future is stolen generation after generation celebrate it. Applauding us, the thieves, until that fateful day, the day the courage of one youthful vigor appeared in the church. That appearance culminated in an energy that galvanized the youths and infected the land with "standing up!" idea.

He pauses to drive home his point. Then continuing:

President: Africa (post-slavery and post-colonial history) has always been of an endemic degeneration of generations in successions. Each generation has always mortgaged the future of the generation coming. Each generation creates chaos and disorder, desperation, hopelessness, anarchy and misery, like mobsters.
Like mobsters, we steal and subtract 90% of Africa's already miserable Gross Domestic Product, each year.
Modestly, Africa's Gross Domestic Product in the last 40 years alone, before most Gen WHY's births, amounts to about 20 trillion US Dollars.

He pauses, with the calculated, duteous tempo of a pastor at a homily for his points to sink in.

President: 90% of 20 trillion US Dollars is 18 trillion US Dollars. We stole well over 18 trillion US Dollars in 40 years.

Pause.

President: We then subtracted from our economy about 80% of the stolen 18 trillion US Dollars. To be clear and without equivocation, of this stolen money we subtracted a total of 14.4 trillion US Dollars from African economy into foreign banks and foreign lands. All done of our own volition, without coercion. Simply put it is suicidal. Of our own volition. Without coercion. Without compulsion.

> *At least 99% of our African leadership, past and present, dead and living were and are thieves.*
> *Like mobsters, we steal and subtract 90% of Africa's already miserable Grande Domestic Products, each year.*
> *Africa's Grande Domestic Product in the last 40 years alone, before any of the Gen WHY's births, amounts to about 20 trillion US Dollars.*
> *90% of 20 trillion US Dollars is 18 trillion US Dollars.*
> *We stole well over 18 trillion US Dollars in 40 years.*
> *We then subtracted from our economy about 80% of the stolen 18 trillion US Dollars.*
> *...we subtracted a total of 14.4trillion US Dollars from African economy into foreign banks and foreign lands. To leverage and enable the White supremacist scum.*
> *All done of our own volition. Without coercion. Simply put, suicidal.*

He pauses again.

Now the Gen WHY are in tortured smirks. Their hearts are forlorn and broken, their faces wreathed in amazement of shame, humiliation, despise and anger.

President: Only Africa's stupidity is capable of such. A stupidity that pales only to stupidity beneath*ness*. The remaining stolen 20% of the sum 3.6 trillion US Dollars is found in Africa, in various forms of troubling, conflicting public and private sector investments. These troubling, conflicting investments are in the form of:

1. Unjustifiable and unaccountable swollen bank accounts;
2. Black market racketeering of money lending and laundering, exchange rate speculation, and counterfeiting;
3. Landed properties, properties
3.a. Properties, luxury homes, real estates, 90% of decent houses found on the African land are owned by less than 1% of the population.
3.b. Land speculations;
3.c. Hotels ownerships;
3.d. Lettable shopping complexes and market stalls

4. Education business
4.a. Private nurseries, schools, institutions, dormitories ownerships;
5. Health care business
5.a. Private clinics and hospitals;
5.b. Pharmaceuticals and their speculations, fake drugs produced and controlled by the Chinese and distributed by the Indians with Africans money;
5.c. Health insurances speculations;
6. Energy business
6.a. Franchise generator businesses;
6.b. Franchise transformer businesses;
6.c. High tension cables businesses;
6.d. Structured moribund energy and sabotage business helped by the Lebanese.
7. Agriculture
7.a. Importations of rice, grains, sugar, salt, wheat, tomatoes, beans, etc;
7.b. Perpetual fertilizer importation businesses;
7.c. Agro-alimentary industries non-existent.
8. Infrastructure business
8.a. Government and their agencies on infrastructure -roads, bridges, highways, airports, seaports, hospitals, educational, railways, public buildings, etc. contracts;
9. Water
9.a. Public water and water purification sabotage;
9.b. Water bottling businesses;
10. Internal revenue business
10.a. Taxes collected and not remitted;
10.b. Taxation favors-waived, renegotiated, cancelled;
11. Petroleum and solid mineral business
11.a. Oil blocs indiscriminately assigned to cronyisms;
11.b. Petroleum production output doctored, no real figures;
11.c. Refineries' lethargic state perpetuity notwithstanding yearly appropriation for repairs. Functionality sabotage;
11.d. Massive importation of refined products;
11.e. Refined products round-tripping;
11.f. Lack of refineries for precious metals;
11.g. Gas flaring; etc. etc.
12. Customs and excise at the ports
12.a. Import duties netted but not remitted to government;
12.b. Indiscriminate import duty waivers;
12.c. Import duties renegotiated, fake surrogate goods declarations.
13. Public administration
13.a. 99% of government staff hardly put in up to three hours of the eight hours daily chore. But they collect full salaries every month end. They are thieves, stealing the peoples' time and money.

13.b.   Government offices and premises are turned into private business areas, including business of praying;

13.c.   They influence contracts, hide files, shuffle the ones they want or ordered to for their own interests of monies.

14.   Borrowing to create external debt and burden you with a gratuitous national debt.

15.   And on and on. This infamous list goes on and on.

These troubling areas of deviated investment by our leadership, obviously, did not meet accountability yesterday.

Gen WHY, we crave your patience. Our analytical effort is to once and for all, hopefully succeed in the demystification of the causes of the continent's nemesis, hazard and mayhem on our progenies, generation after generation.

Gen WHY, now in spasm of unutterable anger, are listening hard, full of expectation, punching their fist in the air.

Gen WHY (voices, off screen): Go on, go on, go on, we are with you President!

President: As you can see, we have problem of energy because the same leadership steal the monies, import and round-trip transformers and invest in the business of generators;

Education for everybody is denied because we in the leadership position are in the business of education for our kids overseas, in the business of private schools at home for a few and in business of ignorance for the masses.

With your monies we impose ignorance on you. We willfully incapacitate your talents and obliterate your personalities and personhood.

Health care for you is a chimera because we are in the business of pilgrimage to hospitals in foreign lands, and in the business of killing our people with importation of fake drugs, and in the business of withering the health infrastructures.

Africa is perennially hungry because we are in the business of sabotaging agriculture and agro-alimentary, sabotaging manufacturing value processing chains and in the business importation of food.

Africa is perennially thirsty for clean water because we are in the business of water bottling and sabotaging public clean water supplies with cholera, dysenteries, bacteria and viruses;

Africa dies perennially from hygiene challenging environment because, we are in the business of perpetuating filths and garbage to prevail mosquitoes, cholera, HIV, venereal diseases, hepatitis, polio, diabetes, obesity, heart failures etc.

Our leadership is perennially in the business of living in foreign lands as reprehensible and appalling thieves in forms of ill-gotten cash, ill-gotten luxury properties, ill-gotten airplanes, of ill-gotten yachts and of ill-gotten exotic cars, illgotten jewelries and watches and in the business of creating and perpetuating misery in Africa.

The President pauses once again for a sip of water.
There is a ponderous eerie silence among the Gen WHY who are listening hard. They are in a voluptuous state of embarrassment, wearing expression of competing emotions of shame, chagrin and indignation at the same time.
That look of shame, chagrin and indignation are real and essential.
Shame gives chagrin its purpose. And chagrin gives indignation its exultation. Then, the President continues.

President: And on and on. Ad infinitum.
Just imagine what a literacy value chain of 90% of your monies, appropriated year in year out for education and training, taken to foreign banks can give you.
Just imagine what value chain industries of 90% of your monies, appropriated for training and skill-acquisitions, taken to foreign banks can give you.
Just imagine what energy value chain of 90% of monies for electric energy, appropriated year in and year out, hidden in foreign banks can give you.
Just imagine what the health value chain of 90% of monies for your healthcare in foreign banks would do for you.
Just imagine what the agro-alimentary value chain of 90% of your monies for agriculture appropriated year in and year out, stolen and hidden in foreign banks can give you.
Just imagine the amount of jobs and employments value chain of 90% of your monies, appropriated for manufacturing and the building industry, stolen and hidden in foreign banks can give you.
Just imagine the wealth, the turnover, the Return on Investment of 20trillion US Dollars invested over a period of 40 years in the afore mentioned sectors of development would have done for the empowerment of Black kind descendants. Just imagine…just imagine …and just imagine the abject shame and craven stupidity we contrive and stage of our own volition. Without coercion.
Since we do these of our volition and without coercion generations after generations, how can we then not come to terms with the ardent truth that our slavery is by our choice?

> *Since we do these of our volition and without coercion, generations after generations, how can we then not come to terms with the ardent truth that our slavery is by our choice?*

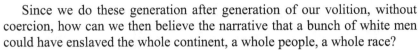

Since we do these generation after generation of our volition, without coercion, how can we then believe the narrative that a bunch of white men could have enslaved the whole continent, a whole people, a whole race?

Since out of our volition, without coercion, we steal our wealth into somebody's else's economy, is it not ridiculous and does it not pale by comparison to think that exertions of guns and gun powder and the chicaneries and the spell of mementoes like bible, chocolates, mirrors, whiskies, gins, vodkas, brandies, etc. etc. etc. enslaved and colonized a whole people, a whole continent in a scouring fit?

The President pauses for his reasoning to sink in.

Now Gen WHY break up in a voluptuous, resounding applause. It's taking the foursome some concerted effort to rein them back to listening postures without missing the key talking points. Buzzo is finally elated. His conclusion on Africa's complicit responsibility and doubts of her innocence of slavery and colonization, and institutional racism seem to find validation and recognition. The President continues.

President: If these lines of thinking offend your long-held point of view on making sense of slavery and colonialism narrative, if you think it's a contest between choice and coercion, let's for once, with cringing and cynical groggy neutrality of the mind consider this:

Let's take the route of the popular belief of coercion that a bunch of white men, let's even give it to you, the irreducible coercion aisle, that the entire white race, with the exertion of the force of arms, invaded our continent enslaving and colonizing us, killing and leaving tyranny in their wake. Let's agree for one moment that this heinous crime was done by coercion.

Won't it be natural and appropriate and best that the descendants of the victims of such appalling acts of crime, coalesce and avenge and revenge slavery and colonialism and tyrannies by all means necessary on the white man and her continent that brought those heinous crimes upon Africa and its people?

Avenge those inflicted untold deaths? Revenge those harrowing suffering and pains? Avenge those untold misery? Take revenge on those infamous, inglorious misgivings that made the western continent of white Europe and America rich and left African continent hallucinating, confused, traumatized and in misery, mayhem in its wake?

Or at worse an atonement? Reparation?

Or at worst an excruciating forgiveness for them in the name of their same God they brought to us to enslave and colonize and incapacitate and loot and destroy?

No? No, the answer is no!

What do African descendants do, what do we do instead?

African descendants honor the slavery memory of their humiliated fathers, of their African-American descendants to this day in perpetual dehumanization at the hands of the White race, by identifying and appropriating the slave and colonial tyrannies and surgically refining them and viciously and inappropriately multiplying those tyrannies inflicted on their fathers by the white man on their own people.

Africa self-inflict, in quick successions, in crescendos, far more harrowing tyrannies from within, replacing one form of slavery tyranny and one form of colonial tyranny from without.

By stealing the entire wealth of their continent into the western banks, they actively enslave and colonize and incapacitate their own people and the entire continent a second time! For the ultimate slavery experience.

Africa enslaved by Africans! Without coercion! Of its own volition! A second time for the ultimate slavery experience!

The President pauses, piercing through the screen to the imaginable contorted faces of Gen WHY, on the other side, on the landscape, in amazement of shock, of grieving shame, sullen, appalled to find understanding.

> *If slavery is not by our choice but by coercion, Won't it be natural and appropriate and soothing that the descendants of the victims of such appalling acts of crime, coalesce and avenge and revenge slavery and colonialism and tyrannies by all means necessary on the white man and her continent that brought those heinous crimes upon Africa and its people?*
> *What do African descendants do instead?*
> *African descendants honor the slavery memorial of their humiliated fathers, of their African-American descendants to this day in perpetual dehumanization at the hands of the white, by identifying and appropriating the slavery and colonial tyrannies and surgically refining them and viciously and inappropriately multiplying those tyrannies inflicted on their fathers by the white man on their own people.*
> *Africa self-inflict, in quick successions, in crescendos, far more harrowing tyrannies from within replacing one form of slavery tyranny and one form of colonial tyranny from without.*
> *By stealing the entire wealth of their continent into the western banks, they actively enslave and colonize and incapacitate their own people and the entire continent a second time. For the ultimate slavery experience.*
> *Africa enslaved by Africans. Without coercion. Of its own volition. Of its own choosing. A second time for the ultimate slavery experience.*

The President (continues).

s

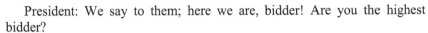
President: We say to them; here we are, bidder! Are you the highest bidder?

We give you our lands, our mineral resources, our arable endowments.

In fact, we give you our descendants. Generation after generation. Forever.

We abhor any value system to create jobs.

We abhor manufacturing.

We love refined and finished and packaged products.

We adore sloth.

We loathe health care system.

We execrate knowledge.

We consort with your luxuries.

We are naturally slaves-disposed. For, we are naturally slaves-disposed.

We are, naturally slaves-inclined. Possessed.

To add to this height of our stupidity is the fact that these monies are hidden in coded bank account numbers. No names. With our demise, I mean, with African leaders' demise, these monies are permanently lost. Not retrievable. Not retraceable to Africa. Lost forever, to the western world.

Is it not time for a whole continent, a whole race to consort with courage in acknowledging and declaring mea culpa, in the sin of our involvement, in actively enslaving our continent, our people, then, yesterday and today?

And then done with this brazen inalienable truth of our self-enslavement by choice, is it not time for a whole continent to pause and ask of its own volition, without coercion, the hard, indisputable question: "are we humans or sub-humans, homo sapiens or homo erectus?"

Are we humans or sub-humans, homo sapiens or homo erectus?

And if we are able to discern and encourage the answer "yes", we are humans, we are homo sapiens, by our volition, without coercion, should we not be ashamed of our homo erectus conduct?

To feel the emotion of shame is essential to the healing of our masochist, selfinduced, cringing, craven stupidity. Come to terms with it and stand up, stand out of it.

Won't it be a thing of pride for a continent to imbibe and refuge in regrets and remorse instead of in willful, blind and bland denial of our facts, in willful removal and negation of our reality, in willful pathological, devious blame on vacuity, and in perpetual seemingly incurable loathsomeness of our stupidity in order to leapfrog her psychological growth and heal and develop and progress our descendants?

> *Should we not be ashamed of our sub-human nature, homos erectus conduct? To feel the emotion of shame is essential to the healing of our masochist, selfinduced-cringing-craven stupidity. Come to terms with it and stand up, stand out of it.*

Won't it be dignifying for our race, and a thing of sublime pride to choose a selfconsciousness of intelligence over this grotesque, inexplicable, ponderous, spiteful, shameful, audacious-millenary stupidity?

Then the President pauses.

Gen WHY's attention is ponderously rapt: there is no next best line of sublime, pristine truth.

Their faces are in a frowning grimace of emotions of fierce hope, of inspiration, fieriness and pride in the voice and words of the President.

Regret and remorse are essential and existential to humility and intelligence.

Remorse gives regret exultation, and both give humility its purpose and intelligence gives humility its reward: the reward is progress and peace and conscience exultation.

> *Regret and remorse are essential and existential to humility and intelligence. Remorse gives regret exultation, and both give humility its purpose, and intelligence gives humility its reward: the reward is progress and peace and conscience exultation.*

Now the President continues.

President: We have lions and gazelles on our land and yet our craven stupidity blinds us from understanding the laws of their nature.

Won't intelligent self-consciousness make us understand that the laws of African nature governing our lions and gazelles are not emotional?

Won't intelligent self-consciousness make us stop being emotional and understand that neither a lion nor a gazelle survives by being emotional?

> *Neither a lion nor a gazelle survives by being emotional. Neither a lion nor a gazelle survives by being emotional. Neither a lion nor a gazelle survives by being emotional. Die and kill to protect and develop and progress and empower your descendants. Die and kill if necessary, to protect and develop and progress and empower your descendants. Die and kill if necessary, to protect and develop and progress and empower your descendants. Just like the white kind. Just like the yellow kind.*

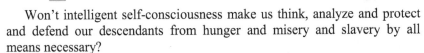

Won't intelligent self-consciousness make us think, analyze and protect and defend our descendants from hunger and misery and slavery by all means necessary?

Just look at the White race, they defy death to develop their descendants.

They die for every technological invention and its advancement. With equal vigor they dehumanize and even kill to protect their families and descendants. No emotions.

The Asians have understood and are doing the same. China's proximity to Africa is a great example.

The Chinese alongside the Indians and the Lebanese are in Africa to die for the kill.

Die and kill to protect and develop and empower and progress your descendants. Die and kill if necessary, to protect and develop and progress and empower your descendants.

Die and kill if necessary, to protect and develop and progress and empower your descendants.

Just like the white kind. Just like the yellow kind.

Won't intelligent self-consciousness make us deploy the God-given human indistinct intellect, to think, to analyze and reflect and rationalize? In sum even in the words of our Gen WHY descendants: "grow our self-consciousness?"

Won't intelligent self-consciousness make us understand, as much as it is humanly capable and possible God, and his ways, and not to confide and consort in the hypocrisy of superstition and mythologies and religion?

For Christians and Muslims of Africa alike, don't we have covenants with Jesus and Prophet Muhammad? Or is it with the idols, the fetishes, and superstition?

Didn't the Holy Bible and the Koran enslave and colonize and annihilate the idols, the fetishes, take us out of darkness, take us into light and give us the possibility of eternal life in Jesus and in Muhammed?

Why so much infidelity? Why so much apostasy? Why so much idolatry and idolization of the devil? Why so much consorting with superstition and coiners of evil? Why avowed heathens, with the Bible and the Korans in our hands?

Won't it be more appropriate to have the books of the devil in our hands, instead?

It's been said and acknowledged that, for any two to work together there must be an agreement.

Didn't we agree to the values and tenets of the Bible and the Koran to be born again and be saved?

In fact, Jesus said "you are forgiven and sanctified. My grace has saved you. Go and sin no more."

He did not say "go and sin more, my grace will save you a second time and another time and all the times you sin purposefully."

How can we take the task in breaking the covenants time and again, the conditio sine qua non, rock of born again and debauch, defraud, mortgage the future of the land and descendants, impoverish them, create mass misery, self-enslave ourselves and hope in perpetual forgiveness of our ways and Heaven?

> *For Christians and Muslims of Africa alike, don't we have covenants with Jesus and prophet Muhammad? Or is it with the Idols, the Fetishes, and Superstition? Didn't the Holy Bible and the Koran enslave and colonize and annihilate the Idols, the Fetishes, take us out of darkness, take us into light and gave us the possibility of eternal life in Jesus and in Muhammed?*
> *Why so much infidelity? Why so much apostasy? Why so much idolatry and idolization of the Devil? Why so much consorting with superstition and coiners of Evil? Why avowed Heathens, with the Bible and the Korans in our hands?*
> *Won't it be appropriate to have the books of the Devil in our hands, instead?*

There is so much stealing, so much debauchery, so much tyranny, so much compulsive meanness, beastliness, so much sodden and dry and brittle complacency, so much deceit and wickedness in God's name, so much dehumanization and demeaning and humiliation of our neighbors, so much hate in contradiction with our covenants with Jesus and Prophet Muhammad in Africa.

There is so much hatred for the covenant of born again and *conditio sine qua non* "love thy neighbor like…".

There is so much hypocrisy of the African Pastors, Imams, men of God.

There is so much validation and recognition and blessings of the stealing, appraisal of the thieves, encouragement of misery and debasing and discouragement of the faithful, of the morally rectitude by these "men of God."

We shout Amen to debauchery. We shout Amen to stealing. We shout Amen to our wants by all means necessary. We shout Amen to our hypocrisy with God. We shout Amen to our wickedness. We shout Amen to misery and to mass misery.

Our Amen to keep our continent in perpetual slavery. Our Amen keeps our Africa in perpetual darkness. Our Amen keeps God away.

Africa despises God. Africa sent God parking. Africa's evil ways make Africa the Canaan for the world.

Our misery speaks for itself. No excuse stands. Words are of no help.

Or maybe these words are indeed, of help:

Indeed, the Bible and the Koran were unjustifiably forced on Africa?

Indeed, idols and fetishes adoration and darkness are the luxuries of Africa?

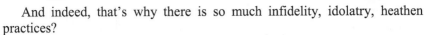

And indeed, that's why there is so much infidelity, idolatry, heathen practices?

And indeed, that's why Africa hates the conquest of Western Christian civilization?

And indeed, that's why Africa hates the progress of Western Christian civilization?

And indeed, that's why Africa loves the pleasures of their tech. and infrastructure? And indeed, that's why Africa craves for the pleasures of the Western Christian civilization, founded on faith in the Bible and rationality, with deepest sense of infidelity, apostasy, idolatry, heathen practices, to the same Bible and rationality? If so, Africa, will remain in misery perpetuity indeed!

Won't intelligent self-consciousness make us understand that our only sure salvation to heaven, if there is heaven, is only by our God's deeds and works with Lord Jesus blessings and help here on earth?

Paraphrasing President J.F. Kennedy: *"the blessings of God, the power of being his image, the rights of being demi-gods. The right and power that God's work, God's will, God's love on earth must truly be ours."*

Won't intelligent self-consciousness make us stop stealing our wealth and moving them into foreign lands, selling our resources and our lands to the highest bidder?

Isn't it slavery, inflicted gratuitously, viciously on ourselves, like masochists in self ridicule?

Won't intelligent self-consciousness over stupidity make us necessarily kill to protect our interest, and above all secure and protect and have the backs of our descendants?

Won't intelligent self-consciousness stop our descendants from a future of condemnation to slavery? From the desperation of forced migration, from the drowning in the seas, from the perils of the deserts, from the contemptuous compassion and from the harrowing humiliation and from self-dejection and from total and scouring hope-illusion on the western streets and here at home?

Won't intelligent self-consciousness give our descendants the keys of freedom and liberty to be at par with their peers always? Instead of condemning them to a future of humiliation and future enslavement at the hand of their peers?

And, absolutely above all an intelligent self-consciousness is the inalienable and ineluctable fact that parents should not be better than their children.

Children must be better than their parents. And children's children better than children-turned parents. And so on ad infinitum.

African Gen WHY let me recognize and validate your sublime self-consciousness by repeating your axiom that humans have birthdays and death days. And that both days are essential to the Lord. They solely belong to him.

The conscientiousness of both days is not revealed to the mind of any being.

No man knows the hour he is born nor the hour he dies.

As he is injected into the world without his knowledge, nor his making and with nothing, so he is ejected without his knowledge, nor his making and with nothing.

Isn't this of a sublime beauty entity?

Now think of the interval between both days? That belongs to man.

It belongs to human endeavor. To his hard work. Not to sloth. To acquire knowledge and wisdom and not ignorance and superstition.

The interval between our birthdays and our death days is to make this place, this world, better than we find it.

Implicitly make our children better than ourselves. Otherwise we have failed.

> *Or maybe these words are indeed, of help:*
> *Indeed, the Bible and the Koran were unjustifiably forced on Africa?*
> *Indeed, idols and fetishes adoration and darkness are the luxuries of Africa?*
> *And indeed, that's why there is so much infidelity, apostasy, heathen?*
> *And indeed, that's why Africa hates the conquest of Western Christian civilization?*
> *And indeed, that's why Africa hates the progress of Western Christian civilization?*
> *And indeed, that's why Africa loves the pleasures of Western Christian technological prowess and infrastructure?*
> *And indeed, that's why Africa craves for the pleasures of the Western Christian civilization, founded on faith in the Bible and rationality, with deepest sense of infidelity, apostasy, to the same Bible and rationality?*
> *If idolization of Africa's idols, and heathen and hypocrisy and irrationality are Africa's chosen luxury, Africa, will remain forever in Misery, indeed!*

The President pauses.

Gen WHY are elated, their faces in unutterable silence of such delicious delight, of such delightful truth and in such fulfilling accord with the President's analysis of facts.

Now the President continues.

President: Gen WHY, thank you all sincerely, deeply. Your forcefulness in value of courage, judgement, candor, integrity, passion, hard work, dedication, dissent, daring, have spurred the land with your supreme standing up credo.

To the extent that your healthy crusade for change challenged the evil in the morass of contending factions of Africa's society.

To the extent that you avoided the trap of partial and discriminatory judgement. To the extent that you sought and enthroned a responsibility of intellectual objectivity and disinterested objective viewpoints.

To these extents you represent the court of last resort. You speak with honesty and truth. And as a court of last resort, you sentenced: *"quit asking what generations before you owe you, but what you owe your generation and the generation your descendants...quit asking what generations before you owe you, but what you owe your generation and the generation your descendants."*

What a lesson in selflessness.

The President pauses once again. Gen WHY feel flattered. They ponderously and unanimously rose to unutterable spasm of proprietary pride and of self-esteem, voluptuously applauding the President and themselves. The President continues.

President: Gen WHY, our ways are old and archaic. Surpassed.

Our situation today is worse than the slave days and colonial days from without. We are a compound of abhorrent stupidity-hypocrisy, scrooge, reprobation, apostate, craven complacency, cowardice.

Our conventional debauchery of politics, our conventional debauchery of religious worships, our conventional debauchery in despotic traditions, use and costumes, our conventional debauchery in services has never met and will never meet the challenges of our people. Generation after generation.

Even though it is a commonly held ground that history repeats itself and human nature never changes; even though this cringing African stupidity never changed even as technology advances; even though the Asians have understood and joined 'the protect thine descendants progressive' field by changing, understanding the game of protecting and advancing their descendants even at the cost of necessarily killing and deceit; even though your 'standing up' has decimated the angels of Africa's stupidity and has dealt a blow to superstition and superstitious beliefs and has exquisitely obliterated the witchdoctors and witchcrafts in a scouring manner, bent the wills of the cultists and the yahoo boys, all in the exploding night; even though primitive stupidity psychologies caved to the wills of accountability; even so, remember that the best antidote you can have to heal Africa is the thinking conscience of the youths.

Gen WHY thinking conscience to keep 'standing up' philosophy-credo shinning from atop the hill of your strength of mind and character, for there would always be thieves, energy suckers, power maniacs, like the stupid Africans, Lebanese, the Indian, the Chinese in your midst, from within and from without, consorts of African stupidity, relentless to tear you down and apart and to keep misery perpetuation. At all cost.

Gen WHY (howling): Out the Lebanese! Out the Indians! Out the Chinese!

President: Gen WHY, at all cost you must remember that for Africa to succeed, success needs the best of women and men.

To that extent bear in mind that it has been said that *"No society can ever be better than the men and the women who compose of it."*

And furthermore, it's been said that "Any Society is a Contract amongst people who make up that Society with their different duties, different chores, and universal rights and the Contract is as good as the signatories and if any of the signatories fails, that's is a rip off to that society."

So, if for example the Army, whose chore of the contract is to provide security; the police, provide protection; President, provide leadership; the cleaner, provide hygiene; the parents provide parenting; the student, study and provide excellence; the politician, provide development; the farmer, provide food security; the Doctor, provide cure; the clergyman instill morality, fails, that failure has ripped its own part of the contract. That failure is the signatory. That signatory is a looter, a plunderer, a pillager. Reprehensible to society.

It's been said that "No society can ever be better than the men and women who compose of it."
And furthermore, any society is a contract amongst people who make up that society with their different duties, different chores, and universal rights and the contract is as good as the signatories and if any of the signatories fails, that's a rip off to that society.

Men and women who can think honestly, think diligently, think passionately, think dedicatedly, think deeply-truthfully, think innocently-impartially, think objectively, think persuasively, think objectively-committedly, exude moral high standards, exude high standard of strength, task-focused and sacrifice.

Your thinking must manifest convincing lines, character, hope, inspiration, justice, ideas to progress forcefully, solely, public common of interest.

So, to our Gen WHY citizens from within and from without our continent and race, as we launch your youth empowerment platform days ahead, if freedom and liberty are the heart of standing up journey, let's task ourselves together with high standards of strength and sacrifice, with good conscience, thinking thoughts and hard work, with God's blessings and power of being his image to make here on earth God's work truly ours. Our

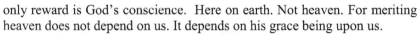

only reward is God's conscience. Here on earth. Not heaven. For meriting heaven does not depend on us. It depends on his grace being upon us.

Our only reward is God's Conscience. In us.

You may further want to take inspiration and strength from the words of Victor Hugo:

"No army can withstand the force of an idea whose time has come."

No army can stand the tide Gen WHY solemn and sublime idea of "standing up."

Trust me, your idea is new. Powerfully new. But key. And yet paraphrasing President J.F. Kennedy:

"Misery is not new to Africa. But what is new is your determined and resolute fierce urgency of now to emerge from misery. What is new is your fierce urgency of now to wipe out hunger, tribulation and humiliation in Africa.

What is new is your fierce urgency of now to create a modern growing economy not in the small fraction of the time it took to build a modern Europe or the United States, not in the smaller time it took to build Japan and Korea and Taiwan and Hong Kong and Singapore, but in the smallest, it is taking to build Dubai, Qatar, China."

Again, Gen WHY paraphrasing Margaret Mead:

"We did not teach you how to think. You thought yourself not just the arduous job of how to think but what to think."

You think "standing up." It is sublime.

And paraphrasing Thomas Jefferson:

"You never put off for tomorrow what you can do today."

You stood up. Even death did not succeed in defying you. You stood up.

'Standing up' is ethereal and has proven formidable and battlefield efficacious to turn the tide of Africa's stupidity.

Standing up is our "new deal." It's the new deal of the land henceforth.

Even though the wake of exploding nights did make excellent victims, seizing the most part of our trillions stashed away in western banks, making them near impossible to willingly and legitimately see the shores of Africa; because those illegitimate accounts are illegitimately coded in numerals. Not in names;

Even though Africa is going to push for a global bank reform to make it a crime for banks to accept and warehouse and launder brazen ill-gotten monies of Africa's nonentities and public servant billionaires, thus taking on the compassionate hypocrisy of the world on one hand and the contemptuous compassion of encouraging, accepting, warehousing, laundering our monies on the other hand;

Nevertheless, the wake of day of accountability has the critical mass for our new deal to hit the ground running.

Gen WHY, together we can't fail to make the most of this 'new deal' moment. If the immediate past mustn't be prologue, we should make the most of this momentum turning 'standing up' opportunity into obligations.

Obligations of the critical mass to create freedoms and rights and duties to liberate our continent from our cringing stupidity, that is beneath stupidity. Obligation against our harrowing slavery and misery. Obligation against Africa's chosen stupidity of self-tyranny, self-imposed poverty and self-imposed disease, humiliation, tribulation, stupidity. In sum a self-imposed institutional self-looting into some others economy and disempowering successions of Africa's descendants. Since words can never break the jinx of our generational misery but deeds can, We need to give answers to:

How do we start?

Where do we start?

What do we start with?

Which do we start with?

When do we start?

So forthwith, from tomorrow here are the "new deal" obligations:

A scouring infrastructure freedom;

A territorial electric energy freedom;

A scouring clean water freedom;

Centerpiece to build schools, build schools, build schools;

Today we make education a fundamental human right;

Centerpiece to build health centers, health centers, health centers;

Today we make health care a fundamental human right;

Centerpiece to build skill centers, build skill centers, build skill centers;

Today we make skill acquisition of our youths a fundamental human right;

A scouring reform of our corrupt institutions of government;

It's a capital offence for men and women of the government, of the National Assembly, of the civil service to own bank accounts or properties overseas; It's a capital crime for "men and women of God" to own properties or bank accounts, but the churches and or the mosques;

A scouring land reforms for agriculture and job creating agro-alimentary value chain system;

Expanding, there would be a ban on our mineral resources from exportation: we can only export at best our semi-finished products. Our partnership will dwell on a value chain system job creating refineries of our mineral resources before exports. It's a fundamental crime for any parents to make kids they cannot take care of;

It is a fundamental crime to live above your means;

Discipline and rule of law are a fundamental requirement of our being;

Make freedom fundamental human rights of citizens and with equal vigor make duties fundamental solemn observations.

Ports infrastructures, federal roads, telecommunications, railways, are to be privatized;

Finally, it's been said that any economy you find the Lebanese and the Indians cannot thrive. Africa should no longer bear the brunt of the collusion and complicities of the Lebanese and the Indians in abating Africa's stealing and misery. The Lebanese and the Indians must end their malevolent complicity or leave Africa!

And hopefully the Chinese will do everything to reverse course from their malevolent complicity, now at its fledgling stage.

Gen WHY are ponderously and voluptuously moved. They stand, most of them in tears to applaud hilariously, the fascinating and hope-inspiring image of the President on the television, who they wish his words could bear the force of a finality that warned and prohibited stupidity and promulgated and enshrined renaissance man credo to endure, obliterating Africa's cringing stupidity, turning it over to the books of development and progress till the end of time. Whenever that is. Hopeful it's imminent. Now.

Gen WHY (shouting as they punch the air): Standing up! Standing up!! Standing up!!!

President (in closing remarks): Let me close by paraphrasing J.F. Kennedy:

"Forthwith let every African generation know, whether old, middle or young, whether a Christian, a Muslim or other faiths, whether one tribe or the other, whether it wishes us well or ill, that African Gen Z have precedents of a just defiance and are ready to pay any price, to bear any burden, to support any hardship, to oppose any foe, to assure the survival and the success of our liberty of choice of standing up to end Africa's stupidity, to end misery, to advance Africa and give dignity to our race. Where ever they may find themselves and in whatever human endeavor, they are engaged in.

God bless you all.

Chapter 2

The entire Gen WHY inner-working committee rose to their feet to an enduring ponderous, thunderous applause.

An applause that lulled even with the exit of the President from the television screen: they readily and promptly brought their attention and applause bearing down on David and Mark.

David and Mark flattered and humbled, are overwhelmed in a wilderness of weeping joyfulness and in assault of tears streaming down their faces.

Then in a surprise move and to everybody's delight amidst fresh applause, Mezzi suddenly sweeps Mark off his feet, hoisting him in the air.

Mezzi: To the youngest gladiator amongst us.

Buzzo: What a beautiful day indeed.

Brett: Phew! Folks what a defining moment that was.

Glenda: I don't know about you. It's like dreaming with your eyes wide open.

Mezzi: "Dream things that never were and say why not."

Glenda: Exactly! Who was that again?

Lynda: Martin Luther King.

Glenda: Look at you. It was said by an Irish man.

Lynda: Who?

Mark: Find out the name. Read! Read!! Read!!! That's why we are here.

Buzzo: Cool. Folks take your sits please. We need to celebrate, except if we are in a ponderous malady of reverie. Lynda, Frank the foods and drinks please. It's a beautiful day indeed. We have a champion indeed in the person of the President.

Meanwhile, everybody slowly takes back their sitting positions, except Lynda and Frank who have hustled off for drinks and snacks.

Meanwhile, the noise of work in progress of the caterpillars, the bulldozers, the humming of the hammers continued and can be heard in the far distance as the youth empowerment platform and the infrastructure around it is being raced to completion.

David: Folks, we have started a revolution that may survive and change the paradigm.

Brett: That may? Please, it's a revolution that must survive. More optimism folks!

Glenda: Bravo! Absolutely I agree! No going back. We have already started giving our lives for our lives.

Brett: We can't be in the business of dreaming the stupidly cowardly dreams of our fathers and father's fathers and their fathers. No, not any more.

Buzzo (stands up applauding): Please ponderous applause to Brett and Glenda for those beautiful lines of conviction, determination and fieriness.

Everybody obliges delightfully.

Buzzo: The President's rhetoric are not just exalting but forceful and credible. His immediate past credentials, immediate temporary precedents, give the generosity of his rhetoric credibility of purpose and exaltation.

David: Thank you Buzzo. That's the situation. My father would rather die for his convictions.

Buzzo: But in so doing, he has involuntarily, dramatically raised our stakes.

Everybody seems to suddenly stutter at those words. Their faces readily twist into a contorted frown of honest and unfeigned amazements. Amazements of wonderment and curiosity.

Brett: I am confused!

Buzzo. How so?

Brett: A whole lot to digest.

Buzzo: Yeah, I will shade some light. But first let me ask you all your takes on the President's speech? Brett?

Brett: Cool. Every of his lines was instructively inspirational and above all rational. But my most important take is "You can only be a slave, only by choice. Not by coercion." Africans are slaves by choice otherwise they would be avenging the evil of slavery. Instead they multiply the evils of slavery and colonialism on self. Amplify their self-slavery, self-effacement...

Glenda (forcefully interjecting): And his argument is overtly convincinglycompelling. If we were and are not slave-disposed, because of our craven stupidity at cringing laziness, how can we be enslaving ourselves today, stealing our monies into their banks, instead of avenging and punishing who, centuries ago enslaved and colonized our grandparents and disfranchised generations of African descendants?

Buzzo: To this day! Cool. Glenda now it's your turn; What's your ultimate take?

Glenda: There is a whole lot. Let me try a summary. When he said "No society can be better than the men and women who compose of it." That means get rid of our stupidity, get rid of the Lebanese, get rid of the Indians, get rid of the Chinese, use our reinvigorated informed self-consciousness to engage the devil we know and make sure our resources are valued before any exports, thus, creating jobs and jobs and jobs and our economic and wealth base.

In the meantime, Laura and Frank are back followed by a caravan of waiters and waitresses carrying trays of food and cartons of drinks and beverages. Foods and beverages are served, and foods are being greedily consumed as the discussion progresses.

Buzzo: Sharp business woman. I like your take. Get rid of our stupidity. Develop the economy with value chains. Create our economic and wealth base. The lack of these is at the heart of the very cause of our misery. Lynda, please your take.

Lynda: For me, the most important take is the acknowledgement and the eulogy for our standing up stance. The eulogy on the value system of our life interval on earth. We are here to make everything better than we find it. We are here to make our children better than ourselves. We are here to make God's deed, ours on earth. Otherwise we have failed as human beings. To that extent Africa has been failing. His eulogy praises and encourages us but, more importantly, at the same time exalts the lost lives of our companions at the Plaza Hill, that life equates to death. Death means life. They are the same...

Lynda got emotional, seized by a sorrowing grief that insinuated in her vocal cod. Gen WHY peers understand and their faces contort in expressions of ineffable ponderous gloominess. A gloominess withered and emptied of words.

Buzzo finds the words and courage to defuse the gloominess. He rises and starts applauding Lynda.

The rest of Gen WHY rises joining him.

Buzzo: Life-death, death-life dichotomy. Beautiful. Can't you all see how much life and how much hope we are breathing into Africa? Could any of us have imagined where we have gotten to already? Please be proud of yourselves and another round of applause to our dead but living heroes at the Plaza Hill.

Instantly eyes turn read overwhelmed. Even so they rise to a thunderous applause.

Buzzo (within the simmering applause): David your take.

Mark and Mezzi (in unison, protesting): No, our takes.

Buzzo: I thought you guys are busy monitoring the takes of our out there on the social media. Your work is a very important indicator of our millions of field Gen WHY opinions and takes out there and we can't rush it. You are going to have the honors of a lot of time of our closing argument. Ok?

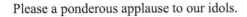

Please a ponderous applause to our idols.

They are ponderously applauded.
Fired up, they reluctantly but fierily get back to their social media chores.

Buzzo: David your take please.
David: The best gift my father gave me is the courage of self-denunciation and renunciation: "We are thieves". Africa's leadership–the monarchy, the politician, the priest, the security services, the bureaucrats, the cabals–past and present are thieves. This courage finally nailed and exalted the veiled poison, the ultimate cause of our stupidity. And it may well define his legacy.
Buzzo: Well said. But I think that may well pale with what he has conferred on today's history. We can say that today is synonymous with the title "The President." Today means Africa's rebirth. The President means rebirth. However it goes forthwith. *The first man who dared "we are the problem for our misery." The first Africa's President who did not blame the Others or Colonialism or Slavery. The First Africa's President who did not deny we have a problem. He dared the identikit and dared the name. He did not swallow the name: "We are, we are, we are our problem of our misery."*
Africa has been a perennial, willful denial, willful blame-shifting phenomenon. And it has incapacitated and hindered our development. Till today. That changes dramatically today thence.

Buzzo pauses and pans the faces. Every face between foods and drinks is in contorted frowns of attentiveness and thoughtfulness.

Buzzo: You, Frank of the unruly herds. What's your take?
Frank: A lot. Just imagine "it's a crime to live above your means" finally?
Just imagine the Lebanese out, finally? The Indians out, finally? The Chinese finally out?
Just imagine equipping and empowering us with skills? Just imagine creating jobs. Just imagine the value chain of our vast resources, producing here at home and exporting? Just imagine free health-care system. Just imagine all these things to turn unruly herds into truly nerds? Just imagine...just imagine...

Everybody rose unsolicitously at the mention of 'unruly herds to truly nerds' to a voluptuous thunderous standing applause of ovation to Frank.
Words cannot describe the value these incorrigible fractious elements brought to this dynamism of the evolving 'standing up' credo revolution.

Reiterating, they crushed the spite of superstition, obliterated superstitious belief, psyched-out the psychosis of pseudo-omnipotence and subdued unaccountability in the exploding night.

The applause is essential. It exalts the memory of Gen WHY's death for life on the Plaza Hill.

As the applause is simmering down, a lone raucous voice from the unruly herds pierces:

Lone raucous voice: We are very hungry. We are very hungry. Just imagine quenching our hunger. The President did not address our hunger. Hunger is predatory and voluptuously effrontery.

A clamor of shouting and shrieks and condemnation started up among the unruly herds.

The rest of the Gen WHY youth crease into an uneasy dense and ponderous silence. Their faces pinched in a solicitous frown. The air suddenly turns uneasy. Taut.

Buzzo (applauding): Beautiful, beautiful take. This is a beautiful take.

David breaks rank, joining Buzzo and started applauding. To everybody's surprise.

David: Please round of applause to this beautiful observation.

The rest reluctantly rose to the urge with hint of conspicuous skepticism.

The moment is arid with insinuation of predatory divisiveness that seems to put to test the charismatic, successful leadership of Buzzo to date.

Buzzo (taking everyone off guard): That beautiful take is predatory. Hunger is predatory and must be dealt a crushing blow. It's a *conditio sine qua non* if we are to succeed. We are in a revolution where we must do our part. The President has offered an olive branch and we must take advantage of it and do our part. We have the solution to hunger. I can see it. Its palpable.

But before let's hear out our golden boys. Mezzi, Mark what are your takes?

The boys are busy, distracted at their computers, immersed in a flurry of tweeting activities amidst discussions and confabulations. Buzzo had to raise the tone of his voice, calling them out.

Buzzo: Ok! Cool ok. Mark your take!

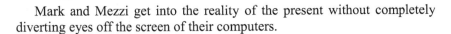

Mark and Mezzi get into the reality of the present without completely diverting eyes off the screen of their computers.

Mark: Yes, my take or their take (pointing at the screen).
Buzzo: Your take first.
Mark: Just imagine education a fundamental human right!

He suddenly jumps out of his seat and seized by a spasm of enthusiastic optimism, started jumping up, doing a virtual geometrical 360degrees circle to his shout and scream of "education."
To everyone's delightful delight, a ponderous applause erupts.

Mark: Education! Education! Education! Education! Education! Education a fundamental human right!

Then he stops, just suddenly as he had started.
The applause hesitantly slows and simmers down. The crowd with their eyes on Mark is expectant.

Mark: That's my take. Now to the take of field Gen WHY... (glimpsing the screen of his computer): "#food a fundamental human right." request has the most of the tweets of field Gen WHY. Education follows, clean water, homes...etc....etc.

The crowd erupts anew in a ponderous shriek and shout of approval, amidst a thunderous applause.

Buzzo appraises and gallantly continues applauding, letting the voluptuous thunderous applause for Mark's 'food, a fundamental right' communique.
Then he slows to a stop. Others reluctantly slow...simmer completely down to the sound of his voice:

Buzzo: Mezzi, your take!
sMezzi (looking melancholic): Everything. Everything the President envisaged. Everything from our idea being the indispensable army no force can withstand to the rights and duties, rights and duties we owe our generation and to our generation's children, to education...to education...to education...to education...to education...to education...to education. The President envisaged a hope system that is voluptuously and ponderously overwhelming. We need to take it to the next level of execution. A deafening level of execution. We must address the emergency of now: the emergency of hunger and thirst. The Gen WHY family is clear on this (pointing at the computer).
Buzzo: Cool...rights and duties...our duties to achieving what we owe our generation and generations our children...education, education,

education, figure out hunger, defeat hunger. Now. Defeat hunger now…and…

The crowd goes into an unsolicited thunderous applause, submerging in its entirety the voice of Buzzo, who could not help but readily join in the exercise of applause.

Buzzo: As I was saying, the stakes have been raised. Our stakes have been raised dramatically.

Glenda: Yeah, our stakes have been raised but we have the stakes within our means.

Buzzo: That's a great poetry. Gen WHY family, you all think we have the stakes within our capability?

Brett: Yeah, I agree. Our family of youths has had willful rejection of fear and favor. A willful self-denial, a selflessness-affliction fit. Our death for life so far, for a catharsis of justice to defeat our degradation and to assert progress.

David: Cool! Buzzo we are curious of your take.

Brett: Right. What's your take, Buzzo?

Buzzo: My take is on rights and duties.

Glenda: Please throw your inspiring light?

Buzzo: Rights and duties are the only weapons to defeat anything. Hunger inclusive.

Gen WHY's faces get into contorted grimaces.

Lynda: With rights and duties we overcome our hunger and thirst?

Glenda: He is always a mystery. How can hunger be overcome by rights and duties?

Now as Buzzo, their idol is about to broach and produce the answers, Gen WHY's attention gets rapt, their faces filled with heightened expectations.

Buzzo: Rights and Duties. Rights and duties are both bankrupt in Africa. We all know it. Right? As kids, pleasures of rights come first. As adults, pleasures of duties come first. In Africa, there are no pleasures of rights for the kids. In Africa, adults do not make any effort at duties, so no right is produced. Rights are denied the children. Rights are called freedoms. Rights to electric energy, rights to education, rights to clean water, rights to health-care, rights to sewerage, rights to food security, rights to dream. Rights to hope, etc.

Any rights depend on duties. And duties produce rights. Right?

> *...Rights and Duties. Rights and duties are both bankrupt in Africa. We all know it. Right?*
> *As kids, pleasures of rights come first. As adults, pleasures of duties come first.*
> *In Africa there are no pleasures of rights for the kids. In Africa adults do not make any effort at duties, so no right is produced. Rights are denied the children.*
> *Rights are called freedoms. Rights to electric energy, rights to education, rights to clean water, rights to health-care, rights to sewerage, rights to food security, rights to dream. Rights to hope etc. Any rights depend on duties. And duties produce rights. Right?*

Buzzo pauses, and scans their rapt grimaced faces and finds their approval Then he continues.

Buzzo: Duties and rights! Gen WHY, we asked for separation on the Plaza Hill because Africa's duties produce no rights for its children. Africa's duties produce misery, hope-hopelessness. And ultimately death.

We asked for separation to debunk the fleeting illusion of our rights.

We separated to concretize "our duties of what we owe ourselves as a generation and the generation our children."

We took our separation. Separation means autonomy.

Autonomy to figure out the grammar of our duties, the logic of our duties, the rhetoric of our duties. The autonomy to produce rights and then duties. Annihilate misery. Dominate our filths and garbage. In sum, dominate our environment.

Buzzo pauses once again peering their faces. Their jaws are dropping. They are listening eagerly hard. They seem intent in not missing any line.

Buzzo: As you all know, we are just at the grammar of our duties. The fundamental idea. The renaissance credo. The renaissance men. The renaissance Gen WHY. The renaissance Gen WHY produced "standing up". The renaissance Gen WHY reached and climbed the Rubicon, sacrificing ultimately for it. And renaissance Gen WHY are not going back from crossing the Rubicon. We are going to cross the Rubicon, Yes?

Brett (applauding): Yes! Yes!

Everybody breaks up in shrieks, shouting and... their fists punching the air.

Buzzo: We are...we are on the second phase of our duties. The logic of our duties. The means. The means. The means to achieve our duties. And unfortunately hunger ponderously insinuates, wedges in. Hunger wants to disrupt and derail the renaissance Gen WHY. Hunger wants to swallow the renaissance Gen WHY with its glorious "standing up."

Hunger is our present and clear lurking danger.

Hunger is predatory. Hunger incapacitates, kills and obliterates.

And hunger raises the stake of our spiritual essence, of who we are, of what we are voluptuously and dramatically.

The question becomes, should predatory hunger stifle, beat and subdue our stake at "standing up" or should predatory hunger exalt it?

Bewildered and confused, silence reigns. A silence of menacing wanting.

It is said that hunger is really predatory. It forges situations. It forces forced aggressiveness, indolent malevolency, feigned deference, complacent evil, among others. It underpins the complex psychology behind pertinacious behavioral aspects of life in Africa: the willful evil isms of survival.

> *Hunger is our present and clear lurking danger.*
> *Hunger wants to disrupt and derail the renaissance Gen WHY.*
> *Hunger is predatory. Hunger is really predatory. It forges situations. It forces forced aggressiveness, indolent malevolency, feigned deference, complacent evil, among others. It underpins the complex psychology behind pertinacious behavioral aspects of life in Africa: the willful evil isms of survival.*
> *Hunger incapacitates, kills and obliterates.*
> *And hunger raises the stake of our spiritual essence, of who we are, of what we are, voluptuously dramatically.*
> *The question becomes, should predatory hunger stifle, beat and subdue our stake at "standing up" or should predatory hunger exalt it?*

Buzzo not deterred, presses on with his persuasive art.

Buzzo: There is more to it folks. To predatory hunger, let's add these extents of mixed realities and imaginations:

To the extent that we are abandoned by fate;

to the extent that we are in the middle of a periled-nowhere: an ocean, a desert; to the extent that we are the lone army the President now counts on; to the extent that we are his life-purpose, his life-legacy;

to the extent that the President can no longer help us: he is, for the absurd, imprisoned by some kismet military coup or worse dead;

to the extent that, for another absurd, the coup plotters hold us in awe; to the extent that they must crush the spite of the President to neutralize us; to the extent that being our hero, we must save him; to the extent that saving him is a 'conditio sine qua non' to obliterate Africa's stupidity

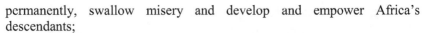
permanently, swallow misery and develop and empower Africa's descendants;

to the extent that our failure spells disaster of ponderous proportion and irremediable repair;

to the extent that ultimately our success would break the jinx of Africa's misery and liberate a whole continent from death of misery;

to these extents the stake cannot be any much higher.

So, Gen WHY family, do we throw in the towel to predatory hunger?

And pass for cringing craven suckers? Pass for losers betraying our duties, producing no rights? Disappointing and burying ourselves and swallowing up the freedoms of our descendants and descendants' descendants, descendants' descendants...forever and ever?

Gen WHY's passions of selflessness ego, of their enthusiasm of heroism, of their life purpose ideals are instantly revamped and animated. They spring to their feet in a clamor of shouting and shrieks and in unison:

Gen WHY: No, no, no, no! Never! Never!!
Buzzo: Then we choose to be good soldiers?
Gen WHY: Yes!
Buzzo: It has been said that: *"What makes a good soldier is his capacity to endure. Not the pain he can inflict." And we will add "to endure the pains and prevail."*
Gen WHY: Endure, prevail! Endure, prevail!!
Buzzo: Please take your sits.

They reluctantly return to their sitting positions.

Buzzo: Do we prefer to be given fish or to fish?
Gen WHY (ponderous and voluptuous in unison): To fish.
Buzzo: Do we prefer how to think or what to think?
Gen WHY: How to think!
Buzzo (radiant with hope): For the one to be given fish and told what to think is enslavement; and for the other to be taught how to fish and how to think is freedom.

Freedom, freedom, freedom, freedom reigns. Long live freedom. Let's toast to hard work, endurance and freedom.

Gen WHY grab their glasses (rise to the toasting): to hard work, to discipline, to consistency, to endurance and to freedom.

Buzzo: It has been said to every problem, there is a solution. Now let's find ours. To the problem of predatory hunger, an unvanquishable solution.

Gen WHY instantly crease into a dense and voluptuous silence. A curious silence full with expectation.

Buzzo: Please raise your hands to answer these questions:

a. If we were to move 100 persons to a distance of 200km from point a to point b, which will be cheaper: the use of two 50-seater buses or 25 four-seater sedans to commute?

Mark trumps everyone at raising of hands.
Buzzo nods him go ahead.

Mark: That's easy. The two buses.
Buzzo: Bravo! (then scanning the Gen WHY crowd): Any dissent?

Gen WHY positive nods, silently validates a consensus.

Frank: The opportunity cost, very evident. The important appraisal of Collectivity.
Buzzo: Bravo! Opportunity cost. The foregoing alternatives. Mr. Prince I did not know you are an economist.

Everybody cracks up, laughing.

Buzzo: Question b.
If we are to give 100 cans of coke to100 persons, which will be cheaper, buying 100 lose cans of coke or buying 8 ¼ dozens of packs of coke?
Laura: Buying 8 ¼ dozens.
Buzzo: Bravo! For same opportunity cost reason. These questions may seem banal, but please note their vigor, their valency, and their important underpin of collectivity over individuality.
The force of collectivity makes about 99% of world's real billionaires and millionaires. *Any person's success at any social problem, the more successful that any person is.* The masses patronize to make their lives bearable. From Bill Gates, Jeff Bezos, Steve Jobs, Warren Buffet, Mr. Ferrari, Mr. Mercedes, Mr. Caterpillar, Mr. Trains, down to Mr. Bicycles, Mr. Tooth picks, Mr. Ketch-up, Mr. mosquito repellent, Mrs. Toning creams etc. They embody, and they substantiate this fact.
The masses, the collective mass of any society make billionaires and millionaires.
Except in Africa…
Glenda: True in Africa the collective mass make men of God billionaires.
Buzzo: Not just men of God, but alongside the politicians and the monarchs. Africa is arid of any success at any social problem. Africa does not have real billionaires. Africa's billionaires and millionaires are miserable. Billionaires and millionaires living amidst their vicious tyrannies and mass-misery contrivances, living in Africa's filths and garbage of environments, devoid of any freedom like power electricity, pipe borne water, education rights, health-care rights, food security rights,

road infrastructure, rail lines, jobs, etc. can't be billionaires and millionaires.

> *Africa is arid of any success at any social problem. Africa does not have real billionaires. Africa's billionaires and millionaires are miserable. Billionaires and millionaires living amidst their vicious tyrannies and mass-misery contrivances, living in Africa's filths and garbage of environments, devoid of any freedom like power electricity, pipe borne water, education rights, healthcare rights, food security rights, road infrastructure, rail lines, jobs, etc. can't be billionaires and millionaires.*

Glenda (interjecting): True! We all, they and us, live in the same misery-ism they create.

Brett: In the same vitrine of darkness, in the same vitrine of infectious undrinkable water, same vitrine of open-air sewer, vitrine of defecation, vitrine of beggars, vitrine of ignorance, vitrine of garbage and filths, the same vitrines of fears and worries and preoccupations and tribulations and hopelessness and anxiety.

Buzzo: Exactly. And the most pathetic, the most deplorable vitrines are Africa's men of God, with their God-forsaken prosperity religion.

They are the most cringing miserable billionaires. Thieves that leverage on our laziness to read, ignorance, on docility, on gullibility to ask WHY and challenge and confront and on weaknesses and the vulnerability of the disadvantaged faithful collectivity. Thieves!

David: It is very tragic. Very unfortunate, indeed. Men with infirmity govern Africa.

Now, Gen WHY break into shouting and shrieking clamor of shame and exquisite hate for Africa's men of infirmity. Especially from among the unruly herds.

Buzzo (with a portentous vigorous voice): The paradox is that our infirmity, the infirmity of the African youths, of us the Gen WHY, pales in comparison to theirs.

In a flash, at those words, a dense and a ponderous silence, full of contemptuous humiliating tantrum expectation, wedges in.

Buzzo scans their faces, pinched in solicitous wrinkling demeanor, gearing up, ready for reproval. Chide homily.

Buzzo: Here we have the Africa's youth badge of shame. Our original sin.

What should puzzle us most: the madness of our infirmity or our ability to endure their inflicted infirmity on us?

> *What should puzzle us most:*
> *The madness of our infirmity or our ability to endure their inflicted infirmity?*
> *The madness of our infirmity or our ability to endure their inflicted infirmity? The madness of our infirmity or our ability to endure their inflicted infirmity?*

The madness of our infirmity crowd-funded the "men of God" in the name of Christ's church. The madness of our infirmity condescends the sum total of Africa's descendants, generation after generation to willfully believe they are collectivelyfunding for heaven, for internal satisfaction, for eternal satisfaction, for heavenly blessings, for heavenly forgiveness? Which?

The madness of our infirmity has the willful blind ability to endure their miserable infirmity. Our infirmity willfully endures their infirmity, that privatized our collective monies by one man–the "man of God". Their infirmity numbs our psyche and our minds.

We make billionaires of "men of God" in Africa through the power of our collective dumb infirmity.

Brett's voice from among the section of the unruly herds pierces the now dreadful eerie silence.

Brett: Truth brother! We are really beneath their infirmity.

Gen WHY (finding their voices, encouraged by the stance of Brett, in unison vigorously repeats after Brett): We are beneath their infirmity indeed.

Buzzo: In Africa it's enough for any fool to appear on the horizon with willful distortion of 'tithe thine' increment old testament tenet for the Jews and 'give out' of abundance, as your heart proposeth of the new testament tenet of the Christians that we fall for it. We fall for it like demented, deranged, unhinged, incapacitated, fools without rationalizing. Without logics. Like craven cringing ignoramus.

> *We the Gen WHY, with our all our degrees, are beneath infirmity indeed. In Africa it's enough for any fool to appear on the horizon with willful distortion of 'tithe thine' increment old testament tenet of the Jews, and 'give out' of abundance, as your heart proposeth of the new testament tenet of the Christians, that we fall for it. We fall for it like demented, deranged, unhinged, ...*

> *...incapacitated, fools without rationalizing. Without logics. Like craven cringing ignoramus.*

Gen WHY (now break in uproar of): Beneath infirmity! Shame on us!

Buzzo: We naively make them billionaires for combined competing reasons of internal satisfaction, for fun of altruism, for atonement of our sins, for God's blessings. For collectivity and collective progress of love they neighbor.

Only to suffer our worst betrayal in the hands of "men of God."

Our monies end up in bank accounts of their choices. They appropriate of our monies in accounts and in luxuries overseas.

Men of God should not have any bank accounts or own properties. Only in Africa such is possible and aspired to.

Had Jesus Christ any bank accounts?

Gen WHY (vigorously): No!

Buzzo: Has the Catholic Pope any bank account?

Gen WHY (vigorously): Hell no!

Buzzo: Has the archbishop of Canterbury any bank account?

Gen WHY: Hell no!

Buzzo: Has the Grand Mufti of mecca any bank account?

Gen WHY: No!

Buzzo: Africa is a land of fear, intimidation and tameness.

The rich fear the poor;

The church and the mosque and the voodoo shrine tame and intimidate the poor;

The poor fear the church and the mosque and the shrine;

The rich fear the potentiality of the coalescing force of the poor;

The poor does not take advantage, out of voluptuous infirmity-gullibility, willful stupidity and ignorance and willful hypocrisy, willful blind fear;

The church and the mosque and the shrine do not rebuke the rich because they are together in debauchery business accord over the poor.

The church and the mosque and the shrine take advantage of the vulnerable and the disadvantaged poor; and we the black kind youths tend to our poverty and misery. Yes?

> *Africa is a land of fear, intimidation and tameness:*
> *The rich fear the poor;*
> *The poor fear the church and the mosque and the shrine;*
> *The rich and the church and the mosque and the shrine fear the potentiality of the coalescing force of the poor;*
> *But the poor, out of voluptuous infirmity of the mind do not take advantage. Their infirmed mind lets the Church and the Mosque and the voodoo Shrine tame and intimidate them...*

> *...The church and the mosque and the shrine do not rebuke the rich because they are together in debauchery business accord over the poor. The church and the mosque and the shrine take advantage of the vulnerable and the disadvantaged poor; and we the Black kind youths tend to our poverty and misery. Yes?*

Gen WHY: Yeah! Beneath infirmity.

Buzzo: Shame on us?

Gen WHY: Beneath infirmity! Shame on us!

Buzzo: Don't we want to be collective billionaires, don't we want our freedom, don't we want to fund our collective needs, our collective bank account, our crowd bank account to defeat misery?

Gen WHY: Yes, that's our choice.

Glenda (interjecting portentously): It's not just a choice! It's our duty!

Brett: Gen WHY, it's not a choice. It's a sacred duty. Our sacred duty.

Gen WHY break out in gruff of threatening determination in their self-importance, shouting: Duty! Duty! Duty!

Buzzo (suddenly diverting, holding their curiosity to a spell): Mezzi, Mark please find out Africa's youth weekly Soda–Coke, Pepsi, etc. spending capacity. Tweet this: "# is there any youth above the age of moron who cannot afford a can of coke on a weekly basis by all means necessary?"

And secondly, let me put the question straight to us gathered here: How many of us cannot afford a can of coke in a week?

Gen WHY: None!

Buzzo: Then are we ready to sacrifice a can of coke in a month for ourselves, for our collective name, for our crowd account, to collectively fund it, that way we have the means to deter and develop. Deter Africa's stupidity and develop our generation and the generation our children and beyond for always?

Gen WHY (ponderously astounding): Yeaaaaaaaaaaaaaah!

Buzzo: Yeah!

Gen WHY (ponderously angrily, punching the air): Yaaaaaaaaaaaaaarrrrrrrrrrrr!

Buzzo: Mark, Mezzi, What's new?

Mark: 92% of the youths above the age of morons can afford at least a coke in a week. Mezzi: And 99% of them want to sacrifice their can of coke every week. Buzzo: Yeah?

Mezzi: *Oui!*

Buzzo: Heeeeh! Heeeeh!! Eeeeee!!! Finally. This is hilarious. Finally, hunger captive.

At those words the already peaking Gen WHY's' air of spell heightens. They are assailed by spasm of unutterable expectations. Their expectation is oppressing.

David: Very interesting.
Buzzo: Now let's do the arithmatics. Are you all here with me?

Gen WHY silently nod their acquiescence.

Buzzo: Who knows the population of the Gen WHY family?
David: Africa 1.6 billion people. The youth constitute about 75%. And 17 % of them are morons.
Mezzi: Precisely 1.2 billion are the family of youths and about 240 million are of morons age bracket.
Buzzo: That leaves us with 960million Gen WHY non-morons.
And how much is a bottle of coke Glenda?
Glenda: About 20 cents of a Dollar.
Buzzo: 20 cents of a Dollar in Africa? Are you sure?
Glenda: Sure, as hell.
Buzzo: That's cheap. Even so, multiplying 20 cents by 960 million will give?
Brett: About 200million US Dollars every week.
David: Multiply that by 4 times in a month.
Gen WHY: Pheeeeeeeeeeewwwwwwwwwwwwww!
Mark: And that's really modest.
Brett: Buzzo, let's hit the ground running.
Lynda: Woooooow! This is numbing. Let's go!
Buzzo (With the air of a proprietary pride): Now you all see our means. The power of Gen WHY family? Do you understand now your power in crowd funding? The power you give to our devious "men of God?"
Gen WHY: Buzzo, Buzzo, Buzzo, Buzzo, Buzzo!
Buzzo: The power you renounced to so naively and so stupidly?

> *...Crowd Funding! Crowd Funding is our means. The power.*
> *Gen WHY, do you all understand now the power you renounced to,*
> *with your infirmity of the mind and give to our devious "men of god"?*

Gen WHY: Buzzo, Buzzo, Buzzo, Buzzo!
Buzzo: You know how much Gen WHY empowerment we can?
How many schools we can? How much skill acquisition we can? How many hospitals we can? How many infrastructures we can? How many factories, value chain transformative factories we can? How much manufacturing, how many jobs, how many houses and homes, how much wealth we can?

Gen WHY: Buzzo, Buzzo, Buzzo…let's go! Let's go. Where is our crowd funding account number…let's hit the ground running?

Buzzo ignores their invocations. He is raising the bar.

Buzzo: Now we can give to ourselves, for the benefit we will derive; For our internal satisfaction; For the amount of jobs, goods and services we will create; For the prestige, for our sense of collective purpose, our self-esteem; For our collective utility; For our collective duties and collective rights to defend, tend and uphold the wealth created;
To alleviate poverty, obliterate misery, create rights and freedom that we owe ourselves and for the generations of our children and beyond in making God's deeds here on earth ours. Until heaven, by favor of mystery of faith belief.
Gen WHY (now in uproar): Account number, account number, account number, account number.

Buzzo, finally got them where he has long wished to have them.

Buzzo: Tomorrow will birth our crowd funding account number.
Gen WHY (in shrieks and shouts): Yeaaaaahhhh!
Buzzo: It just needs statutory government validation.
Gen WHY (yelling): President, President, President!
Buzzo: The President will without doubt give his validation tomorrow.
Brett (perplexed, fixing Buzzo): You really believe in this crowd funding concept?

The air is immediately numbed and wanes into sorrowing doubts and grieving chagrin.
Surprised by this unexpected volte-face of Brett, a ponderous silence swallowed any response. Brett continued.

Brett: Even if it meets the President's validation, what next? You really think these hungry folks would have faith in crowd-funding effort?
Mezzi: On the alternative what else do we have? It's either inalienable faith in ourselves or we remain and rust in misery. Which do you think is easier to choose?
Mark: Have you ever been to our children must play center? Have you ever seen their joy at fries and chips, their happiness inside their commuters and their hopeful pride and dignity in their uniforms? Thanks to the will of funding.
Glenda: Yeah, but funding requires financial stability, a wealth base that you four might have that we don't have for now. Let's face the reality folks.
Brett: Exactly! We don't have financial stability like you do, period!

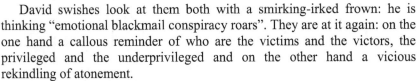

David swishes look at them both with a smirking-irked frown: he is thinking "emotional blackmail conspiracy roars". They are at it again: on the one hand a callous reminder of who are the victims and the victors, the privileged and the underprivileged and on the other hand a vicious rekindling of atonement.

The Status Quo, of which the foursome are by accident heir to should be constantly subjected to consequent emotional blackmail to force reparations. Notwithstanding their efforts and goodwill at "standing up" revolution, atonement not absolution is being asked of them. Not forgiveness.

David (sarcastically retorting to Glenda): Yeah, I see you really traffic in callousness and viciousness. What you are saying is that your financial stability funded the airplanes of the "men of God"?

Glenda: That's not what I am saying…

Mezzi: So, what are you saying? One Dollar a month is somebody's financial stability?

Mark: Shame on us if we waver on this found, sound solution. One Dollar a month?

David (cynical): What's the cost of burial on this land? Is it less than one Dollar? Once again let me put it to you both that you deviate and digress going personal on us. Stop your mischaracterization.

Mezzi: We are talking about the power in the faith of crowd-funding, folks. You don't need financial stability to do that. Just act of faith in ourselves, for an immediate palpable result. Controlled by us. For us. Ours.

Passions and emotions are ponderously animated. Beliefs and words are crossconveyed with gestures of a quasi-finality that warned and foreclosed dialectics. Buzzo notices and steps in muting the situation from escalation.

Buzzo: Okay folks. This animated discussion is a sign of evolving self-consciousness. A quality of thinking, appreciating, climbing. Ingratiating. Let's evolve from here. A great is gone. Toni Morrison died earlier today.

Everybody is caught off guard by this sudden line of diversion of thought.

They fix him with expression of eloquent loss and curiosity.

Buzzo takes in their exquisite numbness and capitalizes on their expectant silence.

Buzzo: She was a writer. A prolific writer. A Nobel laureate. Perhaps the mother of them all. May her soul rest in peace.

And paraphrasing Toni Morrison:

"freeing ourselves would be one thing; but claiming ownership of that freedom would be another."

We asked for separation. We must claim freedom. To claim freedom, we must believe that impossible is nothing for the African Gen WHY's mind.

Africa has failed time and again because of stark aridity of belief-in self value system.

He pauses scanning them with intensity. They meet his eyes.

Buzzo (coldly): And Let me say this: if any of us can't afford one Dollar to feast for three days of each weekend, for four week ends in a month, then the Status Quo's cynical, vicious infirmity pales in comparison to that person's. And such person should be relegated to the realm of Gen WHY's conscience-credo subversion.

Gen WHY, finding their voices readily push back on despondency and doubts. They get back into whim again, yelling and shouting with a proprietary pride.

Gen WHY: We must, we must, we must!

Buzzo: (with a face pinched in a smirking solicitous frown, mumbling to self): Unfortunate sons and daughters of misery, have faith and patience in yourselves. When we are finished with working on ourselves, we would find utmost happiness.

Crowd funding concept as theorized and pushed forward by the foursome has gained acquaintance but has never gained traction among generations of world's youths. It is no different amongst Gen WHY. It has been imagined and fleeting. Ignored, discarded and desecrated, nobody believes it can willfully, consensually and conscientiously happen now.

Everybody, everything seems infected and elated at the same time by the whim-overwhelm of enthusiasm and optimism of crowd-funding indeed.

> *We asked for separation. We must claim freedom. To claim freedom, we must believe that impossible is nothing for the African Gen WHY's mind.*
> *Africa has failed time and again because of stark aridity of belief in self-value system.*
> *And Let me say this: if any of us can't afford 1dollar to feast for 3 days of each weekend, for the 4 consecutive weekends of every month, then the Status quo's cynical, vicious insanity pales in comparison to that person's. And such person should be relegated to the realm of Gen WHY's conscience-credo subversion.*

However, on a closest scanning, the seeming whim-overwhelm of optimism and enthusiasm is not across board. You can notice the eloquent net division of the virtual aisle: Buzzo, David, Mezzi and Mark are pitched

GENERATION WHY'S PERDITION REDEMPTIVE VERSES

on the one side and Brett and Glenda and Lynda and almost all within the rank and file of the unruly herds are on the other side. They have eloquent hints of reluctant measured enthusiasm as they battle ponderous mind-feelings of perplexity, of doubts and of despondency from their within.

Well, they are human beings and doubts and skepticisms are given to remain strongly in their hearts until, this theory wins practicality podium.

After all, doubts and skepticisms and curiosity have been the arms of evolution. The ever-evolving White race has evolved and evolves with it. The Asians are evolving, imitating the Whites' concept. Africans don't want to imitate. They don't want to evolve. Or maybe they can't imitate. They are still homos erectus?

We can infer that: *"Doubts and skepticism and curiosity can be said to be the opium of the evolving minds. And with equal vigor, laziness can be said to be the opium of the retrogressive mind."*

As it has been said that religion is the opium of the masses.

Perhaps something was ponderously left out: *"the ignoble"*. The ignoble poor masses. *Every class of human species enjoys the noble and the ignoble appellation. Like the noble and the ignoble rich, we have the noble and the ignoble poor. The ignoble poor and the ignoble rich are of the same side of the coin. Religion is their opium. Their minds are vulnerably disadvantaged with laziness and cowardliness insanity. Insanity mind set of hateful, of hurtful and of despicable magnitude. Africa has the bane of combined ignoble rich and poor.*

With laziness, comes low self-esteem. Low self-esteem is the product of aridity of evolution: an aridity that hijacks, seizes and swallows any form of progress.

And human beings, every human being has a self-importance indulgence.

And for laziness to be self-important, it traffics in luxury of self-aggrandizement. And the luxury is bombast. And this malign importance traffics dehumanization. In space and time. And the ignoble rich and the ignoble poor are the coiners and givers of this malign self-importance.

Africa is so unfortunate. Africa's very exiguous status quo leadership is of the ignoble rich compared to the West's exiguous noble rich and Africa's majority masses are ignoble poor, compared to the West's majority of noble poor.

The ignoble poor are understandably psyched out and influenced by the life-style of ignoble rich status quo. They idolatrize them and cynically aspire to be like them all the days of their lives.

It's no secret that Africans hate and despise themselves. Their self-importance indulgence is informed by their unutterable desire for the White races' material techno-prowess life style. Just their material life style. Not by the vigor of their intellectual life style. So, they traffic bombast and bombastic insanity to feed selfimportance, dictated by the irrepressible desire for lofty vacuous ostentation of Whites' technological jewels–airplanes, yachts, exotic cars, watches, bespoke clothing, lascivious homes and houses, diamonds, etcetera through hate insanity perpetration and perpetuation.

Hate begets hate.

This cleft of hate-opium is the malign weakness from within as this weakness begets and encourages and contrives gratuitous hate and despise, from without. Africa is not a united family. Africa is a family divided.

Africa's self-hate is the palpable lethal weapon of the others, to loot and pillage her. Their self-hate is the opium that subdues them. Their self-hate is a consequence of Africa's stupidity and their consequent misery and shame.

Africa's masses' faith in Jesus Christ, in Prophet Muhammad, in whatever religion, in any religion, is mainly informed by poverty, misery, in hope of blessings and sinsforgiveness and in ultimate heaven ascendance. In sum in 'by the grace' tenet of the ignoble, not by righteousness, not in "love thy neighbor..." tenet of the nobles. Not in the deeds of God as the only commonality of purpose.

The few, who are graced 'by the grace' in a mass of wealth, vastly through hate thy neighbor maxim insanity, claim self-importance. Self-importance, that is found in their bombastic material life-style of Whiteman's technology jewels, amidst Africa's ignoble poor, in deliberate torture of the ignoble poor. And paradoxically, this self-importance thrives in the luxury of hope of 'by the grace' of last day forgiveness, for heaven ascendance. In sum everything, anything is 'by the grace' insanity.

Conversely, the absolute majority of the masses, hoping to succeed one day, find refuge in faith of 'by the grace' insanity found indistinctly in all forms of religion. Religion becomes the future, the imperative future to hope on, to achieve the selfimportance dictates of material Whiteman's life-style. Or in a worst-case scenario, hope of a heaven ascendance compensation.

In sum in Africa, laziness traffics self-importance indulgence and gives hate its purpose. And the combined hate recipes and elements are abhorrent but essential. They give self-importance indulgence its reward, and self-importance indulgence, dictated by Whiteman's materials, exults hate in heaven, by 'by the grace' reward. Africans have a faith imperativeness for the final day's God's ultimate 'gracing' into heaven, an unsolicited faith. Even if that imperative faith contrives outlandish desecration and profanity by the hands of the devious and debauchery "men of God", it does not matter. It's even justifiable. They have fulfilled their faith imperativeness here on earth to merit heaven. Little does it matter the bombastic terrain life-style of "men of God" that feeds off their imperative faith crowd funding, for their heaven on earth. For them the Lord's Heaven with their promised inheritance is a chimera.

Faith, not poverty, not love, more than hate, more than any commonality of language and religion is the binding factor. Faith is unalienable to coalescing Africans. Africans hate themselves. Africa is so unfortunate to have their combined ignoble rich and poor in the majority.

In reality, only faith, faith in mystery of something, rallies and coalesces Africans. Faith makes them fund. Faith makes them make billionaires of "men of God". Faith makes them tolerate, and accept, and pardon deviousness and debaucheries by men and 'men of God'.

This same faith propensity is hoped would shift the paradigm in the youths, noble and ignoble regardless. This found faith in crowd-funding is essential for Gen WHY survival. It would justify their invested patience, and hope in the future with delayed gratification, it would exalt their dignity and reward their vision and credo.

Buzzo (continuing): I said and I will repeat that the youths of Africa are more infirm than the status quo. We don't believe in crowd funding? What do you all think that revenues of any country is? Isn't revenues made up of taxes–direct and indirect?

David: Yes, they do.

Buzzo: Then you all agree that revenues, which is any state's annual income from which public expenses are met are crowd-funded by the collective taxes paid plus the sum total of the people's natural resources?

Frank: Absolutely yes.

Buzzo: *Africa does not only crowd-fund men of God, we crowd fund politicians and monarchs. The fact that we the masses let the few people we authorize (the government) at a prize (salaries and privileges) to develop our continent with our revenues, loot the revenues without accountability and punishment is why we the masses, the youths of Africa are unfathomably infirm and numb.*

Glenda: Pristine clear.

Frank: *We call our looted revenues "government's money".*

Glenda: Cowardly Cravens. As if any bank were to mess with our monies in its custody, we call them "bank's monies". Indeed, we have been unfathomably very sick in the heads.

Buzzo: So, if we don't believe in crowd-funding to sustain our separation, then who would? The President? The President might love us but he has a relative stake. For now, let us have faith in ourselves. Otherwise, we have everything to lose. Tomorrow our President without doubt will fine-tune our efforts at this idea and sign in validation. That way you all can understand the value, the courage, the candor, the favor, the risk and the love of our President for us. The incredulity of the Status Quo in losing one of theirs, the President, and the scare and the panic and the jealousy and the haplessness of it all explains their violent reaction.

That's why the importance of our alliance with the President. That's why we must prove the lone army he can rely on. We must be good soldiers. We must make him proud. We must complement his efforts. We must succeed.

Yet our efforts through crowd-funding would pale to our efforts of discipline, civility and patriotism.

So, let's take a profound breath for a ponderous critical look at our Gen WHY's mirrors.

> *Faith in Gen WHY's crowd-funding is essential to standing up. Faith in Gen WHY's crowd-funding is essential. Faith in Gen WHY's' crowdfunding is essential. Faith in Gen WHY's crowd-funding is essential. Faith in Gen WHY's crowd-funding is essential. Faith in Gen WHY's crowd-funding is...*

Gen WHY could not fully savor their surprise at yet another sudden unexpected diversion of theme that Mezzi's voice suddenly pierces the air with a message underpinning the theme. A message with a finality that ineluctably warned.

Mezzi: Yes, a deep look at our mirrors. Yes, with no doubt in my mind we will defeat, obliterate and colonize our daily humiliations of hunger and poverty, our daily deprivation and degradation from filth and garbage, and conquer freedom and endure them. But on this path indiscipline is our nemesis. Africa has never developed because of indiscipline. Our parents, their parents, their parents' parents and parents' parents and parents are primitive and not disciplined. Indiscipline is part of our sorrowing heritage. To prove ourselves departing primitivity we must show discipline. If we must succeed, we must have and adhere to code of discipline as a *conditio sine qua non.*

Mark gets out of his seat and started applauding Mezzi.

The Gen WHY crowd finally understands, joins in to a standing applause.

Now the applause slows and ceases as Gen WHY crowd return to their seats with their rapt attention still holding, their faces in attentive listening grimace.

Buzzo: Thank you Mezzi. As you all well know, even the best educated of us lack basic good parenting. Our lazy and ignorant undisciplined parents push us to the confines of the churches, mosques, parties, celebrations, social media, to every ephemeral without the basics and bases of those places.

Most of us are rewarded for doing nothing. Our parents devalue the value of medals. You come first in class, you do your dish, you do your bed you get nothing. Conversely you come last in class you get a medal, gifts, like buying examination papers to pass exams. You get lullaby, if you don't wake up to your daily chores.

> *Yet our efforts through crowd-funding would pale to our efforts at discipline, civility and patriotism.*
> *Indiscipline is our nemesis. Africa has never developed because of indiscipline.*
> *Our parents, their parents, their parents' parents and parents' parents and parents lack civility. They are primitive and undisciplined. That's part of our sorrowing heritage.*
> *As you all well know, even the best educated of us, lack basic good parenting.*
> *Our lazy and ignorant parents push us to the confines of the churches, mosques, parties, celebrations, social media. To every ephemeral, without the basics and bases of those places.*
> *Most of us are rewarded for doing nothing. Our parents devalue the value of medals. You come first in class, you do your dish, you do your bed, you get nothing. Conversely you come last in class you get a medal, gifts, like buying examination papers to pass exams. You don't wake up to your daily chore, you get lullaby as a wake-up call.*

As if lack of parenting is not enough decay, they push us to technologies. Facebook, Instagram, twitter, google, social media world. We seize the opportunity. We put out photos of how our lives are amazing when the contrary is the case. We put out lies, we put out false equivalencies without actually figuring out what they mean. We sound tough behind the screens of social media but we can hardly figure out anything. Social media gives us the dopamine addiction like alcohol, cigarettes, marijuana, opioid, heroine. Before saying good morning or saying our prayers we must check out our phones. Bottom line, we are addicted with the blessings of our parents. They buy us the phones. But not the alcohol, not the cigarettes, not the marijuana, not the heroine. They buy us television times to moron us, to make up their slothfulness and woeful failures in parenting.

If lack of parenting, and push to addiction of technology are not enough for our decay and decapitation, add our hostile miserable environment to them. An environment of ponderous abject hostility – harsh, oppressive, repressive, tyrant, despotic leadership on one part, with cowered, submissive, stupid, gullible, and complacent followership with more vigor on the other, of non-meritocracy, of slavery, of money and material acquisition above any values– of no set values.

Then we wear those veils. Addicted, we imbibe and indulge in superficial relationships with our peers, hypocritical friendships, impatience in everything, willful lying, compulsive cheating, pathological stealing. Gullible. Generation of low self-esteem. We sound tough behind the screens of social media. We are cringing cowards. We take advantage. We are opportunists. Opportunism loyalty, etc. etc. Then stress, social and financial anxiety turn up we crease into confusion, then frustration, then depression.

We find out we are utterly vulnerable and miserable. Abandoned hopelessly to ourselves. We lack the journey of social coping mechanisms to be able to deal with stress, anxiety, depression. Much less their practice. We abjectly lack skilled set values and their practice.

The journey of social coping mechanisms is arduous, tortuous, slow, meandering and long. But regardless, absolutely necessary.

We need the journey of skill set values: passion, hard work, patience, love, sacrifice, joy of life, sadness, respect, compassion, self-esteem, self-confidence, fear of God, fear of society.

Quoting Albert Einstein: *"I fear that the day technology will surpass our human interaction the world will have a generation of idiots."*

Our generation is handed down a reification of societal and Godly moral set of valuesystem. We think God abstract. Depersonalized. We think society is the wild. We grow up in impatience and in indiscipline and in willful blindness and in willful lying and in willful hate, and in willful hypocrisy, and in willful denials, and in willful shamelessness, and in willful remorselessness, and in willful cheating and in willful laziness, and in will cowardice, and in willful ignorance and in willful avariciousness and in willful superficiality and in default blames shifting and in default inexcusable stupid excuses. All ill-gotten and learned from our parents and from our society. We are viciously callous, craven hypocrites, cringing cowards, above anything else. That's why we have suicides on the rise as worst-case scenarios and no deep fulfillment, no joys of life as best-case scenarios. Just waffling through life.

We should and must have the best of ourselves going forward if we must succeed. It is absolutely not for the President but for ourselves. We have more at stake than our parents. We owe that to ourselves, to our children, to the descendants of our children and children's children's children's...children. Ad infinitum.

In the end, we will surely fail if we won't refuse and debunk these vices and decays and imbibe utmost discipline of duties and rights.

And let me conclude by paraphrasing Jim Rohn: *"Discipline, our self-discipline is the bridge between our failure and success, between our misery and joy, between our insanity and sanity, between our goals and accomplishments."*

> *Our generation is handed down a reification of Societal and Godly moral set of value-system. We think God abstract. Depersonalized. We think Society is the wild.*
> *We grow up in impatience and in indiscipline and in willful blindness and in willful lying and in willful denials, and in willful ...*

...shamelessness, and in willful remorselessness, and in willful cheating and in willful laziness and in willful ignorance and in willful avariciousness and in willful superficiality and in default blames shifting and in default inexcusable stupid excuses.
We are viciously callous, craven hypocrites, cringing cowards, above anything else.
That's why we have suicides on the rise as worst-case scenarios and no deep fulfillment, no joys of life as best-case scenarios. Just waffling through life.

VOLUME 8
THE GOVERNANCE

Chapter I

The inner working caucus of Gen WHY, viz David, Buzzo, Mark, Mezzi, Glenda, Brett, Lynda, Laura, Frank are once again seated in the situation room of the President's office, waiting for the President who is yet to arrive.

The President is to officially consume their found alliance, foster it, strengthen it, and together forge a new political, military, economic and psychological leadership and strategies to power the continent out of misery and stupidity.

These women and men seated, waiting and the waited–the President–are of valor and candor.

They are brought together by fate. That fate that is said is predetermined for every human mainly from without. Without human's merits and demerits. Even so most fate are not all kismet. They are from within. Most have been and can be achieved by volition of hard work, of selflessness, of resoluteness in life times. Ultimately conceived within the will of self-consciousness. Like the will of spirit of rebellion of the self-consciousness. The spirit of rebellion that arouses readily, unsolicited to dare, subdue and cross limits and limitation in the White race. The same spirit of rebellion that slumbers, sleeps and is swallowed by fear of the unknown, fear of daring, fear of repression, fear of brute death in the Black race. That spirit of rebellion, in the Black race, that would usually prefer the inevitable, conscious and conscientious slow death, as sentenced by misery, is by some kismet rekindled and valorized by rebel Mezzi.

These men and women ponderously and voluptuously find their rebellious expression, identifying and coalescing with Mezzi.

Most of these men have faced the savagery of hunger but were not ravaged by it. They rebelled.

The unruly herds rebelled to the urge of vicious stealing, callous depredation, cyber thefting, quickest money making within the cultist membership, with their inherent forceful possessions, rapes, rituals. They stuttered, fluttered but held on to valor.

Some have faced the savagery of hypocrisy but were not ravaged by it. They rebelled. Glenda at age 15, had inadvertently asked her family for the palpability of the Lord God. She wanted to feel the Lord. Her family's hypocrisy swallowed their answer. At 16 she had asked her family which God is tenable–African cultist-Oracularwitchery or Pentecostalism-witchery or Islam faith or orthodox faith or Hinduism or what. They once again produced no answers.

At 20, she was subjected to spirituality choice-making, an exercise between her family's two religious extremes–paternal African cultist-witchery and maternal Pentecostalism-witchery. She rebelled against the two, estranging herself.

At 22, yet vulnerable and disadvantaged, undeterred she exploded the night participating in the revolution that obliterated the religious triad extremes of the land, that swallowed her parents and family members, including the chief priestess, her aunt, in its wake. Faithful to valor and candor.

Some have faced the taunting and tempting savagery of bombastic comfort and ferocious humiliation of ill-acquired wealth and its comfort and bombast, but were not ravaged by them. They rebelled.

Mezzi, joined by Buzzo rebelled vehemently and its wake is challenging the conscience of a continent, inspiring their peers to standing up.

Yet others have faced the intoxicating, vicious savageness of absolute power but were not ravaged by it. They rebelled.

The President, of utterly disadvantaged beginning, his poverty-ridden family, unsolicited, fortunately attracted the grace of a missionary school, where he enrolled to become a monk. Sexual promiscuity of some deranged gang of clergies wedged in, insinuating self in his way. He rebelled and was estranged.

His second grace came from an unknown army officer who employed him as a servant. His dedication, hard work, honesty, discipline and loyalty gained him favor and in turn entrance into army school academy where he excelled and passed out impeccably as an army officer.

He refused in its entirety, the corruption and compromise and cronyism within the ranks of the army and their complicity and complacency with the looting, pillagery and kleptomaniacs of the civil society. He rebelled, staging a bloody coup and overthrowing the democratically elected but corrupt government.

As Head of State, he reestablished the rule of law, sense of nationhood, fiscal discipline, moral discipline and order. And suddenly in a pleasant surprise move, he called for election, handing over the government. This act was awesome and ponderously incredible in a continent where power knows no voluntary ceding or transfer.

He retired as a general, retreating from public life at the age of 32.

Just as is obvious and of costume, any good deed is despised and readily obliviated by the society at large in Africa. A society controlled by material possession not by God's deed, good deed or exertion of intelligence nor of integrity of leadership or followers. A society, individually single-minded and systematic in the conduct of their wants and in practice of their businesses of cheating and possessions, by every means possible.

Abandoned and obliviated, he remained sad and totally despondent.

Vulnerable and totally disadvantaged, the politics of Mr. Bombastic Donald George wedged in, convinced him the sky was his limit, with the leverage of his exemplary career and fortitude and proven record; he was needed into leadership role to power off the millennium. Mr. Donald George financed his election, roping him in. He hatefully and embarrassingly put his spiritual essence on the line, unwillinglyhelplessly living out the intoxicating comfort of the savagery of vicious absolute power.

Then, revolutionary Mezzi appears on the horizon. The President finds Mezzi's expressions, pristine and delightfully intoxicating. An awakening to his subdued but latent spiritual instinct. He is rebelling. Comfortably readily crossing the line, identifying vigorously with revolutionary Mezzi and his peers.

These men of candor and valor all crossed the line of rebellion. Thanks to Mezzi the revolutionary.

Mezzi's groggy will was ponderously infectious in its wake. So much so that unsolicitedly, it deployed everyone. They proudly-unsolicitedly identified with Mezzi, braved Rubicon, climbed Rubicon, on the threshold of crossing the line for a catharsis of becoming revolutionaries.

There is a line between a rebel and a revolutionary. Like most things, the line lay in the motive and in the means.

The priceless virtues and solaces of Mezzi's efforts at their 'children must play center' provided the motive. But the means that crossed the line lay in the vicious and ferocious and undeterred exertion that unveiled the African stupidity veils, illuminating and provoking standing up stance that inspired the conscience of his Gen WHY peers, within and without the African continent, making palpable and inexcusable the cringing shamefulness and the humiliating embarrassment and the utter contemptuousness of the Black race.

Now the President enters the situation room taking his sitting position.

He slowly scans everybody's face, finding them of conflicting tortured grimaces and of mixture of expectant competing perplexity, despondency and muted optimism. He settles his gaze on his son Mark.

President: Mark has the egg cracked?
Mark: No Pop! But about to crack. My peers are hungry. And Pop you know that a hungry man is an angry bomb, waiting for the slightest opportunity to detonate.

Everybody cracks up laughing. The tensed air relieving.

President: Mezzi?
Mezzi: Yes, your excellency! Every solution of freedom must ride on a stringent code of discipline and of conduct.
President: It's astounding your level of maturity at critical analysis. Coupled with your precocious extemporariness, given your fledgling age. You hit the problem on the head with the surgical precision of the scalpel. We can't agree any best. Bravo. Brett?

Brett: Mark has said it all. We are hungry and scared of our future. As we plan and program, we would like to live out some fruits and guarantees. Hungry men could turn into angry mobs.

There was an immediate ponderous mixed reaction of shrieks of disapproval and noisy appreciation at the same time. The mixed reactions muted as they came, in a flash. The presence of the President, condescending. It was brief but efficacious. The point was made and lines of cleavage drawn.

However, it seems not to surprise the President, who drew on the lines of the cleavage.

President (in open rebuke): David, why the shriek of disapproval?

David: His has become an incessant ponderous arousal of emotional blackmail and torture.

President: I am heart-broken by your shrieks of disapproval.

Can you all for a moment flip the coin? Even though it's really hard for you to do so. Fortunately for you, you have never had the cause to be famished.

You have never carried the horror and shame and the tribulations and the humiliation and the insecurity of a destitute.

They have and they still do. And nonetheless they, the unruly herds, always on the edge of misery, chose patience for faith in delayed gratification, and over quick ill-gotten gratification conformity of society.

And above all, in their edge of misery, they gave their most beautiful act of faith: generosity. The generosity of the destitute. Their faith beat the spite out of hunger, subdued hunger and conquered the Plaza Hill and the exploding nights.

He pauses and engages in turn, each of the house Gen WHY in an intensive eye- locking fit.

The foursome, refuge in smiling frowns of combined chagrin and remorse and pride. They are essential. Their unsolicited initiative and efforts and stride at standing up justify their pride. But their chagrin and remorse give their humanity, vulnerability, weakness and empathy exultation.

Now the President disengages, fixes Brett and starts applauding him.

Everybody quickly rose to the occasion in ponderous
yelling applause. The applause ceases with reluctance.

The President continues.

Fortunately for you, you have never had the cause to be famished.
You have never carried the horror and shame and the tribulations and
the humiliation and the insecurity of a destitute...
..They have and they still do. And nonetheless they, the unruly ...

> *...herds, always on the edge of misery, chose patience for faith in delayed gratification, and over quick ill-gotten gratification conformity of society.*
> *And above all, in their edge of misery, they gave their most beautiful act of faith: generosity. The generosity of the destitute. Their faith beat the spite out of hunger, subdued hunger and conquered the plaza hill and the exploding nights.*

President: You must all have deepest sympathies and empathies for others' distresses. Besides, you deny your problem, you deny your absolution. Just like Black race does. You identify your problem; you identify your absolution. Just like the White race does. To solve any problem once identified, you must engage it incessantly like Brett until it is solved. Just like the White race. Otherwise the problem will swallow you. And the greatest news is that you are already come so far on that path. Our primitive self-consciousness was not capable of such exertion. You have elevated your self-consciousness to Gen WHY. That's the meaning of Gen WHY. And Brett and the herds are Gen WHY.

So, Brett your worries are the worries of the herds. They are legitimate. Your wrenching method to solving them, awesome. That is the lone winning edge.

You have beaten hunger at the Plaza Hill and subdued it at the exploding nights. You made yourselves good soldiers, not cheap soldiers. You must remain good soldiers. Endurance defines a good soldier. Otherwise you will be cheap betrayals. Glenda?

Glenda (emotional): Your excellency, let me humbly congratulate you sir. You are a rare gem. Really gracious. God bless you sir.

On the last words of Glenda, the rest of Gen WHY get emotional, their eyes lucid, fighting back tears, in unison rose to a thunderous, resounding, ponderous applause. The President is moved by this recognition that seemed honest, pristine and unfeigned. These youths have really insinuated in and gained his heart.

He is determined to make their happiness not a chimera, not a myth. But real.

The youths notice and double down in the applause.

The President could not help but bow in a humble, thankful appreciation.

Gen WHY, now settle back in their seats, giving way to a gradual reluctance silence that settles back in the room.

> *Besides, you deny your problem, you deny your absolution. Just like Black race does. You identify your problem; you identify your absolution. Just like the White race does. To solve any problem ...*

353

CHAPTER 1

> *...once identified, you must engage it incessantly like Brett until it is solved. Just like the White race. Otherwise the problem will swallow you.*

Glenda:(pointedly referencing Brett): However, hungry Africans turning into an angry mob has never been our commonplace. And we all know it. Even though we have blaze-trailed a protest of separation, it might not endure the risk of any tide. A partnership confidently would.

So, it is left to us to make the best of the ferocious urgency of the moment: an enduring partnership with the President.

The President stands up and starts applauding.

President: Please give yourselves a ponderous applause.

They all rose to the applause, voluptuously applauding Glenda.

The President takes back his seating position. The applause simmers and ceases. Then they take back their seats.

President: I am really humbled and inspired. You all inspire me and inject me with invincible spirit of guts. And I am very proud of you. And I want to remain proud of you and more importantly, grateful.

Paraphrasing President Obama: *"change only happens when ordinary people, when the flock, the herds, oppressed and non, get involved...and come together to demand it."*

Indeed, you are the proven pressure from below, and you need the vision from top to inspire and coalesce you.

Let me announce that we are officially here to give birth to our alliance.

Gen WHY rise in thunderous cries and shrieking applause.

President: An alliance to avenge misery. An alliance to subdue and defeat Africa's stupidity with its obliterating shameful scourge of which hunger and misery are the epitome mainstay on our continent. Desperation and filth and garbage allied us to vanquish adversity and hope and purpose would do no less to conquer progress. But before we move forward, let me ask you all if you have reflected on duties and on your duties to succeed?

Gen WHY (almost in unison and looking at Buzzo at the same time): Yes!

President: Buzzo, David?

David: Yes dad, we have made them our priority.

Buzzo: Yes, a *conditio sine qua non* priority. We have them already fast-tracked in our self-consciousness, in our consciences as code of conducts.

President: Bravoes! Awesome! By so doing you all are simply but explicitly, expressing the vow to do the right thing and have others do the

354

right thing. You are solemnly vowing the legacy to take care of yourselves and to take care of each other and the generation of your children?

Gen WHY unabashedly, unsolicitously rose in unison to a thunderous: Hashtag Yeeeeeaaaah!

President: Don't you ever shy away from our ineluctable truth: that Africa is not the problem, Africans are. We are our nemesis.
Don't any of you ever get emotional about this our truth.
To succeed alongside your code and discipline conduct, you must mull over and impress in your minds of mind "who we have been, and who you should not be." And let me give you this conscientious, ineluctable truth to follow you as your inseparable spiritual shadow all the days of your lives. A question and answer recitation within yourselves. Between your conscience and your self-consciousness.
It's going to be your homily. Second in importance to our Lord's prayer. Just as our Lord's prayer is between you and the Lord, with equal vigor, your homily is your soliloquy. You are going to treasure these facts and recite them for the love of yourselves, for your dignity and for the love and the dignity you will hold for generations of your children and thence:
1.   Africa is a continent of misery! Why?
2.   We hate ourselves! But why?
3.   We don't believe in ourselves! But why?
4.   We are of low self-esteem! But why?
5.   We have not advanced humanity in any form or shape! But why?
6.   We Africans are stupid! But why?
7.   We are still very much primitive! But why?
8.   We Africans are slothful! But why?
9.   We have no necessities, it's been peddled! How, with our misery?
10.   Yes, misery is our necessity! How, isn't misery a necessity for invention?
11.   Yes, necessity is the mother of invention, but not for Africans! So why not?
12.   Africa's necessity is misery. Not invention! Then copy. Why not?
13.   To copy is the beginning of evolution. Invent, copy not our necessity! Why?
14.   We have self-consciousness of stupidity. Africa's self-consciousness incarnates stupidity, loves misery, loves primitiveness, loves laziness, loves hate, loves degradation, loves humiliation, loves tribulation, loves being enslaved, loves selfenslavement, loves institutional racism, loves institutional self-looting, loves institutional filth and garbage, loves disempowering her descendants, loves captivity of her continent. Bottomline.
It's been said that: ***imitation begins human evolution. Lack of it is retardation.*** Africa is retarded? We need to evolve, ferociously Change the paradigm. Otherwise we would have proven to be retarded indeed.

Now President pauses and scans their faces in mental notes, amidst absolute stilledsilence. Then the President's voice promptly pierces the air bringing them back to the reality of the present.

President: To date, in my humble opinion, Africa has had four elusive enemies. Avowed enemies of the people. They are everywhere and nowhere at the same time. Enemies that are deadly, retrogressive, hateful, hurtful, harmful, but have our sympathy, our empathy, complicity and compulsive support and liking: willful indolence, willful evil, willful denial and willful scouring corruption.

The culture of willful indolence, of willful evil, of willful denials and willful corruption has shaped us. We compulsively lie, offend, steal, punish and hate and deny. With its very grievous, devious repercussions and perilous propagations and scouring foothold.

And their multiplied grievous, devious repercussions and perilous propagations and traumas and tribulations, and humiliations and misery on our society regardless, has in no way smeared their reiteration.

The President pauses, scanning his interlocutors' attentive faces and finds encouragement. He continues.

President: Africa has been a prison where generations after generations have consciously and hopelessly and pathologically, haplessly abandoned self and awaited self-executions. In fact, every one of us is bereft. There cannot be an illusion of freedom amidst slavery. There cannot be a free African on the African continent.

The illusion of the comfort of ill-gotten wealth regardless.

Just look at us the status quo despots. We just exist. We are a mass of abstracts amidst our people. Africa has not lived. Africa does not live. Africa just exists. Africa just exists in the void. Africa has only survived the test of time of centuries always. Always only by surrendering. Africa has never stood up.

> *Africa has not lived. Africa does not live. Africa just exist in the void. Africa has only survived the test of time of centuries always only by surrendering. Has only survived the test of time of centuries only by surrendering. Only survived the test of time of centuries only by surrendering.*
> *Survived the test of time of centuries only by surrendering. The test of time of centuries only by surrendering. Test of time of centuries only by surrendering.*

Africa never stood up. It never stands up. Instead it surrenders to negative gross domestic products, to negative growth per capita, to below poverty income per capita: about 90% of Africans are below poverty level of $1/day threshold. Africa surrenders to 2% of its ignoble "privileged" thieves, who own property in men. They own 90% of fellow Africans who, they subject to below poverty level, as their properties in men. They wear that medal, including myself.

Africa surrenders to pumping out children into misery. Africa surrenders to a growing young population susceptible to highest rates of adult illiteracy, to maternal mortality, to infant mortality, to disadvantage and peril.

Of this teaming population about 75% is the youth. And 60 % of them is unemployed. The remaining 40% are a mix of gainfully and precariously engaged. A disaster. How did we get here?

Gen WHY are elated with rapt attention. Everybody is expectantly listening very hard. In silence. Their silence does not understand. Their eloquent and stilled silence, expects answers.

President: Africa post-colonialism got here arrogating itself with the function of producer of goods and services, enabler of private enterprises.

Africa became a continent of state-owned enterprises.

African governments instead proved to be bad managers of business enterprises.

And poor and inefficient delivery of basic goods and services to its people.

African governments are able to generate debts, losses and filths and garbage.

It's disheartening and embarrassing the lack of critical infrastructures like power electricity, transportation, telecommunications, schools, hospitals, water to power off and support economic activities of the private sector to this day of the 21st century.

He pauses and scans the tortured chagrined faces of the Millennials. And continues.

President: Once again you will be asking how did we get here.

We got here because African government is a government of cronies and cronyisms. Our Status Quo leadership, with myself of course inclusive, is a government of leadership of cronies, cronyisms and cabals.

We created and have over 100,000 board seats. Over 100,000 board members are beneficiaries of moribund, unproductive state-owned enterprises.

We take the state-owned enterprise into a moribund status, perpetuating that status as we pump repeated ponderous investments in their turn-around maintenances. And we round-trip importation of crude oil refined products, agro-alimentary products, we import sand instead of building materials products for our social fabrics, transformers, fertilizers, etc....etc.

Willful gross incompetence, callous mismanagement, heinous blatant corruption, brazing crippling complacency.

This, to the extent that Africa's vast endowment–mineral wealth, human wealth, artistic wealth, intellectual wealth, the envy of all, are devoted, of our choice, from centuries to centuries to the services of the Europeans, the Americans and their descendants, to the peril of Africa's descendants. Africa is the biblical Canaan.

The President takes a long pause. There is an eerie silence across the aisles. A voluptuous eerie silence of unutterable thoughtfulness, reflections and grieving anxiety for solutions.

The President notices and continues.

President: It is traumatic. I can see trauma in your contorted sad grimaces. I can see unutterable trauma in your sorrowing eyes, conflicted with anguish and pain. The truth that has endured and sustained Africa's misery drama amongst the people, is that everyone seems prepared for the trauma because, no one talks about the trauma. The trauma is numbing. We don't stand up to it. We only surrender. Too often our culture and tradition socialize us to do the easier thing rather than the right thing. It's easier to surrender to the palsy of religion, to the spell of laziness, to the kismet of hopelessness, to the complacency, to the reticence, to the fearful confusion, to the spiritual vacuity essence rather than stand up.

However, it's been said that *most blessings are borne out of danger and most tribulations, desperations, humiliation and miseries give out ray of hope*. So is the fate of our alliance. Our alliance is borne out of danger and must be endured to prevail over the perils of tribulations, desperations, humiliation and miseries.

> *The truth that has endured and sustained Africa's misery drama amongst the people, is that everyone seems prepared for the trauma because, no one talks about the trauma. The trauma is numbing. We don't stand up to it. We only surrender.*
> *Too often our culture and tradition socialize us to do the easier thing rather than the right thing. It's easier to surrender to palsy of religion, to the spell...*

For it's also been said that *the one unchangeable certainty is that nothing, nothing, I repeat nothing is unchangeable.*

So, it is in truth and with ultimate pride that I praise your found confidence. With your found confidence, zeal, enthusiasm, passion, hope, proven heroism and patriotism, I fully entrust your generation the fate of our alliance to prevail over the misery that, for no fault of yours you inherited from a society of despotic hereditary tradition of abject pervasiveness, oppressiveness, repressiveness, decay and despair.

Those words have an immediate soothing effect on their prolonged mind of despondency: Gen WHY crease into spasm of enthusiasm. They shift in their seats. There is a ponderous, unsolicited standing shrieking, yelling ovation that propelled the President to continue.

President: Now that we have refreshed and rummaged a little bit over our embarrassing shameful and urgent situation, our alliance has the central and main objective chore of ferociously-urgently annihilating misery through a sustained poverty reduction and ultimately its eradication, sustainable development, and our progressive integration into the global economy.

So, here is the deal: to prevail on this found misery that is not of your making, our alliance founded on the foundation of standing up credo must be accompanied by social freedom. Some would be immediate and some remote. Some social change must be palpable with immediacy.

You ought to know that "Standing Up" credo and the "day of accountability" racked in so much money and are going to rein in much more through repatriation efforts from the Western banks. I will repeat: post-colonial Africa's leadership (traditionalmonarchic leadership, political leadership, the theocratic leadership) and cronyism and cabals to date have pilfered into the western economy tens of trillions of U.S. Dollars. Hopefully, the West chastising us, justifiably, for our stupidity and our willful underdevelopment of Africa will authorize repatriation. That way they depart from their long-held sickening complicity and crippling hypocrisy of institutional racism and probably hope to find peace in their luxury of self-absolution. Hopefully. With these monies we must confront head-on the social barriers which have for so long blocked economic development and progress here in Africa.

The money is so substantial to produce vigorous macroeconomic and microeconomic duties for equal vibrant privatization and commercialization activities.

...the "day of accountability", racked in so much money and are going to rein in much more through repatriation efforts from the western banks.
Hopefully the west chastising us, justifiably, for our stupidity and our willful underdevelopment of Africa will authorize repatriation. That way they depart from their long-held sickening complicity and crippling hypocrisy and at probably hope to find peace in the luxury of self-absolution. Hopefully.

The President pauses, reaching for his file. As he takes out a stack of documents and holds it up in the air about to continue speaking, he notices Buzzo's hand in the air.

President: Yes Buzzo?
Buzzo: Excellency, you mentioned the words macroeconomy and microeconomy, and the majority of us are at lost at those words. The valency of these combined words to most of us is misery.

Gen WHY break in shouting and shrieks of ponderous consensus. They could not agree any better.
The cry of consensus reluctantly simmers...ceases as Buzzo waves his hands asking for silence.

Buzzo: the Webster dictionary meanings of those words are:
a. Macroeconomics = the branch of economics that studies the overall working of a national economy;
b. Microeconomics = the branch of economics that studies the economy of consumers or households or individual firms.

The President did not blink. Instead he smiles welcoming Buzzo's well thought initiative. He is no novice to economic and financial frameworks of magnitude. Within his career in the military realm, he studied economics and finance within the context of territorial integrity as it impacts defense, surveillance, training and protection.

President: Buzzo, thank you very much. What you just broached is fundamental for any success. Fundamental to our success. Fundamental to future success.
It's easy. Now let's make those words meaningfully palpable.
To make any of you effectively, responsibly productive, important to yourselves and to society in any of your choices of future professional fields and endeavor, society, your parents, government, organizations, etc. must send you to school.
You aspire to be a medical doctor, an engineer, an architect, a nurse, a teacher, a farmer, a banker, a politician, a clergy, a carpenter, an auto-mechanic, an artist, a painter, a musician, a tailor, whatever, you must go to school.

President pauses, scanning their attentive curious faces.

President: Isn't it?
Gen WHY (ponderously in unison): Yes!
President: Cool. So, you agree that society needs to put you in schools to form you?

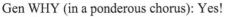

Gen WHY (in a ponderous chorus): Yes!

President: So, society guided by a plan and policy builds schools and school structures from kindergarten to primary education to secondary education to university education, etc., etc. Those structures would comprise of the classrooms, hostels, refectories, teachers' quarters, sports infrastructure, libraries, etc., etc.

Are you all there? What else would society be doing to form you in school?

Glenda: Teachers, books, desks and seats...

Brett: Three square meals...

President: Yes Brett. Even lobsters, if the state can afford them.

The President follows his remarks with a wink. Everybody cracks up with their eyes on Brett.

Laura: Toilets, cleaners, maintenance units, water...lights...

President: Yeah Laura, no more "shut-putting". No throwing of faeces from your dormitory windows. Awful. We need to urbanize the school environment-sewerage, pipe-borne water, power electricity, health center, etc. etc. And what else? David.

David: Transportation...

President: We need roads to schools, we need rail lines to schools, we need means of transportation to schools-buses, trains, bicycles, etcetera. We need power electricity, we need telecommunications-satellite for voice, internet, intranet, for tele-education, etc., etc.

So, these steps meant to form you into productive professionals of different fields of works and similar other steps like:

a. Structural policies to improve and reinforce the private sector, improve the environment for enhanced domestic resource mobilization and increases in business, investment for your employment; strengthening of labor and produce market; improve the quality of private and public services; financial system reforms which help to develop viable banking and non-banking systems, capital markets and financial services, including microfinance.

b. Growth and stabilization through disciplined fiscal and monetary policies that must reduce inflation, improve external fiscal balances, strengthen fiscal discipline, enhance budgetary transparency and efficiency.

c. Sustainable policy and institutional reforms and investment necessary for equitable access to economic resources, particularly to: development of training systems that help increase productivity in both the formal and the informal sectors; capital, credit, land, especially as regards property, rights and uses.

d. Development of rural strategies to develop a framework for participatory decentralized planning, resource allocation and management.

e. Development of strategies to enhance agricultural production and productivity by providing public and private investments for research, supportive rural infrastructure, investing in value chain industries and manufacturing, strengthening of farmers and private sector organization, development of functional agriculture markets.

f. Sustainable development of water resources based on water resources management principles, ensuring equitable and sustainable distribution of shared water resources between their different uses.

g. Sustainable development of power energy based on green technologies ensuring a management principle to guarantee equitable and sustainable generation, effective transmission, equitable distribution of shared energy resources between their different uses.

h. Development of sustainable aqua-culture and fisheries both inland marines resourced within economic exclusive zones.

i. Development of sustainable competitive industrial mining sectors while encouraging private sector involvement and development and investment.

j. Sustainable development of economic and technological infrastructure and services, including transport, telecommunication systems, communication services, and the development of information technology, scientific, technological, and research infrastructure and services, including enhancement, transfer, and absorption of new technologies.

k. Development of business, finance and banking and other service sectors

l. Development of tourism and other social sectors etc., etc., etc.

The President pauses, scanning their faces in a total eerie silence and found they were not bored at all. They are very attentive. He breathes a sigh of relief and continues.

President: All these steps are called macroeconomic structures, structural policies and reforms. They are to be provided by society. Are we making progress?

The President pauses again, scanning their smirking faces in affirmative headnodding gestures.

President: Cool. African society post-colonial system were to provide and to continue providing these infrastructures, policies and reforms through state-owned enterprises—ministry of works, housing and transportations, ministry of education, power authorities, water resources, ministry of communication, health, agriculture etc. etc. But they did not.

These state enterprises are hijacked and are cash-cows for African leadership, their cronies, cronyisms and cabals to your professional formation detriment and peril and disrepair.

Gen WHY rose to a ponderous resounding standing applause. They are wired up and fired up. They have an idea of what is being analyzed and participate activelyusefully in the alliance discussions.

President: So, our alliance is going to have to hit the ground running with investment in economic activities. If we must become attractive to foreign investors for their direct investments, we are to engage head-on, on a mix of macro and microeconomic activities at the same time. And if I may sing it like a song:

Our alliance must support investments in basic infrastructure by the public sector aimed at private sector development, economic growth and poverty eradication.

Our alliance must support investment and private sector development in order to integrate actions and initiative at macro and micro economic levels and promote the search for innovative financing mechanisms including the blending and leveraging of private and public sources for development funding.

Our alliance must pursue a developmental approach through integrated strategies, that incorporate economic, social, cultural, environmental and institutional elements that must aim at achieving rapid and substantial job-creating economic growth, developing the private sector, increasing employment, improving access to productive economic activities and resources, promotion of human and social development, ensuring shared equity of growth and gender equality.

Our alliance must restructure and elevate our villages into sub-urban communities and promote their cultural values into interacting with economic, political and social developmental elements.

Our alliance must promote institutional reforms, policies and development, economic reforms and policies at national, state, and communal levels aimed at creating a favorable environment for investment and the development of a dynamic, viable and competitive private sector and in furtherance aim at promoting public private sector dialogue and co-operation, develop entrepreneurial skills and business culture, development and modernization of mediation and arbitration systems, etc., etc., etc.

These integrative macro/micro economic chores may appear boring, overbearing, alike, interchangeable, repetitive but these are the only steps unsolicitously, *conditio sine qua non* expected of us to power off and become attractive to foreign investments and investors.

Let us agree and sanctify here today that only our most compulsive, driven exertions can make us succeed. Intrinsic, indefatigable, compulsive exertions should be ours, should be our part. Direct foreign investments and assistance would certainly give impulse. Only if there is determination of efforts. No amount of help from without can make us succeed without our compulsive determination of efforts from within. Let us depart from rhetoric to concreteness. If we are to subdue and make our scouring misery captive, we must have a ponderous, competing vital approach that is bold, efficacious and unrelenting at the same time.

Now before we move forward, with your permission, I think it duteous to seek your opinion on democracy.

This elicited prompt, ponderous interest. Their attention is held with almost all hands raised in the air. Laura and Mezzi are the exceptions. Everybody including the President notices.

President: Laura you have no opinion on democracy?

Laura: Excellency, this thing called democracy or by whatever name, is against our people. How can a doctrine, a system, an orientation, a substance decided by the people, and is of the people, become the misery for that same people?

President: Punctilious bruising observation. Thank you. Mezzi?

Mezzi: Sir, I sincerely think that democracy is a beautiful concept as coined and put forward by the ancient Greeks. It does fairly well in the western democracies yet it's not the best thing even there, it's not the best thing anywhere else. In Africa we have its capitulation.

President: Why do you think it's so?

Mezzi: Any functional democracy needs reason. Africa is still primitive. History says Europe fought lengthy, excruciating battles for reason, to grow their once primitive self-consciousness through strenuous determined effort at education of the brain and mind for freedom and for European human rights to bear and endure. Africa is primitive to understand and endure the art of consensus, of compromises and of consensus of compromises.

Democracy in Africa is the vicious lunacy to subdue and humiliate the people and the people's ability in palsy of faith to endure it. It's just beyond and beneath puzzling.

> *Africa is still primitive.*
> *Africa is primitive to understand and endure the art of consensus, of compromises and of consensus of compromises.*
> *Democracy in Africa is the vicious lunacy to subdue and humiliate the people and the people's ability in palsy of faith to endure humiliation.*

The President's face pinches into a competing grimace of pleasure and worry. He remains awed and troubled by this sublime submission of Mezzi. This is no academics. It's deep. It's real and playing and dynamic. What is surprising and troubling is the precocity of the thought in these youthful bodies. These kids are grown men. The grieving shame of the African tribulation has really overwhelmed them with intricacies of life-negativities and hopelessness. When they should've been enfolded in life's endless beauties and fascinations and inspirations and hope to participate and to then express theirs in turn.

President (in mumbles his eyes fixing the infinite void): Reason...primitive...vicious lunacy to subdue...ability...palsy of faith to endure...

Then he recovers. To the reality of the present.

President: Yeah...anybody knows...David how many forms of government do you know?
David: Historically I think they are prevalently eight. We have monarchy, aristocracy, timocracy, oligarchy, theocracy, tyranny, autocracy, democracy.
President: Cool. Many of them. Do you know the main aspect of political power philosophy governing them?
David: All these eight forms have two main aspects of obtaining political power: one is by hereditary succession and the other is by electoral contest.
President: Cool. Miss Glenda which is ours,
do you think?
Glenda: Both!

Mark is quick to call out Glenda with intent of rebuke.

Mark: Common Glenda!

Glenda understands and throws light.

Glenda: Mark, our electoral contest efforts end up in perpetuating the same people in power. Just look around you. Democracy in Africa is a hoax. Always the same people. Equates to a hereditary succession thing, giving us their vicious lunacy...
Brett: Pristine right! Giving us misery. Worse. Democracy in Africa enslaves us. It's like the Western vehicle to continue their tyranny and slavery on Africa from a distance. Mezzi is right. We do nothing but only show the ability to endure. Humiliating. Sad. Shame on our abhorrent primitivity.

The silence turns eerie with palpitation. Mark who is younger than his father's tenure in office is beaten and subdued by the audacity and unfeigned frankness and fierceness of the reality. He creases into a sorrowing sadness. His face puckering with contorted chagrined frown. The President is quick to intervene.

President: Mark, she is right. So, don't be sad. It might seem absurd, but I am transiting, trying to renounce and atone for my evil.

Having said that, I am however amazed by Brett's line '...to continue tyranny and slavery from a distance...'

.

The President fixes the infinite void and then breaks up in a pleasant smile. A smile enfolded with pleasure of serenity and delight. An expansive proprietary smile. Now he recovers and continues.

President: That line is indeed moving. Rekindling. The fear and terror enfolded in that line have held us hostage to date since post-independence colonialism. It has beaten and is beating the spite and defiance out of a whole continent. Everybody, past leaders, the likes of Lumumba, Nkrumah, Nasser, Gadhafi, Said Bare, etc. etc. were removed by assassination at the hands of holders of democracy – the USA and western Europe. It pleases the heart to know that this is no secret to your generation in our effort to forge what might be best to progress you.

Buzzo: I think so indeed. It's imperative that we know this. Africa is a successful western democracy experiment to continue slavery and colonialism from a distance. They have incessantly pillaged and humiliated a people, a continent. In fact, institutional racism and our abhorrent institutional self-looting are their remote controls. They make rich-endowed Africa hungry migrant monsters and their leaders think of solving the problem with speeches and deterrence: "shoot Hispanics, don't let the Jews take our lands, niggers go home to infested Africa. Don't let them replace us." Instead they should have to deal with the hungry migrant monsters on their shores. Every river finds its level. The flow of migrants must find solace. Its futile to think to have it both ways. For 400 years they have pillaged and pleasured. To Africa's peril. Now we need resistance. We need to get us out of primitivity selfconsciousness and find or chart a system to govern ourselves. Malaysia, Singapore, Qatar, even China and Russia regardless of their competing tyrannies are progressing their-not so educated people out of poverty.

> *Democracy in Africa enslaves us. It's like the Western vehicle to continue their tyranny and slavery on Africa from a distance.*
> *I think so indeed. Africa is a successful western democracy experiment to continue slavery and colonialism from a distance. They have incessantly*
> *pillaged and humiliated a people, a continent. In fact, institutional racism and our abhorrent institutional self-looting are their remote controls. They make rich-endowed Africa hungry migrant monsters. And their leaders think of solving the problem with speeches and deterrence: shoot Hispanic; don't let the Jews take our lands; niggers go home to infested Africa; Don't let them replace us, etc. Instead they should have to deal with the hungry migrant monsters on their shores. Every river finds its level.*

President (voluptuously elated): I am fully in this fight and proud of it. Thank you all.

Then he pauses and scans their faces settling on Buzzo. He smiles to him.

President: Only Buzzo can eat this: how many types of government do we have?

Buzzo: That's easy. Basically, three main systems. But before we dwell on that let me again define government to avert equivocations on the mindset of the African youths. *No Society is called government. Society owns government. Society authorizes, through elections, where possible or by usurpation where necessary a group of people, remunerated, contracting them to develop society using society's crowdfunding demand – taxation – a form of tithing plus proceeds from our natural resources called revenue. So, when this group of people loot our revenue diverting it for their private use, giving us misery, we are indeed unfathomably stupid, numb to call our revenue or looted revenue "government's money." Instead of holding them accountable we cowardly submit "Don't worry one day it will be our turn." Our turn to steal our revenue?*

President: *Sacrosanct veritas.*

Frank: Cringing stupidity to say: "One day I will steal my money." It's our money. It's not "government's money", it's ours.

Brett: Just like we did not hold accountable the "men of God" looting our crowd-funding through tithing. Group of men we authorize to serve us become our lords.

Glenda: Insane! Just Imagine not holding the banks accountable if they mess with our monies and we resign calling it "Banks' monies". Beyond stupidity.

Buzzo: Uh, finally we are making progress. However, Excellency, to your question on how many types of government we have, it's about power. It's about the amount of power held by the central government with respect to the state or regional or local governments. And I will explain.

System No. 1;

Unitary system. Here you have the highest level of power centralization. The center sets uniform policy that directs the entire nation. Disregard for local differences. China, France, Japan, UK are excellent examples.

President: Cool. Briefly unitary states create national policies, the same set of laws which are then applied uniformly regardless of geography, location, tribe, language, religion. All local peculiar differences at local levels are overlooked for uniformity of adherence.

And you must know that most absolute monarchies and tyrannies operate under unitary systems. But we have democratic unitary states like France.

The President pauses and scans their rapt faces in mental notes amidst an eerie silence. He thought he found consensus to continue when Mark suddenly pierces.

Mark: Dad you mean France is a democratic tyranny?

President: Within the context of unitary system, yes. Even the UK and I think Japan. No worries. Hold your breaths and follow attentively. We are necessarily heading to understanding the distinctions soon. Buzzo go ahead please.

Buzzo: System No. 2;

Federal system. Here you have medium level of power centralized. The other half is given to the states or regional governments.

So, a federal system has a mix of national and state governments.

The federal government set national policies and laws that the state governments have to apply, tailoring them to their specific needs. They cannot absolutely tailor needs on matters of defense and foreign policy.

USA, Canada, Mexico are great examples.

Then system No. 3;

The confederate system. Here you have low level of power centralization. State or regional governments have almost complete control.

It's a loose relationship among a number of smaller political units. The vast majority of political power rests with the state or regional governments. The central government has very little power. A confederacy is little more than an alliance amongst independent states. The excellent examples are Switzerland and Belgium.

No sooner had Buzzo finished speaking than hands are raised. The President notices and smiles with pleasure.

President: We are gradually getting there. Brett.

Brett: We have UK, as well as France running a unitary tyranny.

President: A unitary system of democracy. In fact, the UK and Japan for example have parliamentary monarchies. There is an electoral contest, the parliament is formed by those contestants of competing political parties who won the majority and they assume office. They in turn nominate/ confirm the prime minister (head of political party that won). The prime minister draws his list of cabinet and the parliament gives their confirmations. Then the prime minister submits his government to the monarchy for approval and blessings.

Then the prime minister inaugurates his government. The same in Japan.

The President pauses, and scans their faces for concurrence.

President: Are we getting there?

Mark: Dad, what of France?

Buzzo: Napoleon Bonaparte killed the king of France.

Mark: Noooo, bad! Really?

Mezzi: France eliminated their king.

Mark (Winking at Glenda): Well sounds good on a second thought. Hereditary succession serves no good. We should have been doing the same thing.

Brett (to Mark): Sharp mind. The exploding night started the process.

President: So, in France they have an executive president instead of the King or the Queen or the Emperor. The rest is the same.

Glenda: So, America has a federal system of democracy with congress at the federal level and replicas at the state levels with Governors?

President: Yes, and powers are shared to a large extent.

The President pauses with expression of delightful pride on his face. Gen WHY seem enough informed for the next level of chore.

President: Let's come to us. Which of the three systems would we recommend for Africa, folks?

Brett: Excellency I don't think we are yet done. We need to analyze China and even Russia.

Buzzo: Bravo Brett! Correct! China, like Qatar, can be described as a unitary system of autocracy, of tyranny if you prefer, with communism dressing where one person makes all the rules with the intent to eradicate poverty.

Each local government council produces representatives to form the national politburo who votes and confirms the intent of the set rules, policies, programs, laws from the autocrat.

Lynda: Like let there be light, and there is light. Everybody to school, and everyone gets education. One child policy and everybody follows. Religion is not a factor. Your religion in your heart. Tribe is not a factor. They seem beautiful and strident.

Laura (in mumbles): Like that one child policy… very bad!

Glenda: Laura! Girls of short memories.

President (trying not to lose ground): What's that?

Brett: Girls, let's leave it there.

Glenda: Excellency, nothing of importance.

All efforts to brush the one child policy aside from the attentive ears of the President failed as Mark, irked took it to another level.

Mark (his voice pitching): We cannot leave it there Mr. Brett. It's a profanation. It's an insult for our 'Kids must play' center. (with eyes fixed on Laura) Mezzi, Laura should come and assist in our 'Kids must play center'. That way she would be conscientious of the suffering, the plights of the kids and the willful unconscientiousness and wickedness of our African parents. Our destitute citizens who can't afford a meal per day are pumping plenty kids.

In Africa making children is an addiction. Equated to a noble addiction. Parenthood anywhere without parenting is a debilitating act and of abhorrent malevolent practice. Africans willfully don't want to broach this argument. Even though parents' relationship with their creed and greed is deeply personal, a societal terror does convince to obey the laws because there are consequences. Otherwise the real noble virtues that progressed society, that gave civilization, that gave freedom and liberty would systematically continue to remain in oblivion in Africa.

President: Laura, you can have as many kids as you want in as much as you can feed them, educate them, parent them. Just consider your own childhood. Has it been clement with you?

He takes a pause fixing Laura. Laura is slow to utter any word, refuging in a defiant silence.

President: Let's not digress yet. We will surely come back to it. Buzzo, please back to system of government.
Buzzo: Russia is a unitary system of autocracy, dictatorship if you want, tyranny with oligarchy code of conduct with electoral contest for a democracy connotation.
President: Buzzo, thank you. You have been an embodiment of encomium. Very brilliant. So now, are we ready to suggest what is good for us in Africa? All things being equal to the extent that no absolute external influence or threat to inform and condescend on our decisions?

The room creases into an eerie silence of a mental wrenching magnitude. Faces are in contortion of expressions. Expressions of expectant delight, regardless.
Expectedly, Mark is the first to brave the silence. He pierces. With expectation to defuse the eerie silence with his very pardonable youthful expression of exuberances.

Mark (almost in mumbles): Our monarchies (the Chiefs, the Obis, the Igwes, the Ezes, the Obas, the Emirs, the Sultans etc.) are ignorant and despotic and kleptomaniacs; our politicians are semi-literates and ignorant and arrogant and avaricious; our priests are semi-literates and arrogant and devious and debaucher; the masses are mostly un-educated, deplorables, destitutes, cowards. A combined bunch of irreprehensible, evil ignoble. We don't need any electoral contest. (raising his voice suddenly) Buzzo, you said it: Africa is primitive. You need educated mind to reason. To understand...how did you put it...yes to understand consensus of compromise.

Buzzo stood up and started applauding Mark. Everybody, including the President, joins in, applauding ponderously.

Mezzi lifts him off his seat and hoisted him on the table. Indeed, there is hope. If this young anagraphy can grapple with these lines of thinking, there is unalienable faith that future generations of Africa can decide for themselves and will stand up with their lives time and again, systematically defending their freedom against any tide of CIA, KGB, MOSSAD, M16, DGSE etc. type -terror and assassinations from within and without. Only to that extent of determination would they be respected; would they be left alone. They would not be dictated to. They would progress, develop their land and they would not be told to go back to infested lands of theirs. They would not be shot at as shooting targets. They would gain respect for themselves and of the others. Everybody settles back to positions. A reluctant silence returns.

President: Remarkable. Amazing. Gracious. Bright light in the tunnel. Glenda.

Glenda: Excellency I think I will yield my time to Buzzo. His self-consciousness is the more informed and the best capable.

Brett: Well said Glenda. I concur. I think we should let him synthesize and suggests what's good for us.

President: Well then, Buzzo to you the honor.

Buzzo: Excellency, I will try. It's been said that democracy goes with reason and autocracy goes with ignorance. So, if I may humbly suggest, given our ignorance of the mind, given our primitivity of the mind, lack of educated minds and mindset, and given the debilitating blunder of willful refusal to educate our minds to be able to recognize, confront and eradicate our stupidity of self-consciousness, I think we need just an illuminated mind. Or if you like, a visionary mind.

This might seem going against the western democracy as we know it. It might seem despotic. Just think of the western democracy as we live it here in Africa. Western democracy has never worked. It will never work. It has been easy to enslave and colonize Africa, have institutional racism and inflict spasm of Phobic-Neurosis and then Object Surrendering Permanence on Africa to self-enslave, self-colonize and institutionalize self-looting, disempower her descendants from generation to generation because of her self-consciousness of ignorance and primitivity, that is fed by her inherent hereditary hierarchic despotic tradition.

Glenda: Truth be said. Our tradition is inherently despotic.

Brett: Awfully so.

Excellency it's been said that democracy goes with reason and autocracy goes with ignorance. So, if I may humbly suggest, given our ignorance of the mind, given our primitivity of mind... I think we need just an illuminated mind. Or if you like a visionary mind...

...Western democracy has never worked. It will never work. It has been easy to enslave and colonize Africa, have institutional racism and inflict spasm of Phobic-Neurosis and then Object Surrendering Permanence on Africa to self-enslave, selfcolonize and institutionalize self-looting, disempower her descendants from generation to generation because of her self-consciousness of ignorance and primitivity, that is fed by her inherent hereditary hierarchic despotic tradition.

Buzzo: Africa therefore has seen the continuation of her naturally inherent despotism by the Western democracy. Western democracy in Africa is simply by despotism. Democracy of despotism. Now we need despotism of democracy. Democracy applied by benevolent illuminated despotism. Just like China. The reform of Africa's despotic tradition is the answer. Democracy of benevolent illuminated dictatorship.

Glenda (scanning the faces of her peers): Awesome! Cerebral!! I think we can't agree any less, huh folks?

There is a ponderous general consensus conveyed by their eloquent silent nods of approval. Buzzo badgers on under the eloquent admiring expectant intense stare of the President.

Africa therefore has seen the continuation of her naturally inherent despotism by the Western democracy. Western democracy in Africa is simply by despotism.
Democracy of despotism. Now we need despotism of democracy.
Democracy applied by benevolent illuminated despotism. Just like China. The reform of Africa's despotic tradition is the answer.
Democracy of benevolent illuminated dictatorship.

Buzzo: An illuminated benevolent dictatorship to dominate our environment making mandatory education, health care, current electricity, pipe borne water, food security, value-chaining our resources, discipline, accountability, rights and duties, punishment for erring, to mention but a few freedoms to power off. Until Africa produces a generation whose self-consciousness knows nothing but the above freedoms as their normalcy, not as a privilege, but an uncompromisable normalcy of way of life we should perhaps not broach the idea of Western democracy in Africa. For you can only give what you have. Or conversely contrive some other system tailored by us to fit us and suit our needs if we are indeed human beings.

At these affirmation Brett rises to his feet, applauding Buzzo. Everyone rises joining him. Buzzo pauses, acknowledging. Then the applause simmers and ceases. Buzzo continues.

> **Until Africa produces a generation whose self-consciousness knows nothing but the above freedoms as their normalcy, not as a privilege, but an uncompromisable, inalienable normalcy, a normalcy of way of life we should perhaps not broach the idea of Western democracy in Africa.**

Buzzo: As I was saying Africa needs a visionary-illuminated benevolent tyrant. An illuminated autocrat to lead a democratic unitary system of transition. A visionary autocrat on top of a democratic unitary system of technocrats. Our diaspora is not arid of such technocrats. Technocrats meritoriously selected within the diaspora of different professional litanies. Though most of them are human faeces out there- cyber thefting, impostors, worse than African home breeds. We trust a concerted sieving effort would find the pundits amidst.

Mezzi: Yeah Buzzo you said it.

Paraphrasing you:

"Any African diasporan who comes back to Africa to loot should have been born a lurid worm. Not a human being. Indeed, the privilege of civilization and the pleasures of civility of the West and the East alike did not pass through the selfconsciousness of such African diasporan. Just like my father and his likes. Their laziness and cowardice of their primitive self-consciousness could not fathom the hard work and its nobility required for civilization and civility. Overwhelmed by it they cannot produce answers and therefore are afraid of "WHY". So, they resign to the lone thing they are used to and capable of giving: filth and garbage"

Brett: Bravo Mezzi! Well coined. Yes, I agree. That's why we need an illuminated benevolent tyrant as our monarch, our president, our leader for prompt accountability.

Glenda: In fact, to that extent if tyranny means what China, Singapore, Qatar are doing, we definitely need somebody like your excellency to fit into that position.

Lynda: That would be utmost Love.

Brett: Indeed.

The president is deadpan. He voluptuously ignores their provocative stimulation. Mark makes it obvious to him.

Mark: Dad did you hear that?

> *A visionary-illuminated benevolent tyrant. An illuminated autocrat to lead a democratic unitary system of transition. A visionary autocrat on top of a democratic unitary system of technocrats. Our diaspora is not arid of such technocrats. Technocrats meritoriously selected within the diaspora of different professional litanies. Though most of them are human faeces out there- cyber thefting, impostors, worse than African home breeds. We trust a concerted sieving effort would find the pundits amidst.*

The President can't feign any more. They have him. He could not help but start blushing and protesting. To no avail, they consider him within the realm of Harriet Beecher Stowe's quote:

"Any mind that is capable of real sorrow is capable of good."

They ignore him and press on.

Gen WHY: Yes President! Yes, yes, yes, yes!

President: I am not hearing you. No, I am not hearing you. I am deaf. I need some rest.

Buzzo: Excellency, that's an understatement. Who else is better than you, my father? Resting and respite would be beautifully sublime after you would have taken us to the promised land.

Mezzi: Yes excellency. You are our Moses. Can you imagine what a delight of hope that would be? What a sublime legacy it would turn out to be? To be the man that lifted off Africa?

David: Dad, the man that lifted off Africa?

Brett: No! That would be belittling: the renaissance African that ever lived!

Mark: Dad indeed! You must give everybody education, healthcare, water, light, jobs and food. Even lobsters (winking at Brett) now. But most importantly give reason to the minds. The minds must be withered of primitivity. So, dad let's give it a try. Dad, there is no time to argue. You must be the exception to filth and garbage. Plaza Hill will bear us witness.

Everybody cracks up. The President does not cave in. The assault of petulance continues.

President: Power corrupts!

Mezzi: Excellency, and you are not arid of applying the breaks.

Buzzo: Correct, power without control is nothing.

Mezzi: Even Mark knows why love is feared so much.

Mark: Dad did you hear that? You've got love. Love trumps power.

Lynda: Yes! Indeed. You incarnate love!

Laura: We have love in you.

President: Okay, okay folks, let me think about it.

374

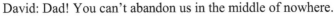
David: Dad! You can't abandon us in the middle of nowhere.
President: You must get groomed to take over.
Buzzo: Absolutely, yes. Who else will groom us?
President: Our alliance would!
Brett: Correct excellency!
President: It needs a period of seasoning.
Brett: Precisely the point Sir. Our alliance would need its seasoning period.
Laura: That's sacrosanct implicit.
Glenda: You taught us patience, perseverance, doggedness, tenacity to conquer. Time is essential…
Mark: Time essential dad. Our alliance is you. No heart breakings dad.
Glenda: Well said.
Mark: no heart-breakings. Excellency there are indeed no two ways about it. You are our Moses. You leading us to the promised land. That's a *conditio sine qua non.*
Gen WHY (yelling in unison) Our Moses! Our Moses!! Our Moses!!!
President (reluctantly conceding): That's okay with me. Folks, I am glad you all remember that Moses never entered the promised land!
Mark: He passed unto them the gift.
Glenda: Precisely, we need that gift from you.
President: Ok, deal. We will try together.

Now Gen WHY erupt in shouts and shrieks of joy that turn out short-lived: The President raises his hand in the air asking for silence. Silence is accorded.

President: It's going to come at two very stringent conditions.

Everybody fixes him with a delighted dread. Waiting for him to make the pronouncement.

President: Firstly, my tenure must be transitory, time-framed at least to the moment the alliance would have made a reliable formidable political class of you.
And secondly, your dedication and loyalty to duty of selfless service is imperative.
Gen WHY (in unison jumping out of their seats): Deal! Deal!! Deal!!!

They seize the room to a ponderous applause, giving consensus to the deal.

President (raising voice): Then let's get down to the business of governance.

The room settles gradually back to a reluctant silence and order.

375

President: Today, I will be dissolving our moribund government. Every local government is going to suggest two of theirs who they think are illuminated benevolent and honest enough to lead and represent them in making their cases. We pick one of them, the most qualified to form the politburo, in sum a working committee. Then together with the working committee we are going to have to appoint experts and professionals, in other words appoint technocrats (mainly from the diaspora) to administer individual government functions, policies, laws, rules, regulations and recommend legislations.

Are you all there?

Gen WHY (in unison): Yes!

President: Now that we have agreed on a political system, let's get finally into governance policies and then programs.

My first policy is a new form of governing alliance: we need a structured governing system of effective checks and balances. *The Gen WHY, Gen WHY and Gen WHY, you will be our shadow government forthwith.*

Gen WHY caught off guards, beyond their expectation from this sweeping unimaginable statement of absolute delight, go into spasm of shrieks and shouts and yelling and howling, in their approval.

The President lulls as he beams with smile watching them with pleasure, waiting for their chants to simmer down. Then the President reluctantly hints at continuing, they cup their mouths in disbelief, reluctantly settling back to silence.

President: You will effectively be involved in the plots, plans, programs, strategy, tendering process up to their adjudications, procurements, implementations, monitoring, commissioning, delivery and payments.

My first policy is a new form of governing alliance: we need a structured governing system of effective checks and balances. The Gen WHY, Gen WHY and Gen WHY, you will be our shadow government forthwith.
You will effectively be involved in the plans, programs, tendering process up to their adjudications, procurements, implementations, monitoring and delivery and payments.

Second, *all state-owned enterprises are abolished henceforth. Dead. They are abolished. Forbidden.*

Our macroeconomic investments are all geared towards and to give impetus to the private sector development. This is for a ripple continuous benefitting economic activities and development effect.

Third, *we need to quantify our mineral wealth, the crude oil, the platinum, the diamond, the gold, the emeralds, the sapphires, the tanzanite, the bauxite, the tantalite, the tin, the uranium, the columbite the iron ore, the rare earth, etc. etc. the list is infinite, of our continent Africa and put them on the stock exchange and have their Initial Public Offers (IPOs).*

With the IPOs we become a nation of stock trading through which monies are raised to develop, industrializing the mines and build our refinery infrastructures.

Fourth, *our agricultural produce like cocoa, palm kernel, cotton, coffee, tea, sheer butter, groundnuts, nuts, fruits, etc. etc. are going to stocks to raise money for their refineries and processing machines and packaging for local and international markets.*

Fifth, *18 months from now the ban on Africa's raw mineral resources and agriculture-alimentary products from exportation go into effect. Eighteen months give our partnership with qualified excellent corporate bodies world over the timeline to develop refineries and processing plants (the value chains) with energy independence, skilling of Africa's workforce within. We must be a producing nation.*

Sixth, *it's forbidden for Africans to have private bank accounts overseas. Foreign accounts can only be for corporate businesses and these business corporate accounts are to be monitored strictly by our central bank institution. Any flagrance would attract death penalty, summary execution.*

Seventh, *we as a people are instituting mutual funds and establishing mutual fund companies and funding them to guarantee the basic human dignity.*

The priests call it sowing of seed, you call it crowd funding and I call it mutual fund and they mean the same thing within the context of our intention. They are essential. Their end justifies their means. Mutual funds at two distinct levels– the "People's" mutual fund, we may also call it the 'basic care', the peoples mutual fund that will guarantee basic education for all, basic health care coverage for all, basic nutrition coverage for all, pensions for all our old beyond 70 years of age, and the second level the "Youths'" mutual fund, guarantees Gen WHY separation, autonomy to develop and progress themselves and their generation and beyond undeterred, in any case.

The eerie silence promptly got fragmented; Gen WHY at those words erupt into a clamor of uproar of yelling, shrieks, shouts that was amazing. An amazement that seemed honest, unfeigned of a ponderous delicious delightfulness. A delicious delightfulness that voluptuously, once again, spitted:

Gen WHY: Moses, Moses, Moses, Moses!

That unfeigned delicious delightfulness entwines standing up, separation and funding expressions into a trinity of existentialism. Funding is existential to separation as separation is to standing up. Each is a justification and hopefully would rein in hoped rewards of making captivity captive and a continent's pride at success forward.

They have been silently in a rapt attention, listening to the posits of the President. Their unsolicited reaction of clamor at the mention of "...guarantee Gen WHY separation... in any case" voluptuously underpins the ineluctability of their inalienable faith in separation. They are decided, but funding sustenance solution as the vehicle is the lone and present dangerous elusive enemy.

Now Buzzo raises his hand to speak, the crowd returns slowly to silence.

Buzzo: Excellency, pardon us but could you shade some light on your "Youths'" mutual fund please.

Mezzi: Yes, Excellency, we are orphaned by curiosity and thirsty of solution.

President: Cool. It needs some time. Let's try. Africa's population is about 1.35 billion but for convenience at calculation *Let's assume Africa's population to be 300 million people. And let's further assume 60% of the 300 million, about 180 million is the population of the youth of age bracket 1 day –35 yrs.* Mark (protesting): Dad a 35year old should not be a youth. What am I then?

Everybody breaks up laughing.

President: We will get to that details soon. Just be patient Mark.

The President pauses, scans their attentive faces and finding approval, he continues.

President: Brett what percentage do we have left?
Brett: 40% left, your excellency.
President: *Bravo. We have 40% left of the 300 million population. That's about 120 million that accounts for adults 36 years and above. In sum of a given African population of 300million we have 60% youths and 40% adults.*
He pauses again scanning their rapt faces.

President: Any questions?
They nod their heads "No." s
President: *Now the 60% youths are divided thus:*

30% in age bracket (1day-18) years and the 30% age (19–35) years brackets. In other words, we have 90 million youths within the age bracket (1day–18) years, who we can call "moronic" youths.

The remaining 90 million within the age bracket (19-35) years, who we can call "age of reason" youths.

And of this "age of reason" youths 30 million are unemployed.

Brett: Only? Excellency, we should be more than that.

President: You might be right. We are in Africa, a land arid of data. However, that seems to be a reasonable assumption. Let's not confuse it within the context of the sum total of 180 million youths. Bear in mind the moronic youths are not yet employable.

Mezzi: Genial. Absolutely right.

President: *So that leaves us with 60 million employed "age of reason" youths. And 30 million unemployed "age of reason" youths to take care of. Here the Gen WHY fit in.*

Buzzo: Excellency 30 million?

President: Buzzo yes. That's coming from the records of the graduating students for the past 15 years bracket matched against employed and non in the labor force.

Buzzo: Right from those who turned 20 from 19 till 35years of age.

Frank: Correct!

President: Are we there?

Then he pauses, scans their faces and finds them full of expectations. He continues.

President: *Of the 40% adults we have 5% above 70 years of age. The pensioners. So, we have 120 million adults of which 15 million are pensioners and 105 million are working. Employed.*

So, we have 105 million working adults and 15 million pensioners to take care of.

Finally, we have the stage set for our mutual fund concept.

Gen WHY expectations are pulsating, peaking, palpable. They are shifting in their seats, longing to hear the soothing dress of separation for independence and autonomy.

President: I need all of you mentally engaged. However, I call on Buzzo, Mark, Brett, Glenda on note taking for comparison after my concept input.

First and foremost, *let's go with the "basic care" mutual fund.* Basic care mutual fund is to take care of basic health care for all, basic education for all, basic children nutrition care at schools and for our destitutes and senior citizens, basic commutation of our moronic and unemployed age of reason Youths, basic pensions, affordable housing scheme, etc. etc.

Here is how.

Africa's average minimum wage is about 100 US Dollars per month. And we have about 80% of this group of the working adult of 105 million. The remaining 25 million working adults have rising salary scales. And accordingly, we are going to contribute to our "basic care" mutual funds thus:

Working pop.	Salary Scale/month	Funding/month	Amount
80,000,000.00	$100	$4	$320m
10,000,000.00	$(200-300)	$10	$100m
5,000,000.00	$(300-500)	$20	$100m
5,000,000.00	$(500-1000)	$50	$250m
2,000,000.00	$(1000-5000)	$100	$200m
2,000,000.00	$(5000-10,000)	$500	$1b
1,000,000.00	$(10,000 & >)	$1000	$1b

The President pauses, scanning their attentive faces; some are engaged in mental notes, others are scribbling. However, they are all listening hard. The President continues.

President: *So, we can see 80 million people with the minimum wage to survive one way or the other with their different professions and must each give $4 every month to mutual fund. That totals $320 million.*

You can see the 10 million lower middle-income class and $100 million mutual fund monthly contribution, 5 million low middle-income class, 5 million middle- income class, 2 million upper middle- income class, 2 million upmost middle- income class and the 1 million super rich.

The President pauses and then:

President: To make sure we are all on the same page, Mark what is the monthly mutual fund contribution of 5 million low middle-income class?
Mark: Uhm…5 million times 50… it's $250m.
President: No! Double check your notes. That's for 5 million of the middle-income class.
Mark: Yeah, sorry. It's $100m.
President: Lynda, what of 2 million upper middle-income class?
Lynda: $200m.
President: Any observations?

Glenda and Brett, their faces in frowning smirk, simultaneously raise their hands.

President: Glenda?
Glenda: Why can't we task the super-rich more?
Mezzi: We are not going to practice communism. It's still a unitary capitalism.

President: Correct Mezzi. They are going to have to pay their super taxes fair share regardless.

In the meantime, Brett has lowered his hand. There is assumed coincidence of intent of questions. President notices and calls him regardless.

President: Brett, what's the total monthly "basic care" mutual fund netted? Brett: $ 2.970 billion. And they are not going to the "men of God".

Everyone cracks up laughing.

President: Now, let's put that monthly amount to use. Brett can we give each of our 15 million pensioners one quarter of minimum wage every month as their minimum dignity care?
Brett: Beautiful, sublime thing sir. Majority are abandoned to selves and immune to hunger and humiliation. What a despicable spectacle.

And he started applauding. Others readily join him. Until it reluctantly slows and ceases.

President: *Can we give each of the 30 million "age of reason" unemployed Youths one quarter of the minimum wage every month with equal vigor?*
Brett*: That will be terrific. Twenty-five Dollars might seem nothing but it's mighty. Terrific for the psyche.*
President: Money is never enough for the ignoble poor. It's to shore them up psychologically. A feel of humanity. That puts them under pressure, never relenting with hard work and perseverance to get out of that sector and join workforce in no time.
Brett: I agree if there were jobs.
President: We are going to create plenty jobs in the next two years that you will never imagine. As we create plenty of jobs, they are going to enjoy commute care, education care, health care, nutrition care, skill acquisition care, etc. Bottomline:
a. We need 15 million multiplied by $25 or the sum of $375 million for our pensioners;
b. 30 million multiplied by $25 or the sum of $750 million for the "age of reason" unemployed youth. For a sum total of $1.125 billion.
So, Buzzo out of a total of $2.970billion of our 'basic care' mutual fund we are spending?
Buzzo: We are spending $1.125 billion
President: *So, we have $1.845 billion left to apportion to other basic cares areas and to mutual investing. And it's every month folks. We raise nearly $3 billion every month.*

They break in an unsolicited ponderous applause. An applause in amazement of shrieks, yelling and shouting.

President: And that's not all. *Now to "Youths'" mutual fund Now of the $180 million youths' family we have 90 million "age of reason" Youths. 60 million (20% of 300 million) are employed and 30 million (10% of 300 million) are unemployed but are receiving "basic care" mutual fund of $25. Naturally plus other 'basic care' benefits.*

> *Money is never enough for the ignoble poor. It's to shore them up psychologically. A feel of humanity. That puts them under pressure, never relenting with hard work and perseverance to get out of that sector and join workforce in no time.*

The President pauses and scans their faces fixing them hard in their eyes. They stand his stare.

President: That way, every one of the "age of reason" Youths, both employed and unemployed will fundraise the minimum wage contribution of $4 a month. Buzzo: Brilliant!
Glenda: This is amazing!
Frank: It's a real thing!
Mezzi: Excellent, amazing. This is it folks. Freedom!
David: What a creative mind dad. Finally, each with a testicular fortitude.
Laura: Beautiful! Even though they would have $21 left in their pockets.
Lynda: Laura, even so they have in addition all other basic cares like commuting care, health care, nutrition care, etc. as they undergo free retraining and skill acquisition exercise to position and qualify them to enter the work force on the jobs that are going to be created in the manufacturing, agriculture, value chain refineries and processing, technology hubs, and services like carpentry, tailoring, etc. sectors.
Mark: Awesome dad. Thank you. You just gifted us the power of surviving. We can now fully separate. No more Moses. You are dismissed.

Everybody cracks up.

President: Yes indeed. You really don't need anybody.

The President pauses, fixing Brett.
Brett seems transfixed by an assault of fear, anxiety and confusion. His face in expression of unutterable agony and sadness. An agony and sadness that seem to recall his life-anguish, life-shame, life-tribulation, life-

humiliation, life-rejection, harrowing pains, excruciating failures, griefs, grieving misery, sorrowing hopelessness, bleeding humiliation by faith in gratification of honesty, that seem finally all vanquished by incredulity? An incredulity that is too numb for excitement and too cold for optimism. He seems on the edge regardless.

The President notices. His companions notice and get curious with their mouths puckering "what the hell, he should be happiest."

President: Brett, what's the matter?
Brett: Excellency, I am numbed.
President: Hold your peace. We are yet to do the math.

Brett breaks down. He can no longer stand up to the whims and caprices of emotional contrast between his familiar and the exceptional. His familiar, excruciating life experience and the exceptional mutual fund powers of separation and freedom. He is overwhelmed by assault of spasm of ponderous tears and voluptuous sobbing.

Brett (finding his voice): Excellency, I am so sorry. But I can't believe this is happening.

He is readily comforted by Buzzo and Glenda sitting by his sides.
The President chagrined and heartbroken started applauding him.
The applause seemed of a sincere and unfeigned empathy.
The rest of Gen WHY readily join him in a ponderous standing applause.
A standing applause, which perpetuity withered and emptied him of tears. He seems pacified. Everybody takes back their seating positions. Gradual silence settles in the room.

President: *"Youths'" mutual fund stands to net $360 million per month.*
In a year you will have $4.32 billion. All this sum goes to Youths' mutual company investment Limited.
Isn't this quite a sum to fund separation and succeed by yourselves in case of force majeure?

Gen WHY erupt in uproar of shrieks and yelling and a hint at dancing.

President (reaches for his glass of water, raising it to Brett): For Brett to lobsters!

At this solicitous, inciteful and baiting remark, the Gen WHY roar anew in a voluptuous clamor of shouting and shrieks in response.
The President watches them in silence of such a delicious delight until the room settles to a reluctant composure and silence.

President: So, summarizing, we will guarantee $25 (which is one quarter of Africa's workers' minimum wage) per month to our 30 million pensioners and to our unemployed youths plus the totality of basic care needs. For their minimum human dignity.

So much so that all employed youths (20% of the 300 million) and unemployed youths (10% of the 300 million) are enabled in equal measure to fund $4 every month to "Youths'" mutual fund. This sum of $4.32 billion is the worst-case scenario because the good news is that it automatically becomes incremental with the goodwill of numerous moron youth with whatever they will and it can attract your peers of world youth over and donors like Bill Gates, Clinton, Oprah, Obama, Warren Buffet, Carter, Bush etc.

The money thus generated yearly is your mutual fund that goes to "Youths'" mutual company for investment portfolio. Investment portal for development. That would be your mutual separation, your medal of freedom and liberty if need be.

You will have so much money, so much money, so much employment, so much development, so much progress, so much well-being, so much wealth, so much overwhelmed with human dignity and happiness that you will become comparable to the state of Qatar and its likes.

Policy number eight: *Any grafting, cronyism, duping of sort, any cyber-theft, any cheating, stealing, any diversion of fund or monies or properties of any proportion, at any level–federal government, state government, local government, community associations, private group, churches, mosques, individuals–would attract death penalty. Immediate death penalty. Summary execution. Hanging and firing squad.*

We are a people of abject, low morality. We are absolutely dishonest. Absolute cheats. Absolute liars, absolute gluttons. Absolute kleptomaniacs. Absolute evil.

Absolutely stupid. Absolutely primitive. Tragically, willfully so!

Since we don't fear God, then we must absolutely have terror of society!

Ninth, *it is forbidden to live above your means. If you can't prove the source of your wealth you will be dispossessed, shamed and excommunicated by a badge of promulgated societal physical symbol like chopping off your left fingers, right arm, plucking off of an eye.*

Tenth, *all monarchies are from now abolished on our land. It is highly risible but of harrowing tragedy that a blind man should lead a herd of blind people. Our monarchy is blind, primitive, ignorant, immoral, retarded, paternal and despotic. A few people materially affluent and the many people materially wretched. This is Africa's monarchical hereditary gift. A gift of hollowness: a vacuity of vicious, despicable, hereditary despotism. Our alliance must bury despotism as it must sow reason. Reason unmakes ignorance. Reason makes it impossible for any mind to unknow knowledge. And knowledge owns individual sovereignty and spreads a suffrage system for their rights of representation. Freedom.*

Eleventh: *As we said, and we reiterate, all men of any religion, all "men of God" must be at least graduates in theology. Christian clergies, Muslim imams, African religion priests, etc. etc.*

They must preach the reality of the books. They cannot interpret, preaching willful falsehood to deviate, distort, coerce, confuse with the willful compulsive intention to debauch and pillage, humiliate, devastate and subdue the faithfuls and society.

Twelfth: *"Men of God" cannot have bank accounts. They should not own material properties nor properties in man. Their congregation shall own bank accounts and shall carter for their welfare. This offence is punishable by death penalty.*

It's high time they live with their inheritance in the Lord.

Africans pray too much. The Lord taught us to pray. In less than five minutes the Lord's prayer is said as Jesus taught us.

Just imagine the time, the man hour Africans subtract from the time-consuming hard work of enabling the brains in order to develop the self-consciousness in disturbing the Lord and more so praying without a plan, program or life goal!

Just imagine the hours spent in night vigil instead of curiosity, instead of reading, empowering the brain to do God's deeds!

Just imagine if God needs us. We need God and yet we willfully disobey God, we willfully are evil, willfully do evil in place of God's deeds to earn his heaven! Just imagine the hours spent in the church instead of resting to recoup for the week of hard work. Didn't God say rest on the seventh day?

No religions should be practiced out of their places of worship. Not in your offices. Not in government offices. Not in the parks. Not in any public places.

All religions preach love. In Africa, all religions practice hate. Too many Africans have a God problem. We ignore the golden rule: "Do unto others …", as we ignore the great commandments: "Love God" and "Love thy neighbor…"

All theologies might come from the same book, but they seem not to hold equal truth and standard. Not only do we have white God versus black God, white Jesus versus black Jesus from without, we have God of the master versus God of the masses from within, here in Africa homeland. Two different Gods in Africa! Everybody studies the same theology, but wound up praying to different Gods. One of wealth, lawlessness, punishment, affluence. The other, of suffering, misery, condemnation, endurance and faith in hope of mystery.

All theologies might come from the same book, but they seem not to hold equal truth. Not only do we have white God versus black God, white Jesus versus black Jesus from without, we have God of the master versus God of the masses from within, here in Africa …

> *...homeland. Two different Gods in Africa! Everybody study the same theology, but wound up praying to different Gods. One of wealth, lawlessness, punishment, affluent. The other, of suffering, misery, condemnation, endurance and faith in hope mystery.*

The President now pauses, scanning their faces swallowed in a dense and ponderous silence. A silence arid of any hint of equivocations. Then he continues.

President: Great Jesus! What a disappointment you have in men. What a desecration, men are capable unto thine bible of love and equality for all. They were not faithful then; they are not now. We are why you regretted ponderously creating man.

It has been said that religion is the opium of the poor masses.

Like the mystery of creation, the mystery of faith in an unknown heaven is ponderously a masterstroke. Mysterious. Maybe that's truly why there is God. This mystery sticks with the poor, the vulnerable, the disadvantaged. It seems as easier to the masses in tribulation as it seems not right in their misery.

Regardless, our alliance should make the love of building heaven on this earth the opium, the religion of the African masses. Make our faith in this palpable reality the lone prerequisite to accede to Lord's eternal heaven.

That is truly the Lord's "love thy neighbor" great commandment. That commandment is not any easier but it's much the right thing.

Thirteenth policy: *We must have a collective, structured edifice for our dears called to the glory of after-life. Just like we have a collective, structured worship places to glorify God in life. We will build cemeteries to host the caskets of the souls of our departed to God. A collective dignifying soave place. A place of wreath to honor them, to communicate with them, to reflect with them, to meditate with them and, a place of intercession, a place for soul searching and solace and answers.*

This will serve other multiple purposes besides.

Mezzi (interjects applauding): Bravo Excellency. Genial. Absolutely genial.

Mark: Yes pop! I love it. Those beautiful flowers. We can visit them, give those living ghosts, flowers, play with them. As they have and perform overseas.

The field Gen WHY are lost at this theme. They have silence of such a minacious dread: Africans build mysteries and mythologies around their dead.

But after what seemed a rapid schooling and sharing of teachings and thoughts, using the phone to swallow answers of cemetery morphologies and typologies, the entire Gen WHY crack up. They seem all to be in amazement of accord that is expressing *"what a twisted place Africa is. What a risible, primitive people. You don't celebrate death, you mourn death. You don't mourn life, you celebrate life,"* and "cemeteries are beautiful with these wreaths that confer humane face and hope and even the beauty of dying and of after-life." At least palpable here on earth.

President (elated): *Cemeteries would truly lay our dead to rest for the passage in the shortest time possible. This in itself would ban the deplorable, despicable celebrations, feasting, eliminates idiotic indebtedness and emotional blackmail of fear, of obligation and of guilt manipulations around our defuncts.*

As it would, more importantly, free the land from our ponderous, irrational, emotional attachments and lease or buy them for:
a. *Development and elevation of our communities to sub-urban precincts;*
b. *Mechanized farming with rippling beneficial consequences.*
c. *Jobs through value- chains and processing activities.*

Gen WHY break out in a howling spasm of ponderous approval. This will truly fasttrack development while stemming migration and at the same time improve greatly an overt and overwhelming life quality.

Meanwhile the President suddenly brings his stare trading them amongst the three females of Gen WHY–Glenda, Lynda, Laura.

Everyone notices and creases into curiosity. An immediate silence settles in the room.

President: All of you know what the acronym FGM is?
Gen WHY (ponderously in unison): Yeah, excellency.
President: Lynda, what's the full meaning of that acronym?
Lynda: Female Genital Mutilation.
President: Brava! And you all know what infibulation is?
Gen WHY (voluptuously in unison): Yessssssssssssssss!
President: FGM and Infibulation bring us to our fourteenth policy: *these atrocious, vicious, useless, primitive practices of unutterable pain, violence, violation, assault, humiliation and life-deprivation and life-sadness are outlawed.*

An immediate spasm of amazement breaks out among Gen WHY. It's a competing amazement of incredulity, joy, happiness and delight.

President: *How can twenty first century Africa deliberately cut the female genitalia and suture the vulva just to prevent sexual intercourse and deny pleasure ordained by nature?*
It is an offence on our land and any flagrant abuse is punishable by death penalty.

The strength of incredulity creases the three-female crowd of Gen WHY into an overwhelm of emotions: they are stilled and too numbed for delightfulness. They are conspicuously-ponderously fighting back tears. Now the tears are streaming on their faces. An ocean of sorrowing tears of grieving shame that can never atone or appease or repair the memory of unutterable viciousness, violation, assault, hurtfulness, hatefulness, humiliation, life-deprivation of the victims at FGM and infibulation. An inconsolable, unspeakable sadness and shame indeed. Everyone including the President notices.

President (started applauding): Please a standing applause to our mother earth.

Every Gen WHY rises to a ponderous, voluptuous applause and embraces of ponderous solidarity and solace.

President: *Our fifteenth policy would be a scouring and peremptory child protection, and prohibition of child marriage on our land henceforth.*

This drew out an instant clamor of shouting, shrieks and yelling among Gen WHY. Mezzi and Mark could not contain their delight at spasm of joy: they jumped atop their tables hugging each other in a dance move. Not done yet, they jump down reaching and embracing the President. What seemed an interminable embrace that surprised and numbed and silenced everyone ensued.
A long eerie hug that mitigated the shame, the horror, the guilt they have to deal with every day at their "children must play center." An embrace that lifted their hearts enfolded with appall, dejection, tribulation, sorrow and misery on the African children's scape but inspires hope of reward in triumph to their groggy endurance, perseverance and fortitude.

Now suddenly Mezzi disengages from the President, forcing Mark to do the same with equal vigor. And we notice that their faces, overwhelmed with spasm of emotions, are streaming with tears.
Gen WHY understand and immediately break out in an astounding ponderous, voluptuous applause as the they walk back to their seats.
The President joins in, in the long applause.
As they take their seats the President re-engages the issue.

President: What beautiful minds we have in these kids. We are very lucky. They are a blessing to humanity. *Indeed, every child must be protected. It will be an unforgivable crime to find on our land any hint of child labor again and child marriage. They must be fed. They must be*

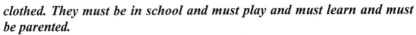

clothed. They must be in school and must play and must learn and must be parented.

Mark and Mezzi (in unison): Yeaaaahhhhh!

Mezzi (excitedly): What would be the punishment for non-compliance, excellency?

President*: The Punishment for abandonment, child labor, lack of parenting or for combination of all? What do you think, folks?*

Their faces crease into contorted, solicitous frowns. A prolonged, ponderous solicitous, frown withered of any answers. The President continues in their gap.

President: I agree, there are no easy answers. Justice should not just be punishment; it is reform. The arduous task of reforming a people. A culture. *They would have life in prison with hard labor. Their hard labor would pay the states' expenses on their kids.*

Brett: Even though they have already committed these crimes out of ignorance and primitivity of the mind?

President: Excellent observation, Brett. It is going forward from today.

We have many of our children already abandoned, in child labor and economic slavery prowling the streets. The state is going to take care of them.

But nine months from today, any fresh flagrant abuse or violation is life in prison with hard labor.

Mezzi: Yes! Impeccable.

Mark: Beautiful.

Glenda: That would help a lot.

Brett: Indeed, it should tremendously curb this awful, reprehensible practice.

President: Strictly entwined to child protection brings us to our next policy approach, our sixteenth*: planned parenthood!*

Gen WHY go ecstatic. An ecstasy of competing rapture, exaltation, transport and raptus. Their venting of emotions is uncontainable. The President watches them silently expressing delight until the room settles to a gradual reluctant silence.

President: *This idea that men and women of Africa just pump out a number of kids they cannot take care of or don't take care of or the both combined is ponderously, irrationally criminal.*

Now a cloud of competing expressions settles in the room: the line is drawn between the agreeables and disagreeables. Buzzo, Mezzi, Mark, David, Brett and Glenda erupt in a vigorous applause. The rest of Gen WHY are watching in silence, their faces in frowns of conflicting expressions of skepticism, doubts, numbness, forlorn, and appall.

President notices and reading the thoughts of the disagreeable, he retorts, irked, raising his voice.

President: Wait, wait, wait a minute...some of you want planned parenthood and unlimited number of kids at the same time? Really?

The air instantly turns taut of such a menacing dread. There seems to be an assault of fear and air of condescension. Words are not proffered. There is an eerie silence. All eyes are trained on the disagreeables, who are wearing distorted frowns of defensive mechanism.

The President regardless, lurches into an audacious critical analysis and whim of such a dreadful delight.

President: I have nothing at stake. The youths have everything at stake. You want to succeed en masse? Don't you?

Gen WHY (finding their voices): Yes!

President: *Now let's do some critical reasoning. Pumping children you cannot take care of is criminal. It's one of the greatest scourge, second to our laziness, and then to our stupidity to our development. Here again the African culture traumatizes us, socializing us to the willful hypocrisy of the easier way instead of the right way.*

The right way is love. If you truly love kids, make ones you ought to take care of. You don't want to see any child a destitute. More so yours that nature obliges you to love and take care of.

Any nation where children outpace development and resources is doomed.

That's part of our dilemma.

We may not want the one-child solution of the Chinese.

We may not want the rational integrity solution of the West.

With equal vigor we should reject our solution of emotional-irrational debauchery. Emotional debauchery that is victim of our cultural principle of emotional blackmail. Where use and costume deploy coercion, fear, motherhood, fatherhood, obligations and guilts to manipulate you to pump out kids without asking the 'tough love' question "mother, father, sister, brother, my friends, inlaws: who and what takes care of the kids?"

He pauses scanning their faces and finds encouragement: the spite of skepticisms and doubt seem crushed. Faces are wrapped in humble expectations.

President: Majority of Africans are interested in everything and committed to nothing. We want to be everywhere but nowhere.

We want good life but not committed to work.

African fathers are interested in fatherhood but a few are committed to it.

African mothers are interested in motherhood but are committed to its excruciating suffering from diligent-delinquent African males' and fathers' willful laziness, cringing cowardice and willful abandonment of chores and responsibilities and of its tribulations and humiliations and desperations and misery.

Bottomline: children are victims.

Within the eerie stilled silence, he pauses and scans the attentive, listening, expectant faces of Gen WHY. And with a tone of voice that conveyed a finality of determination that warned and in a gesture that prohibited, he sentenced:

President: Fatherhood and motherhood or if you wish, fertility, must equate ability of individual resources, availability of emotional, rational, psychological, physical resources to provide and parent any number of kids you pump out.

Buzzo: Excellency, ability of individual resources is not enough deterrent. Kids are costly to parents and to any society. And for our kids to compete and succeed out there, they need quality upbringing.

President: Indeed, even to the extent of having the above-mentioned resources, we can't pump out indiscriminate number of kids. I agree totally.

Glenda: There must be a stringent policy and punishment, otherwise, we won't get out of our misery.

Brett: I agree. We need to make a choice, however difficult, sensitive and excruciating to our desires of heart.

David: Like the one child policy of China?

Laura: That is sheer wickedness for the Africanness in us.

Mezzi: Indeed, any and every Africanness in us that jeopardizes, humiliates, impedes, retrogresses should be discarded.

Mark: Indeed, that's why Gen WHY are here to stay. Dad common make the policy statement.

President: Son, it's a tough one.

Majority of Africans are interested in everything and committed to nothing.
We want to be everywhere but nowhere.
We want good life but not committed to work.
African fathers are interested in fatherhood but a few are committed to it.
African mothers are interested in motherhood but is committed to its excruciating suffering from diligent-delinquent African males' and fathers' willful laziness, cringing cowardice and abandonment of chores and of its tribulations and humiliations and desperations and misery. Bottomline: children are victims.

Buzzo: Indeed, it's a tough one so much so that the Chinese, to maintain one child policy, suppressed lives and imprisoned parents in flagrance…

Glenda: But we all see where China is today and where it is headed to, tearing at progress and at honor and at dignity for its people.

Brett: We just can't have it both ways. I think the most unutterable shame for any parents to bear should be to see their kids in the bondage of their own making.

Buzzo: Indeed, Africans are arid and withered of shame. We must change that at the cost of having to grapple with Chinese-like one child policy.

Lynda: Common, let's not be so mean to motherhood: at least two to three children.

Laura: Two children at least hoping that both are not females.

Every agreeable crack up. Underpinning a ponderous competing expression of elation and resigned despondency. President notices and seizes on the reality.

President: So, Gen WHY, our sixteenth policy is two-child planned parenthood?

Brett: Excellency, as I said earlier on, we can't have it both ways. We are only digging our graves. We will not succeed if we go into the mistake of having kids.

Buzzo: Bravo Brett. Well said. Planned parenthood, two-child policy will be the premium, the way forward after the day we succeed in having our backs first.

Lynda: Having our backs first?

Buzzo: Absolutely yes. No children until we have our backs first. Otherwise unfathomable failure and disappointment for our descendants would this time be coming willfully from us.

The underlying truth sent shivers down their spine. They are assailed by unutterable spasm of competing ponderous confabulations with peculiar scrutiny posited on their female counterparts. Glenda understands and her voice pierces.

Glenda: It makes a lot of sense.

Laura: It makes a lot of sense to take away our rights?

Glenda: It makes a lot of sense our duty to protect that right.

Brett: Well coined Glenda. My childhood was indeed terrible. It's abjectly terrifying to think of any kid without having my back first. I forbid it in its entirety.

Lynda (fighting back tears): So was mine too.

Mezzi: It's even more terrifying and heartbreaking and disconcerting to continue having a landscape, African landscape cynically-willfully littered with orphaned kids.

President (assailed by unalterable chagrin): Africa has been grappling with this willful mistake. No gainsaying that Africa has been in the business of making kids as a respite. Kids outpace resources. So, you need to look yourselves inside out and make this existential hard choice if really you want to heal the Black kind.

Buzzo: Well said Excellency: The existential hard Choice. To heal Black kind Gen WHY must make the existential hard choice for an ultimate sacrifice. We the Gen WHY must have sacrifice as our core value and valor and love. Gen WHY must elevate to the valor of Paused Parenthood. To the suffix '-PP.'

Now the room, seized by the aura of fascination with expectation of the usual pungent extemporaneous truth from their hero Buzzo creases into an eerie silence of rapt attention. They are listening hard.

Buzzo: I am sorry if I must bore you by repeating the obvious. Our self-consciousness mindsets must resolutely, unwaveringly, undauntingly sacrifice their today with its fleeting comfort and happiness temporariness and its illusive dignity – sacrifice their comfort and happiness of looted money of their homes, sacrifice their comfort and happiness of their poverty and misery and laziness and cowardice, sacrifice their comfort and happiness in complacency of misery and dehumanization, sacrifice the comfort and happiness of their obsequiousness and subservience and servility to despotic tradition of their Politicalcraft, of their Monarchycraft, of their Priestcraft , etc., – for their tomorrow with its happiness permanency and dignity.

Gen WHY (the agreeable, applauding): Yes!

Buzzo: Black kind Gen WHY must evolve to Gen WHY-PP. Black kind Gen WHY-PP must recognize the urgency of the towering necessity of having our own backs, by ourselves first above everything else. To heal Black kind, Black kind Gen WHY-PP must sacrifice, must pause parenthood to create our economic and wealth base, value-chain Africa's resources, create our freedoms, dominating our environment, obliterating our filths and garbage in order to "… contribute something mankind can enjoy" before making children. By so doing, have our backs and the backs of the generations of our descendants, empowering them ad infinitum. Indeed, to heal, the Black kind Gen WHY-PP must sacrifice to build its wealth base, dominate its environment before making children. It must sacrifice ultimately' pausing motherhood and fatherhood until it creates its economic and wealth base. It must at prior have its own back and be able to have the back of its Black kind descendants and endure its generation after generation. Gen WHY to Gen WHY-PP is the conditio sine qua non.

Gen WHY concur and rise to a standing ovation: Yes, yes, yes!

Then it simmers and ceases.

Buzzo: If we must succeed and heal! And paraphrasing Lori Deschene: *"Practice the pause. Pause before our humiliation. Pause before our tribulation. Pause before our filth and garbage. Pause before our misery. Pause before our enslavement. Pause before our orphaned children. Pause before outpaced resources by Africa's children. Pause making children. Pause parenthood. Pause have your backs."*

President: (in a subdued voice almost in soliloquy): Well coined Buzzo. Bravo.

Glenda: Paused parenthood! It makes a lot of sense if we must succeed.

Laura (fighting back tears): So, we are implicitly saying good bye to motherhood?

Brett: What a question. It's an obvious no! But paused until we have our backs. You want to be a mother if you don't have your back first?

Lynda (in tears): As painful as pausing motherhood is going to be, I agree it's a conditio sine qua non to succeed and have our backs and then activate parenthood and have the backs of our descendants.

Black kind Gen WHY must evolve to Gen WHY-PP. Black kind Gen WHY-PP must recognize the urgency of the towering necessity of having our own backs, by ourselves first above everything else. To heal Black kind, Black kind Gen WHY-PP must sacrifice, pausing parenthood to create our economic and wealth base, value-chain Africa's resources, create our freedoms, dominating our environment, obliterating our filths and garbage in order to "... contribute something mankind can enjoy" before making children. By so doing have our backs and the backs of the generations of our descendants, empowering them ad infinitum.

It's indeed a moment of heart brokenness. There is a general assault of spasm of a sorrowing grief. So much so that even the agreeable diehard proponents and the silent disagreeable majority alike gave way to their emotions of empathy and solicitude. Everyone is fighting back tears. Lynda and Laura hug each other, profusely crying. Glenda reaches out consoling them.

President (moved, reassuringly): We are witnessing the display of the highest passion of patriotism anywhere. *Your self-abnegation for generation of your descendants, your self-abasement for the absolution of the sins of generations of your progenitors of the Black kind is absolutely sublime. The luxury of your self-consciousness at this courage of sacrifice is beyond astonishment. Y*ou are going to succeed. Your self-consciousness is so ruthlessly honest, ferociously braving, unwaveringly resolute. You will surely break the jinx, dominating Africa's perennial vicious cycle of stupidity and misery and disempowerment of her descendants.

So, Gen WHY, in sum here, today you make solemn the axiom that your generation, the Gen WHY and generations of your descendants will evolve into Generation pause parenthood, the Gen WHY-PP, in order to have your backs before fatherhood and motherhood. And even so, that fatherhood and motherhood must be guarded by the amendment of our sixteenth policy of two-child planned parenthood?

Laura (recovered): Yes! No going back. We must succeed!

Lynda (still in sobs): We must go ahead with this passion. No going back.

Everybody, somewhat relieved but with palpable competing and conflicting emotions, rises to a deafening applause directed at Laura and Lynda.

Glenda: Moving forward excellency, let's get to the laws and punishment! Sir, what would be the punishment for any infringement of the future two-child policy?

President: Imprisonable offence?

Glenda: Sir, prison terms are not enough deterrence. Hard labor in the camps is not enough. Death penalty is way out.

President: Castration?

At the mention of the word, castration, everybody recoils, sinking deeper into their seats. It seems they are suddenly forced into the realization of their intimacy and its sacredness. Their manhood and womanhood and their fertility openly attacked. The thought and terror of the violence, its violation, desecration, profanation got them no doubt reeling and beat their spite into appall, bewilderment and consternation and doubt.

The President understands their eloquent countenance.

President: The theme is without doubt sensitive. You want time out on it to let you ponder more?

Glenda: No excellency. Castration would make us responsible men and women to abide by two-child policy.

The voice of Glenda, that female voice, withered everybody of their assault of spasm of anguish. It gave them courage and catapulted them out of bewilderment, consternation and fear and doubt. It brought them back into the stark reality of their focus: take Africa out of misery. Indeed, they find their voices.

Lynda: Yeah, it will bring much sanity to our funky asses and brains.

Brett: Excellency, we are fine. We must make that hard choice.

Mezzi (in a spasm of incitement): Captivity captive?

Mark: Yeaaaaaaaaaah!

Mezzi: Renaissance credo, standing up?

Laura: Excellency, let's march ahead.

President: *Every woman not more than two kids. Single or married.*

In giving a human face, fairness and effectiveness to this policy, you are going to have to choose amongst the most effective method of contraception out there: combined pills, diaphragm or cap, female condoms, implant, injection, intrauterine devices (IUDs), male condoms, natural family planning, progestogen-only pills, vaginal rings down to the extreme of feminine sterilization and male vasectomy.

There are lots of them out there and anyone you choose will be borne by the state within our basic health care effort.

In summary you will be subjected to castration–forced female sterilization and male vasectomy if you fall within any of the following categories:

1.   A teenager getting pregnant;
2.   The teenage boy or man who impregnates;
3.   A single woman getting pregnant without a job first and a roof;
4.   None of the couple has a job before pregnancy of the female partner;
5.   You make two kids without providing a two-bedroom shelter pre-birth;
6.   You impregnate a woman and renege and abandon her and the kid;
7.   Any proven case of rape;
8.   Any man and woman of any family that does a third kid from one woman.
9.   Each woman of any polygamous home must not have more than two kids.
10. Each man with more than one wife who does not provide a two-bedroom apartment and care and full parenting to each of the wives with their two kids.

These categories will meet castration, hard labor or fines of $20,000 to the state coffers for the cost the state would bear for the fundamental basic cares - education, health, nutrition, etc. etc. of each kid.

These seem to meet everybody's approval. Their facial expressions relaxed, they are enwrapped in crucial mental notes and evaluation within an eerie silence when the subconscious expected voice of Mark pierces.

Mark: Dad, I am beginning to disagree with this policy. You mean I can't even kiss my princess charming anymore…at my fourteen years of age I could be castrated?

Everybody cracks up, reeling with laughter.

President: Sure son, you will be castrated if you don't kiss with your free condoms.

Now everybody cracks up ponderously at the President's humorous retort.

Mark (to his companions): It serves the big boys and girls right to stay in your clothes.

Glenda: I think so. Look at so many teenagers married away to men thrice their ages. Men arid of conscience, capable of unutterable violation of age of innocence.

Mezzi: This evil is mainly a black race thing. Teenagers as young as 12 years getting impregnated and abandoned to their fate in every black community. Look at our African parents, so primitive that they find pride in owning properties in their teenage daughters and sons, sending the one off for prostitution, another for marriage and another for child labor, the other for cyber thefting, drug peddling, scamming and menial jobs....

Buzzo: They don't even broach the argument. Their willful blindness, willful hypocrisy, willful taboos to this debilitating malaise are a normalcy.

Lynda: Indeed, sterilization will rein in to a large extent, this drab of our progress. I sincerely love it.

Laura: Excellency, what if my eventual two kids come out females or males?

President: I am glad you brought that up. You know who Bill Gates is, who President Clinton is, who President Obama is, who the Pope is?

Laura: Yes Excellency. They are famous people. They can afford anything.

President: Brava! These are all the most powerful men on earth. Bill Gates, one of the richest men; any American president is the most powerful on earth; the Pope the most powerful religious leader. None has more than two kids. In fact, the Pope has none. And those other kids are preciously females.

Laura: Quality girls to continue life.

Look at so many teenagers married away to men thrice their ages. Men arid of conscience, capable of unutterable violation of age of innocence.
This evil is mainly a black race thing. Teenagers as young as 12 years getting impregnated and abandoned to their fate in every black community. Look at our African parents, so primitive that they find pride in owning properties in their teenage daughters and sons, sending the one off for prostitution and child labor, the other for cyber thefting, drug peddling, scamming and menial jobs....

President: You just hit the nail: "quality girls." Life is about quality and not quantity. Rich minds make fewer kids and grapple with time to parent them properly. Poor African minds make plenty kids and watch them in misery.

Lynda: They are in the developed world. Advanced minds.

President: Advanced minds. Developed world. If those are the tricks and the magics, let's then advance our minds and develop our world with equal vigor. Let's knock off our primitivity and the consequent mind poverty.

Mezzi: Excellency, one more thing. There is so much rape on this land, there is so much rape that they go undenounced, unreported and hidden and of course unpunished. Unreported for fear of stereotype and being singled out as unworthy for marriage. How do we deal with recognition and identification of rape in order to confront, punish and eradicate?

President: It's a plaque. Sometimes you think that a black man and a black woman are crazed with lust. You wonder if it is the taboo, the hypocrisy of our culture or the complicity and complacency of the lust that tolerate, accept and hide such a heinous, ruinous and debilitating crime. For now, …

Mezzi (interjecting forcefully): President I am glad you mentioned *"crazed with lust."* Those are same exact words hurled at me by my best friend that derided and confused me. And I hoped to find the answers on the African landscape but to no avail. Here I can hardly see couples, young and old indistinctly, holding hands, kissing, in manifestation of affection, of genteel affectations of intimacy and yet there are so many kids.

Everybody's emotion gave way to a voluptuous ponderous laughter. A laughter enwrapped in societal complicit complacency at omerta of intimacy. A laughter entrapped in Africa's tradition of unfathomable code of amorous inhibition.

President (drawling on his laughter): Young man, generally in Africa there are no preambles, no overtures. No love overtures. Marriages are generally arranged without consents. Without consents and consensus of the consorts. We confide in the fate of the choice, the indisputable choice of despotism of our parents on us. For my generation and generations before me this tradition had this hold over us.

Buzzo: That explains it.

President: That explains "crazed with lust"?

Buzzo: Traditional inhibition of any expression of romantic preambles, any prelude of affection, any overtures, any amorous premise to sexual congress. And like everything else in Africa that tradition remains perpetuated to this day.

President: That was precisely the case for my generation.

Buzzo: *So, you were left with guarded uncouth preambles of variegated overtures in the forms of harassment, vulgar words, physical*

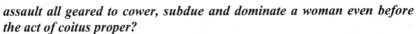

assault all geared to cower, subdue and dominate a woman even before the act of coitus proper?

President (ponderously chagrined*) Appallingly yes. The tradition has never held women to any esteem. Women are simply seen as object of sex, of reproduction and of servitude.*

Buzzo: Yeah, just like everything else, not for the substance. Not for substance of the woman. Africa's self-consciousness is crazed with lust for the cosmetic, for the aesthetic, for the conformity, for the sign, for the superficial. Not for the signified. Not for the substance.

Mezzi: And since every female is naturally endowed with curves and every black woman is exceptionally endowed with prominent, pronounced curves that make them physically more attractive, more appealing and more provocative to the senses of the male hormone...

Buzzo: That, the curves and not the substance of who wears the curves alongside African traditional and cultural validation of ravishment prompt their culturally inhibited testosterones into libidinal overdrive. And since everyman is endowed with tenacious stronger muscles than the female, their libidinal overdrive luxates into "crazed with lust" and it hedges in, expressing violent overtures as a prelude to forced sexual congress on the woman. *An unutterable depraving assault to dominate and possess the woman. Her freedom is trampled and obliterated by African tradition. She comes out physically and psychologically humiliated and violated and confused and dejected and traumatized. The man comes out in validated smugness.*

Mezzi*: A rape.*

President: With the candor of hindsight it's a rape. A willful rape framed by a vicious complicit smugness of African tradition and African male.

Glenda: Worse than a rape: it's dehumanization with unutterable vicious callousness.

Lynda: African men are really sick and sickening. Excellency it's still happening amidst young couples as we speak.

Brett: Growing up in the village it was commonplace.

Glenda: Even right here in our so-called city.

Brett: I have witnessed time and again these lazy husbands and fathers who sit out all day in the village square loafing, beat up their wives who has just come back from the chores of fetching water, or firewood or from the market, then they order them inside their huts and houses only as romantic preamble for forced sexual congress.

Lynda: In fact, Africa is depraved. A continent with unutterable infirmity.

Glenda: Yes, unfathomably depraved. What a way to appraise and reward an African woman who farms, fetches water, fetches firewood, does grocery, cooks, feeds the family, bears children, takes care of them.

Mezzi: These are unutterable sick patients in our midst. Africa is really sad. The tradition is really craven. Elsewhere men, real men are in control of their testosterone. Their self-consciousness respect and protect and dignify their women.

Buzzo: Real tradition and culture evolves to have men build urbanized houses, electrify the houses, pump potable water into the houses, pump cooking gas into the houses, help do groceries for the houses, provide parks and gardens for the household's outdoor respites, express appreciation through bouquet of flowers and holidays…

Glenda: Those are real men. Real men dominate their filths and garbage. Protect their females, give dignity to their family and instead our craven tradition teaches our men the art of laziness and cowardice and validates them to assault and traumatize women. And they willfully, viciously assault. Crazed with lust with the right to assault, validated by a tradition. We simply live in perdition.

Lynda: What a tradition huh? A tradition where the majority of men pride themselves for idling in the shades of trees and not providing shelter for the woman, for not doing the cooking, for the woman doing the cooking, for not providing cooking gas in the kitchen, for the woman fetching fire wood, for not providing pumping water in the homes, for the woman fetching the water from the streams.

Mezzi: Yeah so much so that instead of dominating our filths and garbage their crazed testosterone dominate women. Always the easy way. Crazy, lazy, sickening cowards only capable of sitting under the trees 24/7.

Buzzo: In your opinions why haven't African women reacted, rioted against this age- long condemnation?

Glenda: For pure and abject masochism.

Buzzo: That's punctilious like a scalpel. *Sin of cringing masochism. A child bearing sin of masochism and child rearing self-abasement surrendering permanence for self-absolution cynicism.*

Mezzi: A combined male's and female's unutterable debasing self-consciousness within the realm of Africa's perdition. Africa within the realm of the Devil's abode.

Buzzo: Excellency my second mind boggling question is why would African women marry these unreal, loafing, lazy, coward, cheating, condescending ignorant African patriarchal men?

President: You already phrased the answer. *Africa is a patriarchal realm, where even an inanimate wall that happens to wear the badge of a male organ is a man. And African woman is expected, and even worse is forced by patriarchal despotic tradition to marry this inanimate wall with the badge of a male organ. Or face patriarchal ostracization and the stigma of a prostitute.*

Buzzo: God forsaken cowards. God forsaken misogynic culture and tradition.

Brett: Real culture and tradition dominate their environment with freedoms with progress and with development for their women and their descendants.

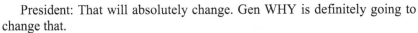
President: That will absolutely change. Gen WHY is definitely going to change that.

Mark (face in contorted disapproval): Dad this "crazed with lust" is a crazy rapist.

Everybody cracks up. Mark ignores them and badgers on.

Mark: Yes dad. Dad even though I have never seen you beat mum, even so you have to do something about this rapist.

President: Yes, I agree totally. First and foremost, our tradition of violence – physical and psychological – on women is forbidden and punishable by law forthwith.

Mark: Great. That's not enough dad.

President: We need to be confronting, identifying and punishing rapists through castration of the actors in order to dissuade them and protect our women, appraising their heroism in their battle of this heinous assault, rehabilitating them in order to eradicate it totally. We hope this first step, will brave the victims into defiance and denouncement.

Glenda: It will help a lot from a psychological standpoint…

Buzzo: And that matters ponderously.

Glenda: To know that it's no more a thing of shame. You have been assaulted and humiliated and you can make recourse. There is a law and there is punishment. You are empowered to denounce for justice and punishment. And avoid reoccurrence.

Laura: Yet, Excellency, that would not be enough deterrence against recurrence, protecting the girls from rape and curb the malaise.

David: Dad, we want annihilation of rape malaise.

Mark: Correct!

Buzzo: I think a rapist needs castration plus a prison term and badge of societal punishment symbol. A rapist destroys the other's life, or at the very best gifts the victim a badge of societal disgrace. And so, the rapist should be made to get worse punishment.

President: Like what?

Buzzo: Chopping their both thumbs off.

Mark (his face in a repulsive frown): Buzzo, that sounds draconian!

President: I think that's fair. Added to castration and prison term with hard labor.

Glenda (fist punching the air): Yes! Yes!! Yes!!!

Everybody joins in punching the air and inundating it in yes, yes, yes! The President fixes them with delight.

President: Now, moving forward, do you have any further fundamental policy statement on your minds?

Mark: Yes dad. What of education, health care, libraries, clean water, lunch for the kids, parks and gardens, games, in short, our Disneyland?

Everybody cracks up once again to the generosity of innocence at spontaneity.

President: I thought we already been through those.

Mark: No Dad. Those are policy statements somewhat elaborated. We need details. Details we can always play and dance to like a favorite song.

Brett: Right! We need every operational detail.

President: Ok. As you well know, words alone can't be enough. Our strength would lie in our determination to make our words and deeds palpable. So, let's take a break for some strength.

Mark: Dad, endurance! You need to be a good soldier.

Everyone cracks up as they rise for a quick break.

Chapter 2

We find them reconvened. Once again positions have been taken. Everyone's seated. With attentive demeanor as the President recommences.

President: Now to details. Operational details.

First let me say that however exalted the rhetoric, Gen WHY hold the key, the power of forcing and transforming the ideas into reality. Your truth must fight the demeaning, dehumanizing society.

Quoting President J.F. Kennedy: *"If our alliance is strong our strength will speak for itself. If we are weak, words will be of no help".*

So, it's with utmost urgency that I will present to you my developmental economic plans, programs with timelines and timeframes that will meet your perusals and dispatch, to enable a roll out of our final blue print.

Shading some quick lights, my steps in order of priority and with some simultaneity of actions would be to commit funds immediately thus:

No. 1. Education, a fundamental human right!

Compulsory basic education. This is the mother of all our battles. We are eradicating illiteracy in all its forms and shapes in keeping with the policy "education a fundamental human right." Everybody in this land must have at least a basic education.

Gen WHY rise to a ponderous applause, breaking out in clamor of portentous voices, wrapped in pride and heroism.

The President with expression of delight acknowledges and continues.

President: That means from nursery to pre-school. That means from pre-school to primary education. That means from primary to secondary education. That means from secondary education to skill-acquisition are compulsory.

And let me repeat: education is a fundamental human right. That means from nursery to pre-school to primary education to secondary education to skill acquisition, are compulsorily compulsory.

Mark (interjecting): Dad, I love that "compulsorily compulsory."

Everybody cracks up with a delighted smile. As the President hints at speaking, a gradual silence settles back in the room.

President: Thank you! Everyone, everybody, every soul must know how to read and write. It's henceforth a crime not to read and write. All parents are warned. Every child, any child ceases to be a toy on our land henceforth.

Apropos to underpin the importance of and avoid equivocations of planned parenthood as it concerns kids, number of kids, resources (private and public) and their welfare, let's refresh. Let me bore you a thousand times for it's absolutely necessary:

–is the present situation where African parents pump out kids without caring for their welfare right? Or

–is it wrong for parents, educated or not, to make any number of children in consonance with taking care of their welfare?

Attentions are fully rhapsodic among the Gen WHY anew. The scourge of this on the African continent and people cannot be overstated. They are giving it the attention it merits.

President: *Is there anyone in this room who does not agree that it should be a crime to just make any child without any plan whatsoever for the child? Or to willfully abandon any child? Or to child-labor? Or that it should not be a crime for any parents or guardian to make property in children? Or to child marriage? Or that it should not be utmost crime to foreclose a child from education?*

The room has creeped into an eerie silence. Everyone is listening hard.

President: Again, we are tying parenthood to a qualitative welfare provision for their two kids.

As I said and let me repeat, the Western countries ride on common sense rational integrity. The West makes children they can take care of strictly - qualitatively. Kids fitted and kitted and well tooled to confront head-on and solve their generational problems, progressing whatever they inherited and innovating and inventing more. We are not restricting motherhood but we are restricting a willful, gratuitous abuse of motherhood that makes our descendants slaves and slaves of their peers within and without.

Population should cease to outpace available resources. It should be the other way around. Growing resources should outpace growing population, like in the West. Again, referencing the Chinese one-child policy, given its positive results, is there anybody who does not see the positive sense in a two-child policy model on our land?

Glenda: Two-child policy is perfect. Since we are the only mammals incapable of imitation…

David: Paraphrasing Sigmund Freud: *"the first form of evolution is imitation…"*

Glenda: Precisely. Instead, we are destructive, our social level is that of drinking, eating, defecating, reproducing… like rats.

President: Now, is there anybody who thinks that castration should not be the punishment and deterrence for abuses and flagrances of two-kids policy and their education and wellbeing?

> *We are not restricting motherhood but we are restricting a willful gratuitous abuse of motherhood that makes our descendants slaves and slaves of their peers within and without.*
> *Now, is there anybody who thinks that castration should not be the punishment and deterrence for abuses and flagrances of two-kids policy and their education and wellbeing?*

Buzzo: Excellency, castration is perfectly in line. Any other option in Africa will fail. We are primitive.

Brett: We are remorseless, arid of conscience…

Glenda: …And shame.

Buzzo: We are lower animals, beneath the concept and practice of reasoning. Our brains are not developed like other two races. They are empty. We don't read. We don't able our brains. We don't enhance our brains. We can't engage critical thinking yet. A few amongst us who can are rejected, humiliated, subdued, trampled upon, disdained, eliminated, killed.

Mezzi: That's why we need an illuminated, benevolent dictatorship. We need our few good men as dictators. Democracy is for the minds that can reason. We need illuminated benevolent dictatorship to lead the primitive herd to the realm of reason.

There is a ponderous applause.

President: Impeccable summary. Please, I urge everyone to look back at our African childhood. We surrender to its trauma because we are traumatized. That in turn makes having children without programming their care the easy thing, a respite, taking refuge. It's not the right thing. It's criminal. It's evil. It's against God's will.

The President then, fixes Mark and gets back in line with his reasoning:

As I was saying, the compulsorily compulsory education churns out *"basic education graduates."* Then follows a ponderous comprehensive aptitudinal selection test of these basic education graduates into these categories:

a. *Graduate university students;*
b. *Graduate polytechnic students;*
c. *Graduate skill- acquisition students.*

The graduate skill-acquisition students are to be skilled in different chores of blue-collar jobs: machine and machinery operators, factory workers, manufacturing, agriculture, industrial, tourism, commerce, etc. etc. all found in the value chain and services system endeavor. Prepared to progress and enhance economic productivity.

The skilled graduates will be equipped to read and understand and use whatever is researched and discovered by the university and polytechnic graduates and trickled down to them for economic productivity and general progress.

For our unfortunate existing illiterate and semi-literate youths, instead we are going to invest in their skill-acquisition in different trades - tailoring, trading, carpentry, iron smelting, driving, etc., etc., for economic productivity.

Concurrently, every existing basic educated, every university and polytechnic graduate is going to have one year of re-orientation and skilling for their employability in a profitable workforce.

Then best brains will be going for post-graduation at home and world over to research on all and sundry. So we can learn, copy, imitate, improve, innovate and invent.

To this end, we will absolutely ponderously embark on two main areas of education infrastructure – physical and human:

a. Physical: refurbish existing schools, upgrade existing schools, build new ones, equip them, abolish private institutions up until basic education.
b. Human: alongside we build capacities - train new teachers and do the re-orientations of existing ones, skill administrators and do the re-sorientations of existing ones.
c. We will build cutting age libraries, libraries, libraries in every nook and corner of our communities.

Any questions?

Four hands are readily raised amongst Gen WHY: Glenda, Laura, Mezzi and Brett.

President: To the ladies first.

Glenda: Excellency, no mention of hostels is made. Our youths live like animals in schools, shot putting and in consort with viruses and bacteria.

President: Correct and noted. It's beneath indecency, the tribulations and inhumanity that lack of hostels subjects our kids to. Even though there is no overt mention of it, it's implicit. Next?

Laura: Excellency, we need toilets in those hostels please. We need with maximum urgency toilets. There is no hint of hygiene. We defecate into plastic bags. We urinate into plastic bags and tie them and haul them from the windows of our hostels into the nights, in sum we shot putting. We have legion of diseases. It's highly embarrassing the level of dirt and indecency and incivility.

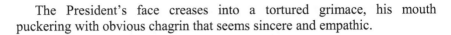

The President's face creases into a tortured grimace, his mouth puckering with obvious chagrin that seems sincere and empathic.

President: Noted. The infamous shot putting, very sad. Thank you very much for your courage. Mezzi?
Mezzi: There are no parks for the kids. Our kids need equipped parks to play and develop their senses.
President: Gotch you! I knew you were going to come after me. Left it out on purpose to make you fume.

Everybody cracks up laughing.

President: Highly predictable. You want to get Mezzi, mess with the welfare of kids. He is a beautiful mind. (then fixing him) rest-assured our kids are going to have perpetual field days, generation after generation. Brett?
Brett: Excellency, I thought nutrition should fall under a fundamental human right?

His Gen WHY peers were taken aback at the umpteenth broaching of hunger by Brett. To that extent almost everyone is berserk at Brett as faces crease into amazement of competing irritation, madness, appall, but to the President's delight. However, it was Buzzo who took the bullish situation by the horn.

Buzzo (fixing Brett with air of melancholy): Brett, we asked for separation, you remember? We fought gallantly. You won the battle of the exploding night. We are working on crossing the Rubicon. The situation made men of us. We should not be having a conversation of anybody's help over hunger. We have been pondering on solutions to dominate hunger by ourselves. And let it be said that we were and are ready to stand without any Status Quo's help necessarily. Even though his excellency came along unsolicitously, exceptionally generous, giving us mutual funds: both basic care and Youths'. Even so, it is said that necessity is the mother of invention. We should be independent thinking, should be literally standing up for God's sake instead of being whining children.

This vigorous, sincere reprimand by Buzzo against self-distrust stuttering Brett wedges self between the vulnerable and the disadvantaged, of memory of unutterable hunger, starvation and tribulation and the fortunate and the advantaged, of memory withered of hunger. The one preoccupied. The other unpreoccupied but empathic and sensitive to the preoccupation and plights and fear of Brett.
The President falls within the empathic group. He knows hunger swallows all the confidence, spite, grit and hope and spits out spasm of fear, anxiety, anguish, hopelessness and self-distrust in any person.

Brett however did not blush. He did not demure. He promptly took defense of himself, retorting back at Buzzo, reiterating his fears. The overwhelm of fears of the Black kind youths: survival!

Brett (fixing Buzzo): Buzzo, I am not a whining child. Far from it. I cannot overstate our dreadfulness at hunger. Hunger is predatory. You may know it but you have never lived it. We trust you regardless. You had already given us crowd funding solution by ourselves. His Excellency has magnanimously given us "basic care" and Youths' Mutual Trust Funds and Investment Companies. Subliminal. Ethereal. However, won't it be nice for every Gen WHY tranquility to give nutrition a fundamental human rights status as well?

Buzzo: Just listen to yourself. Isn't that laughable?

Glenda: It's ridiculous. That way you encourage laziness.

Lynda: Correct, we are fighting our laziness, Mr. Brett.

Mark: He is grossly afraid of something.

President: Well, well, well, Brett has a genuine preoccupation. Its psychological. He has lived there before and wants to put his and peers' fears and anxieties permanently behind.

Brett: Thank you Sir, Excellency. Thank you Sir, for understanding. I am still living there folks.

President: Let me tell you all a story. A real story.

A kid famished found a clergy. In order to permanently eat, he chose to become a monk. He was adopted. He ate abundantly every day. And every night of everyday he hid food under his bed until the clergy found out and told him: lo, this is your house. And every single thing is at your command. And he cried ashamed.

Everybody is rapt, listening very hard in order to make sense of it all.

Mark: So, dad what happened? Did he stop?

President: Sharp boy. That is the very existential question: did he stop or did he continue?

Mark: Dad, go ahead. We don't want to guess.

President: Let me suggest to you by referencing the psychology of Africa's ignoble enriched and the ignoble poor.

Buzzo: He continued.

President: Mark?

Mark (looking at idol Buzzo): He continued.

President: Brett?

Brett: He stopped hiding food.

President: He continued folks. It's psychological. That famished boy is me.

There is a general amazement. A competing amazement of surprise, shock, delight and empathy.

GENERATION WHY'S PERDITION REDEMPTIVE VERSES

President: Africans are largely ignoble. Men and women that compose of the African society are largely famished and ignoble. The men and the women that compose of the African authorities – government, the church, the monarchy are all largely coming from the same coin: ignoble and famished realm. They can never have enough of looting even in an all-out realm of abundance. Its psychological. You don't deny toys to childhood. Every toy denied childhood is every looting perpetuated in adulthood.

> **Every toy denied childhood is every looting perpetuated in adulthood.**

Denial begets denial and looting begets looting. Can you explain Africa's kleptomania and gluttony at excesses of properties, of cars, of jewelries? A debilitating make-up in adulthood for denied toys to their childhood.

Indeed, I stopped looting because of that act of generosity of Mark and Mezzi that day in that church.

That day in that church you understand that only the noble, sublime mind, poor or rich regardless could be capable of such act of generosity.

That day, in that church, looking at them, I felt an unutterable shame that pierced and transfixed me and I transited.

The President gets emotional and loses his voice. He pauses to deal with his tears.

Gen WHY rise in a ponderous applause.

The President recovers, nods "thank you", acknowledging their empathy, their solicitude, recomposes self and continues amidst Gen WHY standing applause. Then the applause slows down and ceases.

President: That's why we must give at least the basics to every child, including toys. Children must play. So that in the end we defeat primitivity. That would in turn guarantee mind enrichment that would scare and defeat looting and avariciousness and kleptomania and abject individual greed and selfishness for contentment, generosity and collectivity, etc.

That's why I repeat to you we need endurance to be good soldiers. Not only would we address the issue of hunger on our land, we will dominate hunger. So please, be patient and have faith in yourselves and self-confidence to make hunger captive, so that in the end and paraphrasing President Kennedy: *"We should not fear hunger nor act out of fear of hunger."*

Mark: Especially Brett. He shall not cart away lobsters selfishly.

Everybody cracks up to a voluptuous, delightful laughter.

The President pauses, scanning their delighted faces and continued.

President: Now moving forward, to point no two.

No. 2. *We need a capillary scouring infrastructure to meet the challenges and the demands of the 21st century economic activities and human mobility in the following categories:*

a. Federal highways and bridges;
b. State roads and bridges;
c. Community roads and bridges;
d. Modern seaports;
e. Modern airports;
f. Sewerage to our cities and communities;
g. Ultra-modern rail transportation system;
h. Refuse collection and treatment.

All federal highways and railways are to be run by private companies. The private companies would build them, create employment, rake in revenues, maintain them and expand on them, building new ones.

The President pauses, scanning their faces once more.

President: Any questions?

Mezzi and Mark raise their hands.

President: Mark?
Mark: Dad, just imagine black engineers constructing our roads. Just imagine black engineers building our cars. Just imagine black engineers building our bicycles, cars, airplanes. just imagine black architects building our skyscrapers, building our schools, building our libraries, our parks, our libraries, building our playgrounds with equipment, our toilets, urbanizing. Huh dad, just imagine black engineers building straight lines, building our sewers, our toys, building everything. Just imagine, that won't be a bad sad dream. Would it?

Everybody cracks up and forlorn and chagrined at the truth of his feelings they applaud. An applause to mitigate Mark's psychological sufferings and desolation and ill-feelings and encourage him somehow.

President: That's the despicable, appalling, immeasurable and inconsolable tragedy. In our history, we have engineers who can't build anything. Our system of education had long broken down.
Most of our youths are graduates. However, their employability remains a discourse on a continent priced on mediocrity of its teachers and colleges and institutions. Exams are scaled through plagiarism and on imposed hand-outs, on sex and on cash inducement and payment.
That's why we need education as a fundamental human right. We need a lot of skill building capacity. From theory to practical. Everyman to his

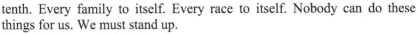

tenth. Every family to itself. Every race to itself. Nobody can do these things for us. We must stand up.

Mezzi?

Mezzi: Excellency, I am extremely glad you mentioned sewerage. The absence of the simplest hygiene in Africa is shocking. Ninety-nine percent of African cities have open air defecation, urination. African urban areas are ghettos. So filthy, so dirty, so repugnant that not even cows are supposed to survive there. One wonders how African children survive these conditions. Yet the Status Quo steal the money and pass through and indeed reside in urbanized Western cities!

Can't we start right away with public toilets and refuse systems?

President: Excellent point. What you realized in "children must play center" is of a ponderous teaching. Those chemical faeces eating toilets and refuse bins are functionally amazing. We are to emulate, replicate and expand on them immediately. To point number three:

> *The absence of the simplest hygiene in Africa is shocking. 99% of African cities have open air defecation, urination. African urban areas are ghettos. So filthy, so dirty, so repugnant that not even cows are supposed to survive there. One wonders how African children survive these conditions. Yet the Status Quo steal the money and pass through and indeed reside in urbanized western cities.*

No. 3. *Energy, energy, energy, energy!*

This is the father of all our battles. Power plants by all available and encompassing green technology means: wind, sun, gas, biogas, etc., in these categories:

a. Power generation (public-private enterprise);
b. Power transmission (at federal, state and community council levels run and maintained by private companies);
c. Power distribution (at federal, state and community council levels run and maintained by private companies).

There should be freedom of electric power. A twenty-four hours light, seven days a week, four weeks per month, fifty-two weeks per year, non-stop.

It's going to be a Public-Private Enterprise, PPE, where government funds them and the private sector builds and runs them, maintains them and expands on them, building new ones.

We have within the time of two years, not more to ban use of generators on our land. I appeal to Africans and their cohorts in the generator business to take note and take advantage and double down their effort to participate in the new green economy. It's an olive branch I am extending to all.

And we can then enable the next point, which is point number 4.

No. 4. *Clean disinfected water must be a fundamental human right.*

Pipe borne, pipe borne, pipe borne water, disinfected water in every home!

We are taking water to every house of every city, town and village.

Hygiene is very important for any human development and upliftment.

These energy and water blueprints have most of the Gen WHY's faces pinched in solicitous frown of disbelief. There was such air of disbelief that swallowed the excitement they felt. So much so that Laura and Lynda already have their hands in the air to ask questions, breaking with the President's questions taking congruous formality format of "any questions?".

The President notices.

President: Lynda?

Lynda: Sir, pardon me, I know it's been said "dream things that were not and say why not..." but you mean that we can have light twenty-four hours a day, for seven days a week, for a month on this our African continent? That we may not have to fetch water from after the rain puddles? Or fight cholera and bacteria? Or we are going to be able to shower, smell decently, feel the comfort of personal hygiene and cleanliness? Feel like human beings? Feel like women?

President: Yes, Lynda. We can. It's been shameful and disturbing: supposed homosapiens playing homo erectus. Willful subjection of its people to subhuman standards by its Status Quo leadership for no justifiable reason whatsoever rather than for stupidity. Primitivity. Laura?

Laura: Excellency, in 20 years of my life I have not used power electricity in my house. In our villages we don't know what it is. We use kerosene lanterns and or candles. Our eyes are gone to the stress and danger of candles and lanterns.

We wake up 5:30a.m every morning of our weekdays to the chore of doing six kilometers, buckets on our heads, to the stream to fetch water to be able to bath and for other domestic uses, breakfast preparation, etc., before going to school. Or to street hawking to raise money. Everyday. Every day, we get to school already tired and sleepy to anything being taught.

Just imagine if I wake up to power electricity. Just imagine if I can study under the light of electric power. Just imagine not being afraid of the night. Just imagine if I don't have to wake up as early as 5:30a.m to walk six kilometers to fetch water. Just imagine going to school not tired and sleepy, just imagine, just imagine....

...Just imagine black engineers constructing our roads. Just imagine black engineers building our cars. Just imagine black engineers building our airplanes, building our skyscrapers, building our ...

> *...schools, building our libraries, our parks, building our bicycles, building our playgrounds with equipment. Huh pop, just imagine black engineers building straight lines, building our sewers, our toilets, urbanizing, building libraries, building everything. Just imagine...*

As Laura transients with a flurry of spasm of "just imagine" expressions, the air is stilled. Everything is stilled into a ponderous and dense sorrowing silence.

Everyone can feel and imagine her troubling air of emotion that is vicious, appalling, callous, heart-broken at the same time.

The weight of this truth and the inescapable responsibility of the African leadership Status Quo, of which the President was part of, in the immediate past, hits and tears him in the face.

The President wanes into a fierce distorted grimace. A grimace of an unutterable sadness. A wilderness of sadness filled with an abject sorrowing shame. A shame that swallowed all tears and denied every understanding, compassion or forgiveness. Now his eyes are overwhelmed as he silently fights back tears. He lowers his head fixing the infinite floor.

Under his immediate past watch, generations of female youths endured the harrowing, silent, hapless destruction of their latent talents. Foreclosed from any of exertion efforts to develop their talents. They have been objects of child bearing and domestic slavery;

Under his watch, the village grew kids that never knew but the fields, the farms, the streams, the streets, scavenging, begging and abuses;

Under his watch the Africa's youths with graduate degrees never could apply what they studied, but were on the infested arid fields of cotton, cocoa, palm trees, groundnuts, arabic gums, mineral fields trying to survive;

Under his watch, Gen WHY emptied of any hope, of any self-esteem, and filled with frustration and exasperation and humiliation, and suffering and fearful confusion turned to cyber thefting, to cultism and cultist killings and sacrifices to make a living. Now ponderous tears are now streaming down the cheeks of the President, these inner working Gen WHY, understand his situation, and even so they watch him silently in transition of self-abasement, of grieving shame and of spasm of anguish.

The President wanes into a distorted grimace. A grimace of an unutterable sadness ...filled with an abject sorrowing shame. A shame that swallowed all tears and denied every understanding, compassion or forgiveness.
Under his immediate past watch, generations of female youths, endured the harrowing, silent, hapless destruction of their latent talents...foreclosed from developing their talents...just objects of ...

> *...child bearing and domestic slavery; ...the village grew kids that never knew but the fields, the farms, the streams, the streets, scavenging, begging and abuse;*
> *...Africa's youths of "graduates" never could apply what they studied, but on the infested arid fields of cotton, cocoa, palm trees, groundnuts...;*
> *...Gen WHY emptied of any hope, of any self-esteem, and filled with frustration and exasperation and humiliation, and suffering and fearful confusion turned to cyber thefting, to cultism and cultist killings and sacrifices to make a living.*

Everyone seemed too numbed for any compassion and too cold for any empathy. After all, it is a necessary stage of a healing process. The President's healing process. Now, Buzzo who could not bear this self-mortifying scene of the repentant President any longer breaks ranks, piercing the eerie silence.

He jumps out of his seat, walks straight to the President, grabs one of the bottles of water in front of him, on his table, fills President's empty glass with water, taps his shoulder and holds the glass up to him.

The President brings his eyes, locking them with Buzzo's, his face in grieving, unutterable sadness. And with contorted expression of chagrin and forlorn, he accepts the water, taking it off Buzzo's hands and forces a smile of gratitude to him.

Then Gen WHY rise to a standing applause. An applause that seemed honest and unfeigned. An applause of towering tacit expression of competing forgiveness, encouragement and appreciation at the same time.

The President drinks the water and finds strength and face to continue.

The embarrassment for his emotional guilt, and for flurry of failed obligations, seem mitigated. At least for now.

President (with air of relief, places back his glass on the table): Thank you all very much.

Buzzo: Excellency, your love and courage are palpable. We appreciate. We love you.

Glenda: Sir, we want to reiterate our love for you. Don't take it. We are a family. A family must come to terms somehow with its remotest ugly past, its past, its present past for reconciliation, if it must endure to a viable future of success.

Brett: I concur. The past must not hold us hostage.

Mark: Dad smile!

Everyone, including the President cracks up: Mark's "Dad smile" is a masterful tension defusing stroke, dropped at the right moment, giving respite and fresh breath to the taut aura. Then the President continued.

President: Let's get to the next point.

No 5: *Value-chains to create abundance of jobs.*

We have already said it before, but it's worth repeating. To create jobs, first and foremost, the exportation of our mineral wealth in its raw state is absolutely banned.

With equal vigor, the same applies to agriculture raw wealth.

There must be a new alliance and partnership with the world for a value chain system. Building refineries, exporting refined products, exporting semi-finished products in ingots, building industries, manufacturing products, enabling our youths at jobs, at skill acquisition and at expertise.

Cocoa needs to be semi-finished before leaving our shores for final chocolate making in Europe. Cotton, gum arabic, peanuts, mangoes, pineapples, shear butter, nuts, etc., etc., are to be valued. And on and on.

We must refine our crude oil for the finished products we need on this continent. Our refineries must optimally function.

Our gas cannot be flaring. We need to harness our gas for energy, cooking, heating our homes.

To these ends, we will be building industrial parks to house clusters of businesses and factories all over our land for the ineluctable, indispensable value chain system for the jobs necessary for our economic progress.

Now to point number 6.

The President brings his stare on Brett and breaks a smile.

President: Mr. Brett, point No. 6 is to make Gen WHY hunger captive.

Almost all rose to uncontainable clamor of shouting and shrieking, expressing contentment, welcoming ponderously President's pronouncement.

President: I want us to consider dedicating ample time to addressing the issue of hunger in the land. Let's treat it with utmost importance that it merits. We push it towards the end of our meeting.

Now to Point number 7.

No. 7. Land reforms: *Land that definitely and ultimately swallows us all is a big deal in Africa.*

An empty land has a marginal value. In fact, land has no value at all until you value it with some developmental investment.

Land ownership and tenure system in Africa are a source of curse, source of illusion, our perpetual scourge of our misery.

We are reforming our land ownership and tenure system to free the lands and consequently liberate the latent imprisoned energy of progress, elevating our communities into sub-urban status.

In this regard, first and foremost, we are going to have to:

a.   Bury our deads with dignity. We need to build structured cemeteries. A common cemetery with tombs that contain coffins for every soul. A

befitting resting place to engage the souls of our afterlife. A meeting place to meditate, think, place flowers and wish and evoke heaven;
b.   Make land leasehold feasible and flexible for mechanized agriculture with farm settlements.

With these two moves firstly, we would have liberated the lands for mechanized farming, mechanized rearing and grazing, etc., etc. Being able to lease these lands for necessary time-periods for mechanized farming by the government and directly made available to the private sector would not only create new employments but would ponderously increase productivity and necessarily feed and benefit our value chain system choice of job creativity and progress efforts.

And secondly, having cemetery fabric to bury our loved ones would afford us an organized, dignifying sanctuary, a sanctuary for the catharsis of our emotional expression visits to our loved ones, visits of floral-love entity of pageantry framing. And we would have besides, removed the hurdles to turn Africa's heart of the people: the African village into befitting modern neighborhoods of 21st century smart communities, and contain, if not eliminate in its entirety, unnecessary urban migration.

No. 8. Basic healthcare:
Basic health care must be a fundamental human right on our land.
Our health care service delivery is, in a best-case scenario in a state of disrepair.
Mezzi: No sir! Excellency, it's non-existent.
Mark: Dad, it's non-existent.
Mezzi: It's disheartening and embarrassing that my cats and dogs and horses have doctors back in America and African children do not.

Most among the Gen WHY go into amazement of competing shocks, disbelief, shame and wonderment. An amazement of a wilderness of grieving shame and unutterable sadness that crushes and withers any doubt and defiance remained in them that Africans have any spiritual essence and any human valency.

Brett: Isn't that for the movies?
Buzzo: Bushman. Watch discovery and health channels and get wired up.
Mezzi: If you have any doubt, why do you think of so much health pilgrimage overseas by the status quo?
President: True. Sacrosanct reality. Those places, healthcare is so commonplace that cows and even domestic rats have doctors and healthcare coverage. And our continent won't give even basic health care coverage to our people. It's simply immoral and pales beneath iniquity.

Now the President goes into a whim of a ponderous audacious *mea-culpa* tantrum that in no way surprised his listeners but underpins his determination for an unalienable atonement.

President: To the extent that we don't have enough medical staff is immoral and beneath iniquity; to the extent that the few we have are being drained by best professional ethics, and best professional practices, and better pay elsewhere is immoral and beneath iniquity; to the extent that we have scanty medical structures and are ill-prepared, ill-equipped, scary and in states of disrepair is immoral and beneath iniquity; to the extent that we don't manufacture even generic drugs and at the same time we let in floods of miscellany of fake drugs, adulterated drugs, killer drugs all by the hands of the Chinese, the Indians and the African Status Quo and its cabal, and are validated by the government is immoral and beneath iniquity; to these extents, with our basic mutual trust fund here is the deal:

a. Every child, every pensioner, everyone, employed and unemployed, living must have basic health care coverage. Americans call it Affordable Care, Italians call it Universal Coverage, Germans call it No Health Left Behind. Call it by whatever name, there must be a scouring healthcare coverage.

To this extent, our mutual trust fund investment company must guarantee:

1. Provision of a scouring state of art hospitals, general, specialized and referrals, cottages, clinics, medical centers including primary health centers on our land;

2. Remuneration of our existing medical staff adequately - properly and provision of residential smart park for them;

3. The training of many, many, many doctors and nurses, arming them with cutting edge techno - skills of the 21st century healthcare services, including and not only telemedicine;

4. That each family must be assigned a medical doctor;

5. That no drugs can be procured without doctor's prescription;

6. That doctors and medical staff are required to be selflessly compassionate in their duties. Any neglect and favors would be met with severe punishment;

7. That it is mandatory for each and every pharmaceutical enterprise to request doctor's prescription for every and any drugs dispensed;

8. That there is death penalty for flagrant violation and pharmaceutical practice and enterprise would be revoked and shut down;

9. That our men and women of food and drug administration are strengthened to perform their duties. Besides, there is death penalty for men and women of food and drugs administration for any adulterated, fake and killer drugs found in our land, as there is a death penalty for the Chinese, Indians and Africans or anybody that exports or imports adulterated, fake and killer drugs to our land;

10. That all generic drugs are to be produced within the space of one year on our land and after which it would be consequently banned.

Now, he pauses, scanning the attentive rapt faces engaged in mental notes.

President: That way, if we work very hard in two years, we would have reduced considerably, if not abolished completely, Africa's medical pilgrimage and its reversal. Are we forgetting any vital issue?

Mark (with expression of repugnant dread): Dad, did we cover malaria, typhoid, polio, vomiting and stooling because every day bears witness to many, many, many kids and the elderly death days?

Me and Mezzi have assisted ponderously in their burials. Indeed, Mezzi financed almost all of the ones we were able to get wind of.

President: You financed and assisted in burials?

Mezzi: Indeed, excruciating and eviscerating vivid images. To see kids, younger, die like flies, their life cut short, is unutterably of permanent withering sorrow. Indelibly, vivid, nightmarish images.

President: Indeed!

Mark: Dad, does Mutual Trust Fund cover their burial expenses as well?

The President is slow to answer. Instead he shudders and then more shuddering. There is a hollowness in his eyes. His face is a contorted frown, puckering a grieving sweating pain. David and Mark notice before any of the group does.

Mark (Alarmed): Dad, are you alright?

President: Yes, I am. Why?

Mark: You are sweating and your eyes are a hollowness, enfeebled, dad.

President (he turns looking away, and sits on the table): Am I?

Mark: Dad, why don't you take a...

Buzzo (Hissing): "sshhiiiiiiihh, silence. He will be fine".

> *Indeed, excruciating and eviscerating vivid images. To see kids, younger, die like nothing, their life cut short, is unutterably of permanent withering sorrowing. Indelibly, vivid, nightmarish images.*

Buzzo is right; the most gracious act of inner healing happens in a psychological silence. A silence that bears, liberating act and produces healings of psychoanalysis dimension.

In fact, the President suddenly recoils in himself, creasing into expression of chagrin and broken-heartedness. They let him fight back spasm of competing shame and guilt. Both are necessary. Guilt gives shame its purpose, and shame gives guilt its reward. The Gen WHY's jury is not just judging his shame but partaking of it, to absolve the guilt of his shame. It's simply ponderously tragic and appalling that, these kids' psyche is already impinged upon with life's odious, mysterious trajectory turning points of ill-luck, will and fate. The deaths narrative of Africa's descendants rest squarely on the Status Quo. The President was part of the status quo yesterday, and he never made life bearable.

Regardless, not pardoning him would be the blind stupidity of cruelty. Cruelty is annihilation of the human race. Pardoning is the survival of love. It is the preservation of, and of persevering the human race.

Gen WHY empathize with his perceived mind of unutterable, unfeigned penitence and respected the silence to help him heal.

Then after what seemed interminable minutes, the President recovers: he turns and forces a fragile, sorrowing smile. The faces of Gen WHY are somewhat reassured. Then they break into a standing applause of understanding and encouragement.

President: (emotional, wiping off tears) Thank you. Thank you.

Now let's finish off, (looking at his watch) we are running late. Let's deal with **program No. 9.**

Mark (with a contorted frown): Running late, deal with program No. 9? Dad, it's almost time for dinner!

Gen WHY go into a roaring spasm, underpinning their consensus. The President watches them with a delighted smile.

President: You don't want to eat fattest?

Mark: No dad, we want to eat fastest!

Everybody cracks up.

The President fixes them to have a hint of their groggy wills and determination. Their determined demeanor tacitly conveys they can hold off hunger a little bit more.

President (smirking): A patient dog folks! A patient dog at endurance folks.

Now to program no 9.

Mezzi: Point No. 9.

President: Correct. Thank You. To point No. 9

No. 9. Transportation and commuting care.

This trans-commute care is through our Mutual Trust Fund Investment Limited.

Bicycle, bicycle, bicycle, bicycle for everyone, everywhere on our land.

A clamor of joy, happiness, jubilation started up among Gen WHY. The President continued.

President: And buses and buses and buses...

Their clamor grew, underpinning ponderously his pronouncement.

President: And trains and trains and trains and trains.

Their clamor is now peaking.

President: Now to the bicycle. We are going to do that through the famous "bike sharing" mechanism. I am sure you are all acquainted with it. It's nothing but:
a. Having bicycle clusters in bicycle stations within vicinities of bus-stops, parks, train stations, in our cities and towns and villages. Yes, our villages are going to be elevated to sub-urban status, with buses serving and plying on them;
b. They are going to have Apps, wired with Isnternet to locate their positions and availabilities at any particular time of the day, on 24/7 basis;
c. You are going to have to have tokens to access and use the bicycles;
d. After usage, you deposit and lock them back in the nearest bicycle station on your app;
e. You are going to have maintenance outposts close to the clusters for any breakdowns and consequent repairs;
f. The bicycle does belong to all of you collectively. You are collective consumers, collective spenders. Be collective caretakers and brothers keeping. Remember this motto: Keep the bicycles better than you find them. Love and discipline. Rights and duties. Rights to use them, duties to keep them better for other users.

The President pauses, scanning their faces in mental notes.

President: If you have any questions on bike-sharing please refer to Buzzo and company for elucidation.
Now the buses. The buses are going to ply every nook and corner of our land thus:
a. We are going to have inter-urban buses, urban buses, suburban buses and countryside neighborhood buses;
b. Each of different bus-sizes for effective quantity and quality service delivery;
c. Each with designated time-frequencies spread in the arc of the 24 hrs;
d. Each with designated bus-stops;
e. Each time-framed;
f. You are going to have mutual trust fund's monthly funded subscriptions for those eligible – the pensioners, the "moronic" Gen WHY, the unemployed of the "age of reason" Gen WHY.
Lastly the trains. Trains, trains and trains.
We are going to build standard gauge for both commuter and commodity trains.
The commuter trains are thus:

a. Normal short distance regional trains that stop in every station of every city, town and suburban areas. People can commute to workplaces, schools, and back every day;

b. Speed intercity trains that stop only in the cities. Punctilious commuter time saving trains;

c. The high-speed trains that run between and stop only in the major cities of high activities, commercial and/or administrative-commercial cities and administrative state capitals. Conquer long distances comfortably in some slick hours. They actually compete comfortably against aeroplanes.

We must develop and enhance the use of trains to transport goods.

Just think of what we stand to gain in doing so:

a. A locomotive would transport about 33 numbers of 30-ton trains at a go. Think about the economy of scale. With a single locomotive you replace 30 trailers that pollute our air, pollute our ears, damage our roads and constantly imperil people's lives;

b. Air and noise pollution drastically reduced and contained;

c. Our roads last longer;

d. Peoples' lives are less imperiled;

e. A lot of time saved for human capital development.

Then to point number 10.

No.10. Affordable houses and their ownership.

We are going to build houses, not huts, not shelters for your outright ownership.

The youths roar to sudden overwhelm of uncontainable joy and happiness. The spite of hunger seems beaten and subdued. Numbed.

Then their uproar suddenly ceases as it came, with equal vigor. They crease back into attentive faces.

President: Indeed. We are going to build many, many, many affordable decent homes.

Glenda: Excellency, we are indeed numbed with such a delight of hope of certainty. Phew! Phew!! Phew!!!

President: For the past 60 years, that is before any of you was born, decolonized Africa has no longer pursued social housing endeavors to give dignity to its people.

Buzzo: That's why there is so much dilapidation everywhere. So much homelessness. So much filth.

President: Indeed, all we have done is buy properties in the West.

Mezzi: And what shameful luxury properties at such shameful outrageous chicanery prizes, of a grotesque, scathing travesty of themselves and Africans.

David: Yeah, a travesty indeed.

President: We are going to urbanize and build mainly one-bedroom, two-bedroom, three-bedroom and 4-bedroom typology bungalows and block of flats. And you are going to own them.

Brett: Excellency, own them?

President: Yes, you are going to own them. Indeed, as we speak, you are the potential off-takers. In a year's time with our developmental programs in full gear, you would have been gainfully employed to own properties, paying them as monthly rentals until you pay them off. Won't that be nice?

Brett: Phew, nice? Extremely wonderful!

Lynda: Beyond wonderful.

Laura: Sublime

Glenda: Awesomeness beyond*ness*.

President: Any architect in this room?

Mezzi: No Excellency. There is none.

Mark: Our architects are not field architects. They are theoretical architects. They build nonsense, incapable for a hut paradigm shift. They are not capable.

Mezzi: They are like our engineers. Theoretical engineers. They don't challenge anything. Just build thatched-houses like our fathers of primitive reasoning. No evolution. Nothing. Well they are Africans. Garbage in garbage out. They don't even try.

President: Challenge tenet! That's the word. We have to challenge everything. I am going to prepare a technical design competition: they are going to design a house with green prerequisites, to be built in a day, post-foundation in cement.

Mezzi: A kind of balloon frame structure. Americans did it. Europeans did it in metal frames.

Buzzo: Africa's balloon frame. That would be encouraging.

President: That's why we are here. The alliance to stand up. We are here to encourage a scouring standing up.

The President pauses, scanning the room.

President: I think we are fully, finally done.

Mark: No dad. To point number 6. At the end, we are to make hunger captive.

President: Correct.

The President now brings his looks on Brett, fixing him. Brett, the most outwardly anxious to make hunger captive and petulant about it, understands and smiles. Then everybody understands and breaks out in delightful laughter, laughing alongside him.

President: Indeed, it will be a round table discussion. If it meets your pleasure, I will host you all to dinner in my house now.

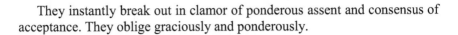

They instantly break out in clamor of ponderous assent and consensus of acceptance. They oblige graciously and ponderously.

President: Common guys, I firmly believe you are now better off for your platform launch next tomorrow.

Gen WHY: Yeeeeaaaaaahh! Platform, platform, platform! Self-consciousness, self-consciousness, self-consciousness! Standing up, standing up, standing up! Renaissance credo, renaissance credo, the self-conscious man, the renaissance Gen WHY, the demi-god at the center of the universe. Standing up...captivity captive..

Chapter 3

Now Gen WHY head out of the meeting room, fired up to honor the dinner invitation of the President. Mark, besides him Mezzi, at the rhythm of platform improvised song, is leading Gen WHY crowd to their private banquet hall reserved for very special occasions. For very special personalities. Everybody else is following behind.

Last of them is the President, alongside Buzzo, talking.

Mark and Mezzi (in unison): Plat, plat, plat...
Gen WHY: Platform, platform, platform!
Mark and Mezzi (in unison): Plat, plat, plat...
Gen WHY: Platform, platform, platform.
Mark and mezzi (in unison): Stand, stand, stand...
Gen WHY: Standing up, standing up, standing up!
Mark and Mezzi (in unison): Stand, stand, stand...
Gen WHY: Standing up, standing up, standing up!
Mezzi: Nigger, Nigger, Nigger...
Gen WHY: Standing up, standing up, standing up!
Mezzi: Nigger, Nigger, Nigger...
Gen WHY: Standing up, standing up, standing up.

Now they arrive at the threshold of the house and the officer on duty swings the door open. They walk into the banquet hall full of people seated and mostly in tete-a-tete amongst and between themselves, waiting to get to the table already set. Among them is the mother of Mezzi and Buzzo, Mrs. Donna George, Mezzi's sweet-heart Jenny, and his friend Tom Bradley. Mark sees Mezzi's mom before anyone else does and shouts in disbelief, expressing his surprise.

Mark: Auntie, Auntie Donna!

As he speeds off to her, every attention was held: heads spinning, bringing their stares trailing Mark's entanglement into the arms of Mezzi's mom.

At the same time Mezzi's eyes casually spots his girlfriend seated beside his mum. He is instantly stilled and numbed. The assault of emotions was enormous. With the emotional shock of disbelief, he is transfixed with his legs glued to his standing position. Jennifer adrenalized,

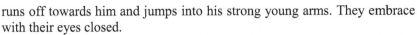

runs off towards him and jumps into his strong young arms. They embrace with their eyes closed.

What their hearts would be saying remains to everyone's imagination. Their world had been torn apart by "Nigger denigration."

They face the ponderous fixations and voluptuous scrutiny of the unexpected intensity of many eyes that seemed more fascinated than curious.

Then they open their eyes enfolding them. You can read their faces in reciprocal surprises, expressing competing and conflicting amazement of the predatory absence and withering abstinence, longings, betrayal, dejection, despair, anxiety, sorrow, grief, wondering, expectation and judgement. Their eyes turn red. Jennifer budges: she started crying.

Only then Mezzi felt the realization and suggestion of sorrow, pain, torment, chagrin, empathy on how he left suddenly for Africa without caring, with apparent vicious callousness, cruel egoism of unforgiving self-pride.

He had unconsciously decided, with the conscientious, impersonal unforgiving callousness and hard-heartedness of the lone-wolf to fight his complacency at his illgotten comfort at life that is entwined with misery and its effrontery and humiliation on the African continent. On its people. On its generations of youths. Down to Gen WHY youths his peers.

Even though, an assault of hatefulness, hurtfulness, rejection, of opiate magnitude overwhelmed his endorphin natural coping mechanism, spurred and shot him callously into Africa, however, in the nightmarish realm of his African fight against misery, orbits the memory of his family, his friends and the constant presence of his girlfriend Jennifer, who has no fault whatsoever.

Jennifer is now in a spasm of a wilderness of unutterable sobbing. It is heart wrenching. Mezzi could no longer stand up to its devastation and desolation.

Convoluted and enfeebled with what his African venture, self-exile, adventure or whatever you may describe it has cost them, cost him, all that was lost, that he hopes to make up to them one day, he started crying.

Paraphrasing, *it's been said that tears begin in the heart, some deny the heart so often, and for so long, that when it finally speaks, we hear not one but a hundred sorrows in the heartbreak. Psychologically, crying they say is a good thing and natural thing: it isn't necessarily weakness but embodies strength or strengthens you. Sometimes into a monster withered of any feeling. But when it gets us, we give way like fallen trees.*

The scene was heart wrenching, as the image of these young innocent fellas express a sublime love in a faraway land of misery. Their image intrudes, pierces the hearts of all present, winning their emotions of sympathy and best wishes.

Mezzi's mom could no longer hold it. Creased and convoluted in a sobbing spasm as well, she goes out, reaches, embracing them.

Then Tom Bradley, fighting back tears, heart-broken and of unutterable chagrin, shouldering the weight of this shebang as the medieval Telamons shouldered the weight of medieval atrocities, with hesitant but determined grave courage, afraid of what Mezzi's reaction could be, reaches out, hesitantly and delicately embracing Mezzi and Jennifer, muttering:

Tom Bradley: Mezz, I am deeply, truly sorry for all the troubles.

It took Mezzi, of what seemed eternal seconds to discern and make sense of the nonconfoundable voice he just heard: he had not seen him. He had no hint he was there. He could not have imagined remotely that voice then, there, in Africa.

His body stiffens. He slowly but delicately started turning his head towards the direction of Tom's voice. As if day-dreaming, he fought his instinct with groggy will to bring his stare to bear in the direction of the voice: lo, there stands Tom Bradley. They lock stare. With his tears. Un attended to. Streaming profusely.

Mezzi immediately lapsed into a reverie of a ponderous recalls. He is seeing the personification of his opiate, the combined morphine, opium and heroin that overwhelmed his endorphin, his natural coping mechanism.

At a killing distance, he has the palpable, unutterable assailant of hate, hurt, rejection, betrayal, hypocrisy, of heart-stabbing that drove him into grieving wilderness of anxiety, sorrow, grief, misery, despair.

That his "Nigger's rage" that got the best of his unprotected, vulnerable mind tilted. A tilt of unutterable viciousness, ferocity, cruelty, hurtfulness and hate, whose audacity created a big cleft, a big hollowness for potentials of inadvertent vulnerabilities of psychosis: infirmities of life-renunciation, suicide, crime, or survival.

He survived it because of the power of his latent cognitive ability. A cognitive ability that willed a finality of solitary and yet vulnerable unarmed voice of love and of strength and of sacrifice and of perseverance and of pride to "stand up. Don't cower. Don't surrender. Don't be a betrayal like your progenies have been to the color of your skin."

It's been said that *opiate takes everything and gives you emptiness in return.*

The emptiness that it gave Mezzi instead, became the blessing that was necessary to spur a Youth, himself to a revolution. Thanks to an overt assault of vicious and ferocious "nigger" inveighs of humiliation and hate. Thanks to Tom Bradley, a revolution of "never again", "never 'nigger' again" was consumed. That assault of pain, that assault of rejection, that assault of hurtfulness, that assault of despair and hollowness is not acceptable again. That was the resolve and the consumption.

And as anger, imperiously and impetuously dissolves into a sorrowing grief, it's time for forgiveness and reconciliation within the realm of their family loop: Mezzi hopes to be understood and forgiven by Jennifer.

Indeed, she has endured unutterable agony, sadness, desolation, tribulations and ultimate loneliness;

He has forgiven Tom Bradley and is of utmost gratitude to him. Standing up would not have been possible without his juvenile misdemeanor geniality at maliciousness and capriciousness;

He has forgiven the perversity of the hypocritical heart of the White powerful woman at the United Nations, his mom, whom she hopes would help Africa develop through only one thing: leaving them alone to their fate, instead of scouring deluding them with restraining hope-forlornness; Let God in heaven decide for his father.

How would a mortal forgive an impenitent soul, his father, who is engulfed by ruthless traffic of pleasure, power, profit and humiliation?

How would a mortal forgive a father, his father, who viciously traffic children from catastrophe of drought to catastrophe of famine to catastrophe of cholera to calamities to hunger to starvation to unutterable agonies and tribulations and abject misery and to death?

How would a mortal forgive a hardened heart, his father's, who makes slaves of Gen WHY and generations of youth before them, escaping from the hands of starving and dying and pleading parents of the African continent, through the perils of the desert and the Mediterranean Sea?

How would a mortal forgive an evil heart, his father's, that is excited with exquisite thrill, giving starving, exhausted, subdued, forlorn and hapless children, as meals to waiting vultures?

His father is in maximum detention center along with other Status Quo subversives, awaiting their fate.

After the President drew the line during a church service, making his choice against misery, he broke with the despotic hereditary Status Quo. He made his intention real with swift obliteration of over one hundred thousand churches and their Priestcraft institution on the land, and in its wake aroused a tsunami of unutterable ill-feeling among the Status Quo— the combined Monarchycraft, Politicalcraft and the Priestcraft. The President became his own man. Astutely apt, he played a masterstroke in military leadership overhaul, and in its wake, strengthening his loyalists: he retired the Status Quo loyalists, replacing them with his own loyalists, promoting same to key positions. He followed up overhauling the combined military defense - the Army, the Navy, the Air Force, general welfare structure, increasing the salaries of their rank and file. He made the case to them of the fierce urgency of now and the unfathomable legacy of their duty of the "now or never" to save and make African children better than they find them. So much so that Status Quo leadership, headed by Mr. George, was rebuffed and refused in their overture to have the military defense, as always has been the case, at their side to suppress and cower Gen WHY, their leadership and the compassionate President from their revolutionary protest of "separation" at the Plaza Hill.

Enfeebled by the ponderous resistance at the Plaza Hill, and frustrated and dejected and in a spasm of assault of abject madness of his mindset of pseudo-omnipotence, Mr. George single-handedly financed and flew in the enormous quantity of cache of weaponry, wedging it in a church compound–the Abode of "men of God", the elusive gathering place of the Status Quo, with the intent to subvert and repress Gen WHY' revolution and overthrow government. The weaponry was the exploding weapons of the exploding night. Mr. George, as always, the indisputable orchestrator of misery and death, was the leader of the treasonable, subversive Status Quo. Only God in heaven can forgive him.

Mezzi, now out of his reverie, in a wilderness of tears, smiles to Tom Bradley. A smile, that in its desolation, devastation and forlornness, and drama seemed unfeigned and sincere.

Then they embrace. A long forgiving embrace that gives forgiveness and reconciliation and focusing a chance. The embrace is essential for the collective world of Gen WHY, for their collectivity tenet, to refocus on their collective arduous fight against their common planet problems. And its defense and protection and endurance for them and for their children's children's children's children's children, ad infinitum.

It's no longer a black world, nor a yellow world, nor a white world. It's a collective world that breaths collectivity: collective air, collective oxygen, collective pollution, collective cancer, collective wants, collective needs, collective problems, collective agony, collective happiness, collective solutions, collective spending, in antithesis to the divisive, hypocritical and fragmented, individualist, cynical, despotic world of the Status Quo.

Reconciliation and focusing are essential for progress of collectivity.

Focusing justifies reconciliation, and progress rewards focusing and exalts collectivity.

The drama overdrive absorbed, a happiest Buzzo started applauding. The crowd joins in. Everybody seemed relieved as they take their seats ready for the sumptuous dinner. Mezzi's puppy appears from nowhere and wags its tail, barking at him.

VOLUME 9

THE HOPE

Chapter 1

The platform. The Gen WHY's prize. The President's medal. Their pride. Their hope.

Today, the day most expected by Gen WHY is finally here.

Today, the day of the platform launch is here. A Gen WHY platform that personifies the purgation of the devil, the devil's son and the evil spirit – the African hereditary hierarchic despotism, with its evil tentacles of the Status Quo is here.

A place conceived from the millenary let down and delusion in Africa's devil son trinity – "men of God," the politicians, the monarchy. A center, an alternative to the church. A center not to defraud and console, not for misery contrivance and paying of tithe and sowing of seed, not to humiliate and subdue and give hope-hopelessness, but for youth empowerment. Gen WHY's empowerment. An African renaissance center. A place of rebirth. A learning and reasoning center. A palpable platform to console and mitigate and defuse the incendiary assault of emotions against the Status Quo and guide and channel the furious emotions, into a positive transformative force, to make their captivity captive. To dominate their filth and garbage. Earn respect.

Africa's descendants have always been perpetually fostered in misery. Generation after generation. Not Gen WHY descendant. These youths, inspired by a leadership, animated by the highest selflessness of liberty, with imbued unforgiving heroic enthusiasm, has staged a contrivance that subdued and crushed the spite and the defiance of hereditary despotism and its vicious and reprehensible misery giving. They separated. They got to Rubicon, climbed it and are fighting fiercely to cross it.

The air is full with expectations: The President is to hold the State of the Union address today on the way forward; the social platforms alongside the radio stations are peaking with beehive of activities and gone haywire, reminiscent of the mood of Gen WHY, with:

#Plat, plat, plat...platform, platform, platform!
#Plat, plat, plat...platform, platform, platform!
#Stand, stand, stand...standing up, standing up, standing up!
#Stand, stand, stand...standing up, standing up, standing up!
#Nigger, Nigger, Nigger...stand up, stand up, stand up!
#Dominance, Dominance, Dominance!
#Dominance, Dominance, Dominance!
#Dominate our Filth and Garbage!

430

#Dominate our Filth and Garbage!
#Captivity…captive!
#Captivity…captive!
#Misery…captive!
#Duty, duty, duty…make descendants better! Make descendants better!
#Duty, duty, duty…descendants better, descendants better, we make our descendants better than ourselves. Better than ourselves!

We are in the middle of cityscape. Now one can identify the Presidential Range Rover, in the middle of the commotion and the crunch of the people at their exertions and struggles to survive. The familiar and the exceptional are voluptuously noted: Lamborghini in the middle of the commuter buses; a Rolls Royce stuck in the middle of puddle of muddy water; men and women squatting, their bare butt to the traffic, defecating, urinating, relieving selves beside the fences of 5-Star Hilton Hotel; herdsmen with their herds, fogging consensually alongside the caravan of a sluggish traffic of cars, buses, and crowd of impoverished pedestrians among them; a majority of dispossessed youths and the anguished, angry, starving freeloaders at their wheel barrows; kids, most with their head pans of "merchandize" are on the streets parading and begging.

The absurdity of this humiliating, inexplicable scene anywhere in the 21st century is defiling. Defiling for any heart with spiritual essence. So much so that the assault of lacerating guiltiness should rout out the politicians, dispossess the monarchies, kill the "men of God", obliterate oracular gods, cleanse superstition, ask Jesus and Mohammad if they are real, remind them of their pent-up just and justice system, rob banks, deploy eruditeness, annihilate stupidity and primitivity and sloth and cowardice to make Africans and the Black Kind mind smart.

Now the Range Rover suddenly slows down and gradually pulls up beside the road that is overlooking a food square. A square defined by a lone tree and stalls of multiple restaurants, with a crowd of men seated under the lone tree busy at something.

Then Tom comes down from the car and without proffering any word to his peers in the car, leaving them in amazement, silently jumps over the trough and walks over, reaching the crowd of men under the lone tree.

In a glimpse he looks the place up taking in the situation, fixes the crowd of men silently, his face sphingine, as he fights off the ever nuisance African flies.

The crowd of men is made up of about eighty percent of men and twenty percent of youth. Five pairs of players are playing at the game of draughts, and they are without doubt so good at their art to have that huge number of spectators. The spectators, most of them on their feet are cheering on, busy at their cigarettes, beers, sodas and food as they fight the nuisance flies and mosquitoes. Few seem to have noticed him. In the meantime, you can't help but notice that Tom has a handkerchief meant to deal with his African sweltering sweat over his mouth and has repeatedly spitted into it, his mucous system obviously irritated, allergic to something. Now he suddenly turns, disengaging from them and heads back to the Range Rover. As he nears the trough, he stops and brings out a fresh handkerchief from his pocket, tying it over his mouth and nose. Then he continued and stops before the trough, stoops down checking it out closely and attentively. Done with it he reenters the Range Rover.

Mezzi: Tom are you okay?
Tom (forcing a smile): Yeah, I got curious of the men under the tree early morning. The stench from the trough is unbearable. I wonder how they breath it unperturbed. Jennifer: What now?
Tom: Mark kindly have your driver back up to about three blocks please. I think we passed a building material mart on our way here.
Mark: Yeah, there is one behind us.

Everybody is silently numbed with curiosity as the driver puts on hazard lights and backs up to the building materials mart, with block making outfit incorporated. Tom checks it out from the car and smiles.

Tom: Mezzi, let's go.
Mezzi: Cool.

Under the watchful eyes of Jennifer and Mark and the driver, Tom and Mezzi in a flash get down from the car and reach over to the building material mart. Tom checks out the place and he quickly negotiates and pays for a bunch of rectangular concrete slabs of 80x40x10 centimeters and squared ones of 80x80x10 cm and 3 biggest aluminum refuse bins with cover amongst the lot. He got them loaded onto two different trucks.
Tom and Mezzi get back to the Range Rover and followed by the two loaded trucks of slabs and refuse bins they drive back to food square with the crowd under the lone tree at draughts.
Now Tom comes down from the car and calls out loudly in the direction of the crowd:

Tom: Hello guys, we got urgent work to do here. I need your help please. Please!

The crowd notices but ignores his call. He tries again.

Tom: Please, please I need your help. Please, please!

His calls fell on deaf ears.
Then Mark joins him and he is recognized by the crowd. And immediately the youth among the crowd started applauding and hailing him as they instantly unite to them, as the men of the crowd continued, unperturbed the draughts spectacle.

Now Mezzi comes down, joining them, arousing an uproar.

The remaining men of the crowd take note and become uncomfortable, and in a flash disband and abandon the square. They are with no hint of doubt sympathizers of the status quo. They do nothing but confuse and mislead and punish the youths.

Everybody gets down to work unloading the slabs and, in a flash, trough was dominated with the rectangular slabs laid over them. The pungent smell is drastically reduced, and some decency of perception installed.

In the meantime, a ponderous, voluptuous crowd has milled and built, from nowhere, full of curiosity, watching the whole shebang.

Then they go over to the food square, landscaped the entire food square with the squared slabs, completely transforming it in a flash, to civility at everyone's surprise and judgement of delight.

Then the three biggest refuse bins are positioned and the filths and garbage swept into them and covered.

The crowd unutterably amazed and grateful, alongside Mezzi and Mark, applaud Tom, who in turn shares the moment of glory by concurrently applauding the youths who helped level out the place with shovels and laid the slabs. The applause slows down, ceases and Tom addresses the crowd.

Tom: Peers, there is a new dawn. You are your government. You see what you achieved right now with your efforts? You must stand up against the laziness and cowardice of your fathers and fathers' fathers. Stop loafing alongside consorts of devil trinity. Stop wasting your time playing draughts and such. You must recognize your filths and garbage, you must confront your filths and garbage, you must eradicate your filth and garbage, in sum you must dominate your environment. Don't sit amidst filth and garbage. You are human beings. Empower yourself, for empowerment as a favor from others is rare. Earn respect. Hard work! Hard work!!

> *...you must eradicate your filth and garbage, in sum you must dominate your environment. Don't sit amidst filth and garbage. You are human beings. Empower yourself, for empowerment as a favor from others is rare. Earn respect. Hard work! Hard work!!*

Mezzi, and Mark moved by pride of what Tom was capable of in little span of time, unite themselves to him and they all head back to the car amidst unyielding ponderous applause from the crowd.

The Range Rover finally pulls away and after a brief drive, veers off into a newly constructed low-trafficked 6-lane road, in the middle of a seeming forest, of a contrasting eerie silence.

Now the car stops. The doors of the car swing open, letting Mezzi, Mark, Tom, Jennifer alight.

Tom and Jennifer glimpse the place over and immediately crease into expressions of amazed, delighted incredulity: the familiarity of the broken complacency of their environment back home in the West recomposes and recompacts.

They scan the faces of Mezzi and Mark looking for answers. Their faces a simper, maliciously hold the answers. They insist, pressing intently for answer and then they understand: It's a park. It's a built park. It's an equipped park. It's the Youths platform.

Impulsively, they break with the group and cross the threshold, walking in. The secret of the park unravels. It's the Youths park. Their platform. Their renaissance self-consciousness credo platform. To imbue and elevate Black kind descendants mind perpetually with mindset of WHY and WHY NOT. Gen WHY youth is trailblazing it. The Gen WHY Platform. For generations of youths to come. Ad infinitum.

Their assault of emotion is so ponderous that they are numbed by it.

Jennifer, delightfully excited, runs back screaming, jumping into the arms of Mezzi. While Tom, creases instead, into a hopping spasm as his eyes roll over the unravelling park.

Jennifer: Wow, wow! This is a combined Harvard, Cambridge, Princeton, Columbus campuses. How did you guys do this?
Mark: It's beautiful, isn't it?
Jennifer: Mezz, this is exceptional!

Jennifer, without waiting for Mezzi's reaction, that is reluctant to express, disengages from his arms, dovetails her fingers into his and drags him into a brisk-walking pace. She wants to contemplate and feel this 'familiar' within the appalling African environment.

Mark is with them, playing the catch-up.

Mezzi: Mark, can you see Tom?
Mark: Tom is long gone. He must be somewhere within, admiring some precinct.

There is no hint of Tom. He is no doubt absorbed and swallowed by the familiar. Now, the trio embark on a tour of the Gen WHY platform. A platform of a concentric of rectangles. Each rectangle, a precinct of peculiar activities.

They find themselves on the outermost rectangle, adjacent to a new cutting-age 6-lane road, that spots on its either-side, a whopping ten-meter breath walkway, voluptuously framed by trees that seem centennial in nature. The trees are not new. The roads, the urbanization, structures, etc., etc. were designed and built around the existing trees and the nature. On the walkways and for the whole length, solar-powered current electricity and refuse bins are strewn everywhere, studded wooden sitting benches are provided, covered structured bus stops are noticeable, with each, a larger than life wall clocks affixed, and a collation of cabins of chemical toilets.

Jennifer (pointing at the cabins): Wow, look at those! That's cool. That is genial. Until now I hadn't given much thought to these cabins. You remember when our last year's boys scouting activity invaded the city of Los Angeles?

Mezzi: Yeah, and we overwhelmed the place. And those cabins saved the hygiene situations for our entire two weeks sojourn.

Mark (to Mezzi): Ah ha! That was where you got the idea. Everybody has been wandering.

Jennifer: The clocks are so large. Are the people mainly astigmatic or myopic?

Mezzi: What a question! We are, especially in the brain. Now both near and far sightedness can't complain any more. Africa's youth must keep to time otherwise we continue perpetuating the misery we find ourselves in.

Mark: Yes time, hard work, patience and perseverance.

Jennifer: This whole thing is amazing. Just look at the peace. The hygiene, the songs of the birds, the lizards, the crickets…this is astounding. Ultimate green. Green architecture. Green architecture indeed.

Jennifer suddenly stops, forcing Mezzi and Mark to do the same. Her face suddenly in a compassionate drawl, short of a sorrowing shame.

Jennifer (in audible mumbles): Those poor women defecating on the road! That was humiliating.

Mark: Yeah, very, very, very sad. A spectacle of indecency and humiliation.

Jennifer: Unutterable sadness. Completely unacceptable.

Mezzi: A sadness withered and emptied of embarrassment it seems.

Jennifer: They just need those toilet cabins strewn on every street.

Mark: But they are used to it.

Mezzi: Mark, common! If you are a human being, you can't be used to that humiliating violation of privacy and civility.

Jennifer (cuddling Mezzi's hair): You've really been through a lot.

These chemical cabins, these refuse systems, these sewerages and level of urbanization should be provided in the city as well. They need some Jesus Christ and Prophet Muhammad to provide them on the streets? Some dignity. There should be some dignity down here.

Mark: That's the fight.

Mezzi: Common, let's keep up with our tour.

Jennifer: Yeah, let's go. Your fight is indeed a noble but harrowing one.

What a question! We are, especially in the brain. Now both near and far sightedness can't complain any more. Africa's youths must keep ...

435

leianwls

CHAPTER 1

> *...in time otherwise we continue perpetuating the misery we find ourselves in.*

They are on the move again. Jennifer seems to crease into a harrowing anguish.

Jennifer: Mezz, I can't imagine your nights.
Mezzi: My nights? Coming to Africa one would think of kissing lions and elephants and zebras. I kissed instead, a litany of pang of miscellaneous misery and the miserable. I was overwhelmed.
Jennifer: My poor Mezz!
Mezzi: I was so angry and desperate that the days wedged me into chores of needs, and duties for the miserable. But the nights were truly wretched and excruciatingly miserable. Listening hard, the darkness sang horrors of misery: starving children, sobbing to conquer sleep; famished adults lamenting; most moment of silences were conveying deaths. These horrors were my night angels. They kept me awake.

Jennifer is too numbed. Her green eyes are fighting tears in vain. She brings her free hand to wipe her tears. Mark notices and offers her a handkerchief. She accepts it and wipes her face.
Now Mezzi stops in his tracks. Jennifer and Mark are forced to stop with him. He embraces her tightly and kisses her. Then, they bury their dejection in the solace of their found proximity, engaging in a long kiss that forgot or ignored Mark's presence. Mark contemplates them with exquisite delight. Now they disengage.

Mezzi: I love you!
Jennifer: I missed you and I am so sorry!
Mark: Cool. Love birds.

Jennifer and Mezzi crack up, breaking into feeble smiles that withered short of laughter.
They started moving again, insinuating themselves into the next precinct in line: the precinct of entertainment, strewn with discotheques, restaurants, bars. In the distance they can see people, torn between activities of culinary and commissioning of the structures and testing out of the sound systems, lights and lightings and sundries. As they get closer, they recognize and pick out Frank and Lynda from among the people.

Lynda: Hey Jennifer!
Jennifer: Hey, how are the gladiators preparing?
Lynda: We are all set for the evening.
Mezzi: Hey Frank, kindly, did you see our friend Tom?
Frank: Sure!

436

Lynda: They were here some moments ago.
Frank: He is in Buzzo's company. They went that way.

Mezzi, Jennifer and Mark trade glances and smiles, finally, fully appeased.

Mezzi: That way?
Frank: Yeah, towards the twin amphitheaters, on commissioning exercise.
Mezzi: Cool. Thank you. Good luck. See you guys later.

The twin contiguous amphitheaters are in the ultimate precinct. It is the point to present, recognize and award excellencies and world class entertainments. A catharsis and sublime center.

En route to the ultimate precinct, they step into the next precinct: precinct of precincts of sports and sporting activities where they met Brett, inspecting and checking things out. This precinct is linked to "children must play center," the ultimate antidote that mitigates Mezzi's psychological distress.

Nothing is lacking for the kids' cognitive growth in this equipped forest.

Jennifer: The children must play center. Your ultimate vision. This makes palpable your great spiritual essences. They will teach and inspire all of us always.
Mark: That's deep. Thank you.
Mezzi: That was too much, short of flattering.
Jennifer: No! I wish I could find the appropriate words. Just think about it: think of anyone your age in this wild world who has dared to do this.
Mezzi: A lot of them, in their own multiple humble ways. Africa makes orphan of its kids. Here you see these orphaned kids prostituting, slaving to feed their siblings and parents. That's ultimate heroism.
Mark: It's the bitter truth. That's our ponderous, harrowing, disgraceful reality.

> *...Africa makes orphan of its kids. Here you see orphaned kids prostituting, slaving to feed their siblings and parents. That's ultimate heroism.*

Jennifer: Yeah. You can't save the entire forest. You are inspiring to saving it.
Mezzi: Thank you. We are all aspiring for a better Africa. That's the fierce urgency.

437

As they march on, now into the penultimate precinct, the precinct of logic, grammar and rhetoric, the ultimate erudition forum, the rarefied cognition cradle, the cradle of Africa's youths' hope, the renaissance credo center, now they walk into Glenda and Lynda, with bags of snacks and sodas in their hands. The sight of those bags and the fragrance of food took them to the realization of their paused hunger and thirst. They look at their watches:

Mark: It's almost time for collation.
Jennifer: Hello all!
Mezzi: Hello ladies!
Glenda: Hello guys. How are you all?
Mark (fixing the bags): Could we have some of those?
Lynda: Yes, but you must follow us.
Mark (in a feeble protest): Again, to the church?

Mezzi bursts into laughter, surprising Jennifer, who does not understand. Glenda's shoulders offer a resigned shrug.

Lynda (piqued): That's not funny, young man!
Mark: Common be clement. You know I was only joking. We are thirsty! Glenda: Yeah! Let's go guys, so we can sit and eat civilly.

They follow Glenda and Lynda and after a brief walk, they turn, cutting into the ultimate precinct: a whole amazing breathtaking, beautiful place opens up to them – the contiguous twin amphitheater. A piece of architectural geniality in the ponderous concentric of rectangles center. Right in the middle of it they could see the silhouettes of David, Tom, and Buzzo seated around a table, discussing and their eyes between papers and the television hanging on the wall.

Delighted and happy, they quickened their walking pace towards them.
Now they are seen and noted back by Tom and the group.
Tom springs to his feet, out of his seat and runs towards them.
He runs straight ending in the arms of Mezzi. They embrace. Then they disengage.

Mezzi: You took off just like that. You were not afraid of the mysteries the African forests could hold?
Tom: No. Far from it. Mezzi, this environment is breathtaking. Carried away by its beauty, suaveness and peace, I acted on that impulse, and before I realized it, I was half way lost. This place is not just so big, it is magnificent and will for all times remain a cynosure of all eyes. Only the lions, the elephants, the antelopes, the zebras amongst others, are conspicuously missing.
Jennifer: Yeah, well said, the environment. And it's larger than Central Park.

Tom: Yeah, very large and curated and beautiful. Then Laura, the girl in charge of etiquette, hygiene and all, saw me.

Tom abruptly stops talking and locks stare with Jennifer, his eyes turning red and watery. Jennifer notices and alarmed she disengages momentarily from Mezzi and reaches out to Tom.

Jennifer: Tom, what's the matter?
Tom (now in tears, finding his voice): And can you guess where exactly she saw me? Jennifer: Where?
Tom (pointing at the vast field between the twin amphitheater): At the memorial ground over there for the fallen Gen WHYs at the Plaza Hill.

Jennifer, shocked and overwhelmed, she brings her stare and locks it with that of Mezzi and instantly broke down in tears.
Mezzi, who hadn't cried in Africa until the arrival of Jennifer, reaches Jennifer, embraces her and overwhelmed conceded to the luxury of his emotions: he started crying like a baby, profusely for a second time.
Mark reaches out, embracing them tightly.
Then they seem to recover a little bit and Mark, now disengages from them.

Tom: Yeah that was where Laura found me paying my respect to their epitaphs with prayers. From there she led me and handed me over to Buzzo after an interminable walk.
Mark: Yeah, this place is all about our business. This is Gen WHY's Central Business District alongside our dead but living heroes, absolutely out of bounds for Status Quo. And soon we will fill it with lions and elephants to crush the Status Quo.

Everybody cracks up.
Now they join Buzzo and David. Within the greeting pleasantries, Glenda and Lynda are already laying the sandwiches, the sodas, biscuits, serviette on the table. They are all seated now and grabbing and grappling with snacks and sodas. The television is on the local channel, silently transmitting images. The State of the Union Address of the President is imminent. Buzzo is intermittently checking his watch.

Buzzo: Jennifer, what's your impression of Mezzi?
Jennifer (surprised by the suddenness of the predatory question): Of Mezzi?
Buzzo: Yeah?
Jennifer (recovers, finding her words): He is an exceptional being. A blessing to humanity. He channeled a predatory anger into achieving this exceptional familiarity. This exceptional wavelet could be the catalyst whose ripple effect will impact a whole continent.

Tom: Well said Jonny. Mezzi positively reacted to my vicious provocation, illinformed by the malicious white supremacist's books and communication organs.

Mezzi: Malicious supremacist's books and organs? No, Tom. Without that your courage at candor, my life would have been an illusion. I would have been lost to a false identity and stupid complacency and beyond imbecile belief that the world is an equal place, *societe' egalitaire*, a fair playing field for everyone.

Then he pauses, looks at Mark and continues.

Mezzi: Then I have my hero here. My friend Mark. Mark is indeed the man. Top. Exceptionally tempered radical of ultimate humor.

Glenda: Yeah, just look at him. You think he can't hurt a fly.

Lynda: He steals the heart away, instead.

David: My little Machiavelli. He changed the heart of our father. That helped.

Mezzi: Helped? Without the President, everything would have been a mirage. Gone into a crashing spasm. At best happening but not so fast in a continent of misery, arid of shame, of remorse, of courage for any revolution.

David: Well, my father is doing nothing exceptional. He is late in doing what the best people have always done, paraphrasing Harriet Beecher Stow:

"It's a matter of taking the side of the weak against the strong, something the best people have always done."

Buzzo: (checking out his watch): Trust me, he is a rare gem especially in this part of the world. Jennifer, what do you think of this place?

Jennifer: It's amazing. Then, finding it within the African bare and naked and unurbanized environment makes it the more exceptional. The question is why everywhere is not like this? Its exceptionality seems cynical.

Tom: Precisely the point. We are in the 21st century, folks. Urbanized environment should be familiar, not exceptional; refuse bins should be familiar, not exceptional; the solar powered lights, the public toilets, the city clocks, the hygiene for human dignity, should all be familiar not exceptional.

The contrast between the familiar and the bare and the naked African environment out there, is exceptionally of a grieving, humiliating shame. An abhorrent, crippling shame and that is to say the least.

If the world's Status Quo is criminal, pillager and heartless, the African Status Quo is cynical. Africa should not, and I repeat should not afford the luxury of not having the backs of her descendants home and abroad. Africa throws her descendants to the mouth of the wolves and feels the ultimate smugness. Shame on Africa!

Jennifer: Folks, just think about the trauma that these deprived, humiliated youths that live over there, would come over here, kiss it, only

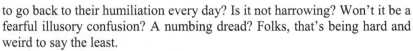

to go back to their humiliation every day? Is it not harrowing? Won't it be a fearful illusory confusion? A numbing dread? Folks, that's being hard and weird to say the least.

Mark: Very true.

The contrast between the familiar and the bare and the naked African environment out there, is exceptionally of a grieving, humiliating shame. An abhorrent crippling shame and that is to say the least. If the world's Status Quo is criminal, pillager and heartless, the African Status Quo is cynical. Africa should not, and I repeat should not afford the luxury of not having the backs of her descendants home and abroad. Africa throw her descendants to the mouth of the wolves and feels the ultimate smugness. Shame on Africa.

Buzzo: Folks, I think it's been said that nothing barely exists without the existence of its opposite. That life is a process of struggle between the opposites – light and darkness, hot and cold, pleasure and displeasure, suffering and enjoyment, sadness and happiness. That looks like irrefutable life trajectory. No life trajectory is a constant. Indeed, we can't be happy 24 hours. You can't be sad 24 hours, you can't eat 24 hours, you can't cry 24 hours. Life is made up of mini-objectives. Keeps changing.

Having said that, this platform is utmost for their pride in their shame and humiliation. Something to reach out and touch. Palpable. Not illusive. In their shame and humiliation something over there, within their reach, palpable will soothe their psyche. Something that will inspire them every minute, that is within their reach, to aspire to, to emulate and copy from. Not imagined.

The whole effort is to have our lives to enfold theirs within the confines of our combined familiar and exceptionality of the familiar, within our triumphs and sorrows, within our pride and shame.

David: That was a deep construct.

Glenda: Jennifer, it's important for us to have this place within reach. Majority of us can only but imagine Milan, New York, Rome, Paris, California, London, Geneva, Venice, Tokyo, Hong Kong, Seoul, Moscow, etc., and their beauty from here in our lifetimes.

Lynda: Yeah having a place of respite, not on some social media, or on some television station, or on some soap opera, right here that looks like your familiar, that can host our portraits for Facebook, Instagram …

Buzzo: So sorry Lynda.

Folks, I think it's been said that nothing barely exists without the existence of its opposite. That life is a process of struggle between …

> *...the opposites–light and darkness, hot and cold, pleasure and displeasure, suffering and enjoying, sadness and happiness. That looks like irrefutable life trajectory. No life trajectory is a constant. Indeed, we can't be happy 24 hours. You can't be sad 24hrs, you can't eat 24 hours, you can't cry 24 hours. Life is made up of miniobjectives. Keeps changing.*

Buzzo, his eyes on the television, goes for the remote control, only to drop it back on the table with a contorted frown. Even though it wasn't yet time for the imminent State of the Union Address, the sudden mutation in transmission on the television had him think of anticipation. This State of the Union Address is as fundamental as their lives going forward. It will confirm the President's guts at love for Gen WHY descendants and their validation.

Buzzo (apologetic): Sorry folks. The sense of our lives hinges on what comes out of that television today.
Mark: Yeah, correct!
Buzzo: And to you Tom: What's the meaning of Nigger?

Tom, who has had to deal with the nastiness of that question time and again, did not blink: he has long been expecting it. Everybody, expectedly creases into attentive rapt composure. It's an open secret that Tom's inveighs spurred Mezzi to the fortunes of their reality of the present. A platitude.

Tom: I have been scolded, then spanked, then systematically, emotionally abused and blackmailed by my father for my legion of "what is a Nigger?" question.
Jennifer: Poor boy!
Tom: What a Nigger is, seems not to have answers.
Mezzi: The answers are swallowed in hate and hypocrisy.
Tom: I am persistently, systematically referenced to history of slavery, colonialism, the compromise, Jim Crow, the lynching – old and present, racial profiling, structured racism explained very well in Martin Luther King's words.
Buzzo: Wow, lucky you. Some historical lessons and updates?
Tom: How I wish...My father is overtly ignorant. He hides his ignorance in the KKK doctrine. In their hate. In their inveighs. In their defiles. In their systematic conspiracy, propaganda. Every day I wake up to his daily homily of: "They are subhumans, coons, human filths, human garbage, parasites, rats, cockroaches, good at nothing."
Buzzo: Poor Tom. What a harrowing, psychological torture.
Jennifer: Unutterable stress and sadness.

Tom: **And when I protest, retorting: "You are not objective. They excel and are excelling in all fields of human endeavor – doctors, engineers, architects, sports, music, theatre, arts, politics, congressmen, a black President ...," he will fire back: "Ignorant, inform yourself on Africa before you open your dirty mouth. Africa has no hospitals, no sewerage, no roads, no running water, no toilets. So how can they have doctors, engineers, architects? They are sub-humans."**

Mezzi: On Africa he is damn right. On descendants African Americans he is not.

Tom: Yeah, in fact my mother, instead, tells him he is not, either way: "Remember that the wealth and well-being of the Whites are thanks to the almost 300 years of their free slave labor and as if that was not enough, their freedom by President Lincoln in 1863 with famine is no freedom." And...

Buzzo: Your mom tells him this historical truth?

Mezzi: Yes, Martin Luther King's "bootstrap of the bootless."

Tom (at a loss): Bootstrap of the bootless?

Buzzo: African American descendants were given freedom without any financial or economic base: No land. No money, no compensation for almost 300 years of slavery, and told they have freedom of hell. What kind of freedom was that?

Sorry, please go ahead.

Tom: Now I get the facts fully. Yes, my mom tells her this truth with alacrity and candor, and on Africa instead she goes "...Africa is a continent of unfortunate circumstances. We are all complicit. We are all responsible for the underdevelopment of African environment. In our environment they excel. You and your KKK are afraid of their latent prowess."

At those words, hell gets lose. It's like a knife driven into his heart...

Buzzo: A knife on his KKK spiritual essence?

Tom: He throws injurious tantrums at my poor mom: "Whore, they only have muscles in the body. They are crazed with lust. Whore, I am sure you are having sex with Niggers, that's why miscreant whores like you elected a Nigger President."

Jennifer: Wow, what a family! Is that what you go through?

Buzzo: What a jealous father you have!

Tom: And I say to him, President Barrack Obama is not a Nigger, whatever Nigger means. He is biracial. He is half our White blood. Just like my friend Mezzi and his brother. Then he gets really furious and goes on tantrum of "One blood drop" doctrine, "the 3/5th compromise," "ranking," "ordering," "White privilege," "White Supremacy," "Negro subjugation in perpetuity." And then he adds: "Your friends know they have nothing to do with Whites. They are by accident. Accident of a casual but cynical sexual congress. They are Niggers. Taunt them, bait them with the name Nigger and see their reaction. I bet you to prove me wrong." And out of cowardice I willfully got drunk, to be able to carry out my father's challenge, calling Mezzi...

Tom, choking, overwhelmed by emotion, is visibly fighting back tears. Buzzo reaches out cuddling his head. Mezzi reaches, hugging him tight to himself. Lynda is refilling his glass with water. Jennifer has tears streaming down her cheeks.

Buzzo: Tom you are a good heart. Let me make you proud aligning you and your mom with the revered Martin Luther King's answer to an NBC reporter's question in May, 1967 to why black Americans face more obstacles and don't get around easily than white European immigrants. I quote:

"White America must see that no other ethnic group has been a slave on American soil.
That is one thing other immigrant groups haven't had to face.
The other thing is that the color became a stigma.
American society made the Negroes' color a stigma.
America freed the slaves in...1863, through the Emancipation
Proclamation of Abraham Lincoln...but gave the slaves no land or nothing in reality...to get started on.
At the same time, America was giving away millions of acres of land...in the West and Midwest, which meant there was a willingness to give to White peasants from Europe...an economic base.
And yet it refused to give its Black peasant who came here involuntarily, in chains, and had worked free for 244 years, any kind of base.
And so, emancipation for the Negro was really freedom to hunger. It was freedom to the winds and rains of heaven.
It was freedom without food to eat or land to cultivate and therefore...it was freedom and famine at the same time.
And when White Americans tell the Negro to lift himself by his own bootstraps...they don't look over the legacy of slavery and segregation.
Now, I believe we ought to do all we can and seek to lift ourselves by our own bootstraps...but it's a cruel jest to say to a bootless man that he ought to lift himself by his own bootstraps. And many Negroes, by the thousands and millions have been left bootless as a result of all these years of oppression...and as a result of a society that deliberately made his color a stigma...and something worthless and degrading."

Tom (shocked and elated): Poor group. It had been from origin a systematic structured racism. And these facts are willfully hidden with cynical complicity.

Buzzo: With cynical complacence complicity of the White kind yes, but they are not willfully hidden. Let's underpin by quoting a Great, a great President, President JF Kennedy:

"This nation was founded by men of many nations and backgrounds. It was founded on the principle that all men are created equal and that the rights of everyman are diminished when the rights of one man are threatened.

It ought to be possible, in short, for every American to enjoy the privileges of being American without regard to his race or his color. In short, every American ought to have the right to be treated, as one would wish his children to be treated.

But this is not the case. 100 years of delay have passed since President Lincoln freed the slaves – yet their heirs, their grandsons, are not fully free.

They are not yet freed from the bonds of injustice. They are not yet freed from social and economic oppression.

And this nation, for all its hopes and all its boasts, will not be fully free until all its citizens are free.

We are confronted primarily with a moral issue. It is as old as the Scriptures and is as clear as the American Constitution.

It cannot be met by repressive police action.

It cannot be left to increased demonstrations in the streets.

It cannot be quieted by token moves or talk. It is a time to act in the Congress, in your state and local legislative body, and above all, in all of our daily lives. Those who do nothing are inviting shame, as well as violence.

Those who act boldly are recognizing right, as well as reality."

Tom: Wow!

Buzzo: You got it now. No excuses for the conscience of the "good" white man.

Tom: And yet nothing happened? And this hate thing is still happening.

Buzzo: Something ponderously happened Tom. They put bullets in President Kennedy's body. Poor man! May his sincere soul rest in perfect peace. And the signified of the bullets is "Silence freedom…Privilege does not share." So, it is totally left to us to fight recognizing, confronting and eradicating this human shame, this injustice with unflinching audacity.

Mezzi: However, yours was a ponderous, courageous act and I will be ever grateful.

David: Just look around what we are achieving, thanks to you.

Glenda: We, unfortunately inherited a difficult world indeed.

Buzzo: The world status quo wants to subject us to their mess for no fault of ours. But we, the world's youths, the world's Gen WHY got to fight to make it right. Anyway, let me give you all what the definition of a Nigger could look like.

445

Everybody lends attentive ear with soothing expectations.

Buzzo: Indeed, I will give you two definitions, one of a Nigger and the other of a Scum. Are you all ready?

They readily but silently nod their heads 'assent.'

Buzzo: *A Nigger is any human being, wherever, of any race, who lets his innate self-consciousness be effaced and be replaced and be dictated to by some conspiracy of subservient self-consciousness essence from anybody, any group, any quarter and is governed by such.*

Buzzo pauses, scanning their faces in mental notes, giving them some seconds to internalize. But Mezzi instantly pierces the air.

Mezzi: In fact, Tom, you refused to be a nNigger! You fought the KKK Scum and scumism in your family and in society until you were overwhelmed, drunk to confront me.

Mezzi winks at those last words. Everybody breaks up laughing.

Mark: Right! Overwhelmed like some cowardly gladiator pushed into Roman colosseum to slug it out.

Buzzo, now badgers on.

Buzzo: *While a Scum is any human being, wherever, of any race, whose conscience is replaced, supplanted with illusional self-consciousness of omnipotence to contrive and impress and impinge conspiracy of subservient self-consciousness essence in another human being, with the sole intent to dehumanize, and disfranchise and pillage and loot and dispossess and possess.*
Tom (fully recovered): Then my father is a Scum.
Mezzi: And mine is a Craven Nigger.

Mezzi and Tom lock stare, concurrently and mutually nodding their heads affirmatively "we concur."

While A scum is any human being, wherever, of any race, whose conscience is replaced, supplanted with self-consciousness of omnipotence to contrive and impress and impinge conspiracy of subservient self-consciousness essence in another human being, with the sole intent to dehumanize, and disfranchise and pillage and loot and dispossess and possess.

Buzzo: In fact, both the Scum, prominently personified by the White's Supremacists the KKK, and the Nigger, prominently personified by the Africa's Status Quo, inflict disavowal, repudiation, denial, pillage, punishment, disdain, ranking, reification of fellow human species. In sum, two categories of ignoble human beings in the business of dehumanizing fellow human beings.

Tom: Yeah, when a man is capable of repudiating himself, his gene. Capable of the cowardice and hypocrisy of coining and enforcing, and upholding and validating an abhorrent 'one-drop rule'-ism. Only a human scum can be capable of that after a sexual congress.

Mezzi: You are in the middle of the capableness of a Nigger. Just look at Negro's environment. An utter disaster of hollowness.

Jennifer: Yeah, a hollowness of harrowing misery. Medieval books misery.

Mezzi: A Nigger's capableness is the passion of gifting filths and garbage.

Glenda: The scum and the Nigger are birds of the same feather.

Tom: I think a Nigger is worse off. How can you be convinced, by any intent of purpose, whatsoever, good or bad, by a fellow human being to give up your birthright, give yourself filth, to live in filth and garbage and to hate yourself?

Buzzo: Well said. That's why a Nigger is a sub-human being. And the scum, the Devil's incarnate. Tom, by the way, what do you think of hate or if you prefer, why do Whites hate Blacks?

Mark: Yes! Why does your race hate us?

Tom: Cool, I am not sure I know all the reasons. I will try to answer to the best of my capacity and knowledge. And I hope everyone here loves candor.

My dad is a proud, outspoken Klansman. Sorry, an avowed White supremacist KKK scum.

Everybody breaks up, laughing. But undistracted Tom badgers on.

> *In fact, both the Scum, prominently personified by the White's Supremacists, the KKK, and the Nigger, prominently personified by the Africa's Status Quo, infringes disavowal, repudiation, denial, pillage, punishment, disdain, ranking, reification of fellow human species. In sum two categories of ignoble human beings in the business of dehumanizing fellow human beings.*

Tom: My mom is hypercritical of KKK, but a Klan's wife. However, my mom represents almost the overriding intrinsic sentiments of the majority of the White race: fairness and goodwill and justice. Even though a luxury of hypocrisy and comfort in silence has the better of their sentiments. That I can guarantee you. And I find myself to be their son.

Mark: You find yourself their son?

Tom: Yes. Mezzi knows. The KKK is a handful of abhorrent cowards, composed of their few well educated, well to do ideologues, powerfully entrenched in our world institutions and the White left-overs who are the dogs on the field.

Mezzi: Educated and have entrenched powers in our institutions?

Tom: Yes, Mezzi. Their ideologues are entrenched in every White governments around the world, in their army, in their police, in the World Bank, in the International Monetary Fund, in the World Health Organization, in World Trade organization, in Food and Agriculture Organization, in the United Nations, in the Food chains, on the Wall Street, in Sport Discipline. In every world's institution.

Everyone is stunned. But not Mezzi. Not Buzzo. Their mom was a pristine malaise.

Tom: Yes. They are a confraternity. You can't imagine the circle of acquaintance of my father, who is a college dropout. They operate in the darkness metaphorically and spatially. Just like the devil, light is their nemesis.

They are the garbage, the scum of the White race, no doubt. Their intrinsic spiritual essence is abjectly afflicted and conflicted with sense of fear, insecurity and hollowness, desperation, jealousy, anger, frustration, hate, subjugation, pillage, destruction of the other kind. Regardless they seem to bend the majority of the White race to their will. The comfort in hypocrisy and in complacent silence and in institutional looting by the White family is been complicit for too long. White family pretend to be far removed from the phenomenon. His Fathers, father's fathers did the same. The only good news is that we, the White Gen Z have open repulsion for this insane, hateful indoctrination. In any case, to live with the KKK-ism is like living in hellfire. Their indoctrination is vicious and ponderous. Their emotional blackmail unfathomable. Their pathological, compulsive defile, coercion and stigmatization within the family of the White race is unutterable. My mother does what she has to.

Mezzi: What?

Tom: Live with it. Tolerate it. Unacceptable to it. Just like almost every White family. People like my mom, who are caught between palpable scum-ism at home and the imagination of Nigger-ism afar, of the African continent, as described and painted by the White supremacist scum and their propaganda machines, are torn to make a choice of what to believe.

Yes, my race hates you, but the question in itself, here in Africa is highly irritating.

Mark: Why so?

Tom: The answer is out there. Seeing is believing. Coming here, everything heard, told, portrayed about Nigger-ism pales and is incredibly and unfortunately palpable. Your environment is the answer. The state of your environment is sub-human. Of unutterable appellations. African Negro did not prove the White supremacists scum wrong. It becomes too easy to side with White supremacist scum-ism. Side with hate and disdain, not just against Nigger-ism, but against the entirety of the Negro kind.

Glenda: Are you sure? You don't hate us for our mineral wealth, our natural endowments?

Tom: 400 years ago, no shadow of doubt. Jealousy and hate gave dehumanization, disposed and possessed what they did not have. Today the West has some mineral resources. So, today the hate is on Nigger-ism. Whether it be White Nigger-ism, as practiced, for example, by the Russian oligarchs and by the leaders of South American countries, or Black Nigger-ism, as we have here in Africa, we should all hate Nigger-ism.

And by the way, maybe, you knew of some of your mineral wealth, but you did not discover any use for your mineral wealth, until the White discovered the use for them. Give it to them for their bravery at curiosity, research, discoveries, inventions and innovations and for their institutional skill at greed, jealousy, exploitation and exclusion and looting contrivances and perpetuity to empower her descendants, all made possible by Africa's stupidity. Africa has had time to amend and develop but does not.

Tom's answer of unutterable reality and truth is swallowed by their eerie defeated silence of unutterable shame.

He continues.

Tom: So, look at it this way if you will: I discover your mineral wealth of which you don't know anything about, and of which, therefore, you have no use for. I need it, of course, and I have the wherewithal to take it. So, why would I tell you about it if I hate you because of it? Won't it be logical to quietly cart it away?

He tells you instead. If he has no morals absolutely, if he does not want you to share in it, why would he tell you and hate you for something you don't want and would not want to know about anyway? He did all these in good faith and a moment later he rips this solemn contract apart because of Africa's stupidity through their abject sloth and cowardice and abject love for cosmetics. Remember black people love glittering finished products. They don't want to participate in making them. They love finished products. They abhor being in charge of creating wealth. Of hard work

Mark: Yeah. It makes sense. A lot of sense.

The answer is out there. Seeing is believing. Coming here, everything heard, told, portrayed about nigger-ism is incredibly and unfortunately palpable. Your environment is the answer. The state of your ...

...environment is sub-human. Of unutterable appellations. Negro did not prove the white supremacists scum wrong. It becomes too easy to side with White supremacist KKK scum-ism. Side with their hate and their disdain, not just against nigger-ism, but against the entirety of the negro kind.

Tom: Does any of us like liabilities? The answer is no. Not even as kids. Liability is failure. Great failure. Degradation, humiliation, racism, classism and hate become easily consequential. You Mezzi, you made me sit up to study hard. You remember? You mocked me. Your mockings made me have shame and shame in turn made me sit up, because I wanted to have your friendship. I wanted to be like you, proud. My mother repeatedly said "Look at your friend Mezzi, how brilliant he is. You should feel shame."

He pauses, engaging and locking stare with Mezzi and then continues.

Tom: I felt jealous and shame. You encouraged and inspired me. You taught me. I walked in your shadows. I listened. I had shame. If I hadn't reacted, you would have discriminated and hated me for my non-reactivity. And probably abandoned me to my fate.

Everyone is listening very hard. Voluptuously collected. Ponderously rapt. They are trying to objectively come to terms with Tom's sense of reasoning.

Tom: Whiteman hates you for your "out there." White man hates you for the things you should and can do but you refused to do.
Just look at your degrading environment. It's beneath what the Klansman thinks. It stinks beyond any imagination. In the 22nd century?
First, my race comes in contact with you, gets jealous of your endowments, natural and physical, and deceives you with the bible, and they write of you and I quote:
"Evangelize the Niggers so that they stay forever in submission to the White colonialists, so they never revolt against the restraints they are undergoing. Recite everyday – 'happy are those who are weeping because the kingdom of God is for them.' Convert always the Blacks by using the whip. Keep their women in nine months of submission to work freely for us. Force them to pay you in sign of recognition – goats, chicken or eggs - every time you visit their villages. And make sure that Niggers never become rich. Sing every day that it's impossible for the rich to enter heaven. Make them pay tax each week at Sunday mass. Use the money supposed for the poor, to build flourishing business centers. Institute a confessional system, which allows you to be good detectives denouncing any Black that has a different consciousness contrary to that of the

decision maker. Teach the Niggers to forget their heroes and to adore only ours. Never present a chair to a Black that comes to visit you. Don't give him more than one cigarette. Never invite him for dinner even if he gives you a chicken every time you arrive at his house."

This was King Léopold II of Belgium, 1883.

Yet, you read the bible he brought you and you adore his interpretation of the bible of you. And yet you did not cast doubt whatsoever in your minds. You refuse to understand that we have a special bible. You are blind to White's special bible shrouded in hypocrisy. You refuse to comprehend that the proclamation of "all men are created equal...and its inalienable rights" is White America's deceptive mechanism to structure and perpetuate structured racism. And you refuse to react to your institutional exclusion and exploitation and humiliation till today.

Instead, like ignoble poor masses, you have an unimaginable strength to endure the betrayal and punishment of your few ignoble rich, who are parasites, like cockroaches and mosquitoes that operate in the darkness. African masses, your sin of unending endurance is even worse. All you can aspire is to be like them?

Gen WHY is stunned to hear this black on white document.

Mark: Where can we find this quote Tom?

Mezzi: It's everywhere in the books, in the libraries. On your phones. On the Internet.

Buzzo: Google the quotes on Africa. It's easy. Reiterating, our greatest sin is not reading.

Yet, you read the bible he brought you and you adore his interpretation of the bible of you. And yet you did not cast doubt whatsoever in your minds. You refuse to understand that we have a special bible. You are blind to White's special bible shrouded in hypocrisy. You refuse to comprehend that the proclamation of "all men are created equal...and its inalienable rights" is White America's deceptive mechanism to structure and perpetuate structured racism. And you refuse to react to your exclusion and exploitation till today. Instead, like ignoble poor masses, you have an unimaginable strength to endure the betrayal and punishment of your few ignoble rich, who are parasites, like cockroaches and mosquitoes that operate in the dark. African masses, your sin of unending endurance is even worse. All you can aspire is to be like them?

Tom: Secondly, he derogates and derides you and I quote:

"Africa has no history and did not contribute to anything that mankind enjoyed." - Georg Friedrich Hegel 1786.

sAnother: *"At this point we leave Africa, not to mention it again. For it is no historical part of the world; it has no movement or development to exhibit...What we properly understand by Africa, is the Unhistorical, Undeveloped Spirit, still involved in the conditions of mere nature, and which had to be presented here only as on the threshold of the World's History."* - Georg Friedrich Hegel 1830.

And yet a collection of other sayings by same Philosopher Hegel:

"The History of the world is none other than the progress of the consciousness of freedom."
"What constitutes a person and gives him rights is not mere consciousness, but self-consciousness."
"Every spirit, once in the world yearns for actualization and self-authentication – to make itself what it can become. This sort of spiritual thriving of the self involves some levels of entanglement of the stream of consciousness with the dialectical order."
"Africa loves the sign, not the signified."
"Africa is therefore a land where consciousness has not yet attained to the realization of any objective existence."
"Therefore, Africa has not reached the level of realizing his own being. He has not yet realized his own person."
"The African is the natural man in his completely wild and untamed state.
"Africa proper is the land of childhood."
-George Fredrich Hegel 1830

Yet another:
"To those who say derogatory things about colonialism, I would say colonialism is a wonderful thing. It spread civilization to Africa. Before it they had no written language, no wheel as we know it, no schools, no hospitals, not even normal clothing." - Ian Smith 1997.

And yet another:
Since the dawn of history, the Negro has owned the continent of Africa – rich beyond the dream of Poet's fancy, crunching acres of diamonds beneath his bare feet. Yet he never picked one up from the dust until a White man showed to him its glittering light. His land swarmed with powerful and docile animals yet he never dreamed a harness...a hunter by necessity, he never made an axe, spear or arrowhead worth preserving beyond the moment of its use. He lived as an ox, content to graze for an hour. In a land of stone and timber he never sawed a foot of lumber, carved a block, or built a house save of broken sticks and mud...for four

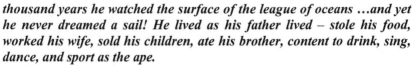

thousand years he watched the surface of the league of oceans ...and yet he never dreamed a sail! He lived as his father lived – stole his food, worked his wife, sold his children, ate his brother, content to drink, sing, dance, and sport as the ape.
-Thomas f. Dixon Jr. 1905

And yet another.

"Ours is one continual struggle against a degradation sought to be inflicted upon us by the Europeans, who desire to degrade us to the level of the raw kaffir, (Nigger) whose occupation is hunting, and whose sole ambition is to collect a certain number of cattle to buy a wife with and, then, pass his life in indolence and nakedness." - Mahatma Gandhi, 1896

Glenda: Gandhi?
Tom: Yes!
Lynda: Mahatma that trained in South Africa?
Tom: Yet another.

"In character and temperament, the typical African of this race-type is a happy, thriftless, excitable person. **Lacking in self-control, discipline, and foresight. Naturally courageous, and naturally courteous and polite, full of personal vanity, with little sense of veracity, fond of music and loving weapons as an oriental loves jewelry.** His thoughts are concentrated on the events and feelings of the moment, and **he suffers little from the apprehension for the future or the grief for the past.** His mind is nearer to the animal world than that of the European or Asiatic, and exhibits something of the animal's placidity and want of desire to rise beyond the state he has reached. Through the ages the African appears to have evolved no organized religious creed, and though some tribes appear to believe in a deity, **the religious sense seldom rises above pantheistic animalism and seems more often to take the form of a vague dread of the supernatural.**

He lacks the power of organization, and is conspicuously deficient in the management and control alike of men or business. He loves the display of power, but fails to realize its responsibility...he will work hard with incentive than most races. He has the courage of the fighting animal – an instinct rather than a moral virtue....in brief, the virtues and defects of this race-type are those of attractive children, **whose confidence when it is won is given ungrudgingly as to an older and wiser superior and without envy**...perhaps the two traits which have impressed me as those **most characteristic of the African native are his lack of apprehension and ability to visualize the future"** – Lord Lugard, 1922.
Tom: And yet another:

"I am inherently gloomy about the prospect of Africa, because all our social policies are based on the fact that their intelligence is the same as ours – whereas all the testing says not really." -James Watson 2007.

The list of derogations is infinite and yet Africa did not, does not react till this day. Can't feel shame.

Mezzi is in unutterable gloominess. These reminders hit him like thunderbolt. The spasm of pains are of unutterable shame. Now he understands the lightness and the goodness of Tom's "Nigger inveighs."

Others seem too numbed to believe and too incredulous and confused for rage. Tom notices and his face is expressing: My man Mezzi needs to heal. He needs to be free from these inherited torments and heal completely.

Tom: Thirdly, he stereotyped you.
In fact, paraphrasing Mr. Brady:
"The transatlantic slave trade committed heinous injustices on the African continent, but the colonial era that came next did the greatest damage. The colonial powers rode on the bed of racial roses prepared by philosophers like Hegel, who provided a basis for modern racism by establishing a role for race in history by correlating a hierarchy of civilizations to a hierarchy of races.

In fact, colonialism oppressed, brainwashed, manipulated, slaughtered, humiliated, subdued and downplayed the African people and culture. Africa has had to contend with the ponderous and excruciating weight of smear of stereotypes with "independence." So much so that instead of reacting, you succumb hating yourself. This is epitomized in your hate for your skin color, your hate for your hair texture, your hate for your Continent. To the extent that you loot your monies away into the Whiteman's banks. These are the bigotries and the contradictions and insanities you struggle with."

He pauses and reaches for his soda, amidst the expression of rage of unutterable thumping anger and spasm of puckering pain and broken heartedness in everybody's penetrating stare on him. He continues, confiding in the miracle of tough love.

Tom: In sum someone appears, deceives you with the bible, you did not stand up; he derogates you, you did not stand up; he subjugates you, you did not stand up; he stereotypes and stigmatizes you, you did not stand up; he derides you, you did not stand up. In all these you prove no sense of shame, no remorse, no pride.

You identify with laziness, personifying it. You identify with cowardice, personifying it. You identify with denial, personifying it and You identify with filth and garbage, personifying them. You identify with liability, personifying it. You identify with complacency, personifying it. All numbing sheer stupidity. You personify stupidity and primitiveness indeed. What option do you think you left him with?

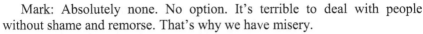

Mark: Absolutely none. No option. It's terrible to deal with people without shame and remorse. That's why we have misery.

Tom: The only option you left him with is to hate you.

He hates you, because he has invented enough, he has given you everything to copy, imitate and innovate and have your own life style. Be independent. And you have a house divide. Not making efforts.

He hates you because you won't have your own life style.

He hates you because he is jealous of his life style.

He hates you, because you are blessed by nature. He is jealous of your blessings.

He hates you because you don't decode nature and your blessings.

He hates you because you are an inveterate, God forsaken consumer, totally inanimate "…not contributing anything that mankind can enjoy."

"…not contributing anything that mankind can enjoy."

In sum someone appears, deceives you with the bible, you did not stand up; he derogates you, you did not stand up; he subjugates you, you did not stand up; he stereotypes and stigmatizes you, you did not stand up; he derides you, you did not stand up. In all these you prove no sense of shame, no remorse, no pride.

You identify with laziness, personifying it. You identify with liability, personifying it. You identify with complacency, personifying it. All numbing sheer stupidity. You personify stupidity. What option do you think you left in him?

The only option you left him with is to hate you.

He hates you, because he has invented enough, he has given you everything to copy, imitate and innovate and have your own life style. Develop yourself. Be independent. Empower your descendants. And you are a house divided. Not making efforts.

He hates you, because you won't have your own life style.

He hates you, because he is jealous of his life style.

He hates you, because you are blessed by nature. He is jealous of your blessings.

He hates you because you don't decode nature and your blessings. He hates you because you are an inveterate, God forsaken consumer, totally inanimate…not contributing anything that mankind can enjoy.

And worst still, at his hate, you take pride in his material life style. Never in his intellectual life style–grammar, logic and rhetoric – that culminates in critical thinking, critical analysis, recognize, research, confront, invent, innovate, empower. At his hate, you take pride in looting and plundering your continent into his banks. At his hate, you take pride in humiliating and enslaving your descendants, generation after generation, in perpetuation.

Mezzi: Yes, what a beautiful construct. The problem is not much of what they did to Black kind, and what they do to Black kind but much of what Black kind did and does to self.

Buzzo: Precisely the problem! The reprehensible, enduring abject inability of not recognizing, not just what they did to us, what they do to us and what they think of us but what we did to us, what we do to us and what we think of us. Black kind could not recognize that they did slavery and colonialism, that they do institutional structured racism and that they think exclude, humiliate, exploit the Black kind to empower their descendants in perpetuity. Black kind, instead went beyond a numbing cynical self-obliteration. Not only did he recognize slavery and colonialism as a beautiful contrivance, he validated them and is trafficking self-slavery and selfcolonialism, institutional structured self-looting, self-pillaging of wealth into White kind banks and prevailing self-exclusion, self-humiliation, self-exploitation and disempowerment of self and dismemberment of her descendants in perpetuity.

Tom: Yes, that's incredibly what I am witnessing.

Lynda: Profanation! Why would he respect us, folks?

Buzzo: The barest minimum duty Africa should do, must do, should have been doing is to have the back of every Black kind sociologically, physiologically and psychologically wherever on this earth. That would truly and ultimately be dominating our stupidity.

Glenda: Our leadership failed. And with equal vigor, the followers.

Tom: Yes, sacrosanct *veritas*! Voluptuous! Followers failed until today. Until you stepped up. You accomplished in three months, what a continent has not accomplished since its existence.

Buzzo: It will continue to be unutterable failure, unfathomable shame, scouring grieving misery until Africa's self-consciousness evolves and recognizes her stupidity, confronts her stupidity, eradicates her stupidity, dominates her environment through infrastructure and value-chains and urbanization, create income, create wealth, endure wealth creativity, empower her descendants, perpetuate descendant's empowerment generation after generation, ad infinitum.

Tom: *It's been said that freedom involves responsibility.*

And paraphrasing President Barack Obama: *"Now this dynamism, of this Country, of this Continent, of this World, is a constant work in progress. We were born with instructions: to form a more perfect union, a more perfect world. Explicit in those words is the idea that we are imperfect, indeed humanity is a failure; that what gives each new generation purpose is to take up the unfinished work of the last and carry it further than anyone might have thought possible. More so when there is unfinished work of humanization."* Indeed, their unfinished work is dehumanizing.

The World status quo – the combined Black kind, White Kind, Yellow kind status quo, the good White Kind, the good Black kind, the good yellow kind – with equal vigor have all failed humanity. They have been

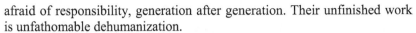

afraid of responsibility, generation after generation. Their unfinished work is unfathomable dehumanization.

Quoting Civil Rights Icon John Lewis: *"If you don't do everything you can to change things, then they will remain the same. You only pass this way once. You have to give it all you have."*

That's what you are doing. You are not afraid. Your generosity of undaunting courage is giving it all you have. Even though you have not been given but utmost generational failures, generational dehumanization, even so you are giving everything you have to change things.

And paraphrasing Michael Jackson's 'Man in the Mirror': *"...A willow deeply scarred, somebody's broken heart, And a washed-out dream...That's why I am starting with me, I am starting with the man in the mirror, I am asking him to take a look at himself and change his ways...make a change ...make the world a better place common, common, man in the mirror... That man in the mirror take that look and make that change..."*,

So, the good White man, the good Yellow man, the good Black man, even though it's tough for privilege to share, you should sacrifice some part of that privileges for a bearable, humane meeting ground.

It's also been said that there is no easy walk to freedom anywhere.

In fact, there is a long walk to Freedom.

And quoting the greatest President of our time, President Nelson Mandela:

"I have learned over the years that when one's mind is made up, this diminishes fear."

You were denied life, generation after generation. You had no choice than conquer fear and embrace freedom and liberty through arduous sacrifice of life, love and time, to make Africa's unutterable humiliation, degradation, tribulations, hopelessness and misery captive. For, yet quoting Michel de Montaigne:

"He who fears he shall suffer, already suffers what he fears."

Yet it's also been said, quoting Philip Randolph:

"Freedom is never given; it is won."

And yet another by Brian Scott Mackenzie:

"Salvation for a race, nation or class must come from within. Freedom is never granted; it is won. Justice is never given it is exacted."

And you are winning, exacting justice. And not only; You are imposing justice.

To these extents, the African youths have broken with the jinx of captivity. To these extents, Africa's Gen WHY have proven the KKK long held view finally wrong.

To these extents, I won my bet on Mezzi's spiritual essence, with my KKK family. To these extents, we, the entire family of the youth of the world, spurred by your audacious resolve at bravery, must rally together with you, to quench the thirst of freedom. We must rally by drinking from the cup of pride and not from the cup of hate, shame, oppression, stereotype and stupidity. So, let me reiterate Buzzo, the solution, the only solution is to recognize, confront and eradicate, dominate African filthy environment to create wealth and empower Black kind descendants by quickly rewriting the script. You have already started rewriting the script. We are in it together. You are not alone. Thank you.

> *And worst still, at his hate you take pride in his material life style.*
> *Never in his intellectual life style.*
> *At his hate, you take pride in looting and plundering your continent into his banks.*
> *At his hate, you take pride in humiliating and enslaving your descendants, generation after generation, in perpetuation.*

An emotional Buzzo, slowly rises and starts applauding him. Every person at that table rises to ponderous applause. An unfeigned, genuine applause, withered of deception, derogation, stereotype, hate and shame, but filled ponderously with pride and hope.

With equal vigor, Tom is finally healed from the imposed torment of his KKK family doctrines. His face finally puckering what seems sincere, excited prideful serenity.

> *No ma! The hate is on Nigger-ism. The act of looting one's own continent, carting it away into Western economy, and gifting its people misery, Whether it be White Nigger-ism, as practiced, for example, by the Russian Oligarchs and by the leaders of South American Countries, or by Black Nigger-ism, as we have here in Africa, we should all hate and upend Nigger-ism in its entirety.*

The combined deception, derogation, stigma, hate, shame and pride are essential – the combined legion of deceptions, derogations and stigmas gave hate their purposes and numbed shame in Status Quo African. And the same combined deceptions, derogations, and stigma, exulted shame instead, in Gen WHY, blacks and whites alike, and shame gave them pride as its reward.

Shame, remorse and pride. Pride should be the reward for shame through the power of remorse!

Finally, the image of the President appears on the television. He is followed by a horde of youths of different anagraphy and military endeavor.

A host of the military personnel are of unfamiliar faces. Evidently newly promoted and appointed to replace the majority of the corrupt military Status Quo.

Buzzo turns on the volume. Attentions are rapt with eyes on the screen. Mezzi and Mark quickly get behind their computers ready to socialize with their peers on the social media platform, their hands, ready to tweet out the pulp of the State of the Union Address, underpinning the President's speeches and remarks on the way forward to make Africa's youths' captivity captive and make Africa's descendants' progress a permanent paradigm shift. s

Now the President takes his seat. The Joint Chief of Defense Staff sits to his left. Further to his left, the Army Chief, the Air Force Chief, the Naval Chief take their positions. To his right seated are the youths. Plenty of kids and teenagers in cluster. The interim Secretary of State and the interim head of cabinet prior to position and appointment confirmations. They are framed by the rest of the youths with the military personnel in a standing fit behind them all. The soldiers look gruesomely fascinating. The stage is set. The entire continent has stopped, at fever pitch, for this moment, with competing amazements of emotions ready to express their utter spasms of assents or dissents.

As the President speaks, Mezzi and Mark are tweeting the "pulp," in real time, to their peers of Gen WHY Family:

> *...what a beautiful construct. The problem is not much of what they did and do to Black kind but much of what Black kind did and does to self. Precisely the problem! The reprehensible, enduring abject inability of not recognizing, not just what they did to us, what they do to us and what they think of us but what we did to us, what we do to us and what we think of us. Not only could Black kind not recognize that they did slavery and colonialism, that they do institutionalized structured racism and that they think exclude, humiliate, exploit the Black kind to empower their descendants in perpetuity, but he instead went beyond a numbing cynical self-obliteration. Not only did he recognize slavery and colonialism as a beautiful contrivance, he validated them and is trafficking self-slavery and self-colonialism, institutionalized structured self-looting, self-pillaging of wealth into White kind banks and prevailing selfexclusion, self-humiliation, self-exploitation and disempowerment of self and dismemberment of her descendants in perpetuity.*

Mezzi: #Democracy has systematically ruined Africa!

Mark: #African democracy is the continuity of slavery and colonialism, by our people, on our people and for some people.

Mezzi: #The ferocious urgency of now: Africa's children got to play. Black kind descendants empowered.

Gen WIIY response is immediate and ponderous: Mezzi's and Mark's computers are overwhelmed by the social-twitter tones, in celebration.

Gen WHY: #Children must play, children must play! We must play, we must play!
Mezzi: # Democracy excludes our kids from playing.
Mark: #Democracy excludes them. Democracy not good for Africa. Very expensive, very classists. Very exclusive. Very illusive. Very elusive. Chicanery!
Gen WHY: #Death to African democracy. Death to destructive democracy.
Mark: #Democracy thrives on reason.
Mezzi: #Democracy loses on ignorance.
Mark: #Africa is ignorant. Blind.
Gen WHY: #Africa's form of democracy equates to misery.
Mark: #China practices no democracy to empower and progress its people.

The barest minimal duty Africa should do, must do, should have been doing is to have the back of every Black kind sociologically, physiologically and psychologically wherever on this earth. That would truly and ultimately be our stupidity dominance.

Mezzi: #China has illuminated benevolent autocracy.
Mark: #Qatar practices no democracy.
Mezzi: #Qatar has a visionary, illuminated autocratic monarchy.
Mark: #Singapore, Malaysia have no western democracy.
Mezzi: #Ignorance thrives with illuminated visionary, benevolent autocracy.
Gen WHY: #Yeah, yeah!
Mark: #Our people are ignorant.
Gen WHY: #Yeah, yeah! Apes, monkeys. Destructive, devious, disruptive.
Mark: # Africa needs education.
Mezzi: #Africa must destroy ignorance.
Gen WHY: #Yeah, sacrosanct truth.
Mezzi: #The best government is that which grows self-consciousness.
Mark: #Africa needs to come out of ignorance.
Mezzi: Africa needs visionary, benevolent autocracy.
Gen WHY: #Yes, yes, yes, yes, yes, yes, yes, yes, yes, yes, yes, yes. Yeeeaaaaaahhhh!
Mezzi: #Africa needs an illuminated, benevolent visionary autocracy.
Gen WHY: The President, the President, the President!

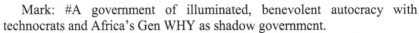
Mark: #A government of illuminated, benevolent autocracy with technocrats and Africa's Gen WHY as shadow government.

Gen WHY: #Yeaaaaaaaaaaaaaaaaaaaaah, yeeaaaaaaaaaaaaaaah!

Mezzi: #Gen WHY would be the government of cheques, checks and balances.

Gen WHY: #Yeeeeeaaaaaaaaaaaaaaaaah!

Mezzi: #Enough with government of talking-crafts, of priest-crafts, of politico-crafts, of monarch-crafts.

Mezzi: #Our children got to play.

Mark: #The government is no more.

Mezzi: # The Presidency, a benevolent autocracy.

Mark: # The parliament is no more.

Mezzi: # The Governors, the local government councilors are no more.

Gen WHY: #Yes, yes, yes, yeeeaaaaaaaaaaaaaaaaaaah!

Mark: #Gen WHY is the government. Gen WHY is our parliament. Gen WHY is our Governors. Gen Why is our local government councilors.

Gen WHY: #Yeeeaaaaahhhhhhh!

Mezzi: #A government dictated to, by the needs of our youths.

Gen WHY: # Wow! Wow!! Wow!!!

Mark: # Compulsory free education.

Gen WHY: #Yes, yes, yes, yes, yes, yes, yes, yes, yes, yes, yes, yes, yes, yes, yes!

Mezzi: #Schools, colleges, research centers, culture, arts, fine arts, theatre, museums, libraries, exhibitions, photography, clothing, etc., etc.

Gen WHY: #Wooooooooooooooooooooooooooooow!

Mark: #Sports and extra-curriculum culture: compulsory reading hobby. One novel a month. At least.

Mezzi: #Healthcare a fundamental human right.

Mark: #Food security a fundamental human right.

Mezzi: #Institutionalized structured cemeteries. Free the lands.

Mark: #Free the lands for mechanized farming.

Gen WHY: #Food, food, food, food, food, foooooooooooooooooood!

Mezzi: #Guarantee constant electric power.

Mark: # Scouring treated pipe-borne water.

Mezzi: #Pipe borne liquified cooking gas in every house.

Mezzi: #Rights and duties.

Gen WHY: #Absolutely.

It will continue to be unutterable failure, unfathomable shame, scouring, grieving misery until Africa recognizes her stupidity, confronts her stupidity, eradicates her stupidity, dominates her environment through infrastructure and value-chains and urbanization, create income, create wealth, endure wealth creativity, empower her descendants, perpetuate descendant's …

> *...empowerment generation after generation, ad infinitum.*

Mark: # Scouring accountability.
Gen WHY: #Absolutely.
Mark: #Laws and discipline and punishments.
Gen WHY: Yes! Yes!! Yes!!!
Mezzi: #Jobs, jobs, jobs. Employment, employment, employment.
Mark: #Value chains, factories, industries, manufacturing.
Gen WHY: #Skill-acquisition! Skill-acquisition!! Skill-acquisition!!!
Mark: #Scouring urbanization and hygiene and decency: Sewerage, refuse bins, public toilets. Parks, parks, equipped parks.
Gen WHY: #Blessings, blessings, blessings!
Mezzi: #Cities of the 21st century. Towns, villages into urban and suburban precincts.
Mark: #Mass housing, houses, houses, houses for everybody.
Mezzi: #Comprehensive commuting, mass transit systems. Railways.
Gen WHY: #Bicycles, bicycles, bicycles. Trains, trains, trains! Buses, buses, buses!
Mark: #Fiscal discipline.
Mezzi: #Secularism for the state.
Mark: #Auster, immediate funerals.
Mezzi: #Prison terms for celebrations and feasting at funerals.
Gen WHY: #Funereal, sepulchral, austere funerals and immediate burials.
Mezzi: #Men of God - Pastors and Imam - must be graduates of theology.
Gen WHY: #Yes, yes, yes, yes. Close the churches, close the mosques.
Mark: #Death penalty for cultism, fetishism.
Gen WHY: #Finally, finally.
Mezzi: #Death penalty for holders of any bank accounts overseas.
Gen WHY: #Yeaaaaaaaaaaaaaaaaaaaaah! Yeaaaaaaaaaaaaaah!!
Mark: #Death penalty for any fraud whatsoever.
Mezzi: # Death penalty for drug trafficking.
Mark: # Castration and life in prison with hardest labor for rapists.
Gen WHY: #Absolutely, absolutely, absolutely.
Mark: #Death penalty for child labor and slavery.
Gen WHY: #Yeeeeeeeeeeeaaaaaaaaaaaaaaaaaaaaaaaaaaaaaaaaaah!
Mark: #Prison terms for parents' lack of parenting.
Mezzi: #Two-child policy.
Gen WHY: #Yes! No more population outpacing our resources.
Mezzi: #Sovereign wealth savings and enhancement.
Mark: #Scouring comprehensive pension scheme for every African senior citizen.
Gen WHY: # Yeassssssssssssssssssssssssssssssss!
Mark: #Make our environment better than we find it.

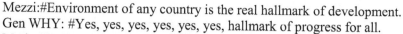

Mezzi:#Environment of any country is the real hallmark of development.

Gen WHY: #Yes, yes, yes, yes, yes, yes, hallmark of progress for all.

Mark: #Hallmark of dignity and respect and love thy neighbor tenet.

Mezzi: #God's deeds on earth ours.

Mark: #Make anything better than we find it.

Mezzi: #A benevolent, visionary, autocratic leadership that feeds every hungry person before feeding self.

Gen WHY: #Yeeeeaaaaaaaaaaaaaaaahhhhhhhhhhhhhhhh.

Mezzi: #A benevolent, autocratic leadership whose hallmark is to live and share the befitting, enabling environment he creates in equal measure with his citizens.

So, let me reiterate Buzzo, the solution, the only solution is recognize, confront, eradicate, dominate African environment to create wealth and empower Black kind descendants by quickly rewriting the script. You have already started rewriting the script, we are in it together. You are not alone.

Gen WHY: #Yeeaaaahhhhhhhhhhhhhhhhhhhhhhhhhhhhhhhhhhhh!

Mezzi: #A benevolent, visionary autocracy that makes each generation of our children better than the generation preceding it.

Mark: #Make our children better than ourselves. Generation after generation.

Mezzi: #For only a benevolent, idealistic autocracy can shift the paradigm.

Mark: #Idealistic visionary: Da Vinci, Edison, Bill Gates, Steve Jobs, etcetera, etcetera.

Mezzi: #Make God's deed on earth ours, to gain heaven.

Gen WHY: #Get up, stand up; get up, stand up; filth dominance. Garbage dominance. Dominate our environment. Captivity captive. Captivity captive. The pride. Captivity captive our pride!

Made in the USA
Columbia, SC
19 March 2024

33273314R00293